Diana Norman was [...] a nurse, and her f[...] *The Times*. She be[gan her writing ...] for a local paper in the East End, and became the youngest reporter on Fleet Street when she joined the *Daily Herald*. While reporting on a visit by the Moscow State Circus, she met a reporter from the *Daily Sketch*, Barry Norman, and later married him. She then worked on *Woman's Mirror* before turning to freelance journalism. She has written four previous novels, including *Daughter of Lîr*, all of which received critical acclaim, and a bestselling biography of Constance Markievicz, *Terrible Beauty*. She lives in Hertfordshire with her husband and two daughters.

The Pirate Queen

Diana Norman

HEADLINE

First published in 1991
by HEADLINE BOOK PUBLISHING PLC

First published in paperback in 1992
by HEADLINE BOOK PUBLISHING PLC

10 9 8 7 6 5 4 3 2

ISBN 0 7472 3825 1

Phototypeset by Intype, London

Printed and bound in Great Britain by
HarperCollins Manufacturing, Glasgow

HEADLINE BOOK PUBLISHING PLC
Headline House
79 Great Titchfield Street
London W1P 7FN

To Trixie

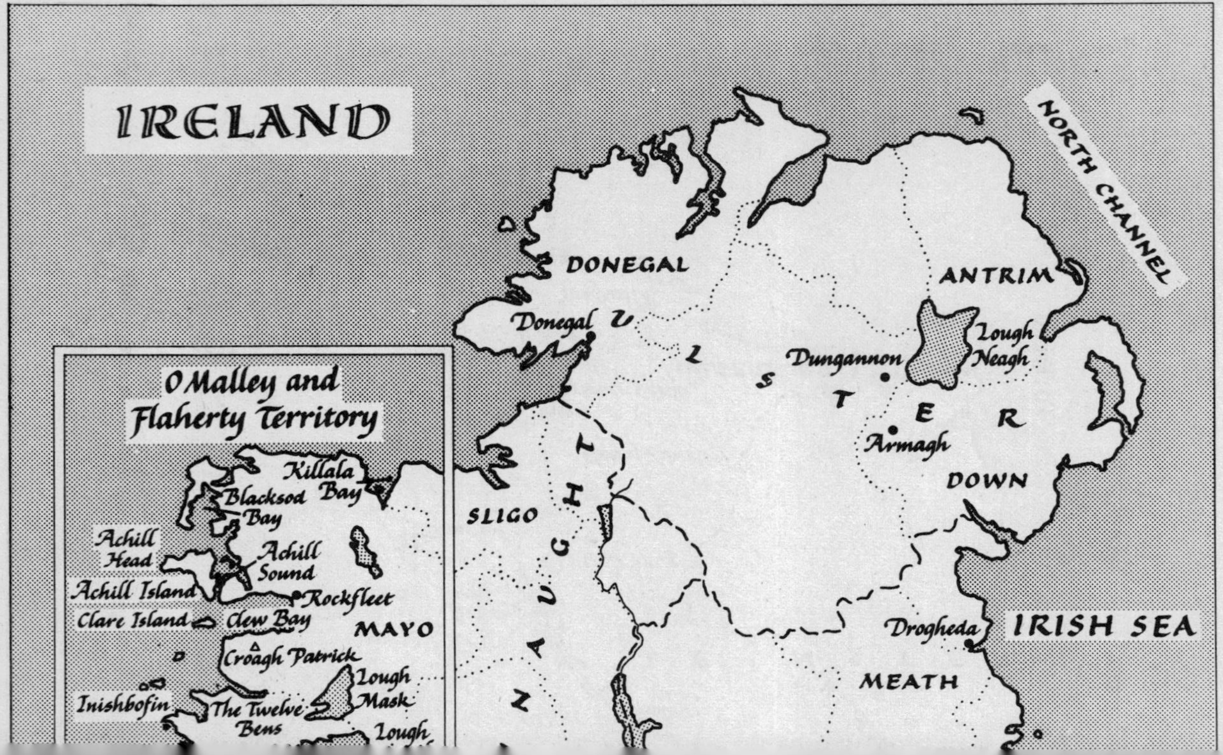
IRELAND
NORTH CHANNEL
DONEGAL
Donegal
ANTRIM
Lough Neagh
Dungannon
U L S T E R
Armagh
DOWN
SLIGO
C O N N A U G H T
IRISH SEA
Drogheda
MEATH
O Malley and Flaherty Territory
Killala Bay
Blacksod Bay
Achill Head
Achill Sound
Achill Island
Rockfleet
Clare Island
Clew Bay
MAYO
Croagh Patrick
Lough Mask
Inishbofin
The Twelve Bens
Lough

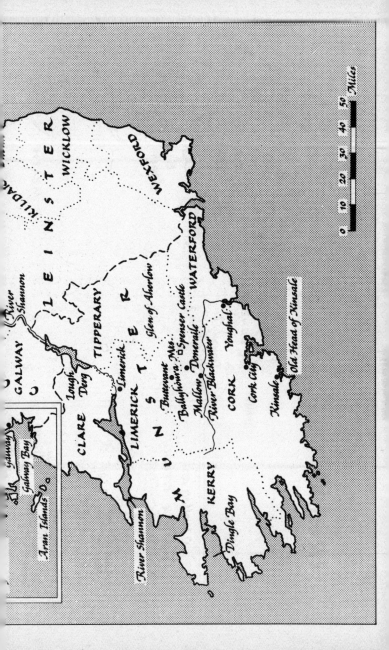

Author's Note

The last twenty years of Elizabeth the First's reign over Ireland were so chaotic and involved so many personalities and clans that, for the sake of clarity, I have kept together leading characters who represented the various prevailing frames of mind. This has involved some playing around with dates and places. For instance, Sir John Perrot's recall was actually in 1588, the year of the Armada, and the execution by Bingham of the pitiful Bourke children was in Ballinrobe, not Galway.

Also, it was the O'Connors who were alleged to have flayed Captain Mackworth, not the MacSheehys, but with so many atrocities committed on both sides during that atrocious war the wrong attribution of one will, I hope, like the other changes, be forgiven in the interests of coherence.

Prologue

In the last hour before she died Maire ni Domnall did what she could to safeguard the future for her only remaining child.

With accustomed authority she ordered her fellow prisoners, already freezing, out of their shirts and shawls and made them knot the clothes together to form a rope. While they were so employed she took the child to a corner.

'Tell me who you are.'

The recital of ancestry took some minutes.

Maire nodded: 'Remember it. Tell me where the treasure is. Softly.'

Whispering, the child gave a location and its cross-bearings.

Maire nodded. 'Remember it.'

'But I should much prefer to stay and die with you, Mother. Please.'

Maire smacked the small hands reaching for her. 'Selfishness, selfishness. Now then, to go back through Munster is impossible.' The child's chance of escape was slight enough as it was, but in the desert the English had made of Munster there would be no chance at all. 'Head for the port and find a ship, preferably one making for the west, but you may have little choice. Pay for your passage with this.' She had managed to conceal her royal gold torque from her captors. She would have bribed them with it to save her life, but she had watched another prisoner try to bargain for his life with a silver box, and the English had said it was stolen and taken it from him and strung him up just the same. She tucked the gold necklet into the child's jerkin which she buttoned with care.

'Now then. Before we get you through, I shall start

1

screaming. It is to attract the guards; you must not think I am afraid.'

For the first time Maire was lying and the child knew it; the last thread of their life unravelled itself and joined the maniacal abnormality which had entangled them. The small face, which had been stiff with terror and courage, began to unlimn. Watching it, Maire nearly gave way herself. She considered whether it was better for them to die together instead of sending the child to face God knew what alone. No, it was not. She tried to think of some last piety with which to give an assurance of the ultimate goodness of God and the unfailing care of the Holy Mother, but she would not lie to the child again. 'Survive,' was all she said.

The watchtower was not a prison and the people had only been kept in it so that the English soldiers, exhausted by hanging so many men, women and children the day before, could have a night's rest before hanging the rest. Nevertheless, its three floors had only arrow slits for windows and even these had a bar newly cemented in the niche before them. With the dagger from her boot Maire had dislodged two stones from the more ancient cement of the slit, and thanked her God that her child had the narrow head and shoulders of their clan.

She placed the rope between the child's hands and put the rest of it between its legs. 'Like shinning down from the yardarm,' she instructed. 'Hang on very tight.' She hauled herself up by the bar and looked out. Sixty feet below a conscientious sentry was pacing out his patrol on this side of the tower, occasionally glancing up. She began to scream. It was easy; stopping would be difficult.

She saw the sentry's head look up towards her. He might not move; he'd heard too many screaming women. But the sound issuing from her mouth released the other prisoners from their hopelessness into the luxury of panic. At once the tower vibrated with terror as if its floors were stacked canteens of beans which whistled in the agitation of boiling.

The sentry began to run towards the steps to the tower door. There was no more time. Maire lifted the child up, forcing its head between the bar and the wall, twisting the seven-year-old body so that the shoulders were presented sideways for the slit. It was difficult to pass the rope beyond the obstruction of the child so that it hung outside, but it was done in time. She glimpsed the face in the moonlight, blood from the small nose running into its mouth. 'Hold very tight, darling.' The endearment nearly undid them both; the child clung, unable to leave her. Maire snarled: 'Survive, didn't I tell you?' The rope swayed as the child slid down the drop that was out of Maire's sight. Doors banged on the lower floors, men shouted above the noise, screams of pain mingled with the hysteria.

A woman clawed at Maire's arm. 'My son too.'

Maire looked down at the boy being held up to her. A typical Munster peasant with a large head. The struggle to get him through would outlast the arrival of the soldiers and tell them where her own child had gone so that they began a pursuit too soon. She nodded. 'In a second.'

There were footfalls on the stairs. Maire felt the rope go slack, saw a tiny shape streak across the yard to the shadow of a cannon mounting, pause and slip over the edge of the hill. She got out her knife and sliced through the knot round the bar so that the rope slithered down to lie unseen at the foot of the tower. She lifted the knife in case the Munster mother should attack her, but there was no fight in the woman. She collapsed, sobbing.

The door opened and soldiers hurled themselves into the room, clubbing and bludgeoning. 'Should I cut my throat now, I wonder,' asked Maire of herself, 'and save the indignity?' But God, if there was a God, was antipathetic to suicide, and having to spend eternity among the inferior classes who inhabited Hell was surely the greater indignity.

The English began hanging the prisoners that night, in case the hysteria developed into a break-out. As she waited in line for the gallows, freed from the burden of her child, Maire had time to be angry and she asked the man in front of her, who spoke English, if he knew why she was being hanged.

'For being a witch, it was said in court,' said the man, absently.

'What does that mean?' asked Maire, who did not recognise the term.

The English-speaker said it meant that somebody had named her as a dangerous woman in order to save

3

themselves from being hanged. 'But I know no one in this area,' protested Maire, as she had protested in untranslated shouts at the mass trial.

The English-speaker shrugged at her as he went up the steps. 'Merely being Irish is enough to hang the lot of us,' he said.

So Maire went to the gallows for a crime of which she was not only guiltless but ignorant. She went furiously, but anonymously. The English had trouble keeping count of their victims, let alone taking their names.

Nevertheless, some six years later, Maire ni Domnall's death came to the attention of Elizabeth I, Queen of England.

Chapter One

An old man, undistinguished except for the chain of office round his neck, shuffled through the petitioners in the gallery who babbled at him but knew better than to pluck his sleeve. 'My lord, will you remind her . . . ?' 'My lord, I've been waiting . . .'

He might have been deaf. Actually his hearing was going a bit, like his eyesight. It wasn't until he was close to the door to the Queen's chamber that he noticed his way was impeded by the Captain of the Guard, six feet of stylised steel armour.

'Who approaches the presence of Her Majesty?' Procedurally the Captain was correct in his challenge, but he knew very well who the old man was. Walter Raleigh liked playing dangerous games. He'd caught the Queen's eye by playing them.

In a sudden silence the petitioners saw the old man pause as if he were confused by the question. Actually he was sympathising with the predicament of this impudent young man and all such young men he had seen come and go over the years. Audacity was what attracted the Queen's favour to them in the first place, but that same audacity inevitably broke them. They never knew when to stop. Had he the energy, he would lecture this one. 'Take heed,' he would say to him, 'it is grey men who survive to become old in this court, the cautious, the dependable, the ones she works to death, which is better than death on the block.' But he did not care enough to say it.

What he did say, mildly, was: 'The Lord Treasurer, summoned by Her Majesty.'

'Pass, my Lord Treasurer.'

Through the doors, through the chamber which separated the gallery from the sanctum and in which the

5

courtiers lounged when off duty, through the inner doors and into the scent which dominated any room she was in nowadays, an Arabic concoction that Hatton had procured for her saying it was the same perfume used by the Queen of Sheba while visiting Solomon, or some such nonsense.

As he bowed – he was excused from kneeling because of his arthritis – he squinted to see who was with her. Black Tom. Deary, deary me, that meant Ireland. He didn't feel up to Ireland this morning. He bowed again: 'My lord Earl of Ormond.'

'My Lord Treasurer.'

Her voice whipped away the niceties. 'The blackamoor, Burghley.'

Her long fingers belonged to the vegetable kingdom, white and elongated as asparagus tips. She kept them still, like her eyes. In someone so animated it was unnerving, deliberately, but Burghley knew every trick in her armoury. Somewhere in his own body, bent at the neck and shoulders as though the chain round them incorporated the weight of its office, there was love for her, if she hadn't exhausted his desire to find it. But the use of 'Burghley' was serious. On good days he was her Spirit. Blackamoor?

'Master Raleigh's blackamoor. Six years ago. You hanged it.'

He remembered. 'I didn't hang it, Phoenix.' (Phoenix was the favoured address this season.) 'I recall the poor thing died in Ireland in some over-zealous executions during the Desmond Wars.'

'Indeed. It appears that at the time they were zealously hanging other people's blackamoors, they also hanged a subject who could have been of use to us.' She cocked her wigged head towards the Earl of Ormond. 'Now that the Lord Treasurer has joined us, you may recount the details.'

As usual she was sharply delineated; hard jewels, starched ruff, pointed stomacher, angular farthingale which today supported a skirt of lemon and green, an acidic shock against the restrained richness of the arras behind her. The older she became and the more intransigent her problems, the more her appearance reassured the public by its decisiveness. It was camouflage to obscure a mind

6

which pondered great decisions with the swiftness of a turtle presented with too many lettuce leaves.

The man who stepped forward, Thomas Butler, 10th Earl of Ormond, was a relief in soft black velvet with his creamy skin a contrast where it appeared through his dark hair and beard. Nevertheless there was a resemblance between himself and the Queen, the same light-blue protuberant eyes, the same shape of face, similar freckles. Three generations back, a Boleyn had married a Butler and provided a mutual ancestor for the two of them. They took pleasure in their cousinship, Elizabeth as much as Black Tom. Though she boasted in public of being her father's daughter, she clung in private to the line of Anne Boleyn. 'My black husband' she called Ormond, one of those endearments of hers which caused the gossip she delighted in. She loved speculation about her sexuality. Privately, Burghley thought, when he thought about it at all, she was a tease. Her hymen was probably as intact as it ever had been, though withering now.

He didn't mind what their relationship was as long as it kept her happy; the Ormonds were Protestant and the only earls of Ireland who had shown consistent loyalty to the English Crown.

'It is a peculiar matter we have here, my lord,' said the Earl, 'and one concerning a Connaught sept, the O'Flaherties. Would you know of them?' Despite a perfect English accent, he had the cadence of an Irishman.

'Is it their name up on the gates of Galway?' asked Burghley. ' "From the wrath of the O'Flaherties Good Lord deliver us?" '

Out of the corner of his vision he saw Elizabeth's lashless eyes glaze intentionally. She resented her Lord Treasurer's mastery of Irish genealogy because her own was sketchy; she flinched from the subject of Ireland and affected boredom with it.

She walked away from them to look out of the great window which was allowing the morning light through in diamond shapes onto the floor.

'The same. Nor has God always delivered Galway from them. A barbaric people. Well now. Some six years ago the tanaist of the O'Flaherties lost his wife.'

7

'She didn't die, Burghley,' called Elizabeth from the window. 'He lost her. Such carelessness.'

'They quarrelled,' went on Black Tom, nodding, 'and the lady left him, taking their two sons and a daughter with her. The O'Flaherty assumed she'd gone back to her own clan.'

'Which was?'

'The O'Connors.'

Burghley pulled his fingers through his beard. The O'Connors were, or certainly had been, the royal clan of Connaught and in a past age had styled themselves Kings of Ireland.

'The O'Flaherty intended to fetch her back when it was convenient to him, the next time he raided O'Connor land.'

The long foot of the present Queen of Ireland could be heard tapping on the floor in irritation at the anarchy of her most westerly subjects.

'When he did, however,' continued Black Tom, 'it was to find that she wasn't there at all, but had taken a ship for Spain.'

With the naming of their vast enemy, an element entered which, by its mass, momentarily altered the room's perspective, looming over the occupants so that they seemed insubstantial and puny, like twigs swirling in a gale. Even the outburst 'Treachery!' from the woman by the window was a bat's squeak.

'Treachery in our sense, ma'am,' the Earl of Ormond said smoothly, 'but not in theirs. These people are not concerned with our quarrel; they trade with Spain, they'd trade for sulphur with the Devil. After a time the O'Flaherty decided on a search, though not so much for his wife as his children. All ships bound from his lands to Spain were ordered to enquire for them, your man even went himself but no trace could he discover. He spent another year in anger, thinking the woman had holed up with some lover out of his reach, though in the meantime he himself had taken another wife.'

There was a snort from the window. 'Barbarians.'

'Then it occurred to him that he should not be so much shamed as concerned that some mischance might have overtaken her and the little ones. It was then that he came to me.' The Earl's eyes flickered towards his cousin and he muttered to Burghley: 'There is a distant kinship between us.'

Burghley nodded. Through what he regarded as the pernicious Irish custom of gossipry, everybody in Ireland was related in some way to everybody else. It once again occurred to him, though he did not point it out, that, through her mother, the Queen of England's veins quite probably shared the same blood as those very clans she despised. Black Tom didn't point it out either.

The aftermath of the Desmond Wars had not provided a helpful environment in which to search for missing persons. Over half of Munster was missing. Some families had run away to escape the war between English authority and the rebel Irish lords, led by the Earl of Desmond, which had lain their country waste; thousands had died of starvation; other thousands had been killed, sometimes by other Irish, most often by the English who had hit on the idea of subduing Munster by depopulating it entirely.

The story of Black Tom's search for the runaway O'Flaherty wife looked like being a long one, and Burghley asked Elizabeth's permission to sit down while it was told. Sometimes she was solicitous for him, but not today. However, he took her sigh as assent and found a chair. His gout was giving him gyp.

Ormond had prosecuted the search through his agents on the Continent and in Ireland, 'having little time myself', but Burghley found himself wondering why such a great earl had prosecuted it all. It would have been more to oblige the Ormonds than the O'Flaherties, he was sure of that. The Lord Treasurer began leafing through that section of his mind which held his knowledge of the west of Ireland and its clans.

'. . . and then it was discovered,' he heard Ormond say, 'that a cog such as is sometimes used by the western clans had been wrecked on a remote part of the Dingle peninsula many years before and that a lady, a child and a sailor had been its only survivors.'

At this point, Ormond said, he had lost heart. The Dingle people adhered, like most of the western coast dwellers, to the time-honoured custom of slaughtering shipwrecked persons who came ashore, in order to claim the wreck for themselves.

9

'But one of my agents happening to be in Cork came across an English settler belonging to the city who had a tale to tell going back to that time. I had him brought to me.'

What the Cork settler had told Ormond was that six years previously he had gone out of that city to witness a mass hanging of rounded-up Irish near a watchtower just along the coast. He'd enjoyed seeing the rebels die, he told Ormond, so that even though some of the hangings took place at night he had stayed there, eating the provisions his wife had packed for him, and watching the entertainment by the light of flares.

What made him remember this hanging above many others he had subsequently seen was that among the hanged there had been a blackamoor, and a red-headed woman.

'The O'Flaherty's wife was red-haired,' said Ormond.

'So are many women,' said Burghley.

'According to report,' said Ormond, 'hers was a special red, a torch, a surprise—'

A red-wigged queen spoke from the window: 'Are we going to be here all day discussing the hair of trollops?'

'Anyway,' said Ormond, hurriedly, 'my settler was intrigued by the way this particular woman died, not pleading nor praying like the others, but spitting and swearing. So intrigued was he that after he had watched her die, he went up to the line of those waiting their turn to be hanged and questioned them about her. He had been in the country long enough to learn something of the Irish language.'

Considering that the waiting line had other things to think about, the settler had done well in getting what information he had. This was that the red-head had consistently protested that she was innocent of whatever it was they accused her of, that she was nobly born, a princess of Ireland, a friend to England.

The figure by the window strode into the men's conversation to confront Burghley. 'Have our representatives in Ireland grown so bold against our person that they hang innocent women?' That she might lose control over her own administration was one of her greatest terrors. 'Why didn't they listen to her at her trial?'

'She had no English,' said Ormond, gently. 'They

10

didn't know what she was saying.'

Quite suddenly Elizabeth's eyes filled with tears. In one of her unpredictable flashes of sympathy, the 'treacherous trollop' had become a fellow woman trapped in horrific circumstances. 'God have mercy on her soul,' she said. 'The justice who condemned her will be recalled to answer for it. What happened to the child?'

'She procured its escape. Some of her companion prisoners saw her give the child a torque—'

'A talk?'

'Torque. An Irish necklet, Majesty. Gold. Then she dropped the child from the window by a rope. My settler was interested enough to make enquiries and discovered that much later a small boy answering to the description of the one in the tower – red-haired like his mother – had been taken aboard a vessel bound for London, but as the ship had already sailed, there was little more he could find out.'

'He could have reported the matter.'

Ormond didn't point out that at the time they were speaking of, famine had spread even to the loyal areas and the Cork settler had been occupied in trying to keep alive in a city where fifty people a day were dying from hunger. But he held his tongue; Elizabeth didn't want to recall the Desmond Wars which had cost her money, men and humiliation, nor did he want to remind her of them. Their relationship had been tried to breaking point in that chaotic period; she had sent in administrators and generals who were ignorant of the Irish situation, who had assumed, quite wrongly, that all the many old English lords, the ones whose families had been in Ireland since the time of Henry II and had not changed their religion during the Reformation, were enemies because they were Catholic and Catholic because they were enemies. It had brought an element of religious war into the country which had not previously been there and which was dangerous. It had forced perfectly loyal men into rebellion against the Crown. In trying to mediate between the two sides, he himself, though a Protestant, and though he had fought against the rebellion as hard as any, had been accused of collusion with the enemy.

So vicious had been the intrigues by some of Elizabeth's officials against him that she'd stripped him of his commission as general in Munster, though she had resisted attempts to arraign him. They were friendly again but with Elizabeth one could never be too careful.

'Well, well,' she said now, tapping him on the arm with her fan, 'we have come to the bottom of the matter and we shall see that those responsible for the poor lady's execution are punished. Does this O'Flaherty know that she is hanged?'

'No, Your Majesty. I thought it better merely to tell him that she had been shipwrecked and leave him to think that she drowned.'

'Much better, much better,' said the Queen. 'We shall send him some token of our sympathy and favour. What do you say, Burghley?'

The Lord Treasurer was watching the Earl of Ormond. 'I think the matter is not quite completed, Phoenix,' he said. 'I imagine the lord Earl is exercising himself over the child.'

'The child? The child? But if we have not heard of him in six years then we must assume that he is perished. Assuming that he landed safely in London, could a friendless small boy, a mere Irish, survive the city?' Elizabeth fawned on her Londoners as they on her, but she had few illusions about the conditions in which they existed.

'But if he did, Majesty . . .' said Ormond.

'If he did, if he did,' said the Queen impatiently. 'If wishes were horses, beggars would ride. What if he did?'

'He would be of considerable use to us,' said Burghley. He hauled himself up. He knew where Black Tom was aiming now, and he was ahead of him. 'If he is alive, he is a contender for the leadership of the O'Flaherties. More than that, he is related to all the great clans of the west, the O'Donnells, the O'Burkes, the O'Connors and such other tribes as might form a bulwark for us in the north and west.' He turned to Ormond. 'Do I mistake the situation?'

'No, my lord, you do not.' The Earl of Ormond eyed the old man with respect. Here was one of the few of Elizabeth's officials who grasped something of Ireland's complexities. A pity he wasn't in charge of it. 'Then there is the grandmother.'

12

'Ah,' said Burghley and clawed his beard again. 'The grandmother.'

Elizabeth was becoming angry at this communion between the two men. 'Grandmother me no grandmothers. Do I understand you wish to find and nourish this urchin because he has a grandmother?'

'No ordinary grandmother, Phoenix. This one is the leader of a great sailing people or, as we might say, a pirate.'

'A woman pirate?'

'A considerable one, Majesty, owing allegiance to no one but herself. She is known to us as Grace O'Malley. If we could gain that allegiance . . .'

Elizabeth swore by God's death. 'Leave the matter, Burghley. Your spies have greater use than to search for some pirate's brat better left in the care of God, if indeed it is not there already. There are enough pirates in our navy without adding unnatural Irishwomen to their number.'

'Nevertheless, great Phoenix, better she be of use to us than to Spain.'

Again the word carried gigantism into the chamber, so that it seemed to lose balance under its tilt.

The Queen planted her legs more firmly on the floor. She always stood straight to her enemies. 'Somewhat late, little man. We seem to have hanged her daughter.'

'Daughter-in-law, Phoenix. A pardonable error, and one of which she is ignorant and which might yet stand us in good stead if we could befriend the child.'

This was the latest policy for dealing with the Irish, to try and foster some of the country's more nobly born children and bring them up as little Englishmen so that when they took over their Irish inheritance they would be sympathetic to England. That was the theory. So far the only one it looked like working on was the young orphaned Hugh O'Neill, whom Sir Henry Sidney had taken under his wing.

But looking for a child in London would mean paying agents and if there was one thing the Queen of England disliked more than any other it was spending money. Her Lord Treasurer saw that, as usual, she would put off making a decision. Her rheumatics were bothering her.

She walked back to the window. Any moment she would dismiss them both.

He said: 'The child is heir to treasure, Majesty.'

He glimpsed Ormond's head jerk up. Deary me, did Black Tom think he didn't know? That was what the man had been after all along, treasure and influence. That was why he had instigated a search for the boy in the first place and why he had only come to ask the Queen's help once he had learned the child was in a city where he, Black Tom, could not possibly find him unassisted. The Earl of Ormond wanted that child. He would let Burghley find him and then offer to foster him. Deary, deary me.

The long shoes paused in the diamonds of sun shining through the great window onto the tiles. Her head went on one side. Her mind scrabbled at locks, threw open chest lids. Her fingers twitched to poke over chalice, pyx, drench themselves in winking carbuncles, mooning pearls, pay her debts and her troops, and cut off with gold the life support of her enemies.

'Treasure?' came the suddenly sweet voice.

'Madam, it is a peculiarity of the grandmother's clan that its chieftains are heir to great treasure. This child may well inherit it.'

'My Lord Treasurer,' said the Queen, 'find this child. The poor boy has suffered much. He needs our protection. Find him. Quickly.'

'Yes, Phoenix.' He bowed with satisfaction to the Earl of Ormond, who opened his mouth and then closed it again. He bowed to the royal back and began to manoeuvre his way out backwards. It hadn't been such a tiring morning after all.

His rear was just approaching the doors, which were opening for him – as usual the Captain of the Guard had been listening to the conversation from the other side – when his name was called by the woman at the window.

'Yes, Majesty?'

'What did you do about Master Walter's blackamoor?'

She never forgot a thing. His unwilling eye was caught by that of the grinning Captain of the Guard. The black moustache and beard curling round the man's mouth always gave the impression that Walter Raleigh was smiling, even when he was not. Burghley held an image of

14

that crisp facial hair in the rictus of a smile as its owner played his part in the greatest massacre ever perpetrated on unarmed men by Englishmen in modern times. Swords had stabbed into the neck and paunch of every member of the Smerwick garrison in Ireland, all of whom had already surrendered, all still pleading for their lives. Admitted, most of them had been Spanish invaders, yet it had not been an episode to bring glory on England's name.

The Lord Treasurer stared up into the face of the Captain of the Guard, imagining it sweating in the effort to kill so large an allocation of human beings.

'The blackamoor, Burghley,' came the voice from the privy chamber.

The Lord Treasurer bowed towards it and nodded to Raleigh. 'I found him another one,' he said.

Burghley shuffled back down the long gallery where the petitioners and courtiers waited and muttered, some of them intriguing against the very man who now passed between them. He could out-plot them all, Raleigh, Ormond, Leicester, even Walsingham. He held too many threads, knew where too many bodies were buried . . .

Back in his office his desk was heaped with letters, commands, complaints, requests for preferment, instructions from his sister on how she was to be buried – and she'd probably outlive the lot of them – reports from his spies, wrangles with the commissariat.

He called one of his scribes and sent him to search among the Irish State Papers. 'Look under the correspondence between Sir William Drury and myself. Six years ago.'

One thing, the Queen would be thwarted in her command to recall the justice who had hanged the O'Flaherty wife. The man responsible had been Sir William Drury, and Sir William Drury was dead. His term in Ireland had killed him. Ireland destroyed them all eventually.

When the papers came, the old man spread them on the table and picked them up one by one, holding them near to his eyes. Eventually he found the reference to the mass trial outside Cork.

'Three hundred and six persons were executed in this sessions,' Sir William had written, 'among which some good ones; two for treason, a blackamoor, and two witches by natural law, for we found no law to try them by in this realm.' The letter went on to the usual commentary on the Irish being dogs, 'and worse than dogs, for dogs do but after their kind, but they degenerate from all humanity . . .'

Lord Burghley stopped reading. His great weariness with all things to do with Ireland was caused not only by the insistence and complexity of the problem it posed, its horrific cost to the Exchequer, nor even by the undoubted savagery of its people, but by the savagery it inspired in every Englishman sent out to deal with it.

Reasonable men stood in his office here in London and listened to his advice on how to govern that country with a firm, wise, and judicious hand, sailed off to it with firm, wise and judicious intentions, and sent back letters incoherent with hatred for its people.

He did not condemn such men. They were not provided with sufficient money to make Ireland peaceful by kindness, nor to commit genocide cleanly and replace its dead population with English settlers. The eternal compromise between these alternatives was an attrition that wore men down and forced them into a cruelty that Lord Burghley would have liked to believe foreign to the English character.

Only the other day he had said to the Queen that he believed the Irish suffered no less badly under English rule than did the people of the Low Countries under the Spanish. He had offered it as an observation, a basis for discussion. But the Queen had been shocked out of reason and had thrown a pomander at his head. She could still amaze him with her ability to feel guilt. He had passed beyond it long ago. There was no blame in anything men did, merely the cupidity of Adam and the slow churn of history presenting sections of the same wheel.

Left to itself the Lord Treasurer's brain would have liked to explore the philosophical sidetrack of whether a country that had no law against witches was too backward to recognise their evil, or too advanced to countenance burning them. But as usual there was too much work to do.

Even so he did not begin right away. Instead, he clambered up onto the windowseat to look on the world outside the court.

From here he could see over the Somerset House gardens, over the lovely river gate to the river itself where the sea-coal barges rowed up to Whitehall and the watermen went back and forth to the south bank in their endless crossings.

On an impulse he pulled down the catch and opened the casement, though his doctor had warned him against damp air. Immediately his nose was assaulted by fresh and foul smells and his ears by noise, birdsong, shouts from rowing boats, church bells ringing in christenings and ringing out the dead, the calls of the street-sellers, all the buzz of a city which had burst its bounds.

He leaned out to peer over the trees to his left and see the spur where Strand Lane spewed people, litter and sewage down to the river. The nobility continually complained of Strand Lane, the only approach for commoners to the Thames between the seven palaces which blocked out the frontage along this stretch. Strand Lane was so . . . common. The Earl of Arundel, who owned the neighbouring palace, annually petitioned the Queen to have the lane closed off, complaining that harlots used it, that his chestnut trees which hung over it were ravaged of their conkers by small boys. Visiting ambassadors walking in the gardens of Somerset House said that it smelled and that rude persons climbed up its wall and jeered at them. But Elizabeth, mindful of 'her commons' and secretly enjoying the discomfiture of the ambassadors, refused to have it closed.

That urchin down there on the lane's bank, making grey pies from the mud of the river, was he the lost Irish child? How old would he be now? Fourteen? Fifteen? Or was he the slightly older boy at the end of the spit who was displaying his sores and begging from passing boats? It was a matter no more important in the Lord Treasurer's scheme of things than a thousand others; the reorganisation of purveying to the royal household, for instance. But it was no less important either.

It was not optimism that led Burghley to persist in trying to bring peace to Ireland by civilising its people. It was desperation. Ireland was dangerous, a vacuum which Spain, sharing its religion, could easily fill.

Burghley wished, and not for the first time, that he could have commanded the past four centuries and

17

avoided the errors with which his predecessors had warped the Irish into an intransigent people. He wished he could have persuaded his Queen out of her negative colonialism, more a policy to keep Spain out than to keep the Irish content. But it would have cost money, and as usual she had cheesepared. False economy, false economy, thought the Lord Treasurer. They were already fighting Spain in the Low Countries. Soon they might be fighting a Spanish invasion here in England. If Ireland broke out at the same time . . .

'Are you all right, my lord?'

He looked round to see the scribes watching him. He had groaned aloud. He shook his head at his chief secretary. 'Armageddon, Percy.'

Percy joined him at the window, interested. 'Where, my lord?'

Burghley ordered the man back to his desk, and returned to his view. 'Am I the only one who can see it?' he asked himself. Well, all he could do was build England's protection with such bricks as Elizabeth allowed him. Young O'Neill was one of them. His upbringing among the Sidneys, that most English of families, at that most English of country manors, Penshurst, seemed to have instilled all the right values in the boy. That would be Ulster safeguarded. Now if he could only do the same in the west; Connaught was the least known factor in the whole imbalance that was Ireland.

He was not sanguine about the story of treasure which had caught the Queen's attention, but if it was possible to find the O'Flaherty boy, then found he must be.

London, though. One hundred thousand people teeming inside its walls and even more overflowing them. The nunnery orphanages which might have taken in the child had gone with the Reformation, leaving a vacuum sucking homeless youngsters into the criminal sewers which underlay and polluted the city and to which even his meanest agents had little recourse. Nevertheless, the Irish pawn must be found.

What did he know of the child, apart from the fact that it was red-haired and had at one time or another owned a golden Irish torque? Well, they could only try. He'd set the search in train today.

The wheeze of his chest reminded him of his doctor's advice and he closed the window, shutting out the smell and noise, and clambered down into the pen-scratched silence of his office.

Chapter Two

It was a wonderful city; at this time it was the most wonderful in the world, not in cleanliness, not in buildings, certainly not in spirituality, but in freedom. Great art had the liberty to flourish in the London anthill and Puritans were at liberty to try and stop it. A man could be a Catholic as long as he wasn't a Papist, but on the whole England had found in Protestantism a religion that suited it and in Elizabeth a queen they could understand.

Despite the fear it was engendering, the threat of Spanish invasion was oddly congenial to the English, giving them a sense of nationhood and providing them with a ready-made national character. Cheeky, was how the English saw themselves, daring, inventive, backs-to-the-wall, nothing to lose, us against a hostile and inferior world.

Ambassadors to the English capital were amazed by the vitality of streets that were overcrowded and insanitary, by the cheerfulness of slums where just to drink the water was a death sentence. They were appalled by the crowds which shouted vulgar approval, and sometimes disapproval, at Elizabeth on her progresses, and the equally vulgar way she shouted back; it was disrespect, it was lese-majesty, it was some new thing being released out of the bottle of England which could never be squeezed back and which, unchecked, might infect the rest of the world.

Londoners were acrobats without benefit of safety net. They could work if there was work. They could starve if there wasn't. Pursued only by equally enterprising diseases, they could grasp the ladder that dangled over their heads and with sufficient wit and ruthlessness, climb to the high wire.

With another sort of wit and another sort of ruthlessness those who didn't do any of these things lived by robbing and tricking all the foregoing.

And if ever there was a sheep to be fleeced, it was the youngster with big green eyes and country dress wandering on a fine Sunday morning along the track which diagonally crossed the three fields belonging to Lincoln's Inn.

His mouth lolled at his fellow strollers and the entertainment about him, at the puppet shows, the sweetmeat sellers and the fire-eaters, as widely as his cheap jallyslops hung on his thin legs. He gawped at a group of young law students whose souls had just been improved by a compulsory two-hour service at the round Temple church and were now being busily unimproved by a dice game with a pedlar. The pedlar was losing and on glancing up at the staring boy, he whispered with relief to his companions: 'Here's another gull for you to pluck, young gentlemen, 'stead of me.'

The students grinned wolfishly at the new bait. 'Join us?' they asked.

Timorous but fascinated, the boy hovered: 'What's that game then?'

The students stifled their delight. 'What's your name?'

'Barbary, sirs.' He beamed at their attention. 'Just down from Norwich with geese and sold them at the Poultry and thinking I'd like to find my fortune in this city.' He spoke with the updrawn sentences of an East Anglian which turned every statement into a question.

'How much did you get for your geese, Barbary of Norwich?'

Proudly, the boy unwrapped a kerchief to show them the three nobles which nestled in its grimy interior. Wellborn as the students were, they were none of them so provided by their fathers that they could afford to pass up a nice sum like three nobles.

Barbary was welcomed, hunkered down beside them, given a swig of ale and had the rules explained to him. Close to, he was even smaller and younger than he'd first seemed, perhaps not even pubescent; his wrists stuck out of his too-short jacket like chicken legs.

The pedlar sighed and got up. 'Stakes too high for a poor working man,' he said. 'Good luck, lad.' He tossed his dice into the newcomer's hands. 'Take these, for they

21

brought none to me.' He shouldered his pack and went his way.

The light summer clouds passed over their bent heads as the dice winked their eyes on the board and the nobles passed, as nobles should, into the hands of the nobility. 'You've lost, Barbary.'

But they'd infected him. He snuffled and begged. He'd wager his jacket, his cap, anything that was his on one last throw.

The soft-hearted of the students was stern: 'Take the goose trail home, Barbary, like the goose you are. London's not for you.'

Still he whimpered and dragged from his none-too-clean neck a tarnished piece of wrought metal which ended in twists. 'I'll wager this, what a lady gave me.'

The thing was passed round. 'It's as base as he is.' But the son of the royal assayer scratched it with his thumb-nail, bit it, widened his eyes and said he would meet the wager with all that he had. The soft-heart refused to play and he was villified. 'You're a woman, Philip.'

Onto the board went the coin they'd come out with, the pedlar's winnings, the three nobles and Barbary's dirty necklet. 'The first to throw two treys wins.'

The dice scattered in spotty variation. Barbary's rolled out of his hand, rattled, teetered and composed themselves into a pair, a neat pair, each with three eyes.

The royal assayer's son snarled. 'Let me see those dice.'

But a figure panted up to them, shouting, and passed them at a run. It was the pedlar and he was yelling: 'Excuse me, gentlemen, but the bulldogs are loose.'

Bulldogs at Lincoln's Inn went on two legs and were no less ferocious than the proctor's dogs the students had left behind at university; no more than those dogs had done did these approve of students who were out of bounds without leave and who, moreover, were gambling. In a second four well-born rumps were heaving themselves over the back wall of their Inn; Barbary, with his winnings, his dice and his necklet, ran in the direction taken by the pedlar, a man who seemed to know where he was going to judge by his corkscrew nips through alleyways and passages so small they could admit only thin persons. Barbary was thin; he kept up.

One after another they ran past Ship Inn and the fashionable drinkers who crowded it since the Queen had given it to dancing Sir Christopher Hatton, but at the far end of Ship Lane fashion stopped. The playing of the minstrels in the Ship's gallery faded, to be replaced by a silence into which the pedlar whistled a phrase of three notes.

Here, where upper storeys overhung the lane and turned it virtually into a tunnel, they were at a portal less exalted than Temple Bar which was parallel to it some hundred yards to the south but more selective in those it allowed through. It was a frontier post demanding a passport. The pedlar, by his whistle, had just displayed it. Those who sounded the passnotes went into a city secret from those who took the Temple Bar route. It was known to its familiars as the 'Bermudas', a place where magisterial writ didn't run, where a system of roads, residences and cut-throughs served their users above ground much as the Roman catacombs had enabled the early Christians to evade their hunters underground.

A person might get into the system without sounding the passnotes, but it was doubtful if he would ever get out.

Hearing Barbary's footfalls behind him, the pedlar turned, grabbed him by his jerkin and hauled him into a doorway.

'Give.' The dice which had been specially made by a gentleman called Bird in Holborn were handed over. So were the three nobles and Barbary's winnings. The necklet was back in place and hidden under his collar. 'Is that all? I reckoned them worth over four pound.'

The students had actually been worth nearer five, but Barbary didn't mention the fact. The pedlar had his original investment and a hundred per cent profit. He'd have to give forty per cent of it to the chief of his Order and most likely he'd spend the rest on drink. Barbary, who disapproved of drunkenness, was saving him from inebriation. He didn't mention that either.

'What did you prig? And don't tell me you didn't, you little filcher.'

Various items which had once belonged to the four students emerged from unexpected parts of Barbary's clothing, a handkerchief, two quills, and two acorns.

'Acorns?' The pedlar cuffed him.

'Oh yes,' said Barbary, and his indignant irony was now in the London accent, 'I could take them out and examine them, couldn't I? Oh yes, they'd have liked that. I thought they was buttons.'

A casement opened over their heads. 'Is that you, Wilkin?' called a female voice. 'Message from the Man for Barbary. He's on the cart and wants a melter.'

'Girl or boy?' asked Wilkin.

'Girl.' Some items of clothing thrown down by the owner of the voice flopped over their shoulders.

'Horse shit,' swore Barbary. 'I hate being a girl.' But in the realm they inhabited a summons from the Upright Man was royal. 'And don't glim. Aren't I humiliated enough?'

As the cap came off his head and a blonde wig went on it and as a panniered skirt covered the jallyslops, the jerkin being replaced by a blue bodice, it wasn't so much humiliation that bothered Barbary as the transfer from a male pocket to a female of a nice little tinderbox which had only minutes ago belonged to the avaricious son of a royal assayer.

The pedlar turned round to face a girl who, reverting to bare feet instead of clogs, was shorter than the boy had been and whose startling green eyes peeped out from fair curls in the essence of innocent femininity. 'Give us a kiss,' he said.

Barbary's rosebud mouth uttered unfeminine phrases. 'Where's the Man?' he shouted up.

'Down Fleet Bridge by now. Hurry, he said.'

Wilkin the pedlar watched Barbary disappear down Grange Alley towards the network which would bring him out at Fleet Ditch, running with the speed of a boy but with the unmistakable hip movement and upheld hands of a girl.

'Lucky he fell in with us,' said Wilkin to himself, 'or he might have become an actor.'

Among the continual entertainment provided by the streets of London the beating of a beggar ranked high, combining as it did the infliction of pain and an uplifting example to the worthy that the unworthy weren't getting away with anything. The beggar tied to the back of the cart and being whipped by two constables as he stumbled in its wake was as unworthy as they came, a sturdy man in his prime whose back might be sprouting his own blood at each cut of the whip but whose facial scabs were daubs of pig's or lamb's blood. Connoisseurs of beggar's tricks pointed out to the less well-informed spectators that the unsightly lumps which deformed the man's neck and arms were of clay and coming off fast, as were his bandages. There wasn't anything wrong with his lungs either; the man's howls rose over the rattle of the cart's wheels on the setts of Ludgate Hill, the laughter of the crowds as they paused to watch him go by and the jeers of small urchins running alongside him. The constables were as lusty as the beggar and laid on their whips with the energy of men who'd discovered more money in the beggar's purse than they earned in a month.

Darting from between the legs of the spectators came a little girl whose clear treble voice dominated even the beggar's shouts. She flung herself at the beggar crying: 'Father, oh father.' One of the constables threw her aside so that she fell into the road, but she picked herself up and ran on, her little hands pressing into steeples of prayer as she begged the constables to spare the man she called father. 'Oh I know he has fallen into evil ways, but he was a good man once.' There was an obstruction of traffic at the top of Lud Hill, as there always was, and the child made good use of the pause, appealing to the constables and crowd alike: 'He was wounded fighting in the Low Countries for our Queen and has since lacked employment, oh pity him, good people.'

Tears splashed down her face and the London crowd, as easily moved to sentimentality as to anger, began to call out to the constables to whip the beggar more kindly.

'He was desperate,' called the little girl, flinging herself at the beggar's waist and falling once more as, less roughly, the constables dislodged her, 'for my mother is dead and he is the sole support of my little crippled brother and me.' The little crippled brother was a melter's classic and the younger constable paused in his whipping. 'I didn't know he had a crippled young 'un.'

'They always have,' said the older constable. 'Get on

with it.' But he was affected by the crowd's change of mood, if not by the wails of the child, and he wielded his whip with less enthusiasm.

Both the beggar and Barbary were estimating with the judgement of experts how much the beggar's back could stand and at what point in the journey across London he would be disabled. There'd merely be stinging pain up to Cheapside, but by Poultry, where they'd be delayed by flocks of duck and geese, the hide thongs would be biting into muscle. By the time they got to their destination, the Tower, the laceration would be irreparable. On the other hand, the growing weariness of the constables' arms would make them grateful for an excuse to ease up.

As they went round Paul's churchyard to Paternoster Close, Barbary, keening with artistry, began looking out for a melter's aid. They needed a clergyman, not a local prelate or canon – they were too bedevilled by London wickedness to have pity on its perpetrators. A nice, innocent out-of-town reverend was what was wanted.

As they passed opposite the north door of the cathedral the sounds of the city were quietened by a waft of vocal incense, holy, beautiful, the mighty *Spem in alium* being practised for the Queen's birthday Mass by Paul's forty-strong choir. For a moment the universe in which Barbary circulated was set against another he did not understand. The strange words that always came into his head at such times dinned 'Hug Adam, shun Eve'. He pondered for the hundredth time on their meaning, and his tears dried: to cry for real was one of the few things Barbary couldn't do.

A jerk of the beggar's head brought him back from wherever he had been, another directed his attention at a clergyman whose ruddy, surprised face and thick boots proclaimed him to be a provincial. Barbary ran up to him and tugged his sleeve: 'The goodness in your brow tells me God will listen to your prayers for my father's soul, though it has fallen into wickedness through ill fortune. Please sir, take pity on his penitence.' Barbary's fluency and accent proclaimed him a girl who had been brought up for better things.

The clergyman was a good aid. The appeal to his and God's higher authority established a recollection of his own worth in a city which had part repelled, part fascinated and totally bewildered him. He trotted alongside the beggar. 'Art thou penitent, my poor man?'

The beggar swore he was to such effect that the clergyman began remonstrating with the constables not to distract the man's attention from penitence by too much whipping. From then on, apart from the occasional flutter of hands and a well-directed whimper, Barbary could coast. The constables grumbled that they were obeying a magistrate's order, but the clergyman pointed out that he was obeying God's, and the journey to the Tower was completed to the drone of the aid's voice and at less than one whip-flick per hundred yards.

At Tower Hill the beggar was transferred to the pillory until dusk. A hanging and quartering the day before made a mere beggar in the pillory small beer and, apart from a desultory cabbage and four rotten eggs, most of those fielded by the brave, pathetic daughter, little was thrown at him. The greatest danger was in being bored to death by the clergyman's preaching which went on for the afternoon until he tired and strode off to do some sightseeing. Down in the river, where masts could be seen packed as close as rushes, the big ships sang their siren song to Barbary. 'Hug Adam, shun Eve,' they sang, and he began to wander towards them in a reverie until the beggar's sharp: 'Don't leave me, daughter,' called him back to duty.

He draped himself pathetically at the foot of the pillory and mentally counted the day's gains. Apart from the tinderbox and his own profit from the dice game, he'd prigged a medal from the younger constable, an apple from a costermonger in Cheap and sixpence from the clergyman. 'Good work, Barbary, my fine fellow.'

The streets began to clear towards dusk and they were alone. 'You took your bloody time,' said the beggar. With his staring head and hands pawed through the holes in the stock board he looked like a dog. In Barbary's opinion that's what he was.

'Saved your fokking back, didn't I? I was dicing some fish at Lincoln's Inn for Wilkin.'

'How much?'

'Two pound and sixpence.'

The Upright Man entered his forty per cent in his capacious mental ledger. 'Not bad,' he said, 'and you make a good pretty dell.' He ran a fat tongue over his lips. 'Pity you ain't.'

'Fokking glad I'm not.' All girls in the Order were handed over to the Upright Man when they were old enough for their first sexual experience, a procedure known as 'breaking', after which they became bawds paying ninety per cent of their earnings to the Man. There was no profit in womanhood, Barbary reckoned. Only the pox.

Behind them the Tower was closing down for the night, booming with the shutting of heavy doors, rattling with keys. Shouted commands indicated the change of guard, and a few men came strolling through the wicket for their night off, giving no more attention to the pilloried beggar than to the tarred heads which topped the high poles above him.

Barbary munched his apple and considered the heads that had been there for as long as he could remember and were now outlined like rotting poppies against the remaining August light. The barn owl which nested high up in the White Tower flapped heavily over the wall and perched on one of them to consider its night manoeuvres, giving the skull a grotesque helmet.

'What'd they do, them heads, Abraham? To be topped like that?'

'Traitors against Her Majesty,' grunted the Man. 'Earl Desmond and his men. Irish rebels. Fry in Hell, the lot of 'em.'

'Krap on 'em.' Of the twelve thousand words which the Renaissance had added to the English language, Barbary used most frequently those which had been brought in by Dutch sailors. Admiring the Queen who had once been threatened with having her own head cut off but had sworn and wriggled and tricked herself out of danger, Barbary was hostile to anyone who wanted to endanger her again. In Barbary's opinion, Elizabeth's accession to the throne had deprived the Order of a useful potential member. In fact, only last week, his eye had been caught by a stall selling cheap plaster casts of the royal profile commemorating the forthcoming royal birthday, and he'd been so moved by patriotism that he'd stolen one.

A respectable figure was puffing up the hill and the

Man raised his head with hope and difficulty; it was time for the constables to come and release him. But it was Cuckold Dick, clutching a stomach not shaped for speed. 'Foll's got a simpler, Abraham,' he panted out. 'We'll be crossbiting in an hour, but he's a big 'un and we might need a clincher. Foll's asking for Barbary.'

'Piss,' said Barbary. 'Must I do everything in this town?'

'You're the best, Barb,' said Cuckold Dick simply. 'Can we have him, Abraham?'

The Man dwelt at length on desertion, on the possibility of being left here all night at the mercy of any passing extremist, on the dereliction of constables who forgot their duty.

Dick cut in: 'The simpler's a rich 'un, Abraham. Gold buckles on his stampers.'

Uprightness struggled in the Upright Man's soul against selfishness, and won. 'Take him.'

'Am I a boy or a girl?' asked Barbary, loping beside Cuckold Dick.

'Boy, Foll says,' Dick told him. 'Choirboy for preference. You got a singing-cheat's rig?'

Barbary's mind scurried rapidly through a wardrobe cached all over the city. 'I got everything,' he said.

The Pudding-in-the-Cloth located in the bewildering back streets of the Bermudas was what was known in Order cant as a 'travelling' tavern, not because of its mobility but because every so often it found it judicious to close itself down and change its name and tenant. But whatever its sign said it was called, its regulars knew it as the Pudding, knew, too, that whoever its official tenant might be, its real landlady was Galloping Betty, the terrifying bulk who supervised its every activity from a carved chair, big enough for a throne, set on a dais at the far end of its main hall.

The tavern was old but spacious – Galloping Betty claimed it had once been a town house of Henry Percy, the 4th Earl of Northumberland. A gallery ran round its upper storey leading off to many private rooms, its kitchen served unfancy but good food, it possessed an excellent cellar and its ale was strong. Less obviously, it contained two cupboards with false backs which led to secret stairways, more exits and entrances than a weevilled cheese and at least one underground passage which came out in another house entirely.

Difficult to find for those who didn't know it, the Pudding was guarded by sentinels who could sniff a magistrate's man at forty paces and misdirect him, as an island set about with lodestones deflects the needle of a compass. The really valued customers were those who only came once and were led to it by devious routes which they could rarely retrace, to be gulled, crossbit, simpled, cozened, versed, barnacled and otherwise parted from their money.

As for the regulars, only the higher ranks of the Order were allowed in. Galloping Betty stamped, sometimes literally, on mere curbers who stole washing, foins who cut purses, and the poorer bawds. These had to do their drinking and practise their illegalities with the common sailors in the stews nearer the river.

'If he be not an artist, let him not near me,' was Galloping Betty's motto; only the Order's aristocracy, the cousiners, the versers, the crossbiters and the beauties were allowed to use the Pudding for their trade. Even the Upright Man had to shed his beggar's rags when he attended the tavern, despite the fact that he took much of its profit.

Barbary's skills had upgraded him to junior status among this excellence and he still experienced pleasure in approaching the Pudding, anticipating the welcoming jerk of Galloping Betty's chins at his entrance, an admission that, young as he was, he had joined the elite of his profession. Besides, it was an attractive place. With its doors and leaded windows open to encourage the circulation of the heavy August night air, it exuded the sounds of bonhomie and a lute. The smell of roasting capon, candles and scent counteracted the stink of the drain which ran outside it.

Poll and Doll sat in one of the casements, not in the vulgar way that common bawds attracted customers – Galloping Betty frowned on that – but laughing and talking, the flash of their white hands as they fanned themselves and the sweetness of their voices a lure. In this light the surfling water on their cheeks made them look fresh and pretty.

Barbary ignored the invitation of the open door, preferring to squeeze down the passageway between it and the next house, which belonged to the Upright Man, and into the yard behind. Here was the backside of the Pudding, a sinkhole where weeds grew between cracked paving and where flies clustered on human ordure and the faeces of the chained, panting, skeletal dog which lay among them.

Barbary ran up a wooden staircase to a first-floor door which led to a storeroom which in turn led to the Pudding's gallery where a watcher could spy through the balustrade at the hall beneath without being espied. The room was crowded, the noise at roistering pitch but no louder. Through the carving, Barbary's eyes reconnoitred the hall in a second, assessing situations, docketing the unknown customers. The fat cove in the corner with Foll would be the simpler to judge from the gold buckles on his shoes. The young conies playing cards with Soth Gard and Harry Agglyntine looked gentry in possession of gelt; well, they wouldn't have it by the time they left. Gybbin was explaining his alchemy to a provincial who seemed capable of believing that gold could be made from goose grease. The two coves Poll and Doll were fascinating elderly merchants; Barbary, who never forgot a face, recognised one as a grocer from Shoreditch. All correct there.

The only person in the room whom Barbary couldn't place, and whom he therefore found disturbing, was the cove with Moll. He was dressed in good black, thin as a barber's cat, a mole on his nose and something on his mind. And it wasn't Moll. The man was acting lechery, pawing at her arm and smiling, but his eyes were roving the room. Barbary could see that Moll was disconcerted. Galloping Betty was regarding him with the suspicion accorded to those whose presence in the Pudding couldn't be accounted for. She didn't know who he was, and he worried her.

Keeping to the shadows so that the simpler shouldn't lay eyes on him prematurely, Barbary moved quietly down the stairs. Down in the hall was somebody he wanted to speak to, someone he always wanted to speak to. Cuckold Dick's arm came out from a darkness to pause him: 'Got the cheats?'

'Yes.' He moved on. All things were 'cheats' in the

31

Order. The canting – its language – reflected a profession in which nothing was what it seemed, a distrustful patois in which rings were famble-cheats, aprons belly-cheats, hats nab-cheats, pigs grunting-cheats, ducks quacking-cheats and a garden or orchard a smell-cheat.

Using the crowded tables as cover, Barbary moved close enough to listen in to Foll and her companion. The simpler was drunk and had got to the can't-we-go-where-we-can-be-alone stage and Foll was countering with if-only-we-could-but-what-of-my-husband in her best never-been-unfaithful-before giggle. Barbary passed on; Foll was his favourite among the beauties, skilled in her trade. In half an hour she'd make her move. He whistled three notes as he slunk past to tell her that he and Cuckold Dick were ready to take their posts. Foll smiled into the simpler's eyes.

Cautiously, Barbary reached his destination and slid onto the floor to sit beside his friend, Robert Betty. 'Who's the foreign cheat? He was marking you.'

'He's been marking everybody. I don't know who he is.' Robert wasn't interested, being intent on a book. 'Long says he's a spy.'

'Who for? Queer Cuffin?' Queer Cuffin was the Chief Magistrate.

'Dunno.' Robert was getting irritable. 'Long says he doesn't know who the fokker is. Cut off, I'm reading.'

'I'm going to read and all. The Jackman's giving me lessons.'

'What in? Ale swilling?'

The Jackman, an ex-monk, had received a pension after the dissolution of his monastery and had ever since been spending it on an attempt to dissolve his liver, an enterprise supplemented by forgery. Barbary devoted much of his lessons to sobering the old man up, but nonetheless the progress he made surprised them both.

Barbary was aggrieved. 'Oh I forgot,' he said, mincing, 'you nosegents is so fokking pure.'

A nosegent was a nun, and the uniform worn by St Olave's Grammar School in Southwark, where Robert Betty was a pupil, so closely resembled the habit once worn by monastics that it contributed to the hell the boy was enduring.

Robert's large hands clamped round Barbary's head

and began banging it against the wall. 'Say sorry.'

'Sorry.'

'Say sorry, my lord Robert.'

'Sorry, my lord Robert.' Robert was dangerous when he was angry, as he was now, and Barbary saw no virtue in pride or stoicism, especially if he was being hurt. Besides, the two of them were as close as brothers. Both were red-headed, though Robert's was a darker, more respectable red than Barbary's, and both were foundlings.

Robert was the elder and his life was the harder because he fought against it, loathing it, contemptuous of the Order, wanting better. His introduction to the Order had been the occasion of a quarrel between the Upright Man and Galloping Betty which had never properly been resolved. It was still legend among the Order members.

'Our Betty's big at the best of times,' Cuckold Dick would say, 'but, Barb, you should have seen her then.' Cuckold Dick had played a commendable part in the story, which was why he retold it often. He it was who'd seen the red-gold cap in a mound of snow that winter's day outside St Benet's near Paul's Quay. He didn't really think it could be gold; miracles didn't happen to Cuckold Dick. But he was an optimist. He went and pulled it out and found the red-gold cap to be hair, beneath which was the face, then the shoulders, then the arms, body and legs of a small child who was quietly getting on with the business of dying. What had kept it alive until then was the sheepskin jerkin and woollen trousers of good quality it was dressed in.

It was while Dick was searching the child for valuables that it began a weak crying and Dick, afraid the St Benet's priest would come out and accuse him of something, shoved the child under his own jerkin and took it to the Pudding to continue the search in comfort.

Being early still, the only person downstairs was the Upright Man and on being consulted he'd immediately suggested cutting the child's left hand off.

'There was logic in it, Barb,' Dick would say anxiously. 'Like he said, the kinchin was dying anyway. Relieve it of its left famble and it could only die the quicker. But if it should survive – and we was going to lavish care on it, Barb – then think what a career would be open to it.'

There was no doubt about that. A begging, handless child attracted sympathy and more money; a begging, handless adult, purporting to be one of Elizabeth's injured veterans, attracted money as a form of guilty reparation from those who knew how heartlessly such men were often abandoned. The Upright Man would take a big percentage of such earnings. But just then had sounded a thundering footstep in the gallery, a shriek, and downstairs came Galloping Betty shouting that the kinchin was her long-lost child who'd had red hair.

'Well, Barb,' Cuckold Dick would always say, 'we all knows as how Galloping Betty has had kinchins in her time and lost most of 'em somehow or other, but this one was only about six or seven and she'd have been past childbearing long before.'

With his usual logic Upright Man pointed this out to Galloping Betty, backing the argument with blows. 'Says he: "Go you, Dick, and get a carving knife and some pitch." But I was held back by Galloping Betty swelling. She gets bigger like. You ever seen an oliphaunt, Barb? Nor me. But imagine one. Imagine something huge, then make it huger. She takes me round the neck and throws me against the wall and she takes the Man and throws him against the other and then she takes the kinchin and puts it in her bosom and challenges us to take it away from her. I wasn't going to, Barb, I can tell you that. And the Man wasn't either. Says he: "Your long-lost kinchin, eh? Have it and the ruffian cly thee." '

Slowly warmed to life in Galloping Betty's bosom, then fed on meat rendered to a pap by Galloping Betty's own gums, the child had lived to be illegally baptised by the Jackman, taking the surname Betty from his acknowl-edged mother and the Christian name Robert after the Earl of Leicester for whom, having seen him once in a procession, Galloping Betty had a romantic fondness.

Nobody showed much curiosity about what circum-stances had brought a little boy near to death in a snow-drift. For one thing, Order etiquette frowned on ques-tions about its members' pasts, a delicacy so deeply ingrained that it was even extended to children. For another, London was littered with abandoned children, some whose parents had come to try and find work in the city and died of its diseases, some whose fathers had gone

34

to the wars leaving them with mothers unable to feed them. Then again, Galloping Betty had discouraged speculation. She had woven her own provenance for young Rob, a hazy myth in which he'd freed himself from kidnappers to return to her, his true mother, and if anybody felt this version lacked a certain authenticity they weren't about to say so.

If young Rob himself remembered much of his early years, he didn't discuss it. Barbary knew that for a long time he suffered from nightmares and gathered that, however much he hated the Order, life within it was still preferable to what had gone before. The acquisition of a child in her dotage brought satisfaction to Galloping Betty, but the Upright Man didn't forgive Robert for his humiliation and did not fail to abuse him verbally and physically whenever he got the chance. The rest of the Order would have been more tolerant of the boy if he'd met them halfway, but as he grew up he became surly and treated both them and their way of life with contempt. The only cheating he showed talent for was at cards, leading some to believe that perhaps he had indeed originated among the gentry. Others said Galloping Betty spoiled him. This she did to such an extent that when the boy made the outrageous suggestion that he receive schooling, she had blackmailed one of her customers who was on the board of St Olave's Grammar School into including Robert among its yearly quota of pupils from the ranks of the 'respectable poor'. Being a late pupil, older than the others and with an inadmissible background, Robert was an outcast there as well. But he persisted in his studies, knowing that they were his only passport to a different and better life.

Apart from Galloping Betty, the only person who loved him was Barbary. Surviving childhood together had given them insights into each other's character available to nobody else and Barbary knew that the outwardly taciturn, surly Robert had an adventurous, amused and amusing side to his spirit.

Left to himself, Barbary wouldn't have questioned the Order training; it was what he knew, he was good at it. It enabled him to take on protective colouring that avoided trouble, and avoiding trouble was as much as Barbary asked of life. In his opinion, Robert's rebellion against it was perverse, a kicking against the pricks, but at the same time he recognised that perversity as admirable, even exotic. And Robert was the one living soul who knew and understood when Barbary 'went into the cherubims' and experienced those strange moments of feeling on seeing a ship or hearing music.

It was at such times that the words 'Hug Adam, shun Eve' came into his head, from far away. He'd asked everybody what they meant, but everybody had a different interpretation. The Jackman said it was a warning against sin.

Robert was similarly enraptured by ships, but his other passion was literature, especially poetry. He spent as much time as he could at the playhouses, having been shown by Barbary the various loose boards in their walls which allowed him in without paying.

As for ships, he explained to Barbary, they were magical to them both because they were transport out of the Order, to far-flung Cathay, to El Dorado, to gold, advancement and fame such as they had given to Robert's heroes, Drake, Hawkins, Raleigh and Frobisher.

Their friendship had been of value to both; Barbary had cheated and stolen double in order to cover up Robert's lacklustre performance, and in return Robert had expanded Barbary's horizons. But now Robert was growing out of the alliance as quickly as he was growing out of his clothes – he was already a head taller than Barbary. His beard sprouted contempt at Barbary's smooth chin and the breaking of his voice mocked Barbary's persistent soprano. He had become a stranger. Frequently, as now, he repulsed Barbary's presence.

Barbary's response to hurt was to pretend to himself and everybody else that he didn't feel it. 'It don't wet Barbary's bib,' he said with dignity – and indeed he had never been seen to cry for real – and moved off to join Cuckold Dick.

Later in the passageway between the Pudding and next door, Barbary changed into his chorister's rig. Keeping out of sight with Cuckold Dick, he could hear Foll's protestations titillate the simpler along the street to the trugging place, which tonight was to be the Upright Man's house. 'But, sir, if my husband should return . . . Hold yourself, sir, for you turn my head with desire. Oh,

36

for my virtue that have been an honest wife till now . . .'
They heard the simpler puffing.

'She'll brim him too soon if she don't watch it,' whispered Barbary.

Dick, who'd crossbit more customers that the sea had herrings, shook his head. 'Trust her.'

'You ever been wed, Dick?' asked Barbary, when the couple had gone into the house. Dick shook his head again – 'Cuckold' indicated his profession, not his marital status.

In the Upright Man's house a bedroom door slammed, and on feet which avoided every squeak in the treads, Cuckold Dick and Barbary climbed the stairs and took up their station outside on the landing. Dick whispered: 'No clinching, Barb, lessen it's called for.' It was the first rule of Order work: when possible keep your face in reserve for another day.

They could hear Foll squeaking and the grunting of the simpler. 'Now, Dick,' begged Barbary. He didn't want poor Foll boarded.

But Dick was an artist. 'I told you and told you, Barb,' he breathed, 'give her time to get his prats bare. A simpler with his hose up's still got advantage.'

He pressed his ear to the door, swaying his hand like a choir conductor, then he gave a downbeat, pulled in a breath and lifted the latch. 'I'm home, my dear. Why, what goes on?'

Peeking through the gap between the door hinges, Barbary saw the simpler's hoisted flag go into immediate droop. Cuckold Dick was as superb as ever, moving from surprise to outrage to incoherent anger. Foll adjusted her bodice and sat firmly on the man's clothes. Sometimes they made a run for it.

But this one, now that he'd got over his first shock, was protesting. He hadn't known the lady was married, she'd led him on.

Barbary adjusted his wig. A clincher was called for. He pattered into the room. 'What is the rumpus, Father? Who is this gentleman? Has he attacked Mother?'

The sight of the bewildered angel, a chorister like his own son – a fact Foll had marked when he'd boasted of it – pierced the simpler with its innocence. The poor lad was tugging at his father's sleeve, as his own boy had done a thousand times. 'Shall we report him to the Arches, Father?' Mention of the Arches, the episcopal court where adultery was punished, and publicised, broke the simpler into a sweat. From then on he was wax.

Cuckold Dick was difficult to pacify. Did the gentleman think his honour as a husband could be bought off by a man who'd dishonested his wife? But gradually, as more and more coins clinked out of the simpler's pockets – Foll, who'd been through them, knew when to give the signal they'd been emptied – it appeared that it could.

The simpler finally made his escape, poorer but of purer resolve. Behind him the broken family wiped its eyes. 'As nice a bite as I ever saw,' said Cuckold Dick, 'and deserving of a drink all round. Better get out of them cheats first, Barb. Just in case.'

When Barbary got down to the street, Robert Betty was waiting for him. 'I need the neck-cheat, Barb. I'm sharping fish tonight.'

'Where?' Robert had begun to go outside the Bermudas to play his card games instead of enticing his victims onto home ground and Barbary thought it unnecessarily risky.

'None of your business. Give.'

Barbary handed the necklet over. It had always been their communal, secret property and had proved itself valuable as a lure in their gaming, earning them extra money that they appropriated for themselves.

'You're a good fellow, Barb. Beneship.' Although he couldn't see his face, Barbary could tell that by relapsing into the abhorred slang of the Order, Robert was apologising for his bad temper.

As he watched the tall figure go off down the street, Barbary saw that even Robert's gait was no longer the Order's. Unless they were cony-catching or versing, Order members never walked like confident men and women; they kept to their toes so they could make a dash for it. But Robert's boots clicked with arrogance, like the gentry's. Nor was he aping. It was as if he were returning to a natural style that was true to his personality. 'Whoever spawned you, lad,' thought Barbary sadly, 'she wasn't one of us.'

He was turning once more into the Pudding when a movement caught the edge of his eye and he looked back. A shadow was following Robert. When Robert turned out of the street, the shadow turned off as well. Barbary trotted silently in the direction they'd taken. Unless he was mistook, the cove who'd been marking Robert in the Pudding was still marking him. 'And what are you up to, barnacle?' wondered Barbary. If Robert didn't want even his best friend to know where he was going, he certainly wouldn't want a stranger in on the secret.

Whoever the barnacle was, he'd followed people before. He was softly shod and he timed his footfalls to coincide with Robert's. Behind him, Barbary timed his to coincide with the barnacle's. Like different-sized dolls controlled by the same puppet master, the three figures moved in concert, each twenty yards apart and heading west.

Because of the pace Robert was setting, they were all going at a lick and it wouldn't be long, Barbary realised, before they were out of the Bermudas. He must act fast. At the next corner he turned off the route the others were taking and pelted down Cutty's Lane into Fenner's Yard, whistling shrilly as he went.

Out of dark doorways figures emerged and followed him. Immediate response to the emergency summoning by one of its members was one of the strictest rules of the Order. 'Rob Betty's got a barnacle,' puffed Barbary as he ran. 'Pick it off him, but no ruffling.' He squinted down Caspar Cut to his left and saw Robert pass its mouth at the other end, followed twenty seconds later by his shadow. 'We can get him just afore Long Acre.'

Robert Betty, still unconscious of what was going on at his rear, stepped into Long Acre via Lamb Court. Behind him the barnacle attempted to do the same, but pillars which had not been there before sprouted across the court's exit. In the poor light they were man-shaped effigies, unmoving, unspeaking, and they did not resemble the sort of men anyone would want to meet of a dark night in a dark alley.

The barnacle paused and looked around, but similar pillars had sprouted at his back. He stepped to one side to pass through the obstruction, but one of the pillars moved to block his way. The barnacle spoke sharply, though there was a crack in his voice: 'Let me pass. I am an officer of the State.'

'Are you, now,' thought Barbary to himself. 'And what does the State want with Rob Betty, I wonder?' He did his wondering in the doorway of the Lamb and watched the impasse at the mouth of its court. The click of Robert's footsteps had faded in the direction of Drury Lane and silence had descended, except for the scuffle of a rat along the edges of the buildings and the shuffle of the barnacle as he tried a feint through the pillars and was stopped once more.

At last Barbary whistled the 'all clear' and the pillars stopped being pillars and scattered, leaving the court to the barnacle and the unseen Barbary, who saw the barnacle's shoulders sag in relief then square as he looked around. At last the man gained sufficient control over his legs to set off again and he ran into Long Acre like a hound trying to retrieve a scent. Barbary watched him cast about and listen, lose hope, and, finally, take the decision to go home.

'And we'd better con where that is, my little State barnacle, hadn't we?' Soundlessly, Barbary loped after him.

Encountering the pillars of Order society had shaken the barnacle's nerve so that he kept glancing behind to see if they pursued him. Only an expert could have followed him without discovery. Barbary was that expert and the challenge to his skill made the pursuit through sleeping London a joy to him. He danced it. The heat of the day had ameliorated into a light warmth that welcomed the movement of his body through it. Stenches were such a natural part of the air that Barbary's nose didn't register them, though it twitched appreciatively at a window box of night-scented stocks as he froze into its shadow to avoid a glance from over the barnacle's shoulder. His mind used the currents of the night to extend itself into the barnacle's brain so that he could sense through them when the barnacle would look round and when he wouldn't, giving Barbary the impression that he controlled the man.

Omnipotence surged through him. He was a hunter, a cat allowing free play to a doomed mouse. He could track the stars to their hiding place in the firmament and they'd never know it. Did the Queen think she governed London? Not tonight. Tonight she had abdicated in favour of Barbary of the Order who could stop men in their tracks when he wanted and release them at a whistle.

'*Nam et ipsa scientia potestas est*,' the Jackman had told him once. If Barbary couldn't remember the Latin, he retained the sentiment. Knowledge is power. There was no one in this quiet city who knew it like Barbary, whose feet had traced every inch of it. He was its king. That barnacle before him, did he know that in this very Shoe Lane along which they were passing, a jump from the steps of Miller Smith's house could take you onto a first-storey windowsill and another would set your arms round a protruding pole of a sack hoist which enabled you by a swing of your legs to surmount the gable and reach the roof? He did not. Earthbound and nervous, the poor barnacle continued east and north while Barbary soared from leads to ridgepole across the roofs, occasionally hanging upside down to make faces only a few feet above the barnacle's head.

If proof were needed that the barnacle didn't know his way well, they were now heading for Clerkenwell, which could have been reached ten minutes earlier. Peeking over the eaves of the Turk's Head, Barbary saw the man pause to get his bearings and then make for Turnmill Lane, stop before a narrow-fronted house and knock on it, da-da-dit-dit-dit. 'Signal,' thought Barbary. 'What a secret little barnacle you are.' A series of leaps and clambers took him to the roof of the house. He heard its door's bars being drawn and the creak as it opened. He waited for a password but to his disappointment there was none. The door closed, leaving the street below him empty. He spent some time crawling from window to window, but they were securely shuttered and he could hear nothing. Whose house was this? The barnacle's? The man's hesitation made it unlikely. Then whose? He could find out. Although this was well outside the Bermudas, there would be some member of the Order who knew. But he would leave his enquiries until tomorrow. 'Done your duty for tonight, Barb.'

He was suddenly exhausted, all power gone. A misery enveloped his back and he felt unusually weighted. He

41

climbed down a lead pipe to reach the ground and set off home, aware that he had a long way to go and lacked the energy for it.

Like many Order members, Barbary lived outside the Bermudas. He had bolt holes where he could pass a night, often without the occupants' knowledge, all over the city, but only one place he could truly call home, and if he was falling ill – and he felt he was – home was where he must be; a sick animal was vulnerable outside its lair.

The problem lay in that his home was on the south side of the river. Barbary knew ways across the Thames which did not involve paying a toll – over London Bridge, under it, hanging illegally onto the painter of a ferry, he'd even swum the river – but they involved an effort which tonight he could not spare. He trudged his way down to the river and then along it, waiting for inspiration. With a shock he realised that the time was the early hours of a new day; there would be no movement on the river this side of the bridge until dawn, and he couldn't wait until then, he was feeling iller by the minute. Pain was dragging at his lower stomach.

Then he remembered a profession whose members used the river in the early hours. A dubious profession, like his own; the Upright Man had once said it ought to be incorporated into the Order. Wearily Barbary forced his legs into a run which took him past the old Blackfriar's monastery and into the wilderness of wharves and quays which lay beyond it. Sure enough, from one of them, dark-clad, dark-visaged men and boys were preparing to launch their barge.

'Give us a crossing, master,' begged Barbary of their chief.

The man hit out at him without a glance in his direction. 'Edge off, fuck-beggar,' he said. Men of his line were not renowned for their honeyed tongue, but this was particularly offensive to Barbary.

'Set yourself this riddle, Barb,' he said aloud. 'When does an empty collier set off from north of the river in darkness? And when is thirty sacks made fifty-six? And would the Cuffin like to know the answer?'

He rose on his toes, prepared to run, as the man looked round. The answer to his riddle was that only false colliers set off in empty barges from the north bank to cross

42

to the south during the day's earliest hours. There they met the true colliers, the charcoal burners from the country, and bought them out, committing the indictable offence of cornering the market. They returned across the river before dawn and re-sacked the coal, filling the bottom of the sacks with dross and only the mouth with good pieces. Adopting the accent and dress of countrymen they then went through the suburbs, selling to the citizenry measures of two and a half bushels of coal dressed up as four. As Barbary had indicated, magistrates were keen to question such men.

Barbary whistled the Order notes while the collier considered his position. Colliers might not belong to the Order, but they were sufficiently on its fringes to recognise its signal and to know, therefore, that they were dealing with a person of consequence.

The collier snarled defeat: 'Get in.'

Barbary crossed the river perched on the stern, well away from the rowers amidships. He chatted to the steersman, the chief collier's son who was an acquaintance of his and whose eyes were frequently blacked by more than coal dust.

A lantern was lit once they got to the south bank and as Barbary was clambering ashore, his acquaintance asked: 'Someone prick you in the prats, Barb? There's blood on your trews.'

Barbary rubbed his rump. 'Got in a ruffle,' he said, 'and sat on the bleeder's head.'

He swaggered until he was out of the colliers' sight and then he began to moan. Pain had come back to his stomach redoubled, but it was agony of mind that made him cry out: 'I never thought it. God, God, what shall I do now?' His voice shifted unseen waterfowl in the lush, soggy-based undergrowth and brought a duck flying out of the reeds, but no comfort from God or man, for this part of Lambeth Marshes was an empty place, as yet no more than partially drained and home to only waterfowlers and outcasts. The few hard paths that ran through it were obscured by August grasses, but Barb's feet knew them of old and carried him mechanically along their tortuous routes towards a slight rise in the landscape where a rushlight burned steadily in the window of a hut, beckoning him home.

Retching with pain, Barbary lurched through the open door and flung himself on the figure which stood inside, knocking it off the balance of its only leg. 'Get off, will you?' it said as it clutched the wall, but Barbary put his head on the man's chest and panted with humiliation and pain.

'Will, oh God, what am I going to do? The monthlies are come upon me. I don't want 'em. I'm finished. Oh Will, they hurt.'

Will Clampett's face became remote, more through embarrassment than surprise. Barbary might not have been expecting the monthlies, but obviously Will had made preparation for their arrival. Disentangling himself, he went to a shelf, took down some tolerably clean linen strips, handed them to Barbary, stumped to the leather curtain which separated Barbary's sleeping quarters from the rest of the hut, lifted it and pointed. Like a dog commanded to its basket, Barbary crawled onto her straw paliasse. The leather curtain swung back into place. A few minutes later it was lifted again and Will handed in a beaker of foul-smelling dark liquid. After that Barbary was left alone.

There would be no further reference to her menstruation. In referring to it at all, Barbary had broken a house rule. Will Clampett would, on rare occasions, discuss firearms, gunpowder, ballistics, metallurgy, the weather, and even, when pressed, their financial situation. Everything else was 'personal' and therefore taboo. Barbary knew the situation, had expected nothing more, but it did little to relieve her loneliness, just as the vile concoction in the beaker didn't do much for her stomach cramps.

She squirmed out the night in oppressive heat and pain, but most of all at the prospect of a future which was, it seemed, to be dominated by a ruthless and totally disbelieved femininity.

Chapter Three

As far as Barbary was concerned, she had been born seven years old.

She had no recollection of time further back than that and only possessed four bits of knowledge about it. That her nationality was probably Hollandish. That she was an orphan. That Will Clampett had found and adopted her while he was a soldier serving Her Majesty Queen Elizabeth in the Low Countries. That she had suffered brain fever which had wiped the slate of her previous memory clean.

She'd come into possession of these slender facts only as she had become older and even then at the rate of one a year on the annual night when Will got drunk. It was always 8 November and he always got drunk. He was a temperate man for the rest of the year, but on 8 November he got drunk. Barbary didn't know why, and she hated it. It wasn't that Will got nasty drunk like the Upright Man, or silly drunk like Cuckold Dick, or incapable drunk like the Jackman, but he became amenable to the extent where he would answer a personal question, and Barbary was always in terror of what the answer to it might be but was compelled to ask it anyway.

She wasn't sure he told her the truth even then. When she'd asked him why she couldn't remember her past and he had said: 'Brain fever. Wiped your memory clean,' he had been wrong. The brain fever, if she'd had brain fever, had wiped nothing, but it had set up a wall of fog in her mind between her life with Will and everything that had happened previously. Behind the fog was something so appalling that her hands sweated whenever circumstances forced her to approach it. 'Don't ask,' Will had told her from the very first, nor had she wanted to. Being in the Order, where nobody asked questions about anybody's past, was a help. Nevertheless there were occasions when the sheer untidiness of being without origin irked her into trying to discover it.

'Where'd you find me, Will?' she'd asked, on 8 November three years previously. Will's head lolled as his eyes roamed the cottage looking for something to fix on and found it in the kettle. 'Low Countries,' he said. It had been a relief in being unexpected. She didn't feel Low Country. That would do for one year. She switched the subject to Will's own past, which was nearly as big a mystery to her as her own. 'That where you got your ammunition leg, Will?'

Will Clampett's loss of his right leg, she knew, occurred when a cannon he was sighting blew up in a war. He'd never told her which war, whether it was land or sea or what.

Will's eyes squinted on the kettle. 'Bastards,' he said, a term he used not for the enemy he'd been fighting but for his own side. Will's bitterness for his Queen and country went deeper even than the average war veteran's. He had lost his leg and, therefore, his peacetime job as a military ironfounder in Her Majesty's service. Other men had been similarly wounded, similarly displaced; the Order was full of crippled beggars who railed against the promises of pension with which they had been waved off to war and which had proved so empty when they'd come hobbling back. But even these men cheered the Queen's appearances, responded to her war speeches by shouting for the enemy's blood, sparkled of eye as they heard the fife and drum. Will didn't.

'Krap on the lot on 'em,' he'd say. 'Her and all,' he'd add, referring to the Queen with a hatred which shocked the patriotic Barbary. But what the hatred stemmed from Barbary had never been able to get out of him. He warned her off now by shaking an unsteady finger. 'Business arrangement,' he reminded her.

He always said that. Their relationship was based on a commercial contract. He'd helped her so she could help him. She'd needed a guardian, he'd needed a fetcher/carrier. If a customer ever asked: 'How do you manage with one leg, my man?' Will would grunt: 'Got one more than you got, anyway.' By which he meant that he had the use of Barbary's.

Owing to his rudeness and the high price of the raw material from which he made his guns, customers were few. It was Barbary's earnings they lived on mostly.

Barbary had been happy enough in her male role as a rising young member of the Order. She'd been happy enough with Will; their business arrangement had grown to mutual trust and eventually, though they never embarrassed themselves by showing it, affection.

There was even happiness behind the fog wall. She didn't pursue it because she was afraid of awakening whatever hideousness lay there with it, but occasionally, usually when she heard music, there was a thinning of the mist, an insubstantial horizon formed itself from the sparkles of a turquoise sea and a voice said: 'Hug Adam, shun Eve.' Then the ship always came into view. It was of a type she had never encountered before, with fifteen pairs of oars and a lateen rig; she had looked for it, hoping it would sail up the Thames one day. When she'd enquired of it among sailors and captains and shipwrights, they had jeered at her description and said no such ship existed except in her imagination.

There had been one sailor, however, a Hanseatic, who'd nodded and said: 'Ja, I saw one like dat once. Great galley, oarship and sail both. Big fokker tried to ram us.'

'Where?'

The man had scratched his head to think, as if being nearly rammed was an everyday occurrence. 'Barbary coast? Ja, Barbary coast. You stay 'way from dere, boy. Pirates. Big fokkers.'

'That's my name. Barbary.'

The sailor had laughed. 'You ain't no Barbar. You little red fokker. These big black fokkers.'

So she was no nearer.

In the beginning, Barbary had not so much chosen to be a boy as had boyhood thrust upon her. Will Clampett, ever uneasy with personal matters, among which he numbered everything to do with the female sex, had kept her for a year in the male clothes in which he had first found her, coping with her growth by cutting them where necessary and inserting crudely stitched patches. With equal lack of expertise he kept her hair cropped.

It was no blame to the Upright Man, therefore, when he looked into the cellar which was their residence – in those days they lived in the Bermudas – that he mistook the sex of the minute tatterdemalion he found there.

'Just the article,' the Upright Man said, and offered Will a penny for the use of his ward in a day's begging. At the time Will was suffering from one of his recurrent bouts of ague and was too delirious to give or withhold his consent. It was a desperate Barbary – they hadn't eaten for two days – who agreed, though even then, young as she was, she held out for a wage of two pennies.

On that day and all the days that followed, her instinct told her to keep her sex a secret. On the road the Upright Man urinated wherever he happened to be when the wish came upon him, and he told Barbary to do the same. 'Get it out, boy,' he grunted, getting his own out, 'give it air,' but she insisted on relieving herself in privacy. 'Will says it's a personal,' she'd piped up when the Upright Man jeered at her. Although Will was a newcomer to the Bermudas, his taciturnity commanded respect, as did his skill making firearms, and the Upright Man was not prepared to offend him even while he scorned him for a 'Puritan', a term of which Barbary was ignorant, since Will either regarded religion as a personal or had none at all.

Barbary was a success as a kinchin co. The brightness of her hair combined with the white of her face to touch hearts and pockets. The Upright Man grumbled that they'd do even better if the boy lacked a famble and had a scar or two, but Will thundered 'No' when it was put to him, so Abraham contented himself by smearing the child's hands and legs with noxious substances like crushed rose-hips, which caused scratching which in turn caused bleeding and had to do.

As she grew older and was drawn deeper into the Order, Barbary blessed the childish intuition which had hidden her sexual organs from the Upright Man. Abraham in his own words was 'partial to 'em younger' which meant he frequently pre-empted his *droit de seigneur* over the nubile girls in his section of the Order and raped them before they reached puberty. His predilection was for the defenceless and since he occasionally buggered the more effeminate and frightened among the boys – he'd been known to look lustfully on good-looking goats – Barbary developed aggression as protective colouring.

Being inarticulate, the Upright Man was daunted by words, so Barbary's language became foul and fluent. While giving her chief no reason to complain of her as an Order member, she showed him she was unafraid by impudence. She swaggered, she boasted, she hawked and spat in a caricature of male bravado. She flirted with the bawds.

She backed all this up by becoming proficient in the art of self-defence. There was no lack of experts to learn from. By the age of ten Barbary could throw a knife and skewer a bumblebee from twenty paces. She knew which part to press on a man's neck to render him unconscious, and which bit between his legs, when kicked, rendered him temporarily useless. Best of all, she knew how to avoid the situations in which these skills became necessary.

Gradually this second, male, nature overtook whatever her real nature might have been and enlarged it. Boyhood conferred the freedom of London on her. She could go where she pleased, released from the lacings and petticoats which cramped other girls' bodies.

Having broken all the rules with success, she had come to believe there were no rules. Whoever governed the universe, Barbary thought, when she thought about it at all, she could cheat it like she cheated everyone else. There'd be an escape from the laws of nature as there were ways of escaping the laws of man. The tidal governments on women, 'having the cousins come to stay' as the bawds called menstruation, must surely pass her by. From the beginning of her time in the Order, she had seen how vulnerable to invasion the female body was. She had heard Goll die in agony after one of Galloping Betty's abortions. She had watched Coll degenerate from a potential beauty to a tired old woman of sixteen, dragging kinchin around the streets. There'd be an exception in Barbary's case, bound to be. They wouldn't wet Barbary's bib. She would go on as she was until she'd risen high in the Order and could kick the Upright Man's arse for him.

Tonight she knew there was no exemption. She'd been nabbed by the celestial Queer Cuffin who'd put out His hand and imposed this humiliating and bloody torture on her. Sentenced her to life.

By morning the pain had lessened, and Barbary's mind ranged its new prison, like the bear in the pit at Southwark, nosing for a way out. She could go on as she was; pad those stubs of breasts she'd pretended hadn't been developing. Get away with it. But for how long? How long before her beardless face became a joke?

Yet there were beardless men. The Jackman was one. Get away with it, get away with it, get away.

For the first time she tried to envisage life outside the Order. Staying in it as a woman was a thought to make her retch. But was it better outside? Barbary squinted into a store of knowledge gathered from observation of market women, poor hard-working sluts that they were, women whose purses she had filched in her cut-purse days, gossip from servants about their mistresses with their forced marriages and their child-bearing and their disagreeable husbands, and decided that there wasn't much to offer her there either.

The only person she'd liked to have been was the Rome-Mort, Queen Elizabeth herself. 'And they ain't going to offer you that position, Barb.'

Well, what?

Dawn came through the leather curtain of her chamber and with it Will's voice: 'You going to stay there all day?'

'What if I am?' yelled Barbary. If womanhood was going to be as enervating as this, she might keep to her bed for ever. Krap on the lot of them. But she got up because she was uncomfortable and hungry.

She went out into the yard at the back of the cottage and cranked up a bucket from the well which went down to a sweeter spring of water than the cattle-trampled streams which ran through the surrounding marshes. She poured some into a ewer for the day's needs and the rest into a bowl so that she could wash out her blood-soaked clout. 'Fokking cousins,' she swore as she washed. 'How long do you come to stay?' She had no idea how long the bleeding could be expected to continue; it occurred to her that it would look odd if, in her male persona, she even asked. She wondered if Will knew, decided he didn't and, anyway, would regard the matter as a personal.

In the distance the late dawn chorus of guns reminded

her that it was Sunday, when the good went to church and wildfowlers came to the marshes to kill birds and make the marsh-dwellers' lives miserable. For years Parliament had tried to stem the use of handguns by increasingly querulous statutes. In Henry VIII's day it had been feared that Englishmen would forget how to use the longbow. Penalty £10 fine. More recent Acts had recognised that the handgun was here to stay but had tried to prohibit the use of hail shot, partly because it was wasteful and killed more birds than a man could eat at any one time, partly because it killed nearly as many Englishmen by accident, but mainly because it required no marksmanship. As the latest statute said: 'It utterly destroyeth the certainty of shooting which in wars is most requisite . . . therefore shall no person under the degree of Lord in Parliament shoot in any place any hail shot or any more pellets than any one at a time.'

This prohibition was no more effective than its predecessors. All degrees of Englishmen, or all those who could afford a gun, came to the marshes to spray pellets like animated pepperpots. Their aim was generally awful. 'Shooting birds that died last summer,' as Will described it.

On this one matter Will took the side of the government. Hail shot was unscientific. The wildfowlers' guns were more likely to injure them than the ducks. Not usually a cruel man, he took vengeful satisfaction on the quite frequent occasions when a wildfowler, bleeding from a missing nose or finger, was helped home by his fellows along the path past Will's cottage, the man's gun having blown up on him. 'You get your money back,' Will would shout after them, 'and use a better gunsmith.'

Will's handguns never blew up. The ones he'd made for Barbary and himself lacked the ornamentation so beloved by wildfowlers – 'tarts' guns' Will called those, with their chasing and inlays – but seven times out of ten the ball they expelled hit what it was aimed at. Will used good metal when he could get it, bored the barrels to perfect straightness, measured out the powder for his cartridges with meticulous care and ensured that each lead ball coming out of the mould he had made himself weighed exactly the same as the last.

Widow Dawkins, the woman who came in every now

and again in an attempt to clean up their cottage and get Will to marry her, urged him continually to make his fortune as a gunsmith. 'Advertile yourself,' she nagged in her thick Bristolian accent. 'Stop living in this squalol.'

Will would do neither. Handguns were no more his interest than self-advertisement. It was true he was working on a mechanism he was going to call the 'Clampett snaphaunce' which would improve the wheel-lock gun by doing away with the use of pyrites, but that was only because the Upright Man was paying him to invent a gun which didn't give the user's position away at night by the glow of its match, as the wheel lock did.

All science fascinated Will. Whenever Barbary heard that there was to be a scientific lecture at Paul's or the Exchange she told Will and Will went to listen, whatever its subject, mathematics, calculus, chemistry, navigation, bookbinding, drainage.

What distressed him was the lack of scientific thinking in the field he knew best, ordnance. For Will's true love was the cannon, a passion Barbary regarded as odd, considering that it was a cannon that had deprived him of a leg.

'The Italians is scientific about artillery,' he said, 'while we'm still hittin' and missin', mostly missin'.' The out-of-date attitude of the English militarists bothered him. Their tradition of chivalry considered close combat more honourable than long-range bombardment. They had even persuaded the Queen against giving the profession of gunmakers its own charter.

In Will's opinion any other form of armament had been redundant for more than a hundred years, ever since the walls of Constantinople had fallen to the guns of Sultan Mohamet II.

There was no patriotism in Will's desire to see cannons improved, merely an angry conviction that improvement was possible and just wasn't being attempted. He had taken the search for cannon betterment on himself. Lacking a foundry, he made small-scale models in his forge. Their cottage floor was a battlefield of miniature bombards, culverin, basilisks and falcons, all of them workable, though some better than others. One of the reasons Will and Barbary had left the Bermudas for the open spaces of Lambeth Marshes was because Will insisted on testing each piece; and though the resulting explosions were small they had inspired hostility from his neighbours.

'Unscientific buggers,' Will had grumbled when their landlord had acceded to complaints and evicted them.

Loyally, Barbary stood up for her guardian against Widow Dawkins' attacks on the state of their cottage. ' "Squalol?" ' she would imitate. 'This ain't squalor, you old bat,' Barbary disliked Widow Dawkins and Widow Dawkins disliked Barbary, 'this is scientific.'

Comfortless was the better word. A table and two stools were the only concessions to human need on view, everywhere else was a clutter of metal. Retorts, scales, measures, quadrants, astrolabes, globes, hammers, borers, chisels, pipes, wires, pulleys, a still – for 8 November – moulds, ingots stood everywhere, giving the impression of an untidy potting shed petrified.

Such cooking as they did, which wasn't much, was carried out in the forge Will had built in the barn next door. Not for Will and Barbary the bread oven which warmed similar cottages, nor the homely cluck of hens. If they needed bread they bought it, if they wanted eggs they took them from the nests of wild duck and geese, if they had an urge for poultry they shot it.

But it wasn't squalor. Barbary knew squalor: she worked in it. Squalor was the Upright Man. Squalor was what the bawds were forced to. She accepted squalor as part of the Order, which was part of the order of life, but that she could recognise it for what it was came from living with Will Clampett. When she heard preachers extolling 'cleanliness of the spirit', Barbary was reminded not of saints, or virginity, or heaven, but of the untidy, rusted, be-metalled cottage in the scruffy Lambeth Marshes. There was cleanliness. When she entered it she left behind the cupidity, lust and foolishness she traded in and climbed onto an island of such purity that, familiar as it was, it remained perpetually exotic.

It contained things she couldn't cheat, a situation she found intriguing. Here was the honesty of mathematics. Here she experienced moments that equalled the most perfect crossbite in mental satisfaction. Here were eternal truths which could be proved, as when Will had helped her to understand Pythagoras' theorem of the circle. Here she became one of the few people in England who knew that a cannon ball did not shoot out in a straight line and then fall down, but that it performed a parabola. Barbary might be having trouble learning to read, but she was aware that a cannon's maximum range was obtainable at an angle of forty-five degrees. Even greater for the expansion of her mind, which tended to believe that foreigners couldn't teach Englishmen anything, was the knowledge that it was an Italian mathematician, Tartaglia, who had discovered these things.

'He had main silly notions,' Will told her, 'and he had great ones. That old Eyetalian invented the gunner's quadrant.'

So divorced from everyday life was the purity of Will's world, the only purity she knew, that Barbary at no point connected it with killing people. Neither did Will. Guns that blew up were what killed people, or took off their legs. Better guns were scientific.

'I'm cutting off, Will,' Barbary called now, and went out. She never told Will where she was going or why, and Will never asked. He disapproved of the Order, although most of the money for his experiments came from Barbary's activities in it as well as the present patronage of the Upright Man.

There was lots to do. The Dummer was ring-falling at Paul's, where the service attracted crowds, and she'd promised to mark for him. The tinder box she'd prigged from the conies at Lincoln's Inn needed getting rid of; she'd have to do some strong bargaining with Dowzabell to get a proper price for it. First, though, was Robert Betty. Tell him he was being marked; find out who his barnacle was.

She was uneasy about that barnacle. A mere magistrate's man they could deal with, but if the barnacle was an agent of the State, like he said, then a new and heavy element had entered the Bermudas and with it overtones of the rack.

It was still early morning but the sun already flexed its muscles to pour down the heat that was turning the Thames sluggish and the city unbearable. Apart from the banging guns in the distance it was quiet in the marshes, ducks and moorhens having taken their broods out of sight into the reeds. She'd be hot in the velvet cap, the velvet doublet and woollen hose she'd chosen to wear today. She'd hooked the entire outfit from a fuller's clothesline in Westminster back in her curbing days and kept it for best. The only reason she wore it now was that its bunched knickers would hide the shape of the new encumbrance between her legs. Barbary paused and shook her fist towards heaven. 'You and your poxy cousins,' she shouted at it.

Her patience was further tried in Southwark as she approached the bridge to see the usual queues of carts and people waiting to get on to it; not as bad as on a weekday, but bad enough. For the thousandth time Barbary wished that Will Clampett's professional pursuits were less explosive and didn't require living in an area which disadvantaged hers. The bridge was undoubtedly one of the great wonders of the world; nowhere else, said Londoners proudly, did a bridge of similar scale span so wide a river as the Thames. But its undoubtedly magnificent three-hundred-and-fifty-yard length wasn't the problem. It was its width. What with the houses which lined both sides of it, and the shops and stalls which lined the frontage of the houses, there were parts of its roadway that were less than twelve feet across, making it one of the world's smallest bottlenecks into one of the world's greatest cities. As the volume of traffic from the Continent across it increased every year, so did the congestion and the bad temper of the traders and foot passengers who used it. You could hear more blasphemy in more different languages on London Bridge than anywhere outside Hell.

Usually Barbary used one of her alternative routes across the river, but today she was reluctant to submit her best clothes to a wet, dirty boat or to the exercise involved in leaping across the starlings which supported the arches at river level.

While she was pondering she was overtaken by a greater worry in catching sight of a stout, respectable-looking man emerging from the bridge. Cuckold Dick. He was so out of context that for a second she couldn't remember who he was; to see him on this side of the bridge was as disconcerting to Barbary as it was to an adulterer when Dick burst in on him. Cuckold Dick was a city man and to set foot outside London's walls made him so nervous that in all the years they'd known each other, Barbary had never seen him south of the river. He was mopping his face and looking around as if the population of Southwark might suddenly turn savage and blow poisoned darts at him.

He sighed with relief when he saw her. 'Bad news, Barb. There's a seek-we out for Rob.'

'A seek-we? For Rob? You mean Rob Betty?'

'Shh.' Dick dug Barbary in the ribs with his elbow. Like most of London he credited Secretary Walsingham with having spies everywhere. The official notifications that the State was seeking a malefactor were posted up in Paul's churchyard and known as 'seek-wes' from their first two Latin words, '*Si quis*', which further down the notice were translated into English: 'If anyone knowing the whereabouts of . . .' Their publication was reserved for top-class offenders like traitors or seditious priests. The most recent seek-we had demanded the handing over of the two recusants, Edmund Campion and Robert Persons, who were on the run and spreading their Catholic doctrine from the shelter of sympathetic households throughout the country. Only a few days before, Campion had been captured at a house in Berkshire and was even now undergoing interrogation in the Tower.

Dick and Barbary joined the queue for the bridge while he told her what he knew, using cant in case they were overheard. The seek-we had been posted up soon after dawn and within minutes news of it had reached the Bermudas and within minutes after that every member of the Order was searching for Robert Betty to warn him. The Order looked after its own.

'No tour of him,' Dick said. 'Cut he libbed the dark-mans at your ken.'

No, Barbary told him, he hadn't spent the night at her place.

'Why'd the cuffins smoke him? Has he contraried?'

'Gerry gan,' snapped Barbary. To go contrary was to turn traitor. Whatever the authorities suspected Rob Betty of having done, she'd stake her life he hadn't betrayed Queen or country. 'He's being barnacled though.' She told Dick about the night's doings as, at last, they crossed the bridge.

'What like barnacle?'

56

'Tall, lank, face to piss vinegar.' Barbary summoned the man who had followed Robert Betty into her mind with absolute clarity and saw what hadn't registered in the stress of following him. 'Swipe me, Dick, he's seven-sided.' The man was blind in one eye.

They made straight for the Pudding-in-a-Cloth.

On the morning after Saturday night revelry the Pudding usually displayed all the animation of a corpse, but this Sunday it thrummed with the activity Galloping Betty was stirring up in the search for her adopted son. Men and women who'd been out since after first light trying to get news of him were returning with what they'd learned, most of it negative. Robert had been keeping his comings and goings secret lately. But there had been one positive contribution.

'Ap Powell says Rob's been sharping at the Prancer down at Greenwich these past nights,' Wilkin told Barbary and Cuckold Dick as they walked into the hubbub. 'Could be he's there yet. He ain't in the City, never trust me.'

Barbary pushed through to Galloping Betty. 'I'll go, Bet.'

Galloping Betty was chastising Ap Powell for not telling her about her son's movements before. 'It's not nice this, Barb,' she grunted.

'I know, Bet,' Barbary said, soothingly. 'We'll get him safe. Let Ap go.'

Betty glanced up at the man held suspended above her head. She chucked him down onto a table and dusted her hands. 'You save him, Barb lad. You love him, same as me.'

'I do, Bet. I will.'

Betty stroked her light beard. 'Come along of me,' she said. They went upstairs together to Betty's bedroom, a place of hanging samite and cobwebs which Betty, who had entertained Saracens in her time, called her 'Hair-reem'. She shifted her massive, carved bed by one of its legs and raised the floorboard it had rested on. From the compartment underneath she took a leather bag. 'Give him this. Swear on the Earl of Leicester and what guts I'll pull out if you don't.'

Barbary swore on her guts and Robert Leicester.

'Tell him to make for France till I can make all vitty

57

again. I'll send a message to Monshewer Pusher.' The Order was partly international and M. Pousser of Calais supplied much of the Pudding's smuggled wine. 'Best for you to go by river.' Betty let the bed drop back on the replaced floorboard and raised her voice so that it carried down the stairs and, for that matter, into Bermondsey: 'Tell Walles I maund his fastest water-cheat.'

Due to the state of the roads which carried heavy traffic to and from Greenwich, it was as quick to get there by river in a skiff as it was on a fast horse, and definitely less noticeable than passing through the tollgates. Walles's oarsmen bent their backs with the energy of men who had been told by Galloping Betty that the skin would be lifted off said backs if they didn't. Walles himself was at the tiller to use to best advantage the currents and banks he knew like the back of his hand. Barbary slumped in the prow, for once unaware of the river life around her.

If Robert Betty had been consorting with the sea captains who spent much of their shore time in Greenwich and Deptford overseeing the outfitting of their ships – and that, Barbary was sure now, was what he had been doing, in the hope of joining them – it might be that he had got into trouble, because the captains were sporadically in serious trouble themselves. Their policy was brutally simple: to win victory and wealth for their country, fame and riches for themselves. It was a policy which often ran counter to that of the Queen, who had other considerations. 'If you can call hers a policy,' Barbary had heard one sea captain grumble. 'More like a veering bloody wind.'

It was an erratic, fitful, blow-hot, blow-cold wind, praising a captain who raided Philip of Spain's treasure ships one day, and the following week imprisoning another for doing exactly the same. Giving an order to sail in the morning and countermanding it that night. She wanted instant results from her fleet yet refused to pay for them, expecting ships to perform without victuals or crew, demanding daring, punishing rashness.

And it was a wind they sailed close to. The radiance which had shone so recently on the golden, globe-circling Francis Drake had sent men like Raleigh, Frobisher and Hawkins mad to outdo him and into dangerous enterprises which might win or lose the Queen's favour, depending on their success. Frobisher had wagered his all on finding gold and the North-West Passage to Cathay. What he'd found was islands of ice and an ore which he'd thought was gold and had turned out to be pyrites. He was still in disgrace.

When the Queen had lifted the sword on Drake's return, nobody had been sure whether it would knight him or strike off his head, so awful had been the insults he had offered to the Spanish during his circumnavigation. Elizabeth had no love for the Spanish, but she was not seeking war with them. Mendoza, the Spanish ambassador to the English court, was still frothing at the mouth. But the *Golden Hind*'s cargo of a million and a half ducats made its captain a hero, not a pirate.

It was likely, thought Barbary, that if Rob had been supping with gentlemen like these he hadn't been using a long enough spoon.

As they neared Deptford the business of the river enchanted her out of her worry. Ignoring the third commandment – all except the fishing boats, which encountered bad luck if they worked on a Sunday – sea-coal barges, a hulk carrying grain and timber from the Baltic, a wine balinger from Brittany tacked their way up to London against what little breeze there was before the tide ebbed.

Past the southern end of the loop in the Thames formed by the Isle of Dogs they were opposite the Royal Dockyards. The slips held the skeletons of keels being built to new, streamlined specifications. A couple of old galleons were being stripped of their ornamental fore- and stern-castles and banked for a bigger broadside of guns. A huge, finished warship, one-hundred-foot keel and weighing eight hundred tons if she was an ounce, floated in the harbour with her sailless complexity of rigging like an aberrant spider's web against the sky, dwarfing with her size and fresh paint the shabby little hundred-tonner alongside. But it was the small ship that was getting the attention. Battered, badly in need of caulking, she had rowing boats encircling her like wasps and her decks were black with sightseers.

As one man, Barbary, Walles and his rowers uncovered their heads and doffed their caps to the *Golden Hind*.

The mile from Deptford to Greenwich was lined with

ships. 'That old clout-head Philip saw this lot,' Walles said, 'he'd know he couldn't beat us.'

A few were preparing to sail, cannons banging and sailors whistling to tempt a fresher wind out of the sky. Barbary's eye was caught by an unfamiliar red and green ensign hanging limply above the poop of a large schooner bearing the name *St Barbara*. 'Whose is that?'

Walles knew everything on the river; he stole his living from it. 'Martin Frobisher's boat, Antonio of Portugal's ensign. Bound for the Azores to wipe the Dons of their gold.' He tapped his forefinger against his nose. 'Only we ain't supposed to know it.'

So Frobisher was trying to get back into the Queen's good books by raiding Spanish shipping from the Portuguese possession of the Azore Islands.

The Azores, thought Barbary. Tropic islands. She populated them with travellers' tales: palm trees, camels, apes and ivory, oliphaunts and mermaids. Would she go off with Frobisher if he asked her nicely to come and bask in the sun and wait for the Spanish plate fleet to pass by? Would she?

He *was* asking her. 'Barbary. Barb. Come aboard.' He changed his mind. 'No, I'll come down to you.'

There was a rope hanging from the ship's taffrail and shinning down it was the seek-we'd Rob Betty, still shouting. He hung just above them by one arm, one bare foot clamped to the ship's side, the other leg and arm splayed in welcome like a starfish. 'Halloo, Barbary. Halloo, Wall.'

'Drunk as a rat,' muttered Walles. Barbary didn't think so, though she'd never seen him like this; Rob was in a state of joy. He showed no surprise at their being there.

'I'm cutting off, Barb. Frobisher's taken me on. We're sailing the Portugal-co to the Azores.' He let himself down so that his feet rested on the thwart next to Barbary, but he clung fast to the rope, grinning at her with more warmth than she'd seen in weeks.

'I'd have said goodbye but Frobisher decided too fast. We're sailing to catch the tide.'

Dumbly, Barbary handed him Galloping Betty's leather bag. He stuffed it in his waistband, barely noticing it. 'I've left a letter for Betty at the sign of the

Prancer. Take it to her, there's a lad.' A thought struck him. 'Come along of us, Barb.'

An angry head stuck itself over the side of the ship and in broad Yorkshire a voice shouted: 'You're not on deck instanter, you rust-pated booger, I'll cut t'bloody rope.'

Sheer happiness suffused Rob Betty. 'Coming, my lord.' Barbary watched him shin up the rope as fast as he'd shinned down. As he reached the taffrail he paused, clawed something from his neck and flipped it down towards the skiff. Barbary put out her hand and caught it. It was the necklet. She put it on. Rob waved and was gone.

The skiff feathered itself out of harm's way as the *St Barbara* moved slowly out into the river, towed by two pinnaces and with only a staysail set.

'Didn't tell him he was seek-we'd then,' commented Walles. Barbary grimaced; in the turmoil of emotion at finding Rob and then seeing him go, perhaps for ever, she'd forgotten why she'd been searching him out in the first place.

'Na,' said Walles. 'No time. Proper Scarborough's warning that was. Asides, he can lie low as good in the Azores as France. Better. Earn himself some prize money.'

She watched the ship limp down the river. Rob was leaving her behind; a relationship which had meant so much to her was being thrown off by Rob with the rest of his past. She was afraid of the pain she began to feel; if she gave way to grief, any sort of grief, some dam would breach and burst into a flood that would sweep her mind away. Wearily, she brushed the pain under a carpet. To be coped with later. His loss. He'd not wet Barbary's bib. She spat grandly. 'Stuff him. And his ship. She's not the one I'm waiting for anyhow.'

'Bring your arse to an anchor. Let's make back.'

In the gap left by the schooner they could see inshore to Greenwich village, huddled round the river edge of the palace grounds and consisting almost entirely of ship's chandlers and inns. It reminded Barbary of Rob's last request. 'Better find the Prancer and get Betty's letter,' she said. 'The lads want refreshment, Wall?'

Walles shook his head. He wanted to get back to the Pool of London before dark, and in the matter of refreshment and his crew, one thing frequently led to another. 'You cut along and get the letter and cut right back.'

Wandering miserably along the quayside, Barbary checked the inn signs for one bearing the outline of a horse. The Nag's Head. That would be the Prancer. Rob was still enough of an Order member not to call anything by its right name.

She was making for the inn's door when it became blocked by two tall figures, one thickset, the other thin. A thickset hand grabbed her shoulder and a thin hand tore her necklet off so roughly that it took some skin with it.

'Red-headed, all right, never redder.' said the thick one.

The thin man was checking the necklet against some information written on a slate. 'Gold.' He bit at the metal. 'Twisted ends. It's him. Robert Betty, I detain you on the orders of Her Majesty, Queen Elizabeth.'

'Get off,' shouted Barbary, wriggling, 'I'm not . . .' She slumped. Jesus, it was serious if the Queen was posting men at all the river ports in order to arrest a young man with red hair and a gold necklet. So they'd got the wrong one, but if it was pointed out they'd got the wrong Robert Betty they'd go on looking for the right one. The rate the schooner was going, thought Barbary, they could still stop her at Tilbury. But if these shifters were kept busy over mistaken identity for an hour or two, Rob would be safely out to sea. She allowed her mouth to sag in bovine ignorance. '. . . guilty of nothing.'

'That's what they all say. Come along now, you're coming back to town.'

'The Bridewell?' asked Barbary. She'd been in Bridewell before. And got out of it.

'The Tower.'

62

Chapter Four

'In accordance to Her Matie's wishes and your instructions, my lord,' wrote Sir Owen Hopton, Lord Lieutenant of the Tower of London, to Lord Treasurer Burghley, 'I have lodged the Prisoner Betty in the poor Princes' Tower in accommodation such as to meet the comfort of a better sort of person. For, though I have held off as you stayed me in examination of him, the general enquiries such as are meet for all who enter here reveal him to seemeth a rapscallion of the lower orders with no knowledge of the Christian catechism nor deserving of it such as I am unused to lodging.

'It pleased him to accuse your agents of mistaking him for this Robert Betty, saying he knows no person of that name and to offer me forty nobles for his release, whereof he assured me certain friends of his would bring it.

'Your pleasure in all things, my lord, yet to expedite the examination and despatch of this person would be to the relief of your humble and most admiring servant, O. Hopton, Kt.'

In effect Sir Owen Hopton was complaining that Prisoner Betty was lowering the tone of the Tower.

The very name of the great, columned colossus crouching over the city might inspire fear in Londoners, but it was a royal palace even if the Queen did not choose to stay in it, her Majesty being sensitive that it was also the site of her mother's execution; it was also an armoury, and the main barracks for the City soldiery, as well as a place of detention. Though its prisoners had been many and accused of various crimes, they had almost invariably been of good birth. Edmund Campion, he who was at

this very moment receiving the attention of the Tower's
rack masters, might be an accursed massing priest, but he
was lettered and courteous. Yet he was lodged in 'Little
Ease', the worst cell in the dungeons where a man could
neither stand nor lie at full length, while a gutter rat
barely speaking the Queen's English was lodged where
royalty had been pleased to await their appointment with
the block.

Sir Owen received a prompt reply from Lord Burghley, but little satisfaction. Reduced to essentials, it said
that Prisoner Betty could stay where he was and sweat it
out. It gave no indication of what, if anything, Prisoner
Betty was accused of, nor how long his sweating must
continue. Knowing the many burdens the Lord Treasurer was carrying, Sir Owen feared it might be a long time.

The Governor was right. Physically, Barbary had never
known such luxury, hadn't dreamed it existed. She had
privacy, so she could go on concealing her sex. Her room
was small but wood-panelled with a four-poster bed and a
mattress, though no other bedding. Underneath the bed
was a chamber pot which a woman servant, accompanied
by the keeper, took away to empty and returned every
morning. There was a chest for clothes, a table and
stool, an aumbry in the wall which contained a bowl and
pitcher. No fireplace, but a brazier, unlit. The window
was minute and high and she had to stand on the stool to
see out of it to the yard below, but it was glazed and the
view was of a well-kept green where richly varied men
and women passed to and fro. Food came regularly;
bread and ale for breakfast, a hot meal in the afternoon
which, if it wasn't of the highest quality, knocked the
spots off anything Will Clampett had ever cooked.

But there were bars inside the window and the room's
door was locked. It was a cell. Unscalable walls and gates,
rearing buildings, vertical drawbridges, iron and stone
made a monstrous Chinese puzzle of which her body in
this small room was the centre. Something stirred behind
the mist in Barbary's mind as she was thrust in and heard
the key turn on her for the first time. This was out of her
class; she couldn't cope with it, it was too big, too grave,
too reminiscent of something evil that dodged just
beyond the edge of her memory. She couldn't cheat this.

Panting, she controlled herself. 'Battle the watch,

Barb.' She'd give it three days and then she'd tell them she wasn't Robert Betty. He'd be far beyond their grasp by then. Friendship could demand no more.

One thing sustained her; the Order knew where she was. The seven-sided barnacle and his mate had brought her to the Tower by river and she'd seen Walles's skiff follow them all the way. She doubted whether even the Order could procure an escape from the Tower, but it made her feel less isolated.

She used cheek to ameliorate her terror. Standing on the stool with her nose to the bars of the window she called familiarly to anyone crossing the green within her vision, or sang them dubious versions of 'Salinger's Round'. When the keepers brought her meals it was to find her lounging like a sultan on the bed. 'Place the vittles on the board, my good man, and don't slop the gravy.'

On the third day she demanded to see the magistrate. 'Old iron britches,' she explained to the bewildered keeper. 'Him what met me when they brought me.'

'If you mean the Governor,' said the keeper, 'he don't come at the beck of any young snot-nose.'

'Snot-nose yourself,' said Barbary, 'and many of 'em. You fetch him. Tell him there's ointment for him, forty nobles to let me go. I got friends.' It was a sum she couldn't imagine anyone turning down. 'Tell him I been wrongful arrested.'

'That's what they all say,' said the keeper.

Her necklet had gone with the seven-sided bastard, and her winnings from the game with the students was in her secret cache back at the cottage on the marshes, but tucked into her trunks was the stolen tinderbox.

She brought the box out and slyly balanced it on her hand. 'This for you if you fetch him,' she said. 'Tell him I'm not Rob Betty.'

'Got one,' said the keeper, 'and he don't care who you are.'

'But I can't stay here, I ain't done nothing,' shouted Barbary, suffocating. 'How long before they let me out?'

The keeper shrugged. 'Most of 'em stay here for years and some of them ain't done much either.'

He went out and the key turned on the other side of the door.

Having bruised her toes kicking the door and torn her fingernails trying to open it and rasped her lungs with screaming, Barbary lay down on the floor, curled up like an imprisoned beast, and surrendered the will to live. Food came and went untouched. The chamber pot was taken away and returned. Keepers tramped in and out on their regular inspection and Barbary's breathing became shallower as her body temperature reduced.

The Governor of the Tower was informed, tutted, and called in the Tower's doctor who prodded the body on the floor with his foot and declared it moribund. 'Remark the hair,' he said. 'It is often the case with this complexion that the humours are drawn into the hair, leaving the body unable to withstand circumstance. We doctors call it incardinitis.'

'Am I to inform the Lord Treasurer that his prisoner is dying of red hair?' demanded Sir Owen irritably.

'In layman's terms, layman's terms,' said the doctor, a man whose gown smelled of too many slopped urine samples. 'We can introduce a moiety of belladonna to stimulate the heart if you wish, but in my opinion the boy will not survive.'

The door slammed and locked behind them, leaving the smell of urine to linger with the echo of the doctor's last word.

A patch of sun came through the window on to the body on the floor and warmed it. Its nose was tickled by a sprig of tun-hoof caught in the rushes, and its hunger awakened by a bowl of congealed soup on the table, still awaiting the return of the prisoner's appetite. The doctor's words lanced round Barbary's unconsciousness with sharp, refreshing pain. 'Survive.' 'Not survive.' Her eyelids moved, then opened. So did her mouth. 'You got that wrong, old pisspot,' whispered Barbary. She was ashamed of herself. She drank the soup.

There were English towns with smaller populations than the Tower's at full complement, and life in all its aspects came through the bars by smells and sounds. Keepers' boots echoing, jingling keys, the night and morning stamp of soldiers drilling, handgun fire, cannons booming outside the armoury, prayers, hymn-singing and sermons. Horses on cobbles, blacksmiths' whoo-up, the

66

sighing of forges, pungency of hot iron on hooves. Bread-baking, brewing, mummers entertaining the married quarters, trumpets, the hoop-la of acrobats. Songs, sack-buts, lutes. Sewage, rain, sun on dust. Men swearing and shouting, giving orders, taking them, children playing, washing flapping in the wind, flags slapping on flagpoles, women gossiping and laughing, the calls of itinerant sellers, meat roasting, porridge boiling, lovers whispering, babies giving their first cry.

The Tower was England, a red-cheeked, sweet-smelling English apple with a worm-hole in its core where a clerk sat beside a rack and recorded the words of the man whose joints were being pulled from their sockets.

The keepers were proud of their Tower. At first they reacted to Barbary like old family retainers whose lord had invited an unmannered guest to the house. Like the Governor, they were used to a higher class of prisoner. But as Barbary's behaviour improved – she'd get nowhere kicking against the pricks – they unbent, some even becoming friendly. "Course you ain't got a fire,' Keeper Pobble told her when the autumn turned cold. 'Fires is extra. Exercise is extra. Writing utensils is extra. Candles is extra. Visits extra. Extra food extra.' He looked at Barbary's numb fingertips. 'But I'll see what's to do with a blanket.'

The least pleasant of the keepers was one she never saw. He came round in the early hours when the Tower was deeply quiet, long after the last check had been made on its prisoners.

Barbary woke up to hear someone at the squint in her door. 'What now?' She hated the squint. She heard breathing. Then whispering. The whisperer wanted her to take her trunks down, it told her what to do when they were down. It told her what happened in the torture chamber, it spoke in rhythmic jerky well-used sentences. Foetid words streamed into the room like a smell.

'God's nails,' sighed Barbary, 'one of them.' The bawds had customers like this. She clambered off her bed and went over to the door. 'Want me feared, do you? Gets you proud beneath your navel, does it? Well, listen to me you beef-headed, mutton-mongering, pizzle-pulling whoreson, I live too close to the woods to be scared by owls. So put that up your pistol and piss it.'

The whispering stopped. Barbary heard disconsolate footfalls retreat down the corridor. She went crossly back to bed. 'Is this what we pay our taxes for?' she asked, who had never paid a tax in her life, and went to sleep.

The whisperer came back, though not to her. She heard him two nights later at the squint on the neighbouring door, same breathing, same filth, but this time echoed by a whimper from within the room itself. She was about to call out to tell her fellow prisoner not to be afraid, when she realised that the whimpering was as rhythmic as the whispers. Barbary spat. 'Two pizzle-pullers.' Well, it was no business of hers how people chose to enjoy themselves.

She had been wondering for some time who her neighbour was. The rest of this storey was unoccupied, but food was carried into the room next to hers and chamberpots were carried out, yet she never heard a word spoken by its occupant.

'Who's next door?' she asked Keeper Viney. Viney was the sort who disliked giving anything, especially information. He said: 'Master Never-No-Mind.' She'd have to wait until Pobble was on duty, or Morgan.

'Don't you worry your head about him, bach,' Keeper Morgan said. 'A mimsy, ailing old boyo, that one. Sulk sulk and whine whine it is with him. Irish, so what do you expect?'

'What's his name?'

'Not even sure he's got one, bach. John, is it? The Earl of Desmond's lad, anyway.'

'What, the traitor earl, him with his head on the pole? What's his son doing here?'

'No harm, that's what. Out of the way of his father's sin. Bring him up a Christian and keep him out of rebellion. Powerful little rebellion in that boy by there, though, mind. Pitiful he is and no one to visit him.'

Barbary was indignant. 'I'm not crowded out with visitors neither.'

'Nothing pitiful about you, bach.' Keeper Morgan, like all the other keepers, never witnessed the moments when Barbary wept with worry for Will Clampett and Rob Betty and moaned for freedom.

Morgan was shutting the door and remaining in the room. Barbary eyed him suspiciously and got ready to fight, but Morgan was being careful. 'Against regulations this is,' he said, 'but there was someone enquiring for you, and asked me very pretty to give you a present.'

Barbary clutched at him. 'Who was it?'

'Now, now. A respectable gentleman. Spoke me very fair when I met him outside, he did.'

Cuckold Dick. Lord bless him. Dick could spot who was bribable and who wasn't at twenty paces. 'What'd he give you?'

Morgan removed his bonnet and took out a nobbled kerchief. 'No harm for you to have something to while away time, the gentleman said. And no harm I saw. Like a bit of game myself, and to hell with bloody Puritans.'

Dice, thought Barbary. Please let it be dice.

It was. Five of them, the best that Master Bird of Holborn could devise and as innocent to the unsuspecting eye as a quintet of young virgins. Nestling among them were two nobles.

'Thank you, Morgan. Thank you very much.'

'That's all right, boyo. Have a game one day, will we?'

'We will,' said Barbary.

When Morgan had gone she rushed the dice to the remaining light and rolled them on her hand. Two of them were normal dice, for general use and known as generals. The other three were squariers, two of them langrets, infinitesimally longer on the forehead than the cater so that they would walk the board without turning up a five or a nine; the other a high-and-low man which was weighted to turn up a sice or an ace when it was wanted, depending on the skill of the thrower.

Barbary jumped on the stool and sang to a darkening sky the praise of Cuckold Dick and her Order. Dice? What dull eye saw them as dice? Dice? These five little cubes were fire and food, light and company. They were extras, money, they were power. Such was their magic that, given time, they would transform themselves into large, beautiful, door-opening keys.

But without the resources of education which would have given her brain nourishment, unused to silence and loneliness, Barbary might have degenerated badly, despite the gift of the dice, if it hadn't been for the visit by Next Door's mother, which occurred soon after.

Barbary had been asleep although it was full morning –

she was becoming slothful – when she woke up to the first sounds of furious activity she'd ever experienced on her floor of the Princes' Tower. A burst of energy had come into it and was raising its voice and stamping its foot.

'Will you look at him,' a woman was shouting. 'Will you just look at that sad boy. Is that a lad in possession of his health? Are you getting him somet'ing for his ear?'

'Madam,' came the voice of the Tower's Lord Lieutenant, 'his ears are costing this country a fortune, to say nothing of his nose and his bowels. Allow me to read the apothecary's list: four ounces of unguent for his ear, four ounces of implaster also for his ear, two purgatives, two perfumed lozenges for his nostrils—'

'And what good are they written down? It's his own body they should be in, not a by-our-lady piece of parchment. And another t'ing, what of his exercise?'

'Madam, he refuses—'

'And his education? Is the claimant to the land of Munster to be brought up a brute beast, tell me that?'

'His lands are forfeit, madam, through the fault of his father, as you well know.' Sir Owen was getting agitated. 'You yourself were fortunate to escape the ultimate punishment.'

'Fortunate? Fortunate? Traipsing after the court and begging me very bread, is that your fortune? Me son in confinement and me daughters in penury, is *that* your fortune? And would you wish your wife less loyal to you than I was to me wayward husband?' The accent became more pronounced with every question mark.

'But I am neither a rebel nor a traitor, madam.'

'You're a damn disobedient servant, so ye are, and so I shall tell Her Majesty who has given orders, *orders*, for my son to be brought up an English gentleman and pity on the poor English gentleman who are brought up in soch a manner.'

She'd got Sir Owen on the run. Barbary listened to his 'doing his bests' and 'under difficult circumstances' retreat down the corridor with the woman in full cry after him. Barbary ran to the window; mothers both frightened and intrigued her. This was one to see.

The green was busy with women going to Aldgate market, but Next Door's mother stood out in the crowd, though she was dressed like a common woman and shabbier than most. Eleanor, Countess of Desmond, might be down on her luck but she radiated a ferocity of purpose which made people get out of her way. Halfway across Barbary's view she stopped and dusted her hands on her skirt. 'Done that,' said Barbary to herself, translating the gesture, 'now for the rest of 'em. You're a proper one, you are. Teach iron to swim, you could.'

By pressing her forehead hard against the bars she squinted along the wall to her left and saw an anaemic hand rise and fall in an unseen wave through next door's bars. 'That your ma?' she shouted to it.

The hand withdrew, but after a time a weak voice said: 'Who are you?'

'Name of Barbary,' shouted Barbary, 'on temporary loan to the Tower. You Irish?'

'Temporary?' asked the voice in tears. 'When are you going out? Why are you here?'

'Don't know to both,' said Barbary, 'but you can take it I'm confident. I got means.'

'Confident,' wept the voice. 'I was confident once.'

'Cut it,' said Barbary. 'With a ma like that? She'll get you out, she will.'

'She got me in. She and my father.' The voice became pettish. 'Why didn't they stay loyal? God damn them both to Hell.'

Barbary was shocked. Like most orphans, she had an idealised view of the parent–child relationship.

Still, there was no denying that with his father's head up on a flagpole, his mother in tatters and begging her bread from the Queen of England, the boy was justified in assuming they'd taken a wrong turning somewhere.

'What's your name?' she asked. 'John, is it?'

But Next Door had exhausted himself and their communion was over for the day. It continued fitfully as the weeks went by, when Next Door felt like it, which wasn't often. His name was not John, it was James, but he refused to answer unless Barbary addressed him as 'my lord', maintaining that if he hadn't been cheated he would now be James FitzGerald, 16th Earl of Desmond, though why he insisted on a title he was ashamed of baffled Barbary.

She obeyed him because she was desperate for conversation and because she had all the English love of titles.

'Wait till I tell the bawds I been chit-chatting with a real live lord,' she said to herself, 'even if I can't see him, and even if he is a half-alive lord.'

There was no doubt the boy had grounds for grievance. When he was eight he had been taken by the English as a hostage for his father's good behaviour. When the Earl rebelled, James had been confined in Dublin Castle before being brought to England and the Tower.

He had been taught that his tribulations were the fault of his parents. Obediently he hated them. His English guardians told him everything Irish was savage and that Roman Catholicism was the religion of anti-Christ, so he abhorred his country, and its people, and expended what little fervour was in his soul on the Protestant faith.

A sweeter nature would have commanded pity, but James was almost repulsively petulant, a fact which didn't surprise Barbary who had seen too many badly treated children in the Order to believe that suffering induced charm. He told Barbary almost proudly that he had been ill on the day he was born. With what she considered misdirected obstinacy he had continued ill ever since. It was the only obstinacy he had. His diseases were his sole claim to attention; without them he would have been ignored. Even his mother, except for short blasts of caring, forgot him. I'd forget him myself, thought Barbary, if he wasn't all there was to talk to.

He was also depressing. He was convinced that sooner rather than later he would die in the Tower. 'Like the Princes,' he told Barbary. 'They died in this very building, perhaps in my very room. Killed by the Plantagenet.'

'There's a lot of it about,' said Barbary warily. Her knowledge of history was minimal.

'Not a disease, ignorance,' sneered James. 'He was their uncle. It will happen to me.' But why he would be murdered or by whom, he didn't seem to know.

It was getting cold. In the mornings the green outside her window was frosted whiter than the sky. Never a warm place, the Tower seemed to stiffen in the winter like an old man's bones. 'Time for some extras, Barb,' said Barbary.

So far, to the surprise of the keepers, she had bought no comforts with the nobles Cuckold Dick had sent her;

instead she had converted them into small change which, during the short gaming sessions she and Keeper Morgan held when he brought her food, she was very slowly losing. Sometimes she won, but more often she lost. It was why Dick had sent the money: so that she could lose. No angler worth his salt went into a dice game to win every time, it discouraged the fish; worse, it made them suspicious. Morgan's success had hooked him.

'Shame to take the money, boyo,' he said, pocketing another collection of pennies.

'Too good for me,' Barbary said, wearily. 'Pity not to have more players so's I could win sometimes.'

'Well,' said the soft-hearted Morgan, 'there's a gathering down in the guardroom some nights. No reason for you not to join in on that. At your own risk, mind.'

Discipline relaxed within the Tower during the winter as officers entrusted with overseeing the night round became reluctant to leave the warmth of their quarters. The Tower's locks, chains, drawbridges maintained its security and within the impervious shell such prisoners as were liked, trusted or rich were allowed the freedom to relieve the tedium of the keepers' night watch by their conversation and their contribution of a flagon. Barbary joined a company which consisted of night-duty keepers, three or four soldiers who dropped in regularly from their comfortless barracks to enjoy the guardroom fire, a couple of well-born recusants, a scholar-publisher named Stokes who had distributed pamphlets against the Queen's marriage to the Duke of Alençon and still hadn't been forgiven, a Captain Askwith, friend to Frobisher, who had sailed too close to the wind, and Sir Philip Efferton, a minor courtier who had got one of the Queen's ladies-in-waiting pregnant and was waiting for Her Majesty to forget it.

It was a jolly gathering. Under normal circumstances, the courtier, the recusants and even the scholar-publisher would have been constrained from hobnobbing with commoners like Morgan, Pobble, the soldiers and especially Barbary, but the reversal of prison imposed a democracy which turned them into back-slapping good fellows.

Usually in their fire-lit, ale-fumed gatherings there were chess games or a hand or two of cards. Sir Philip rendered ballads in his trained tenor and the soldiers responded with semi-pornographic campaign songs.

With the arrival of Barbary, and without the company quite knowing how, the evenings turned into a floating dice game.

Barbary kept it light-hearted. She contributed her version of 'Salinger's Round' to the sing-song. Without giving away the source of her information, she told scurrilous stories about the bawds and their more famous clients.

As she contributed to the entertainment without pushing herself forward or attracting attention by holding back, the dice moved from Barbary's cuff to her palm with the lightness of moonbeams; squariers when it was her turn to throw, generals when it came time to hand on to another player.

With equal delicacy she weighed the company in her mind, assessing who would take loss without suspicion, whom to keep happy with a win and when and how much, all the while allowing her own wins to mount up in sporadic and unspectacular spurts.

She played the game and the company with the skill of a juggler maintaining four balls in the air, so practised that she hardly recognised how skilled it was. Nor did she feel guilt that she was cheating these men; she didn't think about it. She'd made up her mind years ago that if God and society and the law and all the rest of them who condemned the Order as criminal had wanted it different, they should have offered its members an alternative. She hadn't asked to be in the Tower, she hadn't asked to be born. Survival was the game in progress in this guardroom just as it was outside and she was playing it by the only method at her disposal.

'You win, Barbary,' grumbled Keeper Pobble. 'Gets to something when keepers pay out to prisoners.'

'*Quis custodiet ipsos custodes?*' That was Sir Philip showing off his Latin.

'Pay me in coals, Master Pobble,' said Barbary equably. She let the keepers settle their bets in extras which they procured through falsifying the accounts at no charge to themselves. Her cell was becoming cosy.

'What shall I pay you in, Barb?' asked Sir Philip, who'd adopted the modern mannerism of flirting with anything that moved.

'Cash,' said Barbary firmly. 'What was all that fuss down on the green today? Fellow can't sleep without disturbance in this place.'

'Campion,' said Pobble. 'Damn, three and a one. Off to Westminster for his trial. Your throw, Master Askwith. Personally, I'd hang the bastard without it.'

'And so should I,' said Askwith, 'by the Lord. I win, gentlemen. He was in on the Excommunication Bull, sure as God, deny it though he may.'

'Hang the lot on 'em,' said Keeper Dawson. 'Cut their bowels out.' Barbary cocked her head to one side; she listened carefully whenever Dawson spoke. There was something in his voice. 'Telling 'em to assassinate our Queen, the Lucifers. Well, since nobody else looks like moving, I'd better do the rounds.'

'Good man, Dawson.'

Bad man, Dawson, thought Barbary, fondly watching the keeper pick up his lantern. Dawson was the pizzle-puller, she'd bet her winnings on it. When the time was right and after a judicious application of blackmail and bribery, Keeper Dawson was going to assist her out of the Tower; he just didn't know it yet.

She smiled at the company. 'Another game, gentlemen?'

The conversation turned to the concern that nagged them all: their country's security and the threat of Spain. Something dire was about to happen, no doubt of it. The year had seen the great bell of Westminster toll all by itself. There had been the great thunderstorms of June. An eighty-year-old woman had given birth to a monster with a head like a helmet, eight legs and a tail half a yard long. A pack of hunting hounds had clearly been seen in the clouds over Wiltshire, while in Somerset companies of men dressed in black had marched in procession through the sky – Morgan's second cousin had seen it himself.

Sir Philip Efferton became more and more restive as the auguries piled up and lost five shillings to Barbary without noticing it. 'God's wounds, if there is a war and me unable to fight in it,' he burst out. 'Has Her Majesty forgotten me? I'll write another petition, now, this minute. Pobble, light me.' He ran out of the guardroom, with Keeper Pobble hurrying after him.

'Lovely petitions he writes, lovely,' said Morgan. 'Read me one the other day. In tears with it I was. Poetic. Pity you don't write a petition, Barb.'

'Hasn't done him much good,' Barbary pointed out. 'Anyway, I haven't got all me letters yet.'

'Learn then, boy. Young Sir Sulk-whine is getting a tutor, thanks to his mam's urgings. Orders of the Queen to the Governor and four pound four shillings a year for his teaching.'

'Four pound four shillings from the public purse for an Irish rebel's runt to read,' grumbled Stokes. 'I'd letter you for half the price.'

Barbary teetered back on her stool, considering. Her original reason for taking lessons with the Jackman had been to keep some sort of track of the world in which Robert Betty had begun to move. He'd aspired to literacy, therefore she had too. Well, Robert would be coming back one day; she had to think so. And wouldn't he be floundered to find her a scholar? And wouldn't it be cheating on the grandest level to thwart those who kept her confined by advancing herself? Stokes, who was a rash gambler, was in her debt in any case. 'Very well, Master Stokes,' she said, 'I happen to be at leisure this winter.'

That winter more than physical locks were turned for Barbary and other than wooden doors swung open. She was given the run of the Princes' Tower with access to morning lessons in Stokes's cell, to Sir Philip Efferton for dancing instruction in the evening and to share in the afternoon tuition of James, heir to the Earldom of Desmond.

The keepers, Barbary decided, were generously interpreting their gambling debts into this somewhat surprising freedom.

In fact, her education was being connived at on the highest level. Keeper Viney had informed the Governor of the arrangement between Stokes and Barbary and the Governor had written of it to the Lord Treasurer: 'My lord, it seemeth that Prisoner Betty doth aspire to a more gentle condition than befits him in that he would learn to read and letter from another prisoner who is in thrall to him from the vicissitudes of gambling, to wit dice, and has entered into a secret arrangement with him for this teaching. Since your lordship allows much latitude to this person, I dare neither approve nor disapprove the matter until I hear from your lordship how it should proceed.'

In the remorseless roll of official letters onto Lord Burghley's desk the one from Sir Owen Hopton was light relief, giving a flavour of the young prisoner in whom Lord Burghley was taking an increasing interest. He answered it immediately. 'Let all facility be given to the Prisoner Betty that he may zealously pursue learning even while confined so that whomsoever can offer advancement to his mind and spirit let him have access to.' He paused, returned to the letter and added a postscript of genius: 'Let it appear to Betty that this liberty cometh by his own enterprise and is not accorded at our command.'

So Barbary was allowed to pursue her various studies in the belief that she was nipping them from under Authority's nose. Perhaps as Burghley guessed, she wouldn't have stuck to them without it; she had no love of learning for its own sake, but the zest of stealing a march on society, that with it she'd be able to cheat a better class of person, gave a glamour to her lessons which they would otherwise have lacked.

James of Desmond protested when she insinuated herself into his lessons with the tutor, Jennings: 'I'll not be taught with commoners. I'll complain to the Governor. I'll write to my mother. He's *my* tutor, not yours.' Face to face the young earl was even less prepossessing than his conversation had led her to suppose, unhealthy, yellow-skinned and spotty. His cell smelled.

'I'm not prigging your rattle, Ear-Ache,' said Barbary rudely. Increase of freedom was making her big for her boots. 'I'm sitting in. Master Jennings don't mind.' Master Jennings didn't; the two shilling ointment Barbary spread across his palm every week guaranteed it. The Governor, on application, didn't see fit to interfere, and the Countess of Desmond didn't reply to her son's letter, having paid him this year's supply of attention.

But weakly as James was, he was strong on Latin. It was Latin that Jennings was teaching and it was Latin that Barbary mainly wanted to learn in the belief, garnered from sermons overheard at Paul's Cross, that it was the language of high society. Oddly enough, she was more at home with it than with written English, partly because the Jackman, being a Latinist, had taught her its basics and partly because she had no trouble with the situation of the verb in its sentences as if, somewhere else, she had been familiar with it. With James providing competition, she was spurred to beat him and worked hard, squeaking declensions over her slate late into the night.

English, which she took with publisher Stokes, was a different matter. 'Why don't it spell like it sounds?' she complained. 'How can friend be fry-end when it ought to be frend? Latin's got more sense to it.'

Stokes snorted with disgust. 'Latin's day is over. A Popish plot. The vernacular, my boy, English, that's the language of good Christian men. And I don't care a damn how you spell it as long as you use it. Next line on the primer if you please, Master Barbary, and another penny off my gambling debt.'

Not being a schoolmaster, there was no obligation on Stokes to make lessons either uplifting or boring; enthusiasm for the written word consumed him and for the first time it was borne in upon Barbary what a political power it was.

'Didn't I and Stubbs and others use the word to raise the people against Her Majesty's marriage to that Catholic Frenchman?' he chanted. 'And didn't we prevent it?'

'And didn't it chop Stubbs' hand off?' chanted Barbary back at him. 'And didn't it land you in the Tower?'

'Virtue has its martyrs,' Stokes said, amiably. For him his sentence to the Tower was an accolade. It had brought him attention; Puritan churchmen preached against his imprisonment and the printer, John Day, had sent him a copy of the first English edition of Foxe's *Actes and Monuments*, better known as the *Book of Martyrs*, signed with encouraging sentences by the author himself. So it was in the torture chamber of Foxe's prose that Barbary, having conquered her primers, began struggling her way towards literacy, her hair rising to the screams of Protestant saints and her flesh creeping as theirs melted on their bones.

'That would have been me,' said Stokes, almost regretfully, 'under Bloody Mary. God save Her Precious Protestant Majesty Elizabeth.' He bore his Queen no ill will.

'Amen to that,' said Barbary, 'when she sets me free.'

78

There was another kerfuffle down on the green two days later when Campion and two companions for the scaffold, Sherwin and Briant, were tied to hurdles and dragged to Tyburn. Keeper Pobble, who managed to get a front seat, reported on the execution to the dice party that night and showed them his coat where blood splashed it when Campion's entrails were torn out and thrown in the cauldron. 'A fine execution,' he said, 'and deserved. No remorse and stuck to his religion to the last. The Dutchmen were there as well.'

The Dutch jugglers were the rage of London; one was seven foot seven in height, the other a midget who could walk between his legs and dance a galliard, 'though he never had a good foot nor any knee at all' and no arm but a stump on which he could balance a cup and toss it in the air, every time receiving it on said stump.

The sense of what they were missing cast a gloom over the guardhouse and the dice game ended early.

Later that night masked figures arrayed in court dress entered Barbary's cell and hanged Will Clampett by his feet from a beam. His innards streamed out of his nose, leaving his body empty and withered like an autumn leaf which shuddered in the draught and detached itself. Barbary leapt and twisted to catch it before it blew out of the window, but the figures obstructed every move and in one lazy parabola the veined husk that had been Will Clampett swooped between the bars and out of her sight for ever.

Gasping, Barbary sat up in her bed. It had been a dream, but dreams were portents. They had killed Will. That was why there had been no word from him. Will was dead, the one substantial thing in her life had gone out of it. Even if they hadn't killed him, she had; without the money she brought in he would surely have starved to death. 'Oh, Will, don't leave me alone in this awful world.'

And whose faces were behind the masks? Who in hell were 'they' that killed people and put others in prison without reason? And got them used to it.

She sat up. That was what they were doing, getting her to accept it, like they had with the Ear-Ache Earl whose enterprise had been taken away so that he doted on his captors. The weakening by imprisonment had begun, or else why had she left it so long to put the bite on Dawson? Them with their literacy and their wood-panelling and their coals and candles extra.

She scrambled out of bed, picked up her candle holder and beat on the door with it, yelling for the Governor, for freedom, to save Will.

It was Morgan who came eventually to breathe aggrieved platitudes through the squint. 'Now, Barb bach, is this nice? Will's asleep, whoever he is, and the Governor, and me, with your permission. The Queen's Majesty keeps you here – I don't know why, either – and the Queen's Majesty will let you go in her own blessed time. Sleep now, or no extras. Dawson? You won't see him for a bit. Transferred he is to the Catholic cells. Crowded out down there, bach, with the names Campion and the others gave out under torment.'

'What do you want to get out for?' asked Stokes at the morning's lesson. 'This is your university, boy, and a bloody sight more comfortable than some, believe me. You've got a brain, lad, use it.'

But when his pardon came through ten days later the publisher left the university of the Tower of London without a goodbye or a backward glance.

In place of English, Barbary, her equilibrium recovered, a little more defiance gone out of her, took up lessons in navigation with Captain Askwith.

Askwith's crime had been to board a ship belonging to His Catholic Majesty Philip of Spain, whom Elizabeth was even yet trying to placate. As Askwith said: 'If she'd had damned ducats aboard her I'd be knighted. Know what she was carrying? Leaves. Cargo of roots and leaves, I ask you. Threw the lot overboard.'

But if Captain Askwith was a poor judge of cargo, he was an experienced navigator and through him Barbary's spirit sailed to the seas of flying fish and great stars.

She learned to read a sea card, the stars, and a staff and astrolabe, but most of all she learned admiration for the courage of English adventurers and great-hearted ships.

In late spring, just as she was becoming reconciled to her imprisonment, the summons came to deliver her out of it.

Chapter Five

They took Barbary out of the Tower at night and by Traitors' Gate. A generation before, another red-headed girl had been brought into the Tower by that same route in order not to attract the attention of the streets.

Just as the Princess Elizabeth had been afraid of being put to death inside the Tower, Barbary was afraid of being put to death outside it. Without knowing that she was doing so, she reacted as Elizabeth had done. She made a fuss. If they were going to get rid of her, there would at least be people who knew about it.

She had to be bumped down the steps to the rowing boat and when she wasn't shouting, she was whistling the Order pass notes. They had to haul her into the boat. It was as she was being rowed under the portcullis of the Gate that she heard three answering notes coming from somewhere along the bank.

Barbary looked at the size of the two liveried men who formed her escort, added it to the muscle power of the four oarsmen, and decided against escape. She whistled for rescue. 'Too dangerous,' was the answer. 'We'll watch you. Bene darkmans.'

A good night to you and many of 'em, thought Barbary and spat. The Order had failed her while she was in the Tower; it was failing her out of it.

It was a beautiful, spring-scented night but to Barbary it was doomladen; the high, full moon, her friend on many escapades, focused its light only on symbols of death, glinting on the halberds of her escort, a cross in a waterside cemetery and on the heads of dead pirates licked by the tide along the Wapping sea wall.

'Where are you taking me?' she shouted at the men in the boat and sank back when they made no answer. 'And why?' There was no hope of finding that out; these men

81

wouldn't know. Keeper Pobble who'd woken her up and accompanied her to the water steps hadn't known. 'Interrogation, I expect,' he'd said. 'Tell the truth now, Barbary, and shame the Devil. No harm can come if you tell the truth.'

'They tell me what truth they want and I'll tell it,' she'd assured him. She looked back to the massive shape of the Tower still blocking out the stars. Poor old Pobble, she'd miss him, and Morgan and all the others she'd been able to manipulate. Compared to the God-knew-what that lay ahead of her on this black river, the Tower looked like home. Well, keep the bib dry. She pulled her cap firmly down on her head. 'Wouldn't drop me off at Lambeth Marshes, I suppose?'

The bank of lights coming up on the starboard bow were the windows of Greenwich Palace. For a second Barbary thought they were going to free her after all and that some insane rule insisted they let her go in the same place that they'd picked her up. Instead she was rowed to the port side of a vessel moored at the palace's water steps. She recognised it; every citizen along the Thames knew the royal barges.

God help, thought Barbary. She looked up at the elaborate stern cabin to see if the royal pennant was flying above it. It wasn't.

She was made to scramble up a rope ladder and heaved over the brass taffrail between the rowers who were in their places, oars aloft. The moonlight made the royal livery colourless, but she smelled the metallic smell of the gold braid which emblazoned it. She was hurried along the deck and down some steps to the cabin.

Part of her hoped and part of her dreaded that the Queen would be in it. It would be like seeing God. Instead the cabin bustled with clerks transforming what was almost a state room into an office, settling desks into place, unpacking writing implements, opening chests, selecting manuscripts. She was plonked on a stool facing the largest desk. A voice said: 'Tell them to cast off.'

'Cast off, cast off.' The order was repeated up the steps and along the unseen deck above. The cabin cleared, leaving Barbary, with a guard behind her, looking at two desks behind each of which sat an old man. She recognised them both and in the recognition was flattened.

One of them, the older, was the self-effacing but inevitable shadow behind the Queen in every royal procession, the Lord Treasurer Burghley. The other was not so familiar on the London streets, but the Order made it compulsory for its members to know who he was. Early in her apprenticeship the Upright Man had taken Barbary to the gates of a house in Seething Lane to wait until she got a glimpse of its owner. 'Burn that man's h'image into your glaziers,' the Upright Man told her, 'for if ever you offends him nor any of his people, I'll cut them same glaziers out your head and use 'em for marbles.'

Barbary's glaziers had widened. There weren't many people the Upright Man was afraid of. 'Who is he, Abraham?'

The Upright Man spat. 'He's the rack, that's what he is. He's as everywhere as the pox. Glim his smell-cheat. That smell-cheat can sniff out the Queen's enemies all over England, all over the world. Once sniffed, they're cindered.'

'But we're not enemies of the Rome-Mort, Abraham.'

The Upright Man cuffed her head. 'That, you little bastard's why we don't tangle with Mr Secretary Walsingham.'

And I done it, God help, thought Barbary. Tangled with Mr Secretary and the Lord High Treasurer of England. The queerest of all cuffins. But how did I do it? The barge began moving and the cabin lanterns hanging over the desks swayed in the sweep-stop, sweep-stop motion engendered by thirty oars rowing in unison. Their light shone on the desks and on something on the desk of the Secretary: the necklet.

Barbary panicked. The krap thing. It was that bloody necklet caused all her and Rob Betty's trouble. It was stolen, must be. Years ago, long before they'd acquired it. It must have belonged to somebody great, maybe the Queen herself and at long last Her Majesty's nose in the shape of Walsingham had caught up with it. What was the penalty for prigging the Queen's neck-cheat? Hanging? Quartering? She'd always been wary of the necklet. Now it had become unfamiliar; somebody had cleaned it so that its curves and twists glowed in barbaric opposition to the tasteful chains of office round the old men's necks.

All the sounds around her were rhythmic; the deep beat of the time drum, the clunk of the rowlocks on deck, and the scratch of quills in the cabin – both the old men were writing. No word was spoken.

Despite her terror, Barbary realised something. They were trying to sweat her. She blinked. They might be gentry, but they were using the old Flemish bite ploy, sweating the cony. Doing it effective, and all.

The necklace grew bigger in the swinging light and glowed a deeper gold.

'Is this yours?'

Barbary jumped; Mr Secretary Walsingham had spoken. He was tapping the necklet. His very face, now that it was turned to her, was terrible; it was thin and agonised with temper and pain.

She tried to control her breathing and prevaricated: 'Can't say it is.'

'Did no one ever tell you to doff your cap to your elders and betters?' asked Walsingham irritably.

'Can't say they did,' said Barbary, still cautious.

'Do it.'

Reluctantly Barbary took off her cap. There hadn't been time for one of Pobble's haircuts; her summons to interrogation had come too quickly, so her hair was curlier and longer than she'd have liked. Dragged by her cap it stood up and out from her head. Its colour was alarming, catching what light there was in the cabin and making everything else darker by its intensity.

Lord Burghley thought: A burning bush. He was reminded of a tree at Theobald's which surprised him every autumn by its deepening red. Each day until the leaves fell off he would think, It can't get redder, and each day it did. He glanced away from the boy and then looked back, to be amazed once more. The hair appeared to have drained all colour from the thin face which, the Lord Treasurer noted, was beardless, making the boy only thirteen, fourteen perhaps. He looked older, a result, no doubt, of the depraved life these street urchins led. He sighed at such depravity, but the sigh was automatic. He found it difficult in his old age to feel disapproval; he found it difficult in his old age to feel anything. Besides, if the boy were venal, so much the better. It was a relief when Walsingham told the boy to re-cover.

'Now then, what is your name?'

'Harry Smith, your worship,' said Barbary cheerfully. 'Market trader of Cheapside. At your service.'

'Also known as Jim Pettit, Harry of Holborn and Barbary Clampett,' snapped Secretary Walsingham. 'Falsehood is useless.'

'What you ask for then?' Impertinence was the only way she could fight off the fear that threatened to disintegrate her.

So far Lord Treasurer Burghley hadn't said a word, which made him almost as frightening as Walsingham. His face was very old indeed with a long straight beard but, for all its wrinkles, it was forgettable. Suspicion, Puritanism and urinary troubles had made Walsingham's face sharply memorable, but all Burghley's experience had taken expression out of his rather than etched it in. His eyes were hung round with drapes of skin and looked out on everything, good and bad, with abstracted disinterest. The only comfortingly human weakness was in his hands which were greenish-white against the beautiful velvet of his gown and had the same swelling of the joints as the Jackman's had. Occasionally he rubbed the palm of one hand against the thumb joint of the other, just as the Jackman did.

You got the gout, my old Treasurer. She was getting her wits back. They *were* using the Flemish bite, by God. After the sweating came the hatchet and pap routine. Walsingham the hatchet, Burghley the pap. The one putting on the frightener, the other reassuring. She'd seen it a hundred times. Done it a few, too. All right, in some way she didn't understand she and Rob were in trouble with these very queer cuffins. But somewhere, faintly, at the back of everything, was the scent of fish.

The Lord Treasurer spoke for the first time. Kindly, like a good pap should: 'Pour the young man some wine.'

Wine was poured into a very nice goblet – she could have got a couple of nobles for it – and the aroma of fish became stronger.

'I should like to tell you a story, Master Barbary,' said the Lord Treasurer. His voice was as neutral as the rest of him. 'It concerns a young prince of Ireland who some years ago became lost after a shipwreck.' He decided there was no need to mention inessentials like hanged mothers at this stage. 'It was thought he had died. But, a while ago, we received information that he was alive somewhere in London, unknown and unknowing as to his background.'

Barbary nodded. Perhaps the wine was drugged. Perhaps these two old men liked young boys for you-know-what. They'd start talking dirty any moment, or expose themselves.

'Her woman's heart being moved by this young prince's plight, our great Queen asked me and my lord Secretary here to set a search in train for him. All we had to go on was that he possessed red hair and a torque. Like this one.'

'There you are then,' said Barbary. Could she make the door before they nabbed her?

'And one of my lord Secretary's agents discovered just such a young man at an inn in an area of the City known as the Bermudas. He attempted to follow the young man but lost him.'

'Incompetence,' said Barbary heartily. 'You boot that agent's arse, your worship. But just because the young man got the necklet, it don't mean he stole it. Perhaps he found it.'

'Master Barbary,' said the Lord Treasurer with patience, 'you mistake me. The torque or necklet was a clue to the young man, not the young man to the torque.'

'Right,' said Barbary. Her eyes measured the distance to the cabin door. She could be on the deck and over the side before they could say God Help Us.

'We issued what, I believe, is vulgarly known as a "seek-we" for this young man. We posted agents to look for him at the ports. The Pool, Deptford. Greenwich.'

'Ah,' said Barbary, 'I expect your men saw him throw me the necklet from the boat. I can explain that. "Give this to Her Majesty," he said to me, his very words, "Give—"'

'*Forget the necklet.*'

The shout startled them both into staring at Mr Secretary Walsingham who had made it. Blowing hard, he reached for a green bottle of physic that stood on his desk and poured himself a dose. 'By the Lord, Burghley,' he said, 'one forgets how irritating the cunning of the criminal classes can be.'

Lord Burghley nodded reassurance at his colleague and then at his victim. 'Forget the necklet, Master Barbary,' he said quietly. 'We do not believe it to be stolen and even if it were we should not proceed with the matter. No harm will come to Robert Betty through our hands. Nor to you. Do you understand that?'

Comprehension arrived in the green eyes and with it surprise: 'Rob's not Irish; he's English as you or me.'

The Lord Treasurer sighed with relief. They'd said the boy was intelligent; he was quick as well, once he stopped looking at things from the criminal point of view. 'Our information is that he is a foundling. Nothing is known of where he was born.'

How'd he know all this? Had Sir Secretary torn it out of Galloping Betty? Bribed it out of the Upright Man? The Order didn't part with information about its own just for the asking. Well, but, Rob Betty? An Irish royal? Never. 'What you want this prince for anyway?'

'We wish to restore him to the estate that is rightfully his,' said Lord Burghley carefully.

In course you do, in course you do, you lying old Treasurer. The smell of fish was very strong now. The buggers wanted this Irish prince for their own purposes. Nobody did nothing for nobody without a motive. This might be the Queen of England's barge, but it had a whiff of the Bermudas. She was on home territory. A cousiner among cousins, a cony-catcher among cony-catchers.

If they'd known it, the faces of the Lord High Treasurer of England and Barbary Clampett at that moment, separated by a desk and sixty years, looked not unalike. Masks of indifference. Tricksters' faces. 'Missed him, then, din't you?' Barbary said. 'The boat sailed and him on it.'

'No.' It was the acidic voice of Secretary Walsingham. 'We didn't miss him. We found him on the quayside at Greenwich. A young man with red hair and a golden torque. We've been keeping him safe in the Tower.'

Eventually, to bring the boy to coherence, the guard had

to slap him. The Lord Treasurer shook his head to stop Walsingham slapping him as well. Nervousness, greed, ambition he had anticipated, but he had not expected that the guttersnipe would react by kicking his legs around and laughing himself sick. Did the boy know something they didn't?

Barbary fought for control and wiped her eyes. It was serious really. Her, an Irish prince, God help us. Where did they get them from?

She sobered up. It *was* serious: if she'd really been a boy, if she'd qualified sexually for the role of this royal bog-trotter, she'd be panicking now at being forced into something that boded no good. As it was she held the winning card. She could get out of the situation any time she liked. She could show her hand – well, not her hand but, given the decencies, another part of her anatomy – and prove she wasn't a male, Irish or otherwise.

Not yet, though. First she'd see what profit was in it.

Her eyes met the curtained eyes of Lord Burghley across the desk. He was the one she related to, as she was meant to. But in any case her instinct told her that he was the prime mover behind the whole business. I know you know I'm not this lost prince of yours. You know I know you know it. Walsingham's men saw Rob throw me the neck-cheat. Therefore, you got a powerful reason for wanting to produce this prince and you'll use any ringer to do it. Rob Betty for choice but with him gone, me.

She was reminded of Matt the Clapper who discovered his wife had been left money only a few days after he'd done her in, and made Foll pretend to be her and claim it. Lord Treasurer of England you may be, she thought, but you're doing a Matt the Clapper or my name's not Barbary Clampett.

'What'd I do as this Irish prince then?'

'Claim your rightful inheritance.'

There you are. Matt the Clapper. 'And hand it over to you, I suppose?'

She heard Walsingham hiss: 'Why are we wasting our time with this sewage rat?' The Lord Treasurer sighed again. He had a lot of work ahead of him; he could have managed the whole business more amiably without the presence of his colleague, indeed he had been surprised when Walsingham had asked to come along on the journey, although he supposed the Secretary had his own, personal affairs to settle at the house to which they were going. Walsingham had very little patience with Burghley's plan for this boy, had very little patience with Ireland come to that, his sympathy lying more with the exterminate-the-lot-of-them school of thought.

Lord Burghley said gently: 'My son, you are the heir to vast tracts of land, the leader of a people who have fallen into error. We wish merely that they be reunited to their gracious sovereign and yours, Her Majesty, Queen Elizabeth, to serve her in peace and amity. As their leader and her loyal subject, you shall bring them back into her fold.'

'Oh,' said Barbary. Politics. Still, there'd be gelt to be got somewhere before she made her escape. She'd play along for now. But first she'd better know what cards these old buggers held in their hands. She said: 'Begging your pardon, your worship, but I'm not Irish. I'm Low Countries. My foster father served there. He found me there.'

Secretary Walsingham intervened: 'Clampett served in Ireland. He found you *there*.'

'He knows where he served, don't he?'

'He is lying.'

It was the first occasion on which she experienced history being rewritten. It took her breath away. Lying was her very own art form, but this was something else, a fact erased to be replaced by a political expedient.

Let's see how far you'll go, old Secretary: 'I don't want to be Irish. Suppose I won't do it. What'd you do then?' She hunched her shoulders.

The Lord Treasurer returned to his writing; this was Walsingham's field. The Queen's Secretary said: 'We should have to suppose that your sympathies did not lie with your country. We should have to suppose that they had been alienated by a baleful influence, someone who had preached sedition to you during your bringing up.'

Will? Was it Will he'd got trapped in all those syllables?

'Guard, Master Barbary would profit by some air. Take him on deck.'

She was lifted bodily from her chair and shoved out of the cabin and up its steps. Up on deck the air was delicately scented; the moonlight polished the river and the ranks of rowers. They had stopped rowing. She had been so occupied down in the cabin that she hadn't noticed the cessation of the boat's movement. The barge had been tied up at a landing place on the starboard bank, the taffrail gate opened and a gangplank put in place. The guard jerked Barbary towards it. On the bank, where a lane led up from the river, some men holding lighted cressets clustered round a gibbet. Usually such gibbets suspended the iron-banded corpse of some river-side malefactor which emitted a stinking warning against evil-doing on every passing breeze. Although this one was empty, it wasn't going to be for long. Two ropes were being slung over it. There was going to be a double hanging.

Funny time for a hanging. Barbary began to pant. 'Who're the swingers?' Was one of them to be her? The guard neither answered nor moved. The Maytime bank was unreal, a stage. The flickering lights by the gibbet distorted the gasping faces of the men who were now being hauled up by the ropes, whose hands clawed and whose legs kicked. One was Cuckold Dick. The other man had only one leg to kick; his left stuck out at stiff angles, being artificial.

'Will,' screamed Barbary. The guard picked her up by her belt so that in her struggle to get down the gangplank to reach Dick and Will she found herself swimming in the air. She swam and kicked and fought as she was carried back into the cabin and slammed onto the floor. She tried to get up to reach the door but was slammed down again. She crawled towards the Lord Treasurer, a shrieking, weeping petitioner. 'Stop it. Tell 'em. I'll do anything. Don't hang them.'

'Hang who?' enquired the Lord Treasurer kindly.

'I'm begging,' wept Barbary.

The Lord Treasurer addressed a servant who'd been in the shadows. 'My compliments to the captain and ask if anyone is being hanged.' Barbary struggled to get back on deck, but her guard held her firm. Through the nightmare she heard the repeat: 'Being hanged? Being hanged?'

'Will,' she screamed.

There was an arhythmic step on the stairs down into the cabin and a sailor limped into the room. He was pushing a whey-faced Cuckold Dick before him. 'Yes, my lord?'

'Are you hanging anyone, Master Corbet? This young man seems under the impression that an execution is in progress.'

'Execution, my lord?' Master Corbet grinned at Barbary, 'No, my lord. Her Majesty wouldn't like it, it being her own barge like. We only stopped to change the rowers.'

'Stopped to change the rowers,' confided the Lord Treasurer to Barbary. Mr Secretary Walsingham waved the captain to take Cuckold Dick away. Before he left, Master Corbet grinned again at Barbary. He cocked his head to one side, extended his tongue and jerked at an invisible halter.

'It wasn't Will, Barb,' said Cuckold Dick with difficulty from the doorway. Barbary nodded. The sailor had an ammunition leg. She could see it as he left. Acting out a hanging in the moonlight he would have looked very much like Will Clampett.

'You see?' said the Lord Treasurer to Barbary. Barbary nodded. She got up off the floor and dragged herself back to her chair. The barge was under way again as if its rhythm had never been interrupted and as if her heart was being unreasonable in not beating in time to its oars. She wiped the snivel off her nose with her sleeve. She felt little ill-will towards the Treasurer behind the desk, not even to the bastard Walsingham. They were both Authority and in the world she moved in Authority was as capricious as violent weather, holding the right to impose torture and death, always had, always would. As soon expect compassion from a hurricane.

She'd asked and Authority'd answered and the card it held was a winner. A cruncher. It said it could hang Dick or Will any time it wanted. Dick for his crossbiting and Will for treason maybe, or talking sedition – and God knows he did, though it was just his way. You couldn't trump that one. She'd asked and Authority had drawn her a picture as clear as the portrait of the Queen hanging on the bulkhead. Lord High Treasurer of England and Lord High Secretary of England they might be, but they were no different from the Upright Man really, just better dressed.

She took in a shuddering breath. 'Where *is* Will, if you'll pardon my asking?'

'You refer to Master Clampett?' asked the Lord Treasurer, as if the subject hadn't come up before. 'I flatter me provision has been made for him that, if he'd had choice, the man could have made no better for himself. He has been put to work in a cannon foundry. You shall see him soon enough, for the foundry belongs to the gentleman to whom you will be squire, Sir Henry Sidney.'

'Squire?'

'Most certainly. Having found you at last we must fit you for your new estate, as we have done with other Irish nobles, apprentice you in the ways of kingship so that when you assume your place at the head of your people you can lead them into proper obedience to the Queen who is their sovereign and yours. You have no memory of Ireland it seems . . .'

Not bloody surprising either, thought Barbary, never having been there.

'. . . and must be reminded of its customs.'

Barbary, thought Barbary, they're going to make you an actor. And after all you done to keep yourself decent. Walsingham had long gone back to his writing. The field was now Burghley's.

'You must be acquainted with power and how to use it for the glorification of God and Her Majesty. Riches shall be yours . . .'

If she'd known her Bible better Barbary might have realised she was being taken to the top of an exceeding high mountain to be shown all the kingdoms – well, one kingdom – of the world, and the glory of them. And if, in enumerating the castles, tributes and estates which would be Prince Barbary's, the Lord Treasurer raised images of English places like Nonsuch, the Tower, and Burghley House alongside English-type manors with rosy-cheeked, cap-doffing tenantry, stableyards, orchards and dairy-maids, then perhaps his own ignorance of a country he had never visited was as much to blame as Barbary's. Perhaps.

As she listened, Barbary calculated. You think you got me, old Treasurer. And maybe you have. And maybe, when the Queen's chief minister offers me riches, I don't mind being got. Not when he holds what cards he does, and not when I got an ace hidden up me trunks meself. All right, old man, for Will and Dick and for some profit I'll play along for now.

She saw Burghley glance at the hourglass on his desk. 'But we must not overwhelm our young prince.' He stood up and coughed to indicate that Walsingham should join him in his salute. Walsingham hissed as he did so.

The Lord Treasurer of England and the Queen's Secretary bowed to Barbary Clampett of Lambeth Marshes, whom they were leading into deception, by whom they were being deceived, and with whom, side by side, they were setting out to deceive the people of Ireland.

With equal ceremony, Barbary got up and bowed back.

For a moment the two chief tricksters, the old and the young, highest in the land and the lowest, were touched by the admiration which only professionals can feel for each other. Barbary winked at the Lord Treasurer: 'You ever thought of taking up cony-catching, your worship?'

They let her join Cuckold Dick on deck where he sat on a hawser, rubbing his neck, still managing to look respectable, like a merchant who'd been hard done by. As ever, his face was calm as a plate of porridge, which it resembled and out of which his small eyes looked on the world with uncondemnatory acceptance. Born in prison to a mother who was later hanged for killing her pimp, he had, he always said, lost the faculty of surprise very early. To Barbary he had seemed part of the natural scenery of her life, she hadn't really considered him. The fierce protective affection his vulnerability now inspired in her was a revelation.

And he had been hard done by. His aldermanic girth had been reduced by being imprisoned without charge in the Bridewell for nearly as long as Barbary had been in the Tower. 'Couple of shoulder-tappers picked me up just after I oiled that warden to give you the dice,' he told her. 'Wanted to know all about you and Rob, how old, born where, what parents, the whole Jesse Tree. Well, I didn't know, did I, Barb? And what I did, I wasn't telling, though they was so powerful anxious to find out they breeched me.'

A breeching was a flogging. 'I'm sorry, Dick.'

'Not your fault, Barb. What they got, they got from

the Upright Man. Brought in a week after, he was, and it was him blew you. They promised to breech him if he didn't.' He looked at her apologetically on Abraham's behalf. 'You can see it from his side, Barb. He'd only recent had the cart tail as you know, and his stripes was still sore.' Dick rarely saw wrong in anybody, not because he was liberal but because he was that despair of the Church, a man colour blind to the whiteness of good and the blackness of evil. His own refusal to give information about his friends he did not regard as high-principled or courageous but merely a matter of being able to withstand the pain at the time, whereas the Upright Man could not.

'Go on.'

'That's it. Next thing I was on this water-cheat, next thing after that I was dancing the gallows' waltz.'

There was no questions as to what she was doing here, what he was, why he had endured a mock hanging on a bank of the Thames on this lovely night. Things happened and there it was, just another instalment of the dark saga that was his life.

Nevertheless Barbary, keeping an eye on the rowers to see that none of them listened, told him. She owed him that much and anyway she had a desperate need to confide in someone. She told him everything.

'You're a female?'

'Yes.'

'Been one all this time?'

'Yes.'

'Well, watch us apples swim.'

He was surprised, but he adjusted his image of her without too much effort, and without affecting his attitude towards her. For a man who made his living by acting sexual jealousy and passion, he had little enough in his make-up. Looking back, Barbary realised that Cuckold Dick's relationship with the bawds, come to that the men and boys of the Order, had always been platonic. What was remarkable, she thought, was that this asexuality had been unremarked. Dick's acceptance of other people's foibles was so thorough as to make his own seem natural.

'Do you think they'd let me get off now, Barb?' He was becoming increasingly uneasy the further he was swept away from his home territory.

'I asked.' He'd served their purpose as an Awful Warning to her, so why couldn't he be freed?

'What'd they say?'

'They said you'd have to be found honest employment.'

There was silence as they reflected on the novelty of the idea. The moon was setting and the time drum had lengthened its beat so that the rowing could keep within the bounds of the look-out's vision. They were heading into darkness.

'Dick.'

'What?'

'How'd you fancy becoming apprenticed to an apprentice Irish prince?'

Chapter Six

If there was an Elizabethan Eden it was Penshurst. The manor was at that moment in the possession of the finest of their generation, a focus of the noblest aspiration of which England was capable, gathering place for its best minds. There was no canker here; what you saw was what there was, and all of it beautiful.

Barbary saw it first at night. She and Lord Treasurer Burghley and Mr Secretary Walsingham disembarked at its river steps, where she was parted from Cuckold Dick, who was sent off to take up a position in the servants' quarters. The guests were put into sedan chairs. It was a new experience for Barbary, but nervousness spoiled the fun of it. She leaned out of the chair's window to watch Cuckold Dick being led away through the trees like a man picking his way among volcanic lava. He hated countryside, and this was as deep a countryside as he'd ever encountered. But here, in the park, it had been civilised. Still with her head out of the swaying chair, Barbary saw that sheep had obediently nibbled the grass to carpet length, oaks and beeches had been protected by railings to grow to statuesque proportions, their lower branches spreading just above man-height. Under one of the biggest oaks a silvery herd of deer posed long enough for a spell to be broken when they vanished in suspended bounds.

After a while they were decanted from the chairs into a glade. Down an avenue of trees leading into it approached what seemed, in the distance, to be mobile snowdrops. A whisper like water grew into chatter and laughter and the notes of a mandolin. The snowdrops became lanterns and people in pale silk and satin, indolent and magnificent strollers who at that moment imprinted an image on Barbary's mind so lovely that time and disillusion were not to tarnish it.

Closer, she saw they were glorious but mad. They all held jewelled masks, several men were knights in armour, some of the ladies had wings attached to the backs of their dresses, there were dwarves with antlers growing out of their caps. An enormous dog carried a yoked collar which gave him an extra head on each side of his real one.

A tall, stout man stepped forward to bellow an elaborate welcome, exchanging bows with the Lord Treasurer and the Secretary. Barbary heard Lord Burghley murmur: 'How's it going?'

The big man dropped his voice. 'So far so good. Not a cross word out of her. Is this him?'

Lord Burghley's hand pushed Barbary forward. 'My lord, may I present our Prince of Connaught, also known as Master Barbary Clampett. Master Clampett, this is Sir Henry Sidney.'

Sir Henry surveyed Barbary without enthusiasm. 'Are you sure?'

'His background fits. He had the torque. Experts have examined it and judge it as true royal Irish from those parts.' Burghley pushed Barbary again, gently. 'Show my lord.'

Barbary's grubby neck had regained the necklet. She took it off and held it out, remembering to take her cap off at the same time.

Sir Henry gestured to a link boy to hold a lantern closer and looked from Barbary to the necklet and back again. 'They all look alike to me.'

Torques or Irish? wondered Barbary.

Sir Henry nodded at her. 'Welcome, Donal mac Owen O'Flaherty, and may we be as true foster father and son as were Tyrone and I to each other.'

'We'll give it a try, eh?' said Barbary politely.

Sir Henry's tufted eyebrows went up and Walsingham hissed. Burghley said hastily: 'He has been brought up in the rudery of the commons, as I explained in my letter. But he is quick to learn.'

'He'd better be. Does he know he's to meet the Queen?' He beckoned to one of the women. 'My dear, here is another wild Irish for you to tame. Donal, I present you to your liege lady and foster mother, Lady Sidney.'

'Call me Barbary, lady,' said Barbary, bowing.

Lady Sidney held her mask away from her face to nod, and revealed that she had no face. Despite the Lord Treasurer's warning grip on her shoulder, Barbary yelped. Beneath the woman's jewelled cap there was nothing, blackness, a face-shaped hole in the universe. Out of it came words: 'She's waiting, Henry.'

Sir Henry nodded. 'We're in the middle of a fantastical,' he said to Burghley, who indicated sympathy. Sir Henry stood back and shouted at the top of his considerable voice, 'My Lords, you are well come into the land of Faerie, among enchantments and chivalry, gods and goddesses, demons and full dreadful hobgoblins. Yet we, its denizens, are sore bereft, for the Queen of this place, our Belphoebe, the Virgin of our souls, has been spirited away and we cannot find her.'

Barbary heard Lord Burghley sigh; it had been a long journey and for most of it he had been at work. However . . . He raised his voice to an artificial level: 'What news is this that pierces me? Our Faerie Queen lost? Let search be set in train.'

As Barbary watched, the Lord Treasurer of England, the Queen's Secretary, assorted nobility, adventurers, scholars and poets began running around expressing pantomimic concern as they peered under bushes. Battle the watch, Barb, she said to herself, you've landed among lunatics. She reached out and caught the liripipe of a dwarf skipping by. 'Who you all looking for, Shorty?'

The dwarf put his tongue out. 'The Queen, of course.'

'The real Queen? Of England?'

'Of course. And don't call me Shorty, rustyballocks.' He ran off.

'She's over there,' Barbary shouted after him. It was obvious where Her Majesty was. A white satin shoe with a diamond-encrusted buckle was sticking out from behind a beech. Barbary shifted her position so that she could get a better view and saw that the shoe belonged to someone who was concealed in a cushioned bower apparently made out of flowers. The Queen? The Queen. Barbary, whose idea of playing a game was restricted to cards or dice, was amazed. Is this what the Governor of the Faith got up to off duty?

She grabbed at a tall young man who was passing. 'She's over there.'

He looked down at her with amusement. 'Shut up.'

Barbary retired and sat down on the grass to listen to the over-agonised shouts: 'Phoebus, come back to us. Reveal yourself, O sun of our eyes.' She watched the Lord High Treasurer shaking boughs as if the Queen had perched herself up on branches. She saw a transformed Mr Secretary Walsingham baying: 'Where are you, O Diana,' all the while avoiding looking towards the bower. She watched a giggling maid of honour taken behind some bushes by a very good-looking, very tall and dark, steel-armoured knight. She began to doze off.

She opened her eyes to shouts and barking. The dog with three heads had taken up position in front of the bower. Its two artificial heads were beginning to droop and the one in the middle mournfully regarded the young courtier who'd told Barbary to shut up. He had drawn his sword at the dog and was addressing it as 'Cerberus' during the course of a long poem. At the end of it he raised his sword and the dog lay down. The courtier stepped over it and handed out the Queen, who said: 'Well delivered, Sir Philip.'

Trumpets blasted, cheers sounded, a lady-in-waiting who'd got over-excited burst into tears and everybody knelt down and began proffering the Queen presents.

There was feasting after that. Hidden musicians among the trees played as the guests ate. Tables under trees from which dangled lanterns in crystal stars and moons were spread with food that Barbary had not imagined possible. Unable to appreciate how great an honour was being paid her, she was seated at the Queen's table, though well down the far end. For most of the meal she gawped, in between stuffing her mouth as full as possible as fast as possible on the Order's principle that you got it while it was going. A maid of honour on her left – it was the one who'd gone behind the bushes – was as curious about Barbary as Barbary was about the other guests. 'Who are you?' she asked.

'Important,' answered Barbary. 'Who's everybody else?'

It was a stunning list. The fair-haired man running to fat up the top of the table was Robert, Earl of Leicester,

Galloping Betty's hero and Lady Sidney's brother. There were bishops, Sidneys as thick as rabbits – the one who'd told Barbary to shut up was Sir Philip, eldest son of the house. Barbary fitted faces to what had been household names. Sir Christopher Hatton, a good-looker, drank too much.

'Who's that dangerous one? With the earring.'

The maid of honour giggled. 'Sir Walter Raleigh.' He was the one she'd gone with behind the bushes. Barbary could see why.

'Why's that Lady Sidney got no face?'

'Ah, poor lady. She nursed Her Majesty through the smallpox but then contracted the infection herself. The scars are honourable but, they say, dreadful. Now she wears a mask to cover what was once most fair.'

The better light showed Lady Sidney's mask, a tight-fitting shape of black velvet gashed at the mouth and eyes. Watching food disappear into it, which it did sparingly and with neatness, was horribly fascinating. The eyes continually checked the guests and food supply like a good hostess's should but they did it so slowly as to make the terrible mask even more sinister. In fact, Barbary realised after a while, the creep of her gaze came from exhaustion. The Queen sat near Lady Sidney, talked to her, but never once looked into the mask. There's some debts don't bear regarding, thought Barbary.

But compelling as Lady Sidney's non-face was, it was the Queen's who got most of Barbary's attention. That's the Queen, she kept telling herself. That *is* The Queen. She might have been disappointed; the face, for all its animation, was lined, the hair was definitely a wig and the behaviour was disgraceful. Barbary had known bawds comport themselves better. Lashless lids fluttered, the snow white hands coquetted – Barbary could have sworn she saw one of them reach over and goose Sir Christopher Hatton. At one point Her Majesty, shouting Latin couplets at Sir Walter Raleigh, backed them up by throwing rolls of bread down the table. Barbary put it all down to the mystery of regal fun.

She had never seen an unbounded woman before; even Galloping Betty had been subject to the Upright Man. But when they had made Elizabeth Queen, they had unleashed a spirit that was virtually uncontrollable. Intelligence, ego, style whipped out on a scale that the world couldn't reconcile to womanhood because no woman had ever shown it before. 'She's a better man than any of them,' was the Order's verdict on its Queen, echoing a belief that Elizabeth had a masculine soul, which was held right up the social scale, even by Elizabeth herself.

Barbary was spellbound. The power of the night came out of Elizabeth. It was her personality that suspended them all in this ridiculous magic, made viable by some appalling, addictive element that gave them their reason for being. Barbary saw the diners, even the gravest ones, vying like children to catch the Queen's attention. Their compliments were so flowery as to be ludicrous, but it wasn't only time-serving; they were desperate for her approval, the men wanting it with something that approached lust. You're worth treacling, you are, Barbary thought. There's not another like you.

When Lord Burghley beckoned her to the top of the table and the moment had come to be introduced to this phenomenon, Barbary's legs had trouble carrying her across the grass.

'So here's our Irish foundling,' said the Faerie Queen. 'Small, isn't it?'

'Large enough for our purposes, ma'am,' murmured Burghley.

Barbary knelt and took off her cap.

'Also it seems to be on fire. Should we douse it?' The witticism brought shrieks of sycophantic laughter from the listening courtiers. Sir Christopher Hatton handed a glass of wine to his Queen as an extinguisher.

Barbary looked up into a face that had been painted as thickly as Folly's at the Pudding-in-a-Cloth, and with less artistry, but which still compelled her to try and make her mark. 'Don't put me out yet, Your Majesty.'

'Should I not? You, who joined with the most lawless in my city.'

While briefing Barbary, Burghley had said this would be a tricky moment; all monarchs were unsettled by lawlessness, Elizabeth most of all. Barbary answered, as Burghley had told her to: 'Madam, forgive me. I had to survive.'

'Ah.' It was an appeal the greatest survivor of them all

101

never dismissed. 'And what recompense shall I have for not putting out your light?' The Queen held the glass threateningly over Barbary's bared head.

Again Burghley had told her what to say. 'Poor gifts, Your Majesty, but all I have – my heart, my soul and my loyalty.'

'You Irish have offered them before,' said Elizabeth grimly.

'Well, but you see,' Barbary was getting chatty, 'they was Irish Irish, I expect. Now me, Your Majesty, I'm English Irish. Different again.'

'And will you make your people love me?' She'd put down the glass.

'Buggers me, Your Majesty,' said Barbary, 'how they could do anything else.'

The Queen looked round at a table that had gone suddenly still. 'Buggersmee,' she said, 'an unfamiliar word. What does the lad mean?'

Sir Henry Sidney cleared his throat. 'A derivative of "boggart", Your Majesty, a pigmy sprite of Irish superstition; obviously the boy retained the word from his lost childhood.'

'Boggart, boggart, boggart,' savoured the Queen. 'Pigmy sprite. It suits him. Very well, Master Boggart, I shall accept your gifts.' She glanced round with sudden malice. 'Richer than many I have received this evening, I think.' She turned back to Barbary. 'And shall you be my own little boggart and spirit your tribe back to obedience?'

'That I will, Your Majesty.'

'Then, Burghley, equip him as befits a prince. He has our favour.'

The interview was over. Lord Burghley wiped his forehead. There had been some nasty moments, but it had gone better than he had hoped. The boy had won himself the accolade of a nickname. Nobody, unless it was the Irish themselves, would dare question his credentials now. He'd even wormed his way into the royal purse. And the entire Land of Faerie, Burghley thought ruefully, couldn't produce a greater wonder than that.

The Queen's visit to Penshurst, which had already lasted two days, continued for a critical three more. Any royal stay over five days put the host, unless he was very rich indeed, into financial difficulty. Seven could mean bankruptcy. The Lord Chamberlain was often bribed to suggest that she stay somewhere else. Sir Henry's joviality became more studied as the Queen, who had indicated that she would leave in three, put off her departure, but there was no stinting of hospitality. There were more fantasticals, there was hunting, falconry, a pageant, recitations, poetry readings – the last three all extolling the virtues of the Queen – a bear-baiting, some extremely lewd jesters, and a sermon on Sunday by a young local parson against 'the vanity in decking the body too finely'. Halfway through he seemed to realise that an audience which included a queen who possessed three thousand dresses and spent £405 a year on spangles was not receptive to the theme, and ran dry before he reached the end of his text. There was a masque, a ball, a tourney and a competition to judge which lady was the most beautiful and therefore most fitted to be Queen of the May. Elizabeth won it.

Only she remained inexhaustible. She led the hunt. She listened intently to every oration for the orator to make an error in his Latin or Greek. She danced until dawn. She capped poets' lines with couplets of her own.

Servants began to stagger. There were panics in the kitchens, where catering on such a vast scale was causing supplies to run short, from which Lady Sidney emerged calmly but with rings round her eyes nearly as black as her mask. While the Queen's attention was engaged elsewhere, her courtiers took turns to steal away and have a nap. The Earl of Leicester pleaded a cold so that he could spend a day in bed. Involuntary moans came from the Lord Treasurer at the inflammation of his gout. The sanitary arrangements were strained to the limit and the scent of perfumes and potpourris was underlaid by the stink of sewage.

Even Barbary, to whom each entertainment was a discovery of wonders, began to flag. This was partly due to the sleeping arrangements which had to accommodate more than seventy extra people, not to mention their squires, grooms and body servants. The Queen naturally occupied what was usually Sir Henry and Lady Sidney's bedroom, though she slept in her own bed, which always went with her on a progress. The Earl of Leicester had the next best, the Lord Treasurer and Secretary Walsingham shared the next, and after that it was a free for all in a pecking order in which, Barbary discovered, an Irish prince, even one of whom great things were expected, did not rank high. After two nights of sharing a bed in a crowded tent in the grounds with three male courtiers, she sought out Sir Philip Sidney, the eldest son of the house, with whom she was forming a friendship. 'Here,' she said, 'I got promised a room to myself.' It was the one concession she'd held out for, and gained, when she and Lord Burghley had discussed the terms of her apprenticeship. A room to herself and Cuckold Dick as her particular servant.

Sir Philip raised his elegant eyebrows. 'The Order of Beggars provided a suite for all its members, did it?'

True, Barbary had slept in worse places, she'd slept in places rats found unwholesome, but none of them had risked the revelation of her sex, whereas here her fellow bedmates were beginning to demand that she change into a nightshirt when she retired instead of sleeping in her day clothes. One, who'd become violently insistent about it, she'd had to kick in the prats.

'I was promised,' she said doggedly. 'Why can't I have a billet in the village, like Sir Walter?'

'Master Raleigh,' said Sir Philip, his lip curling as all the Sidneys' did when the Queen's Captain of the Guard was about or mentioned, 'has been accommodated elsewhere because we didn't want all our female servants impregnated at one time. It causes staff problems. However, our promise to you shall be redeemed, O copper-nobbed foster brother.' Barbary amused him. 'A cottage in the grounds is to be put at your disposal. In the meantime it may not have escaped your notice that we are in the middle of a visitation.'

'When's she going?'

'God knows. Hold your patience until she does.'

'Can't I sleep in the servants' hut?' A large barn had been put up especially to accommodate the overflow of retainers. Cuckold Dick was in there, with a nice straw pallet all to himself.

'No, you can't. Allow your low mind to absorb the fact that you are now of high degree, an English gentleman of

Irish princely extraction, if that's not a contradiction in terms, and one to whom our blessed Queen, God help her, has taken a fancy. Rank carries discomfort. I don't know why you're complaining; I'm sleeping in a vat in the dairy.'

The Queen had taken such a fancy to Barbary that 'Master Boggart's' phraseology became the immediate rage; courtiers could be heard referring to their legs as 'pestles' and their handkerchiefs as 'wipers', or using 'pigsney' as a term of endearment. As they took the air together on Barbary's second evening at Penshurst, Elizabeth commented on the fineness of the night. 'A night to run off with another man's wife,' agreed Barbary, surprised to find that the phrase evinced mirth from the Queen, as well as a whack of mock reproof from her fan. Within minutes everybody was repeating it.

But there was no doubt that being the Queen's pet was wearing, demanding attendance on parade every moment of Her Majesty's long and energetic day, besides constant sharpening of the wits to keep Elizabeth amused. Barbary had to keep reminding herself to what undreamed heights she had risen and to resist the temptation to fall down and sleep. She was given a complete new outfit of clothes to wear while others were being made to the Queen's own specifications – 'gentle colours, Master Boggart, that will make friends with your hair'.

Her good offices were sought. The young cleric took Barbary aside to ask her to help him regain the Queen's regard after the misjudged sermon, and begged her to accept a 'gratification' for doing so. The gratification turned out to be a purse containing five angels. The Countess of Oxford, who felt she had offended the Queen by praising the married state too warmly, gave Barbary a pearl brooch for her hat that she might smooth the way for her return to royal favour. Sir Walter Raleigh suggested Barbary capitalise on her new position by borrowing money to invest in one of the ships he was sending on another venture to the New World. A poet, Edmund Spenser, a protégé of Raleigh's, begged most respectfully to dedicate a sonnet to her.

Barbary accepted the gifts, said 'Certainly' to all requests and took no action. As she said to Cuckold Dick, in one of the brief moments they had together, 'I'm not making their shoes till I know the length of their feet.'

Dick, too, was finding Penshurst financially rewarding. Although cards and dice were not his speciality, he was still a master-gambler compared to the servants to whom he was introducing new games. 'I don't even have to grim 'em,' he told Barbary, almost aggrieved at there being no necessity to cheat. 'Money for old rope, this is.' But he advised making a run for it. 'There's too much grass, Barb,' he said uneasily. 'Let's get back to the streets. Streets is natural. Goose-turd green wherever you look, makes me ill.'

'Goose-that-lays-the-golden-eggs green this is,' said Barbary. 'We can't go yet. It's Will would suffer.'

Cuckold Dick had managed to slip away and visit nearby Robertsbridge where Will was employed. His visit temporarily allayed Barbary's fears for Will as it allayed Will's fears for Barbary, though Dick reported that the ironworks closely resembled Hell. 'Steam, sulphur and rumblings,' he said, 'but old Will's happy as a dog in a doublet. The cannon master thinks the world on him.'

Barbary could imagine it. Once he knew she was safe, Will would be able to apply himself to his passion without troubling himself as to how or why he had been uprooted from the Lambeth Marshes to a factory in deepest Kent.

'Barb, I still think we ought to leg it,' Cuckold Dick persisted.

'Leg it then.' Barbary was impatient. The entertainment this afternoon was a tourney, and it promised to be spectacular. 'But while they're pissing money against my wall, I'm staying.' She slapped him on the back. 'Battle the watch, Dick. This is clover, and we're in it.'

He watched her figure in its dandy new suit of masareene blue run towards the house. 'Clover's green, Barb,' he muttered, 'I don't like it.'

The way in which Barbary was capitalising on her popularity was by gathering intelligence. The Order always took great care to keep itself informed about the political situation, who was in, who was out, who had power, what laws were going on the statute books, who was bribable, who incorruptible. 'When you're after the cheese,' the Upright Man would say, 'it pays to know where the traps are.' If she was to spend time in the Sidney establishment, she too needed to know what was what. There was no lack of informants; the court seethed with gossip.

Mr Secretary Walsingham, she learned, was here to try and arrange a marriage between his daughter, Frances, and the young Sir Philip Sidney. Sir Philip, said the courtiers, was in love with another, but she was married.

Sir Henry Sidney, she learned too, had been out of favour with the Queen for some years and the present royal visit was in the nature of a reconciliation. Sir Henry had incurred the Queen's wrath during his term as Lord Deputy of Ireland during some of its worst rebellions by reputedly dealing too gently with the rebels and, even worse, spending too much of the Queen's money.

The use of harsher methods by subsequent Lord Deputies spending just as much money had only promoted even greater rebellion, thereby causing the Queen to reconsider her original condemnation and giving the Earl of Leicester the opportunity to persuade her to put her relationship with his brother-in-law on a sweeter footing and pay Sir Henry this dubious honour of a visit.

It was going well. Excellent gauges of the royal temperature that they were, the courtiers reported that Elizabeth was genuinely enjoying herself. The Sidneys were back in favour.

Barbary was relieved to hear it. You don't want to be apprenticed to a family of losers, Barb, she told herself.

The Queen's actual departure seemed nearly as long as her stay. Sir Henry, Lady Sidney, their household, the guests to whom they wished to say farewell stood or sat on their horses at Penshurst's gates for nearly three hours while Elizabeth listened to a loyal address from the local Mayor on behalf of a large crowd which had gathered in the lane to get a glimpse of her. She distributed alms, touched the scrofulous and accepted gifts from her people, many of them just bunches of flowers, with more grace than she had accepted the jewels and gold of her courtiers.

Last night she had stood on top of a painted wooden castle, the 'Fortress of Perfect Beauty', playing the part of Virtue though the front of her dress was open showing her bosom, and pelting with petalled bombs the attacking forces of Desire (Sir Philip Sidney) and his foster children (the Earl of Leicester and Sir Christopher Hatton) as they tried to assail the Fortress from scaling ladders decorated with flowers. She had screamed with pleasure and mock fright at the firework display – Sir Henry had hired the Italian firework expert, Ridolfo, for this final lavishness.

Now it was raining, dampening her wig and spotting her white cloak, but royalty had descended on her. She was patient, attentive to the boring Mayor, gentle and gracious to her commons. A rustic choir insisted on singing their much-rehearsed 'Come Again' so many times that its listeners got to know it by heart. Barbary saw three women and a man go into a faint at being in the Queen's presence. Ailing children were held up above the heads of the crowd to benefit from her gaze. Some of the people were hysterical. It did not matter that the Virgin Mary, whom their grandparents had worshipped, had been set aside by the new religion. Here she was, replaced, accessible in their midst.

Barbary's heart surged with adoration. Impossible that she should have hob-nobbed so familiarly with this deity. Impossible and wonderful.

The previous night the Queen had suggested taking Barbary back to London with her, and for a moment Barbary hoped wildly, but Burghley argued against it and won, though only just. 'Our young prince needs schooling, Phoebus.'

'Is our court so unlettered, Burghley, that he cannot receive it there?'

The Lord Treasurer swallowed, and leaned closer. 'You are the greatest scholar of our age, madam, but even you cannot protect him from the jealousies and intrigues to which he might be subject.'

Elizabeth nodded and turned to Barbary. 'It appears we must part for now, Master Boggart.' She became the frail little woman. 'I am so set about with plots by those who hate me that for your own safety you must remain here. Pray God that intrigue does not invade this so-called sanctuary and that I leave you among friends, not enemies.' The long royal hands cupped Barbary's face and the royal lips kissed her forehead. 'Be true to me, my Boggart.'

In the rain, watching her Queen, Babary vowed again,

as she had vowed then, to be Queen Elizabeth's loyal subject for the rest of her life.

The sixth rendering of 'Come Again' arrived at its close, and before the choir could begin a seventh, Elizabeth urged her horse forward, thanked her people, and the royal progress towards London had begun.

The Sidney household, Barbary in its midst, ambled back up the avenue, past trampled flower beds and lawns churned to mud. 'Are we ruined, Henry?' Lady Sidney asked. She was swaying in the saddle with tiredness.

'Nearly, sweetheart. I shall have to borrow.'

Lady Sidney moaned.

'And for all that, I have offended her,' continued Sir Henry. 'This morning she asked me to go back to Ireland.'

'Oh God, not again. You told her no?'

'I told her no, unless I went on my own terms. With the title of Lord Lieutenant, not Lord Deputy. She must retract having called me too costly a servant – costly, by God, when I spent my own money to feed her army which she thinks can provision on thin air. She must send me with enough money to do the job properly, and publicly admit that I was the best Governor of that country she ever had. There's more to ruling Ireland than hanging rebels.'

'She won't do it.'

'No. We are out of favour again.'

A sob came out of the black mask. 'How can she? How can she?'

Sir Henry put out a hand to steady his wife. 'The ingratitude of princes, my dear. She owes us too much to bear. You, more than me.' He looked around at the dilapidation of his estate and his stoic dignity cracked. 'And I gave her fireworks,' he snarled.

Chapter Seven

'He kicked you *where*, Master Harington?'

'Between the legs, mistress.' Harington's eyes were still watering. 'For mere correction of his hand, which is vile, he attacked me like a devil.'

The black mask turned on an unrepentant Barbary, who shouted: 'He came for me with that stick thing.' In Barbary's book assault was assault.

'It is a rod,' came the voice from the mask, 'and, by God, you shall be ruled by it. No pupil shall injure his master in this house. Bend over.'

Under the gaze of the mask, Barbary's bottom received Tutor Harington's revenge . . .

'Get him on that 'oss, lads.'

Screaming, Barbary fought three stable boys at once: 'I'm not getting on that fokker. It kicks.' Order training had not included the equestrian arts.

'It don't kick. Get on it.'

'No.'

The head groom expired. 'The mistress said you was to learn 'orsemanship, and 'orsemanship you'll bloody learn. I thought you Irish was supposed to be good with 'orse-flesh. Now get *on* it . . .'

'What do I have to kneel for? No other bugger kneels at dinner.'

'You are Sir Henry's squire,' explained Thomas the Chamberlain, tonelessly. 'It is your duty and privilege to proffer your knight and his guests the fingerbowl that they may cleanse their fingers.'

Disgustedly, Barbary slapped the napkin over her shoulder and rehearsed shoving the slopping bowl at the Chamberlain. 'Why can't they suck 'em like everybody else. . . ?'

* * *

'I've told you and told you, Boggart. Use the point. In rapier work you use the point, you don't slash it like a damned scimitar. I can be under your guard on the instant. Like that.'

Barbary removed the rapier point from her doublet. 'Waste of bloody time, this.'

Sir Philip Sidney closed his eyes in a prayer for patience and opened them. 'You are receiving lessons in swordsmanship from, I may say without vainglory, one of the masters of the art. Hardly a waste of time. Suppose a Spaniard were to come at you, sword at the ready. What would you do?'

'Shoot him . . .'

'It's no good, Henry,' reported Lady Sidney.

'Have patience, my dear. O'Neill was as wild when he first came to us.'

'O'Neill had nobility, however barbaric. This . . . this . . . boy is a mannerless ruffian, a vandal. He has been in the gutter too long to be saved.'

'Harington reports well on his reading. And on his Latin and navigation.'

'Then let him navigate himself somewhere else. Back to the swine pens he came from. He is a disruption, Henry. He *spat* at Betsy when she tried to bath him. His language is disgusting. He has no more knowledge of his catechism than a heathen and I am afraid of his corrupting the staff. As for that awful servant of his . . .' Sweating with agitation and the heat of the June day, Lady Sidney removed her mask to wipe her face. Sir Henry got up and went to the window. She had been beautiful when he married her.

'One thing, my dear,' he said, 'there seems no taint of immorality; none of what went on between O'Neill and the dairymaid.'

Lady Sidney huffed. Seducing dairymaids was an aristocratic prerogative. She would not condone it but she could cope with it. Her own brother, Leicester, Robert, her second son . . . it was what dairymaids were for. She'd be less repulsed by Master Barbary if he showed some such tendency, though she would not say so to her husband who, having a lesser pedigree than her own, did not appreciate the *laissez faire* of the elite.

Sir Henry's bulk loomed over her, blocking out the

111

sun. 'The boy will stay, Mary. Though Elizabeth might deny it, I am a loyal servant of England, and if I can shape this boy to England's purposes as I shaped O'Neill, I shall have served her well.'

But I've got to shape his manners, thought his wife. 'Yes, Henry.'

'And Philip likes him.' He saw Mary Sidney's cavitied face soften before she tied the mask back on. At the door of the library she turned back. 'Ireland,' she said, 'nothing but ruin from it. I wish it to Perdition.'

Sir Henry banged his fist on his desk. Nobody understood, not even his own wife. He controlled his voice. 'If it goes there, my dear, England goes with it.'

'Either we leg it soon, Barb,' said Cuckold Dick, inexpertly dabbing salve on Barbary's weals, 'or your arse'll be corrugated.'

Barbary clenched her teeth. She was dismayed by her ineptness in adapting herself to life among the Sidneys, but she found herself at such a disadvantage in this alien culture that she instinctively battled against it and, inevitably, was losing.

She cricked her head round to snarl, 'You salving that skin or grating it?'

'Never said I was a lady's maid, Barb.'

She dropped back. Losing. That was the rub. If she legged it now she'd be losing. Unacquainted with excellence, she reasoned that she'd be missing opportunity, education, the chance of riches. Besides, there was the threat of the gallows literally hanging over Will and Dick.

'We leg it,' she said, 'and they catch us, they'll trine you and Will. Maybe me. We stay.'

Cuckold Dick sighed. Such initiative as he had operated only within a tightly organised structure, which was why he'd been so worthy a member of the Order. Now that he was marooned outside it, the only regulation he could work to was laid down by Barbary. If she said they stayed, they stayed.

Barbary wriggled her trunks up, then got off the bed and went to look out of the window. They hadn't, after all, given her a cottage in the grounds. Instead she and Dick had the two rooms over the archway into the courtyard at the side of the house. The window behind her looked out onto a cobbled courtyard with urns of geraniums and mounting blocks. From this window she could see Lady Sidney's herb garden and the park. What was natural was lovely, what was man-made, as in her room here, was of simple good taste.

'What's wrong with it?' she asked out loud. 'And me?'

There was an element here at Penshurst that an element in herself resisted, and she couldn't fathom why. She'd felt at ease with the Queen of England, she felt she'd weighed up Lord Burghley, even Walsingham. But the Sidneys, being neither tricksters nor victims, the only people she really understood, baffled her. They had a completeness which gave her no mental handhold to use on them.

Behind her came Dick's mild voice: 'Heard this preacher once, Barb, talking about some cony who was kicking against the pricks.'

'Like I kicked Harington?'

'Not that sort of prick. More a hedge with thorns sticking out.'

'And?'

'Well, the preacher said it didn't do him no good. All he was doing was getting scratched. Like you, Barb. You're kicking against the pricks.'

'So?'

'Well, don't. Go along the hedge, like, not through it. Bend a bit. You're bright, Barb. Best crossbiter's aid I ever had. What's it conies say we are? Dissemblers. That's what you got to do, dissemble.'

She turned round to him. He'd regained weight and was in the brown, belted gown provided by the Queen. She'd once thought his appearance the acme of respectibility; now she saw it was seedy, with foodstains down his front and dandruff in his hair. I wouldn't change him, she defied unseen Sidneys, not for gold with knobs on. He was her link with the life of the Order, the only person, apart from Will, to know she was female and more comfortable in the knowledge than Will; his sexual neutrality was so complete that she could bare her backside for him to salve with no embarrassment at all. And he was right.

'You're not so green as you're cabbage-looking,' she told him. 'I can treacle 'em, can't I? Lead 'em on?'

'None better, Barb.'

Then that's how she would cope with it. She was a trickster, so she'd trick. Pretend, play-act, bow with the wind. She couldn't understand how, with all her training, she'd been such a fool as to battle; as long as she hung on to the knowledge that they were just so many more conies to be caught, these Sidneys wouldn't overwhelm her. 'Battle the watch, eh Dick?'

She turned back to the view from the window to where the park stretched away in sunlit glades stippled by the great beeches. Some watch.

It was simple. Her ear picked up their phraseology, she shaped her mouth to use it as they used it. She aped Sir Philip's walk, table manners, his address to the servants. With Lady Sidney she showed an interest in herbs and flowers, with Sir Henry she probed politely into politics. She charmed Betts, the parson, by requesting instruction in the Faith. On Sundays she kept her eyes down and read her Bible.

'There is an improvement, Henry. The boy is showing signs of civilisation. Even Harington reports submission to discipline – I had already suggested a less rigorous use of the rod.'

'Very wise, my dear. The Irish will respond as long as the iron fist is in the velvet glove. Never one without the other. How many times have I told Elizabeth, not one without the other.'

'You're right, Henry.'

Sir Henry Sidney nodded. He knew he was. O'Neill had proved it.

Long afterwards, when Barbary remembered Penshurst, it was as a background to some image of Philip Sidney. Philip playing tennis. Philip drawing a bow at the archery butts in Long Meadow. The stables illuminated by a shaft of sun coming down through the hay-speckled air to wash Philip in light as he rubbed the blaze of his favourite war horse. Philip's pom-pommed shoes crossing twice in mid-air before landing from a leap that, in Barbary's opinion, made other dancers look ridiculous but not him. Philip illuminating Caesar's Commentaries out of the greyness that Harington made of them. Philip sucking a piece of hay and teaching her, of all things, Turkish politics.

114

Most of all she remembered their visits to Gamage Copse, a hangar of beech trees which had been made a sanctuary for the park's fallow deer and where they would cluster round and feed from the hand. Philip, lace-collared, lace-cuffed, gartered above the knee, leaning negligently against a green trunk, talking or reading her his latest poem to Penelope Rich:

> When Cupid, having me, his slave, descried
> In Mars's livery prancing in the press:
> What now, Sir Fool! said he – I would no less:
> Look here, I say! I look'd, and Stella spied,
> Who, hard by, made a window send forth light.

'I haven't finished it yet, but it promises well, eh young Boggart?'

Barbary sighed. 'It's not as bad as "Arcadia", but it's still krap.'

Sir Philip Sidney rolled up his manuscript and hit Barbary on the head with it. 'I am rewarded for casting my pearls before unlettered swine.'

'Nobody else will listen to them. Why don't you do more like "My love has my heart and I have his"? That was good.'

'This is the modern style.'

'Over-elaboration,' she was learning the vocabulary, 'like bloody Spenser.' She had taken against Edmund Spenser on the night she'd had to sit and listen to that poet recite an interminable something he called 'Shephearde's Calendar'. Lady Sidney had kept pinching her every time her head nodded. 'Him and his iambics.'

'You're a Philistine, Boggart.' As much as he could be on a day when the bees thrummed in the thyme and beech leaves made penny-shaped shadows in the sunlight, Philip was disapproving. 'Cloth-maker's son he may be, but Spenser will be a great poet. Greater even than me.' He cocked his fair head in judgement on his last sentence and decided against it. 'Or perhaps not.' His humour came back as he unrolled the scroll and considered his poem again. '*She* will like it. Oh God, Boggart, what agony it is to love without attaining. "Desiring nought but how to kill Desire." '

'If she wasn't married, you probably wouldn't desire

her,' said Barbary. Philip winked at her and began a dissertation on Aristotle.

Sitting on the grass and watching him, Barbary resisted the temptation to hug his ankles. She wasn't in love with him, but if God ever needed a deputy she reckoned Philip Sidney would do.

She supposed he had faults. He believed that no one without the bluest of blue blood should hold authority, yet he addressed beggars as his equal. He hated Roman Catholicism – he'd happened to be in Paris on St Bartholomew's Eve, an appalled witness to the massacre of the Huguenots – but numbered Catholics among his friends.

Only Elizabeth refused to hitch this star to her wagon. Perhaps because he'd admonished her against a Catholic marriage, more probably because she was frightened of being eclipsed, she kept him kicking his heels at home, using his undeniable talent as a diplomat only on the most minor occasions, forbidding him to go off and explore the New World, as he wanted to.

And that was all right by Barbary because it meant she had his company and, with it, all the company of poets and mathematicians and ill-tempered philosophers and important and strange men and women his presence attracted. While Penshurst contained Philip Sidney, the world came to Penshurst.

His voice interrupted the reverie into which Aristotle and the scent of grass were sending her. 'Did I tell you I once met your grandmother?'

She stretched and yawned. She didn't have a grandmother. 'Sir Henry said you'd received her in Connaught or somewhere. He seemed to think she was a battleaxe.'

'Perhaps.'

She looked up at him, attracted by a timbre in his voice. One of the deer was nuzzling at his sleeve, leaving its slime on his coat. 'Wasn't she a battleaxe?'

'Oh yes.' He scratched the deer between its stubs of antlers. 'I think in the end that to have quiet in Ireland we must kill all the Irish, but do you know, Boggart, there was something to her. I was reminded of Elizabeth.'

'The Queen?'

'Our own dear Queen. One momentary chime of the same bell. Faults by the bushel, and a quality to quicken the blood.'

116

'Well, well,' said Barbary. She was unused to a mention of the Irish that didn't traduce them. 'I'll tell Her Majesty you're equating her with an Irish pirate, shall I?'

'An Irish pirate with a treacherous grandson. Now if you will mount that amble-pad you call a horse, we'll go home for dinner.' To get Barbary used to riding, Sir Henry had been forced to send out for a pony to which, ordinarily, he wouldn't have given stable room. It had a leg at each corner of a square body and a tendency to doze while walking. Philip said he'd met more exciting stick-insects. Barbary called it Spenser.

She was now dissembling so well that she was considered sufficiently civilised to move on to the crux of her education: lessons with Sir Henry Sidney on Ireland.

Sir Henry's purpose, like Lord Burghley's, was to turn Ireland into another England, same divisions into counties, same administration, ruled by the same Common Law.

In this they were being liberal. Ireland was too close. England could neither risk its falling into the hands of a foreign power nor, which might turn out to be the same thing, its independence. It must be an English colony. Harsher men advocated the genocide of its rebellious people and their replacement by English settlers. Burghley and Sidney stopped short of this, partly from humanity and partly because they didn't believe it to be practical.

If they could have kidnapped every baby boy likely to turn out an Irish leader and brought him to England to train in English ways, they would have done so, convinced that once he saw the superiority of the English system over his own he would return to his country full of zeal to begin its Anglicisation.

They were bewildered that it wasn't Anglicised already.

'You see, my boy,' Sir Henry told Barbary, 'many of the Irish barons are the descendants of Normans who invaded and partly conquered Ireland in the twelfth century. One would have expected them to develop as this, their mother country, developed. '

'Why didn't they?' asked Barbary.

'If I knew the answer to that,' said Sir Henry, 'there

would be no Irish problem. Myself, I believe there to be some infection in the Irish air which turns men native. Even Englishmen who gained lordship over there as recently as the last century or two are now indistinguishable from the true Irish with their cloaks and their wild hair and no stirrups to their horses.'

Barbary had no opinion of the Irish herself. For as long as she remembered she had been told they were treacherous and ignorant, and believed it. Such Irish men and women as had attached themselves to the Order had reinforced this belief by being more degraded than its lowest of low members. They were invariably drunk and lachrymose with homesickness. From the superiority of his uprightness, the Upright Man had called them 'Papist shit' and used them like dogs, which had served them right for being Irish.

'D'you hear the one about the Irishman and the hen?' she asked Sir Henry. She saw at once she'd made a mistake in manners. Irish jokes were low and Sir Henry did not subscribe to them. She was confused by his refusal to join in the general view of the Irish as sub-human. As far as Sir Henry was concerned, they were merely 'in error'. Not to have had the advantage of Roman invasion had been their first error, which had been compounded by their refusal of Norman rule and had gradually led to the greatest error of all, their obstinacy in clinging to the Roman Catholic faith when England had shown them the way to Protestantism. 'A people who walk in darkness.'

'Though indeed,' he added, 'the churchmen who were sent to bring them the light were not good examples. Nor do I think they would have clung to Papism if we had not mistakenly persecuted them for it. It was their way of retaining their Celtic nationality. The quarrel between us is not basically religious, though it has become so. It is the age-old misunderstanding between Celt and Anglo-Saxon.'

Sir Henry's true hatred was for the English settlers who ruled in Dublin. 'Backbiters and bigots.' They had made his job as the Queen's Deputy in Ireland a burden with their opposition to his every reform.

And that, with a confusing picture of a country divided into areas which were dominated by Old Irish, Old English, Ango-Irish and new English, was Barbary's education on Ireland.

Everything changed with the coming of the O'Neill.

That day she and Philip and Philip's best friend, Fulke Greville, had gone to Gamage Copse to enjoy the St Luke's Little Summer which was making the October glorious. Philip and Fulke had strolled away through the trees, arguing abstractions, and Barbary was ploughing through Philip's translation of Xenophon for an examination Harington was setting the following week.

It didn't seem momentous that she had chosen to sit under a beech with a pile of its leaves as a back rest, nor that her legs were covered with her cloak against the first nip in the autumn air. But she had taken off her cap and the colour of the leaves matched her short hair and gave the impression of extending it so that a wave of it apparently flowed round her head. To a first glance the spread cloak looked like a skirt.

The earth thrummed with vibration from hooves. A very large horse cut out the sun and a voice said: 'Now why is a pretty young woman wasting her lovely eyes on a book?'

She was up in a moment, slamming her cap back on her head, stamping her boots and swearing in the masculine.

Philip and Fulke came up at a run and threw themselves into slapping the new arrival on the back. 'Hugh, may I present a countryman of yours, Master O'Flaherty, better known as Boggart. Boggart, this is the Earl of Tyrone.'

Hugh O'Neill twirled off his hat in an ornamental bow. 'Desolated,' he said, 'to have insulted this lively young gentleman by taking him for a dryad. Blame it on me ageing eyes.'

There was nothing wrong with his eyes which were dark, though his hair and beard were red. They weren't ageing either.

'Hugh,' said Philip, 'why are you speaking in that ghastly accent after all the trouble we had beating it out of you?'

The O'Neill smiled. 'My dear fellow,' he drawled, in perfect upper-class English, 'you must give a pagan time to adjust. I'm straight off the boat.'

119

'A long stay, I trust. This is always your home.'

They got on their horses and set off at a walk back to the house, three of them talking, Barbary silent and bringing up the rear. There was a whiff of the alien about this O'Neill. He wasn't quite right. Gaudy as Elizabethan court dress was, his went a shade too far, literally. His crimson doublet was over-bright, over-pinked and over-slashed, its peascod belly stood out an inch too far over what was otherwise a slim waist. His black and gold trunk hose was outrageously bombasted and his silver Dutch cloak had too many blue tassels. Barbary, having spent enough time with the Sidneys to know what was tasteful and what was not, jeered at this provincial caricature aping the *dernier cri*, because that was better than the discomfort of feeling that the apes of the *dernier cri* were being caricatured by this provincial.

Discomfort was the word for the presence of this young man, and not just because for a moment he had acknowledged her as female. Thoughts at odds to what he was saying glided behind his eyes like the fins of sharks. He reminded her of cony-catchers at work. There had been a second back there that had established an odd recognition between them. 'And when I trust you,' she told the Earl of Tyrone's back, 'will be when two Sundays come together.'

At that moment the O'Neill wheeled his horse. 'I see it,' he shouted, spreading his arms to her. 'No doubt of it. Heir to the O'Flaherties, with the looks of the O'Connors and the colouring of the O'Malleys.'

'Have you had your spies out again, Hugh?' asked Philip. 'Boggart's supposed to be incognito just now.'

'He's to be a surprise to my poor countrymen, is he?' The O'Neill grinned. 'And a surprise he will be. No, no spies. Your father wrote to me. He thinks the young gentleman will need an ally in Ireland.' He gestured to Philip and Fulke. 'Go ahead to your lofty purposes,' he said, 'while we bog Irish bring up the rear, as we should. We will commune, Master Boggart and I.'

He slowed his horse to Spenser's pace so that the other two went ahead. Again Barbary was uncomfortable. The ease with which he had apparently accepted her as heir to the O'Flaherties was nearly as unsettling as if he had challenged her imposture. Did he truly believe she was a royal Irishman? Was he in cahoots with Burghley? Was he playing some game of his own?

'How's the training going?' he was asking companionably. 'Has Harington graduated from the bum-beating school of philosophy? Is Sir Henry still advising God on where he went wrong?'

Her lips twitched, but she refused to be drawn into a confederacy. 'I am learning a great deal,' she said.

'So did I,' he said, 'so did I.' Every damn thing he said resounded with double meaning. 'And what's your given name?' he asked. 'Even in Ireland we don't christen a baby Boggart.' It was a reasonable question; there was no excuse for not answering it, but each piece of given information drew her deeper into some baffling conspiracy.

'Barbary,' she said. 'Jesus, what's the matter?'

Hugh O'Neill had fallen forward onto his horse's neck, banging his head against it. She put out her hand to help him, and felt his shoulders shaking. The bastard was silently, helplessly, laughing.

'Will you shut up?' she hissed. 'Shut up,' and immediately was even crosser for the alliance her rudeness made with his.

'Barbary.' He wiped his eyes on his horse's mane. 'Isn't that the fine name, and common on the west coast of Ireland.'

He was mocking her. Furiously, she tore away the upper hook and eye of her doublet and whipped out the necklet. 'You want proof?' she shouted at him. 'Here's proof.'

He turned it in his hands, no longer laughing, making it seem that he was exchanging secrets with the thing. He nodded as he handed it back to her. 'When I was a boy,' he said, 'I saw it round the neck of your mother.'

He was going to say something else or had said it. Barbary's mind blinked. They were in the avenue that led to Penshurst house and in that one subliminal second the flanking trees became leafless and ugly, the house a ruin.

O'Neill said, or was going to say: 'I'm told the English hanged her.'

There was a feast to welcome Hugh O'Neill back to his foster home. As usual Penshurst was entertaining other visitors; a secretary to the King of Navarre, Dr Dee the Queen's scientist and magician, a Venetian botanist, Baron Alasco of Poland whom Philip had met on his Grand Tour, assorted poets, courtiers on leave and Mary, the Sidneys' eldest daughter who was now the pregnant Countess of Pembroke.

The jewels, metal-threaded ruffs and embroideries of the aristocracy at the top of the table graded further down into the unglittered, less fashionable cassocks of the merchants and higher servants, until, like a partly unsloughed snakeskin, it reached the dull russet and home-made linen of the peasantry whom Sir Henry, with his immaculate courtesy, always invited to his festive table.

Barbary was excused the duties of squire and sat in honour next to the Countess, across the table from the Earl of Tyrone. Sir Henry was out to reminisce with the O'Neill and wanted his new protégé to hear at first hand the advantages attendant on eschewing Irish savagery for the refinement of Renaissance England. Since his voice was loud and commanded attention, everybody else could hear too.

'Make this lord here your exemplar, Master Barbary,' he boomed. 'Regard him now, yet when I found him he was no better than a horseboy hiding in the bogs of Dungannon, hunted by his uncle, Shane O'Neill, Shane the Grand Disturber, who had already killed Hugh's father and cut the throat of his brother. Such was the ignoble feuding of the O'Neills of Ulster.'

'Barbarians,' smiled O'Neill up and down the table and Barbary wondered that nobody else noticed his knuckles were as white as his teeth.

'I hope, sirrah, that Shane's heirs are kept under control so that they cannot now threaten your position,' said Sir Henry.

'They have been suppressed, my lord,' said the O'Neill and smiled again and Barbary, still watching his hands, saw them gripe as if he had tracked Shane's children down one by one and with those same hands torn out their throats.

'And here he now is,' expounded Sir Henry, 'the undoubted lord of the north of Ireland, Her Majesty's trusted servant, friend to her friends, and as good an

Englishman as ever turned his weapons into plough-shares.' There was a great deal more of this as Sir Henry demonstrated, without actually boasting, the Pygmalion role he had played in turning the rude clay of this Irish-man into a desirable Elizabethan. And all the time Hugh O'Neill smiled as Galatea might have smiled.

The light coming through the tracery of the tall win-dows dimmed and servants lit candelabra on the table and applied tapers to the torches on the walls, deepening colours and scenting the hall with rosemary and resin.

Barbary kept blinking, trying to dislodge the flash of mental image which had distorted the proportions of Penshurst that afternoon and which still warped every-thing she saw, so that the walls of this hall where she had learned reason and manners lacked symmetry, bloating Sir Henry's handsome red face, insisting that Lady Sid-ney's mask covered a grinning skull. She tried to believe some baleful influence emanating from Dr Dee, the Queen's necromancer, had turned this night abnormal when it should be like other nights. Or that it was a trick of the flickering light.

She knew it was neither; it was that ginger-headed, dark-eyed man sitting across from her who had brought something from Ireland with him that had infected her, and only her, so that her surroundings seemed diseased.

He was saying regretfully: 'I could wish Her Majesty trusted my advice and yours, Sir Henry, on the adminis-tration of Munster. Have you seen this?' He passed over a piece of paper on which there was dense printing and heavy capitals in the manner of a fly sheet.

Sir Henry called for his spectacles and read it. ' "A Note of the Benefit that may grow in short time to the younger Houses of Gentlemen if they do accept Her Majesty's offer to undertake the Settlement of Munster . . . to be the chief lord of a great seignory . . . homage . . . corn, cattle. The Plot offers many advan-tages to the younger children and kinsfolk of gentlemen of good families and those of inferior calling and degree . . . To preserve the English nature of the under-taking none shall marry but with persons born of English parents . . . no mere Irish are to be permitted in any family there, nor land rented to them, to employ them, nor shelter them . . . a goodly land." '

He looked up. 'This is madness. Unless Munster has changed since last I saw it—'

'It is a wasteland still,' said the O'Neill, 'just as it was after the Desmond rebellion, eight hundred thousand acres of starvation. And how it is to be tilled without the "mere Irish" I do not know.' He added casually, 'And Sir Walter Raleigh is to get forty-two thousand acres of it.'

Sir Henry stared. 'Forty-two *thousand*?'

'From Lismore to Youghal.' The O'Neill shrugged. 'After all, he did lay down his cloak for the Queen to step on.'

Sir Henry's fist hit the table and made the plates and tankards jump. 'Madness,' he shouted. Lady Sidney put out a hand to stop any treasonable statement, but he shook it off. 'I told her not to do it like this, I told her.'

'Never mind, Sir Henry,' said O'Neill. 'Good Sir Walter may have trouble enjoying his acres. Some of them are, or rather were, the MacSheehys' ancestral land.'

Sir Henry recovered with difficulty. 'The MacSheehys,' he muttered, and then he remembered. 'The Mac-Sheehys,' he said again and a look of amusement passed between him and the Earl of Tyrone. 'He has my prayers.'

'What I am afraid of,' said the O'Neill, 'is another rebellion. It may be feasible to fill up the void of Munster with English settlers, it may not. You and I know it isn't exactly Somerset, or Kent. But to displace the native population from a quarter of Ireland . . .'

'Madness,' repeated Sir Henry. He lifted his hand: 'However, do not interfere, my boy. Ulster is enough for you to cope with.' He had spoken.

The O'Neill bowed in his seat and changed the subject. 'I fear that I must be on my way tomorrow.'

There were protests from around the table. Lady Sidney said: 'But my dear boy, we hoped you would stay.'

O'Neill kissed his hand to her and shook his head. 'This is a buying spree; I am off to London to purchase tableware, tapestries and other good English things. I want to turn Dungannon into a typical English manor, re-create Penshurst in Ulster. And I want Lord Burghley's permission to import some lead. As you know, there is a special embargo on lead for Ireland in case it is turned into rebellious bullets, but I need it to roof my Dungannon Penshurst.'

He stood up. 'Before I go, may I propose a toast as a loyal Irishman to Her Glorious Majesty and to the adornment of her realm, the family Sidney.' He raised his glass: 'To Queen Elizabeth, may the worms eat her flesh while she is still living. And to you, my dear Sidneys, may your stinking patronage choke you.'

Gradually Barbary unstiffened her neck and looked first up and then down the table. Sir Henry was smiling and lifting his glass. Beside her the Countess of Pembroke was saying, 'How charming.' Down the length of the table unperturbed, jolly men and women were uttering 'The Queen, God bless her' and 'To the Sidneys'. Everything was normal; it was she who had gone mad.

Desperately she looked up at the O'Neill to find him gazing at her. He nodded. 'I see the young gentleman remembers his Irish,' he said.

Eventually the Countess beside her said: 'Father, Master Barbary is not feeling well. I recommend fresh air for him.' To Barbary she said: 'Shall I come with you?'

Barbary shook her head. Sir Henry gave his permission for her to leave the table and she slipped out of the hall which was becoming uproarious as the O'Neill told funny stories against his countrymen: '. . . And Patrick said: "Bejasus, I can't tell you how many miles it is from Waterford to Cork, but it's eighteen miles from Cork to Waterford."' She could hear the laughter as she went down the terrace steps to the yew walk where the long shadows of the hedges made geometric shapes in the moonlight.

She hadn't understood him. She *could not* have understood him. It was some inflection in his voice as he spoke the Irish that must have indicated to her the terrible meaning. She could not have recognised the words. If she'd picked up the sense of one here or there it was because she knew a little Shelta, the patois used by Irish members of the Order and sometimes by the Order itself.

Behind her she heard tables being moved in the hall and musicians striking up as the company prepared for dancing. She moved away from the sound and held her head as she walked. Out here nightingales were singing but they could not restore normality. 'Oh God,' she said out loud, 'I am Barbary Clampett. I'm not Irish.'

'You are,' said a shadow.

She screamed at it: 'Get away from me.' He was standing in her path with his fantastic clothes made black and white by the moon.

'You understood.'

'I didn't. I didn't.' She turned away from him, illogical in her panic. 'I'll tell them.'

She heard him say: 'They're too sure of themselves. They wouldn't believe you.'

She knew they wouldn't. In her mind she said to Sir Henry: 'The Earl of Tyrone has offered you and the Queen the grossest insult,' and heard the words bounce off his impregnable self-assurance like peas rattling against armour. She could have wept at the Sidneys' certainty of their own rightness. 'You've no right to hurt them.' The music was in its stride now, tinny with distance, but audible.

'Oh, I have.' He came closer and took her fingertips in his, raising them. 'I have a million rights, all of them dead in Ireland. That's a nice measure they're playing.' He was walking her between the yew shapes, their two hands raised. They were dancing. She jerked her hand away, but he went on, one elbow akimbo, the other arm elegant in the air as if she still accompanied him.

At the end of the stave he turned and advanced back to her, his high-heeled shoes with their over-large buckles pointing in time to the music. His hand took hers again and, because she could no longer fight the night's improbability, she didn't pull away. 'They're good people,' she said, helplessly.

'That's what makes them dangerous.' He was skipping now in the most intricate part of the galliard; Barbary's lessons with the dance tutor had not advanced so far even if she had felt like skipping, which she did not. She stood while he jigged round her, flirting his long fingers. 'They tell me your foster father works in the cannon foundry. That may be useful to Ulster. If it comes to it.'

He was a weasel gyrating round a bird. She tore her eyes away from him to look around, to reassure herself that the grass was in place and not overhead, that the stars weren't twinkling out of the ground, that this was solid, English, Penshurst. 'Don't talk to me,' she screeched at him. 'Will wouldn't . . . we wouldn't help you, you shitpot traitor.' All these years she had prided herself on her swearing and now in her great need it was inadequate. Yet she couldn't tear herself away. 'You're mad, you are. You're mad.' She spotted their leggy shadows stretching across the walk. 'You're unnatural. Look at you trying to dance with a boy.'

In the house the drums crashed. The O'Neill leaped in the air, crossed his feet and landed close to her. 'But I'm not, am I?'

She backed away from him until a hedge stopped her. He paced with her. 'I'm dancing with as great a dissembler as myself, aren't I?' The music went back to the start of another round; she was beginning to hate it. But when he held out his hand this time, she took it, mesmerised, and together they paraded down the walk. 'You see, *Master* Barbary, I was interested to see this new young chieftain the English had invented to inflict on Ulster's western flank. And see him I did, sitting under a tree.' They turned and began the parade back. 'And I saw that for once, know it or not, the English weren't cheating anybody. They couldn't have invented the nose of him, nor the skin, nor the hair, and definitely not the eyes.'

The drums crashed again and his hands came out to span her waist, throwing her in the air and catching her.

'But the English weren't seeing what I saw. And the question was then, was it poor old Hugh who was blind? Or the English?'

'I think I'll sit this one out,' said Barbary. 'I'm going back.'

'You'll stay and you'll dance.' His fingers were on hers like pincers. She stayed and she danced.

'And so, politely, I asked this young chieftain's name. And he told me. It was Barbary, he said.'

They twirled. She spat. 'And what's wrong with that?'

'Nothing. It's a fine name. And common on the very west coast of Ireland to which this young chieftain lays claim.' He smiled. 'Among girls.'

He threw her up in the air again but this time, as he caught her, he kissed her. It wasn't a romantic kiss, it was an induction; his tongue probed her mouth as his hands went down her waist, over her hips and under her buttocks, to prove to both of them that he'd guessed right, a tribal thing, a welcoming and an initiation. Nevertheless it moved parts of Barbary's mind and body that she had not known were moveable, or even there.

He released her. The music from the house had stopped, leaving the nightingales in command. 'We'll be in contact again, Master Barbary,' he said. She watched him swagger away up the walk to the lights of the house. Then she sat down because her legs weren't feeling very strong.

The next morning Barbary informed the tutor Harington that she was taking the day off.

'You shall not,' he said. 'Today is for mathematics.'

When she told him where to stuff his mathematics he threatened her with the rod. She took it, broke it and handed it back. 'I'm taking the day off,' she repeated clearly. 'I had a bad night.'

In the stables she crisply ordered a groom to saddle Spenser and then surprised that lethargic pony by spurring him into a trot across the parkland north towards the church.

'Bad night' had been an understatement. All through it the events of the previous day and evening had re-enacted themselves in the solitude of her room like the aftershocks of an earthquake so that each time exhaustion sent her into a doze she was jerked out of it by another wave of mental and physical tumult as if her brain could only absorb O'Neill's revelations one at a time and had just reacted to the next in the series. There had been so many of them that they warred for priority of concern.

That the poor Sidneys had nurtured a viper in their bosom was as nothing to the fact that she had joined that same viper in complicity. Was it treason to dance with a traitor? It was if you didn't inform those against whom he was planning treason. At one point in the dreadful night she had got up, wrapped a cloak round herself and set off for Philip's room to tell him everything she knew. But in the corridor the assertive eyes of Sidneys and Dudleys had stared down at her from their stiff-necked portraits, unprepared to take the word of a guttersnipe against that of an earl, Irish though he might be. Class was a stronger bonding than race. O'Neill was Philip's boyhood friend;

his Boggart was a newly arrived, and imposed, acquisition.

She'd wavered about in the corridor, moving forward, stepping back, longing to rejoin the clean conviction of England against the dirty foreigners, to strike a patriotic blow for Queen Elizabeth, to know again where she stood.

But she didn't know where she stood. The O'Neill had destroyed that happy certainty. Suppose that she herself was one of those dirty foreigners? In the end she'd crept back to her room.

She'd been left with only one move. She had to see Will. The fog wall that had protected her sanity for so long was shifting; it was a fine day to everybody else's view, the sun warming piles of leaves that had been crisped by early frost, rose-hips sprinkling the hedges with bright red, dew glissading up and down spiders' webs, but Barbary's eyes saw it through a mist. 'The English hanged her,' was being twittered by blackbirds. A countrywoman with a yoke of milk pails curtseyed to her as she passed the lodge and called pleasantly: 'Good day, Master Barbary. I'm told the English hanged her.'

Hanged who? They hanged all sorts. They'd hanged Mary Cutpurse for killing her baby. Whoever she was, she'd probably deserved it. She wasn't Barbary's mother, Barbary didn't have a mother. Then why was somebody's mother hanging from the neck at the back of Barbary's mind?

Only Will knew for certain. She'd never had the courage to ask him before, but now she had to. Almost reluctantly, she admitted to herself that the courage to face the answer, if she got one, had been given her by the O'Neill.

She hadn't seen him before leaving the house, for which she was thankful. A sprinkling of that gentleman went a very long way. He was too disturbing and she pitied any women with whom he became involved. Nevertheless, he had been the herald of a new concept, a promise that womanhood, though a disaster, might contain its own delights. For all her worries, Barbary found herself grinning.

And there had been something else. That tongue in her mouth last night, his hands, his bloody impertinence, his duplicity, the whole complication of the man, had tasted of another country. It was a terrible country, full of idiots and murder and sudden death, and he had come out of it jaunty. He'd joked and betrayed. The devious bastard was the most daring man she'd ever met. The woman hanging in the back of Barbary's mind had the same quality, a plotter and fighter. It was time to make her acquaintance.

The larger Kent towns, especially the ports, loathed the iron foundries and furnaces which were springing up all over the Wealden countryside, mainly because they used so much charcoal. Regular complaints were sent to the Queen from loyal citizens wailing that the woods of Old England were disappearing fast, that soon there would be scant timber for the building of houses, water mills, bridges, ships, gunstocks, barrels, arrows. Hunting would end for ever.

Barbary had been with Sir Henry at court when weeping merchants had petitioned him to close down his foundry at Robertsbridge. Sir Henry's answer was not only that he would not close it down, but that he was enlarging another at Panningridge. 'If Spain comes against us,' he told them, 'your wooden walls will need cannon to mount on them. And if you knew aught of iron-founding you would know that birch makes a better charcoal than oak.'

The Panningridge project was due to the advent of Will Clampett. Barbary sometimes wondered whether Sir Henry would have so readily agreed to take her as his squire/protégé if Will hadn't been part of the bargain. Recognising the man's ability, leg or no leg, Sir Henry had quickly promoted him to cannon master and recently moved him from Robertsbridge to Panningridge where he was modernising the existing forge.

Barbary had been delighted by the honour to Will and the fact that Panningridge was only a mile or so away. Sir Henry was delighted that he could soon sell first-class ordnance to his country. Will was in a seventh heaven.

It took a specialised eye to see heaven in Panningridge; most people would have consigned it lower down. Its clear, brown stream, a tributary of the Eden, had once formed a deep, wooded ravine but, for all Sir Henry's protestations that he was not raping the woods, the great trees had gone, to be replaced by scrub. The upper end of the stream had been dammed into a pen pond large enough to qualify as a lake; below it stood the furnace which, with its water wheel, looked not unlike a mill except for the lobster-pot-shaped chimney which stood beside it belching smoke and fire. Will's two new furnaces for the casting of cannon were being built to his own design; scaffolding stood thirty feet high round objects like fat obelisks. Among the weeds were stacks of iron sows shaped like canoes, piles of charcoal and bricks.

Most satanic of all was the noise. The valley roared with the sounds of rushing water, grinding wheels, fire, and vast, water-operated hammers, whose thud could be heard at Penshurst. All iron foundry men went deaf sooner or later.

Spenser always balked at going too close, so Barbary left him in the pasture grazed by the foundry's oxen and crunched her way up the cinder track. It was hard on the feet, but roads leading to ironworks had to be tough to take the tons of wood which went into them and the tons of iron which came out. One of the legitimate grievances against the foundries was the havoc done to the highways by their enormously heavy, ox-drawn wagons.

She saw a familiar face and yelled at it. 'Matthew, where's Will?'

Matthew doffed his 'skull', the foundry worker's tin hat, and mouthed: 'Morning, Maister Barbary.' He pointed. Wincing, Barbary walked towards the obelisks where Will, the cannon master, was rowing with the iron master, Henri D'Arras, though how each was making the other hear him was a mystery. D'Arras, who'd been imported by Sir Henry – the French were experts in iron smelting – was using his stubby hands with Gallic emphasis, Will was thumping his wooden leg. Barbary had to pull at their sleeves to be noticed.

'Trouble?' she asked Will when she'd dragged him far enough away for a screech to be audible.

'He knows his iron, that Frog,' shouted Will. 'What he don't know is his cannon. Wants to cast 'em unbored. Old-fashioned. Unreliable. Nowadays we makes a bore mould and casts round it.'

'I want to talk to you.'

The places where they could talk were limited not only by the noise but by the fact that Will's leg tended to stick in soft earth. They kept to the track until it turned a hill and then went up a dry path into woods where the thick multiple trunks of coppiced hornbeam absorbed the noise of the valley and they could hear birdsong again. Will was silent, preoccupied with the problems he'd left behind him. They chose a glade surrounded by sweet chestnuts and sat down, Will on an old stump, Barbary among the ferns.

'Things have happened, Will.' She gave him an edited version of the O'Neill's visit. When she'd finished she looked up at him. 'It's time I knew,' she said.

He'd taken off his hat to rub his scalp, a sign he was disturbed, and his curly greying hair stuck up on the top of his head. He stared down at his ammunition leg and said nothing; not as if he was refusing to tell her the truth, but because doing so would necessitate speaking of the personal for which he didn't have the vocabulary. She helped him out to show him she was ready: 'I am Irish, aren't I?'

He nodded. Barbary closed her eyes in a rush of misery; she had hoped hard that he would not confirm it. Well, they were on course now: no going back. 'Is that where you found me?'

He nodded again.

'Will,' said Barbary in desperation, 'if this is going to be ask-the-question-hear-the-answer it's going to take a fokking long time. Tell me.'

He frowned at her sideways – he'd never liked her swearing – but what he saw in her face demanded response. He turned his eyes back to his wooden leg and kept them there. 'Master Jack Wingfield's Ordnance,' he said.

'That was your company in Ireland?'

He nodded. 'Whole cannon, demi-cannon, some culverin . . .' He was going to bog himself down in technical details where he felt safer. Barbary moved him on.

'And you were a gunner?'

He was, him and Little Bill, his co-gunner, with five gunners' mates and five boys, the team in charge of laying and firing the huge, unwieldy cannon royal they called the 'Mousetrap', partly because her breech-loading took off unwary fingers and partly because the name was a euphemism for the female pudenda. She needed seven pairs of oxen to drag her. She weighed eight thousand pounds, fired seventy-four-pound shot from a bore of 8.54 inches and was a bitch to manoeuvre over the wet Irish terrain. 'Orders from the Lord Deputy,' Will said. 'Join up with his besieging force at a place called Smerwick on the south-west coast.'

Who was the Lord Deputy of Ireland then? Barbary did a quick calculation. Sir Henry? No, Will was going back eight or more years; it would have been Sir Henry's successor, Lord Grey of Wilton. She didn't dare interrupt for details like this; Will was beginning to speak, not to her, perhaps to something that had been waiting for him to talk for nearly a decade, but anyway speaking. It was almost in note form, like a man jotting in his diary, but the phrases were effective enough for her to follow him. 'Mud up to the hocks, ours and the oxen's . . . Never saw the natives, except skeletons and corpses . . . Not a cow lowing in the fields, not a sheep, not a pig . . . Enemy always out of sight . . . Yelping in the woods . . . Our men started to disappear.' She began to go with him through the war-exhausted Munster landscape where a soldier in the column could call to a friend in the mist, only to find he'd gone.

'Four hundred in our detachment when we started, about half that when we got to Smerwick. Two of my boys missing. Didn't see them again.'

He raised his head to Barbary, suddenly remembering her. 'Your Spenser was there.'

Instinctively Barbary looked towards the field where she had left him. Spenser? Will meant Edmund Spenser, but it was nearly as incongruous to imagine the enthusiastic poet who had sent her to sleep in those surroundings as it was her pony. Again she didn't dare ask for explanation.

Smerwick stood near the tip of Europe's most westerly peninsula. It was there that what was thought to be a vanguard of a Spanish invading army had landed to help the Irish rebels in their fight. They had shut themselves up in a fort on a barren, windswept point of land jutting into the Atlantic, ready to join up with the rebel Earl of Desmond's army and sweep the English from the land of Ireland.

'They was a year too late,' Will said. 'Desmond didn't have no army now. Couldn't have fed it if he had. Our commons was short enough, he was starving.'

But there the Spanish were, seven hundred of them, crowded into a formidable fortress and the Pope's banner flying from its walls. The ocean was smashing the rocks below them, the English navy out at sea cutting off their retreat, and Grey's army standing between them and the rest of Ireland.

The moment Wingfield and his artillery arrived, Grey set them to bombarding the fort. 'Monday it was, the seventh of November,' said Will. 'We began firing at dawn. Captain Zouche and Captain Raleigh was warding the trenches against light attack . . .'

'Sir Walter Raleigh?'

He didn't hear her, his ears filled with the crash of loading and firing. 'Their return fire killed Captain Wingfield.' Will was quiet for a moment. 'By two o'clock of the afternoon we'd silenced their sakers, by three o'clock whole sections of their earthworks was collapsed on top of them. No more casualties our side, 'cept that John Cheke who was Lord Burghley's nephew. Came galloping up on his horse, waving a sword like an amateur to get a ball on his head.' Will grunted. 'We heard Grey itching his britches because the Lord Treasurer's nevvy was killed and dictating a letter that the boy'd made "so divine a confession of his faith as no divine in Her Majesty's realm could match it". That boy never had no time for confession, not with his brains spurted.'

By evening on the Monday the Smerwick garrison had surrendered. 'Some of their officers came out to parley. Turned out they wasn't Spanish at all, Italians, mostly, and Basques, all sent by the Pope, the old bastard, to defend the Catholics of Ireland. Poor, draggly things the lot of them.'

The commander of the garrison was a Bolognese, Sebastiano di San Joseppi, who asked for guarantees of safe conduct. 'Grey wouldn't give him any. Said him and his men was pirates. San Joseppi said he wasn't no more a pirate than Drake was when he burned Cadiz, the which made Grey powerful angry.'

In the cold and wet the victorious but exposed English soldiers watched the parley. At one point San Joseppi fell to his knees and pleaded for the lives of his men. There were women in the fort, he said, Irish camp followers who had harmed nobody. Could they go free? Grey remained adamant. The garrison must surrender at its discretion.

'At its discretion,' repeated Will, 'meaning no quarter.'

There was nothing San Joseppi could do; the garrison had been without water for forty-eight hours. 'A fort without a well,' snorted Will. 'Amateurs.' Nevertheless, as the Bolognese went back to lead out his men, he'd looked hopeful, unable to believe the English wouldn't show mercy at the last.

'They came out dragging the Pope's banner, crying "Misery-cord", or so it sounded, and begging for water. The Irish among them was silent. They knew it was misery-cord for them. Some of the women, though, they pleaded their bellies and maybe some of them was pregnant, I don't know.'

The foreign troops were stripped of their armour and weapons and sent back inside the fort. Gallows were hastily erected outside it and the Irish men and women hanged at once. 'Excepting three priests as was with them,' Will said. 'Those three died slow.'

It was so still in the glade that a red squirrel flowed down the trunk of one of the trees, scrabbled in the leaf mould, picked up a chestnut and scambered off with it, unaware of human presence. Barbary doubted if Will saw it.

'Grey used us artillery men, leaving the pikemen ready in case there was still an Irish attack on the rear,' he said at last, suddenly. 'Two parties, one led by Captain Mackworth, one by Captain Raleigh. There was six hundred of the enemy in the fort. There'd be two hundred of us, so he said, and all we had to do was go in and kill three each, hew and paunch. Not to think on them as surrendered soldiers but captured pirates, like to the Papishes who'd murdered good Protestant men, women and children on St Bartholomew's Eve. Serving the Queen and God, we'd be, with reward to be expected here and on high. Spirits was handed round. That Spenser spouted poetry at us.'

Will wasn't questioning the orders. He attached himself to Captain Raleigh who, like him, was a Devon man and spoke his language. 'Took a pike and followed him in, shouting for Good Queen Bess.

'They ran when they saw us, but it was a small fort and they piled up at one end. We made those as would sit down and then a thrust to the neck and another one low into the belly, dragging up and out. Hew and paunch. They didn't die straightways, but they didn't get up again. The others wouldn't stay still and we had to run after them. The officers used the sword. Captain Mackworth, he was a man to steer clear of, a dirty bastard. And he laughed. Captain Raleigh went at it workmanlike.'

It took hours. 'Either there was more of them or less of us, but we killed more than three each.' They killed so many each that the iron of their pikes blunted and it took an increasingly heavy thrust, or more than one, to penetrate. Their arms tired. 'And we slipped on the blood. And the ones we hadn't got screamed, and the ones we had got coughed. That was the thing later, the coughing. Couldn't work out why they coughed so much. Then there was only one left, a boy, and he just sat and waited. Captain Mackworth wanted to play with him, but Captain Raleigh cut his head off immediate.'

Barbary thought of when she and other urchins had run alongside the scarlet and blue columns marching through the streets of London in time to the irresistible sound of fife and drum on their way to the embarking point for war abroad. Bannerets flicking in the breeze, cuirasses glinting, bishops blessing them, women waving, God with them, glory ahead. She had cheered.

And ever since she'd known him, Will had got drunk on 8 November.

'After that we were ordered down the coast to Youghal to beat off an Irish attack. And that was where the Mousetrap blew up.'

Little Billy, Will's co-gunner, had been killed in the explosion along with two mates and a boy. A piece of metal had sheared off Will's leg. Since his unit was now without a commander and since Grey, thanks to Elizabeth's cheeseparing, had been forced to dispense with the luxury of army surgeons, Will had been lucky to receive any attention at all. He found out later that he owed his life to Captain Raleigh who'd taken pity on a fellow Devonian and tourniqueted Will himself, had him shipped further down the coast out of the way of Irish attack and paid for a doctor to attend him. When Will became sensible again to things other than pain, he'd found himself in a cottage overlooking the Irish port of Kinsale.

'And that's where it all got mixed up.' Up to that point the situation had been clear. What had been done at Smerwick had been war, the responsibility of his commanders, not his. It was war in which England equalled right, Ireland equalled wrong. Protestantism versus Catholicism. Anglo-Saxon good versus Celtic bad. But . . . 'O'Kelly, he called himself, said he was hereditary physician to some clan or other. And his wife, Mary. Good people, looked after me something wonderful. He put moss on my leg for the infection, then when it was better rubbed it with spirit to harden the stump. Caring, my God, they cared for me.'

And they regarded themselves as loyal subjects of Her Majesty Queen Elizabeth, and the little town of Kinsale was full of others like themselves. 'All good subjects of the Queen, and as Irish as shamrocks.' And Catholic. To Will's horror he had found himself lying on a bed over which was an idolatrous statuette of the Virgin Mary. A priest had called and swung a censer over him. Like the rest of Munster, even though it was in the Pale and under English protection, Kinsale was starving, but there had always been food for Will.

They had dragged his bed to the window so that he could look out as he got better and watch the boats coming in and out of the harbour. And that was when he'd had his revelation, his light on the Damascus road; everything had changed for him.

Barbary waited for a recital of the momentous, a vision, an angel, the word of God, but when it came it was anti-climactic.

'I saw the soil was red,' said Will simply.

On the south coast of Devon, and especially around the tiny fishing hamlet of Oddicombe where he'd been born, the iron-rich soil is flamboyantly red. Gaudy red cliffs run like a curtain wall against the sea, ploughs leave long red furrows in the earth which turn brick-coloured as it dries, ingraining red dust into the folds of the ploughmen's necks. Devonians grow used to it yet never take it for granted and see the beauty around them as a sign that God loves their country above all others. When, as he'd accompanied his cannon through the damp waste of Munster, Will had encouraged himself by the thought that he was doing it for England, into his mind had come the emphatic tapestry of God's own land. Its symbolism had warmed him. When the Irish women, pale and screaming, had been strung up, it had been because God was not on their side as he was on the side of the rosy-cheeked women back home. When Captain Walter Raleigh had hailed him into the fort to kill foreigners, the man's Devonian burr had sounded rich with assurance and familiarity. In a sense Will had killed for a landscape.

But now, as he looked out of a Papist's window in an alien country, he saw the same landscape. The sea of Kinsale was as blue, the stone of the harbour walls was as grey, the hills nearly as red as back home. It resembled Brixham where Will's father had sailed his catches to the fish market. When the Papist doctor came in from digging the turnips in his garden, his red-dusted hands shook red earth off the vegetables before giving them to his wife to stew. God whose blood had coloured English Devon had equally coloured this part of Irish Munster.

'I'd been tricked, do you see,' said Will to his ammunition leg. 'We weren't special back home, or if we was, they was just as special in Ireland.' They might speak another language and worship in another form but God took no notice of these minor differences and had made their lands alike. Perhaps even in Spain and Italy there were parts with red soil. At their deepest derivation all men were the same.

This new and appalling internationalism seemed so self-evident to Will then that he believed the leaders of all countries with their superior education must be aware of it. Yet still they egged on the ignorant with slogans and flag-waving and patriotism for their own ends. 'Who profited?' he said, suddenly raising his head and looking at Barbary for the first time. 'Not the poor buggers who followed them. Not us, dead and left behind.'

Raleigh knew, Grey knew, Queen Elizabeth knew.

They got the profit. Their enemy the Earl of Desmond knew and if he wasn't getting the profit it wasn't through lack of trying. They reduced to a simple 'Kill the enemy' the diversity of sameness that God had seen fit to introduce and to which this damned Catholic Irish doctor, who had saved Will's English Protestant life, was a testimony. They imperilled the souls of their instruments. On their behalf Will had killed defenceless men and been a party to stringing up innocent women. He had offended against God. His reward had been the loss of a leg and abandonment.

'A judgement on me,' he said. But those on whom God's judgement should have fallen far heavier were flourishing and rewarded.

In the glade the sun was overhead now and Barbary stared up at spear-shaped leaves so translucent that the shadow of chestnut clusters still unfallen could be seen through them. She was restive. Will's personal had turned out so personal that she wished she hadn't probed. She didn't understand his philosophy; the world around her rested on the demarcation of classes and countries, goodness and badness, them and us. She tried to shift him on: 'Let's get to me, Will.' But she had set something in train that had to complete its journey. Will didn't hear her.

As the pain of his healing wound receded, his dreams became terrible, so close to delirium that he dreaded going to sleep. He didn't dream pictures, he dreamed sounds which made inchoate shapes. Huge chokings advanced to asphyxiate him and a thin stick of a cough beat and beat until he woke up screaming. He wanted to get away from Ireland like a murderer wants to run away from his crime; his pity for it and his guilt repulsed him, the kindness of the doctor and his wife were repellent.

'We heard Desmond was dead. A clan he'd despoiled killed him. Cut off his head and sent it to Dublin who sent it to the Queen. The war was over, but they kept on hanging.'

The doctor padded Will's stump and carved a wooden leg to fit it from a piece of bog oak. Will's hand went to the acorn-cup-like top of his ammunition leg. 'This one.'

To Barbary that leg had been an old friend. When Will was not wearing it, it had stood in the corner of their cottage, as familiar as a broom. She'd made jokes about it. And all along it had been alien. Like Will was. Like she was. 'Are we getting to me or not?' She had caught Will's horror and wanted the story over.

When he was at last mobile he'd offered to do some fishing for the family and, because the harbour was over-fished by too many hungry people, he had managed to make a rest for his wooden leg against the thwart of a rowing boat to give him purchase to row along the coast in search of richer waters. Out in the boat he was a better man. He re-accustomed his hands to the details of fishing. There were small moments of triumph when the lines bobbed and he could haul in fish. Above all, being away from land enabled him to consider what he should do with the rest of his life. The army had made no enquiries about him; he doubted if it knew or cared whether he was still alive. Raleigh had not come back to see if he'd survived and anyway was not an officer of his unit; having discharged his kindness, he'd gone back to England to find favour with the Queen. 'But even if the Lord Treasurer had bobbed up out of them waves with a pension in his hand, I'd a spat in his eye,' said Will. 'Taken the pension, mind, and spat in his eye after.' His bitterness had nothing to do with his abandonment, veterans of war were always abandoned by their country and he should have expected no better. It was because Authority, from Elizabeth down, had led him into a sin he would never be rid of. He didn't care if he never saw England again, but he couldn't stay in Ireland, the land he had sinned against, either.

Then, one day when he was spinning for mackerel among a shoal that had gone in close to shore, he saw some soldiers searching along the cliff top. They were English troops; Will recognised the military livery of their bright blue base coats which made them such excellent targets for Irish snipers. 'Bloody prancing bluebells,' he said. They were stabbing into gorse bushes with their pikes and sweeping aside bracken.

Will saw what they couldn't. Twenty feet below them a small boy was clinging crabwise to the cliff face. Though he was dressed in buff jerkin and trousers, the colour of his hair clashed marigold against the brick shade of the cliff, making him as easy a target as the soldiers. As Will watched, he lost one handhold and swung down like a pendulum, dislodging puffs of red earth. Will's eyes went instantly back to the soldiers; there would have been the sound of dislodged pebbles, but they hadn't heard, they were too busy calling to each other. Now they were calling to him. He feathered in closer to the beach and cupped a hand to his ear. 'Fugitive, fu-gi-tive,' they were yelling, confident that all foreigners could understand English if it was shouted slowly enough. 'Seen him, Paddy?'

The boy had scrabbled another handhold and had his head twisted round, watching Will. He was very small. Will pointed towards Kinsale. 'Saw somebody hiding by the river,' he shouted. Assured by Will's English accent of his good faith, they began running towards the Bandon.

Will beckoned to the boy and pointed to his boat. Slowly the boy completed the descent, every so often stopping to rest his head against the cliff face, as if to stop it swimming. When at last his legs reached the horizontal, they crumpled and he fell. He began to crawl over the beach towards the boat. One of the soldiers was running back along the cliff top and now the child was in the open, but there was nothing Will could do except make hurrying gestures; his manoeuvrability was still minimal. The soldier began to yell to the others to come back, and began to climb down the cliff.

Will knew what he was going to do, even if he didn't know how he was going to do it. That child crawling towards him so weakly but so doggedly was the expiation of his sin. If he could save that one small morsel from this boiling pot he would have one entry on the credit side of his soul's ledger. He had never in his life wanted something so much as he wanted this little boy not to join the pile of corpses that was Ireland.

The first soldier was on the beach now, others swarming down the cliff. The boy was splashing into the water's edge. He could swim well, that was one thing; the water had revived him. Will began to throw his catch at the pursuer. A well-fleshed mackerel hit the man's face, knocking his helmet off and making him pause. Will leant over the thwart and scraped the boy into the boat. Then he was rowing as he'd never rowed before. Somebody on the beach was loading a flintlock but Will, with his contempt for army small arms, doubted if it was a danger. Anyway, by the time it was fired they were out of range and he could turn his attention to the child. The boy was panting with more than exertion, his face so white that his freckles looked dark green.

Will was prompted into using one of the few Irish phrases he knew: 'What's your name?'

The child's eyes were closing. 'Barbary,' it said.

'I reckon it was lucky I asked then,' Will said to his ammunition leg, 'for you went into a stupor after that, the which lasted weeks and when you come to you didn't remember a blessed thing. I'd might have had to name you myself.'

Barbary shook herself and took a deep breath. 'What would you have called me?'

Will's face went very grave as it always did when he was going to make a joke. 'Mackerel.' He had a new lightness about him; the shadow that the Smerwick episode had left in his memory had been faced for the first time and, through the process of recounting, dissipated. Words had given it shape, hung it out to dry, and he had become fluent to the point of volubility.

But in abandoning the taciturnity which had made him seem so wise when Barbary was growing up, he had revealed himself as a different man to the one who had been her prop; a man of errors and guilts and nightmares, more vulnerable, braver, and definitely more complex. She could have wished the old one back; this one needed re-assessing, and she was suddenly too tired to do it. 'What happened after that?'

'There was a Bristol boat in the harbour, seen it on my way out. Captain was a Devon man and took us aboard there and then. Five shilling for our passage back to England and no questions asked.'

By this time the child's breathing was giving cause for concern. The captain's wife and Will had stripped off its clothes, uncovering first the torque and then the sex of the child. It had taken a bit of readjustment for Will the bachelor to realise he had burdened himself with a girl, but it had become unimportant in the fight to save the child's life.

'The which we did, though you wasn't intent on it,' he

said. What had weighed on him was that he had not gone back to say goodbye and thank you to the doctor who had saved *his* life. 'Wasn't possible,' he said. 'The soldiers was on the look-out for ye, more for the torque than anything, I reckoned. And good man though he was, he'd like have betrayed you.'

Suddenly he put out his hand and touched Barbary's arm. 'Don't you go back there, now, not after all the trouble I had getting you out.'

Barbary could safely promise him that. It wasn't a question of going back, anyway, not when she still couldn't remember having been there in the first place. Will's recital had done nothing to nudge her memory. The woman hanging at the back of her mind was still a dark shape in darker shadow. 'So you can't tell me if I am who they say I am?'

Will shook his head. 'They'll say anything.'

They walked back towards the ironworks, Will more lively than she'd ever known him. Her debt to him was greater than she'd dreamed; he hadn't just taken her in, he had saved her life and risked his own to do it. She knew she ought to feel more grateful than ever, but she wasn't. What she felt was illness; every time the subject of Ireland came up, some new and awful knowledge accrued to her. She had been healthy until touched by that leper hand; now everything was diseased. The process of disorientation begun last night by the O'Neill had been completed by Will so that her own self was unfamiliar to her. 'Who are you?' she screamed to it, so suddenly that the yell animated Spenser into a twitch of the ears. Who was that child who had crawled into Will Clampett's boat? Why had it been escaping from English soldiers with an Irish torque round its neck?

She couldn't remember. The fog wall between the woman she was now and the child she had been was as thick as ever. No part of Will's story had touched a responding memory. It had touched something – she was twanging with a vibration of horror, sick with it – but the fog remained impenetrable. And she was glad of it. She didn't want to remember.

God Almighty. Suppose she was this missing Irish heir? Suppose Lord Burghley and Walsingham had accidentally got it right and she was this O'Flaherty? Well she couldn't be. She was female. They'd got that much wrong, so maybe they'd got it all wrong. She was convinced they'd picked her out of the streets because she fitted the role they wanted her to play in Ireland, not because they were sure they had the right person.

'Battle the watch, Barb.' Take it calmly. She was no worse off now than she had been when she thought she was a Hollander rescued by Will from the Lowland wars. All right, it looked now as if she was a Paddy, rescued from the Irish wars. But what difference did it make? The real Barbary, the one she had become since she was old enough to remember, was still the same, formed by Will and the Order, still belonging to the dear, crime-ridden streets of London, still English, still a loyal subject of Her Majesty Queen Elizabeth.

Survivor that she was, Barbary thrust away mind-destroying discomfort in order to keep her mental feet on solid ground. She rejected the disconcerting O'Neill as too alien to have any validity. She made herself try and forget the new, vulnerable Will Clampett she had just listened to as an aberration, reinstating him as he always had been. That glimpse he had given her of an England which was as barbarous as the Inquisition, that was, well, that wasn't the England she knew. So what if it killed defenceless foreigners? Foreigners deserved it for not being English in the first place.

She clawed herself back into the familiar, using time as if it were sand, brushing it back to cover the nastiness revealed by one of its slips. She piled it over the most terrible enlightenment of all, that those dear, crime-ridden streets of London were no longer home to a mind that had been stretched by the learning, poetry and books the Sidneys of Penshurst had given her.

She took a deep breath and felt better. She'd go back. She'd find a way to become Barbary of the Order again. Back to the Pudding and normality. Somehow she'd take Will and Cuckold Dick and dive into that happy underground where this new and troublesome situation couldn't touch her, back to the world of good, honest conying.

She was still puzzling over how this was to be achieved when she arrived back at Penshurst, and found that her future had already been decided.

Chapter Eight

The people loading themselves, their families and possessions onto the ships in Bristol harbour were the undertakers. They were also coopers, masons, farmers, blacksmiths, bakers, brewers and carpenters, but their common denominator lay in their undertaking to hold Crown lands in Ireland of Her Majesty Queen Elizabeth.

By creating an English shireland out of Munster's wilderness they could own more land than the squires they used to serve, and they were making a lot of noise about it. The quaysides dinned with shipmasters explaining at the tops of their voices that there was no room in their holds for the cisterns, beds, cauldrons, sheepdogs, milch cows, mattresses and portraits – and in one instance a senile grandfather lying comatose and ready in his coffin – and with the undertakers equally forcibly maintaining they wouldn't leave them behind.

Commissioners' agents moved through the crowds quantifying the milk and honey that awaited the undertakers and giving them conflicting reminders that 'the better sort of Irish are very civil, hospitable, of good faith and bodily constitution' but that none of the settlers were to marry or employ them.

From the upper window of the Golden Hind tavern the Lord Treasurer of England looked down on the chaos with concern. 'I had hoped to see more gentry, some younger scions of our nobler houses taking up the enterprise.'

'Shit scared,' said the man beside him. His voice was as big as the rest of him. It rattled the inn's pewter mugs hanging on their dresser hooks. People on the quayside stopped quarrelling to look up. 'We've made such a urinal of Ireland as no gentleman will even piss in it.'

Lord Burghley tried not to look pained. Sir John

145

Perrot was an embarrassment but a necessary embarrassment. There had been no Lord Deputy of Ireland since Grey on his latest tour had been recalled in disgrace and, with many misgivings, Elizabeth had been persuaded to send Sir John to take up the post. He knew Ireland and for some reason the Irish liked him, as they liked all eccentrics; or perhaps, thought Burghley, because he is unique in liking them.

He proclaimed, loudly, that he was the bastard son of Henry VIII. With his red beard and girth he looked the image of the old king, and possessed all his father's appetites. He was crude in his habits and language and made the Queen's eyes glaze over by persisting in addressing her as 'sister', which was as nothing to what he called her when she crossed him. But he was unorthodox and generous and if anybody could heal the scars left by the Desmond Wars – a task Lord Burghley feared was impossible – he could.

Already he was booming his policy to the young man who stood beside him. 'No peasant henceforward to be called a churl, no churl to be called a serf or receive unchristian punishment from his master. Eh, my young lord, what about that? You Irish lordlings have done as much harm to your own people as we have. Shall we turn the Irish peasants into good English franklins and yeomen? Root out old oppressions, eh? What say you?'

'Gawd help us, Sir John,' said Barbary in broad Cockney, 'you're taking all the fun out of lordship.'

She got a slap on the back that nearly knocked her out of the window. 'Ha, ha,' roared Sir John, 'I like you, young O'Flaherty. We can do business together.' He turned to the fourth member of their party. 'What say you, Sir Richard? Shall we bring humour to Ireland, eh? No oppression where there's laughter, what say you?'

Sir Richard Bingham's lips didn't suggest acquaintance with laughter. From the look of them the only event he'd found funny was the death of his mother.

Barbary didn't think she and Sir Richard were going to get on. Yet soon, when the tide turned, she would be embarking with him and Sir John for Dublin, and from Dublin she and Sir Richard would be travelling across Ireland to the west where he was the Lord President of Connaught, and where she was supposed to begin her career as a leader of the western clans. In a pig's eye, she thought.

She hadn't intended getting as far as this even, but the summons from Lord Burghley had arrived on Penshurst's threshold in the shape of a secretary and two men-at-arms. Less than an hour later she was on her way to Chatham to catch the boat which had brought her to Bristol where the fleet for Dublin was waiting to sail. Her packing had been done for her; what little time she'd had at her disposal had been taken up with goodbyes and thank yous and last-minute advice from Sir Henry Sidney.

She'd been moved by Sir Henry's farewell present to her: a clinking purse and the pony, Spenser, 'though God trust the Irish do not take him as an example of English horseflesh'.

There hadn't been a moment when she could have escaped, and with Will Clampett still a hostage for her good behaviour she didn't dare to. Her comfort was that Sir Henry's regard for his cannon master would oppose any harm to him. There'd been no time to say goodbye to Will, but Philip had promised to explain to him on her behalf.

There hadn't even been time to decide what to do about Cuckold Dick. They'd discussed it as they rode together to Chatham. 'You've been a prize to stay this long, Dick. Time to go back to the Bermudas.'

'Don't like the thought of you alone among the Irish, though, Barb.'

'I won't be for long. I've got a plan.' She'd only just thought of it.

'You're a one for the plans, Barb,' said Dick admiringly. 'What?'

'Pirate. I'll go for a pirate. With all the sweeteners I got from them who wanted me to treacle the Queen, and Sir Henry gave me five guineas, I've got enough gelt to buy into a ship. I'll con more out of Burghley before I'm older, see if I don't. Then when I get to Dublin I'll cut off, get a passage back to England, pick up Will and cross the Channel before they know it. Join the Sea Beggars, maybe. Will's an asset, see. With his knowledge of cannon, any privateer'd be glad to take us.'

She was working it out as she went along, but she was

147

charmed by the logic of the idea which would solve all her confusions. She might even afford her own boat; she knew enough sea dogs in the docks of London to make up a crew. It could be done. This supposed grandmother of hers in Ireland was a pirate, so there was a precedent for a woman captain. The seven seas. Mermaids. Be her own woman, sail her own boat. For the first time since she'd left the Bermudas she experienced the cherubims. They'd never come to her at Penshurst, but now as she sniffed the salt of the Kent coast she heard music and saw again a mental image of the strange galley standing out to sea, waiting for her. Again a voice commanded: 'Hug Adam, shun Eve.'

Cuckold Dick was silent, bumping like a sack of turnips on his trotting horse. 'No call for expert crossbiting in the pirate trade, I suppose, Barb?'

'Hardly any.'

He nodded. 'And so much as crossing the Fleet bridge gets me seasick.'

She was touched that he was even bothering with excuses. 'I'll be right, Dick. And so should you be, with all that money you conied out of Penshurst. No, you go on back to the Upright Man.' She hadn't meant the thought to depress him but could see it did; Abraham was an unpredictable master and Cuckold Dick had lived soft these past months. Yet she knew the thought of Ireland depressed him even more. It depressed her.

'Well, but, Barb,' Dick said, 'I'll come along as far as Bristol. Always wanted to see the West Country.'

'You hate the country, you liar.'

'Well, but.'

They had finally said goodbye a few minutes ago down on the quay. She could see him from the window, loitering furtively by some bales, waiting for the ship to sail so that he could wave it out of sight. She wished he'd go. Sir Philip Sidney, Will Clampett and Cuckold Dick, she thought, as disparate a trio as could be found in a month of Sundays, but it wrenched her to leave each one.

Lord Treasurer Burghley had met her on the quay. 'There have been events,' he told her. 'Also it seemed advisable that you should travel with the newly appointed administrators of Ireland since they will be the two men most nearly concerned with furthering our plans.'

'I'll need money,' said Barbary bluntly.

The Lord Treasurer knew no Irish agent who didn't. Ireland ate money. The Pyrrhic victory of the Desmond Wars had alone cost Elizabeth half a million pounds, as she pointed out daily. Still, the rapacious clans would be more likely to accept this young man as their leader if he returned to them showering gifts. 'This should cover travelling expenses,' he said. 'This' was a nicely heavy purse. 'And the Queen has graciously provided a chest of trinkets wherewith you shall reward various of your people for their duty to her.' Tawdry trinkets at that, he thought, some of the least tasteful gifts made to Elizabeth to mark her visit to boroughs and guilds, but they'd probably delight the natives.

Barbary smiled beautifully at him.

'I have put it in the care of Sir Richard Bingham who will account to Her Majesty for every penny, as you shall account to him.'

Barbary's smile had weakened. Now that she'd met the man, she abandoned hope for the chest. As soon try to cony a rat trap out of its cheese.

Sir Richard was saying: 'I have faith the Irish will respond better to fear than to humour, Sir John.'

'You would,' said Sir John, rudely. He turned away from the window to the table which was piled with food. 'Shall we eat, gentlemen? What say you to a last breakfast? Who knows when we'll see its like again. Report gives that there is starvation even in Dublin.'

'The report is true,' said the Lord Treasurer. 'Most unfortunate. The Irish are saying that if the English can't feed them, what is the use of submission? It has led to further rebellion.' He turned to Barbary.'I fear the authorities have had to restrain your grandmother. She is awaiting trial in Dublin Castle.'

'Grace O'Malley in prison?' said Sir John Perrot, spraying pieces of capon. 'She'll not like it. A fine woman. I was there when she came with her clan to tender their allegiance. The O'Malleys were the last to do so, what about that? A hellcat to conquer but a fine woman for all that. Fine pair of tits.'

Purse went Sir Richard's lips. 'If she swore allegiance to the Crown and has since rebelled, the slut should hang.'

A ham bone slammed on the table with a force that made its crockery skip into the air. 'God's balls, man,' shouted Sir John. 'Is the noose your remedy for everything? Enough to hanging. There'll be no more of it.'

The Lord Treasurer closed his eyes. It happened every time, whoever was chosen. If the administrators of Ireland had spent as much energy on fighting Earl Desmond as on fighting each other, the war wouldn't have lasted a week.

To his relief an interruption arrived through the door at that moment, a woman trailing luggage, a toddler, a depressed-looking girl servant, and domestic problems. Was this the right room? Were they the right gentlemen? A trunk with her best bed linen of finest weave was missing. Servants nowadays. The baby had but recently recovered from the quinsies; she herself was again in an interesting condition and therefore would they promise her the ship would not go up and down too much. Her husband would express his gratitude when they got to Dublin. Who was he? But they must know Master Edmund Spenser, recently appointed Deputy Clerk to Munster? And a rising poet. The Queen had personally praised his work, had she not told them of it?

Barbary had never encountered someone of such physical insignificance who could so agitate the very air as Machabyas 'Maccabee' Spenser. She was very little, brown, with downy black hair on her top lip, and the chaos she exuded kept people around her constantly off balance. But there was a vulnerability to her which brought protection from the well-mannered. The Lord High Treasurer of England set her a chair while the Lord Deputy of Ireland relieved her of the child to drip best ale into its mouth from his own fingers. Only Sir Richard was unmoved and unmoving, except for a thinning of the lips when Mistress Spenser invited him to stop over at 'Spenser Castle' on his journey to the west.

'A castle, madam?'

'Indeed, Sir Richard. Three thousand acres that march with our good friend Sir Walter Raleigh.' If she was hoping to impress them with the connection, she was disappointed; as usual the name of the Queen's latest favourite evinced a distancing in his competitors.

While the knights were engaged with Mistress Spenser,

Lord Burghley drew Barbary outside onto the landing. 'One last matter, my son, on which Her Majesty has asked me to command you. It may be that, indeed it is known that, the clan O'Malley has amassed some sort of treasure. Doubtless piratically gained from Her Majesty's high seas. It should be clearly understood that this treasure is the property of the Crown and must be returned.'

Perhaps Burghley saw the reflection of gelt flickering in Barbary's eyes, for he put a warning, arthritic hand on her shoulder. 'Sir Richard has been apprised of it and will assist you in its recovery. We have offered your grandmother a pardon in exchange for details of the treasure's whereabouts but so far she has refused to divulge them. Sir John will permit you access to her in prison and you are to gain her trust as her heir, telling her she will escape the gallows only if she passes the secret on to you.'

'And will she? Escape the gallows, I mean?'

Lord Burghley shrugged. 'Under Sir John's regime of moderation it seems that she will.' The grip on Barbary's shoulder tightened. 'Remember that we hold your pledge of Master Clampett for your good behaviour and that you have the Queen's love. Aid her in this matter of the treasure as in all else, and you shall not be the loser.'

Barbary was still calculating the ploys necessary to cony information from an imprisoned woman pirate, treasure out of wild Irish and non-interference from Sir Richard Bingham as they boarded.

The *Elizabeth Gallant*'s name was more impressive than her appearance. She was styled a warship, though the only warlike things about her were her high, old-fashioned fore- and stern-castles. She was small, as broad as she was long and stank of her last cargo, hides. Sir John Perrot didn't take to her, shouting at Lord Burghley, whose Treasury had provided her: 'A warship do you say? Last damned war she saw was the War of the Roses. A fine figure I'll cut arriving in Dublin in this worm bucket.'

But all true galleons were confined to port, ready to defend England from the Armada that Spain was threatening to send against her, which was another sore point with Sir John. 'They should be out on the high seas attacking the bloody Spaniard's ships before they get to us. Is that sister of mine so quake-buttocked that she must defend rather than attack?'

Barbary looked round Bristol's immense harbour and decided that, worm bucket though the *Elizabeth Gallant* might be, she was a safer bet for the crossing than the collection of traders and tubs, some of them not even decked, which were to take the undertakers over. She also had a hold capacious enough to accommodate the piles of equipment, the retinue of servants, grooms and horses Sir John was taking with him, as well as Sir Richard's smaller train.

Sir John recoiled at the sight of Barbary's Spenser tethered among his own chargers and hunters. 'God's balls, what's that?'

Barbary had to admit the pony didn't look his best; he hadn't enjoyed the journey so far and was sulking at being below decks. She brazened it out. 'Mine,' she said, 'and I'm sorry, Sir John, but he's not for sale.'

'I wouldn't offer for him,' the Lord Deputy assured her, 'if he crapped gold through a trumpet.'

Finding all Mistress Spenser's missing luggage and settling her, the miserable servant Barker and her baby in the sterncastle cabin tested Sir John's patience. 'I've provisioned armies in less time.' But eventually he gave permission for his ensign to be hoisted and instructed the captain to set sail or, as he put it, 'Set this haystack under way.'

Barbary stood with the others at the taffrail, searching the quayside for a last glimpse of Cuckold Dick. Although she had tried to put out of her mind the Irish dimension that had attached itself to her past, this moment brought the full realisation that she was leaving everything she knew for a land where bad things had happened to the child she had once been. She was being returned to the place that lay behind the fog wall and, fully as she intended to leave it as soon as possible, she was frightened. England had never seemed dearer, and dearer still was Cuckold Dick. She was at the point of apprehension where her mind chose one event as a portent. If it happened she would have good luck; if it did not, she was heading for disaster. The portent she had picked on was a farewell wave from Cuckold Dick, but she couldn't see him.

Lord Burghley was standing on the quay as if willing the seeds of Munster's plantation to succeed by watching them blow out of sight towards their seed-bed. Along the other quays crowds cheered the rest of the fleet on its way, but nowhere could she see a brown-clad, drooping, pot-bellied crossbiter.

By her side at the taffrail a figure was contemplating a diminishing Bristol as gloomily as she was. 'Ireland better be worth it,' it said.

Barbary sighed in agreement, then jumped round, 'You old scobberlotcher, you swapping great shifter.'

'Couldn't let you go by your own, Barb,' said Cuckold Dick calmly. 'I didn't like the cut of that Sir Bingham. A vinegar-pisser if ever I saw one.'

'I don't like him much myself,' said Barbary, patting him, 'but you're still an old scobberlotcher.' She was overwhelmed with affection and relief. The portent had turned out excellent.

Three hours out from Lundy, Cuckold Dick began wishing he hadn't come, but by that time they were all wishing they hadn't come. The Irish Sea caught sight of the forty or so little English ships and grew furious, its cloud brows knitting into a mass of blackness that advanced on them at gale force. The old fashion of *Elizabeth Gallant*'s rig didn't allow her to sail close to the wind and she heeled over on each tack as if dodging the colossal boots of some escapee from a giants' Bedlam who stamped, screamed and tore its clothing. The sea seemed to alter its mass and hit the deck in solid chunks that made the planks tremble, only then dissipating into water that streamed back under the taffrail and down the scuppers. In the stern-castle cabin Maccabee Spenser clung onto her screaming baby and Sir John, who was clinging onto a rafter and swearing. The Spenser servant, Barker, had rolled herself into ball. In between bouts of vomiting, Cuckold Dick was re-acquainting with his existence a God he'd ignored for years. Barbary had jammed herself into a corner and was wishing fervently that she had Dick's unsuspected command of prayer. Her eyes caught sight of Sir Richard's face and stayed on it; the man's lips were compressed but of all the passengers in the cabin he was the least afraid. Somebody had told her he'd once captained his own ship brilliantly. His eyes met hers and

153

passed on with disinterest, but she kept her gaze latched onto him for comfort. A swine, but a brave swine.

The cabin door crashed open and a sailor stood in its frame, the water he'd brought in with him slopping about his bare feet. 'Captain's compliments,' he shouted above the wind and the baby, 'horses and cargo loose in the hold. Need every man to help.' Barbary's hope fastened on him; like Sir Richard he looked concerned without panic. Perhaps sailors had their peace always made ready with God, just in case. She wished hers was, but she still wasn't sure who He was. She realised what the man was saying; he wanted them to go out on deck, into that; this was what men did, had to do, and for these purposes she was a man.

Cuckold Dick tried to rise, vomited again and was contemptuously pressed back by Sir Richard's boot. He would be useless. Sir John Perrot disengaged Maccabee's clutching fingers, transferring them to the cabin's fixed table. His worry for his horses outweighed the weather. Barbary caught hold of his belt and with Sir Richard bringing up the rear they struggled onto the deck into the insanity of the wind and sea. For a moment Barbary remembered the rest of the fleet and wondered what was happening to passengers in the undecked boats; it was impossible to see. Then her own survival commanded her attention.

A line had been rigged between the cabin and the mainmast, but even clinging to this their feet kept being swept to one side so that they sprawled in the swirling water like drunks, staggered a yard or two and sprawled again. The rain was almost horizontal and lashed against their eyes. The sailor just stopped Sir John falling down the part-opened hatch over the hold. Between them he and Barbary steadied the Lord Deputy onto the ladder and he climbed down. The screams of men and horses down there vied with the screaming wind. The sailor jerked his thumb at Barbary to get onto the ladder. She knelt down, still clinging to the line with one hand, groping for the ladder rungs with the other. When she felt the rungs, she let go of the line. It was in that moment, before she could hold with both hands, that *Elizabeth Gallant* bucked as a giant wave came over her port bow. Barbary's free hand reached for Sir Richard's, but it wasn't there. Time slowed between the second when she was about to fall and the second she actually did so, and she was able to think quite clearly: 'That man will be the death of me.' Then her head struck the edge of the hatch and she dropped twenty feet, one leg breaking as it hit the floor of the hold.

There was pain. There was noise, even more atrocious than the pain. The noise retreated but the pain went on, interleaving itself with a voice: 'Lantern. Set it myself. Planking. Strip his clothes off. He'll get the ague.'

Semi-conscious, but aware at deep level of the danger, Barbary began to fight. She tried to scream that she was all right, her clothes must stay on, but the pain and the voice were inexorable. So were the hands that pulled and unbuttoned. 'Stop struggling, lad. No time for modesty. Get a knife to his shirt. And the trunks. There.'

She'd had nightmares about nakedness. Was this another one? She heard the silence, felt draught on her body, the appalling exposure. She heard the gasps. A laugh. 'Great God. He's a girl.'

In the palace at Whitehall Queen Elizabeth's long, asparagus fingers showed their bones as they ripped up the communication from Ireland. 'I'll have his head. Her head. I'll give her Master Boggart, the unnatural trollop. Jesus. Was there ever a prince so smitten by the snares of traitors as I am.'

The two men in the room with her cautiously stayed on their knees, assessing her anger.

'I blame you, Burghley.'

The Lord Treasurer had known she would. He had thirty years' experience of the Queen's angers with which to judge this one. Definitely below the display at the revelation of Leicester's marriage to Lettice Knollys – she had gone nearly mad – and well below her outburst of screaming and crying when they'd rushed through the execution of Mary, Queen of Scots, and she'd been appalled at what the rest of the world would think of her. No, this one was a stamping teeth-grinder roughly equivalent to the time when Catherine de Medici had told the world that Elizabeth was too old to marry the Duke of Anjou. This, like that, was a nostril-flarer, a thrower. It was temper, pure and simple, because she had been made a fool of. He could cope with it.

'And you, Ormond. What plot are you hatching against me that initiated the search for this . . . this harlot?'

Black Tom bent his head as strips of the letter were thrown onto his shoulders and fluttered harmlessly to the floor. 'No plot, cousin, I assumed . . . we all assumed that it was one of the boys who had survived the shipwreck, not their sister.'

'You assumed. You assumed. Because we are the weaker sex, you assume we cannot survive life's vicissitudes. But we can. I can. Even with your bungling. I shall see you both out yet.' She leaned her face down close to theirs, so that they could see the cracks in the paint round her mouth and smell her remaining teeth. 'I want her racked, Burghley.'

'Could I suggest, Phoenix—'

'Suggest me no suggestions, little man. Was the fellow Crumpet in on this deception?'

'Clampett, Majesty. I fear he must have been.'

'Rack him as well.'

They stayed on their knees while she stalked about. Allow her a minute to enjoy cracking Boggart's bones, then begin the damage limitation. After the minute was up, Black Tom said gently: 'Great Queen, this Master – Mistress – Barbary can still be of use. Obviously, if she is not the grandson of the O'Malley woman, she is the granddaughter and therefore may still have recourse to the treasure.'

The magic word slowed her down, as it had slowed her before. The Lord Treasurer picked up the ball: 'And she is now marriageable property, Phoenix. We can find her a reliable English husband who would then have claim to the O'Malley-O'Flaherty lands.'

She whipped round maliciously. 'I've caught you out, little man. Under Irish law women cannot inherit property, you said so yourself. Therefore her husband cannot claim it.'

'Your memory is faultless, Phoenix. But, since we are establishing English Common Law in Ireland, it is our rule and custom that must prevail, not theirs.'

She narrowed her eyes. 'The creature made me a laughing stock.'

They knew her well. The Earl of Ormond rose and

helped the Lord Treasurer to his feet. The worst was over. 'Impossible, Majesty. You are the sun and the moon. And who is to know what she did? Thank God it happened before we introduced her to the clans as their prince. Her existence has been kept quiet. The man Clampett will say nothing for his own sake, and hers. The Sidneys were as taken in as I was myself, and will not broadcast the fact. Sir John Perrot keeps her secretly in his own house while he awaits your instructions.'

They dripped logic on her wounded pride until she was mollified. 'Well, well, arrange it how you will. Just procure me that treasure.' As they bowed themselves out she was positively smiling. 'After all,' she said, 'the young freak made an even bigger fool of you than she did of me.'

The Captain of the Guard looked thoughtful as he opened and closed the doors of the royal chambers to them. The Lord Treasurer hoped that Raleigh had heard every word and been tempted by the carrot he had dangled. It was a considerable carrot, after all; an heiress to treasure, access to Irish lands and power that made even Sir Walter's vast present estate look small. It was a prize that might induce this overweening pirate into rashness. 'Go and marry her, my son,' willed Lord Burghley, silently. 'Try and make yourself King of Connaught, King of Ireland. That handsome head would look its handsomest stuck on a pole.'

Beside him the Earl of Ormond was swearing. 'Are your agents blind, Burghley, that they can't tell prick from pussy? I was made a fool of in there. And me only satisfaction is that, like Herself said, you're a bigger one.' He walked off to salve his Hibernian dignity, leaving the Lord Treasurer to hobble back to his office alone.

Deary, deary me. This preoccupation with whether or not one looked a fool, what did it matter? He had long outlived worry about whether people laughed at him or not. He'd survived bigger jokes than this one.

But now, as he passed one of the tall passage windows, he saw what a joke it was. From here, above the Privy Stairs at the bend of the Thames, he could look downriver past the frontages of the Strand palaces and glimpse Somerset House where he had been on that day. The head of Master Barbary came vividly into his mind's eye with its freckles, its astonishing hair, its trickster's eyes. He put it onto a female body and was surprised by a rush of admiration for the unquenchable daring of the human spirit. 'I fear it will go hard with you now, young madam,' he said to it, 'but you conied us all.' For the first time in years his chest contracted with amusement. He was still wheezing with it when he returned to his desk, and the clerk Percy became so alarmed that he ran for the medicine chest and a bottle of balsam.

She knew how a man must feel after castration: humiliated and lessened; cast out from the lords of creation's marvellous company. The magic cloak that protected her had been stripped off, revealing shameful incompleteness underneath. Her courage had gone; it cowered at the end of the tunnel into her body, afraid of intruders.

She'd gone to pieces. She lay on the bed in the attic of Sir John Perrot's quarters in Dublin Castle, her head sticking out of Sir John's nightshirt as out of a tent, and refused to eat.

'Come on now, Barb,' begged Cuckold Dick, 'have some of this nice jelly. Got carragreen or some such in it, so the cook said. Make you a big strong . . . lady.' He tried to edge the spoon between Barbary's lips and got showered with carragheen soup as she spat it out. 'That's not nice, is it? What good's it going to do? I don't like this any more than you, but we got to lump it.' Actually, he was as terrified as she was, and as lonely. A helpless, panicking Barbary left him leaderless.

The door was flung open by Sir John, carrying clothes. 'How are we today?'

Cuckold Dick said apologetically they weren't so well. 'Our head still aches, Sir John.'

'Lucky to have a head to ache, my girl. Judging from Burghley's reply to my letter, the Queen's impulse is to cut if off and Burghley says if you don't find her the O'Malley treasure, she will. What about that, eh? You shall have until that leg mends, Mistress Barbary, and then we confront your grandmother with you. For your sake I hope she co-operates in the enterprise. What say you?'

He didn't wait for an answer, which Barbary wasn't giving him anyway, but flung the clothes down on a chest. 'You,' he said to Cuckold Dick. 'Get her into those. Got 'em from Mistress Spenser. You'll be staying with the Spensers from now on. That pious old fart, Archbishop Loftus, has heard word I'm keeping a mistress in the attic and is already complaining to Burghley of my improprieties. I'll give him improprieties. God's testicles, I'd forgotten what an envious, backbiting hellhole Dublin was. How's the leg?'

He flung back the bedclothes and raised the nightshirt. Barbary's hands clamped a fold of it firmly between her legs, causing Sir John to snort. 'Good God, girl, too late for that, I've seen it.' He poked at the cast, found it firm, and wriggled Barbary's toes. 'I spared you from damned butchering doctors at least. What do they know of broken limbs? I've had more breaks on the hunting field than hot dinners, and set most of 'em meself. It shall be as good as new, what do you say to that?'

If Barbary had been less depressed she might have said thank you. Cuckold Dick was full of praise for the way that, after her fall, Sir John restored order in the hold, pronounced the break in Barbary's shinbone a clean one, yanked the leg until the two ends fitted and then clamped it between two pieces of planking, all before she had recovered consciousness and in a boat that had, in Cuckold Dick's opinion, been trying to toss itself into Hell.

When at last the *Elizabeth Gallant* limped into Howth harbour Sir John ordered his servants to go ashore and obtain comfrey root. The Lord Chancellor, the Mayor and Corporation of Dublin, and all the other civil and military notables, having ridden hastily from the city in full regalia to welcome the new representative of their Queen, had to wait; the Lord Deputy designate was busy pouring pasted comfrey root onto an encasement of splints round the broken leg of a miserable, red-headed young woman. The cast had dried into a plaster that itched furiously but held the leg like a clamp. Sir John flicked it. 'Hard as the Devil's dick,' he said. 'We'll find you some crutches.'

He rummaged among the clothes on the chest and brought out a canvas-wrapped parcel, chucking it onto her bed. 'Came for you by messenger from Penshurst,' he said. At the door he turned and winked at her: 'I'll say this,' he said, 'you've got the prettiest little red parsley-bed as I've seen in a month of Sundays,' and went out.

'You might've said you was grateful, Barb,' admonished Dick. 'We can't have too many friends in that class.'

'I *am* bloody grateful,' Barbary shouted at him, 'but he wouldn't have mentioned my Mary-Jane if I'd been a boy, would he?' That was it. Sir John's attitude towards her had changed from the well-met bonhomie he'd used to her at first, to a nudging, knowing, vaguely hostile patronage now she was a girl. It had nothing to do with her imposture. The English apothecary who'd been called in to check her leg, and who had no idea who she was, displayed the same attitude. His examining hand had wandered too far up her thigh, considering the break was in her shin. He'd only desisted when Barbary told him: 'Go any higher and I'll break your fokking wrist.' Womanhood apparently meant being open to insult.

Cuckold Dick was struggling with the parcel. 'Letter with it,' he said. 'Read it, Barb.'

It was from Sir Philip Sidney and began: 'Dear and worthy Boggart,' so presumably it had been written before the news of her change of sex had reached him. She scanned it. 'He says Will is turning out cannon like a warren produces rabbits and what's in the box is from him, with his love. Philip says Will says after use it's to go back to him for refurbishment.'

'What's he mean?'

'Philip doesn't say. He *does* say he's going to marry Frances Walsingham, having decided after all that she is his only true love. So much for Penelope Rich. He wants the Queen to let him go to fight in the Low Countries.'

'God keep the good gentleman safe.'

'Amen to that. Let's see what's in the box.'

There was a layer of russet wool which Barbary recognised as part of Will's old jerkin. Below that was straw and nestling in it . . . 'Oh, God bless you, Will.' It was a handgun.

'Powerful strange-looking object,' said Cuckold Dick. 'What is it?'

'Bless him, oh, bless him. It's the Clampett snaphaunce. I knew he could do it.' It *was* strange-looking, being the only one of its kind in the world, as far as Barbary knew. Dutch poachers were credited with the recent invention of something similar, a wheel lock using flint on steel rather than pyrites, because they were dissatisfied with the glow from the matchlocks giving their position away at night. But Will had taken the idea, refined it and, with precision craftsmanship, produced a version eighteen inches long. Its stock curved downwards and, typically Will, was unornamented. Underneath the steel barrel two hooks held a miniature rammer and mop. A string of small wooden cylinders like a clumsy necklace held the cartridges, tiny sausages, each containing exactly the same weight of powder and ball as the next.

Dick picked one out and pressed the stiff paper at its ball end. 'Bit pea-sized, Barb,' he said. 'You won't stop a cavalry charge with that.'

Barbary peered down the barrel at the rifling. 'Maybe not, but the next bugger who insults me'll get the shock of his life.' Her morale was back. As Dick said, the Clampett would be useless at long range against armour, it wouldn't even do for wildfowling – unless the bird sat still while she got up close. But that wasn't its function. It was personal defence, her own secret weapon; carefully aimed, it could drop a man at a dozen paces. And that, Barbary knew, was what Will, concerned for her safety in Ireland, had intended it for. They'd taken away her manhood; Will Clampett's gun had given it back.

She puffed out her breath. 'Let's get those bloody clothes on.'

The difficulty was not the comfrey cast on her leg, though it didn't help, but the fact that neither she nor Cuckold Dick knew about women's attire. If anything, Dick was the better guesser.

'I don't credit that bit for the leg, Barb. I think it's a sleeve.'

'A sleeve? How can it be a sleeve? I got a bloody sleeve on already.'

'And these wood bits in here, Barb. They goes to the front, not your back.'

Barbary stared at the wooden stays with horror. 'They look like they're out of the Inquisition.'

Eventually most of the sections had been assembled, and they were left puzzling at what was left over – a long, stuffed, bolster-like roll. 'It's a draught excluder,' said Barbary, hopefully. 'It got into this lot by mistake.'

Cuckold Dick considered it, and then her. 'That skirt don't look right, Barb. I credit this is the bum-roll what sticks it out from underneath like. We got to start again.'

'Krap.'

Eventually the roll-farthingale was positioned. 'How do I look?'

Dick walked round her. Even to his unpractised eye the clothes Maccabee Spenser had sent over were a job lot, and intended for somebody bigger than Barbary. The skirt was moderately fashionable, though made from a plebeian fustian, the high-necked bodice was of rich apricot-coloured velvet, but had seen good wear and was rubbed over the stays. Her hood belonged to another period altogether, being of the type favoured by the late, unlamented Bloody Mary. Its rigid gable roof, side pieces and back curtain covered every scrap of Barbary's hair.

'One laugh, Dick, and I'll shoot you,' she said. 'Is it that bad?'

She looked diminished, overwhelmed by the alien clothes, suddenly deprived of colour by the hood; only her green eyes fought back.

'You won't frighten the horses, Barb, but that's about all.'

She hopped back to the bed. Despite the over-large items, every inch of her felt pinched and restricted. 'I can't stand this,' she said, 'I can't. What am I going to do?'

'Not much until that leg's mended,' said Dick. 'After that, well, that old besom in the cells down below still knows where there's treasure, and we're still the best there is in the cony-catching line. And there's piracy.'

She nodded. He was a comfort.

The last item from Mistress Spenser's ragbag lay on the bed, a long, old-fashioned muff made out of rabbits whose skin might not have had the mange while they were alive, but did now. Barbary picked it up, tore a rip in its lining, and slid the Clampett snaphaunce inside. It just fitted. 'All right, womanhood. I'm ready for you.'

Chapter Nine

After two weeks of living with the Spensers, Barbary decided that womanhood had even less to recommend it than she'd thought.

Edmund himself was not the problem, he was kept too busy with his clerkships up at the Castle, the centre of Dublin's administration, while at home he paid Barbary scant attention. He didn't seem to recognise her as the Boggart he'd met at Penshurst, much to her relief. The problem was his little Maccabee, the well-intentioned, ubiquitous, constantly busy, ever-twitching Maccabee; Maccabee who talked as if in terror that God might stop her mouth at any moment, which Barbary began to pray He would.

At first Maccabee treated her lodger with distaste. She couldn't remember under what name and title Barbary had been introduced to her on the boat, but she knew it was as a male, that she had been discovered to be female, that the authorities were shocked by it, and therefore so was Maccabee. There was talk of disgrace. Why had Sir John thought fit to quarter such a person on the Spensers' God-fearing family? This continued until Edmund came home after an interview with Sir John Perrot to say that they would be receiving rent for Barbary. 'I'm given to understand our guest is an agent of the State,' he said, bowing faintly in Barbary's direction. 'Where necessary she is to be introduced as your cousin. We must treat her well, my dear. Sir John hopes you will teach her the requisites of domestic life in which she is lacking.'

That instruction, Barbary came to feel, was a mistake. Her stock with Maccabee had undoubtedly risen, but so had Maccabee's need to boost her own. She exulted in possessing skills that Barbary did not. From then on it was: 'Oh, can't you cook? Now you sit there, poor soul, and watch me make a flummery. First two calves' feet boiled for their jelly . . .' Or it was: 'Oh, can't you sew? Then here's how to turn a seam . . .'

It wasn't that Barbary didn't want to learn these things, though she found them hideously dull, but that Maccabee's relentless instruction continued from the moment she got up until she went to bed. Barbary, who had once been independent, with time to herself, now had none. It was like being manacled to an ants' nest. Maccabee was the one who expelled energy all day, but it was Barbary who went to bed feeling that she'd been bled by too many leeches.

Maccabee's dedication to teaching Barbary 'the requisites of domestic life', was equalled only by her dedication to the memory of her father, the wool merchant Chylde, whose qualities and importance Maccabee never ceased to impress on Barbary.

Barbary got very tired of the Merchant Chylde. 'My father, the Merchant Chylde,' she mimicked as Cuckold Dick helped her up the stairs to her room in the attics – attics seemed to be her portion in Dublin – 'he had a thousand oliphaunts, you know, and ate every one of them. Oh, can't you cook oliphaunt? Stay there, my soul, and I'll get a skillet . . .'

'She means well, Barb,' said Cuckold Dick.

'She means to drive me mad, that's what she means. Why in hell did Edmund marry her?'

'Needhams, I think, Barb. She says he was a struggling poet when she met him. And she was the Merchant Chylde's only kinchin so she probably got a nice little inheritance. Anyway, she seems to make his chimney smoke.' The attics he and Barbary and the servant Barker occupied were over the Spensers' bedroom and the sound of sexual rompings frequently issued up through the floorboards to disturb those trying to sleep above.

'No accounting for taste.'

Cuckold Dick went back downstairs to sit with Maccabee as he usually did for a couple of hours in the evenings, before going off to the tavern he was beginning to frequent. He said he was 'paying his politeness', and rather enjoyed it. Nobody had explained Dick's presence, Barbary just having introduced him as 'my friend', and Maccabee, presumably believing him to be another agent of the State, interpreted his usual mournful amiability as wisdom. She consulted him on everything from child-rearing to entertaining; his replies were necessarily guarded, but as Maccabee didn't listen to them in any case, they got on excellently. It was difficult to bore Dick, and he found Maccabee's deference a novel experience.

Barbary struggled onto a high stool set by the attic's tiny window so that she could look out. This was the moment she looked forward to all day, away from Macca-bee's remorseless assault on her eardrums. It wasn't peaceful exactly. Edmund Spenser was renting one of the tall, thin, lathe and plaster houses which fronted the city wall along Wood Quay, the busiest and noisiest part of Dublin. From here she looked down onto the artery of the Liffey. On this dark, November evening it was lit with flares and dinned with activity. Even the three fer-ries within her view couldn't cope with the traffic to and from the other, north, bank and watermen looking very like the watermen of the Thames and crying the same 'Westward ho', 'Eastward ho' rowed up and down the ebbing tide. From Fishamble Street next door, which ran towards the river, stallholders were exchanging news of the day's selling as they swept fish-guts and scales down the slip into the Liffey before shutting up for the night.

Upriver to her left the torches on Old Bridge showed the people leaving the city for their homes on the north bank. In front of her, ships were still unloading by the light of flares, jammed three or four deep out into the Pool so that shipmasters were remonstrating with dockers who had to clamber over their decks in order to get at the cargo in holds beyond, disputes which Barbary enjoyed overhearing.

What unsettled her was that many of the exchanges were in Irish, and that she understood them. Edmund, being interested in the native poetry, had hired an Irish-speaking clerk from the Castle to come to his home twice a week and teach him the language. Although there was an ancient statute, dating from an earlier English admin-istration of Ireland, which forbade the Irish themselves to speak Irish, Edmund interpreted it as not applying to a scholar like himself. 'Even her Gracious Majesty has taken instruction in the tongue,' he said, 'therefore it behoves us, who settle here, to do the same,' insisting that the entire family, Barbary included, should attend the lessons with him in the parlour.

His own progress was slow but painstaking, Catherine's somewhat better, while Maccabee's was non-existent. It was Barbary's which was so extraordinarily fast that it terrified her. Unlike the others, she had no trouble getting her tongue round Irish pronunciation; it took to the syllables like a snake released into grass. She hardly had to glance at the words and phrases set for homework to have them instantly secured in her mind where they joined others that floated up, unbidden from a memory she hadn't known she possessed. It was uncanny, as if a ghost was whispering secrets in her ear.

She hid her unwanted expertise from the others and sat through the lessons in sullen silence. But she couldn't hide it from herself. Here was confirmation of what Will Clampett had told her. Like it or not, she was Irish. The Irish language lay behind the fog wall, as intimately a part of her as her intestines. It had been no fluke when she'd understood those outrageous words the O'Neill had used to toast the Queen and Sidneys at Penshurst. God help her, she and Hugh O'Neill were of the same race.

She began to wonder how she became so proficient in English, and decided that, since Will had not mentioned her as being unable to speak it, her unknown parents had been bilingual, as so many Dubliners were.

But they had not been Dubliners, of that she was positive. The city was completely unfamiliar to her, and surely she would have remembered it if she had spent her early childhood in it.

It enabled her to go on trying to ignore the revelations of her Irishness, to persist in being Barbary of the Order, trickster extraordinary, attempting to extricate herself with profit from a difficult situation. The Barbary of Penshurst, who had once sworn loyalty to the Queen of England, had paled into the background. It was difficult to retain loyalty for a woman who was threatening one's head. As soon as she could, she'd investigate this business of the treasure, filch it, and try her new proposed career as a pirate. Until then she was in thrall to her broken leg, Maccabee and Dublin.

Believing, like the typical Cockneys they were, that

London was God's own capital city and all others were provincial and inferior imitations, she and Cuckold Dick had been prepared to sneer at Dublin, but Barbary was beginning to be impressed, while Dick had already fallen in love. 'Imagine the Bermudas with a brogue, Barb, and you've got it.' Even from this window she could see what he meant; it was like a small-scale London and different. Its wharves and streets had the same overcrowding and enterprise, the same men and women sold brooms and mousetraps, she heard the same English calls, 'Buy my dish of great smelts', 'A hassock for your pew', 'New oysters', 'Whiting, maids, whiting', 'Rock samphire', 'Hot, fine oatcake', and all in an Irish accent. The smell of wood and coal fires, so reminiscent of London, mingled with the scent of peat and drifted up into an air that gave a special outline to the roofscapes. She longed to get out and explore it, away from Maccabee.

Being the main city of the Pale – the areas of Ireland amenable to English administration – Dublin had escaped much of the famine caused by the Desmond Wars, though wolves and plague had prowled the streets during the worst times. The uneasy peace of the last few years had given it breathing space in which to recover, and the influx of the undertakers was bringing back its prosperity. Yet there was still famine in the city. Only yesterday evening, Edmund had come home to report that Treasurer Wallop's stables had caught fire in mysterious circumstances, and several of his horses had burned to death.

'The mere Irish fell on the carcases in the instant,' he told Maccabee, 'gnawing at the half-cooked flesh.'

'Who *are* the mere Irish?' asked Barbary. She found the strata of Dublin society confusing. There seemed to be Old Irish, Old Anglo-Irish, old-established English, all of them contemptuous of the newly arrived English, who in turn looked down on the lowest order of all, the mere Irish.

'Scum,' answered Edmund, shortly.

The bastards better not eat Spenser, she thought, and had an idea.

The next morning Cuckold Dick was despatched to fetch the pony from the Castle stables. 'That's a nice horse,' said Maccabee whose judgement of horseflesh was

as unreliable as her judgement of people. 'My father, the
Merchant Chylde—'

'Get me up,' Barbary told Cuckold Dick. If she could
swing the damned cast over . . .

'My soul, you're not going to ride him, are you? It
would be most unwise with that leg . . . Edmund
wouldn't—'

'We have State business to attend to,' Barbary said
loftily, having managed the mount. Why hadn't she
thought of this escape before? 'We'll be back for dinner.'
No more embroidery, no more flummery, no more Merchant Chylde.

Carefully, with Cuckold Dick at her side to protect her
leg from the traffic, she allowed Spenser to pick his way
through the activity of Wood Quay.

Immediately, a group of dockers shouted to her, 'A
fine, soft morning for your complexion, mistress.' Barbary frowned at them.

Cuckold Dick, beginning to pick up local customs,
murmured: 'They mean "Good day".'

'Why don't they say good day then?' She felt edgy and
exposed to insult in her female clothing. Anyway, it
wasn't fine at all, it was drizzling.

Following the city wall up towards Dames Gate, past
the windmills, she was informed time and again by men
and women that it was a fine, soft morning, a morning to
rinse the Liffey, a morning to put water in the ale. 'These
are still "good days" are they?' she asked Dick.

'They like words, Barb.'

There must be something in the air, she decided, that
infected those who breathed it with chronic love of language and curiosity. The greetings were often followed
up by questions. 'And how did you get your poor, green
leg, mistress?' They seemed to know everything about
everybody else. Told she was Maccabee Spenser's cousin,
they asked: 'And wasn't there a strange happening on the
ship the lady came in on?' Barbary said she had been too
seasick to notice, which led to a general discussion on
seasickness cures which mysteriously but invariably led
on to the political situation.

'They're a friendly lot,' Cuckold Dick said, 'brew a
nice drop of ale and all.' There were more taverns to the
acre than Barbary remembered in London. Cuckold Dick

said the ale was good but different. 'Browner, like the Liffey.' While she was still bedridden he had gone out one night with a couple of Sir John's footmen and been introduced to another drink called 'whiskeva' or something, so he told her, white and shaking, the next morning. 'Don't you touch it, Barb. It's an Irish plot. The captains forbid it to their soldiers, they say it bloody near lost 'em the war.' But she noticed that didn't stop him going out to sample it again.

Most of the taverns were crowded with soldiers. The captains and captain-generals were gorgeously accoutred, but the men were a ragbag. Their only common denominator was their weapons and the red cross of St George sewn to the backs of their cloaks. Occasionally a band was in uniform because its commissioning officer had supplemented the Treasurer-at-War's allowance to enable his men to look like soldiers. Generally, however, contractors to the army had undercut their competitors by providing such shoddy cloth that the men had bought, stolen, or borrowed civilian jerkins merely to keep themselves warm and any resemblance to the uniform patterns kept in the Wardrobe Office in London was purely coincidental. Most were conscripts who hadn't wanted to be soldiers in the first place, even for eightpence a day, and certainly not soldiers in Ireland. The volunteers either hoped to make money by plunder, or had criminal records that made England too warm for them.

Dublin's other surfeit, besides taverns, was in churches; Benedictine, Cistercian, Dominicans, Arrouasians, they had been emptied by the Reformation and their walls were being quarried for the new buildings that were going up everywhere. Barbary saw one lovely polygonal abbey in use as a stable. At an ancient nunnery, workmen were carrying carved panelling and ornaments out into the street and throwing them onto a bonfire. What drew her notice was a crowd of men and women silently ringing the fire and staring at an object licked by the flames. As she passed she saw what it was, a full-sized wooden statue of the Virgin Mary.

Already she knew who were 'mere Irish', you could tell them by the patched, voluminous, woollen cloaks fringed with fur that all of them, men and women, kept wrapped round their lean bodies as they loped through the streets, scavenging, begging, or asking for work in painful English. These were the natives who had been driven into the city by starvation outside it. They were the sub-class, the human dogs who moved through the crowds as if in a dimension of their own, aware only of food or each other. She felt contempt. There was nothing so low in London; even the Order wouldn't admit human detritus like these.

A barber standing underneath the pink and white pole of his trade suddenly leapt at one of them, a male who'd been pushing a barrow past his shop. 'That's not legal,' the barber shouted. Barbary pulled on Spenser's reins to watch. What wasn't legal? Pushing a barrow?

The mere Irish let go of the handles and slowly turned to face the angry barber, who was considerably smaller than he was, and who pointed at the Irishman's hair as he shouted. 'That. That glib of yours. Not legal.'

The barrow-pusher's hair hung down over his face, his eyes peering out through the thick strands like a wild cat's out of a clump of ferns. The barber reached up and gathered up the long fringe, which, Barbary presumed, was the offending 'glib', brought up his other hand containing large scissors and, in one practised movement, cut the hair across. He turned to the crowd that had gathered, throwing the hair into the gutter. 'They've no right, no right. Against statute it is. Damned bastards.' He hurried back into his shop.

The Irishman said nothing. He turned back to his barrow and trundled it off, but for one second Barbary glimpsed the exposed eyes, and shuddered. Some of the crowd laughed, one man picked up a round of horse manure and threw it after him. But the barber, thought Barbary, as she kicked Spenser into motion again, he hadn't been laughing, his had been the anger of the uneasy.

Later, she found that unease everywhere. The Pale was afraid. It had conquered the natives, but not got rid of them and, like conquerors everywhere, it credited them with hidden, mystical powers. The traditional Irish glib was forbidden because it was a symbol of the secrecy with which the Pale felt the natives worked against it, worshipping with their forbidden priests in caves, plotting with witchcraft in the hills which surrounded Dublin and beyond into the wild countryside where English law ran out. For all its learning, its inns of court, the schools of philosophy, the residences and the summer palaces of its chief administrators, Dublin was a frontier town.

Barbary liked it, she decided; it was invigorating, and its hint of fear made it oddly exotic.

They rambled out of the city to Hogges Green where the Dubliners went to play skittles and bowls or practise their archery at the butts. It was a large area of open country, grazed by sheep and edged by the ever-present Liffey. Spenser liked water and took it into his head to go down to the tide edge. Barbary dropped the reins and relaxed, enjoying the smell of the estuary, the seagulls and waders. For the first time there was no human noise around her. Except for a child who was crying somewhere. The sound was coming from a clump of alders on the bank. Annoyed that humanity was intruding even out here, she might have ridden past, except that there was a note to the crying that disturbed her, and an activity under the alders that made her curious.

She urged Spenser towards it. In a gap between two trees a woman was being raped. A soldier was standing by, watching, holding a struggling little boy. The woman was silent, but she was kicking, trying to dislodge the soldier who was on her, heaving, pinioning her arms with his own.

Always, afterwards, Barbary remembered the face of the child. She drew her pistol out of her muff and aimed it at the watching soldier. 'Get him off her,' she said. She called over her shoulder to Cuckold Dick: 'Go and get the watch.'

She hadn't time to load the pistol, but the soldier didn't like it. He didn't like the look in Barbary's eye either. He kicked his companion, who jerked himself out of the woman and looked round, into the barrel of the Clampett snaphaunce. Grabbing his trunks up, he got to his feet and the two men ran off.

The woman lay where she was for a moment and then scrambled towards the child, holding him and murmuring in Irish. She was a typical mere Irish, tall, thin and good-looking. Her face was bruised. She glanced at Barbary, nodded, picked the boy up and began to limp away.

'Stay here,' commanded Barbary. 'The watch will need a description of those men.'

The woman looked at her curiously, trying to understand the English words. She said slowly: 'You'll be new here. No, they were kind men.'

'Kind? *Kind?*'

The woman came up to her, putting her face up to Barbary's as if she was going to tell her something of importance. 'The kind ones,' she said, 'are the ones who don't kill you after.'

Barbary let her go. The two constables of the watch who came up with Cuckold Dick some minutes later were unimpressed by the story. 'You wouldn't understand, mistress, being a respectable lady and one that's new here. She wasn't being forced at all, not at all, so don't distress yourself. That sort, they ask for it. She was probably doing it for pay, if you'll pardon the expression. What's that grand word for them?'

'Sex mad,' suggested his companion.

'Licentious, that's what it is. Them women have no morals at all, so don't be worrying about it. How did you get your poor, green leg now?'

They accompanied her back to the city walls, talking all the way. She shook them off at Dames Bridge and turned down for Wood Quay. The damned woman and her child had soured her day out, she was tired and her leg was beginning to hurt.

It was then that a man who'd been lounging against a wall, watching her, came forward. 'Mistress Barbary? My master would be grateful if you'd call on him. I'll lead you to his house.'

Barbary looked at him suspiciously. The fellow was in splendid livery but it had no emblazonery on it. This was probably a summons from Sir John, but you couldn't be too careful. 'Who is he?'

The man looked around at the people passing by. 'Well, now, I was not to mention the name, ears being everywhere, but if I was to lead the little pony, perhaps you'd be looking at the back of my gauntlet.'

Barbary looked at it, reining Spenser in. Embroidered on the back of the glove was a red hand cut off at the wrist. 'So?'

'Ah, Jesus,' said the man, shuffling his feet with irritation. 'Are you coming or not?'

'Very polite,' said Barbary. She looked at Cuckold

Dick. 'Do we go?' She knew she would; she was intrigued, and anything was better than an afternoon with Maccabee Spenser.

'Always got the Clampett, Barb.'

Their route this time took them towards a richer part of the city where the English administrators and lords like Ormond and Tyrone, the rich and loyal Irish, had their town residences. On the way they passed the King's Inns, the crazily timbered houses from the time of Henry VIII, which were occupied by the legal profession. If anybody was flourishing in Dublin it was the lawyers, Barbary decided. Black-gowned figures with ear flaps on their caps scurried to and from court with their clerks following, carrying small hills of rolled documents. Edmund Spenser had said that the settlement of Munster was proving more complicated than its planners in London had envisaged. Irish and Anglo-Irish were contesting grants of their land to the undertakers, and while the court battles went on and the lawyers grew rich, the poor undertakers themselves were having to wait in Dublin until their licences were approved, and their money was running out.

A man Barbary recognised from the quay at Bristol – he was the one who'd been accompanied by the grandfather in the coffin – was hanging onto the arm of one of the lawyers. 'I wanted to get my winter corn in.'

The lawyer dislodged him. 'My dear man, I expect a settlement any day. You can sow it in spring when you get there, can't you?'

The farmer watched him bustle off. 'They call it winter corn because it goes in in winter,' he shouted. 'How'm we going to live?' But that wasn't the lawyer's problem.

Though they went in through a side gate, the servant with the red hand on his gauntlet led them along a walk of rose trees to the courtyard of an impressive house, a Palladian frontage with a balustraded flight of steps leading up to the front door from a courtyard guarded by stone hounds. The servant helped Barbary off Spenser but instead of putting her down, carried her up the steps and into the house, calling over his shoulder to a groom: 'Look to the small nag, will you?' Cuckold Dick followed them into a flagged hall and then through double doors into a large room, so like the salon at Penshurst that

Barbary was momentarily disorientated. Tall windows, screens, carved desk, carved mantel over the massive fire, similar firedogs, even the same Dutch bowls of potpourri. The servant lowered her into a large chair and left.

A man looked up from the desk. 'Saints defend us, what *are* you wearing?'

'Oh, it's you,' said Barbary, rudely. 'How the hell did you know I was here? I'm not dancing today, I can tell you that.'

'Make your mind easy,' said the Earl of Tyrone. 'If I wanted to dance with scarecrows I've got them back in Ulster. Will you take that bloody fireplace off your head?'

Barbary grinned and took it off, feeling lighter – and not just from losing the weight of the hood. All the fascination and sense of risk which Ireland had engendered in her since her arrival was personified in this man. He was less fantastically dressed today, black velvet, white lace pointing; no longer posturing for the English aristocracy.

He got up to fetch a tapestried footstool and put it carefully under her foot. 'How did you get your poor green leg?'

'Your Irish Sea tossed me down the hold of the ship coming over. The bastards undressed me while I was in a faint.'

'Fun for them,' he said, 'but it wasn't the sea. That was Ireland wanting the truth of you. You're a woman here. You can't cheat Ireland like you cheated England.'

That's all you know, Barbary thought. Let me get my hands on that treasure and I'm away from both of them. Aloud she said: 'What do you want?'

The O'Neill jerked his head at Cuckold Dick standing by the door. 'You, out.'

'You stay,' said Barbary. 'Dick knows all about you. I tell him everything.'

'Does he now? Do you?' He walked back to his desk and poured two glasses of wine, gave one to her and sat down. 'Have you considered my little proposition?'

'What little proposition?'

'Guns, woman, the guns. I want you to persuade your friend Master Clampett to do business with me.'

She was sorry he was so insane, though he had lost the ability to shock her; among the walls and yew hedges of

174

Penshurst his treachery had seemed momentous, here he was just a mad Irishman. But she wanted to prolong the interview; he was better company than Maccabee and she'd like to know a lot more about him. Deliberately, she yawned at him.

He flinched. 'Will you oblige me by never doing that again?'

This was new; his voice had gone thin with dislike. Stepped beyond the mark, had she? Chit of a girl annoys the great lord by over-familiarity? She almost welcomed the change, even as she resented it; at last she knew where she was, where he put her, and this terrifying intimacy of his was just an attempt to charm her into doing what he wanted.

She became more pert than ever. 'Insolence, was it?'

'It was time-wasting.' He came up to her, standing between her and the window so that the afternoon sun outlined his black figure and shone through his ginger hair; she had the impression of a lighthouse. 'Sooner or later, you are going to get me those guns and sooner would suit me best.'

She didn't say she couldn't if she wanted to. She was too experienced a card player to reveal her hand when she didn't know his. 'Why should I?'

'For the same reason I want them. Come on, O'Flaherty. Where's your patriotism?'

'Where's yours?' she shouted back at him. 'You're the Queen's subject. You want to fight for Ireland against her, you get your own bloody guns.'

He looked down at her as if amazed. 'Fight for Ireland? You think I want to fight for Ireland?'

She was confused. 'What are we talking about?'

He went back to the window and pointed beyond it, still looking at her. 'You think I want to avenge those skeletons out there? Get justice for the scum of Munster? Fight for the True Faith? I stood by and watched while Elizabeth and Desmond reduced Munster until there was nothing for its people to eat but grass. Ask your Edmund Spenser, he was there taking notes, the bastard. The corpses had green stains round their mouths. They died on a diet of shamrock.'

He put his hands on his desk and leaned towards her. 'Do you know who killed Desmond at the end?'

She shook her head.

'An Irishman. His name was Moriarty. He was a small farmer and he was cross because Desmond's men had stolen his cow. He went out looking for it in the Phantom Mountains and came across a hunted, broken old man sleeping in a hut and cut off his head. So perished the great Earl of Desmond. Don't talk to me about Ireland. There's no such thing.'

She looked around for help at the familiar furnishings, but this wasn't Penshurst. She didn't want any part of it.

'Who am I, O'Flaherty?'

Dick would have to get her out of here in a minute. 'The Earl of Tyrone, my lord.'

'You're right. I am the Earl of Tyrone. That bitch over in England thought up the title herself and gave it to me. And very happy I'd be as Tyrone. I like England, I like its ways. I even like Elizabeth.' He picked up an ornamented dagger from his desk and flipped it so that it stuck into the panelling of the wall. He stretched before walking over to pull it out, musing. 'My next wife will be English,' he said. 'Nobility, I think. Blue blood, apple cheeks and nice with the table napkins.'

'Yes, my lord.' She didn't take her eyes off him. He was pointing the dagger at her.

'But who else am I?'

'I don't know, my lord.'

'I am the O'Neill. *The* O'Neill. I eat with my fingers in the open air at tables made out of tussocks and my milk comes out of dirty pails and my hereditary harper sings me songs that were old a thousand years ago. And great savages called O'Donnell stride up to me and say: "O'Neill of Ulster, we call on you as the aid of our ancestors to help us. The English adventurers have come to Dundalk and taken our ancient castles and ravished our women." And who answers them, O'Neill or Tyrone?'

He crossed the room and knelt in front of her, taking her wine cup and holding her hands in his own. His eyes were darker than she'd thought, and the pale skin of his face more freckled. It had tears on it. 'Who answers?'

'I don't know.'

He drew in a deep breath and got up, briskly. 'Well, as a matter of fact, the Earl of Tyrone did. "Hang on, old

176

fellow," he said, "I'll just go and ask them nicely in Dublin." '

'And did you?'

'Yes, I did. The Earl of Tyrone did. And Sir Jolly Jack Perrot says: "Yes, Tyrone, those English adventurers are naughty, unauthorised men. But they are English. And just in case your Irish O'Donnells move against them, I've taken their chief's son, Red Hugh O'Donnell, by a trick and I've put him in prison as a hostage for their good behaviour." And what does Tyrone say? He says: "Oh, right ho." '

He sobbed as he turned and smiled at her. 'But what Sir Jolly Jack doesn't realise, or doesn't care is that young Red Hugh is the brother to one of the wives I have when I'm wearing my O'Neill hat. He is my brother-in-law, my vassal from time immemorial. He is a foolhardy, hot-headed young pain in the arse, but he happens to trust me.'

He closed his eyes. 'So there he is, in Dublin prison along with his friends, Conn O'Hagan and Art O'Neill.' He opened them. 'And your grandmother.'

No grandmother of mine, no grandmother. Nothing to do with me. I don't want to be involved with you or your aliens. Let me go away.

'But I'm dealing with that,' said O'Neill, brisk again. 'What I am trying to demonstrate is how difficult Elizabeth makes it to be her loyal subject *and* a Gaelic chieftain. One day I may have to choose, and I may choose wrong. And if I choose wrong my people are not going to be reduced to eating shit and shamrocks. We'll go out like true Celts, blowing the Saxon to Hell along with us.' He smoothed her hair back from her face. 'And that's why I need guns.'

'Please,' said Barbary, desperately, 'I'm not your man . . . woman. Admitted I was found in Ireland, but there were orphans swimming around the place like minnows. I could be anybody. I don't feel Irish. I don't want to feel Irish. Ulster-Munster hocus-pocus, it's not my business. I'm a cony-catcher. That's what I'm good at. Stop telling me things. How do you know I won't go to Sir John and tell him?'

'Ah, Connaught, Connaught,' sighed the O'Neill. 'I am Ulster. I have known you for two thousand years. I have married you, fought you, killed you, we have danced together to the tune of one blood. I am your Ard Rí, your High King. You won't betray me.'

'No,' said Barbary, 'I won't. And I won't get you guns either.'

'Oh yes, you will.' He smiled down at her. 'You stay in Ireland long enough and they'll force you to choose. And you'll choose wrong. And that's when I get my guns.'

He told a servant to take Spenser back to the Castle stables and sent her home in a satin-quilted sedan chair. He didn't say goodbye, he just said: 'And for the love of God, will you find something decent to wear.'

It was still only afternoon, though it seemed a century later, when she got back to the house on Wood Quay and crutched herself up the stairs to her attic, leaving Cuckold Dick to explain to a Maccabee already impressed by the sedan chair that the State business had been so tiring that Barbary must be left alone until morning.

The exhaustion was mental, as if her mind had been abused. Why, though? He'd been serious enough, the poor mad sod, but she hadn't; she'd no more than flirted, a sort of investigation really, a look at his cards. Then why this response? It wasn't his atrocity stories of Irish people; they weren't *her* people.

'He treats you like you were important, that's all.'

So did Lord Burghley.

'Yes, but Burghley wanted something of me.'

O'Neill wants guns.

'Yes, but O'Neill asks as if he's calling on some ancient debt, deep commanding deep.'

Krap on him.

She went to sleep and dreamed her face had turned green.

In the morning she stayed in the attic, telling Maccabee she had to discuss yesterday's State business with Cuckold Dick. It was an excuse of endless usage. The attic was grey and very cold, a reflection of the weather outside, much of which seemed to be blowing through the ill-fitting window. There was less activity down on the quay as the threat of a bad winter kept more and more ships away. But it was still preferable to Maccabee's parlour.

'What did you think of him yesterday, Dick?'

He sat on the end of her bed, brushing dandruff off his doublet as he considered. 'What I think, Barb, is he's going to spring that O'Donald, or whatever his name is, and all the rest in Dublin Castle. And I think, Barb, if we're going after that treasure, it better be now.'

She gaped at him. He'd cut through all the atavism, the attraction, the atrocity, and reached the nub. He'd listened for only what concerned the matter in hand. And he was right. 'But I'm dealing with that,' O'Neill had said; his pride or his honour or whatever the Irish nobility called it wouldn't allow his friend O'Donnell to stay in gaol. He'd get him out and, probably, the others with him. Including Grace O'Malley.

'Dick,' she said, 'have I ever told you you're not the fool you look?'

They spent the rest of the morning working out ploys, happy to be back on sure ground and using their skills again. Counterfeit crank, the whipjack, the palliard, ruffling, esen-dropping, every traditional way of couzening the location of her treasure out of Grace O'Malley was considered, and discarded. They had one advantage unique in their experience: they had the authorities on their side, up to a point. After that point they had to couzen them as well.

'As I see it, Barb, we spring her out of the queer-ken, and then cony it out of her.'

'No, the cony first. Why spring her at all?'

'Well, she's your grandmother, Barb.' He drew back because her face had become distorted. Love him as she did, she nearly spat at him.

'You stupid bastard. I've told you, haven't I? These people are nothing to do with me. They're . . . they're disgusting. They kill each other, they die and keep on dying. Like animals. They're filth, losers. They're a joke.'

'All right, Barb, all right.'

'It's not all right. She's no grandmother of mine, don't you understand? She's some stinking old Irish trug and I won't have her. I won't have her.'

'All right, Barb. Don't blow your stack. All right.'

She unclenched her fists. 'All right. But that's how it is.'

He sat hunched and unresentful until she'd stopped

shaking. 'So,' he said, 'what we got to do is, we got to cony the whereabouts out of her while she's still in the clamps. And for that she's got to think you're her long-lost kinchin – I know you're not, Barb, I'm just saying.'

She was discouraged. 'Not likely, is it? Kinchin or not, these Irish betray their own mothers. There's heads of rebels as thick as lollipops up at the Castle that got sold to the Lord Deputy by other Irishmen. She'd reckon I'd steal the treasure anyway.'

'She might, Barb,' said Dick gently, 'if she thought she was going to hang and the secret go with her.'

'She ain't.'

'She don't know that. Remember how John Graye the Little got hisself put into the Clink so's he could cony Swanders out of the whereabouts of the pearls he'd lifted from Lady Hoby's ken? Told Swanders he was going to marry Swanders' sister, and as how Swanders was going to hang wouldn't he like to testament the pearls first? Remember?'

'Swanders hanged anyway.'

'Barb, concentrate.'

She pulled herself together and thought about it, then leaned over and patted his knee. 'You're getting on my nerves,' she said, 'being right all the time. Now then . . .'

The next day a large wicker hamper of clothes arrived 'For Mistress Barbary', brought by a porter who didn't give his name nor that of the sender. There was no chance of opening it quietly; Maccabee was beside herself with manic accounts of the birthday surprises provided for her by the late Merchant Chylde.

'I haven't got a birthday,' said Barbary.

'You have now, Barb,' said Dick. 'Look at these duds.'

Even to Barbary, who wasn't susceptible to female fashion, the items in the hamper were mouth-watering. The largest was a gown of orange-tawney velvet, its V-shaped stomacher so thickly embroidered in white, yellow and gold it was impossible to guess at the base material. There was a hat, silk knitted stockings, pumps, a pair of Spanish leather buskins lined with lamb's wool, garters, girdles, muff, gloves, cloak, handkerchief, petti-coats – and a gold chain with a locket. While the others were occupied with exclaiming and unpacking, Barbary opened the locket, shut it quickly and hung it round her neck.

Maccabee translated her envy into taking charge of Barbary's attiring. Cuckold Dick was sent away, Barker made to hover in a corner, and Barbary endured what seemed hours while Maccabee showed off a knowledge of style which she had certainly never applied to her own clothes.

The stomacher was more restricting to the bosom than the wooden stays of Maccabee's hand-out but, Barbary felt, even though she was not yet permitted to look in a mirror, more fun. 'Bit low, though, isn't it?' she asked nervously. She was showing bits of her frontage that had never been on display before.

'Then we'll put in the partlet.'

'What's a partlet?'

'Oh, my soul, don't you know what a partlet is . . . And this is the ruff, we call it a rebato. Now this is a girdle, nice bit of metalwork, and it should have hangings; here they are, a pomander and a mirror. Now this is *the* latest version of the court bonnet. We call it a "pipkin".'

Whatever it was called, it was the sauciest bit of headgear Barbary had ever seen, a tiny, round piece of felt in popinjay green with an ostrich feather held on by a gold clip. Beneath it her hair was stuffed into a caul of gold thread.

'Have you got a lover?' asked Maccabee suspiciously. 'Who could have sent these things? Let's see what's in the locket.' She shut it in disappointment. 'Empty.'

It was empty because the oval bit of card that fitted it was hidden up Barbary's sleeve. There was no writing on the card, no portrait, just an inked drawing of the Red Hand of Ulster.

Well,' said Maccabee reluctantly, 'I suppose you'd better see yourself. Barker, fetch the mirror.'

She wasn't given long in front of it. 'Female vanity is abhorrent to the Lord,' Maccabee said and snatched it away, but in those few seconds Barbary saw not standard beauty, but an audacity of colour and form that trapped the eye and kept it. The blazing creature in the mirror cocked her head with its rakish hat at Barbary. ''Swelp me,' it said, 'I'm *it*.'

'That will do,' said Maccabee. 'Whoever sent them obviously meant them for wear at Sir John's investiture. Take them off.'

'I'm going to show Dick,' said Barbary. Even on crutches the creature in the mirror moved differently, upright, swaying the stiff folds of velvet which hung from its hips and back, its neck held high to avoid the prickles of the ruff. The outfit wasn't brand new, she could smell the perfume of whichever of O'Neill's wives or mistresses had worn it before, and felt gratitude to her, allied as she was in a new sisterhood of stylish women.

Before she could reach Cuckold Dick's door Maccabee called to her: 'I believe I know who sent the gown, Cousin Barbary.' There was a new, coquettish tone to her voice.

Barbary leaned over the stairwell. 'Who?'

'Wouldn't you like to know?' Maccabee was bridling with her idea and couldn't keep it. 'I've just thought. Sir Walter.'

'Oh.' Sir Walter Raleigh was visiting his estates in Ireland at the moment, and the Spensers were so enamoured of their patron that they were inclined to attribute every good, even fine weather, to his beneficence. Barbary was relieved that the real donor was unguessed at, but curious as to why Maccabee should think Sir Walter Raleigh would be showering gifts on a woman he'd hardly seemed to notice. 'What the hell for?'

'I've told you about that word, cousin. Because,' Maccabee wriggled her shoulders, 'because Edmund says you're allied to an Irish noble house and might be marriageable property.'

'Marriageable property?' It was ludicrous. 'He wouldn't be allowed to marry me. The Queen would kill him if he married anybody. Good thing she doesn't know about Alice Goold and her baby down in Lismore.'

'That's just gossip,' said Maccabee crossly, who had herself imparted it to Barbary. 'Well, I think he's interested and I think he sent the gown.'

Barbary let her go on thinking it, and swung through the door of Dick's attic and propped herself against the wall, prinking the puffed tops of her sleeves: 'How's this to knock 'em off the perch?' Then she stopped. 'Oh Dick, don't.' Appallingly, he'd begun to cry. She hopped

182

across the room and plumped on the bed to sit beside him and take his hand.

'Never had no mother, Barb,' he said, wiping his nose on his hand.

'I know. I know.'

'If I had've, I'd want her to look like you do now.'

She tried not to laugh. Or cry. She sat with him until he'd got over it, her arm round his shoulders, dandruff falling on her orange-tawney velvet.

That night in her dream she was all green; green skin, green hair, green clothes, indistinguishable from the grass of the field in which she was pinioned. Somebody was ploughing the field and heavy hooves were plodding in her direction. She kept shouting to the ploughman that she was there. He saw her, but shouted back, 'Marriageable property,' and set the team forward over her.

Sir John Perrot's investiture as Lord Deputy of Ireland took place in St Patrick's Cathedral amid scenes of grandeur and farce. The ceremony had been delayed because Treasurer Wallop had taken its most important symbol, the Sword of State, home with him and it took time to fetch it back. Archbishop Loftus, not a military man, got the pieces of ritual armour mixed up as he placed them on the Lord Deputy, and was accordingly sworn at. The Master of the Rolls had trouble deciphering the Queen's letters patent and umm-ed and ah-ed all through his reading of them.

The lords and ladies, burghers and burghers' wives of Dublin didn't mind; they had come to show off their best robes and hats and, except when commanded to be still in the name of the Lord, milled about chatting. The trumpets and choir and the cathedral itself were splendid.

Barbary sat on a stool just inside the Lady Chapel which now had a bust of Elizabeth in what had once been the Virgin Mary's niche. As the lords of Ireland trooped through the nave to take their seats in the choir, she spotted O'Neill among them, pompously grave-faced as the rest. She caught his eye – in the orange-tawney she was catching a lot of eyes – and bowed her pipkinned head. He turned away as if he'd never seen her, but not before one eyelid had batted down.

The next day Barbary had a private interview with the

new Lord Deputy and outlined as much of her plan as she was prepared to give him. He was blustery. 'Stratagems and wiles, the Devil take us,' he said. 'I tell you, mistress, if that sister of mine had not commanded this enterprise I should have nothing to do with your feminine treachery.'

She wasn't having that. 'Feminine treachery my arse. I'm told Red Hugh O'Donnell was tricked aboard a ship and kidnapped on your orders, Sir John. What sort of wile was that?'

'Political,' he said and grinned at her. He was a big man in more ways than physical and could always be disarmed by a show of spirit. 'Those Ulster tribes must learn the lesson that I am in command of this country. Not the O'Donnells, not Tyrone. Me. What say you? The spies are reporting odd stories about Tyrone. Questioning his loyalty. If I don't keep Ulster to heel I'll have my own administration ripping my throat out and the whole damned slaughter will begin all over again. Already Wallop is writing to Burghley that I've gone native because I won't countenance more hangings. What would you have, eh?'

The treasure, thought Barbary, and the hell with the lot of you. She said: 'When can this plaster come off? I can't do much with this contraption on my leg.'

'Third week of Advent.'

'Very well. And we're agreed on my stratagem, Sir John?'

'Yes, you hussy, we are. And, mistress, see that it succeeds. Elizabeth has set her heart on that treasure, money-grubbing besom that she is. In that bonnet, yours is too pretty a head to lie in some executioner's basket.'

'I'm grateful for your encouragement, Sir John.'

The prospect of being a prison warder gave Cuckold Dick sleepless nights. 'Are you sure I can do this, Barb?'

'Dick, you've been in more queer-ken than I've had hot dinners. You know how the key-turners talk. You know how the bastards think. You can do it.'

'All right, Barb, but you promise me. Promise me they'll never hear about this back in the Bermudas.'

She missed him when he took up his post at the Castle. For one thing, his absence left her more open than ever to Maccabee's verbal attrition. But it was necessary for him to be accepted as part of the Dublin prison scene before she appeared on it, and she couldn't play her part until her leg was properly mended. Besides, she wanted Dick to keep an eye open for any attempt by O'Neill to engineer the prisoners' escape. Her odd relationship with O'Neill was one she valued, but not enough to be deprived of treasure for it.

'Where has Master Dick gone?' Maccabee asked, who missed him too.

'He didn't tell me.'

Nobody was to know of the plan except Sir John Perrot. In Dublin secrets had the quality of eels and tended to wriggle away from those who held them. Philip Sydney had told her that what enraged Sir Henry when he was Lord Deputy was that the Irish frequently knew the contents of State despatches from England before he did. Trusting only Sir John Perrot with knowledge of the arrangement was a safeguard, but it was also a risk. Barbary woke up sweating at the thought that Sir John might drop dead while she was incarcerated, and she'd have to serve the sentence for a crime of which, for once, she was innocent.

The days crawled by. No confessing Christian, Barbary decided, had ever longed for the advent of his Lord as she did now. The weather got colder. There was ice on her washbasin when she woke up, shivering, in the mornings. Down on Wood Quay the dockers swore warm oaths as their fingers fumbled with frozen bolts and ropes.

Only one incident interrupted the dreary tenor of Spenser life. The servant Barker disappeared. She went out to buy hot pies from the stall on the bridge and never came back. Maccabee and Barbary went looking for her. Edmund instituted enquiries among the watch and issued a fly-sticker giving her description, but she was never found.

To Barbary's surprise Maccabee, whose relationship with the girl had been conducted mainly in shrieks, displayed not just shock and irritation but genuine grief, and went daily to church to pray for Barker's safety and return.

'First Master Dick and now Barker,' she wept. 'They

say the mere Irish are abducting people and eating them.'

'They're hungry enough,' said Barbary.

'Cousin, don't be bad. You don't really think so?'

'No.' Privately, she feared that Barker had been assaulted and thrown in the Liffey. Or had seen a chance of escape from drudgery and gone off with a soldier. She didn't express the first possibility and nothing would convince Maccabee that Barker had gone off on her own volition, so they were left with the cannibal theory which turned Maccabee's fear of the mere Irish into downright hatred.

With the loss of Barker, and until Maccabee could hire another servant, Barbary had to help out more than before, especially in amusing the Spensers' child, Catherine. She was intimidated by this chore at first, never having had to do with small children. Catherine, however, was a grave, obedient toddler and listened intelligently while Barbary told her the story of how Well-Arrayed Richard had fallen in the vat of porridge while burgling the lavender-maker's ken, or sang her the Pudding-in-a-Cloth's more respectable drinking songs.

'What's that you're playing?' Maccabee asked, coming in unexpectedly from shopping.

'Cousin Barby's showing me the Three Card Trick,' piped Catherine.

'We don't know that one, do we?' said Maccabee. 'It's kind of Cousin Barbary to play games with you, isn't it? Perhaps after dinner we'll all play it.'

At last the English apothecary was called in to remove the comfrey cast. He did it warily, his hands sticking strictly to their job, and pronounced Barbary's leg perfectly mended.

Barbary took Maccabee to one side. 'I have to go away on State affairs for a while,' she said. 'I wish to leave my good clothes here until I come back,' God knew if she would see those delights again, but business was business, 'and if possible I don't wish anyone to know that I have gone. Can you keep it a secret?'

'I can keep secrets,' said Maccabee with dignity. 'Haven't I told everyone that you are my cousin?' She began to cry. 'And indeed I was glad to do it, for apart from dear Edmund and Catherine I have no relatives. Must you go?'

Damn the woman, thought Barbary as she went up to her attic to pack, why can't she stay uniformly awful? Why does she have to be touching now?'

Into the wicker hamper went all her finery. She was reluctant to part with O'Neill's locket, but if she knew prisons, and she did, it would be stolen. She slipped the piece of card bearing the Red Hand of Ulster out of it and tucked it in her pocket. She'd wear the cloak he sent, though; the only certainty about the next few days was that she would be very, very cold. And the buskins. She put on a pair of Maccabee's woollen socks and pulled the boots over them. A bit large. She took them off and put on another pair of socks. Now they fitted well enough. The muff. Gawd, she'd have to leave the Clampett behind; her fellow prisoners would assume she'd been searched and she wouldn't be able to explain away a snaphaunce pistol. How could she explain away the torque? Well, she'd think of something; she had to have that. It was part of the plan.

She waited until it was dark and crept downstairs. Through the door of the parlour she heard Edmund saying: 'But my dear woman, the Three Card Trick is a notorious gambling game . . .' Definitely it was time she went.

She eased back the bolts on the door and went out. The cold gripped her like an enemy. Geometric shapes of white in the dark water showed there was ice in the Liffey and it was beginning to snow, flakes hissing as they touched the flare on Prickett's Tower. She turned right and right again into Fishamble Street. For all her apprehension and the weather, it was liberating to be walking freely again; there was nobody about except some mere Irish crouched against chimney stacks and for the sheer joy of movement she began to run. Left into Cowe Lane, past the Pillory and into Austin Lane which ran parallel to the Castle's western wall. Somebody was sheltering in its shadow with a lantern.

'Took your time, Barb,' said Cuckold Dick. 'Nearly froze me nutmegs off.'

'Where are they?'

'Bermingham Tower. Up there.' He pointed to a round shape appearing and disappearing as the moon rode the snow clouds. Most of it was concealed by the Castle's turret. Both were incorporated into the city wall. 'It's a bugger, Barb. Back of the tower there's the river Poddle. When we go, we got to get across that, lessen we find a boat. Even the first time won't be easy.'

There were to be two escapes. She had planned the first with Sir John Perrot. She was to be arrested and put alongside the Irish prisoners, the warders to be unaware that she was Sir John's agent. With Warder Dick's connivance, she would get herself and her fellow detainees out of the castle. The ploy was to convince Grace O'Malley that she, Barbary, was her grandchild and gain her confidence. When, according to plan, they were immediately captured and re-arrested and Grace was facing execution, Barbary was confident that she could cony the whereabouts of the treasure out of the woman, just as John Graye the Little had conied the goodies out of Swanders in similar circumstances. 'Or my name's not Barbary Clampett.'

Where Sir John's plan and Barbary's plan diverged was in the projected second escape, the one Sir John didn't know about, which was to take place the moment Barbary knew where the treasure was. It would feature only Cuckold Dick and herself, who would then decamp, secure the treasure, sail back to England, pick up Will, and begin a new life. 'On a tropic island, Dick,' she'd said, 'oliphaunts, and mermaids and coconut palms.'

Dick had been more doubtful. 'Sounds good, Barb, but there's some rough edges.'

Barbary, however, desperate to extricate herself from Ireland, had been confident that the rough edges would smooth out as they approached them. Now, here, in the cold, under the looming towers of Dublin Castle, the edges were looking not just rough but jagged. However, the die was cast.

'Windows?'

'Two, both backing onto the Poddle. It's not nice, Barb. They're not all in together like the good old queerken back home. Separate cells, no glim lessen they buy it, not much pannam and peck neither.'

'Perrot keeping them short?'

'Not him. The screws. Same old story, selling the prisoners' food. They don't like the mere Irish, Barb, I can tell you. But our lot's getting cash from somewhere.

They been stripped. Nothing. But the other day she was eating best porridge. Take my oath, one of the screws is in cahoots with 'em, but I don't know which.'

'O'Neill?'

'No sign. But I don't like it, Barb. They got something under their nab-cheats. They're powerful cheerful for folk in Needhams like they are.'

'Got the rope?'

'Brand new.'

'It better be. Let's get going.'

Cuckold Dick left her. Their conversation had frozen her feet. She stamped them, then walked on up Austin's Gate and stood looking up at the turret which hid the Bermingham Tower from this angle, getting colder and colder as she waited for the Lord Deputy's agents to come and arrest her.

'What's the charge?' shouted the night keeper over Barbary's screamed cursing.

'Treason and spying,' shouted back the head keeper, holding fast to Barbary's right arm, while a third keeper held her left. 'Agents just brought her in. Hold her, she has the muscles, for all her size. Why they couldn't keep her till morning. Waking me at this hour. Be quiet, you slut.' He punched Barbary in the eye. With her good eye she absorbed the geography of the room. It took up the entire floor of the tower, but a third of it had been bricked off to form six cells, each with its own door in which were open squints. From the darkness of four squints, eyes were watching her.

'Search her?'

'Just feel for weapons. I want my bed. But I'll have the boots for my collection. I know a young lady who'd fit 'em. Take 'em off her, Jack.'

The night keeper advanced on Barbary and got a kick in the stomach that whooped the air out of his lungs. The head keeper punched her again, this time on the jaw and she went limp. When she came round the boots had gone, and so had her cloak. The head keeper had both. He leered at her: 'Nice warm rooms in this hostelry,' he said. 'We wouldn't want you to suffer the over-heating now, would we?' The other two sniggered. Prison-warder humour, Barbary decided, didn't improve this side of the

Irish Sea. 'Put her in Number Five. They'll examine her in a day or two.'

She was pitched into one of the cells. She lay, hurting, for a bit.

Still, so far so good. The onlookers in the cells wouldn't be able to doubt the authenticity of the head keeper's punches. She couldn't doubt them herself. Carefully she put her fingers to her eye and touched obtruded flesh. The Order would say she was in half mourning – full mourning was two black eyes. Well, she'd had her eyes blacked before. And they'd overlooked the torque – the watchers in the cells had seen them overlook the torque. Good. The only hitch was that the O'Malley woman wouldn't have glimpsed her hair, one of the proofs of her supposed pedigree. Through all her struggles Maccabee's damned gabled hood had stuck obstinately over her head.

She got up and began investigating her cell, mainly by touch since only miserable light came through the squint from where the night keeper with rushlight and tiny brazier sat on the other side of the tower room. The cell was about seven foot long and shaped like a wedge of cheese, of which the door formed the narrow end. A wooden shelf ran along one side to serve as table and bed. On it was a wooden pillow, a blanket stiff with dirt and a pail which, her nose told her, had served previous inmates as a chamber pot and not been cleaned since. Apart from some none-too-fresh straw on the floor, that was it. No window, but everything she touched was freezing. What the temperature fell to in the cells with windows was something she didn't like to contemplate.

There was murmuring outside. She went to the squint and pushed her face against it sideways, peering to the left, where she could just see the doors of the other cells. Her one good eye opened wide. Her fellow prisoners were playing cards. One of them had attached a stick to a bricklayer's hod in which was a dog-eared pack of cards and hands reaching through the squints were passing it back and forth so that each player could pick up or discard. The game was some sort of primero.

Their conversation was as unstressed as if they were sitting round a gaming table. It was in Irish, but so much of her knowledge of the language had returned to her by now that she could understand almost every word. All the reaching hands looked masculine. She tried identifying Grace O'Malley by voice, but their tones were getting softer, almost lulling. Across the room the night keeper was wriggling down under a blanket in his wicker chair. They wouldn't start to question her until he fell asleep; Irish or English, no prisoners worth their salt gained or gave information in the hearing of their gaoler.

With the confidence of aristocrats they were playing for huge sums. 'A thousand crowns,' said the nearest voice – that would be Number Four, a man. Even pitched sotto the voice had an explosive energy. 'A thousand to shame the Devil.'

'The only shame,' drawled another male voice further down – Number One or Number Two – 'is to take your money. The O'Donnells never learn caution. I wager two thousand.'

'Caution? Caution?' hissed Number Four – from O'Neill's description it could only be young Red Hugh. 'Wash the dirty word from your mouth. Caution is for women. Ah, now, I'm sorry, Granny. I'll be cautious in me coffin.'

'And it's me will be putting you in it. Will we get on with the damned game? I raise another thousand.' That was Number Three or Two. The whisper was hoarse and aggressive, but it came from a female throat. Barbary had found Grace O'Malley.

They bantered softer and softer. She could feel their eyes on the night keeper, whose chin had slumped. In a minute he was snoring.

'Number Five?' It was the drawl of Number One or Two, who'd accused Red Hugh of incaution and bet even more, a sleepy voice. Speaking English.

'Yes?' she said.

'Our apologies for the welcome. Over-lively, we thought. Would you have a name?'

She allowed her breath to catch, as if she'd been crying but was now being brave. 'It was Barbary Clampett. Now it's Barbary O'Flaherty. I think.' Let them prove it for themselves. Cony-catcher's law.

There was a silence. The night keeper's rushlight was guttering. From long practice of keeping watch his head jerked up, he lit a new rush and went back to sleep. They waited until his snoring was regular.

'Allow me to introduce you. The silent one on my left here is Art O'Neill. On my right is the Lady Granuaile O'Malley. The violent gentleman on your left is Red Hugh, tanaist to the Clan O'Donnell. I am Conn O'Hagan and tanaist to the O'Hagans. If it's of interest to you, I have a bad cold. Too many draughts here. We're going to speak to the servants about it.'

She allowed a sob to escape her. 'Grace O'Malley?'

Red Hugh took over. His voice hit her ear with energy from a couple of feet away. 'So the Saxons call her. What's it to you?'

'They say I'm her granddaughter.'

There was another silence. Red Hugh's whisper hit her again: 'Who says?'

He was interrupted by Conn O'Hagan. 'Should we not let the little lady explain in her own way? Sure, she's got a story to tell.'

She didn't like the way he put it and, anyway, she hadn't wanted that; better if they got it out of her, question by question. In fact, she was beginning to dislike Master O'Hagan. A treacler if ever she'd met one. However, make a beginning and then plead fatigue. Leave them wanting more. Cony-catcher's law.

So she told them and, as planned, she told them the truth; not all of it, and with a slight bend to what there was, but the truth. Cony-catcher's law: if it's verifiable, tell it. She began with her capture by the Lord Treasurer's agents and the interview with Burghley. She left out the fact that Burghley didn't care whether or not she was the O'Flaherty heir and had only picked her up because she fitted the role. They must not think her credentials questionable. 'They thought I was a boy, you see, the heir, and they wanted to train me, like they'd trained O'Neill.'

'What do you know of the O'Neill?' That was Red Hugh, angry.

'He's my friend. He recognised me as the lost grandchild.'

Silence again. 'We wouldn't want to question your word,' came the smarmy voice of the O'Hagan, the bastard. 'But most people know who they are. Would you have an explanation for why you didn't?'

192

'Later. I can't talk any more now. I need to sleep.' Her eye and jaw ached and she was very, very tired. She piled as much straw on the shelf as she could and burrowed into it, pulling her knees up under her skirt and arranging the curtain of Maccabee's hood round her neck and face, grateful that it was so awful the keeper hadn't wanted to steal it as well. She fought sleep for as long as she could and listened; they might begin talking about her among themselves. They didn't, it would have been impossible for her not to hear them, but she had an uneasy feeling that somehow they were communicating. Presumably they had been in alliance all their lives and here in prison they had formed the almost mystical bond of the isolated. O'Hagan had constantly used the 'we'. They would know each other's minds in a way that totally excluded her. Well, sod 'em. It wasn't their company she was after. She fell asleep.

There was no dawn. The only sign that day had begun was a changeover of keepers. Thumping sounds from the other cells indicated that the prisoners were trying to exercise warmth back into their bodies.

She began jumping up and down, longing for breakfast. It didn't come for about two hours, and when it did it consisted of one hunk of bread and a beaker of water. The only cheering thing was that it was Cuckold Dick who brought it; she glimpsed his face, stolid and dull, as he pushed it through the squint of her door.

It was a long day. She heard Grace O'Malley tell Art O'Neill that it was snowing hard – obviously hers was one of the cells with a window. That was one very tough old girl, Barbary decided. Her few comments were foul-mouthed and caustic, but, though her sufferings must be intense, they contained no complaint. A different age and a different sex from the others, they still treated her as an integral part of their strange brotherhood. None of them complained, except Conn O'Hagan, who moaned about the service and his cold, but she noticed an anxiety for Art O'Neill. He rarely spoke and was plainly unwell, but neither he nor the others mentioned it. They spent the day in incessant games of cards and their equally incessant banter.

Once again, when the night keeper came on, he was lullabied to sleep by gambling calls that came softer and softer. Barbary braced herself.

'Number Five?'

'Yes?'

'Are you better?' It was the bloody O'Hagan again.

'Yes.'

'That's good, that's very good. You were in the middle of a story last night, and as we Irish love stories we were wondering if you'd continue.'

'What do you want to know?'

'Well, sure, we'd be interested in hearing how you lost your memory.'

Again she told them some of the truth. Born at seven years old. The fog wall that hid the previous years. Trying to explain the inexplicable and surprised to find how much she resented exposing to these aliens deep matters she had never told anyone before. There was humiliation in it. That treasure better be worth all this trouble. She made no mention of the strange ship that came to her in the cherubims, nor the voice which commanded her to hug Adam and shun Eve – that went too deep. She gave them what and when Will had told her about finding her at Kinsale, but left out his part in the Smerwick massacre; he had killed these people's allies.

They were quiet while they digested it all. Again she was sure they were communicating, but it wasn't out loud.

'This necklet as you call it,' it was the hoarse whisper of Grace O'Malley, 'have you got it on you?'

'Yes.' She took it off and held it through the bars. A hand, Red Hugh's, took it from hers and passed it down the line. There was a long, low moan from Grace O'Malley's cell. 'It is the torque. It's Maire ni Domnall's own royal torque. The child is who she says she is. And me thinking they were all drowned dead. Mother of God be praised for her mercy. She's given me back me grand-daughter.'

Squinting through, Barbary saw a hand stretching out as if desperate to touch her. 'Oh, my child's child.'

She reached out her own hand as far as she could. 'Grandmother!' As sweet a versing as she'd ever done. She felt the old triumph, mixed with something else she didn't have time to analyse.

The men were still holding back, still questioning, but

their suspicion was shaken by Grace's muttered prayers of thanksgiving.

'What for were you arrested?' asked Red Hugh.

'They were so angry after the accident, when they found I was female. The Lord Deputy said the Queen wanted me executed, but he's not a cruel man.'

'Kindness itself, the bastard,' said Red Hugh.

'He put me in the charge of a man called Edmund Spenser until my leg mended.'

'The clerk who pretends to poetry?' It was Conn O'Hagan, who pretended to poetry himself. 'An English poet, and isn't that the contradiction in terms.'

Why didn't they shut their pipes while she concentrated. There was still a long way to go. 'Sort of house arrest,' she continued, 'while they made up their minds what to do with me. But I was so lonely and miserable. Mistress Spenser treated me as a servant. My only relative in the world was the grandmother I'd not seen. She'd take me in, I thought, give me a home, if she was free. So soon as my leg was well I started loitering around the Castle, asking questions, trying to find out where they were keeping her to see if I could get her out.'

A triumphant cry came from Grace's cell. 'There speaks the true O'Malley. Ah, me own child's child. Me brave girl.'

'Shhh.' She'd woken up the keeper. He swore and flung an empty tankard at the cells. 'Cut it, you Irish bitch.' They had to wait until he'd grumbled himself back to sleep.

'I would have too,' Barbary said quietly, 'if they hadn't arrested me, suspecting what I was planning.'

'Would have what? Got your grandmother out of here?'

'I think so. There's a keeper, the one that brought the breakfast . . .'

'He's new.'

'Is he? Well, he's a rogue. I recognised him. I'm sure it's the man. It was in London and he was being whipped at a cart's tail.'

Ignorant savages that they were, they'd think London as small as Dublin; everyone acquainted with everyone else. 'I was going to put the bite . . . I was going to threaten to expose him if he didn't help me get Grandmother away.'

'Ah, the brains of me darling girl.'

'Granuaile.' They were warning the silly old cow not to wake the keeper again.

'But what if he *is* a rogue?' came the soft whisper of O'Hagan. 'They're all rogues. Have you not met their clergy, Mistress O'Flaherty? They must be lovely gentlemen when they start out from England to bring the light of the new faith into our darkness. But a terrible thing happens when they're halfway across the Irish Sea. Sure, the bad sea fairies spirit them away and replace them with loose-living, drink-swilling crap-hounds. Now isn't it unkind of the fairies to do that?'

The man was touched in the head. She'd met butterflies with more concentration. It was Red Hugh who got the point: 'If the bastard's a rogue, he'll be open to bribe.'

Barbary relaxed for the first time that night. They were caught. She'd got them. In the pot with parsley. She slid down the door to sit with the relief, listening to them taking over.

'What'll we bribe him with?'

'The torque, man, the torque. He'll not reject gold.'

'Ah, now, must I give up me poor dead daughter-in-law's torque to a Saxon? . . . I'll do it. Next time he comes on duty.'

'I've got to sleep,' Barbary called gently. 'Goodnight, Grandmother. God keep you.' God keep the treasure.

'Goodnight, darling girl. I'll have you in me arms soon.'

'Is there anything we should ask Mistress O'Flaherty before she sleeps. Art, you've not commented on the plan. Have you a question?'

Art's voice came faintly: 'Ask her where she got that hat.'

It was a bad night. She kept waking to bouts of uncontrollable shaking which was mainly the cold, but also nerves. It had gone very easy. Too easy? No, they were conied. But why, now they accepted her as one of themselves, did they persist in talking to her in English? She'd told them her Irish was rusty, as it still was a bit. But there was something . . .

The day keeper was Cuckold Dick. She winced when she saw him; it was too soon, it would look too pat. It wasn't what they'd arranged. Something was wrong, or, more likely, he didn't want her to stay in these conditions any longer. As it was, there was no chance for Red Hugh to put the bite on because there was activity in the room nearly all day. An intruder had been spotted in the Castle, down by Store Tower where they kept the arms. The place was in an uproar with the search for the man; keepers, guards, soldiers pounding up and down the stairs, thumping along the leads of the roof, shouting, calling into the cell room of the Bermingham Tower to have a warm by the keeper's brazier and swap the latest rumour. Their breakfast was overlooked, and Barbary had to bite her lip to stop herself moaning from the cramps in her stomach.

'Are we to have nothing to eat?' Red Hugh shouted at Cuckold Dick.

Dick, very properly, shouted back: 'Fuck off, Irish.'

By the afternoon things had quietened down. It was then that O'Hagan and Red Hugh began their bite. For amateurs they did well; a layman's version of the hatchet and pap routine, just like Burghley and Walsingham had put the bite on her; O'Hagan the pap, Red Hugh O'Donnell the hatchet. And a nasty hatchet. 'You're a convicted rogue, so you are, and if your own English don't have your balls, there are Irish who will.'

O'Hagan: 'Leave the poor man, Hugh. If he does us this favour, he'll be paid with gold, and no one to know where he got it.'

Dick was a credit to his profession; defiant, then surly, then whining. She was proud of him. Yes, well, he supposed he could get a rope, but he'd want the gold first.

'After. When we see it hanging outside our window.' O'Hagan was suddenly forceful. 'And we want it now.'

'Now?' Dick showed genuine alarm. This wasn't the plan. He didn't like it. Barbary didn't either.

'Now,' Red Hugh shouted. 'Don't you speak your own fucking language? Undo these locks and go and get it now. Better still, take it up on the roof and tie it to a crenel. And tie it tight.'

'They'd know it was me . . .'

'Ach, tell them the intruder attacked you. Blame it on him. Do it.'

'The night keeper. He'll be coming on duty in a minute.'

'I'll attend to the night keeper. *Do it.* My cell first.'

Dick fumbled with the keys at his belt and went to Barbary's cell door, the typical, stupid warder held to routine. As he opened her door there was a shave of a second while his eyes met Barbary's. His said: 'Let them out and we've lost control.' Hers replied: 'Leave them in and we've lost the treasure.'

He moved off down the line to unlock Red Hugh and the man came out of it like a bull, his long, carroty hair and beard surging with the force of his movements. 'Give me the keys. Go and get the rope. Hurry.'

'Get his boots first,' called Grace O'Malley.

Obediently, Dick leaned down and began taking off his boots. Red Hugh pushed him onto his backside and pulled them. He tore the ring of keys off Cuckold Dick's belt and rushed to Grace O'Malley's cell, fumbling with the lock and dancing with impatience on his big, prehensile bare feet. 'Get the rope,' he shouted over his shoulder. Dick went out.

Grace was saying, 'Hurry, hurry.' O'Hagan was clutching the edges of his squint and shaking the door, gripped by the panic.

Grace was loose, a big woman with long hair striped like a red and grey badger. She took the keys and control from O'Donnell. 'Stand to the door. He'll be here in a minute.' She took no notice of Barbary, concentrating immediately on O'Hagan's cell. Barbary crossed to the keeper's table and picked up the rush-holder – she'd be in charge of the light at least. O'Hagan emerged, another tall man. Were they giants, these Irish? Their shadows crossed and re-crossed like the branches of wind-whipped trees. Nobody came out of Art O'Neill's cell, and Grace and O'Hagan went into it to see to him.

'Hush now.' Red Hugh was crouching by the door to the steps leading up from the lower floors. They could hear footfalls coming up. The latch lifted and the night keeper came in with whatever passed among gaolers for a merry quip on his lips. It was never finished. Red Hugh grabbed the man by the shoulders and knocked his head against the door jamb with a force that damaged both.

'Boots,' called Grace from Art's cell.

O'Donnell dragged the keeper by his collar into the centre of the room and dropped him. 'Gag and tie him,' he told Barbary, 'and take his boots.'

She dropped down by the unconscious man and tied his hands lightly with his own belt. He wouldn't be waking up for some time, if he ever did. Cony-catcher's law: no violence. They hanged you for violence. Carefully she tied her handkerchief across his mouth, making sure his nose was unobstructed. His breathing was terrible. She began struggling with the man's boots.

'The rope's here already,' called Grace. She was still in Art's cell.

Barbary blinked. That was quick work on Dick's part. It was only seconds since he'd left the room. Wouldn't they suspect that he'd had the rope ready? Still fighting to get the keeper's boots off, she glanced across the room. There was a movement in Grace's empty, open cell. A white division to the small window. A rope had come down and was hanging outside it. Two ropes? Dick was overdoing it. What was happening?

She left the keeper and went to the door of Art's cell. They were putting Dick's boots on the feet of a man slumped against the shelf. Grace was carefully tying a blanket round him. 'Can you make it, Art, do you think?'

The man nodded. 'Don't leave me behind.'

O'Hagan stretched. 'I think I'd better go first,' he said. 'Me cold, you know. I can't stay in this draught any longer.' The bastard would be gabbing at his own funeral, but he was brave. Whoever went first had to be brave.

'You,' Grace was addressing her, 'get all the other blankets and throw them down. Carefully. We don't want them in the river.'

Barbary nodded. She went into O'Hagan's windowless cell, grabbing the blanket, then into Grace's. She'd left the rushlight behind. Moonlight was coming in through the window, shining on the rope, outlining the cleft of the window. Voices babbled behind her, but in here it was silent.

Barbary stopped, her eyes were on the window and the rope. 'No,' she said, 'I won't. Mother, I won't.' She was a child but the child had knowledge of the future now. With the benefit of adult perspective it looked out into the darkness, knew the insupportable agony awaiting it at the foot of the tower and knew that it was better to stay here and die than go through that loss again. It had died out there, died from grief.

O'Donnell came into the cell with the rushlight, swearing because she hadn't thrown down the blankets. She didn't hear him. He held the light to her face. 'For what are you crying? This is no time. Afraid? Are you afraid? Jesus God, wait there. I'll get your blanket.'

He came back and threw the blankets out of the window, leaning out. 'Are you down, Conn?'

A voice came from a long way below: 'I'm down. Will you hurry?'

O'Donnell reached for Barbary and pulled her to the window. 'Out.'

'Mother,' screamed Barbary. 'Mother.'

'Will you hush your noise? I'll get Granuaile.' He pushed Barbary out of his way, so that she fell to her knees by the shelf. He put the rushlight by her. 'A fine time to want your mother,' he grumbled, and went out.

She could hear them in another time and another space helping Art through the window and onto the rope. 'Oh God,' she prayed, 'God help me. Give me back my mother.'

He didn't do that, He did something else. Through the wall of the cell He sent her the ship of the cherubims. It floated indomitable and dearly familiar on the stone sea, its oars moving in the swaying rushlight. A heavy hand fell on her shoulder and a voice said: 'Get up, girl. This is no time to be afraid. Follow me down.' It wasn't the voice that had falsely moaned from Grace's cell. This was clear, familiar, like the ship. It was the voice that had said: 'Hug Adam. Shun Eve.'

The ship faded so that only its skeleton was left where Grace O'Malley had scratched its shape on the wall. The rusty nail she had used to score it into the stone lay by the rush-holder.

Barbary's head whipped round and saw her grandmother's face at the window, her big hands round the rope. 'Follow me down, girl. Don't be afraid.'

Obediently, she got up and went to the window. 'Yes, Grandmother.' She watched Granuaile's badgered head moving down and down. To her right, O'Donnell and his friend were both on their rope, Art supported by the casket of Red Hugh's big body and arms.

'Now, girl.' The familiar voice floated up to her. 'Don't be afraid. Follow me down.'

'Yes, Grandmother.'

She climbed onto the window ledge, held the rope and, swinging out, wrapped her legs round it. Cold air and the necessity to survive brought her wits back. There was a drop of a hundred feet at the end of her toes; she couldn't see ground, just the black river waiting to take her in. She grinned: 'You won't get me. I belong elsewhere.' She belonged. She was climbing down to her roots, that tough old besom, those men. Irish, after all. A pity, but roots were roots. Where was Cuckold Dick? He was roots, as well. The rope burned her feet and her hands, but she'd clambered enough rigging on the Thames in her time. They wouldn't wet Barbary's bib. Irish Barbary's bib. She would hug her grandmother when she got to her, tell her, get enfolded by the maternity that she'd ached for and hadn't known she'd needed so badly.

Her feet touched ground, she turned round and opened her mouth and somebody put a gag in it. Her grandmother tied Barbary's hands behind her. 'I told you I'd have you in my arms soon, you little whore.'

Above them, her rope snaked down from the crenels of the roof. O'Hagan had a knife, Cuckold Dick's knife, and cut off a section. Grace O'Malley tied it round Barbary's waist and then, with O'Hagan, went to help Red Hugh and Art reach the ground. The second rope fell from the crenels.

'Gggg,' said Barbary. She tossed her head up and down, like a horse. She arched her body, threw it against Grace's. 'Gggther.'

'Take her,' Grace said to O'Hagan. 'I'll kill the bitch if she touches me again. Throw those ropes in the river.'

O'Hagan's hands clamped on her shoulders, his breath steaming across the top of her hair. 'She means it. And a pity to kill a pretty hostage.'

She hit her head against his shoulders, tears of frustration and rage popping from her eyes. 'I'm attending to that,' O'Neill had said and of all the fokking, shit-arsed, bloody nights, this was the one he'd chosen to do it. This was *his* arranged escape, not hers. Some warder was in

O'Neill's pay. But, ignorant of Barbary's plans, the O'Neill hadn't thought of telling them that there was a young woman in town whom he believed to be Grace O'Malley's grandchild. And it was the truth. She *was*. She knew it now. She, Barbary Clampett, really was the person she'd told Grace she was. She'd perpetrated the greatest conying of her career, only to find now that it was no conying at all.

They hadn't believed her. At no point had they believed her. Cony-catcher caught. To them she was a spy, but they'd gone along with her because she would help the escape and be a good hostage. They'd treacled her, that old bugger Grace weeping, and pretending, but in fact refusing to believe that one of the grandchildren she must have grieved over for so many years had been resurrected in the shape of a Cockney girl.

Oh Jesus. What had they done with Cuckold Dick?

They were putting boots on, adjusting blankets. They began moving, O'Hagan putting his knee in her back every time she faltered. Her feet in their socks were gathering ice and squeaked on the frozen top layer of snow. Art was being piggy-backed, his arms round Red Hugh's neck. They turned west where the river ran on their left, running quietly as if too cold to make a noise. The turret wall loomed silently over them. They reached the corner where she'd been arrested. Where were the sentries? If everything went according to plan, they would all have been re-arrested at this point, taken to Sir John Perrot and all but her – excused because of her youth – condemned to hang. On their way back up to the cells, Grace O'Malley, according to the plan, would utter broken words like: 'I must die, my child, but you at least can live as a true O'Malley. The treasure is hidden in the . . .'

'Will you hold the cow?' demanded the real Grace O'Malley as Barbary threw herself against her once more. She must warn them. Any moment they would run into the trap she herself had set for them. What a clowning, somersaulting sodding mess it was. Again she threw herself at the woman who had gagged and bound her. She jerked her head to try and indicate where the sentries were. O'Hagan dragged her back before Grace could hit her. They moved on. There were no sentries, although somebody was standing in the shadow of the wall. Red Hugh went up to him. Whoever it was kept his voice down. She could hear O'Donnell, though. He said: 'Well done. Thank himself for us. What did you do with the day keeper?' That was Cuckold Dick. She strained to hear the answer. Mumble mumble. 'Give the man gold,' said O'Donnell. 'I promised him. I'll not break my word to a bloody Saxon.' She nearly collapsed with relief. Dick was alive at least.

'Now give me your boots,' O'Donnell was saying. Mumble mumble. 'Well, it's not as far as we're going. And your cloak while you're about it.'

They were off again, skirting the city wall, past St Nicholas Gate. Snowflakes stuck to their eyelids, making it difficult to see. Here and there a diffused glow showed in a window slit, but nobody was fool enough to be out on such a night. They crossed a meadow, a bridge, into country with only an occasional building. They were heading for the hills. Somebody would discover their escape soon and the hunt would be on. She glanced behind her and saw their footprints filling up, the ones further back already vanishing. But how far did these lunatics think they could get without horses in this weather? How long before that indomitable old woman dropped from exhaustion? How long before Art O'Neill froze to death? How long before she did?

Were they going to kill her once they were safe and had no use for a hostage? They wouldn't need to. All they had to do was leave her and walk away. She'd be dead within the hour. She was dying now. She was dying a fool's death because she deserved it. God, hadn't she had enough clues as to who she was? Why had she fought it so long? Was it so terrible a thing to be Irish? Yes, it was. And if she needed proof of how terrible, here the Irish were fleeing through snow to their deaths.

They began to climb. O'Hagan gave the rope to Grace O'Malley and took the lead.

Somewhere a wolf howled. O'Hagan lifted his head and howled back. 'A Wicklow wolf,' he said, 'come to lead me back to my own territory. There's a hut ahead.'

A hump in the whiteness turned into a thatched hut. It was deserted, but to exchange freezing snow for freezing dryness felt like luxury. They were rubbing Art's feet and hands. O'Hagan felt his way round the walls and cried out that there were some hides in a corner. They were bustling, re-dressing, making plans, speaking in Irish.

'Do we go on?'

'No, stay the night here. Art can't go on.'

'I'm all right, I tell you.'

Their voices moved in and out of her head, sometimes making sense, sometimes not.

'We can't stay here. They'll pursue in the morning. We'd not outrun it.'

'We go then.'

One voice came through clear. O'Hagan's. 'She stays here, Granuaile.' Argument. 'She's no boots. She'll die.'

'She's not fit to live. Taking our names in vain. Laying claim to the drowned.'

'Was that Maire's torque?'

'It could have been anybody's. There's a thousand like it.'

'She stays here.'

'She'd only be a burden if we took her.'

'Ach, the hell with her.'

They were leaving. There was a thump in the wall to her left, and one shape came back to kneel beside her. 'If you feel along to your left,' said Conn O'Hagan, 'you'll discover something to your advantage, as the lawyers say.' She was lifted and woolly material, a fleece, wrapped round her. 'There's more hides in the corner. Get angry, Saxon. It's anger helps you survive. I know.' She felt the knuckles of his hand rub gently against her cheek. 'I don't know why you move me,' he said, 'but you do.'

She heard the rasping squeak of their boots in the snow and craned her neck to see through the window's broken shutter the four shapes enfolded in whiteness. She felt to her left and discovered the sickle that O'Hagan had driven through the stones of the wall. She watched the snowflakes fall during the long, tricky, painful business of rubbing the rope round her wrists through against the sickle's blade. She felt no anger against those who'd left her here. She would have given her soul to go with them.

Chapter Ten

The year just beginning had been prophesied as disastrous. Actually each year that arrived was prophesied as disastrous by some crackpot somewhere, but the coming of 1588 carried more forewarnings by seers with better credentials than most.

Regiomontanus, for instance, the mathematician who had provided Columbus with his astronomical tables, had predicted that the world would end in 1588, or, at the very least, suffer upheavals which would dwindle empires.

He didn't predict which empires, but everywhere rulers struggled to reassure subjects that it wouldn't be theirs. Queen Elizabeth was so nervous she had forbidden almanac compilers to allude to Regiomontanus.

There was more than superstition behind her unease. Her agents' antennae were directed towards the monastery-palace laid out in the gridiron pattern on the edge of the Guadarramas thirty miles from Madrid. Here a tireless man who had sworn to punish Elizabeth for her heresy and the murder of Mary of the Scots, and to re-establish the True Faith in her country, worked scrupulously on the finishing details of the Armada he was sending against her.

It was a curious example of public perception that Philip of Spain, at that moment pouring four million ducats into the risky enterprise of an invasion of England, had the reputation of being a colossus of caution, while Elizabeth, his sister-in-law, was seen by her people as charmingly capricious, yet was hoarding her ships like a miser. Her admirals and captains implored her to let them set sail, carry the war to the enemy, gun the Armada out of the seas before it arrived to gun them. But Elizabeth refused to let them move out of port. She wouldn't even let Drake carry out what he called target practice and what she called 'wasting shot'. Ships at sea were expensive, whereas ships at home remained undamaged, their sailors eating fresh food on half pay.

It was not a good time for telling the Queen about an escape of Irish prisoners, especially as the chance of treasure had gone with them. Lord Burghley's arthritic feet lagged more slowly than ever as he entered the royal presence at Greenwich to give her the news in Sir John Perrot's letter.

'It appears, Phoenix, that Mistress Barbary tried her best to trick the whereabouts of the treasure out of Mistress O'Malley, but was tricked in her turn. They left her to die in a hut in Wicklow where, by the mercy of God, our people found her in time.' He waited for the onslaught. She stood with her back to him, watching the Thames as if from here she could look out for the Armada. She had grown calmer as the crisis escalated. She didn't turn round, but a flick of her fingers indicated that he had permission to sit.

Her voice when it came was reflective. 'My entire annual revenue is somewhat less than Philip of Spain draws from his duchy of Milan.'

'I know, Phoenix.'

'And now no treasure from Ireland,' she continued.

'I'm afraid not, my Phoenix.' He flinched as she turned round.

'Lackaday,' was what she said, 'I suppose we'll have to do without it.' Her eyes were cheerful. She had floored him and she knew it. She loved being unexpected. 'And what shall we do with that Boggart person? Hang it?'

He gathered his wits. 'I still maintain there would be advantage in marrying her off to the right man.'

She sighed. 'Marriage, marriage. Do you know that Tyrone has written asking permission to marry the daughter of my Marshal in Ireland, Mabel Bagenal?'

'Yes, Majesty.'

'And that Sir Nicholas has written saying that he'd rather see her dead than married to an Irish Catholic?'

'I suspected he would, Majesty.'

'Well?'

It was a tricky matter. 'I confess to a certain unease about the Earl of Tyrone, Phoenix, but on the surface

206

there is no reason for refusing the match. The girl is willing, I gather, and, Irish or not, he is her superior in rank. Indeed, to refuse him might cause trouble.'

'Trouble,' she said. 'We are about to be beset by the biggest fleet the world has ever seen, and there might be trouble from a disappointed suitor.'

'A suitor who might ally himself with the sender of that fleet.'

She tutted. She was amazing him with her mildness. She turned back to the window, as if the Armada might creep up the Thames unless she kept her eye on it. 'When it comes, Spirit, I shall take my place with the army at Tilbury.'

'Oh, Majesty, I beg you—'

'Burghley.' It was a snap. 'I have to be in the thick of it. I have to be. My subjects must not think that because their prince has the body of a woman she lacks the heart of a king.'

He found himself sobbing; if his knees had let him he would have grovelled to the hem of her gown. Countless times she had driven him mad, frequently insulted him, and always worked him like a dog, but in moments like these he knew that he loved her because when it came to it she had greatness that surpassed any he had known.

'As for these marryings,' she said, 'there's too much of it about. Let them wait.'

'Her Matie is greatly displeased at the failure of Mistress Barbary to locate the treasure,' wrote Lord Burghley to Sir John Perrot, 'yet she is to be permitted to live for, under Common Law, the woman is natural heir to a turbulent princedom of Connaught, and should a husband of proven loyalty be found for her as would bring discipline and calm to that unhappy people, there may yet be some gain. Let the woman be close confined until there is resolve to the matter.'

'Which,' snorted Sir John Perrot over the letter, 'shows how much you know of the Irish, little man.' Sneaking English rule into Ireland by way of intermarriage had never worked. Strongbow, Ireland's first Norman invader, had married the Princess of Leinster, but had still been obliged to make his conquest by the sword. Under the Brehon Code women could not inherit, so the

Irish ignored the claim of foreign husbands. If anything, it fell out the other way, foreign husbands being absorbed into their wives' culture. Within a couple of generations the descendants of Strongbow's invaders had adopted the saffron shirt, abandoned riding with stirrups and generally become more Irish than the Irish. His sister could choose a husband for Barbary O'Flaherty, but if she thought he could rule western Connaught, however proven his loyalty, she would need to think again. Well, well, there was no advising the royal bitch.

In his own mind Sir John was not sure whether Barbary had connived at the escape of Grace O'Malley, O'Donnell and the others, or whether the spurious escape which they had arranged had coincided with a real one arranged by someone else. Certainly it was a long and suspicious coincidence, but on the other hand, what had the girl gained except, from the look of her, her own death? Sir John, never a man to take orders, decided that Barbary was sufficiently closely confined by the illness that was wasting her and put her back into the care of the reluctant Spensers.

The Spensers weren't pleased. 'My dear one, should you not speak to Sir John?' quivered Maccabee. 'It is a disgrace to treat you like this, as if our home were some wayfarers' hostel. Are we to be compensated for our hospitality? Are you to receive enhancement at the Castle? Who *is* Barbary really? What happened? Why must she be put on us?'

'A leper,' said her husband with gloom, 'must put up with lepers. Sir John hates me, I have felt it.'

Maccabee shook her head in sympathy; it was a wonder to her that her husband, so clever, his poetry acknowledged by the Queen, was always passed over for high office. He didn't even have a royal pension, as many lesser poets did. Too honest, her Edmund. Too good for his own good. However, she had been over that ground before. 'But what has Barbary done? Is it disgraceful?'

Castle clerks usually knew what was going on, but this time only that Barbary had been somehow implicated in the escape of the prisoners could be gleaned from a miasma of rumour. 'Some say the Lord Deputy himself helped them to get away,' said Edmund. 'It would not surprise me, considering his laxity towards the Irish.

Others say the Earl of Tyrone had a part in the escape, which again wouldn't surprise me. However, I have it from Sir John's secretary that Barbary, adventuress though she is, has her worth in the marriage market. So once more you must nurse her with care, my dear.'

'But no gentleman, surely . . . not after she paraded as a man . . . such an unsavoury reputation.'

'*Quis nisi mentis inops oblatum repuit aurum?*' asked her husband.

'I'm sure, my dear. What does it mean?'

'That virtue is of no account nowadays if set beside the opportunity for riches and power.'

'Barbary? Rich?'

'There is no harm if we tell our patron of what goes on. We owe him that. He shall make up his own mind. I will say no more, Maccabee, but should she tell you anything when and if she recovers . . .'

'I will inform you at once, my dear.'

'And I shall inform Sir Walter.'

The whole matter was academic. The girl seemed to be dying.

Barbary's constitution had proved tough just as long as her mental geography had been based on the certainty of herself planted like a flag in the middle of an inner circle, which was the Order, contained in an outer circle which was England. Like some dyed-in-the-wool cartographer, she had designated everything else Here-Be-Dragons country. Now events, like modern explorers, had redrawn the map and altered the landscape of her mind.

The hypothermia she was suffering from when the pursuit discovered her was not serious, hardly worse than that of Cuckold Dick, who had been knocked unconscious by the escapers' accomplice and left lying on the open roof of Bermingham Tower. What was dangerous was her lack of will to fight it, the gaol fever which followed it, and the congestion of the lungs which followed that.

She was reliving grief. The fog wall had blown away in that cell in Dublin Castle and the terror that had lain behind it, waiting to wrack her, rampaged through her delirium. Her mother. She had left her mother to hang. Maire's face looked into hers and said: 'Survive.'

'But I should much prefer to stay and die with you, Mother.'

Maire's face became stern. 'Survive,' she said.

But she didn't want to survive, not without Maire, not if survival meant hiding in unfamiliar streets, pursued by men who wanted to kill her. I should much prefer to stay and die with you, Mother.

She screamed for the mother the English had hanged, feeling only now the agony of pity and loss that the fog wall had protected her from all this time.

It was a double loss. Time and again, in her fever, the little drawing of a ship scratched onto a stone cell wall became alive and rowed towards her to take her back to where she now knew she truly belonged, to western Ireland and her grandmother. Time and again she tried to clamber aboard it but that same grandmother kept pushing her back in the sea. 'Get away from me, you little whore.'

'It's me, Grandmother. I'm telling the truth this time.'

But the ship sailed away, leaving her to drown.

Maccabee attended to her, sometimes enthusiastically when she was trying out a new physic to improve her patient, exasperatedly when it didn't. The real nursing, the turning, washing, feeding, soothing, was done by Cuckold Dick. His presence was the one solid thing in Barbary's limbo. She clung to it and slowly dragged herself away from death into a consciousness that seemed little better.

She lay, thin and exhausted, in her attic bed and stared out at a pointless life. Not English. Rejected Irish. Not enough energy and wit to be either. A cony-caught conycatcher. Tears of inertia and shame and grief kept coming out of her eyes. She wanted her mother.

'Carragheen soup, Barb,' said Dick, spooning it into her. 'Don't wet the bib, Barb. We'll find that treasure yet.'

'Treasure?' whispered Barbary, 'Oh. Treasure. I know where it is. I just don't want it any more.'

At the door Maccabee, who had been about to enter the attic, turned back and went downstairs to her husband.

Some days later, still weak and uninterested, she was

washed and her hair brushed by Maccabee's new woman servant, arrayed in Maccabee's best nightcap and second-best nightgown with a shawl over it. Dick carried her downstairs and laid her on the settle in the parlour under a patchwork quilt.

People who had never called on the Spensers began to call then. Fine horses halted outside the door of Wood Quay and well-dressed men dismounted and told their servants to knock on it. Poor Maccabee had to hire a second maidservant because she was forced to spend so much time chaperoning Barbary during their visits. They were the sort of men Lord Burghley had wished to see on the quayside at Bristol boarding ships for Ireland. But these men were in Ireland already, their fathers had led the way as soldiers and administrators. Already their families owned chunks of Munster; they loved the land, if not its people, and they wanted more. Barbary kept being woken up from fitful naps to be introduced to names that were an inventory of new Ireland, St Leger, Wallop, Maltby, Bagenal, Fitzwilliam, Fenton, Gardner. The faces were those of speculators.

They looked her over, but their talk was of the new Lord Deputy, whom they were learning to hate. He was creating chaos. The man didn't know how to deal with the Irish. He wanted – imagine it – an equable tax system, he defended Irish land rights against good English undertakers. He'd actually knocked down Sir Henry Norris for opposing him. In the very chamber of Dublin's Parliament. He'd sworn to do the same for Archbishop Loftus, had called that worthy cleric an ungodly bastard for not carrying the Word to the Irish, as if the Irish could understand it if he did. How could he preach to a nation whose language could include a phrase like 'Div dav duv uv ooh', a phonetic version of the Irish phrase meaning, 'The black ox ate the raw egg'? Sir John was a drunk, a blasphemer, possibly even – they lowered their voices – a traitor.

Barbary hardly heard them, aware only that they made her tired. She was glad when they went. 'I don't know what it is,' she said wearily to Cuckold Dick when he carried her upstairs after the Bagenal brothers had gone home, 'but in that parlour I feel like somebody's lunch.'

'About time you caught on,' said Dick, aggrievedly for

him. 'I been telling you and telling you, Barb. They're suitors. The Spensers don't like it. Got you earmarked for Sir Walter, I reckon. But word's out you're worth something.'

'Worth something?'

He plonked her on her bed. 'Latch on, Barb. They're eyeing you up like the favourite at Smithfield. I heard John Bingham's put in a bid already. If the Queen takes it up you'll soon find Sir Richard's your brother-in-law, and then where'll you be?'

The full extent of the danger hit her at last. Worth something. They thought she was politically and financially valuable. She'd been laid out on a slab for buyers. She'd be bought and used, made an excuse for the appropriation of land. Personally dominated, bedded, impregnated. She was more frightened than at any time in her life.

She caught Dick's sleeve. 'Get me out.'

His doughy face was concerned. 'Where, though, Barb? You ain't been looking out the window but the weather's krap awful. Seas are closed and we wouldn't get no boat.'

She tugged at him again and again. 'Get me out. Get me out.'

That night she dreamed she was in a cage and the bars of the cage were men's penises.

Other men came, and one woman. Barbary hadn't met Mabel Bagenal before, but Maccabee had been full of the latest gossip about her and the request the Earl of Tyrone had made to the Queen for her hand. Barbary found herself greeting with interest the girl O'Neill had decided was sufficiently apple-cheeked, napkin-using and aristocratic to qualify as the English wife he wanted. Mabel was all those things as well as being very young and very pretty. Her clothes were stunning and Barbary, with her new appreciation of fashion, studied with pleasure Mabel's tall, crowned hat with its jewelled hatband, the sleeveless velvet blue gown which complimented her fair hair and blue eyes, the diaphanous ruff and sleeves of her kirtle. She had all the mannerisms of court – it was rumoured that the Queen might make her a maid of honour, if she didn't marry, of course. Once she'd paid her courtesies she dismissed Maccabee with the cruel confidence of the well-bred: 'I am sure you must have things to do in the kitchen. Mistress Barbary shall entertain me well enough.'

When Maccabee obediently retired, Mabel drew her stool close to Barbary's settle, her chubby face full of secrets. 'I know all about you,' she said. 'You-know-who has told me. He wishes me to tell you he is sorry that you were caught up in you-know-what, but he had to get them away.'

Barbary blinked. O'Neill must have limitless trust in this girl to tell her about his part in the prisoners' escape; she was, after all, daughter to the Queen's Marshal in Ireland and her brothers ranked high in the Queen's army.

'Isn't he bold?' breathed Mabel. 'What daring he has.'

Barbary caught hold of her hand. 'Has he heard if they got away?' There had been a terrible furore over the escape but no real news of the escapers since the snow had swallowed them. Rumour had at one and the same time flown them to Spain and frozen them dead.

'He told me yesterday he'd got news. One of them died of the cold. Mistress Barbary, you are hurting my hand.'

'Which one?'

Mabel Bagenal rubbed her fingers. 'Now which one was it? He did tell me.' Obviously the fate of the escapers concerned her only so far as they were pieces in the game being played by the man she loved. 'One of the minor O'Neills. That's it. Art O'Neill froze to death, Red Hugh just lost a couple of toes.'

'The others made it back safely?'

'Yes. So did Red Hugh.'

Barbary let out her breath. They'd gone to their earths; Grace O'Malley to her seaboard kingdom in Connaught, Red Hugh to Ulster, Conn O'Hagan to the fastnesses of his Wicklow Mountains, Art to his grave. Three of them alive, no doubt to cause more trouble to the Crown, but alive. They'd got away. Joy went through her. Grace was safe, Conn O'Hagan was safe . . .

'I'm told you're thinking of marriage,' Mabel said, smiling. 'My brother has asked me to speak well of him to you. He is greatly attracted.'

'Tell him not to bank on it,' said Barbary, but Mabel had introduced the subject of marriage only in order to speak of her own.

'Why do you think Her Majesty is delaying her permission?'

Barbary could think of several reasons; Mabel's father's opposition to the match, O'Neill's Catholicism. 'Perhaps she suspects O'Neill,' she said.

Mabel's big blue eyes widened. 'Of what?'

'Well, you know what.'

'Oh that. But he had to help his vassal.' Obviously to Mabel the treasonable act of aiding political prisoners to escape from the Queen's gaol was a philanthropic lark. 'Hugh's no traitor. He loves his country.'

Which country? Barbary was sorry for the girl, just to mention O'Neill thrilled her; it was why she'd come, to talk to someone who knew how daring her lover was. At home she wouldn't be allowed to mention his name. But did she realise what she was in love with? How could a girl of the Protestant gentry know the cleft in O'Neill's soul? Barbary could guess at it because she had a cleft in her own, but even she couldn't plumb the depths of the man, never would, didn't want to. 'Have you been to his home in Ulster?' she asked.

Mabel grinned. 'Father would go for his whip if I even thought about it.' She stopped smiling. 'Why? Have you?'

Barbary reassured her. 'No. But I was born Irish and I remember things. They're not English.' It was hard to find words because impressions of that long-ago time came in confusions too fleeting to be put into language, and touched baser senses like hearing and smell. 'Music,' she said, 'and cow manure.' The rampagingly bucolic mixed up with sea and spirituality. Warring with the Clanrickards and the Joyces because that was what they were there for. Cruelty and cherubims, intellect and arthritis. There was no common root, prehistory contained no Trojan War, no familiar legend of Arthur, only alien, mythical gods. These things were O'Neill's. They were also Barbary's, and even she found them uncomfortable. 'You'd hate the life,' she finished, lamely.

'But that's what's so beautiful about him,' Mabel said. 'His poetry is so wild and sad and lovely and different. It's . . . it's enlarged, and yet he's so kind.' Looking at the girl, Barbary saw ecstasy. Wherever Mabel went from here would be a descent from a plane

Barbary's whole existence had never reached.

'All right,' she said abruptly. 'Just remember you're in love with the O'Neill as well as the Earl of Tyrone.'

After Mabel had gone Barbary wondered why she had inflicted home truths on the girl. Honesty, especially brutal honesty, wasn't usually her line, but Mabel had offered her friendship and she'd felt she owed her something for the offer. She'd never had a female friend of her own age; she discounted Maccabee and the bawds. The O'Neill inspired many conflicting emotions in her but she knew that, win or lose him, Mabel was headed for grief.

Maccabee was out when the next visitor called, another male. Barbary heard a deep voice at the front door and turned her face to the wall. How many of these bastards were there? At least with Maccabee away this one would have to survey the goods while Cuckold Dick looked on as chaperone. That'd teach him. She heard Cuckold Dick come into the room and hiss: 'Another suitor, Barb.'

'Tell him to sod off.'

'You might think different about this one, Barb.' There was an oddness in his voice that made Barbary turn round. He was in the doorway, looking like a shell-game man about to reveal the pea. He was pushed aside by somebody who had to bend his head to enter the room. A lot of men had stood in that doorway, mostly young, a few handsome, all resolute on advancing themselves, but none had set the air tingling with triumph behind them and the intent of triumph to come like this one. His clothes weren't as magnificent as some but the steel gorget beneath the ruff round his neck was a proper battle accoutrement, not merely a civilian's sign of masculinity. His cloak was over one shoulder and a pearl drop in his left earlobe. With his pickdevant beard he looked a younger version of Raleigh, less dark – there was a reddish tinge to his hair – equally superb. Just the eyes were different; they held command and confidence, but where Raleigh had enough of those qualities to be careless of them, this young man husbanded them with ineradicable wariness; he'd earned them, he hadn't been born with them. It was when she reached the eyes that Barbary recognised the boy she'd grown up with.

'It's Rob, Barb,' shouted Cuckold Dick, tears pouring

down his cheeks. 'It's Rob Betty.'

Now lettest thou thy servant depart in peace. Simeon of the New Testament had awaited the consolation of Israel; Barbary, she knew now, had awaited the consolation of Rob Betty. The days of their friendship swept in to wrap her in a comfort that made the intervening time contrastingly bitter. Now there were three of them to share the good bad old memories of the Order and speak the intimate language of that extraordinary university. She had longed for him, he was here. And grown into himself to become the handsomest man she'd ever seen.

'Oh, Rob.'

'Barb?' He saw the curls of hair beneath her cap, the second-best nightgown, the new femininity, but he was having trouble with them. 'Raleigh said it was you turned into a girl. I couldn't believe it.'

'How did Raleigh know?' She didn't really care, it was just something to say as he crossed the floor and knelt by the settle to peer at her.

'Are you really female?' he asked. He smelled of perfume and Rob and salt-ingrained leather. 'You're not catching some cony with this?'

'Rob,' she said reproachfully, and found herself fluttering her eyelashes. 'I've always been a mort.'

'Why? Why fool me like that?'

Bless him, did he think she'd impersonated a boy just to deceive *him*? 'I didn't want the Upright Man breaking me like he broke Foll and the others.'

'But you could have told *me*. Weren't we friends?'

Bless him, bless him. 'Aren't we friends still? I'm in sore need of one, Rob, I can tell you that.' Though she tried, she found it difficult to convince him of how natural the assumption of a male role had come to be, to the point where she had barely acknowledged her true sex to herself, let alone anyone else. He seemed to think it had been duplicitous of her.

'You always did fit in with the Order,' he said, and she saw that his hatred for his past life had grown rather than diminished since he'd been away from it.

'It kept us both alive, didn't it?' Amazing, they'd been apart, undergoing volcanic changes, and here they were snapping at each other just as they had on their last night together at the Pudding. But the spat warmed her; it indicated the intimacy of people who knew each other too well to watch their manners. Unless in Cuckold Dick's company, she'd been unable to relax like this since she came to Ireland.

'Anyway,' she said, 'it's your fokking fault I'm in this position. The powers-that-be thought *you* were the prince of the O'Flaherties. They only took me for second best.' She told him everything that had happened since he'd escaped that fate by the skin of his teeth. The Tower, Lord Burghley, Penshurst. 'I bloody near became the Queen of England's favourite.' He was fascinated now, occasionally laughing, showing beautiful white teeth. 'Oh, yes, Master Betty, I've mingled with the great since you saw me last.' She told him about the boat to Ireland, how her sex was discovered, Sir John, the plot to get the treasure, and its failure.

He kept screwing up his eyes as if trying to adjust his vision of her out of the old focus and into the new. It must be difficult for him, she thought; somebody he's known all his life turning into somebody else. As difficult as it was for her to come to terms with an unexpected nationality.

'And are you really this O'Whatever?' he asked. 'Or is this just another cony-catch?'

'I wish it was.' And she did. Viewed from the complexity which now embroiled her, Order life was imbued with a sunny simplicity. 'She'd scratched the shape of a ship on the wall of her cell. It was out of my cherubims. I knew it. Ironic, ain't it? I was conying her and all the time I was telling the truth – and she still thinks it was a cony.'

'So you know where the treasure is?'

There was something in his voice. 'Leave it, Rob,' she said, sharply. 'You don't want it. Believe me.' She couldn't remember with what words her mother had sworn her to secrecy but they bound her. To tell would be to betray something her soul instinctively guarded, too precious to the clan women. Clan women? Where were these shibboleths coming from? In these last few days they had welled up as if from something deeper than her own memory, more like a primaeval haunting.

He got up and walked away from her and she was afraid he was cross until he said: 'I envy you.'

217

She was astonished. 'What for? Did you want to be this Irish prince then?'

'Good God, no.' That was an insult. To be a low-born English adventurer measured several classes above the Irish aristocracy as far as Rob was concerned. 'No, but you know who you are, even if it *is* Irish. And your people didn't abandon you, not deliberately.'

'Did yours?' This was ground they'd never trodden. She'd never dared to ask what he recalled of the time before the Order took him up.

He shrugged. 'Yes. And the hell with it.' It was still forbidden territory. He drew up a stool near her settle to bring her up to date with his own doings, but he had to get up again and stride about because it was such a grand story. 'God, Barbary, but it's been a man's life and an *honest* life. All the filth of the Order blown away in a clean sea wind.' He glanced at her. 'And nobody knows it ever clung to me. I am the son of a poor but respectable tailor now dead.'

'With a poor but respectable mother?'

'Also dead.'

Poor but disreputable Galloping Betty, thought Barbary, sloughed off without a twinge of pain. Will he slough me off too? 'Tell me,' she said.

She absorbed the details later; at the time she was too busy absorbing him and his splendour as he strode about the room, making it very small and cluttered, to take in more than the gist. Piracy and slaving was what it boiled down to, this manly, honest life. She frowned for one minute as he described the slaves. 'Savages, not men. Animal functions, animal minds.' She had heard the mere Irish described by some of her suitors in just those terms and when it came to it she was mere Irish herself. But he swept her on. He'd swarmed the ladder of promotion like rigging. 'Jesu, but I am a fine seaman.' Attacking Spanish treasure ships under Frobisher had given him prize money, which he'd invested in part share of a ship which he had sailed for Hawkins who was too busily engaged in overhauling Her Majesty's fleet at home to take a personal part in the trade he'd set up in slaves from West Africa. 'There's riches in it, Barbary, but oh Lord the stink. And if you're unlucky the death rate can wipe out your profit.' With the money from that he'd gone in for a bigger ship and joined Carew's enterprise, sailing to Virginia and bringing back tobacco and potatoes to Carew's cousin, Sir Walter Raleigh, in Ireland, where he had succumbed to Raleigh's spell.

'I'm his man now, Barbary. We'll fall or rise together, and if I judge character, it will be to rise. How the Queen can bother with those frisking courtiers when she has him to advise her . . . He could rule the world, Barbary. He could rule Ireland for her and there'd be no rebellion by the bastards then. They wouldn't escape Lord Deputy Raleigh like they escaped fat old Perrot.'

He fell quiet, his elbow resting on the high mantel over the fire, and studied her. 'It was Raleigh told me about you. I would have looked for you anyway, but Raleigh said as how there was this young rapscallion called Barbary Clampett who'd turned into an Irish heiress.' He cocked his head on one side. 'I like the result.'

'Do you, Rob? Do you?' She was thrilled. 'But how did Raleigh know? I'm supposed to be a secret to all but the Queer Cuffin.'

He winced. 'I wish you'd not use cant. We're out of the Order now.'

'But how did Raleigh know?'

'Good God, isn't he Captain of the Queen's Guard? And one of her favourites? There's not much he doesn't know.' Abruptly he took up his cloak. 'I must go. I'm supposed to be about his business.'

She went into a panic. 'Don't go, Rob. Take me with you. I can't stay here. They're trying to marry me off. They say I'm marriageable property.' She struggled up to her feet, but swayed. She was still weak.

Something moved in Rob's face and she realised that for the first time, in showing weakness, she had become truly feminine for him. Gently, he pushed her back on the settle. 'Sweetheart, I'll be back.'

Nobody had called her sweetheart before. Dumbly, she watched him swirl his cloak round him. As he got to the door he turned and said: 'Since first I saw your face I resolved to honour and renown ye. If now I be disdained, I wish my heart had never known ye.'

Barbary swallowed.

'I forgot to say,' he said, finishing her off by a wink, 'I'd become a poet since we last met. Good, ain't it?' He grinned. 'The change of gender suits you. Keep it for when I come back.'

He went, leaving a woman who until now had remained unwooed at a time when she was ready for wooing, to whom love poetry was something directed at others, who had never thought of herself as desirable.

'Oh Jesus.' She'd always loved him. She'd thought she loved him as a brother, but she didn't think it was legal to think about brothers the way she was now feeling about Rob Betty.

He came often after that, welcomed by the Spensers because he was a friend of Sir Walter Raleigh's, and welcomed by Barbary to whom he was spring and summer. Every time he came through the door, Maccabee's parlour became a place of energy and excitement, transformed by his traveller's tales into a rocking ship or an African coast. The world had opened up for him and he'd had the wit and courage to take advantage of it. All the frustrated ambition which had made him a surly adolescent had been freed to allow full tilt to the charm and humour she'd seen in glimpses when they were children. Her bad dreams went and were replaced by images of his magnificent throat, his long legs in their beautiful boots, the stretch of his body when he put his arms behind his head.

She had no time for her many problems, only for trying to assess whether he was as infatuated with her as she with him. Sometimes she thought he was, or why did he come so often? But something she wanted to find in him eluded her.

On the few occasions they were alone together he was eager to hear what she could remember of her Irish childhood. Did she recall her father? What had been his status? How much land had he owned? She was reluctant to talk about it, partly because she didn't know – 'I was only a kinchin, Rob' – partly because of a mental prohibition that made her feel she was betraying some ancient loyalty, and partly because she wanted to recall their times in the Order instead.

But this he wouldn't. 'Those days are dead.' He got cross when she talked cant, wanting to keep his new vision of her as a woman. 'You're a lady, don't spoil yourself.' So she assumed a different personality for him;

softly spoken, gentle, unemphatic. It made her character-less, she felt, but he responded to it with warmth, and his appreciation was so wonderful that her independence evaporated under the sun of it. But she still kept the secret of the treasure, and one other thing. In response to some warning she saw no reason for, but obeyed, she repressed the meetings she'd had with the O'Neill. The deep, ambivalent mingling of her soul with that Irish-man's was unsayable, especially as Rob frequently voiced distrust and contempt for Irish lords.

Then came the day when Rob brought Sir Walter Raleigh to visit, sending Edmund and Maccabee into paroxysms of hospitality. 'Take this chair by the fire, Sir Walter.' 'Another capon, Sir Walter.' Mary, the new servant, was kept on the go between kitchen and parlour fetching Maccabee's best refreshments.

It was difficult to associate this sophisticated, gor-geously apparelled courtier with the man in Will's story who had hewed and paunched helpless men by the hun-dred at Smerwick. No good thinking about it either; like everything else Will had told her, that knowledge had to be consigned to the place that had once been behind the fog wall; a time out of life, horrific and mystical, nothing to do with the present.

She wondered if he'd remember the night of the Penshurst fantastical or whether he'd been too busy taking maids of honour behind the bushes to notice her. He remembered. He kissed her hand, giving her a wicked wink. 'A magnificent transformation, Mistress Boggart, from elf to Queen of Faerie.'

She couldn't help winking back. He was a bit magnifi-cent himself. Killer he might have been, but it was small wonder Rob had modelled himself on the man.

For all he was a Devonian with a thick accent, he had the sharpness that reminded her of the London streets. He took the stage, eclipsing even Rob, who was happy enough to play second fiddle. While they listened to what was being done on his estates at Lismore and Youghal in the south of Ireland, and the strange-sounding plants he'd shipped from the New World for their gardens, Barbary watched Rob watching Raleigh and knew that, even if Rob came to love her as she loved him, she would

221

never receive the adoration he extended to his hero.

She jumped as he turned the conversation to her. 'You're a true maid of Connaught, mistress, with your fiery hair and spirit. 'Tis a pity you'm to be given off to some old administrator as'll not appreciate either.'

Terror. 'What administrator?'

Infuriatingly, Raleigh produced a long, thin tube of silver with a bowl at one end, to which he set fire while sucking the other. Barbary was so frightened she barely noticed. 'What administrator?'

Smoke came out of Sir Walter's mouth. 'There, there, maid. Don't be frit. I shouldn't have said, seemingly, but word is you'm to be used to bring your clan back under Her Majesty's dominion. Connaught's a wild land, as beautiful as you are, and 'tis time English writ ran there in fact as well as name. 'Twould need a doughty man with your help to do it, yet there's none but weaklings at court nowadays.'

Married off. Sent back to that strange time and place with a stranger, *as* a stranger, to subdue it. 'I'm not fokking marrying anybody,' she said. Could they marry her off against her will? Raleigh's shrug was not reassuring, nor were stories she'd heard in the past of heiresses being married, want to or not, to their father's choice. 'Fokking hell,' she said, hopelessly, not caring that Rob shot her a disapproving glance. 'Are you sure?'

'That's what they'm saying at court.'

At that moment Mary, entering the room from the door behind Raleigh's chair with two tankards of ale, saw the smoke issuing from the front of this valued guest and emptied one of the tankards over his head. Amid the recriminations, the confusion, moppings and apologies, only Raleigh kept a resigned calm. 'People do keep doing that,' he said.

As his host and hostess, still apologising, saw him to the door, he suggested: 'Let Master Rob take the maid to her room. She'm not too viddy.'

Viddy Barbary was not. Rob had to carry her up the stairs and she clung to his neck, begging him to take her away. 'I don't want to get married. I don't want Connaught or any of it. I want to go home. Rob, take me home.'

He set her down gently on the bed and cupped her face in his hands. He'd never been kinder. 'You could marry me,' he said.

Marry him, her love. Be rescued from her rock by this Perseus. 'Risk it,' he was saying. 'We'll marry now, before they can stop us. I'll be the one who helps you win this kingdom of yours from the savages. Make it an Eden where we can be king and queen.'

He was wonderful. 'But the Rome-Mort'd punish you.'

'The Queen,' he said, and kissed her. 'Not the Rome-Mort, the Queen. And Raleigh can win her over, he can do anything with her.'

There was one last proviso. 'She's not a savage, though, Rob. She's my grandmother.'

He took her by the shoulders and shook her. 'Where's your romance, woman? Stop quibbling. Will you marry me or not?'

He must want her. He was the one taking the risk, the appalling risk, of marrying her without the Queen's consent. He wanted her and she wanted very much, very much, to be wanted. 'Yes, Rob,' she said.

It didn't surprise Barbary that Raleigh and the Spensers were prepared to dare the Queen's displeasure by conniving at her marriage, but this was because she was so surprised at herself and the level of thrill which kept her feet suspended from base ground that she had no room for any more.

Raleigh himself procured the licence from some Bishop's Commissary. Edmund Spenser had always intended to resign his post at the Castle and undertake possession of an estate down in Munster's Awberg Valley not too far from Raleigh's vast acres, and this was a good time to do so – before Sir John Perrot found out that the girl who had been put in his charge had been married off with his complicity.

She and Rob, to her relief, were not to go and claim her clan lands yet awhile. With his prize money, Rob had bought an estate which marched alongside the Spensers' and they were to get this into working order before they moved on to the more chancy enterprise in Connaught. They were all to set off within the week in a wagon train with the rest of the undertakers. There was much heigh-ho-ing and nonny-no-ing for the life of soil and toil away from the corruption of court and castle. Shepherds' pipes and flocks figured large in the conversation. Spenser harped on about the idyll of a couple of rustics called Corydon and Phyllida.

'Are you happy to become a shepherdess, sweetheart?' Rob asked.

'Yes,' she said. 'Sweetheart.' Yes to being a proper woman, a wife like other women were. Yes to baking bread. Yes, yes to Rob and the stride of his thigh boots, yes to his smooth neck rising from its ruff, to the light hairs on his forearm when he rolled up his shirtsleeve. Yes to being as much in love as Mabel Bagenal, who had caused reverberation throughout this country and England by not waiting for the Queen's permission to marry the man she loved and running off with him.

They were married in the afternoon three days later in Maccabee and Edmund Spenser's parlour by Master Tobias Bildon, a reverend gentleman careless in his personal and religious habits, who hiccuped the necessary words and put out his hand immediately for the five pounds Rob was paying him for his services. The witnesses were Sir Walter Raleigh, the Spensers, Mary their servant, and Cuckold Dick. Rob's tokens to his wife were a ring and a bale of assorted silks taken from a Spanish galleon.

Maccabee had outdone herself on the wedding supper, partly to catch the attention of Sir Walter and partly out of genuine enthusiasm for the occasion. They began with a cod's head in a sauce of oysters and pickled shrimps decorated with parsley, red cabbage and preserved burberries, and moved on to stewed pigeons and a collar of pig with mustard and sugar served with spinach tart. The wines, which were excellent, were a gift from Raleigh himself.

They were on the syllabub and junkets when Rob rose waveringly to his feet and announced that his wife had acquired not just one new name, but two. 'Let you, my dear,' he said, toasting Barbary, 'henceforth be known as Margaret. Margaret Betty.' He leaned down to her. 'Barbary has an outlandish sound to it, smacks of boyishness and . . . and the past. Margaret, that's a sweet, pretty name for a sweet, pretty wife. Let you be Margaret.'

Barbary leaned forward on her fist to squint at the idea through a haze. It looked back at her squarely, a solid name with no risk to it, an English name growing daisies, a name that kindly served out ale to its labourers cutting hay in the meadow and gave orders to dairymaids. 'I'll have it,' she said, 'so long as no bugger calls me Betty Betty.'

Raleigh laughed at that, so everybody laughed, except Rob who looked discomfited. 'Margaret doesn't swear,' he said.

There was the usual uproariousness as Maccabee and Mary escorted Barbary to the attic and the men poured wine and advice into Rob before leading him up. Cuckold Dick was beside himself, showering everybody with wheat and barley, tying horseshoes to Rob's boots and trying to outdo Raleigh in a duel of barely articulate but filthy jokes.

In the attic, Barbary hugged Maccabee with gratitude; what the woman had done here had not been to impress Raleigh, but from the genuine sentimental benevolence of a wife to a bride. The shutters were open to a pattering rain that was ushering in the thaw, and a weak moon shone on a double bed strewn with herbs and with white ribbon tied in lovers' knots on the pillows. A candle of scented beeswax was burning on the clothes press.

Maccabee helped her off with her clothes and tucked her into bed. 'There's dried marigold leaves in the mattress, that's for constancy in love,' she said. 'And don't tell Rob, but there's some rosemary in there as well.'

'What's that for?'

Maccabee giggled. 'Rosemary flourishes where the woman wears the trousers. May God bless your bed this night, Margaret.' She went out.

As she waited for Rob, Barbary had none of the wedding night nerves that a virgin was supposed to have. It wasn't the wine; she saw no reason for them. Sermons on the Puritan view of sex in marriage, as a function for the begetting of children and never as a source of enjoyment, had thundered into the ears of other girls but had left Barbary guilt-free because she hadn't been in a church to hear them. If anyone had influenced her attitude to copulation it had been the bawds to whom it had been such an everyday, or often-a-day, activity that their casual references to it had robbed it of the burden it carried for a hell-fearing Christian miss. Barbary was prepared for a wonderful melding of bodies or a rumbustious slap and tickle, or any combination of the two. If she shivered it was from chill and anticipation.

She heard his step on the stairs and the last-minute rudery of the men calling up after him. The door opened and he stood there in the candle- and moonlight with his shirt open at the neck. His face was concentrating as if on some problem. Would he finish his poem to her? One line of it and she would melt. He didn't look at her, but crossed to the shutters and closed them, came over to the bed and blew out the candle. 'Rob,' she said, 'I love you.' She heard him undressing briskly, almost businesslike. He got into bed and she opened her arms to his big, warm body, putting her face to his to kiss him. It wasn't there, it was out of reach as he arched over her; no kisses, no fondling, no words, straight down to the main event, the penis into the vagina. 'Ow,' she said.

The shutters hadn't quite obliterated the moon; she could see his face. His eyes were closed, intent on his own business. 'Ow, Rob,' she said again. He opened his eyes reluctantly, saw her, seemed to get cross and turned her over so that he could finish the function from the back. Which he did, with more enthusiasm but with minimal effect for her. After a quick, breathy climax, he heaved himself off her and turned on his side away from her.

'Is that it?' squeaked Barbary. Oddly enough, her immediate reaction was indignation. She couldn't believe he'd been so rude; what she'd just experienced was sexual discourtesy. She hammered on his back. 'Is that it? Why, Rob?' Was that her wedding night, that . . . that *exercise* he'd performed?

Then into her disappointed surprise flooded misery such as she'd never hoped to feel, and she sank back, shaking. She had been wronged; she couldn't say she'd been assaulted, or raped, but the cruelty of both was there. It wasn't her he'd had sex with; it wasn't the sexual act at all as she'd been led to understand it, just some task Rob had imposed on himself and might as well have carried out alone.

She thought she'd experienced despair in the Tower,

226

but she hadn't. She had still been able to scheme and plan in the Tower; she couldn't scheme her way out of this comfortless, desolate lack of love. This was despair. For he didn't love her, he had just told her as much. She had wanted him to and made the want into belief. What a fool.

She got out of bed and went to the window, stripping her mental landscape of the flowers and blossomed trees with which she had dressed it and investigating the crags that were left. 'Who told you to marry me, Rob?' she asked. 'Was it Raleigh?'

Chapter Eleven

If they could have discussed it, Barbary felt, they could still have rescued something that approximated to a tolerable marriage, but Rob refused. There was nothing wrong. Why must she harp on these things? Damned women were always talking slops. Of course he loved her. They were happy. Nobody had suggested he marry her for gain. Was she sick to think such a thing? There was nothing *wrong*. He had more important matters to think about.

She was still sure that this wedding had been suggested to him by Raleigh. Sir Walter was not prepared to marry her himself but by pointing out its advantages to Rob, his acolyte, he would give himself a controlling interest in the enterprise to take over the O'Flaherty-O'Malley lands.

And Rob's ambition to be the power over great estates had convinced him that Barbary was desirable. For he almost loved her, she was convinced of that. Rob was a surprisingly honest man, and not so lost to greed that he would have married her without feeling any affection. Perhaps he'd even made himself believe he loved her – desire following his ambition. Perhaps his reaction to the wedding night had been as big a disappointment to him as to her.

But affection, this almost love, was no good to Barbary. She lost character again, becoming unsure of herself, bewildered and unhappy as she waited for Rob to fall in love with her. He had to. Sooner or later.

There was a lot to do; agricultural implements and seed to be purchased, supplies to see them through spring. The instability of Munster's economy after the Desmond Wars devastation left the area still underpopulated and stock unavailable. In its good days it had been possible to purchase sixty milking cows, three hundred ewes, twenty pigs and a good plough team for one hundred pounds. Fifty pounds a year enabled a man to keep up a house and life style that in England would have cost a lord four times as much. Edmund, Rob and the undertakers were out to re-create the paradise Munster had once been.

The problem was lack of labour. The only unemployed in Dublin were the starving mere Irish and these the settlers were forbidden by royal decree to take on. Raleigh promised to send some of his men over from Youghal once Rob had taken possession of his estates and with that they had to be content.

'Just as well we've got Cuckold Dick,' said Barbary. 'We're going to need all the help we can get. Not that I can see him haymaking or milking cows.' She looked round the parlour, where she and Rob had been making lists. 'Where is he? I haven't seen him today.'

'I sent him packing,' said Rob. 'Gave him two guineas and told him to be off. He's not coming with us.'

'What did you say?' asked Barbary quietly. She could not credit she had heard him right.

'Margaret, it is time you realised where I am headed. We are going to be gentry in Munster, lord and lady of a manor. Then we shall go on. Raleigh will persuade the Queen to forgive my marrying you without permission when we subdue your lands in Connaught in her name. Raise your eyes to what awaits us. Forget the old life. It never existed. And I am not taking into the new one a remnant who looks and talks like what he is, a mountebank.'

'That mountebank,' said Barbary, 'happens to be the best friend I have. He saved my life. I love him.' She got up. 'I'm going to find him.'

'Sit down, Margaret.'

'No.'

'You shall not go.' Rob stood up and barred her way to the door.

She tried to push past him, terrified at the thought of how abandoned Dick must feel, how abandoned she felt in the artificiality of the life Rob was making for her. It was *lonely*. She couldn't live in it without Cuckold Dick.

She whirled up in the air and came down across her husband's knee. He was spanking her backside. 'I. Am. Master. Here,' he was puffing. 'Time. You. Learned. To.

Obey.' In all the grief, anger and humiliation, she sensed Maccabee coming into the room and immediately going back out again. She was hauled upright and pulled upstairs. Even as she struggled, and partly it was why she struggled, she knew that Rob was being artificial in this too, obeying some standard of behaviour that wasn't natural to him but which he thought conformed to the life of proper men. She was pushed into their attic and heard the door close and lock, and Rob's footsteps going steadfastly downstairs.

Rob unlocked the attic door an hour later, having designated that amount of time as sufficient for his wife to see the error of her ways, and found himself staring down the barrel of a Clampett snaphaunce.

'Sit down, Rob. We're going to have a talk.'

He sat down. He knew she wouldn't shoot him, but the gun had transferred authority. You can't deny the personality of someone holding a primed snaphaunce, however different you might wish that personality to be.

'I don't want you to call me Margaret any more,' said Barbary mildly; she had been doing a lot of thinking. 'I ain't Margaret. I'm Barbary. If I wasn't Barbary I'd be no precious use to you because I wouldn't be inheriting anything. You can be Lord Rob or whoever you like, but I'm going to be myself. That's one thing.' She didn't ask him if he agreed; she no longer cared if he did or didn't. Now that marriage had turned into adversity the old Barbary was back, bib unwetted.

'The other thing is, Dick might be a mountebank, and me a cony-catcher, but you're a canter yourself. On a scale him and me never dreamed of. You tricked me into marriage.' She raised the gun towards his mouth which had opened to speak. 'I don't want to discuss it, I just want it out in the open. Whatever you like to pretend to outsiders, this is an Order marriage, and you ever cony me again and we go the dead donkey.' Divorce among Order members was as casual as the marriages and consisted of both parties standing by a dead horse or donkey saying 'I renounce you' and walking away. She stood up. 'Now I'm going to find Dick, and if he wants to come with us he's coming with us.'

Dick was in his favourite tavern, the Anchor, along the quay. He was sitting by himself staring into a tankard of ale. She sat down beside him and put one of her hands over his. He sighed. 'If he don't, he don't,' he said.

'You don't go, I don't go,' Barbary told him. 'Where'd I be without you?'

'That's daft, Barb. He's your cove.'

'He versed me for the gelt.' Gentry might marry for gain, but Order members married because they wanted each other, however briefly.

'He loves you in his way. Even if he don't know it.'

'In his way,' she said bitterly. He certainly withheld his love when she was the real Barbary and was only affectionate when she adopted the character of what she had begun to think of as a milksop. Their nights together were still unpleasant. God knew who he made love to, Barbary thought, but it wasn't her. Their sexual encounters left her humiliated and lonely. But she supposed Dick was right. For better for worse, Rob was her cove now.

'What'll you do?' she asked. 'Go back to England?' The thought made her miserable.

Cuckold Dick scratched his head, showering dandruff. 'Reckoned I'd stay on a bit,' he said. 'The landlady here's a bene mort. Remember Davy Jones, the counterfeit crank? Turns out she's his cousin. It's a small world, Barb. She's offered me a libbege.'

Barbary looked around. The Anchor was smaller and less well appointed than the Pudding-in-a-Cloth, but, now that she examined it, the clientele came from the same mould as the Pudding's. The dice were falling as well for a man and a woman on the next table who were playing a noisy game with a couple of seamen as they had for Dick the Dicer back home. The motherly-looking woman at a table across the room was sewing while she watched the men around her play cards. From time to time she also glanced in the looking-glass on the wall behind two of the players and what she saw there seemed to make her needle ply sometimes fast, sometimes slow.

Barbary turned back to Cuckold Dick. 'You old sod,' she said.

Dick nodded modestly. 'Home from home. And Barb, you remember that younker of Lord O'Neill's? The one with the hand on his glove? Popped in the other day and gave me a bung of gold. Just like that.'

She nodded. So the escapees from the Castle had got word to the O'Neill and paid their debt.

'And he said,' continued Dick, casually, 'as there'd be more where that came from if I was to keep me hearing-cheats open for anything as affects O'Neill.'

'What'd O'Neill want another spy for?' asked Barbary. 'He's got enough friends to tell him what's going on in this town.' She'd learned from Spenser that the city's old guard were cleaving close to O'Neill now that Sir John Perrot, their pet hate, was voicing his suspicion that the Earl was a traitor. It was one of those situations that made an assessment of Irish politics impossibly difficult. Here were the conservative Anglo-Irish Protestant colonists backing a Catholic Irishman against their own Queen's representative whom they disliked because he backed Catholic Irishmen in general. Out here, one remove from the sharp divides of England, concepts of patriotism, loyalty, treachery, were not so clear-cut. To Dick, amoral and apolitical as he was, they were downright fuzzy. 'You be careful, Dick.'

'I'll be all right, Barb.' Tears rolled down his cheeks as he smiled cheerfully at her. 'Don't you worry about me. You're the one going among the savages.'

Sightless from her own tears she grinned at him. 'Eat them for breakfast,' she said. She couldn't say goodbye. She got up and went briskly outside, walked briskly along the quay until she came to a deep deserted doorway and went in it to sob. So this was marriage, this friendless institution cutting you off from everything dear and familiar. For that moment she saw her husband as an enemy who had won the first battle of what looked like being a protracted war. She sobbed again. Well, he wouldn't win 'em all. She wiped her face and set off again, not to the Spenser residence but to Dublin Castle stables.

Two days later the undertakers from England left Dublin to take up their estates in Munster. An escort of soldiers went with them. At the head of the long train of carts and riders were Sir Walter Raleigh and his two protégés, Edmund Spenser and Rob Betty with their families, their goods ensconced in a better-class wagon than the rest of the train and their persons up on better horseflesh – except for Master Betty's wife who, to Master Betty's obvious displeasure, was mounted on a slow, square, lugubrious pony which definitely let the side down.

The officer in charge of the escort accompanying the undertakers into Munster announced himself to be Captain Humfrey Mackworth.

Captain Mackworth? Captain Mackworth? Barbary remembered Will Clampett's account of his Irish war. The Captain Mackworth who, assisted by Captain Walter Raleigh, had slaughtered the surrendered Spanish garrison at Smerwick?

The same. She heard Edmund Spenser mutter: 'Are you wise to be returning to Munster? The Irish have long memories,' and Mackworth reply: 'Long memories, but short lives.'

He was a jolly-looking, round-faced man whose only visible scar was an old cut puckering his left eye into a somewhat saucy wink, the result of a hunting accident in his youth. Watching him and Raleigh ride together companionably at the head of the column, Barbary wondered if the remembered shrieks of unarmed men troubled their dark moments, and decided it did not. The memory had been excused and excised. They were undisturbed by the fear of reprisals either by men or by God. How was it that Will Clampett, so much more ignorant, so much less imaginative certainly than Raleigh, could suffer guilt for his part in the massacre and these two men, who had led it, were untroubled? Perhaps it was that Will had no vanity and could allow that he was a sinner, while Raleigh's arrogance made him invulnerable to self-doubt.

Mackworth, she decided after some study, was just a bastard. But an efficient bastard. Keeping some one hundred wagons, with their attendant families and livestock, rolling together over Irish tracks took some doing.

His instructions on the first day were clear: 'When we get beyond the Pale, nobody, nobody at all, is to leave the train. When we reach your various destinations you will disperse in groups. No family to live alone in any of the homesteads until each one has been made defensible and a system of warning beacons set up. Understood?'

'Excuse me, Captain.' It was Ellis, former Bristol pig farmer, who had emerged as spokesman for the undertakers.

'Excuse me, but why's the precautions? We thought as how the Munster Irish was put down.'

Captain Mackworth said: 'Pacified, Master Ellis, pacified. The only sure way of suppressing the Irish is to hang them man, woman and child.'

'Excuse me, Captain, but what's wrong with that?' There was a laugh from his fellows among whom Ellis had established himself as a wit.

Mackworth winked his already winking eye. 'Nothing at all, Master Ellis. I am an advocate of it, not to say a practitioner. But our lords and masters in England and Dublin, never having been in the front line themselves, want us to love the Irish. Pat them on the head. Tuck them up in bed at night.'

'So they can kill us in ours?' It was a woman who shouted, the shrillness in her voice showing she was nervous.

Mackworth rallied her. 'They'll not do that, mistress. Too afraid of us. Just never turn your back on 'em. You'll be safe enough. Trust God and Humfrey Mackworth.'

Both inspired confidence during the drive through Anglicised Leinster. An early spring sun shone on sheep and peaceable shepherds as the wagon train rolled over the grass plain of the Curragh which had once known the sweep of St Bridget's chariot. Mackworth organised encampments for the undertakers near villages where the water was sweet, English spoken and Elizabeth acknowledged as ruler. For Raleigh, the Spensers, Rob and Barbary there was lodging in great houses, the finest of all being the Ormond castle at Kilkenny. 'Where will we find the servants,' worried Maccabee, 'if Castle Spenser is as big as this?' Edmund reassured her that it was not, but she went on asking the question.

From the way it had been spoken of in Dublin, Barbary had the impression that the Pale was an actual fence, some sort of chestnut paling running through hill and valley to separate civilised English Ireland from a Celtic wilderness full of savages. There was no fence, no wall, no ditch. But though the demarcation between loyal Ireland and unsafe Ireland might be invisible, she was aware they'd crossed it. Something altered. She saw Mackworth quietly order his men to string out and form a phalanx along each side of the wagons. In the military cart the shot began loading their arquebuses. The pikemen became more alert. When a pheasant clattered out of a nearby wood they snapped their heads towards it and marched with their eyes on the spot it had come from. She watched Rob and Raleigh casually ease their cloaks away from their sword hilts.

That night the gentry stayed with the train and encamped with the commoners. Rob, Raleigh and Mackworth strolled outside the circle of wagons, keeping the sentries up to scratch while the Spensers and Barbary sat on stools outside their pavilion and watched little Catherine playing in firelight with the other children. Maccabee was in conversation with Ellis, one of the few people who listened to her fantastical servant problems and he only in order that she should listen to him. Either pig farming had shaped Ellis's looks and demeanour or his looks and demeanour had predestined him for the trade. His face was suffused, his eyes glared and his nose upturned to show bushy, aggressive nostrils. He attacked every subject with the authority of the pig ignorant and rejoiced in an age that presented men like him with opportunity for advancement. Elizabeth – he called her 'that good old girl' – had been raised to the throne, Desmond overthrown, Munster made available for settlement, all so that Ellis might flourish. 'That good old girl understands Ellis and Ellis understands her.' Poets, philosophers, scholars were out of their depth; it was Ellis, down-to-earth, spade's-a-spade Ellis, farmer's son and farmer, who would hold true communion with Elizabeth Regina if ever they met. Having wintered in Dublin he had become knowledgeable on the entire Irish question. 'Lazy buggers, pardon my French. Need someone as knows how to drive 'em. Touch of the lash and they'll work my fields well enough. They've not come across Ellis before. Ellis'll surprise 'em.'

What surprised Barbary was that Ellis's wife was pretty, uncowed and apparently approved of him, while his two sons, whom he'd sent to grammar school, seemed amused and intelligent.

'Well, my soul,' Maccabee was saying delightedly, 'don't you know we're forbidden to use Irish labour? Though how I'm to run Castle Spenser . . .'

'Can't be done,' returned Ellis. 'That good old girl, she's got to say "No Irish" but she knows and Ellis knows it can't be done. What she means is "Don't raise 'em." Use 'em like you'd train cows if there wasn't no plough team. But don't raise 'em above what you find 'em. They don't know no different, don't want no different. We understand 'em, that good old girl and Ellis.'

A drizzle hissed on the incandescent logs of the central fire. The undertakers sat on, as if by staying awake they could outface whatever it was that lay in the blackness beyond the light. Deciding she'd feel better with the Clampett, Barbary went into the pavilion to prime it. Rob entered while she was doing it. On the trek they'd hardly communicated; their sexual encounters had been stopped by having to share beds with other people – a relief for Barbary and, she felt, for Rob as well. 'Rob,' she said suddenly, 'it ain't that I'm agin being rich. I want to get on as much as you. I just can't put on the swank any more.'

He didn't look at her. 'It never bothered you when you were crossbiting.'

'Yes, well. I can't do that any more either.' Her trickery had left her, perhaps when she'd found she was an amateur compared with Burghley and his ilk, perhaps when she'd ended up versing her own grandmother, perhaps at the loss of Cuckold Dick, perhaps with the discovery that her marriage had been the biggest trick of all.

Surprisingly, Rob said: 'Raleigh likes you.' There was puzzlement in his voice, and calculation. If Raleigh, courtier, adventurer, great sea captain, could take to Barbary there might be no harm for her to stay as she was.

Yes, well, thought Barbary, he would. He's aware of women, he wants to conquer them all. And sure enough of himself to appreciate a character, an odd'un like me. But you, Rob Betty, you're rigid in your insecurity. You've got to conform and I've got to conform for you. And I won't. There's no trickery left.

The next day they passed the Rock of Cashel. It silenced even Ellis who, until then, had jeered at Irish churches. 'What they do, knit 'em?' he'd said every time they glimpsed the angular little buildings of multi-coloured stone which nestled like abandoned pot-holders in the valleys. He was quiet for an hour as they moved across the plain dominated by the cathedral on its outcrop, squinting back to see if it had stopped being intimidating. 'Bloody Papist, St Patrick,' he said, when it finally went into the mist.

As they came near the Golden Vale the countryside became more like England, but an England deserted for ten years. Hedges put in by undertakers of the First Munster Plantation had been left to sprout into banks of ragged bushes, untended by the Irish to whom the segregation of land was an alien concept. English-type farmhouses still stood in ruins, thatch burned off, cindered rafters exposed. Areas of forest that the English had begun to assart were going back to the wild. An old sawpit still had a partially logged oak across it where the Irish enemy had fallen on an English woodfeller before he could finish the job.

But the mud churning beneath the hooves of their horses was rich, and the sun, appearing and disappearing between chasing clouds, shone on pasture of a scarcely believable green.

'Didn't the Irish farm it?' Barbary asked of Edmund Spenser.

'Only primitively,' he told her. 'A pastoral race. Nomads, taking their cattle to the high ranges in summer and to the valleys in winter.' He spoke like an historian on an extinct people but his eyes searched the track ahead and his hand fidgeted inexpertly with the hilt of his sword.

The calling began as they edged through the Glen of Aherlow.

Attempts to clear the forest which had sheltered Desmond and his army for so long had been abandoned. Saplings and the stumps of a thousand trees had resprouted now that the sheep which should have nibbled them away had themselves been eaten. The trees formed cover between the steep hills towering over the south side of the track; to the north was marsh. Rain dripped off the leaves to join the streams which splashed down towards a wagon train suddenly diminished by the unexpected size of the mountains.

A fluted call from high up on their left was answered from bushes on their right. It came again, behind them.

Again, this time in front. Maccabee cocked her head. 'I can't place that bird, Captain. Irish, I suppose?'

Mackworth waved to his men to keep the wagons close together. 'The green-crested cutthroat, ma'am. Commonly called the MacSheehy.'

'Really? There seem a lot of them round here.'

'Too many, mistress. Time for you ladies to get under cover from the rain.'

Barbary helped Maccabee into the wagon and settled her on a bed of bales. Her estimation of Spenser's wife was rising; she might be too stupid to recognise danger when she heard it, but the cheerfulness with which she was enduring this journey into unknown territory with her baby due any day showed courage of a high order. She sat Catherine near her mother and diverted her attention from outside with games of cat's cradle until the child slept, then crawled to the opening.

The bird-like calls had stopped; so had genuine bird song. Harness and wheels creaked, a baby near the back of the train was crying, streams rushed, but all these noises were absorbed into a landscape otherwise so silent it might have been dead. Alongside, men marched without talking, their shoulders rigid with attention, eyes scouring the defile.

Then, somewhere high up, a new call began. It started in the lower register and ululated upwards, in a louder and louder crescendo, until it reached the scream of a maniac. It broke off, leaving its echo ricocheting back and forth across the glen. The woods erupted with frightened birds, rooks circled cawing over their heads, magpies rat-tatted alarms, pigeons blundered up out of the branches.

'What was that?' called Maccabee.

Barbary blew out her breath. 'Irish calling the cows home, Maccy. Try and sleep.'

The world around them settled again, then from a clump of trees ahead came the low moan that began another call, this time louder, more insane. It looped across the pass like a thrown rope uncoiling. Some of the front pikemen broke ranks and ran towards the copse, Mackworth shouting angrily at them to come back. Barbary could see them jabbing with their pikes at branches and clumps of fern and sympathised with their need to throw off fear by activity. Eventually Mackworth's barks of command recalled them and she watched them lope sullenly back to the column. She counted them as they came, three, four, five. There had been six.

'Where's Crane?' demanded Mackworth. The men looked round at each other, bewildered, turned to go back.

Mackworth stopped them with his sword. 'I'll run through the next man that leaves the wagons.'

'But Crane, Captain. He was with us a minute ago.'

'Crane's gone. Forget him. Get in line.'

Another call was beginning. It was joined by another, then another, mingling screams until the train was entangled in whips of sound that scarred the brain.

'Lot of cows,' muttered Maccabee sleepily.

Barbary primed the Clampett. The green-crested cut-throats wouldn't get her and Maccy and Catherine as easily as they'd got Crane. Rob and Raleigh were wheeling their horses to go to protect the back of the column. At that moment they looked like versions of the same man, both faces intent, not with pleasure, certainly not with fear, but with interest in the situation and their own reaction to it. They're showing off, thought Barbary, and doing it well. Rob caught her eye and she gave him the Order's thumbs up at which he grinned for once. Well, if the only time we can make contact is in moments of danger, it's going to be a funny marriage.

Pebbles came bouncing down some scree. Captain Mackworth danced his horse out of the way as a boulder tumbled after them and rolled over the spot where he'd been, hitting a pack mule and breaking its leg. Mackworth called for an arquebus to shoot it, and himself helped to tear off the panniers. 'Courage,' he was shouting, as the wagons moved on. 'They think they can frighten us.'

'You mean they're not sure?' asked Barbary. She was getting cross as well as frightened. The mule might have been her pony.

There were screams of agony – Crane? – howls that ended in the giggles of the insane. Barbary leaned down to put a hand over Catherine's exposed ear and heard the canvas of the wagon tear. A spear point was sticking through where her head had been. Even that was less terrifying than the noise. It was assault, aural artillery. They were bracketed. The whole valley reverberated with the sound of hatred, poison gas streaming through holes in the mountains, a forest of shrieking trees.

Barbary stopped being cross, flattened herself into the bales and gave herself up to terror.

A kindly god had made an end to the pass and towards the end of the longest afternoon of their lives they reached it, less three undertakers, two killed by spears and one small boy by a slingshot. Another slingshot had broken the arm of one of Ellis's sons and another pikeman had disappeared, nobody knew how. Some of the stock had died nastily and a hen coop had been broken, releasing its occupants to the wild.

The undertakers felt they had been through a major battle; Captain Mackworth assured them it was a mere skirmish, the MacSheehys showing nuisance value. He was invigorated, almost proud. She heard him tell Raleigh: 'I have been well and truly announced back to Munster.' She supposed he knew best, but what had happened in the Glen of Aherlow seemed to her more impersonal and terrible, the hatred of a landscape for its new possessors.

The next two days were rain, darkness and fatigue. Mackworth insisted the entire train accompany each group of undertakers to their settlement. 'For one thing to ensure that each of you knows where the others are situated.' They crossed and re-crossed the swollen Blackwater. All the bridges were down, some through disrepair, others deliberately destroyed. Even when they found a ford, there was difficulty urging the wagon teams into tumultuous water, and more difficulty getting them out.

Barbary lost count of the times she got soaked to the skin as she helped families carry their belongings into farmhouses and cottages while soldiers nailed canvas to roofless ceilings to provide some shelter from the rain. The undertakers were silent and exhausted. The land they had come to was grey with drizzle and, as they already knew, hostile, but their determination to settle in it had grown with their adversity. As one family, the Biddlecombes, stared round the ruin they were going to live in, a small child burst into tears: 'I want to go home.'

240

His mother smacked him: 'This *is* home.'

In intensifying rain the rest of the wagon train moved west to the valley of the Awbeg around which the remaining undertakers, including the Spensers, were to settle. Blinded by the drizzle, without signposts, and in what appeared to be abandoned countryside, it was not surprising that even the assured Captain Mackworth kept losing his way. He wouldn't admit it. Every decent road they struck he said: 'Ah ha, this leads to Mallow in the minute.' It didn't. It led to small collections of cottages where the inhabitants, dragged into the rain by Mackworth's soldiers, insisted it was Michelstown. At Buttevant they said it was Buttevant. At Doneraile, Doneraile.

'Nonsense,' shouted Mackworth, 'this is Mallow.'

'Doneraile, your worship.'

'I tell you it's Mallow. You savages don't know your own damn location.'

'Your worship's sure to be right then. And all these years us thinking it was Doneraile.' The next minute the Irishman sprawled in the mud from a whack by Captain Mackworth's fist.

'Insolence,' puffed Mackworth. 'Ah ha, there's light ahead. I knew I was right.'

The light was torches held by a search party of horsemen and soldiers. 'God's breath, Mackworth,' said a tall man from a tall horse. 'What are you doing in Doneraile?'

The insolent Irishman and his family were evicted while Mackworth, Raleigh, Spenser and Rob went into conference in his cottage with the tall man. Barbary, furious with fatigue and the new delay, helped Maccabee and Catherine down from the wagon and followed the others inside to dry. The cottage smelled of peat, goats, cooking oats and wet cloaks steaming from the fire which cast even bigger shadows than the big men who were dwarfing its one room and its only indigenous occupant, a baby in a wicker cradle.

They didn't intimidate Barbary. 'These ladies need hot drink and vittles,' she announced, shepherding them towards the fire. The tall man stood up politely and Barbary plonked Maccabee onto his vacant stool. 'And they needs 'em now.'

'For Lord's sake, woman,' hissed Rob, 'this is the Lord President of Munster.'

241

'Then he can organise hot drink and vittles,' snapped Barbary. She had come to the end of her tether; what concerned her more was that Maccabee, who looked very white, had come to the end of hers.

The tall man bowed. 'John Norris at your service, mistress.' He went to the door and called for one of his lieutenants to bring brandy, and himself ladled out some porridge from the cauldron into a bowl for Maccabee and Catherine. He was huge, dark-complexioned, grizzled and ugly. His nose was flattened (an injury sustained while quelling an army riot), his right hand crippled (a musketball during the battle of Nordhorn in Flanders), and he limped (a thigh smashed by shrapnel at Malines). But the battering, while it had physically malformed Sir John Norris, had hammered into his soul a rare concern for others. He was also susceptible to beauty. As Barbary unwound her sopping travelling veil from her head and shook her head near the fire to dry it, Sir John's chin went up in surprise.

Barbary took to him. Feeling she'd been over-harsh, she said in her best Penshurst voice: 'Kind of you, my lord, to come looking for us.' Now she thought about it, it was extraordinary that a man who commanded a quarter of Ireland had done so.

'If I'd known such ladies were in distress,' Sir John told her earnestly, 'I would have been out the sooner. It was at the behest of the Queen that I came at all.'

Raleigh, always unsettled when an attractive woman's attention was commanded by anybody but him, stepped in. 'My Lord President is sent to take us away from you, mistress.' Maccabee and Barbary stared at him, then at Sir John.

Rob said: 'It's the Armada. There's news that it's ready to sail. Raleigh and I are ordered back at once. Sir Walter's promised me command of his *Speedswift*.' He spoke with the reverberative hush of an Arthurian knight glimpsing the Holy Grail. Barbary, his undertaking, his plans for a kingdom in Connaught, were unremembered. He was refastening his cloak as he spoke, desperate to be off. The Armada might endanger England, but at that moment he could have kissed Philip of Spain's foot for giving him the chance to tilt for glory.

The two wives in the room threw themselves on their

husbands. 'Me too,' begged Barbary. 'Rob, I can fight the Armada too.' The idea of escape overwhelmed her.

'Not you,' begged Maccabee of Edmund. 'Dear husband, don't leave me.'

Both men were embarrassed; Rob because Barbary was being unseemly in front of great men, Edmund because nobody had even suggested he should go.

The President of Munster saved the situation with tact. 'England needs her women and her poets,' he said. 'Let us who can do nothing else go kill the Don. If the Armada invades Ireland we shall have you in reserve.'

Barbary dropped back. She was going to be imprisoned in rain and domesticity and danger.

They were to leave right away, Sir John Norris to oversee the English land fortifications, Rob and Sir Walter to put the finishing touches to fitting out the *Speedswift* and the *Ark Raleigh*. Courteously Sir John offered his home, Mallow Castle, where his brother, Thomas, who was to take over the running of Munster in his absence, also lived. 'He and my sister-in-law would be delighted. Kilcolman is no place for you at the moment. We heard there had been MacSheehy activity there, but I fear we have been too busy to investigate.'

But at this suggestion Maccabee went into hysterics. Despite all the devastation she had seen she still retained a grand and fully furnished image of her home-to-be. Her son – she was sure it would be a boy – must be born a Spenser in Spenser Castle. How could they suggest anything else? The birth was days away, plenty of time to make any little repair to the place.

Barbary dragged herself out of her depression. Maccabee needed her; probably the only person in the world who did. She didn't know much about pregnancy, but Maccy's shape suggested the baby was imminent. Mary, the servant, was an experienced midwife, the Ellises would be living with them until Spenser Castle had been fortified, and Mrs Ellis had had two children of her own. And wasn't Baby Jesus born in some sort of country hut? Perhaps they could manage. She caught Edmund's eye and nodded encouragement.

Edmund said: 'I think, my lord, that there is no sense in delaying our settlement.'

The lord President nodded. 'I'll send some of these

men with you.' Rob, not sure how the gentry took leave of their wives, told Barbary to be dutiful, hesitated, then kissed her hand. Raleigh kissed her on the cheek, hard.

She stood in the small doorway to wave them off. Rob looked superb, like all men going off to war, and in that moment she loved him over again, for all that he had tricked her and was deserting her, just for his beauty. War for him meant lack of complication. He would be brave, a man among men, boasting perhaps of the little wife who waited for him back home with no mention of the fact that their marriage was an emotional disaster. You lucky bastard, she thought. Why didn't women have the wit to invent war? He blew her a kiss at the last, the moment giving a pang to his feeling for her, as it gave a pang to hers for him. But he was relieved to be going, and although it left her to cope with darkness, rain, Maccabee, Ireland and the Irish, his departure meant equal relief for her. At least the real Barbary could deal with them in her own way.

Even with directions and fresh horses, Kilcolman eluded them for hours. 'Straight down the Doneraile road,' Sir John Norris had said. But the Doneraile road wasn't straight. 'Bloody Irish,' grumbled Barbary, forgetting she was one of them, 'wouldn't know a straight road if it bit 'em in the arse.' A thunderstorm, unable to make them wetter, aided them in lightning flashes which gave momentary glimpses of their location.

'Look for turrets,' Maccabee kept saying. 'There'll be turrets.' There were hills, the Ballyhouras, on their right, there were trees, there was mud, but turrets were lacking.

At last a dismal dawn revealed two jagged stumps they had passed time and again in the night to be the ruins of gateposts. An overgrown track inclined gently, muddily, upwards. They followed it and stopped. Edmund said nothing. Ellis said: 'That's the only one-storey castle I ever seen.' Maccabee began to cry. Barbary, light-headed with fatigue, began to laugh so much she nearly fell off Spenser.

Tumbledown walls fringed a large, natural mound. On this side of it stood the stump of a tower that had once formed a gatehouse. Across the rise was another stump, this time two-storeyed. That it had once been a tall keep was evident from the blocks of stone lying scattered around it. But in the middle of the mound was what had once been a sizeable house, perhaps even a castle – it was impossible to tell because somebody, a lot of somebodies, had taken it apart stone by stone so that now it was just an enormous heap of granite rubble.

The whole place looked ridiculous. The gate-tower was a ruin, but enough remained of the keep to make it look as if it was trying to stand on tiptoe to see over the bailey walls.

Edmund got down from his horse and stood with his back to it, facing the wagons. He was pale but in that moment he had a dignity and courage Barbary hadn't suspected. 'My dear,' he said to Maccabee, 'welcome to what will be Spenser Castle.'

Barbary stopped laughing. Maccabee stopped crying and announced she was in labour. From the Ballyhoura hills came a moan rising to the ululating howl that told them they had been located by the enemy.

Chapter Twelve

The Armada bore down on England in crescent formation, like a scythe. With no other nation to help, the English fleet went out to meet it and joined battle on 31 July. For ten days the fight veered back and forth, the huge, soldier-packed Spanish ships trying to grapple, the English with better ships and better guns dodging out of boarding reach, pumping out cannon balls at a faster rate than the enemy, using the tide races and currents they knew so well.

After ten days the English gained an ally. As if He had been waiting to see which side looked like winning, God in the form of a wind puffed out His cheeks and blew against the Armada. The Spanish could not beat the English and God. They were forced up the North Sea to face the 750-league journey home round the stormy, unknown waters of Scotland and Ireland in battered ships running out of provisions.

The worst losses were in Ireland. Connaught's Governor, Sir Richard Bingham, worried about holding his unruly coast against these possible invaders, gave orders that all Spaniards coming ashore were to be killed on sight, as was any Irishman who aided them. The sea and rocks of Donegal, Mayo, Clare and Kerry did most of his job for him. As many as seventeen ships may have gone down, most of them with the loss of all hands. At loyal Galway the entire crew of the *Falcòn Blanco Mediano* was executed on Bingham's gallows. Here and there in the remote parts a few survivors were clubbed to death, like seals, for what they wore, being regarded by wild shore-dwellers as just another offering from the sea. Several hundred Spaniards, however, were helped by the Irish at the risk of their own lives and delivered safely to Scotland.

Nevertheless the superb seamanship and administration of the Spanish Admiral, Medina Sidonia, brought two-thirds of the Armada back to Spain.

The English fleet was jubilant, as it had a right to be, the Spanish downcast. But neither side yet regarded the battle as decisive. Meticulously, Philip of Spain enquired, read every report, and started making plans for a new Armada that would avoid the mistakes of the last. The English commanders pleaded with Elizabeth not to disband a navy that might yet be required to fight off another invasion. The war was by no means over.

Rob Betty distinguished himself during the battle of the Armada. The *Speedswift* went in to attack Sidonia's own ship, the *San Martin*, like an angry and agile wasp. On 5 August, during a lull in the fight, Rob was called aboard the flagship and knighted by Admiral Howard with other brave men, including Hawkins and Frobisher.

So it was an exultant *Sir* Robert Betty who wrote to Barbary after it was all over. He could not yet return to Ireland; he was joining Drake and Sir John Norris in an expedition which would follow up the victory while the Spanish were still recovering. They were to go to Lisbon, destroying any Armada stragglers they found there or on the way, take Lisbon and, finally, the Azores, from which they could intercept Spanish treasure ships from the New World.

'Be assured, my dear wife,' he wrote, 'this venture will be as successful as the last, for God is pleased to smile on our Great Queen. Already Her Sacred Majesty hath in her turn smiled on me with the gift of the manor of Kerswell in Devon which is rich in pasture. In her goodness she hath confirmed me in the estate of Hap Hazard in Ireland in which regard I urge you, my dear wife, to see to the appointment thereof against my return or, if you be not able, to be guided by Master Spenser in the choice of some excellent Englishman to whose capacity as steward for some reasonable wage the building of the manor thereof may be entrusted. Sir Walter Raleigh is to recommend to Her Majesty our venture in Connaught whereof I have great hope on my return. He has further in his goodness undertaken to press Her Majesty that she overlook your offences against her that one day you may bask in the favour of her prosperity as does your loving husband. For this encompassing, be virtuous, dutiful and zealous that all may go forward to our greatness.'

It struck Barbary and she realised it must have struck Rob, that he needn't have married her at all. The 'venture into Connaught' was no longer necessary to bring him lands and the attention of the Queen; his own courage had done it for him. 'You should have waited, Robby.' Still, he couldn't un-marry her. She hoped for his sake he could get Elizabeth to overlook his wife's 'offences' so that he could proceed to that greatness he wanted so much.

But blow me, she thought, I'm *Lady* Betty. At that moment the one person she wanted to share the news with was Cuckold Dick. He'd split himself laughing.

As for those instructions about the Hap Hazard estate, Rob had no idea what conditions were like here in Munster. The shortage of workers was crippling, even worse than the MacSheehys, and they were bad enough. Danger may have temporarily receded from England, but here it was ever-present. Captain Mackworth kept driving the MacSheehys away, but now and again their call would echo over the Awbeg Valley to tell the undertakers they hadn't gone far. A cow would be killed, a horse hamstrung, an unwary Englishman killed tilling his fields.

Here in Ireland the system of beacons was kept in readiness for firing so that one beleaguered English household could call for help against the attack. Every time they restacked the Spenser beacon with dry kindling, Edmund would pause and thank God they hadn't had cause to fire it. Barbary supposed she was grateful but she was too numb with fatigue to feel it.

People said you couldn't die of hard work, but in those first months at Kilcolman, Barbary thought she might. Mrs Ellis delivered Maccabee's baby boy. Ellis and sons made the place defensible and reconstructed enough of the keep to be habitable. Then all four of them left to begin work on Ellis's own land at Doneraile. Mary the servant also left, to join her husband on his settlement. The two soldiers whom Edmund had persuaded Mackworth to lend him to guard the place did only that, apart from eating. It was Barbary who was left with the cooking, washing, cleaning, who watered and fed the stock, who looked after Catherine and tended Maccabee and the baby.

Continually she swore at the labour and herself for doing it. 'These fambles,' she said, shaking her roughened fists at Edmund, 'was never made for work.' It was a form of protest against her position to throw off Penshurst manners and revert to Order cant, see Edmund's eyes widen in shock when she swore, but he didn't dare reproach her. 'I am grateful,' he kept saying. 'I don't know what we would do without you.'

Barbary didn't either. She stayed because at the moment there seemed nowhere else to go and she worked because if she didn't there would be chaos at Kilcolman and Maccabee would suffer. It had been a difficult birth and Maccabee was not pulling round. Her milk was just sufficient, but she was weak, not only physically but mentally. She seemed vague, cried a lot and took little interest in either the baby or what was happening around her. Edmund spent most of his time in those early days desperately scouring the surrounding villages for domestic and agricultural labour. Eventually he came up with Rosh.

Rosh did not promise well. True, the woman was big and moderately young, but she had one muscular arm protectively round the shoulders of a frail old man and the other on the head of a grubby boy.

'Edmund,' said Barbary between her teeth. 'Three, I said. Able-bodied, I said. Not one and hangers-on. Throw her back.'

'She was all I could get, Barbary,' said Edmund. 'They speak English. The boy's strong for his age and the old man should be able to tell me the legends of his people.'

'Oh good,' snapped Barbary. 'I was afraid the old fart might be useful round the house.'

'Will you listen to the music-less mouth of the bitch,' said the woman to her father in Irish. 'Doesn't she know no man ever wore a scarf as warm as his daughter's arm round his neck?'

Barbary turned on her in the same language. 'Well, suppose you take it off his neck and put it in this fokking washtub.' Haggling with traders in the local markets had taken away her inhibitions about speaking Irish, and given her a command of the vernacular.

249

It had not been a propitious start, yet within the week Barbary would have shot anyone who tried to take Rosh away from her. The woman's capacity for work was only outdone by her willingness to do it. An axe wielded by her reduced trees to logs and logs to kindling within minutes. Sheets, baby cloths, petticoats went into the stream dirty and blanched as if in fear of her fists. Her spade cut perfect bricks of peat out of the bog down the hill and turned the uneven tussocks at the back of the bailey into a neat square of tilth in which the herbs and vegetables she planted came up standing smartly to attention.

The marvel's one failing lay in her cooking of which the household had expected great things, only to be disappointed when it turned out to be as awful as Barbary's.

Her name was Roisín, pronounced Rosheen. Her father's name was Duibhdáleithe; it meant 'black man of the two sides' and its pronunciation defeated the English. Edmund Anglicised it into Dudley. The old man appeared not to mind. He was courteous and worked as hard as his frailty allowed, but he was absent; his opinions and emotions were elsewhere in some previous age where Irish greatness still existed. Rosh said he had been the *reacaire* to his clan's *ollámh dana*, but she said it with hopeless pride, knowing they wouldn't understand what a dignity that was and that to the English he was just a homeless old mere Irish. Only Edmund pricked up his ears. 'A reciter of a chief poet, by the Lord,' he said and from then on sat down with the old man almost every night and made him recount the myths that clung to the hills and valleys around them.

It irritated Barbary to see the men sitting when there was so much work to be done. 'If the old bugger could weave as fast as he prattles we'd have something to show for it.' But her own hands would fall in her lap as the old man began the stories in his sing-song voice, his remoteness cutting out the medium between listener and story so that there were nights when the household hunted with Finn Mac Cool over the Ballyhouras they could see from their window, and heard the blast of his Fianna's horn sounding from the Galtees only a little further away. He always began in the same way:

Three sorrows of story-telling fill me with pity,
the telling of them grates on the ear;
the woe of the Children of Turenn –
sorrowful to hear.

And the Children of Lîr, bird-shaped;
a curse on the mouth that told their doom:
Conn, Fiacra, Finola and Aed –
the second gloom.

And the Children of Usnach, shield of men,
who fell by force and cunning craft –
Naisi, and Ainle and Ardan
There cracks the heart.

It cracked Barbary's. Memories from her childhood came
unbidden as she listened. She had sat on her mother's
knee and heard these stories from another *reacaire*,
enfolded in not just her mother's warmth but that of the
people who encircled them, listening. There had been a
companionship that put the Order's in the shade, her
body part of a greater body encompassing the blood and
thought of its components. The old man's voice took her
further than the Galtees, it took her to the land of the
cherubims.

Seeing her wipe away tears Rosh asked: 'If you're
Irish, why are you serving these Gauls?' She said it
sharply in the first aggression she'd shown.

'They're not foreigners to me and I'm not serving, you
bog-trotter,' said Barbary, 'I'm helping. For that matter,
why are you?'

Rosh shrugged: 'Any man can lose his hat in a fairy
wind.' She was always saying things like that. She had
the largest collection of meaningless proverbs Barbary
had ever heard. 'An oak is often split by a wedge from its
branch,' she'd say, or 'When you get lime on your boots
it's hard to get off,' or 'A Clare man will sleep in your ear
and build a nest in the other.' Such profundities appeared
to have comforted her through bad times, though she
never mentioned her past. The only glimpse Barbary got
of it indicated horror. It came through Catherine who
gained it from the boy, Lal. (His name was Laoighseach
but to everyone's relief Rosh called him Lal.) He was a

251

silent child of about nine, going on thirty-five thought Barbary – with a face that had closed down all expression. The one person among the English he communicated with was Catherine, and only then when nobody else was about.

'They won't hang Sylvestris, will they?' demanded Catherine anxiously of Barbary. Sylvestris was the new baby's name, Edmund being enchanted just then by the woodland that surrounded them.

Barbary picked her up. 'They certainly won't. Why?'

'Lal says they hanged all *his* brothers. He showed me on Peggy.' From behind her back Catherine produced her wooden doll, dangling from her fingers by a thong round its neck.

Barbary disentangled the small fingers and ripped the thong off. 'Nobody's going to hang anybody.' She looked over at Rosh, who was watching, and immediately looked away again. There were some things shouldn't be seen in another woman's eyes.

Gradually life at Kilcolman improved. Masons from Raleigh's estate at Lismore arrived and rebuilt the keep and the gatehouse to their full four storeys, then began work on the large stone manor that would crown the hill. Labourers, two loyal Irishmen from Youghal, the rest mere Irish, were hired and given plots of land on the estate, the mere Irish having smaller plots than the loyal. A steward and more house servants were acquired. Clutches of farm cottages sprang up along the banks of the Bregoge which ran through the estate, where they could be seen from the gatehouse, yet not offend anyone looking out from the windows of the manor. A dairy was begun, stables, kennels. Spenser pigs grunted in the woodland, Spenser sheep roamed the Ballyhouras, Spenser cattle grazed the water meadows. Hedges were planted.

Edmund, Barbary realised, was trying to create an Irish Penshurst. The wages he had to pay out to the mere Irish were paltry, while his income from the Irish tenancies he owned in other parts of Munster was making him richer than he'd ever been before. He modelled himself on Sir Henry Sidney and strode his fields talking knowledgeably of virgates, ploughlands, ox gangs and yield. The knowledge actually came from Ellis who was making a success of his farm at Doneraile, although his treatment of his labourers was such that every so often a couple would escape its tyranny by running away to join the MacSheehys.

Barbary's dislike of Ellis grew the more she knew him but the man was indispensable. Kilcolman estate would not have got the start it did without Ellis's instructions on what to plant, where and when. Edmund was a figurehead, it was Ellis who gave the commands and Barbary who saw they were carried out. But gradually, and to her relief, the responsibilities which had rested on her shoulders were shifted onto O'Mahony, Edmund's new farm steward, who had worked for Raleigh. The only function she retained was looking after the hens and ducks, and that was because she liked it.

Eventually there came a Sunday in late September when she woke up and realised that, apart from feeding the hens, she had nothing to do. She'd got out of bed ready to start the day before it came to her that it stretched in front of her, whole and uncommitted. Abby, the cook, was in charge in the kitchen, her daughter Lucy had the linen cupboard under control. Rosh had only yesterday beeswaxed the new floors in the house, as well as polishing everything else that stood still. Maccabee was well enough to dress Sylvestris, and, anyway, Catherine could help her. There were still no men to spare to start building Hap Hazard so she didn't have to oversee that.

She went to the northern arrow slit and leaned against its slope to look out. The moment the gatehouse of Spenser Castle had been finished, Barbary had claimed its top floor as her living quarters. Another one to accommodate a porter was being built on the opposite side of the steep drive. The entrance to Spenser Castle was going to have grandeur.

'But my dear cousin,' Edmund protested, 'you must have your own room here, in the house with us.'

She was working like a dog: she was entitled to her own kennel. 'I want that one.' He could hardly refuse her and he didn't. The ground floor of the tower contained a large well, while supplies in case of possible siege were stacked on the first floor into which the gatehouse's only door opened to the bailey. The upper storeys were empty and in the top one Barbary made her home. Edmund gave her hangings to take the chill off the walls, a bed, table, stools, a brazier and a clothes press. She cut rushes to put on the floor. It was inconvenient, was investigated by the occasional bat, and would verge on the icy when winter came, and she loved it.

Maccabee couldn't understand the move. 'Why are you leaving me?'

'I'm only a spit away, Maccy.' She paused in her packing. 'But you know, when the masons are finished here they're going to start on building Rob's manor.' She thought of the land called 'Hap Hazard' five miles away, which they were to undertake, as Rob's only. It was Kilcolman, into which she had put so much work, that she felt was hers quite as much as the Spensers'. 'And when that's finished I'll have to move over there.'

Maccabee burst into tears. 'You mustn't leave me. I don't like it here. I'm so frightened.'

Barbary felt her trembling against her arm. 'It's just the namelesses, Maccy. You're not frit of them old Mac-Sheehys?'

'It's the forest. The forest frightens me.'

At the bottom of the drive to the house was the track to Doneraile and on the other side of it deeply forested land dipped down before rising again to become the foothills of the equally wooded Ballyhouras. Edmund grandly called it the 'Deer Park' and had hired gangs to thin out its enormous beech, oak and ash and clear the spaces between of clogging undergrowth. They were making slow progress and had so far penetrated less than a hundred yards, so that most of the interior was still primaeval. What or who made the eccentric tracks that weaved through it nobody knew. Since that first day when they'd heard the calling that had pursued them through the Glen of Aherlow, it had echoed to only non-human sound, the bark of deer and foxes and a mixture of birdsong as dense as its canopy. Deep in it might be sinister, but the cleared edges were lightly dappled and a storehouse of good things. Rosh and Barbary were watching the ripening of its hazelnuts and blackberries with predatory eyes.

There was no doubt, though, that Maccabee, who had stood the rigours of the trek into Munster so well, had not been herself since she arrived at Kilcolman. All her irritating chatter, her busy-ness had faded and left her nervous and dependent. Barbary blamed the birth, but Maccabee attributed her unreasonable terror – what Barbary called the 'namelesses' – to the countryside that enfolded her.

Barbary liked it. It wasn't the land of her cherubims, but as she stood looking out on it from the windows of her tower that Sunday morning she felt an affinity with it. To the north, and very close, were the dark Ballyhouras. To the south, further away, were the Nagle mountains. The smudges visible eastward on clear days were the hills of Waterford and, westward, the mountains of Kerry. The mound her gatehouse guarded was one of several pretty hills. Defensible walls now surrounded its base, like a circlet round a high-domed head. On the top of the head was growing the castellated shell of what would soon be a fine house dominating the surrounding countryside.

One day there would be an ornamental garden leading down from it to the Bregoge, a tributary of the Awbeg, but at the moment the slope was of rough, goose-cropped grass. Further off, where the land rose again, was an odd lake, crescent-shaped, as if a new moon had come hurtling down from the sky and crashed into the earth. This side of the lake was marshy and full of frogs whose croaking dominated the night sounds and drove Edmund mad when he was trying to compose his poetry. Interruption to his muse was one of the few things that provoked him to outward anger. Barbary had heard him shout out of his window last night: 'I'll see to your choking, you devils. I'll have you drained.'

Always trying to change things, Edmund, thought Barbary as she dressed. Trying to create England out of an Irish landscape. Altering names, insisting on calling the Awbeg the 'Mulla', and belittling the high peak of the Ballyhouras into the 'Old Mole'. It was all something to do with the fantastical epic poem he was working on which would, he hoped, finally bring him the Queen's recognition since she was the allegorical heroine of it. Barbary had no time for allegory, mainly because she didn't understand the allusions.

And poor Abby in the kitchen who was really called Gobinet, and Lucy who was Luighseach, had to be given

255

Anglicised names in case a Dublin official came enquiring into why Irish labour was being employed. Why couldn't the English admit they were in a foreign country? Because doing so would remind them that it didn't really belong to them?

Personally, she liked it as it was. And today the sun shone on it. The Armada had been beaten off and the expedition to the Azores would keep Rob with his demands away for another year at least. She was free and there was no work to do. She turned back into her room, shook her fist at the bat which had come back in the night and hung upside down from a corner beam looking at her from its aggressive little eyes, hauled her mattress and bedding to the window to air, went down the tower's stairway to the first floor, out of the door and down the steps.

She climbed the incline to the house. Lal was holding Edmund's horse so that his master could mount. 'Ah, Lady Betty, my dear,' said Edmund, always formal in the presence of servants. 'Just in time to accompany me to church.'

On one of the parcels of land held by Edmund was the all-Irish hamlet of Effin with its tiny church. Since the outlawing of Roman Catholicism in Ireland, only a handful of loyal Irish attended it, and they did so reluctantly, since owing allegiance to Elizabeth did not mean in their eyes that they had to practise her religion. The churchman responsible for its service was an Englishman, Prebendary Chadwick, but, like so many of the Protestant ministers in Ireland, Prebendary Chadwick was too busy grabbing land of his own to try and secure the hearts and minds of the Irish. He collected tithes from the parishioners, of course, but until Edmund had arrived and dutifully attempted to fill the gap, no service had been held at Effin for three years.

'I ain't coming, Edmund,' said Barbary evenly. It was an old argument.

The poet put on his responsible look. 'I request it, cousin,' he said. 'We live among the most barbarous people in the world. We must show them an example.'

'I'm one of them barbarians, Edmund.' And so's that boy standing there, she thought, listening to every word.

It flustered him to be reminded she was Irish. 'I regard

you as one of us,' he said. 'And you're no Papist.'

'No, I'm not. And I'm not coming to church neither. I'm taking Sylvestris for some air.'

'How can these people find the True Path unless they see us, their betters, following it?'

Barbary shrugged. It wasn't her problem. 'Are you going to call in on Tadg O'Lyne on the way back?' Tadg was a distinguished, blind, old Irish poet who lived in part of the ruins of Ballybeg Abbey.

Edmund became defensive. 'I might.' Then enthusiasm took over. 'You know, cousin, these Irish poets have much to teach us in cadence and good invention.'

'You stayed overnight with him the last time . . .'

'We had much to talk about.'

'. . . and a spear was put through his cow the next day.'

'Coincidence,' said Edmund.

'The same coincidence as burned down his barn when you stayed the night the time before that?'

'I'm not responsible for the MacSheehys and their terror.'

It was Rosh who had begged Barbary to dissuade Edmund from visiting the old poet. Finding the English farms well defended, and the reprisals carried out by Captain Mackworth too painful, the MacSheehys were now dissuading their fellow Irish from fraternising with the enemy by killing the stock of anyone who entertained an Englishman in his house. Barbary doubted if they were winning the hearts and minds of their people any better than the undertakers were.

She wagged her finger at Edmund. 'It won't fadge, Edmund. You're taking advantage. Rosh says poor old Tadg can't refuse you lodging because it's against his honour. She says it's tradition and he'd rather die than not be hospitable. But he don't like it, and I don't blame him.'

Edmund's lips tightened and he mounted his horse. 'You can tell Rosh that it is not up to an Irish slut to teach manners to an English gentleman.'

Barbary watched him ride off, a thin, stiff-necked but curiously nebulous figure. There were so many bits to Edmund they seemed patched on, as if he'd borrowed them from people he admired. What lay underneath and

257

whether it was worth discovering, she had no idea, except that it was stubborn. He'd go to Tadg's sure as eggs were eggs to learn the poetic art of a people he called barbarian, and sure as eggs were eggs one of Tadg's few remaining animals would be killed next day because of him. 'You're a dandiprat, Edmund,' she said under her breath. 'What's worse, you're a hammer-headed dandiprat.'

She spent a pleasant day playing with Catherine and Sylvestris in the sun. At first Catherine, who had a lot of her father in her, said: 'You shouldn't take his swaddling clothes off. His limbs won't grow straight.'

'Who's a little drabbit, then,' crooned Barbary, releasing Sylvestris from the last of his binders. 'The Irish don't swaddle their young 'uns, and their limbs go straight enough.'

Catherine cocked her head on one side. 'That's true. Can I take my stays off?'

'Yes.'

'And paddle in the lough?'

'Yes.' The open-air attitude of the Irish produced healthier children, for all their poverty, than did English confinement. In fact, Barbary thought, the Irish were healthier altogether for all that their diet included a lot of green stuff – young nettles, comfrey, sorrel, fat-hen and all wild herbs. The meat-eating English scoffed at them and called them 'grass-eaters', but Barbary compared the stunted growth of Maccabee, Edmund and Catherine, and even herself, to the thin but tall and strong-limbed Irish servants, and decided that grass-eating had its benefits.

It was such an unusually lazy day that by the time everybody else had retired to bed, which they did just before sunset, Barbary, for once, was startlingly awake. She leaned against the jamb of her westerly window, her foot tapping for something interesting to do while her mind grumbled at the lack of purpose and excitement in her life. The sunset turned every tree into a beckoning shadow and warmed the scent of evening adventure so that it drifted up from the grass, up the stones of Spenser walls to tantalise the nostrils of the red-headed, still very young, woman who stood there.

It was then that she saw a flicker at the very edge of her right-hand view. Low rays of the sun were in her eyes, but definitely something human-sized had moved. Quickly she crossed over to her east window. From here she could look over the bawn where the cattle had been enclosed for the night. She counted them. All present and correct. None with a spear through its neck.

To the right of the cattle pens was the raised wooden hen house. She listened; she knew enough of hen behaviour now to interpret the low clucking coming from it as the sound of undisturbed birds settling down for a good sleep. Nothing wrong there. She went to the north arrow slit to scan the ground that fell away below her towards the Ballyhouras. It had been cleared so as to give no cover to an enemy creeping across it but the hummocks in it cast shadows. One of the shadows detached itself and hurried over to the next, where it paused. It was Rosh. What's more, it was Rosh carrying the egg basket which Barbary herself had given to Lal this morning to collect the day's layings, and in which, when he'd finished, had been an unusually small clutch. 'Not laying so well today,' he'd told her. In her surprise that he'd spoken at all – for him this was garrulity – she'd not questioned the statement. 'But it wasn't bible, was it?' she realised now. 'You and your ma filched the rest of them eggs and now she's off on her ten toes with 'em. But where to?'

Barbary didn't give a dump for the eggs. Rosh could have them. Had got them. What she minded was not knowing what was going on. Ever since settling at Kilcolman she'd been aware that the English were excluded from the native life of the countryside. In mysterious ways the Irish communicated with it and each other. For instance, how had Rosh, who until today had not been known to leave the estate, been aware that the Mac-Sheehys were persecuting Tadg O'Lyne, the poet, four miles away?

But it was more than that. On certain nights, which were no feasts recognised by the English, faraway pipes and flutes and laughter taunted the ears of the under-takers. The estate owners would make angrily towards the sound, for to hear music and secret laughter was as unsettling as to hear the hated, hating, screech of the MacSheehys. They never found anything. Some trampled grass perhaps. On their return they would investigate the servants' quarters, and discover each man, woman and child beatifically keeping the right bed and snoring. Somewhere, somehow, life in which the English had no part was being lived. They began to believe in the fairy world of Irish myth. The Pooka invaded their nightmares. It bothered them.

Most of all it bothered Barbary. She who had been part of the secrecy of London's underworld resented being cut off from this one. It was dangerous not to know what was going on and, anyway, it itched her curiosity until she screamed to scratch it with an answer. Rosh knew the answer. And Rosh was going to lead her to it.

She moved like lightning. But she was Barbary of the Order again, and she didn't rush out of her tower into a darkening, hostile countryside without precautions. She threw the string of the muff in which she kept the Clampett snaphaunce over her neck – a muff might look incongruous in this weather, but the Irish were too eccentric themselves to notice eccentricity – and she flipped her shawl over and over until it was a fat roll which she tied round her head, giving its outline the approximate shape of an Irishwoman's headgear. She could now prattle Irish as good as Rosh's and if she met a MacSheehy she'd give him the rough side of it. And if that didn't do for him, she'd shoot him.

An instant later she was out of the tower. The great gates had been barred for the night. The walls were high, but Barbary had seen them built. At the back of the bawn was a stretch of the original retaining wall, from the days when Kilcolman had belonged to the Earl of Desmond. It retained fissures that nimble toes might use for purchase. She ran for the bawn, through the cattle pens and behind the hen house. Then she saw that nimble toes would not be needed for climbing. Rosh hadn't gone over the wall, she'd gone underneath it. There was a hole in the ground at the foot of the wall. Set to the side of it was an old well cover and a pile of manured litter from the cattle pens which usually concealed it. The entrance was only a little wider than that to a badger sett, just big enough to allow a slim human body to slide into the tunnel which, she found as she pushed herself through it, sloped steeply down and then steeply up, leading under the wall to the world outside.

She pulled aside the branches of a low bramble bush which concealed the outside entrance to the tunnel, heaved herself out and was immediately running low across the ground to the 'Deer Park' and the trees into which Rosh had already disappeared. As she entered the edge she listened and followed the sound of feet brushing leaves along a track that led into the interior. A fat harvest moon was taking its place in a sky still glowing pale from the remnants of the sunset, but it was dark under the canopy that grew thicker as she moved forward and her ears kept being cheated by the rustlings of what she hoped were merely the woodland's animals going about their nightly business. Rosh was going at the unhesitating pace of someone who knew the way like the back of her hand. Luckily, it was a slowish pace – she wasn't risking the eggs. And she had no suspicion she was being barnacled, and barnacled, what's more, by a mistress of the craft. Barbary grinned. Penshurst, marriage, maturity had fallen away. The old intoxication was back, the cony-catcher was on the loose again. This track was an alley, the branches her rooftops. It just smelled better than the Bermudas.

She made up the distance and spotted the tall, skirted shape and instantly adjusted her pace so that her shoes touched the ground exactly in time with Rosh's.

And what's for extra, she told herself, for once I'm on the side of law. It's Rosh who's the prigger and me the priggee. Whatever Rosh was going to do next was probably illegal as well. Everything the Irish did, unless the English permitted it, was illegal: speaking their own language, practising their own religion, wearing their hair this way, putting on their clothes that way.

The wonder that it hadn't come to her before was almost as great as the realisation itself. For a fraction of a moment she missed the movement of Rosh's step and had to freeze as the woman glanced over her shoulder before going on. The mere Irish *were* the Order. They were surviving against crushing authority, just as the Order survived. Rosh was her as she had been. She had been Rosh as she was now, hunted, stealthy, knavish. She was shadowing herself.

I won't peach on you, whatever it is, she promised mentally. But I've got to *know* whatever it is.

They were climbing now, the scent of bracken becoming forceful. The steep rise allowed the moon entry under the trees, but Rosh was too intent on keeping her basket level to look behind. The track was heading for the summit of Edmund's 'Old Mole'. Barbary was getting tired when at last Rosh paused. She heard the Irishwoman mutter a thanksgiving before she moved down a steep slope out of Barbary's sight. Barbary gained a vantage point and looked after her. Below, the trees ran out into a grassy dip between the hills, and in the clearing there was fluttering light and the movement of people. Barbary sniffed. The light was coming from candles, but not ordinary tallow candles; she was smelling beeswax.

Barbary grimaced. Was *that* what Rosh was up to? If she was, it wasn't only illegal, it was so dangerous that the thought of being caught just watching it made the palms of her hands sweat. She had to find out, but she wanted cover, nice thick cover, preferably armour-plated. She cautiously circled the rim of the dip before she spotted the nearest thing to an armour-plated hide the forest had to offer. It was a yew tree. She took the shawl from round her head and tied it about her waist. Barbary knew about yew trees. They were the only trees she did know about. Every cemetery in London had one. She knew they scratched you to hell but that, if they were old, like this one, they had gaps in their interior which allowed a small person who had a high threshold of pain to hide within them. She'd avoided more than one pursuit by availing herself of a yew tree's hospitality.

Making use of this one's hospitality meant crawling a yard downwards across open ground, but it was under shade and the people in the clearing were too busy to notice her. Gritting her teeth, she squirmed under the low branches, found a gap and undulated upwards into it, removing barbs from her hair and ear. Gingerly she parted the stems in front of her and looked through a tunnel of yew at the scene below.

She'd been right. This was a ceremony which could only be lit by beeswax candles because bees were reckoned to be virginal creatures, untainted by the sexual act, like their patron saint, the Virgin Mary. A white cloth covered a bumpy, natural altar on which the candles were standing round a battered tin plate. Two boys were robing a tall man, putting a white cope over his head. A hundred or more Irish men and women were in the dell. Where had they all come from?

Dolly worshippers. Papishes. Catholics. Romans.

She was about to see a Mass.

She felt the prurient curiosity she'd experienced when she and Rob, both very young, peeked through a crack in the floor of the Pudding-in-a-Cloth to try and discover what it actually was that Foll did for her clients.

Protestant propaganda hinted at eroticism, human sacrifice, the Devil rampant and naked presiding over idolatry. She couldn't see the Devil. She couldn't see much. Just the priest, now robed, a careworn man in the candlelight. There was still some light in the sky, but the figures gathering before him wore the fur collars of their Irish cloaks high round the lower part of their faces. She recognised Rosh and the two O'Dwyer boys who worked for Ellis. Wasn't that Patrick, one of Edmund's estate workers? And his wife? Here and there were figures that resembled men and women she'd met at Mallow market but she couldn't envisage feeling a compulsion to put herself in the danger these people were risking. Captain Mackworth hunted down priests with more zest than he hunted the MacSheehys, which was saying something. If he was caught, that white-coped man there would be cut apart still living. The rest would hang, if they weren't burned. And all for a ritual. What possessed them?

They were afraid. They bloody should be. They kept glancing at the encircling trees, just as Order men on their way to a robbery scanned the streets for constables of the watch. Rosh waved to an oak on the far side of the dell and an arm high up in it waved back. At least they'd posted a look-out. Lucky he hadn't spotted her wriggling into the yew tree.

The basket of eggs was lying on the ground with other goodies, a ham, a bundle of onions, more baskets. Offerings. Supplies for a priest on the run.

They were kneeling now. The priest was chanting in Irish, not Latin, and he wasn't keeping his voice down either. Typical devil-dodger. They all talked like God was deaf.

'Holy, Holy, Holy, Lord God of Hosts.'

Her lips mouthed the words before her brain caught up

with what she was doing. Jesus God, she knew what to say. As easily as those people in the dell, she could make the responses. She was a Papist. Had been a Papist. Of course. She was Irish. She hadn't connected. Somewhere in the land of the cherubims she'd been taught to kneel like these, pray like these. She clenched her teeth against the rhythm of the words, and jerked her eyes away from the dell as the priest went into the Prayer of Humble Approach.

Under the tree where the look-out was posted something moved. She strained her eyes to see what it was. Something moved behind her yew. Infinitely slowly, tearing her cheek against the thorns, she twisted her head round and saw the moonlit glint of a breastplate.

Mackworth was here. Mackworth and soldiers. Jesus. Mary. Mother of God, don't let them see me. Don't let them see me. Don't let them see me. With terror for herself came terror for the people in the dell. Protect them. Warn them. Mary, Mother of God, keep them from these soldiers' swords. Connected now to the faith of her childhood she used its phrases in her extremity of fear.

There was a movement on her right. They were surrounding the dell. Any moment Mackworth would give the signal and he'd be down on those kneeling souls like a wolf on sheep.

There was a loud clapping of wings as a pheasant trailing droppings and feathers came flying out of the bushes to her right where it had been disturbed. The worshippers in the dell looked up, got up, began to run. She heard Mackworth's voice – she knew it well – 'Charge!' Soldiers began spilling out of the trees. She heard the one behind her break into a heavy run, saw his back as he pelted down the slope.

Her wits came back. Escape. The pheasant had spoiled Mackworth's manouevre. The soldiers hadn't completed their pincer movement; half the dell, the half that lay to the west, was clear of them. The Irish were running in that direction. She saw a woman fall and prayed it wasn't Rosh. A child was going back to help his mother up. Leave her. She's as good as dead.

Go? Stay? Go. When they'd finished chasing, the soldiers would come back to the scene of the crime, spread out and search for stragglers. They'd have lanterns. Go then. And go in the direction they'd come from.

There was screaming from the dell, but Barbary was wriggling out of her tree, her snaphaunce was in her hand, and she was stealing from tree to tree as she'd once slipped through the shadows of London's streets.

The next four hours were a nightmare of sliding, falling, running, lying still, listening, peering, wondering where the hell she was, and hating. Hating the Irish for their perversity in sticking to their religion: 'What's it bloody matter, anyway?' Hating the English: 'Why don't they leave the poor fokkers alone?' Hating Mackworth: 'He loves it.' Hating her surroundings: 'Bally-bloody-houras.'

One of the Order expressions for being in trouble was 'in the briars'; for the first time that night she knew what it meant literally. Barbed arms dragged her down into them, toothed tendrils curled into her legs, her skirt. She cursed and tore her way through, less frightened now of Mackworth than of disappearing for ever into the maw of this forest.

Her thousandth – or was it two thousandth? – fall tipped her into cleared space, her hands clawing water and mud. She'd found the bank of a river. Wiping her eyes she saw the dim shape of a bridge and beyond it a steep track edged by houses. Doneraile. She was at Doneraile, two miles from home. Even then she wasn't safe. The road to Kilcolman, usually a dead place at night, was waking up to hoofbeats and the drum of marching feet. Every soldier in Munster must be out. She had to make her way back through fields and copses.

The brambles over the tunnel under the wall were still as she'd left them. On the other side the cover had not been replaced. Rosh hadn't come back.

She had no capacity left to feel worried about anything except how to cover the distance to her tower and bed. Some people wanted salvation: she wanted her bed. Spenser Castle had no sign of life as she staggered through its grounds. She reached her bed, fell onto it, and slept.

With the peevishness of a soul summoned to Hell, Barbary woke up to someone pounding the knocker of the gates. 'No,' she said, 'Oh no.' But the Devil summoned on.

She opened one eye. Light was only attempting her east window. As she squinted, her bat came fluttering back from its night's foray and hung itself resentfully in its corner. It was dawn, just. She'd had barely two hours' sleep.

She heard Nup, the Anglo-Irish ex-soldier who was now Spenser Castle's porter, gardener, odd-job man and lodged in the new gatehouse opposite hers, grumble his way to the squint, draw it back to see who was there, and begin the de-barring of the gates.

The voice which last night had ordered the charge on the Mass said: 'My duty to Master Spenser and permission to search his premises. We're after an escaped priest thought to be in this vicinity.' Captain Mackworth wasn't asking, he was demanding.

She really woke then. So the priest had got away? She stung all over. She raised her hands and saw the backs were scored back and forth with dried blood. Her dress, which she'd slept in, was good as shredded. She got up and peered into her mirror; every lock of her hair was having a stand-up fight with the others. Luckily the only other scratch on her face was the yew tree's, but if Mackworth saw her now he'd know she'd spent the night abroad. She tore off her clothes, finding new wounds.

While she re-dressed she dodged from window to window. There were a lot of soldiers with Mackworth, but the search was being held up by a night-shirted Edmund affronted at this intrusion into the dignity of his new home. Mackworth was explaining and pointing to the Ballyhouras. '. . . savages held a Mass last night . . . some damned priest from Spain . . . got away . . . apprehended some . . . dangling from the gibbets in Mallow.'

Rosh. Oh Jesus, had they got Rosh? Then, from the eastern window, she saw her. She was coming out of the hen house. Relieved, Barbary failed to notice for a moment that Rosh was acting oddly, even for someone who had been up all night attending an illegal gathering and escaping from English soldiers. Then she did. The woman was pale, understandably, but why, with the danger over, was she still so gripped with fear that she looked shiftily about? Why latch the hen house door so carefully? Why – it was out of all sense – why, now it was daylight, had she forgotten to let the hens out?

Barbary dropped her hands onto the sill and groaned. Oh, Rosh. Rosh, you roaring pillock. You perfect, mutton-headed, pestle-pated *pillock*. You got the priest in there.

She turned away and began pulling a comb through her hair. None of her concern. Rosh could stuff hen houses with a thousand patricos, it was nothing to her. He'd be found, sure as eggs, but it was his and Rosh's neck would stretch, not hers. Old Nick and ninepence to her.

She heard voices from the bawn and went back to the window. Mackworth had gone up to the house with Edmund, but one of his soldiers was searching through the cattle pens, and had hailed Rosh. And Rosh, niggle-witted heifer that she was, wasn't answering. She was still standing with her back to the hen house door as if a sudden drop of temperature had frozen her there.

'Hey, nocky,' the soldier was saying to her, 'what you got in that eaves.' He was a Londoner. Only Cockneys called a hen house an eaves.

Barbary groaned again. She was going to regret this. She leaned out of the window and twanged her old accent into shape. 'Hey, you. Mud-crusher. What you want?'

The soldier looked up at the perky red-head in the window and grinned. 'Last time I was called mud-crusher, I was home.'

'I'll mud-crush you, you go unsettling my cacklers. Stay there, I'm coming down.'

She whipped up her torn dress in case they searched her tower while she was gone, bundled it over her hands like dirty washing and ran down the stairs. The infantry-man was leaning on his pike with pleased expectancy. Rosh hadn't moved a muscle. 'What they call you, then, carrot-nob?'

'They call me *Lady* Betty,' said Barbary. 'Wife to *Sir* Robert Betty. Heard of him, have you?'

The names of the Armada heroes had been toasted by drinking Englishmen in taverns from the Low Countries to Connaught. 'Great man,' said the soldier. He winked. 'And lucky.'

Barbary winked back. 'Whitecross?'

'Next door. Golden Lane. And wondering why I left it.'

Barbary nodded. 'Know it well. Now then, what's with my cacklers?' As she spoke she wandered to a point where she could see the ground between the hen house and the wall. A pile of cattle litter covered the tunnel.

'Orders,' said the soldier. 'There's a Papist loose. Got to search every out-house and all Irish shacks, and Madam Midnight there's acting suspicious.'

'Thick as pig shit,' said Barbary, 'like all Paddies. Still and all, you're not tramping around my eaves in those clumping great excruciators. Them birds get the pip as soon as look at you.' She held out the worst of her hands to the soldier. 'And that cock in there's a tiger. Look what he done to my hand.' The soldier quailed. 'You go and look under that hay in the byre,' she continued. '*I'll* search here.' She gave him no time to object, but snapped at Rosh: 'Open that door.' Rosh came to and opened it. The soldier moved off to the byre.

Barbary stepped in and drew the door half closed behind her. As hen houses went, this one was big; the late Earl of Desmond, or whoever ran the castle for him, had obviously gone in for poultry on a large scale. The Spensers' thirty hens were lost in the wide-slatted perches which ran its twenty-foot length. She moved in semi-darkness through the farinaceous, green-yellow smell of hen turds, relieved here and there by a chink in the planking of the walls letting in the dawn. 'Chook-chook,' she said pleasantly, loud enough for the soldier to hear her. 'Chook-chook.' She was nervous. Priests were queer cattle and the thought of one lying in here somewhere, waiting, was unattractive. The hens were nervous as well, displeasedly settling feathers as if they'd been ruffled by recent disturbance. They increased their clucking, telling her it was time they were in daylight. 'Chook-chook.' She stepped backward, suppressing a whimper, as the cock flapped up from her feet to a rafter and rasped into his morning call. She'd told the truth about him. The bird was a black-hearted bugger, likely to fly at you with his talons up for your eyes. She shuffled past him. 'One move, Double-guts, and tomorrow's Christmas.'

There was something dripping, a slow, irregular drip. 'Chook-chook.' A pool with a black sheen was by her foot and as she looked, it rippled from another drip. Reluctantly, wishing she was elsewhere, she raised her head. Fingers nearly touched her nose. A human arm was acting as a drainpipe for the blood seeping down it to gather in the half-closed hand and well over onto the ground.

Priest's blood. Papist blood. She swallowed. If he was losing it at this rate he wouldn't be a priest much longer, he'd be dead. She stepped onto the lower perch and raised herself up to get a glimpse of the face turned towards her. It was white and unconscious. And it wasn't the priest's.

Barbary looked at it for some time. 'Chook-' she said to it slowly, 'chook.'

She turned and went briskly to the door, opened it wide and began ushering the hens out. Rosh gave her a glance, but Barbary ignored it. Double-guts erupted into the sunlight, handsome and wicked, with the hens stepping bandily after him. She left the door open.

Over the byre the soldier glanced nervously up at Double-guts who'd landed on its roof to crow. 'Nothing?'

'Nothing. You?'

'Nah. Roast-a-stone, this is. He's in some paddy hut somewhere. But the Captain'll get the shifter, rest on that. The Captain hates priests worse'n MacSheehys.'

She stretched. 'Better see to his breakfast then. Wouldn't say no to some inner lining yourself, would you?'

'Lady,' said the soldier warmly, 'you're a prize. My belly thinks me throat's cut.'

Barbary nodded and shoved Rosh forward. 'The kitchen, masterpiece,' she told her, 'and see if you can get a proper English breakfast for a proper English gentleman.'

As Rosh stumbled past the soldier he dragged at her arm. 'Say "thump".'

'They can't,' said Barbary involuntarily. 'The sound's not in their language.'

'I like hearing 'em try. Come on, masterpiece. "Thhhump." '

'Tump,' said Rosh.

Barbary's hands, wrapped in her dress, inflicted more damage on it. She winked at the soldier as Rosh made her getaway. 'Hopeless,' she said. 'But her black pudding's near as good as Mother Bunch's.'

'Mother Bunch's,' said the soldier with longing. They walked up to the house together, swapping memories of London. Barbary heard him report to Mackworth that the bawn had been checked and was clear. She caught up with Rosh in the smoke house, where the Irishwoman was trying to lift a flitch of bacon off a hook with hands weak from trembling. Barbary helped her. Her own hands shook, but she was invigorated by her conying. Beautiful it had been. Like the face in the hen house.

Rosh dropped the flitch to the floor and collapsed onto it. 'For what did you do it?'

'They'd have trined you else.' She jerked an invisible rope round her neck. 'And him. Come on, we must hurry.'

'Who is he?'

Barbary stopped to stare at her. 'Don't you know?'

Rosh shook her head. 'He was a stranger. He came with the priest. When we ran, he held back and fought two of them to keep them off. But he's terrible wounded. He was asking for you, and the English were everywhere so we brought him here. And anyway, didn't the feller save my life?'

Barbary nodded slowly. 'He saved mine once. His name's O'Hagan.' She shook herself. 'And he's dying. The moment the coast's clear, get down to that bawn and stem the bleeding. Got any stuff for it?'

'Bog moss,' said Rosh, 'We use bog moss to stop putrefying.'

'Gawd help us. Well, it'll have to do. After dark we'll move him. Get him away from here.'

'He's broken his ankle. He was too big for the tunnel and he had to climb the wall. He fainted and fell off.'

'Jesus.' This was sheer Irish carelessness. 'We'll get him to my tower then. That's nearest. And burn this.' She passed over her poor dress. 'Now, for Chrissake, move.'

'Well, I hope you get him, Humfrey,' Edmund was saying. 'Nevertheless, these Popish priests are willing to come out of Spain by dangerous travel here where they know peril of death awaits them and no reward or riches are to be found, and this only to draw the people to the Church of Rome.' He was on his hobby-horse, emboldened by sitting at the head of his long oak board offering hospitality. 'Whereas our idle ministers like Prebendary Chadwick have the living of the country open to them, no pain, no peril, but do nothing for God's harvest. Prebendary Chadwick nestles by his mistress's side . . .'

Captain Mackworth stuck his knife into a fat piece of bacon. 'Prebendary Chadwick is nevertheless a Christian, Edmund.'

Shut your pipes, screamed Barbary's nerves at the two of them. And you, you belly-swagging bastard footwobbler, will you get out of here?

Aloud she said: 'More ham, Captain? It is our own sweet-cured.' With Maccabee merely a depressed presence at the table, she had to be hostess.

Mackworth took more ham, more ale, more everything. 'When do you start rebuilding the Hap Hazard estate, ma'am?' The question was aggressive. Mackworth rejoiced in not being a lady's man, which meant that most of the time he ignored women, and verged on the insulting when he didn't.

Edmund said: 'We are fortunate that Lady Betty is delaying her project and looking after us during my wife's indisposition.'

'Fortunate indeed,' sneered Mackworth.

Swipe me, Barbary realised, he thinks Edmund and me are doing the naughty. You dog-bolt, you Nebuchadnezzar. If there was a thousand priests hidden round this house I wouldn't hand them to you. It struck her that Mackworth's suspicion was fortunate. The man's dog nose had sniffed out something wrong in the house. He wasn't dragging out the breakfast through greed but because his animal instinct told him that Barbary had something to hide. He'd been looking at her squint-eyed ever since she'd sat down. She calmed herself. Better for him to think she was niggling that dandiprat Edmund than guess the truth.

At long last she stood at the gateway and mouthed goodbyes and good lucks in their hunt to him and his soldiers, and turned away as they cantered out of sight – to endure the longest day of her life. Nothing could be done for the body in the hen house in daylight, except to ensure that nobody found it. Every minute was another drop of blood out of his body. Occasion after occasion she and Rosh tried to snatch a word together, and every blessed time somebody or something intervened to prevent it. She saw Rosh put the hens away towards evening, but even then it wasn't until after household prayers that the Irishwoman, passing close to Barbary on her way to bed, hissed: 'Stopped the bleeding,' and Barbary hissed back: 'When all's quiet.'

Edmund and Maccabee slept at the back of the house, overlooking the crescent-shaped lake. Bedrooms for guests – of whom, thank God, there were none – were at the front, overlooking the gatehouses and the bawn, but so did the children's rooms, and the servants' attics. As Barbary slunk down the steps from her tower and into the gardens, it was like entering a stage lit by the moon's chandelier. The yew tree walk that Edmund had planted in the hope that it would one day rival Penshurst's was a pathetic waist-high frill which emphasised, rather than concealed, to the watching windows that overlooked it, her progress along it.

It was a relief to get through the gate to the bawn and be hidden by its walls. Rosh was waiting for her. They didn't speak. The hens put up a squawking when they went in, but settled down when they smelled who was disturbing them. The body hadn't moved. 'Is he dead?' But if it was dead, it still retained warmth.

They pushed and pulled at it, until it flopped onto Rosh's shoulders, and then flopped to the floor as the Irishwoman gave way under its weight. With no room to go two abreast, they took one end each and staggered with it between the shelves until they were outside, but even that short distance brought home the knowledge that they could not carry it all the way to the gatehouse.

'What'll we do?'

'We'll have to drag him. One arm each.'

'But his poor leg.'

'It's his poor leg or his poor neck. And our poor necks for that matter. Get that bloody arm and drag.'

She had to blot out what pain and damage they were inflicting on the man, blot out that he was a man at all. Think of him as an object, bumping along behind them. It wasn't easy when she noticed that the object was

272

leaving a trail of blood behind it. Nor when it started to moan in full sight and hearing of the manor's windows.

Getting the body up the outside steps to the gatehouse took a quarter of an hour, and twice as long up the narrow, twisting staircase to Barbary's top room. By the time they'd stretched it, twisted it, and got it onto Barbary's bed, they were half dead themselves. They slumped down onto the floor and closed their eyes.

'He'll not survive this.'

'Sod him.'

For four days the body on Barbary's bed had the depersonalised demands of a baby's. She and Rosh washed it and kept it warm; when it could swallow they stuffed milk into it at one end and cleaned up the results from the other. The wound had been caused by a sword thrust through the right ribs; it seemed to have pierced none of the vital organs and, incredibly, Rosh's dreadful bog moss was keeping it clean. The ankle was blue and swollen, and would take a good six weeks to mend if the body could make up enough of its lost blood to live at all.

'Will it?' asked Barbary. 'He's horrible white.'

Rosh shrugged. 'The apple will fall on the head that's under it.' Her proverbs had returned with the recovery of her nerve.

'Is that good or bad?'

'Ach, there's always hope. All's not lost that's in the floodmark.'

They cut his hair and shaved off his beard because Rosh said they sapped strength, leaving the pallid, suffering face more vulnerable than ever.

Barbary had never had a human being physically dependent on her before. Come to that, she'd not been acquainted with male nudity before; Rob equated undress with degradation and anyway preferred copulation in the dark. The body of the man in her bed was an anatomy lesson in long muscles, bones and interesting bits, a relief map of masculinity. Rosh unashamedly thought it beautiful. 'He's a grand-looking fellow, so he is,' she said.

'Is he?'

Rosh rolled her eyes. 'Don't pretend you've not noticed. I'd not mind if it was my bed he was in.'

'I wish it was.'

Her compassion was for the body's helplessness rather than its beauty, and compassion was something she wasn't used to and would much rather be without. It worried her by day as she went about her duties at the house. By night it entered the uncomfortable sleep she took on a makeshift bed on the floor. One night Captain Mackworth climbed through the window to get at the body on the bed and she jerked awake to protect it. In the sweating, panting moment of realisation after the nightmare, she had to raise a rushlight to see that her patient was still there. There was no comfort in the fact that he was, remote and defenceless as ever. She'd never felt so lonely, so terrified for another human soul. Mothers of babies must feel like this. 'But I'm not your bloody mother,' she told the figure on the bed. She resented the unwanted commitment. 'You're nothing to me, you bald-rib.'

Neither was the hunted priest anything to her, but she grieved when Captain Mackworth caught him.

Her fear wasn't helped by Edmund's account of the priest's execution at Mallow. Mackworth had broken the man's legs and arms and kept him three days without water before allowing the law to administer what was by then almost the mercy of hanging, drawing and quartering.

'I'm sorry,' she said to Rosh when the Irishwoman slipped over, as she did every night, with food and fresh bog moss.

Rosh didn't answer. 'There'll be a frost tonight,' she said. 'I've brought some kindling for the brazier. Himself will need to keep warm.'

Just before she went out, she turned. 'Be sorry for the good Captain,' she said.

Barbary lit the brazier. The air coming through the arrow slit had a nip in it already. She had pushed the bed under the slit so that in leaning over it she was hidden from the window. Nup's easterly window was on exactly the same level as her westerly one; she didn't want him or his wife looking across the intervening space and wondering why she was spooning food into what should have been a bare pillow. Although all the windows, except the arrow slit, were glazed, the gatehouse had no shutters.

Only that morning Edmund had offered to rectify the omission and send up a workman to install them and she'd been hard put to find a reason that would satisfy him as to why he shouldn't. In the end she'd said she wouldn't use them anyway. 'Don't like being under hatches.' It had been one in a relentless and wearing series of difficulties. 'You don't half give me trouble,' she said to the body on the bed as she got into her night smock and brushed her hair. She warmed the liquid mess Rosh had prepared for the patient, raised his head and began feeding him. He was swallowing better.

She stopped. His eyes had opened and were staring up at her in puzzlement. She'd got so used to his being insensible it was a shock.

'Hello,' she said.

He frowned, and then relaxed. 'Wine,' he said, and went to sleep.

Next morning in the kitchen as she helped with the autumn salting, she whispered to Rosh: 'He's better. He asked for wine.'

Rosh was pleased. 'And isn't that typical of the nobility? Wine he says. How are we to get wine, I'd like to know.' Edmund's steward had the key to the cellar and ensured it was kept for special occasions.

'I'll steal some.' The indication that her patient was recovering had energised Barbary; she could have stolen diamonds out of the royal crown.

'Why not just ask for it?'

Barbary stared. 'Ask for it?' She played with the novel idea, exploring possibilities, and went to find Edmund. She bumped into him on his way to the kitchens. 'I've been thinking, Edmund,' she said, 'that I should begin educating myself. Would you lend me a book I could read?'

He was delighted. 'My dear cousin, I have just the thing to enlarge the enquiring mind.'

'And Edmund, would it be possible for me to have a flask of wine? It would warm my blood while I tackle the words.'

Within minutes she was equipped with a book – she noticed it was one of Edmund's own works – and permission to ask the steward for wine.

'Now what was it I was doing?' Edmund tapped his

275

forehead. 'Ah yes. Cousin, would you be good enough on your return to the kitchen to tell Abby that there will be a guest for dinner. Captain Mackworth honours us again.'

'What for?'

The poet blinked. 'He is engaged on another search. You may not remember, but in the hunt for the priest two of our soldiers were killed by a wood kern. The Captain is not one to overlook the death of his men. He's despatched the priest, he wants the kern. He believes him to be injured and still in the neighbourhood.' As Barbary turned away, Edmund added: 'There will be no need to feed the soldiers this time, cousin. Hospitality to the Captain is quite enough; we cannot extend it to the whole army.'

Would they search the gatehouse? What excuse could she give for refusing her permission? Could she refuse? Would they search anyway? Get him away before they came?

She answered the last question as she asked it. She couldn't. Remembering how hideous transferring him from the hen house had been, she dare not subject him to that again just as he was recovering.

She gave the message to Abby, and found that Rosh had gone out to the orchard to pick the last of the apples. She joined her under the trees and gabbled out her news. To her amazement, the Irishwoman remained calm. 'There's no need to go to the Sceiligs if you smile till next Shrove.'

Barbary shook her. 'What the hell does that mean?'

'It means wait and see. The Captain may not come.'

'Of course he'll come. You can bet on the bastard.'

'I wouldn't. *Beidh lá eile ag an baorach.* He may not come.'

And he didn't. The day took a year off Barbary's life, but by the end of it Captain Mackworth had not arrived. Some of his soldiers called in just before dark; they didn't search for the wood kern, being too busy searching the woods for the Captain himself. He had entered them with a small patrol and disappeared.

As she took herself slowly to the gatehouse for the night, Barbary mulled over Rosh's '*Beidh lá eile ag an baorach*'. It meant: 'The underdog will have his day', and she didn't like the sound of it.

The body on the bed was still asleep, but the unconsciousness was not so comatose. He woke up as she fed him, swallowing obediently but wanting to go back to sleep. She wished *she* could, but she must stay awake in case Captain Mackworth turned up after all. She got out Edmund's book and sat down close to the brazier with it. 'The Shepheardes Calendar,' she read, 'by Edmund Spenser. January. Aegloga Prima (what the hell's that?). "A shepheardes boy, no better do him call/When Winters wastful spight was almost spent,/All in a sunneshine day, as did befall,/Led forth his flock that had bene long spent . . ." '

'Wine,' said the body on the bed.

Barbary reached for the wine flask, but a movement of her patient's head stopped her. 'The colour of your hair,' he said. 'Been worrying me. Not just red. Wine in it.' He was asleep again.

Barbary shook him. 'Come back. There's more to worry about than the colour of my bloody hair.' Just for that moment, O'Hagan, and not an insensible figure, had been in the room, his voice familiar and her loneliness gone. 'Come back, you.' It was useless. Saying that much had used up what energy he had. She pulled the covers closer about his neck, and went to the mirror. It was true, her hair was darkening as she was getting older. Refracted now against the firelight, it still looked appallingly red, and it still made passers-by look at her twice, but perhaps there was some new shade . . . She preened at her reflection. 'Wine,' she said.

277

Chapter Thirteen

He was not an easy convalescent. He might have been brave fighting Mackworth's soldiers, but on the first day of his recovery he showed he was a coward about having his wound dressed and taking the blood-humouring medicine Rosh compounded for him out of raw liver and herbs. On the second day he asked for his sword, his clothes and a horse to get him away from this damned place. By the time Rosh and Barbary had told him to hush, that his requests were impossible and that he couldn't get away from this place, damned as it might be, he'd fallen asleep once more.

On the third day the fuss he made about Barbary having to carry his chamber pot out to the midden for emptying turned into a full-scale quarrel. 'I'll not be shamed in this manner. Let the woman do it.'

'Her name,' said Barbary, 'is Rosh. And why's it less shaming to have her do it, may I ask?'

'She's a servant. It's a job for the lower orders.'

Barbary was infuriated. 'She risked trining for you, Lord Muck and Muck. Lower orders, indeed. I was lower orders than she is, and even I reckon I'm a cut above an ungrateful Irish traitor.'

'Traitor? You call me a traitor?' He pulled himself up and swung his feet over the bed. 'I'm out of this hole.' She saw him wince as his bad ankle felt his weight, but on one foot he stood up and steadied himself by a hand on a rafter. He was very tall. She watched him sway and knew the room was circling round him. She poked a finger in his chest and he fell back on the bed.

'See?' she said, picked up the chamber pot and stumped out.

When she got back he was sulking with his face to the wall. 'I should have let you freeze, you damned Saxon.'

'You're only here because you didn't. For that matter, why are you here?' But he was sleeping like a log. She studied his face. Where was that concern which had saved her life in the Wicklow hut? Not in this man, for sure, with his thin cheeks and peevish disposition. Rosh, whom he patronised, constantly made excuses for him: 'Don't blame the lad. It's a terrible thing for a lord of the hills like him to be crippled in a tiny room at the mercy of women.'

And Barbary had answered: 'He could have been cooped in Mallow Castle at the mercy of the executioner if it hadn't been for women.' He'd certainly shown courage, fighting to defend the priest. But with only inglorious women to display it to, his courage had gone. 'You pull yourself together,' she said to her sleeping patient.

She spent that night on the floor by his bed but made plans to move down to the room below next day for decency's sake. It was bad enough if she was discovered to be harbouring a traitor; she needn't have it thought she'd slept with one as well. Each flight of the gatehouse's staircase had its own door which could be bolted, so no visitors could come on her unawares and wonder why she was now on the third storey rather than the fourth. She'd ask Edmund for some more furniture. Take that old settle out of the barn and at nights make up her bed on it. That's what she'd do.

The next morning he was improved in health and somewhat improved in manners. 'I am grateful,' he said, stiffly. 'Send the woman to me and I'll thank her too.'

'Her name,' hissed Barbary, 'is Rosh. And she's got better things to do than run every time you lift a finger.'

'Indeed she has. She could cook me some decent food for a start. I'm hungry.'

She cut through the arrogance. 'What are you doing here, O'Hagan?'

He shuffled himself into a sitting position, wincing pitifully. 'Being uncomfortable.' Sighing, Barbary put another pillow behind his back. He settled himself and said: 'Actually, in part I was looking for you. We were hoping to persuade you to procure us some guns.'

'Who's we?'

'The O'Neill, the O'Donnell and myself.'

'So you don't think I'm an English spy any more?'

'The O'Neill says you are not, that you are Barbary O'Flaherty who fell into Saxon hands as a child and managed to survive by trickery and theft. I fear we cannot convince Granuaile O'Malley of that, however. She still thinks you're an imposter.'

'And what does O'Donnell think?'

'The O'Donnell never thinks. He acts. An impulsive man, the O'Donnell.'

'And what do you think?'

'In view of the fact that you are saving my life, I am forced to believe the O'Neill.' He closed his eyes for a moment. He was getting tired again. 'What about those guns?'

They had a cheek, coming here, demanding guns, putting her to unbelievable inconvenience, not to mention danger, them and their careless assumptions. 'Well, damn your impudence. You and O'Neill *and* your O'Donnell. I'm married now. I'm a respectable married woman.' It wasn't much of a marriage, but no Irish Tom, Dick or Harry was going to get her to abandon it for the asking. 'I love my husband. Dearly. He's a hero of the Armada Battle. Knighted by Admiral Howard. Rewarded by the Queen. Personally. Why the hell do you think I'd help his enemies? Even if I could. Which I can't.'

'Ach, I told the O'Neill it would be a waste of time.' He looked as if finding that it was had grim satisfaction for him. 'But he insisted I give you a message.'

'What?'

O'Hagan closed his eyes again. 'He said: "I told her once that she would make a wrong choice. It may be that she has made one. Now it may be that she would want to make another." '

So they'd sat there, these Irishmen, and discussed her marriage. How dare they. How *dare* they. How did O'Neill know it had been a mistake? Cuckold Dick. He'd told him. Or perhaps Dick had just said that he'd been dismissed from Rob's employment, and O'Neill had drawn the inference, like the damned inference-drawer he was.

She said slowly, with careful enunciation, 'You can go back to your O'Neill and you can tell him he's mistaken. And you can tell him I wouldn't get guns for a quake-buttocked, rabbit-sucking bastard like him if I was told

280

to by the Angel Gabriel. And you can tell him to stop his arse with *that* oyster.'

She slammed out.

O'Hagan regarded the ceiling. 'O'Neill,' he said to it, 'it appears you are a quake-buttocked bastard.' He smiled. 'But you're not as wrong as I thought you were.'

The door crashed open. A puce-faced red-head said: 'And that goes for you and all.' The door crashed to.

She stayed furious all morning, refusing to find an excuse to go back to the gatehouse with provisions. How dare they try and drag her in. She might be Irish-born, she might be miserable in her marriage, but that didn't put her in their camp. She didn't belong to them.

By afternoon her anger was fading and the old question came back: Where *did* she belong? With Rob and his pretensions? With Spensers, Mackworths and Raleighs? Could she return to being an unquestioning English patriot now that she'd viewed England from Ireland? No. From here the Irish Sea leached out glory and glitter and left England's crown resting on the skull of a conqueror.

She thought bitterly that if she belonged anywhere it was in the universal sub-class of Rosh and Cuckold Dick and the Order, even with the dreadful MacSheehys, the bottom-of-the-heap people who had to squirm and steal and lie and kill to avoid complete obliteration. And she'd been torn away from even that to be put in a no man's land all her own.

'You don't play with me any more,' complained Catherine. 'You're not there all the time.'

'I'm not, am I? All right, we'll go nutting.'

'When?'

'Now. We'll go and tell your ma.'

It was true she had been neglecting the children, though it wasn't due only to the secret in her gatehouse. Autumn had brought so much to do with its gathering, slaughtering, preserving and pickling. Edmund had insisted on all the customs of an English harvest so that she had also been initiated into the mystery of corn-dolly making, while in the fields mystified Irish labourers had been taught by English labourers to sing: 'Well a-cut. Well a-bound./Well a-zot upon the ground./We-ha-neck! We-ha-neck! Hurrah! Hurrah! Hurrah!' to the last sheaf brought home.

The house was still full of workmen as Edmund read-
ied it for the social occasions he would hold in it during
the winter months. It was very much a provincial manor,
but linenfold panelling was being installed in the hall and
a tapestry had been ordered from Flanders.

As luxury grew up around Maccabee, making a buffer
between her and the namelesses in the woods, she grew
more confident. With Barbary so busy she had been
forced to take on more responsibility for Sylvestris and
that it was doing her good showed in the way she was
beginning to agitate. 'If Edmund intends to hold a ball
and the Norrises and the St Legers come, we must learn
the new steps, though where we are to find a dancing
master . . . Oh, my soul, you don't dance at *all*? I shall
begin to teach you this very evening.'

'Tomorrow, Maccy.'

Catherine and Barbary strapped panniers onto pony
Spenser and, hand in hand, ambled over the north stub-
bled fields where geese were feeding. As if to make up for
the gales of spring and summer, the weather had become
luxuriant, the nip at nights colouring leaves so that in the
warmth of day the woods were peppered in saffrons and
russets which enhanced the slanting light. Among the
hazel trees the usual nut-gatherers' obsession gripped the
two of them. It was hypnotic to brush away the thin grass
and find brown-shaded nuts in their frilled cases.

'It's like hunting for treasure, isn't it?'

'Better. You can't eat treasure.' The Order should hear
her now.

They half filled the panniers. 'Shall we try for some
chestnuts?'

Barbary squinted at the sky; there was still an hour or
more of good light left. 'We won't go too far in.' They
moved deeper to where the sweet-chestnut trees formed
natural glades with their transparent, finger-spaced leaves
high up on the tall trunks. A disturbed red squirrel
flowed away through the branches. They were too early.
There were hundreds of clusters on the ground but few of
them had split open. They hadn't brought gloves so they
competed in kicking the hedgehog-spiked balls off their
shoes into the baskets.

'There's a lot of crows about today,' said Catherine.

Barbary raised her head. There were. 'Catherine. We'd

better go home.' She said it gently, trying to keep her breathing under control. She stood up straight and walked towards the girl. The child mustn't look behind her. God, don't let her look behind her. 'We must go home now,' she said again. She reached Catherine and put a hand on her neck and guided her gently to the edge of the glade. 'You run on and unhitch the pony. Run fast. I'll catch you.'

She watched the child out of sight and, unwillingly, turned back. She couldn't have seen what she had seen. It might be a scarecrow against the tree.

Captain Mackworth's round face grinned at her and winked a reassuring eye. They'd left the head intact so that he could be recognised. The rest of him had been flayed. The only skin on the body hung in flaps or formed white worms that clung against the raw, bulging flesh. Where his private parts had been was dried blood, turned blacker by massing flies. Given confidence by her stillness, two crows left the circling flock and landed on the scarecrow's shoulders.

She turned and walked quietly away. Out of the glade she began to run. She snatched Catherine's hand and, with Spenser bouncing his panniers behind them, ran until they had nothing above them but sky, away from leaves which dappled the sun onto monstrosities.

'Did you tell anybody?' asked O'Hagan.

'Of course I told somebody. Think I was going to leave it there for some other child to find? Or Maccabee? I told Edmund. And he's ridden into Mallow to tell Norris and the garrison.'

She'd had to guide Edmund to the glade so that he could see for himself; but she hadn't gone any further. She'd heard him scream and call on his God. She had recovered some of her wits by then. Yes, she thought, barbarians did this. But only days ago you stood in Mallow's marketplace and watched another man being cut to pieces. Did you scream then?

And now O'Hagan, who had grieved for the death of the priest when she'd told him about it, was as unmoved by the soldier's death as Edmund had been by the priest's.

He was biting his lip. 'There'll be reprisals.'

'Yes, there'll be reprisals,' she snarled at him. 'That's what you all want, isn't it? It's a game. You split that man open, I'll skin this one.'

She was shaking. She tried to pour herself some wine, but slopped it. She'd prided herself on having a strong stomach, but this atrocious tit-for-tat was proving too much for it.

He snarled back, 'If it's a game, we didn't want to play. And it's *our* bloody ground. That's MacSheehy land out there, not Spenser's. For hundreds of years MacSheehy land. They hunted it, fished it, farmed it. Where Spensers and Norrises and St Legers will sit by their fires this winter, MacSheehys sat not long ago. By what right did you take it from them?'

She still wanted somebody to pay for the body on the tree, and there was only him. 'Edmund says it's your own bloody fault. If you Irish had banded into a nation instead of fighting each other . . . you needed to be civilised.'

'And our laws to be changed, and our hair to be cut, and our language to be taken away and our religion to be banned. Showing us what a lovely faith Protestantism is by hanging and burning us for not believing in it. Sure, you Saxons have done us a favour.'

She said sullenly: 'Savages.'

They fell silent. They had exhausted themselves blaming each other for what neither was responsible. She tried again for the wine and this time managed to pour straight. She gulped it down and sat huddling the beaker in her two hands.

He said more quietly: 'Maybe the MacSheehys were never people you'd want to take home to mother. But they weren't savages. The English have made them that.'

She wanted to go down to her bed, but she was reluctant to face the dark. She heard him say: 'But I'm sorry you had to see it.'

She looked up at him suspiciously.

'Edmund Spenser is right,' he said. 'We were ripe for conquering. Why we couldn't be left to kill each other in peace I'll never know, but for sure we were tribes, not a country. Even the poor Desmond fought only for Munster. But O'Neill now.' He eyed her. 'The O'Neill is something new. For all his faults, your man could make Ireland a nation.'

She had been right to be suspicious. He was merely being reasonable in order to peddle O'Neill to her.

She said: 'Are you going to talk all night?'

He lost his temper again. 'Are you going to get us those guns?'

'After *today*?' She couldn't believe him. 'I wouldn't trust any of you buggers, Irish or English, with so much as a sodding hatpin.'

The manner of Captain Mackworth's death as much as the death itself caused terror among the undertakers. They were inured to living with apprehension, to watching out for themselves and their stock when they heard the screeches from the forest, to going armed, sensing when the MacSheehys had retired to their fast-nesses in the hills and when they were on the prowl. It was the background against which they lived and the price they were prepared to pay for colonising the Golden Vale of Munster. But the scraps of flesh and bone tied to a tree was a reminder that the price could go higher.

Not for the first time they wrote to their Queen in England expressing their fear and demanding better military protection. As always, nothing came of it.

Watching an enraged garrison march out from Mallow Castle on the punitive expedition to put paid to the MacSheehys once and for all, they didn't know whether to cheer it on or demand that it stayed put to protect them from further outrages.

Edmund Spenser was particularly exposed. Had the MacSheehys killed the Captain because he'd been zealous in hunting down them and their priest? Or had they put him to death in remembrance of the six hundred men he'd slaughtered at Smerwick? If it had been a reprisal for Smerwick, then Sir Walter Raleigh was another man in danger, and so was Edmund who, while he had not taken part in the actual massacre, had stood by while it was done and publicly defended the Lord Deputy who'd ordered it.

Pale and worried, he justified it again over the dinner table in conversation with Ellis who, like many of the outlying undertakers, had decided to evacuate his land

285

for the period of the emergency and move into his neighbour's more defensible manor. 'Back home they called Lord Grey a bloody man for ordering it, and said he regarded the lives of Her Majesty's Irish subjects no more than dogs'.'

Ellis belched. ''S what they are.'

Edmund Spenser's eyes were fixed. 'In the famine the Irish came creeping out of the woods and glens on their hands because their legs wouldn't support them. Anatomies of death, crying like ghosts from the grave, falling on carrion if they could find it. If they found a plot of watercress or shamrock they flocked to it as on a feast until they couldn't eat it any more. In a short time there were almost none of them left and the country was empty of man or beast.'

''S only way,' said Ellis, his thick hands ripping the leg off another capon. 'Teach 'em. Cruel to be kind. Make a short end of it. 'S only way.'

Edmund's eyes refocused. 'Oh yes,' he said, 'it's the only way.' The ghosts the poet had raised were still in the room; Barbary watched wraiths against the new linenfold panelling stare at the loaded table; she saw Edmund re-seeing them and crying for them and being prepared in another part of his complicated soul to see them starve again.

'Only good Irishman a dead Irishman,' said Ellis.

'The only way,' said Edmund Spenser.

Having Ellis in the house was the worst part of the emergency as far as Barbary was concerned. The man's presence was ubiquitous, loud, hectoring, inquisitive. She had to walk him round the estate so that he could see how and where the crops and cattle were being disposed. As they neared her gatehouse, he expected to be invited in. 'What's up there then?'

'My apartments,' said Barbary. 'My *private* apartments.'

He passed on reluctantly. 'Done well for yourself.'

The man was unlikeable and unliked, but he could boast of friendship with families like the Norrises and St Legers and it looked increasingly probable that he would soon be Mayor of Mallow. It wasn't so much that he had bridged the class divide of Munster society as assaulted it, and it gave way to him not only because he was becoming increasingly rich, but also because he voiced his uninhibited hatred and contempt for the Irish as patriotism and he wrong-footed anybody who might have had a more liberal view into the camp of those who were 'soft' on England's true enemy. 'Give the buggers an inch and they'll rebel again,' he kept saying. 'We must keep our foot on their necks.' And the killing of Captain Mackworth had silenced the soft and raised Ellis to the status of prophet.

'That's the potato field,' said Barbary.

'You don't eat them foreign things,' said Ellis, more as a statement than a question. 'Only fit for the Irish, them.' Sir Walter's strange tuber from the New World had grown successfully on his Youghal estate and was gradually spreading through Munster, though mainly among the mere Irish. Its value to them was the ease of growing it. With no livestock and few tools of their own, they could dig two parallel ditches, throwing the excavated earth into the middle with manure and have a self-draining bed that needed little more attention. Half an acre, even of poor soil – and usually poor soil was what they had – could support an entire family for a year. The potato didn't need threshing or grinding. To cook it only needed a pot and a peat fire.

'Lazy-bed farming,' scoffed Ellis, 'that's what I call it. Suits lazy Irish. They're all growing it in their plots, lazy bastards.'

'Don't give them time to grow much else, do you?' retorted Barbary. It was well known that Ellis's terms of employment for his Irish serfs bordered on slavery.

'That I don't,' grinned Ellis. 'Lash the buggers into being busy. Keeps their minds off rebellion. Potatoes is good enough for them. They don't need civilised food. Ellis knows.'

By the time they'd finished the tour, Barbary was having a pleasant fantasy in which she procured a cannon from Will, and blew Ellis up with it. The crudity with which he and the other undertakers expressed their hatred and fear for the Irish sent her up to her gatehouse at nights prepared to sympathise with the man who was imprisoned in it. But within minutes sympathy went. His rudeness exasperated her into defending the indefensible. She couldn't think what was the matter with the man, but his bad temper was infectious and they had fallen into a rut of mutual recrimination.

Tonight she found him reading Edmund's 'Shepheardes Calendar'. He flung it to the end of the bed as she came in. 'I'm in no mood for English pastorals. Get me some Greek. Get me the *Iliad*, for God's sake.'

'I'll get you the back of my hand,' she told him. She put down the food she'd brought and picked up the book, smoothing out its pages. 'He's a great poet, Edmund. Everybody says so. Who are you to chuck him about?'

'An English poet is a contradiction in terms,' he said. 'Is that his wife who goes to pick herbs every morning?'

'Yes.'

He nodded. 'She reminds me of a little hedgehog I had once,' he said, and looked sideways at her, 'though it lacked the moustache.'

He was trying to bait her, but she'd taken in a greater enormity. 'Jesus, have you been looking out of the window?'

'What else is there to do?'

'What else . . . You careless bastard, do you know what could happen to me if you're seen here?' In her panic she clutched her hair.

She heard him say: 'I'd not let anything happen to you,' and for the first time the voice was the voice she'd heard in the Wicklow hut, but when she pushed back her hair to look at him he was gnawing on a piece of chicken and complaining, 'Not enough salt.'

She took a deep breath; if he wasn't going to break out of this quarrelling mode they'd got locked into, she'd have to. 'Look, O'Hagan,' she said reasonably, 'you want to be out of here and, believe me, I want you out of here. But Rosh risked her life and I risked my life and my reputation getting you up here. It'll be as big a risk getting you down, but with one of your stamps . . . feet . . . not working, the risk gets extra. We need the dice loaded in our favour when we go, and I'm not making a move until they are. Is that fair?'

There was an alteration in his face, almost a defeat, as if he'd given way to an inevitability. She'd breached a wall, but there was something in the look of him now which made her uneasily aware that in doing it she'd freed him of irritation and released something more forceful.

'And when will my stamp be better?' He seemed amused.

'Another week or so, Rosh says.'

He said: 'It's not been easy. I've begun talking to the bat.'

She smiled. 'I've talked to it a bit myself.'

'Ah, but the damned thing's begun to talk back.'

'And what does it say?'

'Not to look out of the window.'

She'd won. 'Good. Then let's get that wound dressed.' She knew the contours of the wound like a general knows his battleground, she had watched it diminish like a beaten enemy but tonight, for the first time, she was uncomfortable with it, self-conscious when she put her arms round him to pass the bandage across his back, aware of his skin and the line of his breastbone where it made a dip beneath his throat, wishing he was complaining like he usually did instead of watching her.

He said: 'About your reputation. If they catch me I'm prepared to go to the gallows swearing you are not my type.'

'Thank you very much. And what is your type, may I ask?'

'Oh, soft, dark-haired, compliant, fragile women, grateful to me for noticing them. Not women with hair like a toasted carrot.'

'Good then.' The bandage had to be passed round his back twice. She felt giddy.

'I like tall, rounded women with poetry in their souls. Graceful women. Not bossy women who swear like a docker.' The words were getting softer and moving the muscles of his throat. 'Not women who are short and skinny with crafty eyes. Not Saxon tricksters with hearts like lions and freckles on their noses who save a man's life at the risk of their own.'

She fumbled the tying of the bandage. His eyes were on hers; he had dark lashes and stubble was growing on the pale skin of his jaw and if he went on like this she would be past help. She managed the knot and sat back. 'That's good then,' she said again. She got up, wondering if her legs would carry her to the door. They did. Just.

289

His voice reached her as she lifted the latch. 'And if the pleasure of caring for me has worn thin from time to time, it's because being in the company of a woman like that is very trying to a man in bed.'

She went out, shut the door behind her and leaned against it, trying to clear her head of murmured negatives that wafted through it like the far-off chant of sirens. They wove her to the door so that she had to pull herself away from it to descend the steps. 'God damn the man.' They wooed her off the hard bed of the settle to sit at the window where they joined the night sounds in the moonlight. 'God damn him to Hell.'

He wanted her as she was, Barbary Clampett, not as Rob had wanted some totally different woman. Him and his damned words that made you throb to get close to him.

The words wreathed themselves round the fidelity in her soul to undermine it, like ivy creeping into mortar. But fidelity was strong, not to Rob, her husband, though it encompassed him as part of the upbringing where loyalty was the only moral principle that mattered, and betrayal the only crime. That it would be adultery was unimportant, but by committing it she would be abandoning the part of England that mattered to her. The body of that man upstairs was its enemy, Rob's enemy; it was dangerous, it was Ireland. It was the only sin that mattered, defection.

In the morning she dragged Rosh out of the kitchen to the orchard. 'You give him his feed tonight,' she said. 'I'm done with him and his insults.'

Rosh was not deceived. 'Will you stop knauvshaling the poor man and get into his bed where you belong. And him struggling for his honour not to want you there.'

Barbary stiffened: 'Who's this Honour?'

'Ach, it's a code the nobility has. You're his hostess, and married, and he thinks you love your husband and is as blind as the bat on the roofbeam.'

She said automatically, 'I do love my husband. Dearly.'

Rosh shrugged. 'Sure, we all love our husbands, but that's no reason for denying a launchy man like that, nor it is.'

'You're disgusting.'

'And you're forgetful. Isn't it today we're going to the fair?'

She had forgotten. She'd been looking forward to the Mallow Autumn Fair. The Spensers, including Catherine and herself, were going to spend the night at an inn in the town so that Edmund and Ellis could have a clear day to look over the horses and cattle they wanted to buy. Edmund, being an indulgent employer, had given permission for most of the house servants and some of the outdoor staff to accompany them.

In her memory, fairs were an amalgam of wonders and danger. Fake mermaids, dancing bears, jugglers, fire-eaters, sweatmeat stalls, conies by the hundred asking to be conied. Faces as familiar to her as her own which must be passed without a flicker of recognition on either side; Jackman in his persona as Dr Cabal, the quacksalver, shouting his cure-alls in Latin to attract the serious punters, the bawds in all their splendour with Cuckold Dick lurking in the background, the Upright Man bleeding from every disgusting pore. The thread of rogues to which she belonged running through the careless crowds and the sharp eyes of the constables. Great days.

But when she went into the hall she found that Maccabee was ill. 'Of course I can go to the fair, Edmund,' she was saying, but her face was yellow and after a minute's protestation she sank into her chair.

Edmund drew Barbary aside. '*Would* you stay with her? You are so good, cousin, I should be much relieved . . . Should I leave more staff behind, do you think? The place will be undermanned.'

'Edmund, the MacSheehys are on the run with a garrison of soldiers up their arse; they're not likely to double back and call in here for supper.'

She sent Rosh to the gatehouse with a day's supply of food and settled down to devote herself to Maccabee and Sylvestris in a house so unusually quiet that they could hear the sound of Abby, the only servant in it, flapping her pastry onto the board in the kitchen. After some rest and attention, Maccy recovered enough to insist on Barbary having another attempt at needlework. 'You will never be a true lady without this skill, cousin. Now this is how to do a French knot.' Barbary's fingers, which could pick a lock and a pocket, massacred the stitch while her thoughts consigned the French and their knots to hell and wandered off to the gatehouse.

So that was the cause of his bad temper all this time. In his strange Irish mind it was more honourable to be rude to his hostess than to seduce her. Damn him. If he wanted to make love to her, why the hell didn't he go ahead and do it? She was affronted, forgetting that her own peculiar loyalty had drawn her back from the brink. Him and his honour.

She was almost relieved that Maccabee didn't want to be left for the night. Barbary clambered into Edmund's side of the Spenser four-poster bed and listened to Maccabee chatter herself to sleep. There was a restlessness about. She was restless, Maccabee was restless, and outside the shuttered windows something disquieted the forest and filled Barbary's dreams with the squeals of rabbits torn by foxes and the scream of foxes torn by rabbits.

There was knocking on the front door. 'Stay there, Maccy. I'll go.' What damned time was it? She struggled into a cloak and slippers, cursing herself for leaving her snaphaunce over in the gatehouse. Downstairs she heard unfamiliar voices. What the hell was Nup doing opening the gates without her permission?

She pulled back the bolts and turned the great key. Against a sky that was showing reluctant light stood the tall figure of Sir Thomas Norris, the Lord Deputy of Munster, and, mopping with apology, the much smaller figure of Nup. 'I'm sorry, mistress, sorry. I'd opened the gates afore—'

Sir Thomas cut him short by stepping into the hall and shutting the door on him. His cloak was muddy and he smelled of sweat. 'The fact of the matter is, Lady Betty, that your noddle of a gatekeeper opened to some of my men who were demanding admittance. My officers are rounding them up now and we shall be away from here within the minute. You must forgive them; I fear they are drunk, but they have this night performed such a service to Her Majesty . . .'

Barbary rubbed her eyes. 'Take it slower, my lord, will you?' There was none of the link between her and this man that she'd felt for his brother. Sir John Norris and Rob had their fortunes tied up together in their mutual

292

expedition against the Spaniards, and she and the Norrises met occasionally to swap any news of the expedition which came their way, but Sir Thomas, a conventional man, found her baffling.

Tonight, however, Sir Thomas, exhausted but uplifted, was more forthcoming. 'We found the Mac-Sheehys' camp.'

'Lovely.' She remembered that she was hostess. 'Do you want some wine or something? What are you doing here then?'

He wouldn't stop, and his explanation was gabbled. He had to leave.

His men were running riot, small fault with them, but he must take them back to Mallow before they got out of hand. He'd gone before she'd grasped what it was all about. She caught his last words: 'We'll be back on the morrow. Stay indoors until then.'

She bolted the door behind him, went up to tell Maccabee that there was nothing to be frightened of, and looked out of the bedroom window. All was quiet at the back of the house, but there were shouts, howlings and general mayhem going on at the front. She could hear it.

'What are they doing round my cattle pens?' she demanded. 'Stay put, Maccy. I'll go and see to the buggers.'

What worried her most was what was happening at the gatehouse. At the door she paused to take stock. The lawn was full of soldiers uproariously drunk, a couple were chasing hens, others were flinging themselves on the ground as they tried to tackle some of the piglets who'd been loosed from the sty, and were being attacked in their turn by a furious sow. One was riding Colossus, the Kerry bull which Edmund had recently purchased at a high price to improve the quality of his herd, and Colossus, though slow-witted, was beginning to resent the indignity.

Whatever else they'd discovered at the MacSheehy camp, the men had got at its liquor store and now were after food; the army in Ireland was permanently short of provisions. Well, they'd come to the wrong manor. A part of Barbary was in every grass-blade of Spenser Castle and she wasn't about to have it sacked by a load of booze-crazed foot-sloggers.

Officers were trying to restore order with the flat of their swords, urged on by commands from the bellowing Sir Thomas. Barbary set off across the lawn to fetch her snaphaunce, only pausing to put out a foot and trip up a soldier running after a hen. He fell and was collared by a captain.

It was quieter down by the gatehouse, and all sound blotted out when she saw that its door was open, a hole surrounded by splinters where its lock had been. The lock was still attached to the frame, having proved stronger than its surrounding wood. Whoever had broken in was still climbing the steps. Looking up she saw the wobble of light from a lantern on the walls, heard metal clatter against stone. She went up faster than she'd ever done, desperate to get to the top before whoever-it-was. She didn't make it in time. Somebody rattled the top door and then banged on it. She heard: 'Lady Betty, Lady Betty, give us a kiss.' It was a Cockney, it was Mud-crusher, the soldier she'd tricked away from the hen house. He was drunk and he saw her. He swayed above her on the top step, the lantern casting upwards to make his face ugly and desperate. 'You give us a kiss,' he shouted at her. There were tears on his cheeks. 'I'm a hero now and all. Done proud. They done it to us, we done it to them. You give us a kiss.'

'You'll kiss the gunner's daughter afore you're done,' she told him. 'Come on down.' But he'd passed beyond her influence; it came to her for the first time that he, that all of them, had taken part in something so terrible that being flogged at a gunwheel, the penalty for insubordination, was a diminished threat.

Suddenly he realised the door he'd been trying to open was bolted on the inside. 'Who you got in there, lady? You sarding someone? Got a pike for your pin-cushion, have you?'

'Come down,' begged Barbary. Jesus, don't let O'Hagan interfere.

The soldier put the lantern down, leaving his hands free to reach for her. 'Standing on your pantables, and all the time putting horns on poor old Sir Rob, eh?'

The door behind him swung open. 'No,' said O'Hagan, 'she isn't.' The range of the lantern showed the soldier's feet leaving the step. She heard a crack, saw the feet regain the step to be followed by the rest of his body.

She was terrified. 'You've never killed him.'

'I refrained,' said O'Hagan, 'from the pleasure. I'll push, you pull.'

'I could have managed,' Barbary shouted at him.

'Now you don't have to,' he shouted back. 'Will you get the bastard downstairs?'

Somehow, with O'Hagan using one foot and one arm, Mud-crusher was bumped down to the main door. 'Suppose he tells when he comes to?' she asked.

'When he does he'll not remember.'

'I'll cope now. Just get back upstairs.'

The officers had restored something like order; apart from a few strays, most of the men had been rounded up. She called a captain she vaguely recognised and Mud-crusher was carried off in an untidy but fast-sobering column that was being marched out of the gates.

When at last they'd all gone it was light, or as light as it would get in weather that had turned overcast, and Barbary, Abby, a chastened Nup, and Maccabee, who refused to stay indoors, could see the damage. The herb garden was ruined, the newly planted yew hedges were trampled, hens and pigs were all over the place. Worst of all, Colossus was missing. Offended at his misuse he had wandered out of the gates in the furore and there was no sign of him. Barbary gave instructions. 'Nup, go and get some cottagers to help. Maccy and Abby, you round up the pigs. I'll go after Colossus.'

But indignation had restored strength to Maccabee. 'That is Edmund's very expensive bull,' she said. 'I'll get him.'

There wasn't time to argue; it might take two of them anyway. 'We'll both go.'

The back fields had been ploughed and they had to walk along a balk, wetting their slippers and ankles in the grass.

They wandered into the three-dimensional grey of woods that had shed their personality along with their leaves. Trunks and branches were greasy, the fallen leaves beneath their feet wetly treacherous. 'Coom, coom, Colossus,' they called and heard their voices peter out into moist silence.

'This way,' said Barbary, following a trail. 'Something's

kicked up the mould here.' Maccabee didn't move. She was staring round her like a sightseer, except that her hands were over her ears as if to block out intolerable sound. Barbary watched her, not wanting to look, aware that at the edge of her vision the shape of the glade was wrong; all round, to the back, front, sides, its branches bore fruit, enormous ragged pears that hung from bent stalks. The last clear thought before she surrendered to her eyes was: Should have known. They'd hang them here. Where Mackworth hung. Oh God, so many.

There were no men, except old ones. The garrison had found the MacSheehy camp but not the MacSheehy enemy, not the MacSheehys who had flayed Mackworth. They had found the home camp, the wives, mothers, sisters, daughters, small sons, grandmothers and grandfathers. And the garrison had brought them here and hanged them all. Hard work, work in shifts, three or four men to each rope. So much rope. So much straining as they pulled. So much screaming, so many struggles for so long.

This had happened to her mother.

There were scores of hanging bodies, perhaps hundreds; they overflowed into other glades where they made dark nuclei in the midst. Little bodies, big bodies, all with their heads on one side as if they were shy at being found in this condition. Her mother had looked like this. Barbary stood in an architecture of death, pendicles arranged at different heights, clusters where a branch was big enough, single bodies placed almost artistically at random. A child's bare feet, gracefully pointed, were near her shoulder. She swung away and faced a pair of muddy moccasins. This head was grey, but it bent at the same angle as the gold one behind her; one lined, one chubby, they shared the same look, slack, indifferent. All the faces were the same, it was the feet that had the individuality. An old woman's with bunions, an old man's with rheumatism and knotted veins, a stout but small pair of boots beneath a petticoat, toddler's feet, little toes, a townsworth of people who had walked and run on the good earth, now quietly suspended above it.

Someone was moaning, either her or Maccabee. Maccabee was kneeling by the worst thing in the world. Barbary saw it, rejected seeing it. She whimpered as she went down on her knees to it, touched it, just in case.

The men who had done this had lost their hold on the most basic imperative of their lives. The baby hung from its mother. They had hanged the woman in the act of giving birth. They had known because she was stripped; they'd hanged her between the contraction which pushed the baby into the world and the contraction which would have expelled the afterbirth; the child hung from the mother by the cord at its navel.

Oh God, obliterate this crime against genesis. Obliterate the men who committed it. Obliterate me for having seen it. But there was no God.

Maccabee said clearly: 'They'll tell.'

Hunched so as not to brush against the bodies, they tiptoed out of the woods as if afraid of waking what they left behind them. 'They'll tell,' said Maccabee again. Tell who? A non-existent St Peter as they crowded through his non-existent gates?

Barbary put Maccabee to bed, called Abby to watch over her, and went downstairs to stand in some space, the hall, the kitchen, she didn't know, wasn't aware that she was standing at all. It was as if she had been hanged as well; she was suspended, bloodless. Somewhere down on the ground soldiers and officers were justifying what they'd done. Do it to them before they do it to us. Not people, smell different, don't feel as we feel, sub-human, not us-es. But it was too late for her. She and the baby and the mother were connected by that umbilical cord, part of a huge, corporate womb and the violence done to it had violated the whole world. She had been violated.

Knowing that it was impossible for her to know it, she knew nevertheless that in the forest she had been made barren.

Later that day she walked over to the gatehouse and up its steps. She opened the door and looked at the man on the bed. 'You can tell the O'Neill I'll get his guns for him,' she said.

He had been reading. He scrambled up and she went to him.

She told him a little, not much, not anything about the mother and the baby. She had fits of shuddering she couldn't control. He held her for a long time, just held

297

her, soothing her as a mother with an injured child. 'There, there, Cushlamochree. Quiet now, my brave girl. There, there, pulse of my heart.'

She had no more fellow feeling for the Irish than before, no more sense of her own Irishness; even pity for Ireland had not overwhelmed her. But from this moment on, she knew, she would support the side of its people because the imbalance of the scale against them was too monstrously weighted to be borne. She would support them from an impulse resembling the involuntary reaching of hands to straighten a lopsided picture. She would do it, if she could, because it had to be done.

The ridiculous things he was saying so gently began to get through to her. 'Quiet now, pulse of my heart.' She could feel the pulse of his heart. In the wasteland she was lost in, this cricket ticked out its insistence on living. Concepts like honour and loyalty were irrelevancies. Not to be dead was what counted, not to be cold or alone. The only warmth and companionship she knew had been in this room all these weeks. Her own body ticked into life.

'About damned time,' he said and he wasn't holding her like a mother now.

It wasn't at all like sex with Rob. He looked at her, spoke to her, mostly in Irish. Everything sophisticated and moody had gone, leaving his face defenceless. Her body and soul had held a gap and he filled them both, like the fitting of mortice into tenon by some beautiful carpenter. A tight fit, so that the rest of her wrinkled up in a huge and joyful orgasm. 'Gawd help us,' she said, when she could speak. 'What was that?'

'Me,' he said, panting modestly.

'Well, do it again.'

'You know nothing of the male constitution, woman.' He collapsed back onto the bed and put his arm round her, so that they lay staring up at the darkening ceiling together. The bat stared back. 'Oh God, that I have to do penance for this.'

'You have to do what?' She sat up and could only just see his face.

He said: 'I would hear you coming up the steps and wait to see you in the doorway. *Is mo chen in maiten bán.* Come into my dark oratory, be welcome the bright morn, *is mo chen, a muingel mass*, white-necked and gold-bedecked. You were dawn to me, Saxon. But it's still a sin.'

She was appalled. 'I'm not a sin. I'm not a sin.' She was hammering on his shoulders. Sin hung out there in the forest. How could sin be juicy and warm and *fitting*?

He caught her hands. 'You are the bravest woman with the reddest hair I have ever known,' he said, 'but you are married.'

A damned devil-dodger. All the light had withdrawn from the room now and he had gone with it into shadows where she couldn't follow, leaving just his bones in the bed. There were too many facets to him for her to be sure of who he was; the kindness, the mockery, the courage, the bad temper, the hypochondria, the lover and now the Catholic. She would accept them, any of them, but he had to apologise to God for loving her at all.

'I don't understand,' she said wearily. 'You're foreign.'

'Irish,' he said. 'I'm Irish.'

There was noise outside, Edmund's voice shouting for Nup to open the gates. Tiredly, she slipped away from his detaining arm, out of the bed to dress and go back into the cold.

Edmund and the others had heard about the hangings from Sir Thomas Norris and when they'd passed along the road by the woods they'd seen the bodies being taken away on carts.

Edmund was cross with her. 'Sir Thomas told you to stay indoors,' he chided her. 'Not a sight for ladies and their susceptibilities. Tragic, but inevitable. They must be taught a lesson. I fear it may have sent my poor wife mad.'

It had killed her. Maccabee began to die immediately, turning yellower and yellower. Barbary didn't go back to the gatehouse because Maccy grew restive when she was out of sight. She stayed in the Spensers' room, taking it in turns with Edmund to sit with her, trying to persuade her to take the doctor's nostrums, to calm her. But she was in terror. 'They'll tell,' she kept saying, clutching at Barbary.

'Tell who, Maccy? Who will they tell? Tell what?' But if that remoteness which the dead in the wood had possessed contained a secret, Maccy died with it, in too much pain to pass it on.

Rosh and Barbary washed her, put her in her best clothes, shut the once-busy little mouth, tied the linen band that would keep it from falling open and settled the small hands on her breast. 'Oh, Maccy. Goodbye.'

Edmund cried easily over the body of his wife, Catherine with a desperation that produced almost as great a desperation in Barbary. The pitying maternalism she had contracted in the forest wouldn't leave her. She picked the girl up and felt the child's bony little frame relax totally into grief against her. 'There, there, pigsney, don't cry.' How idiotic. Why shouldn't you cry? What is there to stop crying for? Cling on. Human warmth's the only thing worth having in this world of dead bodies. I'll go back to the gatehouse soon where human warmth is waiting for me, and I'll cony O'Hagan away from his God if it's the last thing I do.

When Catherine had sobbed herself to sleep, Barbary bent and kissed her and went to the gatehouse. Rosh was coming down the stairs. 'Thank God you're here. He's going tonight.'

'Going?' She felt cold. Being without volition, he had seemed a sort of present that she could pick up or not, go back to any moment she wanted. 'He can't go.'

'He's got to stop the MacSheehys. If they'll listen to anybody, they'll listen to him. They're planning to attack Mallow Castle.'

She pushed past Rosh, who called after her: 'I'll see if the coast's clear.'

He was sitting on the bed, pulling on his boots. Rosh must have stitched together the one they had slit to his ankle, as she had mended and cleaned his doublet, shirt, hose and trunks. He was no longer her patient, but a tall and presentable Tudor gentleman. 'The MacSheehys are planning to get the rest of themselves killed,' he said. 'And now is not the time. If there's to be another rising it must be all Ireland's, and not before Ireland's ready.'

He stood up, testing his ankle. 'That's what I was doing.' He looked sharply at her. 'When I was so rudely interrupted. That's what I was doing, organising the clans.'

He'd already left her. They might never have shared a

bed. He was paying her back for all those dependent weeks by showing her he was independent of her now, that she was only a very small part of his plans. Not consciously, perhaps, but he was. He could go, and confess his sin and gain absolution or whatever these dolly-worshippers gained, and be spotless white the next time he wanted to colt with a woman. Well, go, and the Devil and ninepence go with you.

He came nearer, studying her face. 'I'm sorry the little woman is dead. Is there anything I can do?'

Not now, my lad, not ever. 'No, thank you.'

'You never need me, do you?'

'I don't need anybody.' She stuck out her hand as she would in saying goodbye to a stranger. He shrugged and kissed it.

'My eternal gratitude, mistress. Don't bother to see me out.'

She didn't. She stood in the doorway and watched him pass down the curve of the stairway. He was limping piteously. 'Me ankle's still giving me pain,' he called up to her. If his whole leg had collapsed like a rotten pea-stick, she wouldn't have lifted a finger.

She heard his footfalls pause. 'About the guns,' he called, 'you'll be contacted.'

'I'll hold my breath,' she hissed and heard her words snake down the stairwell after him.

Suddenly he was chasing back up the stairs. He reached her, grabbed her and kissed her. 'Hold it on that, woman.'

By the time she'd gathered the pieces of herself that had melted all over the stairway, he'd gone. She went back into the room and watched him hobble towards the bawn and out of sight. No sound came from the dark house where Maccy was laid out on her bed.

There was a wasteland around her again, and no cricket ticking away in it. But he'd done one thing, the Irish bastard, he'd made her so bloody angry that she could cope with it.

Chapter Fourteen

The smoke from Sir Walter Raleigh's long, silver pipe puffed out into the early summer air towards the crescent lake. His tobacco case was made of gold. Edmund's pipe, like the one Sir Walter had also given Barbary, was of whale ivory and had gone out long ago. It lay beside him on the window seat as he read:

> Of warlike puissaunce in ages spent,
> Be thou, fair Britomart, whose praise I write,
> But of all wisdome be thou precedent,
> O sovereign Queen, whose praise I would indite
> But ah, my rhymes too rude and rugged are,
> When in so high an object they do light . . .

He looked up from his manuscript. 'Not too fulsome, do you think?'

Raleigh took his pipe from his mouth. 'Can't be,' he said.

Sitting in her chair, wrestling with a seam on Catherine's new skirt, Barbary raised her eyes to heaven. There was no virtue, no ideal of beauty, no compassion and grace that Edmund hadn't heaped on that ill-tempered, vain, grand old woman, the Queen of England. One character had not been enough to encompass all the flattery – Barbary had stopped asking when the Faerie Queen was actually going to appear in 'The Faerie Queen'; Britomart, Belphoebe, Mercilla were all manifestations of her perfections.

For days now Edmund's voice had droned away until the hall reverberated with nine-line stanzas. The servants dusted away words, cooked words, words fell out of the cushions when they were shaken. And all the time, Raleigh listened and smoked and nodded. During an interval when Edmund had gone off for a pee, Barbary took the opportunity to ask: 'Is it good then, this poem?'

Raleigh answered with sincerity: 'It rises above anything yet produced under the name of poetry in England.'

She couldn't see it. All this knight errantry was irrelevance as far as she was concerned; there hadn't been much chivalry in the streets where she'd grown up; she didn't see it manifested in Ireland. It didn't get on with the story. Every time Edmund got to a good bit he stopped; palaces, landscapes, pageants, feasts were taken to pieces and every part likened to something else. Champions duelled until she didn't give a dump who won.

'Oh well,' she said, resignedly, 'I suppose you know.' After all, Raleigh was reckoned as a nifty poet himself.

But she still couldn't work out why he was putting in days on it. She had to; she was, if only temporarily, the hostess. But Raleigh the adventurer, man of action, lover of the Queen? What was he doing, lounging around an Irish backwater, listening to an allegory, however great, that threatened to go on for ever?

He had brought her letters from Rob, who was still having a high time raiding Spanish shipping. Like his other letters they carried detailed instructions for their new home. The building of Hap Hazard was going well, with Raleigh's help and advice. Rob wanted it to be modern, a mansion rather than a castle, brick rather than stone, herring-bone style, crazy with black beams, white plaster and elaborate chimneys. 'For I have faith that Ireland shall be at peace now, and battlements unnecessary,' he wrote. Barbary shrugged her shoulders and passed his orders on to the masons. Certainly these last few months had been peaceful. There hadn't been so much as a cattle raid by the MacSheehys. Spring planting had gone ahead with growing confidence that revolt had been frightened out of the rebels. 'Root and branched 'em,' crowed Ellis. 'Dogs fall quiet iffen you kill the pups and bitches.'

'The dogs fall quiet iffen they're waiting their chance,' thought Barbary, and for Rob's sake ordered a high wall to be built round Hap Hazard; it spoiled its lighthearted charm but would give some protection when the storm broke.

She commanded the work of the rammers, wallers, brickers and paviours without enthusiasm. She had no intention of ever living at Hap Hazard, but seeing to its completion was the last thing she could do for Rob before she left him. For her the marriage had dissolved at the moment she had seen the baby and mother in the woods. There had been the great divide. It was when Ireland had become vulnerable and she had switched allegiance from Rob who sided with everything English. She would never see him again. Anyway, he'd never loved her and she, she realised now, had never really loved him. Love was what she had discovered with O'Hagan. And she wouldn't see him again either. She tried to put him out of her mind, insisting to herself that he had been an interlude that was over. Him and his religion.

Where she was going to go and what she would do when she went was not apparent. 'About the guns,' O'Hagan had said, 'you will be contacted.' She was waiting for the contact, and until then inertia and the pull of affection for the place and for Catherine and Sylvestris kept her at Spenser Castle. Edmund had begged her to stay on for the children's sake 'until I can make other arrangements'. It had caused gossip among the undertakers, and Lady Norris, Sir Thomas's wife, who disapproved of Barbary, had actually told Edmund that his children should be in the care of someone more conversant with the 'gentilities'. But Edmund, with one of those stubborn quirks which saved him from total conformity, refused. They were happy with his 'cousin'; he liked his children to be happy.

When he had company, as now, Barbary moved out of the gatehouse and into the castle to act as hostess. Raleigh's stay had caused a lot of work for everybody; they had invited half Munster to various festivities for his entertainment. What surprised her was that the servants hadn't minded; they had enjoyed the unaccustomed excitement, and were charmed by Raleigh himself, who had handed out clay pipes and tobacco to every one of them, saying that the smoke would cure them, like hams, against the ageing process. He acquainted himself with their names and personal history, and flirted shamelessly with the women, young and old. He had done more than flirt with Lucy, the cook's daughter. Searching the orchard for a hen that had gone broody, Barbary had heard puffing and squeaking coming from behind a tree. Investigation had shown Lucy, with her skirts and legs up, and Sir Walter, with trunks down, standing against the tree in the act of what the Order called 'doing a perpendicular'. Since it was obviously not rape, Barbary had walked away. Later she got Raleigh on his own and scolded him. 'You stop sarding my girls, you mutton-monger,' she said. 'They're good girls, and Edmund don't want a nursery full of little Raleighs.'

Raleigh was undiscomfited. 'Don't 'ee fret, my beauty.' With Barbary he relaxed into deep Devonshire, partly to point up her own refusal to use better-class English with him, and partly as a familiarity. 'She'll come to no harm for a bit of loving, and if so she do have a babby, I'll care for 'un. 'Tis lonely here for a lusty lad.' His black eye-brows had twitched an invitation which she'd ignored.

Then why does he stay? She couldn't work it out. There was an Earl of Essex, a new Earl of Essex, arrived at court to bewitch the Queen. Raleigh was amusing about how jealous the young man was of his own position in the royal bosom, but he dwelled on the matter too long and too often to conceal his own raging jealousy of this rival.

So why are you here and not safeguarding your back at court? Barbary raised her head as Edmund's voice rang out. Raleigh took his pipe from his mouth. 'Good Shepherd Edmund,' he said – it was their little joke that they were Theocritan shepherds in a pastoral ruled by Goddess Elizabeth – 'here's too mighty a poem to be hid in this Irish forest. Come back with me to place this jewel you have wrought into the crown of England. Display it to the world, as it do deserve to be.'

'Come to England, you mean?' asked Edmund.

'I do.'

'To court? But Sir Walter, good Shepherd Walter I mean, they don't like me at court. Burghley hates me.'

Raleigh spat out of the window. 'Burghley's an old man. The Queen's our prize. A royal poem for a royal mistress, my lover. Boldness.'

Edmund wriggled. Boldness wasn't his forte, but he was afire with the idea, Barbary could see. She also saw at last what Raleigh was about. He wasn't going to go back empty-handed to fight young Essex for the Queen's affection. He was taking presents which would tempt Elizabeth from his rival. He would hand her the wonders from a New World, tobacco, the potato. And he would hand her 'The Faerie Queen', a poem which could sate even that old harpy's thirst for flattery. 'You saucebox,' she thought, with grudging admiration. 'Straight as a ram's horn you are.' Well, for Edmund's sake she hoped it was as great a poem as Raleigh thought it was and that the Queen would enjoy it more than she had.

Later that morning Edmund joined her in the kitchen and took her out to the gardens. 'Shall I do it, cousin?'

'Be a proper fool not to, Edmund.'

'I have been thinking for some time that Catherine and Sylvestris should be exposed to English ways. I could join my sister. I have hesitated to bring her here with . . . you know.' His hand indicated the Ballyhouras and the sleeping presence of the MacSheehys. 'You must come with us, cousin. Neither I nor the children can do without you.'

Can I let them go? Will they be unhappy? Will the sister realise how gentle they are, how easily hurt? But there are other children here who are being hurt already, unborn children who are destined to be hurt, babies . . . 'No, Edmund. I stay here.'

He took the refusal happily enough. 'Of course, there is Hap Hazard to be completed.'

When he left her, she was joined by Raleigh. 'A sweet, pretty morning, Mistress Barbary.'

Leaves had newly unfurled from the bud, catkins hung in suspended showers, lambs were gambolling on the hills and the forest was a contrast of greens filled with bird-song. 'What of it?' she asked suspiciously. It was always necessary to keep Raleigh at a remove, to remind herself that he was a killer; the man vibrated with energy, sexual, intellectual, elemental. She could understand Lucy being overwhelmed by it. Physically, he and Rob and O'Hagan were alike, Rob actually modelling his manner and ambition on him. The difference between Raleigh and O'Hagan, she thought, was that the Irishman was civilised and Raleigh, for all his learning and wit, was not. O'Hagan was held by ancient custom and culture;

Raleigh was rootless. He had no limits. He was a product of his age; unweighted by any tradition of the past, he could soar to the highest peak, and commit any crime to get there. But he could also fall. She wouldn't want to bet on which it would be.

'What are you going to do?' he was asking her.

'What about?'

'Your inheritance, maid.' He pointed his pipe westward. 'There's princedoms for the winning out there, and even so that you're not a lad, you're like the Queen, you have the heart and stomach of a prince. Rob and I were planning to win yours for ye. But seeing as how we're so occupied, perhaps you should go see for yourself how the land do lie. Present yourself to your granny, like. No harm in it.'

'Ware hawk, thought Barbary. Aloud she said: 'What's up?'

There was a flash of white teeth in his ferocious black facial hair. 'Bingham's up,' he said, 'our Governor of Connaught. He's a many-sided gentleman, seemingly. Gamekeeper, poacher and butcher. Unless and we're watchful, he'll have it all. Don't you have nothing to do with him until so be as Rob and I get there. The land's mazed; Os and Macs fighting each other *and* Bingham, separate and together. Rob'll need to know who's friend, who's foe. 'Tisn't a job for most maids, but you can do it, I reckon.'

'Spy it out?'

He drew a beautiful handkerchief from his sleeve, dabbed his eyes with it and adopted a falsetto: 'Oh dear Granny, take me in for I am your little grand-babby as was lost.'

'She thinks I'm a trickster.'

'Then trick 'un.'

The green eyes and the black eyes were lit with mutual understanding. 'What a pair of cony-catchers we'd have made,' she thought. In essence, he was using her for his purposes as much as he'd used Lucy, but the idea was still attractive. If it hadn't been for the mother and baby, she'd have gone along with it, and turned it to her own advantage, not his. She might yet.

'I'll see,' she told him. The rest of the stroll was taken

up with his persuasion and instructions. If she went, she was to contact his men at Youghal, who would go with her as protection . . .

'Do you come falconing tomorrow?' he asked. 'Every soul with a bird will be there. It's Sir Thomas Norris's welcome for my Lord of Tyrone.'

The O'Neill was at Mallow? Then falconing she would go. It looked as if her contact had arrived.

Raleigh was right. Practically the entire population of the Blackwater and Awbeg valleys had turned out to join Sir Thomas's falconing party. As an exercise in falconry it looked like being a disaster. The crowd, the shouts, the horn-blowing, the barking of dogs, the neighing of horses was enough to frighten the surrounding countryside bird-less. The provincial nobility and those aspiring to the nobility were dressed to kill, a beautiful, clashing caval-cade of colour, with each rider apparently growing a carved log from his/her wrist which, every so often, sprouted wings and flapped its annoyance at the disorder.

The hawks' hoods and jesses were as rich as their owners' clothing. Raleigh's white Norwegian peregrine, which he carried with nonchalant ease, was in gold and silver. Ellis's arm was showing signs of falconer's droop under the weight of a vulgarly flashy gerfalcon, usually a king's bird.

The Irish, however downtrodden, could never resist a sporting occasion and had turned out to let the side down with their patched clothes, their pet kestrels, their mongrel dogs and their subversive Celtic comments.

Barbary had been introduced to various forms of the chase, stag, boar, hare and falconry, at Penshurst. She hadn't taken to it then and she wasn't taking to it now. She looked at the bird on her wrist, a merlin that Sir Thomas Norris had insisted on lending her: 'One more gripe, you moth-eaten mouse-catcher, and you're baked with bay leaves.' Such occasions, in her opinion, brought out the worst in everybody. Those on good horseflesh despised those who weren't; her own poor old Spenser was beneath contempt. Those who were on foot despised those on horses. Those who were familiar with hunting parlance used it to exclude those like her and Ellis who weren't and talked loudly about 'bowesses', 'disclosing', 'eyer' and 'timbering', being in turn despised by the mews servants who regarded everybody else as a bunch of bloody amateurs.

In the crush of the meet at Mallow Castle she'd caught a glimpse of the O'Neill but if he'd seen her he did not show it. Now she trailed resentfully after the cavalcade as it wound along the Blackwater bank. Catherine, who was falconing socially for the first time, came cantering back, a sparrowhawk on her small wrist. 'Hurry up, cousin, you'll miss the branching. Oh, isn't this wonderful?'

'Lovely,' said Barbary grimly. 'You go on. I'll see you at the picnic.' There was to be a mass open-air banquet later for the Norris's guests at Ballybeg Abbey, seven and a half miles away.

Catherine cantered off. Soon Barbary and Spenser were ambling along alone. Not quite alone. A man in livery popped out of some bushes and took Spenser's bridle. 'I'll show you where there's game, mistress.' She looked down at the man's cap and then his gauntlet. It was embroidered with the Red Hand of Ulster. They turned off left into hills.

The O'Neill sat in a clearing on a backed camp stool drinking wine and talking to a man, similarly seated, across a brazier which was cooking pigeon breasts. Further away a servant was flying his peregrine for him at partridge which were being flushed out of the undergrowth by a string of beaters, all in Ulster livery.

Spenser, who liked frequent stops and hadn't had one for four miles, sank to his knees, making Barbary's dismount an undignified scramble. The O'Neill helped her up. 'A pony with devotional habits,' he said. 'Do you mean to wear the bird round your neck?'

Barbary untangled the merlin and handed it over with relief. 'Bloody thing keeps pooping on my arm.' She had been tense about seeing the O'Neill again; in retrospect he was alarming and there had been times when she was scared at having committed herself to the banner of so chancy a man. What she had forgotten was the familiarity with which they could communicate; there were whole seas to O'Neill which were unnavigable to her, but they had a channel to themselves. He was still dressing like a popinjay but he'd aged; not through wrinkling – there were no lines – but the very lack of lines, its deliberate blankness in repose, was mummifying all youth out of his face.

'Allow me to introduce Murrough MacSheehy,' he said.

She had never thought to see a MacSheehy, never wanted to. They roamed round the edge of her imagination dressed in pelts, wolf-shaped people. A stocky man looked back at her, round-faced, respectable, the sort of man you'd be happy to order your groceries from, unless you looked into his eyes and saw hatred so habitual that it had become passionless. She supposed he ate, drank, made love, but she saw that for him these would be extraordinary things to do; the natural function for this man was hating.

'Murrough, this is the lady you are to escort when the time comes.'

The MacSheehy's acknowledgement was minimal. 'We know her,' he said. God, had they been watching her?

To her relief, he went off to join the falconers down the hill.

'Escort me where?' She'd as soon be escorted by Death, reaping hook and all.

'To Connaught.' He led her to a stool and called for wine.

'Connaught? I thought you wanted guns.'

The O'Neill sat himself down, crossed his legs and smiled at her. 'Who changed your mind for you? O'Hagan?'

'Have you seen him?' she asked before she could stop herself and realised from his damned, patronising smile that he'd not only seen O'Hagan, he'd sent him in the first place.

'You bastard,' she said, 'you gave him orders, didn't you? He was to seduce me so that I'd get drawn in.' Jesus wept, wasn't there one man in the world who wasn't trying to trick something out of somebody else?

'And did he?' He leaned forward, prurient and interested. He really didn't know. It was a comfort.

'What did he tell you?'

He sulked and sat back. 'Nothing, except that you'd agreed to get my guns. I gather you nursed him. And if you knew O'Hagan better, you'd know he wasn't the man to give that sort of order to.'

No. But you'd hoped, you slippery sod. However, the day had regained the sun. She grinned at him. 'How's Mabel?' Few people had seen Mabel Bagenal since she'd eloped with the O'Neill, riding pillion on a wild gallop into the night to be married at a Protestant service by a bewildered Bishop of Meath, who later explained that he'd done it to protect the girl's reputation.

O'Neill's face went blank. The question was outside their channel. 'The Countess of Tyrone is well,' he said. He allowed the snub some air and then relented to add: 'It's her damned brother is the problem. He protests to the Queen, to Burghley. He accuses me of bigamy, he raids my borders. You'd think I'd cuckolded the man.'

She shook her head. 'You don't half take chances, O'Neill.' She'd heard enough argument among the English to know that the number who doubted his loyalty was growing. 'Jesus, any moment one of that falconing lot could have blundered in here and seen you chatting to a MacSheehy. I'm not getting no guns for them, I can tell you. I saw what they did to Mackworth.'

'And I gather you saw the reprisal for it.'

She looked away, and in doing so noticed a look-out posted in one of the trees and that servants who were apparently taking their ease were facing outwards, like sentries. They'd done this before. Wherever O'Neill went, ostensibly socialising with English Irish, he was secretly meeting with their enemy. This camp was just one knot in a net he was preparing all over Ireland.

'Barbary,' he said, and his voice throbbed, 'I have no idea of war. As I trust in Almighty God, I have no idea of it. I want to be Gaelic chieftain of my people as my ancestors were. I want to serve Queen Elizabeth as her loyal subject. But there is no trust in any of us. She won't trust me when I'm Gaelic. My Gaels won't trust me when I'm English. I am a rope tugged by young O'Donnell who wants me to save Donegal and Connaught from the terrible man the English have put there to rule it, and I am tugged by Elizabeth to ride against O'Donnell. I can't trust her not to invade Ulster one day and take it away from me, as she took the Awbeg Valley away from Mac-Sheehy. But I tell you this, I'll not be turned into my own woods to live like an outlaw as MacSheehy has been.'

311

He put out his hand and covered one of hers. 'I'll not go to war, Barbary, but I must be prepared for it.'

She looked into his wet eyes. He cried easily, like Edmund. But she believed him. She believed him because he believed it. Balance was all they could aim for; imbalance was not allowing babies to be born.

'I know,' she said. 'What do you want me to do?'

He brushed away his tears. 'First you must be accepted by your grandmother. I need Granuaile O'Malley. For such a small island we are lamentably short on seafarers. There's the O'Sullivans in the south-west, and the O'Flaherties and the O'Malleys in Connaught. And the greatest of these, thanks to your grandmother, are the O'Malleys. It's her ships will bring the guns to Ulster.'

Burghley, Rob, Raleigh and now the O'Neill, nearly all the men in her life wanted her in Connaught for their differing reasons. Well, she couldn't fight them all.

'Will she accept me?'

'I've talked to her. She says you must a pass a test.'

'What test?'

The O'Neill looked uneasy. 'I don't know. That is a doorful of a woman. She said to me: "She shall be given the tide, a curragh and a landfall. If she comes safe ashore she is an O'Malley. If she does not . . ."' He peered at Barbary: '*Are* you her granddaughter?'

She went back to the cell at Dublin Castle and saw the ship scratched on the wall come to life. 'Yes.'

'You'd better be.'

'Why? What if I'm not?'

The O'Neill coughed apologetically. 'She said: "If she does not, the sea will drown her and her lie."'

The young summer was held for a moment in a cuckoo's call further down the hill. The beaters moved towards the sound, shouting. As the cuckoo flew out of its tree, O'Neill's falconer unleashed his peregrine. It gained height above the low-flying grey bird, stooped and landed on its back, taking it to earth.

The O'Neill was put out. 'Now why did they do that? It's bad luck to kill a cuckoo.'

'Is it?' said Barbary flatly. 'How about red-headed women?'

'Ach, it's bad luck to kill them too.' He turned to her. 'Do you go?'

She considered. She wasn't a wife any more, she wasn't a lover, or a mother. She wasn't English, she didn't feel Irish. She had grown out of the Order. She belonged nowhere. The land of the cherubims was the only possible home she had left, and gun-running for O'Neill the only occupation. Both were likely to prove deadly.

'Why not?' she said.

The O'Neill kissed her hand. 'God go with you. The MacSheehy will guide you through to Connaught, and I've made arrangement with the clans to let you through. You'll be safe under my writ. But would you like a friend to go with you?' He shouted down the hill. 'Send that man up here.'

'What friend?' It's O'Hagan, she thought. He's ordered O'Hagan to go with me. I'm getting O'Hagan back.

Then she saw who it was. She sat down on the camp stool and leaned back in contentment. Coming up the hill, shambling and portly, was Cuckold Dick.

313

Chapter Fifteen

When she saw Edmund and the children off on their journey to England, Barbary had to wrench Catherine's hands away from her neck to get her into the wagon. It was like wrenching her own flesh. 'You be a good girl, pigsney,' she said, trying to sound cheerful. 'Do as your aunty tells you. You'll like London.'

'Will you come and see me there?'

'That I will.' If I live.

She hugged Sylvestris. How would they get on without her? Would their aunt understand them as she did? Would Edmund, so often abstracted, remember that Catherine was frightened of the dark and Sylvestris was sick if given eggs?

She watched the wagon sway off down the road, returning the wave of Catherine's handkerchief, listening to Sylvestris's crying becoming fainter, wondering why women were so eager to have children if this agony was an inherent part of it.

The house was empty without them, though all the servants and estate workers were being retained to keep the place going for when Edmund returned. He was a comparatively wealthy man now, and could afford two establishments.

She and Cuckold Dick were to begin their own journey the next day. She bade no goodbyes. Only Rosh knew where they were going and she, if asked, was to answer: 'Lady Betty has gone away and didn't say where.'

She gave much thought to what she should write in explanation to Rob. I'm leaving you because this is a loveless marriage we're in, and I was tricked into it anyway? I've given my body and soul to another man? I've gone over to the Irish?

Eventually she decided not to write at all. Although she owed him nothing, she didn't want to hurt him and, she thought, he'd suffer less social damage from a wife who'd just disappeared than a wife who had committed adultery with and defected to his enemy.

Perhaps he'd think she had done what Raleigh had suggested, and gone to Connaught to spy the land for him. Perhaps he'd think she'd gone back to the Order. He could take his choice.

She was careful in packing her saddlebags to include nothing that Rob had bought and realised as she did so that he had bought her very little, except the ring and bale of silk he had pillaged from a Spanish galleon for a wedding present. She parcelled them up and left them with a note for Edmund telling him to hand them on. Poor old Rob, we didn't give each other a lot. Well, she'd done her best in overseeing the rebuilding of Hap Hazard; she'd done that much for him.

At dawn the next morning Cuckold Dick, on a horse given him by the O'Neill, and Barbary on Spenser, rode down the drive and into the Deer Park. Barbary hadn't been among its trees since the day she and Maccabee had stood among the hanged bodies, the day of the mother and baby.

This morning it was refreshed with buds and catkins, with delicate, pale daffodils growing among the new grass, but Barbary kept her eyes straight ahead. It wouldn't ever be spring in these woods for her, nor for the man who waited for them and who, without greeting, turned his horse and led them towards the Ballyhouras.

They were handed on like parcels along a route which had no road recognisable as such. Sometimes it was a green lane between high banks, sometimes no more than a badger track through the centre of forests from whose edges came the distant sound of crashing trees and the chop of the undertaker's axe. They slept in huts belonging to a dispossessed people, hidden in woods and without a fire, given food and a courteous but unsmiling welcome.

Only the MacSheehy accompanied them, but they were directed by unseen guardians. Twice, once in the Slieve-felims, and once near the Shannon, which they crossed at

315

night on a battered and illegal ferry, a whistle came out of the air, and they had to take cover while patrols from Limerick went by.

Barbary wasn't sure which suffered most from the relentless going, pony Spenser or Cuckold Dick. Of the two, Dick complained the less, but his unease at being exposed to so much air and space was obvious. The fact that he was looking leaner and brown didn't ameliorate her guilt; fitness was unnatural to a personality only truly at home in the unhealth of a crowded city.

'Why'd you come?' she asked him sharply. 'You could have gone back to the Bermudas long since.'

'Didn't mind Dublin, Barb,' Dick said. 'I done a lovely crossbite on a cove for the O'Neill. Worked it with Janey, the landlady at the Anchor.'

Barbary was interested. 'Why'd the O'Neill want him bit?'

'Dubbams. Information. The cove was a nunquam, messenger, for the Rome-Mort.'

The O'Neill, it seemed, had found Cuckold Dick a useful addition to his espionage service. Dick could recount the entire political situation in Dublin; who was in, who out, who was backing Sir John Perrot's attempt to be fair to the Irish – hardly anybody – the O'Neill's precarious position with the Queen. But he retailed it all without emphasis, taking no side with his employer O'Neill, nor with his Queen, as if he were giving details of the weather. He was the most un-judgemental man Barbary knew; as patriotic as he was sexual, which was not at all, a watching victim of the life around him. If he could have spoken the language, Barbary thought, he would have been equally at home in the criminal quarter of Cathay as in London's Bermudas. He was a citizen of the underworld. What combination of his battered emotions had involved him with herself, she couldn't guess; she was just grateful that it had dragged him into this alien environment to be with her.

'The O'Neill said you'd need me, Barb.'

'And don't I just.' This journey with the unspeaking MacSheehy into an unknown and possibly dangerous past would have been insupportable without him.

Just as when they had crossed the Pale on the way to Munster, they were aware of the change when they crossed the border into non-Anglicised Connaught. For one thing the country shook itself out of its gentility, raising the hills to mountains, streams tilting into waterfalls. For another, the frontier was marked by hangings. Not that they passed through frontier posts, there were no frontier posts as such, but when they looked down from their vantage point at a crossroads it was to see it studded with occupied gibbets. And further on, where they crossed a stream at a concealed ford, they found that the Lord Deputy's soldiers had been before them and that the trees overhanging the stream bent with the weight of corpses. Like a gamekeeper decorating his fences with dead crows, stoats and magpies to frighten away other predators, Bingham was showing the Irish what he did to rebels.

But within a day's ride it became obvious that though he intended his fringe of corpses as a warning, Bingham had in fact marked the point at which English rule ran out. This was Irish Ireland, no sense of oppression, no deadness. A string of horsemen came galloping down a mountain towards them as free as running foxes, stirrupless, saffron shirts billowing, illegal glibs streaming backwards with the speed of the going, illegal wolfhounds loping at their horses' sides.

'From the O'Neill,' shouted the MacSheehy quickly. 'We have the O'Neill's permission.'

'And who's O'Neill of Ulster to permit travellers through Connaught?' But they were friendly, prepared to assist O'Neill as an ally as long as it was clear that this was their territory. They surrounded them, questioning, laughing, their voices raised to carry on the breeze for all to hear, and Barbary realised that Connaught had not yet been conquered or, if it had, it didn't know it. These were O'Kellys. For the sake of peace and quiet, their chiefs had gone through a ritual submission to Elizabeth's representative, Sir Henry Sidney, years before at Galway, as had most of the Connaught clans, but it no more affected their lives than a new moon. For the first time she was encountering free Irishmen.

They insisted that the travellers be entertained at their 'booley', for a feast outside the long, low, wooden pavilions they built every summer up in the mountains so that their cattle could graze on the high grass, and they could hunt.

Barbary, trained to the English view of the Irish as nomadic herdsmen, was unprepared for the sophistication of the meal she and the others sat down to that evening. True, they were in the open air, seated on tussocks at a long plank table, and the smoke from the fires where beef, mutton and venison turned on spits watered her eyes, and, true, the feasters tended to lean down and wipe the grease from their hands on ferns, or their wolf-hounds, but the food, and the hospitality were as fine as at any Penshurst dinner.

Brigh O'Kelly, the hostess, talked philosophy from behind a plate of oatcakes so high that it nearly obscured her and at the same time piled mountains of food on her guests' plates, while her sons and daughters, on bended knee proffering ale or *usquebaugh*, were equally intent on drowning the gold-chased chalices they drank from. A tall, comely woman, dressed in a beautiful *leine*, the traditional linen smock, with a gold torque and earrings, Brigh O'Kelly had the same all-noticing calm of Lady Sidney. 'Try a few of me honeyed onions with your beef now. And how is Elizabeth, daughter of Henry? Is she well with her?'

Cuckold Dick, to whom the question was addressed, bemusedly assured her that the Queen of England was in good health.

'That's great, that's great. We heard she'd had the smallpox . . .'

They were ten years out of date. 'Should I be sending her some of me buttermilk potion for her skin, do you think?'

Cuckold Dick being at a loss, Barbary assured her that the Queen would be grateful.

Cormac O'Kelly shouted from his end of the table: 'And what about a nice wolfhound for her hunting, would she like one of them as well?'

Yes, said Barbary, Her Majesty would like a nice wolf-hound. They made no mention of Deputy Bingham, whose over-enthusiastic use of the gallows in those parts of Connaught he could reach they obviously regarded as bad manners, but they held no ill will for Queen Elizabeth.

Barbary saw the MacSheehy looking at these, his fellow Irish, with the hatred of a soul from Hell regarding the

318

blessed. But he remained as silent as ever. The chasm between his experience of Elizabeth's rule and theirs – they talked of the English as if they were just a newly emerged clan – was too great to be bridged. They'd learn.

God preserve them from it, thought Barbary suddenly, looking at the interesting, interested faces around her, imagining their joy in their land, their life style, in each other, blanked out; the myths they enjoyed weeping over at this moment – the harper was singing the 'Children of Lîr' – replaced by repetitions of death to inspire generations into hatred and revenge. Keep them innocent and free.

She slept in Cormac and Brigh's long house that night, between sheets and white blankets on a pile of rushes. 'Nobody ever caught cold sleeping on sweet new rushes,' Brigh said.

Obviously they knew she had some connection with Grace O'Malley, and were dying to know more, but at no point had they asked her. Curiosity into a guest's business was bad form.

The next day they wanted to take her hunting, and it was only reluctantly, at her insistence, that they let her go. Even then she was escorted through the mountains to the edge of their tribal land where she and the others were handed over to the next clan, the O'Dalys. It was actually done under a flag of truce. 'We're at war with the O'Dalys, sorrow fly away with them. The bastards have been at our herds. But you'll be safe enough, thieves of the world though they are. They respect the O'Neill.'

All the Connaught clans, it seemed, respected the O'Neill, though whether they respected him enough to sink their differences and band together when the time came, thought Barbary, was another matter.

From then on travel was slow, partly because the terrain became wilder but mainly because Connaught clans could not receive a newcomer into their land without entertainment. There was a feast of welcome in every new territory. Sometimes it was held outdoors, sometimes in castles built on crags, or on an island in a lough. It was always noisy – the free Irish were incapable of eating without the accompaniment of harpers and singers – friendly, and crowded.

Cuckold Dick regained some of his natural bloating,

and groaned with hangover as they set off the following morning. 'I'll never touch bloody whiskey again, Barb.'

'Until the next time.' She couldn't stand *usquebaugh* herself and in order to save her hosts' feelings surreptitiously emptied it under the table, soaking various wolfhounds in the process.

As they went further north and west they found they were no longer under the aegis of O'Neill, but a deity known as 'Herself'. Joyces handed them over to MacJordans and MacJordans to Clanrickards with the instruction: 'Travellers to be escorted to Herself.' O'Neill's writ had run out and that of Grace O'Malley had taken over. It was something, thought Barbary, for a woman to command such a title among clans as powerful as these. For they were very powerful clans indeed, no longer pure Irish but descendants of Norman knights, De Burgo, Dexter, Prendergast, who conquered Ireland in the twelfth century and then absorbed themselves into its culture, becoming Bourke, MacJordan, MacMorris, gone native while still retaining a sense of superiority and a wider contact with the rest of the world. Their castles were big, gloomy and medieval; they feasted Barbary lying on couches in halls as big as Westminster's. They dressed Irish, had adopted Irish names, spoke Irish, but ('Jesus, Barb, look at them fart-catchers') splendidly dressed footmen stood behind the couches.

On the morning following the feast at the grandest castle of all, belonging to MacOliverus, as Barbary was being accompanied by MacOliverus women down turret steps to the great hall, ready to ride off with her escort to the next destination – and wondering when this interesting but interminable journey would be over – she passed Cuckold Dick and heard the whisper: ''Ware hawk.'

She excused herself to the ladies, pretending she had forgotten something back upstairs, and joined Dick in a window recess. 'What?'

'We're too far north, Barb.'

'Eh?'

He looked worried. 'Do you know where we are?'

'No.' She'd stopped asking the names of locations. She looked out of the narrow loophole, glimpsing a colossal view of mountains and a bright blue lough nestling in the middle of them.

'Nor me. But, Barb. We're too far north. O'Malley territory's over there somewhere.' He waggled his hand through the arrow slit in a south-westerly direction. 'I found out. This MacOliverus is a chief of Clan MacWilliam, right?'

She nodded.

'Now there's two parts to Clan MacWilliam. The Lower MacWilliam and the Upper MacWilliam. I know because O'Neill told me afore I set off. "When you gets to the Upper MacWilliam," he says, "you'll be a day's ride to Grace O'Malley's land." '

'So?'

'This MacOliverus is the Lower MacWilliam. Last night somebody addressed him as MacWilliam Iochtarach, and that means Lower, don't it?'

'All right, but if this is Lower MacWilliam ken, the next stop north'll be Upper MacWilliam and we'll be oatmeal.'

Dick shook a doleful head. 'This is Ireland, Barb. Upper and Lower's got bugger all to do with geography, nor logic neither. Lower MacWilliam's more north of the Upper. The cove as I sat next to last night was trying to explain it. We've passed the Upper MacWilliam. We been taken too far.'

Barbary drew in her breath. 'Where's that shite MacSheehy?'

'Gone.'

'Gone?'

'And never called me mother. We're in the brown stuff, Barb.'

She handed him her muff. 'Load the Clampett, then come on down. Me and MacOliverus is having a talk. I'll upper his lowers for him.'

But the handsome MacOliverus was unfazed by her questioning.

'Beautiful lady, it's Herself's very own castle you'll be at this very own night. At Carrickahowley. Well, it's sort of her castle. Temporarily, if you see what I mean. And her very own son waiting there to greet you.'

'O'Flaherty?' For one confused second she thought he must mean her father.

'No, no. Bourke. Tibbot. Tibbot of the Ships. And agog to see you.'

321

Tibbot? Bourke? She remembered no Tibbot Bourke. As she mounted Spenser, Dick was waiting at her side to pass up her muff before getting on his own horse.

Whatever was up – and something was, her nose was sniffing fish – there was damn all she could do about it. The escort was too big, and it was guiding her through a landscape so bewildered by bog, precipice and river that she and Dick couldn't hope to find their own way in it. Was Grace O'Malley still so suspicious of her? Did some quirk of Connaught clan politics, already more confusing to her even than the landscape, want her hostage? Or dead?

She rode all day with one hand on Spenser's reins and the other hidden round the butt of the Clampett.

But as evening came on, her nose began to smell a different scent than fish. Compounded with weed and brine and space, it sidled up on her like an acquaintance once seen years ago, afraid she wouldn't remember. A subliminal picture blinked into her brain. A shore and on it a rectangular tower and beyond the tower the flat, limitless surface of the sea. Her head whipped to her left, pointing like a dog's. Hills, just hills. The track they were on meandered dully between grass and heather, trying to pretend that it was a typical Connaught road, that the little beaten paths heading westward off it led to yet more sheep-cropped hills. The track was lying. It was throwing strangers off the scent, but Barbary's nose knew the scent from way back.

Somewhere just beyond those hills to the left, where the paths went, was the sea.

Why were they keeping her away from the sea? Her sea. The iodine content of her body awoke to that mysterious substance present in the water over the hill; just as every drop in the ocean answers to the force that creates the tide, Barbary's blood responded to a gravitational pull.

'Is it this turn to Carrickahowley?' her escorts were asking each other, 'or is it further on?' They hadn't been keeping her from the sea; they were lost, as the track intended they should be. The shoreline over those hills was a secret.

Barbary watched a skein of greylag geese pass overhead going west on long, unhurried wingbeats. Hardly aware she was doing it, she headed Spenser down one of the paths to follow them.

'We'll say goodbye then.' Behind her, uncertain voices bade her farewell as if relieved that she'd taken the initiative. She was going where they didn't want to go. She didn't hear them.

'Wait, Barb. Where you going? We'll be stranded.'

They were, literally, stranded. The track threaded between two hills and opened out into a stream-riven, flat expanse of grass and rock on which rabbits were enjoying the pleasantness of the evening. Rowan and hawthorn trees cast long shadows over close-nibbled turf that had been lent a viscous emerald green by the sunset. There were hills on both sides of the view, but down its middle, curved like a hand with fingers extended towards her, was sparkling clear water. And interrupting the low, golden light, sturdy as a giant with his legs slightly apart as he looked out to sea, was the black outline of a tower.

She had been born here. Or if not here, somewhere just like it. A tower, hills, water, were the constituents from which she was assembled.

'. . . 'Ware hawk, 'ware hawk. For Chrissake, Barb. 'Ware *hawk*.' Cuckold Dick was pulling at her arm. She dragged her eyes away to concentrate on the here and now, which was lanced with the shadows of armed men, about ten of them, closing in from behind and from the low buildings which stood across the stream adjacent to the tower.

'What do you want?' she asked crossly, as they encircled her. She hadn't got time for fear or dealing with it; she was too busy with the other emotions this place held.

They were odd Irishmen, now she came to look at them, if Irish was what they were. They were smartly defined in English iron helmets, short cloaks and had a blazon on the front of their tunics. Squinting into the dying sun, she could just make out the quarterings. One contained a lion and another a black cat.

'Well?' she shouted at them. Whatever they'd been expecting, it wasn't irritation. Their leader, a man with an English sword on his belt, glanced towards the tower at a loss. The door in its dark side opened and somebody huge came down the steps, making the sign of the cross.

323

'God and His saints be praised we got you here,' he said. If he'd just rescued her from drowning, he couldn't have taken more credit for her safety.

His relief sounded spontaneous, but Dick whispered: 'He's been watching from the tower these five minutes.'

With her in the sun and him in the shade of the tower, she couldn't make the figure out, except that it spoke English with the fruity, exaggerated care of one trying to disown a natural Irish accent. 'I am Theobold Bourke,' it said. 'Welcome to Rockfleet Castle, cousin. Come in, come in.'

Even when she'd been ushered into the hall of the tower and servants had scurried to put a flame to the resined torches in the sconces, she couldn't make him out. She never really did.

He was enormous, over six foot and wide with it. At the moment his height made his bulk impressive, but any more lateral growth was going to land him in the category of the obese.

'I'm supposed to be meeting someone called Tibbot somewhere called Carrickahowley,' said Barbary peevishly. She was resentful at leaving the images on the shore, and being dwarfed never improved her temper.

'So you have, my dear girl. Carrickahowley is the Irish for this castle, but I prefer the English version, Rockfleet. I am Theobald Bourke, known to the Irish as Tibbot of the Ships.' He used the word 'Irish' as if patting an unkempt head, but, for all his care, he pronounced Theobald 'T'eobald'.

'Oh yes?'

'Ah hah,' he boomed, as at a triumph. 'We're displaying a gap in our knowledge, aren't we? If we are Mistress O'Flaherty we should know of me.' He lowered his big head and put up a finger in mock interrogation. 'Grace O'Malley? Your grandmother? Married Richard Bourke? Gave birth to Tibbot Bourke? Eh? I'd be your uncle, wouldn't I? Your Uncle Tibbot.'

He *was* a gap in her knowledge. She knew no Uncle Tibbot. She stared up into his face and saw with a shock that, for all his girth, for all the loud superiority, Uncle Tibbot was very young, younger than she was. Aided by his size and his deep voice, he'd opted to by-pass youth for the style and grandeur of an English middle-aged

324

gentleman, but his eyes let him down. They darted about and blinked too often in adolescent suspicion of being found out.

She smiled back at him. 'That would be after my childish departure from the Irish scene, would it, Uncle?'

Inside the grown-up armour, a little boy sulked, then changed tack. 'You'll be hungry.' He clicked his fingers, commanding a servant to take their cloaks. He nodded distantly at Cuckold Dick to indicate that he wasn't the class of person he usually entertained and drew out a chair at the table for Barbary to sit, pointing to Dick's place and shouting for the first dishes.

She tore her eyes off him to look around. The flame from the sconces threw light on excellent furniture and tapestries, all in the English style. The only typically Irish adornment was a gruesomely lifelike crucifixion in wood. Whatever else he had abandoned, Tibbot of the Ships kept to the faith of his birth.

She was unsettled by four of his soldiers ranging themselves round the walls with spears in their hands, like statues. Ornamental perhaps, but they made her spine tickle.

Like the hall, the table was the most elegant she'd seen since Penshurst, laid with an enormous gold salt – Cuckold Dick had been placed below it – gold candlesticks, gold plates, gold goblets, wreaths of cowslips, linen napkins. A servant placed a charger in front of Tibbot containing a long, unappetising-looking grey fish, decorated with prawns. 'Now I think this will surprise you,' he said, cutting into it with the dedication of a chirurgeon. 'It's lamprey. An acquisition I brought to Sir Richard Bingham's table for which he has always been grateful.'

'You've dined with Bingham?'

Again the jubilant 'Ah hah. As a lad I was fostered in his household. Didn't they tell you that in Dublin?'

So he was another of the young chieftains the English had attempted to anglicise by rearing them in noble English households. And to better effect in his case than O'Neill's. Where the O'Neill aped English manners as a form of profanity, Tibbot found them congenial.

'Now don't be put off by its look,' he said, sliding a slice of lamprey onto her plate, 'nor that poor old Henry the First died of a surfeit.' He spread out his fat fingers to lick them. 'It's ambrosia.'

If he could surfeit Henry the First, whoever he was, perhaps he was going to surfeit her, whatever that meant, and it sounded nasty. She didn't like the way there were only the three of them at table. She didn't like the soldiers round the walls. 'And I don't trust you, Beefbelly, further'n I could throw you.' Hungry as she was, she didn't touch the lamprey until her host had taken his first bite. She heard Dick whisper sadly to himself: 'It's eel. And it ain't jellied.'

A servant poured them wine. 'A nice little sack I picked up in Spain,' said Tibbot of the Ships.

If they sat discussing pan and peck all night, she'd never find out what was going on. 'The MacSheehy was supposed to be taking me to Grace O'Malley,' she said.

'Yes. I sent him a small . . . *pourboire*, asking him to bring you here instead.'

So the MacSheehy had accepted a bribe to disobey the O'Neill and let her fall into the hands of this possibly dangerous uncle. She'd never liked the MacSheehy and, obviously, he hadn't liked her much either.

'This is Bourke territory, my girl. And you can thank your stars for that.' His face tightened. 'Of course, Herself would say it was hers. She married Father to get all the land on this side of the bay. Married him and sent him off on a trading trip to Spain, and when he sailed back, wouldn't let him land. Said she'd only married him for one year certain.' He pointed a colossal, agitated arm upwards: 'Stood up there, leaned over the parapet and shouted: "I divorce you." ' He was spurting bits of lamprey into his beard. 'She kept the castle, of course.'

This 'one year certain', after which wife or husband could simply withdraw from a marriage, more than anything else separated Irish society from mainland Europe. It scandalised the English. Grace's use of it scandalised her son. He wanted Barbary to register shock, but she was used to similar arrangements in the Order, and was thinking how well it would suit her and Rob.

She needed to place this new, giant uncle and his motive for bringing her here, apparently to save her from some terrible fate at the hands of his mother. Barbary got a mental picture of Grace rampaging Connaught, looking for her granddaughter, cutlass upraised – and didn't believe it. Why this uneasy, extraordinary meal? The lamprey had been replaced by cooked swan, its feathered head and neck wired to rise lifelike out of the meat. Keep him talking. How much does he know? Learn. The soldiers round the walls indicated her life depended on it.

He was back on food, a favourite subject, pouring wine for them both.

'I stole a cook from Genoa on my last voyage. The climate didn't suit him and he died, but not before he'd passed on some of his skill. Admire Italian cuisine, do you?'

'Never met him. Why'd you bring me here?'

He waved his knife at her. 'It was a damned near thing. Herself's on Clare just now, so we can get you away before she knows you've been.'

'Why?'

'Why?' He sat back. 'Good God, woman, she'll kill you.'

'Why?'

'Because she didn't manage it in Dublin, that's why. Because she thinks you're an imposter. Because, God forgive me, she's an uncivilised woman.' He crossed himself. More wine for the two of them. Cuckold Dick was left to pour his own. Which he did.

So he knew what had happened in Dublin Castle. But he didn't know, bless his porky britches, what had since transpired between O'Neill and Grace O'Malley, and that Barbary was to be given a chance to prove her identity. He wasn't that much in the confidence of either. Unless, of course, Grace O'Malley didn't intend to give her a chance at all, but had tricked O'Neill into putting this hated imposter into her power. Who was lying?

The swan went, a glazed boar's head with an apple in its jaws came in. Barbary's stomach was starting to revolt. With the absolute concentration he gave to food, Tibbot began carving. Barbary picked up her newly filled goblet, looking for a handy wolfhound, didn't find one, and poured her wine into the rushes.

He continued to recount atrocity stories about his mother. 'Shall I tell you why they call her the Dark Lady of Doona? She had this lover,' his full cheeks went tight again, 'one of many. Anyway, he got killed out hunting

327

by the MacMahons of Ballycroy. And she sailed to the MacMahon stronghold of Doona and she slaughtered them. All of them.'

'And kept the castle.'

Tibbot nodded. He was getting drunk. 'She kept the castle.'

Roast peacock next, its spread tail giving Barbary another screen behind which to pour away another goblet of wine. The atrocities went on. Grace and piracy. 'Sent more good men to the bottom than I've had hot dinners. What sort of woman is that?' Grace and gambling. 'She cheats. I swear the bitch cheats.'

Venison with antlers stuck into it. Atrocity. Wine. Veal and mutton pie with a live skylark pinioned to the crust. Atrocity. Wine. The rushes round Barbary's feet were sopping. Her Uncle Tibbot stretched his arms across the table, looking at her with venom. 'Do you know how old I was when she took me on my first pirate raid? Five. That's how old. I was frightened by the guns. You would be, wouldn't you? At five? And I clung to the back of her skirt. Do you know what she said? She said: "Are you trying to crawl back into the place you came from?" That's what she said.' His mouth was puckered, tears rolling down his cheeks. He heaved himself up. 'I'm going to piss.'

She watched him blunder out with something like compassion. Loves her, hates her, envies her, fears her. Poor old Beef-belly.

Dick reached casually for the wine: 'Clampett cocked, Barb?'

She crumbled some bread: 'Trained right on his nutmegs.' It had been pointed ready through the muff on her lap the whole meal, waiting for one move from the spearmen. Her back was stiff with tension. She'd grown old in this damned room while that tortured tub of lard went through his performance to scare her off.

She could hear him relieving himself out on the steps, then the sound of vomiting. Above the flickering sconces, a high window was letting in moonlight. The soldiers tensed as she left her place and clambered up on the chest beneath the window to look out.

The hand of water was silvered by the moon, still beckoning her. The bay, he'd called it. This would be one of the hidden inlets of Clew Bay. Beyond the turn of the hill – there was a stag outlined against its smooth top – the water curved out into that huge, magical expanse which flowed into other secret inlets with other towers. She'd been born in one of them. Not here, she knew now, but one of them . . .

'What are you looking at?'

Offguard, she said: 'Waiting for the ship.'

'What ship?' Tibbot shoved her out of the way to look, then relaxed. 'There's nothing there.' He'd sobered up a bit. He held out his hand like a courtier to help her back to her place. 'So you see why we must return you to the Pale, quickly.'

'What does she think I want?' What do *you* think I want?

'Whatever you can get. But, my dear Mistress Barbary,' he jeered at the name, 'there's nothing you *can* get. Whatever they advised you in England, women here can inherit nothing.'

She nodded. He was giving himself away nicely. 'Except the treasure.'

'What do you know about the treasure?' His hand had gone to his sword hilt. The soldiers shifted.

She recited: ' "The ceremony of the Kishta is for the noble women of the Two Owels and the female fruit of their womb." ' She was showing her hand because it was time to show it; she was sick of the table's masculine meatiness, the disguising, this derivative meal, this derivative man. She kept her hand tight on the butt of the Clampett. 'I've come home, Uncle Tibbot.'

Absorbing that she was truly his niece took time because he had been so sure she wasn't. She saw it touch astonishment, jealousy and finally, a deep atavism. He was Irish through his bones, and the Irish tanaist was a wolf that killed all rivals. 'You stupid, interfering whore.' He'd stood up and was leaning like a huge mattress over the table. 'I'll not have you here. She's *my* mother. What's hers is mine.' It was terrible, a child's 'She loves me best' coming from a man's throat.

She cowered back and took the Clampett out of the muff. He stared at it and she thought she'd have to shoot him. But he wasn't a fool, whatever else he was.

He sucked in breath. 'My dear lady, no need for that.'

He collapsed back in his chair and collected himself well. She was proud of him. 'What I am trying to say in my rough way,' he said quietly, 'is that there's nothing but grief for you here. Herself is a savage living a savage's life. Look at you now, a dainty English lady, used to English ways.' Did he think all dainty English ladies carried a handgun? 'Herself will never learn it, but you know and I know that our future lies in acknowledging England's supremacy. Gaelic Ireland is dead.'

'And you wouldn't fight for it?'

'I did.' The answer surprised her. 'When the other Bourke clans rebelled I went to war against the English. And lost.'

'What if there was another rebellion? What if all Ireland rebelled?'

He put his elbow on the table and rested his big jowls on his hand, smiling. 'I believe in keeping my options open.' It was the most honest thing he'd said all night. She found herself smiling back.

He became brisk. 'Bed for you, little lady. We'll talk in the morning. Your servant can sleep with my men. Cathal, light Mistress Barbary to her rest.'

'My servant, as you call him, sleeps across my door.'

He shrugged, and bade her an avuncular goodnight. The man who'd waited at table took a flare from a sconce and led the way up the tower's narrow, curving staircase to an upper storey. Halfway up, in the darkest section between the moonlit loopholes, he stumbled, dropped the torch which went out, stumbled again in the blackness so that his foot slipped backwards and caught Barbary on her shoulder; she fell back and sideways, slithering down two steps into Cuckold Dick who lost his footing but, filling more of the staircase's width than Barbary, managed to wedge his spread arms into a fence that stopped the two of them from breaking their necks.

It was over quickly. What took longer were anxious calls from Uncle Tibbot at the bottom of the stairs, slobbered apologies from the servant, before Barbary and Dick, rubbing their bruises, were able to limp into her room, bolt the door, and realise what a nasty incident it had been.

Dick stayed at the door with his ear against it. 'Way

out there, Barb?' He pointed to the window.

She looked out and down, to a sheer drop. 'No.'

The room overlooked the inlet. She stayed at the window, breathing fast, trying to dispel her shakes. What was it with her and towers that her worst moments, and her best, occurred in them? A long way down, on the ground, just out of her sight, a whip was swishing back and forth, and someone was moaning as it hit.

'They're lashing that bastard stumbler,' she said over her shoulder. 'Because he nearly killed us? Or because he didn't?'

'We was Amy-ed all right,' Dick said. Ever since Queen Elizabeth's favourite, the Earl of Leicester, had been unencumbered of his wife by her convenient accident, the act of pushing someone downstairs, or of being pushed, had become known in Order cant as an 'Amy Robsart'.

Barbary gave way to her shaking legs and slid down to the floor. 'Why, though? If he wanted us worm-meat, whyn't he just spear us clean and quick? Why that fokking awful meal?'

'It was marvellous tasty, Barb,' said Dick with the air of a man giving credit where it was due. 'Making an impression. Your Uncle Tibbot can't weigh you any more'n you can weigh him. He reckons the Rome-Mort sent you, and he don't want to upset the English. Wants to stay palsy with Bingham.'

'Why the Amy Robsart, then?'

'He's Irish, Barb. He don't think straight. Shit-scared you was going to take something away from him. But I tell you this, Barb, he's a likely lad. Give him a few more years and he'll swadder with the best.' Dick shook his head, as one who sees a protégé's brilliant potential. 'What an Upright Man he'd make then.'

He made her lie down on the bed while he took first guard duty. For a moment or two Barbary's eyes stayed on the moonlit window; for all the evening's vicissitudes, for all that the best they could expect of the next day – if they survived it at all – was to be escorted back on the long journey they had already made, she could not rid herself of the certainty that the view outside was going to produce something wonderful. Its particular combination

331

of land and water was so acutely personal to her it couldn't, surely, witness her destruction without coming to her aid.

'Barb.' Dick's whisper cut into her last sleep. She'd been waiting for it. Good or bad, she'd known it would come. 'Barb. Come and see.'

The moon was still up, contrasted into a wan disc by the sun beginning to rise out of sight behind the tower. Light touched the top of hills and the furthest edge of sleek water. The view was full of everything early, tide, fresh leaf, new grass, the first calls of oystercatcher and curlew bobbing in the shallows, terns skimming the unbroken surface.

And into the inlet was coming its missing piece. The ship. It should always have been there. The breathless morning obviated a sail, so the slanting yardarm was empty, leaving the hull's symmetry uncluttered except for the oars on each side rising and falling in a beat of matchstick wings. At this distance they flapped so delicately there was no sense of propulsion, the ship just grew in size.

Barbary sobbed.

The tower look-out was late seeing it, but now there was a shout: 'Herself's coming!' Boots sounded up and down the staircase outside their door, somebody hammered on it: 'Come out.' Dick shook his head. Spears started thudding into the wood, but they had piled most of the room's furniture against the door during the night, and after a few tries there was silence.

The ship's unearthliness was dispelled as it approached; Barbary could see the sweating backs of rowers bending to and fro, the sea-stained, wooden figurehead of a woman's torso at its bow, but with detail came the music, a drum beating the rowers into time, a chant. The oarsmen were singing. They always had.

With its shallow draught the galley was able to approach right up to the rock plinth on which the tower stood. A man in the bow shouted: 'We've come for the Protestant woman, Tibbot.'

From above her head – he was standing on the roof of the tower – Tibbot shouted back: 'What woman?'

The man in the prow grinned and pointed at Barbary's window. 'The wee one there, waving like a windmill.

Herself expected her at Murrisk. You'll smell Hell for this.'

She didn't care he'd called her 'Protestant', which in his sense meant anything of inferior quality. She didn't care, she didn't care. She was leaping up and down. 'Don't go without me.'

From above, a chastened Tibbot called: 'Don't tell Herself, Cull.'

Cull jumped ashore, followed by some of the rowers. 'Ah now, Tibbot, just let the wee girl go.' Dick was pulling away the furniture from the door.

Cull met her on the steps, a weatherbeaten, capable-looking man whose eyes widened at the sight of her hair.

'There's two of us,' she told him, joyfully. 'Oh, and our mounts.'

He was not friendly. 'Herself's expecting the one of you,' he said, 'not a damned entourage. Get into the galley.'

It had been a bad night and a dawnful of emotion. 'You think I'm leaving my friend and my horse with that bastard Tibbot,' she raged, 'you bloody think again. He'd cook 'em. I come here willing.' Shaking, she pulled the Clampett out of the muff. 'Want me unwilling?'

He didn't look at the gun, being too busy staring at her with a peculiar look on his face. At last he turned away and gave an order: 'Prepare horse stays.'

Tibbot emerged from the tower, full of aplomb. 'Are you off, then, cousin?' He turned to Cull. 'Where are you going with her?'

'She's for the Test,' Cull said shortly, moving off.

Tibbot of the Ships took his niece's hands in his. 'My poor girl. My poor, poor girl. I warned you.' Cull was shouting with impatience from the galley. Tibbot put his head down to give her an avuncular kiss on the cheek. 'Shun Adam, hug Eve,' he whispered.

Barbary drew a deep, grateful breath. 'Thank you, Uncle.'

A moment later she followed Cuckold Dick and Spenser along a gangplank into the cherubims.

Chapter Sixteen

On the map of Ireland the O'Neill had given to Barbary, the west coast looked like a tattered flag streaming out into the Atlantic with bits shredding off the ragged end from the blow of an easterly wind. The reality was the other way round. The bits were islands, scores of inhospitable pieces of rock which had refused to go under the Atlantic as it surged on its westerly way to lacerate the land.

On this day they floated greeny-brown out of a sapphire sea. The men at the oars of the galley were singing the 'Oro and Welcome Home', just in case Barbary was who she claimed to be; if she wasn't she wouldn't understand it and would soon be dead anyway, so no harm to sing her to her funeral. The 'chunk' of the oars went in time to the song.

Rowing was so much their second nature that they made it look easy to speed a galley against the wind, though it wasn't. Cuckold Dick and Barbary faced them in the stern. They weren't a pretty view. Every one of them had the neck, shoulders and arms of an ogre. In contrast, their legs looked weedy when they stood up, though they were as muscled as most men's. An over-abundance of scars and broken noses made Cuckold Dick uneasy. 'I bet their mothers were polite to 'em,' he murmured to Barbary. 'If they had mothers.'

Barbary wasn't seeing what he saw; more than a decade of years had washed out of her eyes allowing everything she looked at to be touched with the glittering unexpectedness it had held for her as a child. These men, or men very like them, had not seemed brutal then and didn't now. Their faces were landscapes of home, just as the shapes of Croagh Patrick and the Twelve Pins behind her were home, just as the salt of this wind and this sea was part of the saline in her own veins. She struggled, like Odysseus against his ropes, not to call out to these villainous-looking sirens, to the seagulls, to the mermaids and dolphins of her kingdom: 'It *is* me. I'm back. Oh God, I'm back.' They wouldn't believe her. She had to prove it.

She had been allowed to rest at Murrisk, where a grumpy, seasick Spenser had been put ashore and, with Dick's horse, installed in a hilly meadow more to his liking. Then the galley had rowed out into Clew Bay where every one of the little islands, locked into it like a petrified school of whales, possessed that far-off familiarity to the child within her who had shrimped the pools of their beaches. Now, out here on the open sea, the bigger islands sent their names and personalities pulsing across the waves to her, like pleas to come and land. Out to starboard, Clare, not Clare Island, just Clare, crouched lion-fashion at the bay's entrance. A castle, a mountain, a chant in a church. Hold Clare, young Barbary, and no ship enters or passes unless you allow it passage. Clare is power.

Coming to port was Caher, small, wedge-shaped, containing an appalling holiness. 'Dip oars to Caher,' whispered Barbary, a second before Cull shouted: 'Dip oars to Caher.' Eighteen pairs of oars rose, streaming water, and dipped in reverence. Inishturk, the Island of the Boar, walled with cliffs. Ahead Inishbofin, the island of the ghostly white cow, hiding with its bulk the Sound between it and its calf, Inishark – and the place of her ordeal.

Cuckold Dick was gaining confidence from the brightness. 'Well, Barb, not a bad day for it. Bit of a chop, but nothing we can't handle.'

She patted his knee. He had no idea. Bit of a chop, bless him. The smoothness of the rowing and the skill of Cull at the galley's two tillers were making light of a very considerable swell. Here in the stern they were sheltered by the banks of oarsmen, but the galley's pennant was streaming in a straight line. Better get his safety established before he saw what test Grace O'Malley had set her. 'I'm making the landing alone, Dick. One of her conditions.' It wasn't, but no reason for them both to come to a watery end.

Dick looked suspicious. 'You scrimming me?'

'No.' Her invigoration was masking her fear.

The men had stopped singing, and a spare rower was beating the great drum at his feet, gradually quickening the stroke. Don't hurry for me.

There were other ships in the Sound, three small galleons, some hookers, and a couple more galleys, part of Grace O'Malley's vast fleet hiding in the inlets like hermit crabs, waiting to reach out and grab passing merchant-ships. A couple of yawls were fishing. The Sound was virtually invulnerable to pursuit; its rocks and reefs could tear the bottom out of those who didn't know them. The families who lived on Bofin were all involved in Grace's pirate trade and most of them were lining the vantage points to get a glimpse of Barbary's ordeal; what concerned Herself concerned them.

If you had to die it was a fine day for it; even better for living. Shags stood along the spines of rock ledges in untidy knobbles, waiting their chance to dive. Spits of sand were white under the sun, the rocks had become grey-brown, green-grey, black-green, any colour as long as it was rock, the Sound was a downland of swell on which white heads grazed like sheep around the half-tide shoal.

Dick was becoming less easy as he eyed the spume along the shoreline. 'Where's this landing then, Barb?'

'There.' It was just in sight, a reef like a lower jaw of rotten teeth centring on the two pillars of rock against which the Atlantic dashed itself, furious at their impudence in daring to impede it.

'Them? You got to get between them two rocks?'

Cull saw her pointing and leaned down to her. 'Did you know? Are you yourself then?'

'Yes.' He'd treated her kindly ever since her outburst at Rockfleet. She'd heard him muttering to the stroke oar: 'Threatened me, she did. And the spit of Herself as she did it.'

He nodded. 'I thought when I saw the hair. I thought to meself: "It wasn't from the wind she caught *that*." But Herself won't have it, and a bad day she's chosen to prove it. Do you know the trick of it? I swore I'd not tell and she'd have the skin off me.'

She was beginning to gasp with fear. 'I bloody hope so.'

The oars had come to rest and the two anchors were splashed overboard. 'Herself's in the haven waiting you.' They lowered a small curragh over the side and opened the taffrail gate so that she could clamber down into it. It was bobbing like a leaf. The galley crew watched her, interested but uncommitted, though one or two of them called out a blessing. Only Cull's face was worried. He handed down the oars. 'May God open the gap for you.'

At the last moment there was a bump in the curragh and Cuckold Dick settled himself in the stern. 'Get out,' she shouted.

'You need the ballast,' he shouted back. She needed a lot of things, courage, skill, memory; what she didn't need was the responsibility of drowning her dearest friend. But she was glad of him; the curragh was too light. Dick was peering over its side. 'What's it made of?'

'Leather.'

His shoulders began to droop as if he had plumbed the depths of Irish madness. She began to row. 'When we . . . get there . . . be ready. To shift. Where I tell you.'

He was looking over her shoulder to the rock pillars. 'Can't be done, Barb,' he said, loudly and reasonably. 'Let's go home.'

She glanced behind her. From here the angle put the rocks so close as to preclude an eel. The sea lifted before the interruption so that the surface of the small bay beyond looked *lower*. Was she remembering right? Eve was the straight one to starboard, Adam leaned in a topple towards her. Both of them had spray skirts that shot up to their waists and back. 'Bigger than . . . it looks,' she puffed. 'But don't cough.'

They couldn't talk any more. The clash of sea on rock was drowning all sound. A seagull flew past with its beak open to show the red of its mouth but its call was lost in the noise. The race that made this place murderous was tugging them faster and faster to the pillars and she let it take them, praying that she could get out of it at the right moment.

Shun Adam, hug Eve. Shun Eve, hug Adam. Christ, which was it? What had Tibbot said? She'd done this before, but her grandmother had been in the stern then, and the wind had been a light breeze. 'Pull, young

Barbary. Let's see if you're a true O'Malley with you.'
Where was the old besom now? Standing on the beach
beyond the pillars waiting for her granddaughter's body
to come ashore in slices?

They were towed at increasing speed past a high shelf
of rock on which an enormous seal was watching them
with voluptuous indolence. Was that Herself? A seal-
woman grandmother? More than likely.

Close now. The curragh was too light, resting on the
water like a puffin. 'Shun Adam, hug Eve,' Tibbot had
said. She could hear his whisper in the undertow. She
was truly grateful to him; you could bank on Uncle
Tibbot to put you wrong. Her trust was in the voice from
the cherubims. 'Hug Adam, shun Eve.' She shook wet
hair out of her eyes to glance back. They were lifted up.
Down. Up Christ, they were *above* the rocks. NOW.

She tossed her head to the right and Dick leaned hard
to port. She wrenched her arms, pulling, the water like a
solid rock against her oar. Shun Eve. Eve, you bitch, who
named you? Here's Adam, a jagged piece of work, but
what you saw went straight down to the bottom; it was
Eve with vicious crinoline spread out beneath the surface
in snags that shredded a boat's bottom. Eve sucked you
to her. They rose for the last time. Abandon hope. Abandon sanity. Abandon ship. She saw Dick screaming.
Shun. SHUN the shame of Eve. Pull. PULL, young
Barbary. She pulled obediently, desperately, and was in
the friendly current that threaded them under the leaning
Adam and into the bay's calm water.

The thunder stopped. She could hear a curlew fluting
and Dick being sick. Her head was on her knees, her
arms gone; she couldn't row ever again. She didn't have
to. The impetus of the current had carried them to the
beach and somebody tall was dragging the curragh's prow
onto the pebbles.

'Why didn't you say?' asked Grace O'Malley.

They sailed back to Clare in the flagship blasphemously
called the *Grace of God*. The wind sang high incon-
sequential notes in the rigging and, as they glided into
harbour, dropped, as if it had been summoned by
Grainne O'Malley for the purposes of the ordeal and
could now dispense with itself. The inhabitants of the

338

white cottages around Clare's harbour cheered her into it, as the inhabitants of Bofin had cheered her out of theirs. Hands reached down to Barbary to pull her up the steps to the quay, patting her. 'There now, and welcome home, Barbary O'Malley.' So she was an O'Malley. Would the O'Flaherties want to put her to an ordeal to prove she was an O'Flaherty? Well, they could stuff themselves: she wasn't going through that again. She had completed herself. She'd never felt so complete in her life.

An old woman shook her fist at Grace. 'And didn't I tell you, Granuaile? Wasn't she in me dream? Look at the hair on her. And you risking her dear life.'

Grace looked down at the crone, 'Go sell yourself for dogmeat,' and strode on up the slope to her castle. There had been barely a word of welcome from her, certainly no apology for having left her true granddaughter to die in a Wicklow hut.

Dick touched Barbary's arm. 'Overcome with emotion, eh?'

Barbary grinned back at him. 'Broken up with it.' She'd have felt insecure if Grace had been. Exhilarated, she had found the grandmother who was the substance of these bare, ungiving rocks. No lullabying pap had been fed to her by this woman; swim or drown, sail or wreck, grab or go under – the tenets Barbary had survived by all these years came from Grace O'Malley.

Cuckold Dick shook his head admiringly: 'What an Upright Man *she'd* make.'

The castle overlooked the harbour from a rocky rise on its southern side. It was typical of the O'Malley castles, mainly a rectangular keep three storeys high, castellated, harmonious and uncomfortable. Again, Barbary experienced an exchange of familiarity, a hound on guard wanting to greet its young mistress but not daring to disobey the old.

There was a deputation at the door. Barbary's feet left the ground as she was handed from hug to hug. 'Will you be remembering Katty? Ach, the times you've piddled on my knees.' 'It's Manus. Manus, that gave you the little puppy and the measles.'

Among the crowd was a Spaniard, a beautiful young man, Spanish from the crown of his hat to the stained but gilded pom-poms on his shoes, whose beard tickled

Barbary's hand as he kissed it and whose name he huffed at her in carefully enunciated but incomprehensible aspirates.

Bemused, Barbary watched him hurry up the castle stairs after Grace O'Malley. 'That's Don Howsyourfather,' said Manus, Grace's steward. 'He was aboard a Gaulish ship, the *Gran Grin*, that foundered in the bay.'

Barbary stared at him. The *Gran Grin* had been part of the Armada fleet. Rob had mentioned it in his letters. 'Only him?'

'Ah well, he was the best looking, and, do you see, Dowdarra Roe O'Malley, Herself's kinsman, got to the rest of the crew first and he didn't fancy any of them.'

'So what happened to them?'

'Ah well,' said Manus, 'they wouldn't surrender, you understand.' He brightened up. 'But Herself saved Don Howsyourfather.' He thought for a moment, then added: 'And a fine chest with gold in it. And some doublets for Mass. Some good braid. Some goblets. And a grand little canary in a cage.'

She had stepped back in time to a kingdom of rock and sea centring on itself. Bourkes, Clanrickards, O'Connors, O'Flaherties made up the list of allies and enemies. Foreigners were men from Ulster and Munster. Other nationalities were just Gauls, that is, non Gaels, amorphous beings who were irrelevant except to be robbed or killed. That Spanish interest and theirs coincided meant nothing; Spaniards were Gauls and of no more value than fish. Don Howsyourfather had been lucky.

She would have to talk with her grandmother about the political facts of life.

There was no need for Clare Castle's windows to command the sea; such a sophisticated system of signals and runners covered this part of Connaught's coastline that if so much as an unaccountable rowing boat surfaced in the fifty-odd miles of passage between Blacksod Bay and Slyne Head, Grace would know of it in plenty of time to challenge it, demand 'pilotage' – a euphemism for protection money – or sink it. Instead the well-lit upper room of the castle had a view of the harbour, across Clew Bay to the shore and mountains of the mainland.

It had none of the style of Tibbot's tower at Rockfleet; no style at all. It was a hotch-potch of furnishings. A fine, carved chair, a massive Spanish bed with Flemish hangings, an equally massive, brassbound chest, several lobster pots and coiled ropes, a rack of muskets, some eel glaives, a prie-dieu which was being used as a clothes-hanger, a canary in a cage. A huge, rusty iron chain was attached to the bedpost, running across the floor to the window where it stretched over the landing stage into the water, its other end being padlocked to the *Grace of God* out in the bay. If anybody tried to steal her flagship in the night, Grace was going to know about it.

Today it also had a monk hanging from his ankles by a rope attached to a hook in the ceiling. The canary was singing, the monk was swearing.

Grace O'Malley settled herself in the big chair. The rest wriggled their backsides into coils of rope. Manus remained standing and unhappy. 'Can the Father come down now, Grainne Weale?'

'How long's he been up?'

'Since this morning, poor man.'

Barbary studied the monk, a Cistercian, and decided Manus was lying; if the man had been hanging by his heels for that many hours he would be showing other signs of distress than anger. Somebody had taken care to put wadding under the ropes so that they would not chafe his flesh; a similar decency had tied his robe to his knees so that his saintliness was not jeopardised further than his bare legs.

Grace regarded him with disfavour. 'Will you remember me now?'

'I bloody won't,' shouted the monk.

Barbary watched her grandmother rise, take hold of the monk's neck and raise him by it so that his arched head could look out of the window. 'Who rules what you see?'

'Am I denying it, you damned woman?'

She shook him. 'Who rules the sea? Who took Doona Castle? Who escaped from the Saxons? Who is consulted by every chieftain from Clare to Donegal including the O'Neill? Who commands the biggest fleet the world has ever seen? Who pays your bloody wages?'

The monk sulked. 'You do.'

She shook him again. 'Then remember me.'

'I won't.'

341

Cuckold Dick's mouth was open. 'How can he forget her?'

Barbary shook her head. 'I don't think it's that.'

Manus joined their whispering. 'It's the Annals of Clare. He'll not write Herself into them. It has the history of the O'Malley area known as Two Owls, and the name of every O'Malley since St Patrick went up Cruachan Aigli, but he'll not include Granuaile.'

'Leave a bit of a gap, won't she?' asked Dick, fascinated.

'Ah, but she has a bad right to remembrance, being a woman.'

Grace O'Malley swung the monk's head round in Barbary's direction. 'Will you see it's not going to end with me? There's my *tanaist*.'

She had declared Barbary heir to her pirate empire.

Barbary closed her eyes and then opened them to see the monk beaming on her. 'Did you pass the test then?'

'Pleased to meet you,' she said.

'Delighted,' said the monk. 'Welcome with congratulations. And you'll not be remembered either.'

'Why not?'

The monk's answer was firmly reasonable, though Grace had now let go of him so that his head was again swinging inches from the floor. 'It's against nature, do you see. There should be no women chieftains. God wouldn't want it remembered that Eve could outdo Adam.'

It was impasse, and one likely, from the manner in which Grace O'Malley had just picked up a knife, to end in blood. Barbary made her first intervention as heir designate. 'Grandmother, I can read and write. I'll write whatever you want. I'll remember you.'

There was a general intake of breath. Female literacy was obviously rare in these parts. 'God bless the hearers,' said Manus. 'Your woman's a scholar.'

There was a blur of steel as the knife cut through the rope and the monk tumbled onto the floor. 'Out,' Grace told him. 'Cross me again and I'll make you scratch where you don't itch.' The monk scrambled to the door and disappeared.

The feast to welcome Barbary was eaten at long tables outside on the quay and was what Manus described as a 'flahoolagh', meaning chieftain-like. It went on, and off, for two days. As each sheep, venison and ox were carved off the roasting spits, others took their place; the long tables were hidden by dishes of stirabout – oatmeal flavoured with honey and butter – a dozen types of fish, bowls of watercress, leeks and hazelnuts which were refilled as they emptied.

The food was less ornamented than on English boards, and Tibbot's, but it was well cooked and fresh. There was enough wine, mead and ale to fill the harbour but it was the *usquebaugh*, light golden and smoky smooth, that commanded Cuckold Dick's superlatives as he slid under the table for the last time, still begging Manus to tell him the secret of its manufacture. Even Barbary ventured a glass or two.

The sound of pipes over the water announced the arrival of ships carrying the great men of Connaught to the feast for Grainne Weale's granddaughter. MacWilliams, Bourkes, O'Flaherties, Joyces, MacJordans, MacEdmunds, O'Connors, each full title was announced by their hereditary poets to the accompaniment of harps, as their golden-cloaked owners stepped ashore. It was an impressive gauge of Grace's power, Barbary realised, that she could summon men representing septs and clans as anciently important as these, though undoubtedly curiosity had played as big a part in their coming as diplomatic expediency. They wanted to see if this new woman was big enough to fill the shoes of the old, or if, when Grace O'Malley died, they could move in on the kingdom she had carved out for herself. And how in hell *had* she carved it out? There were no rules of succession under which a woman could succeed to monarchy or chieftainship here as there were in England. Elizabeth's path to the throne hadn't been easy, but there had been precedent for it; there was none for Grace's. Elizabeth had been supported by influential parties; nobody backed Grace, who had faced opposition, incredulity and that greatest of Irish obstructions, custom. Admittedly, her empire had been gained by battle, plunder and piracy. But so had Elizabeth's.

As she watched her grandmother greet and be greeted by these great chieftains, Barbary searched for the resemblance that Philip Sidney had found between the amazing pair of women. They were about the same age, though Grace, who was taller and thick-bodied, looked the elder with her undyed, red and grey hair and her untouched, weathered skin. She was handsome in a way consistent with her sixty years, whereas Elizabeth could look forty in a flattering light and a raddled crone in a bad one.

Elizabeth had charm; Grace, as far as Barbary could see, had none, but then the barren Elizabeth constantly had to insist that she was feminine, whereas Grace had enough children to prove it for her.

Still, Philip had been right. There was something . . . They were *racketeers*. That's what it was. Dick had seen it at once. If they'd been born to the Order, both would have risen to the top; if they'd been born to trade, they would be successful merchant venturers. If Elizabeth had been an O'Malley, she now would be where Grace was, and Grace, born to Anne Boleyn, would have made Queen of England, because they believed in their own right to power and had the huckster's gift of making others believe it with them. They were manipulators, cony-catchers. They played the only game in town, the game men had invented, and beat men at it.

The chieftains at her grandmother's board kept the same nervously appraising eye on Grace that courtiers kept on Elizabeth, and for the same reason: they didn't know what she would do next. They were out for treaties, alliances, the use of her ships and men: The O'Connors wanted to move against the O'Donnells – would she help? The Lower MacWilliamship was unexpectedly vacant – which of the contenders to the title was she going to support? And Grace, to the contentment of her grand-daughter's cony-catching soul, wheeled and dealed for one person's advantage, her own.

There was little exchange between the two of them. Apart from making sure that the chieftains did Barbary honour, Grace paid her hardly any attention, except to lean over from time to time and bark out matters she felt the girl should know.

'Did ye hear the English have hanged Owen O'Flaherty?'

'Oh?'

From behind his place at the back of Barbary's chair, Manus whispered: 'Herself's eldest. Your father.'

'Oh.' She couldn't remember him. Somewhere in the shadows of her mind was a man who sang of his prowess in battle. Perhaps that was him. She'd never know now. The English had done a good job in orphaning her.

Grace seemed to be taking it well. But then loss was to be expected in Gaelic society. Very few of these chieftains round the table had achieved their position without assassinating someone with a better right to it. Grace's husband, Donal-of-the-Battles O'Flaherty, had murdered Walter-the-Tall Bourke, a candidate to the MacWilliamship, to oblige his sister, who was Walter's stepmother and wanted the title for her own son. Nobody seemed to have minded too much.

Barbary whispered to Manus: 'What happened to my grandfather?'

'Donal of the Battles? Ach, the Joyces killed him.'

'Oh.' For all their disregard for life, which they took in the firm belief that they sent their victim to a better one, they were innocent as the dawn. To them the English were merely another clan with nasty habits. What they regarded as a purely ritual submission to Elizabeth had entitled the Queen of England to regard herself as their Ard Rí, but High Kings had come and gone in their long history without making much difference. Nor had Elizabeth made any difference. Her troops still couldn't penetrate Connaught in safety. Her father had ordered the abolition of monasteries, but monasteries still flourished. The monk Grace had hung from his heels did not exist as far as the English were concerned; the title to his monastic land was marked down as belonging to a certain James Garvey Esq., a worthy English undertaker. But James Garvey Esq. had never dared visit it, and its monks still chanted their Cistercian rule within its walls, acknowledging only the Pope. The O'Malleys upheld them, and occasionally persecuted them, as they had since the early saints built their beehive cells on the hillside of Knockmore a thousand years before.

And despite their continual warring, perhaps because of it, these chieftains and their people lived in balance. They never hunted another species to extinction, they replanted what wood they cut down. The English word 'landowner' had no translation into Irish because they did not understand the concept. Land was shared by even the meanest member of the clan; something everybody occupied temporarily. Assassination was private enterprise, but it was also a sin and they did penance for it, there was no such thing as a legal execution. A murderer must compensate his victim's family under a law which also gave very considerable rights to women. Irish society, in its own particular way, was harmonious.

And they were proud of it. Instead of questioning Barbary on her knowledge of England, its plans and the disposition of its forces, the chieftains courteously ignored that she'd ever been there, as if she'd been abducted by savages and it would be bad form to expose her shame.

The sun was setting out to sea and for one moment coloured everything, animate and inanimate, into saffron. The sheep and horses on the hillside, the hill itself, the water of the harbour and the cottages above it, the men's beards and jewels, the harps of the poets, Grace's hair and face, the glorious chalices on the table, all were washed in a dying gold. Barbary wanted the air to solidify so that these people could be preserved in its amber. They had so little time left before they and their strange culture disappeared for ever. The thought, and the whiskey, brought tears to her eyes. She had found her home, and it was doomed.

'Did ye hear of me marriage and divorce to Richard-an-Iarainn?'

She looked blearily at her grandmother. 'Tibbot's father?'

Grace nodded. 'Iron Dick.'

She tried to concentrate. 'And had he?' she asked.

Grace O'Malley stared at her and then, for the first time, made physical contact with her granddaughter; she slapped her on the back and laughed until the tears fell down her face.

From then on the relationship eased. They stood together on the quay in the dark and watched the chieftains rowed unsteadily back to their ships by torchlight, their calls and the music of their harpers echoing back across the water.

'Tibbot-ne-Long didn't come,' said Grace as they went up to her tower room for a nightcap. It was a statement of fact, not a request for sympathy. Informing this woman

346

that her son had tried to kill her granddaughter was more than Barbary had been able to find it in herself to do. Grace's anger that he had kidnapped her had been considerable enough; as punishment she had sent a force to Rockfleet to 'fine' some of Tibbot's cattle and horses into her own herds. Barbary settled herself in a coil of rope and said, truthfully: 'He's a strange one.'

'Fostered by the English,' said Grace in explanation. 'His father's doing. I was against it. No good ever came from the Saxon.' She looked speculatively at Barbary. 'And in the end didn't they use him as hostage? That I had to go and submit to prison?'

So that was why Grace had landed up in Dublin Castle. To save her son. Tibbot hadn't seen fit to mention it.

'For all that, he'll get the Lower MacWilliamship,' Grace said, 'or I'll know the reason why.'

The guests to the feast had brought the news that MacOliverus, the Lower Macwilliam, he who had sent Barbary into Tibbot's hands, had been killed in a hunting accident. One of the biggest chieftainships in Connaught was up for grabs. If Tibbot wanted it – and his mother was backing him – Barbary felt sympathy for anyone standing in the way.

She yawned. She was tired but reluctant to interrupt this new intimacy her grandmother was showing her. Ever since she'd passed the test, she had basked in Grace's acceptance, but not in Grace's confidence. Only tonight had there been a thaw; perhaps it was because she'd made the old girl laugh with her dirty joke.

'And until I can see what's what with the MacWilliamship,' said Grace, 'I'll not be sailing to get the O'Neill his guns.'

Ah. So that was it. Implicit was not only Grace's ambition for her son, but a distrust of the O'Neill, and Barbary, and a war not of her choosing. 'No good ever came from the Saxon.' It was time to teach her grandmother the facts of life.

But first. 'I brought you some presents,' she said and retrieved from her travelling case a box of tobacco and the whale-ivory pipe Raleigh had given her.

Grace picked up the pipe and studied it. 'And where do I stick this?'

Barbary grinned. 'There's a joke to that in England.'

'There's a joke to it here,' said Grace.

Barbary filled the pipe, lit it, pulled, coughed – she couldn't take to the habit, although she'd tried – and handed it to her grandmother. Grace didn't say thank you, 'I burn me weeds on rubbish dumps,' but she didn't cough. She sat back in her chair, her fingers curled about the pipe as if they'd fallen into accustomed grooves, drawing on it as naturally as a baby sucking mother's milk. There was a sense of encounter; Paris had set eyes on Helen, Hannibal on an elephant. It was love at first puff.

'Now, look,' said Barbary. 'If the English conquer Connaught and Ulster, there won't be no MacWilliamship.' She began to paint the wide political picture. She used words like 'banding together', 'common enemy', 'patriotism', and saw them swirl away out of the window with Grace's pipe smoke. She was lyrical on a united Ireland under the leadership of the O'Neill, of Gaelic children being born to freedom. 'And that's why O'Neill wants cannon,' she finished.

'How much?'

'Very much. I told you.'

Grace spat. 'I mean, how much will he pay?'

'Pay? You don't pay for your own survival.' She went into it all again.

Grace smoked and listened and at the end of it said: 'Is that what they taught you in that Order of yours?'

'It's what I learned since.'

Her grandmother nodded. 'It's horse-shit. If the O'Neill wants guns transported, he pays for it. The English paid me two hundred pounds for similar services rendered. I'd need as much from him.'

Barbary blinked. 'You served the English?'

'I did.'

'I thought you said no good came from the Saxon. Didn't they put you in prison? Trine your own son?'

'No reason not to take their money.'

'It was O'Neill got you out of prison.'

'No reason not to take his either.'

Barbary sank back in her chair. 'You baffle me.'

'Do I now? Well, you'll learn.' Grace looked sideways at her granddaughter. 'Tell the O'Neill two hundred pounds and I'll think about it. But not till harvest.'

Barbary jumped. A voice, the voice of Don Howsyour-father, had sounded sleepily from behind the curtains of the great bed. 'Do you come to bed, my little apple?'

Startled in her belief that sex petered out at thirty, and even more by the thought that her grandmother was anyone's little apple, Barbary said goodnight to her. Grace nodded, still finishing her pipe.

'Well,' asked Barbary of the moon as she went down the slope outside the castle to the house overlooking the harbour which Grace had given her for her own, 'why shouldn't the old masterpiece niggle at her age if she wants to?' If the Queen of England could still pull in lovers, why not Grace of the Ships? Power, that aphrodisiac which attracted beautiful women to authoritative men, however old, was as effective when the sexes were reversed.

And how had Grace got that power? By being the complete survivor, eschewing patriotism, sentiment, principle. The only weakness she had, and the one that had put her into prison, was love for her son.

Barbary addressed the moon again. 'Bloody love,' she said. 'What good is it?'

The harbour that had been saffron an hour or so ago was emptied in a moonlight with the soft shine of pewter. The sea patted the edge of the sand invitingly. Taking off her shoes and stockings, she went for a paddle, in the need to become immersed in the elusive, wonderful night. Tiny waves washed longings back and forth, to have been in this place for ever, to stay for ever in this place, for this place to have for ever. For another bed with a man in it, in another tower, in another part of Ireland, in another time.

'It'll take time,' she told Cuckold Dick. 'Even if O'Neill pays her for carrying his guns, Herself won't leave Connaught just now with the MacWilliamship at stake. I'll talk her round eventually. Until then, Dick, my old herring, it looks as if we're in the pirate trade.'

Dick said nervously: 'It can't be that bad, can it, Barb? It's only the Order with seaweed.'

But it wasn't.

Chapter Seventeen

The Hollandish carrack was equipped each side with four demi-culverin, having sacrificed artillery for cargo space. What she lacked in guns she made up for in speed, manoeuvrability and sheer cheek. Probably because English patrols of the Channel had cramped her style, she'd arrived off Galway the previous week and crippled two merchantmen bound for Bristol, relieved them of their freight and sent them to the bottom. Now, having escaped the wrath of the English navy stationed at Galway, she was sailing north to find pickings in other waters. Grace O'Malley's waters.

Barbary was ordered aboard the *Grace of God*. 'It'll be a grand experience for ye,' said her grandmother. 'I'll mince those Dutchmen into dog vomit.'

'Grand' was not the word Barbary would have chosen. While appreciating the theory that Grace O'Malley's credibility depended on reducing foreign piracy along her own coastline, she suspected she was not going to enjoy the practice. But at this stage she was less afraid of battle than of offending her grandmother. The deck lifted easily under her feet as *Grace of God* swept out of the Sound under full canvas into the sunlight of a fine, blowing day. For once Barbary's spirits failed to rise to the ship's *joie de vivre*.

She wished Cuckold Dick was with her, but two days ago his piratical career had ended before it started. They'd been aboard the galley, one hour out from Clare and bearing down on a naive little Scottish merchantmen whose captain had not seen the necessity to call in and pay 'pilotage' to Grace O'Malley. Dick was explaining to Cull why he, Dick, was not feeling so well. 'Gawd, Cull,' he said, 'but I was foxed last night.' 'Fox-drunk' was an Order phrase and Dick translated it literally. Grace, standing on the galley's poop, froze. Cull swore. The stroke oars stopped rowing, and a ragged shock wave spread along the banked rowers so that oars struck out at all angles while the galley floundered.

Grace O'Malley turned slowly to Dick. 'What did he say?'

Cuckold Dick moved to safety behind Barbary. 'I only said I was drunk last night, Barb.'

Cull shook his head: 'Your man said the word.'

'What word? What's he done?'

Grace rasped: 'Return galley.' The starboard oars dipped, turning the galley back the way she had come, her crew all the time looking fit to kill at Dick. 'And indeed,' Cull told Barbary later, 'without he was a friend of yours, he'd have been over the side. It's the Devil's luck to mention the little red gentleman on board a Connaught ship.'

'Fox, you mean?' She knew sailors were superstitious but this was ridiculous. Cull covered his ears.

Grace watched the Scottish merchantman pass unmolested along her coast with the air of one seeing her children eaten. Nobody explained, possibly because they didn't know, why mention of a fox was fatal to marine enterprise in Connaught, but Dick was banned from the fleet.

And bully for him, thought Barbary. Wish I was. The look-out in the crow's nest had just yelled 'Enemy in sight' at a tiny break on the horizon, and Grace had ordered the cannon run out. In the three hours it took to overhaul the carrack, Barbary reflected on the selectivity of courage; she could be brave, had been brave, in various circumstances, but she didn't think battle at sea was going to be one of them, especially as she had no function in it. Grace on the quarterdeck was showing all the fear of a woman about to box a small boy's ears for his impudence; the crew's anticipation of prize money was obviously greater than their anticipation of death or wounds.

Barbary went down to the gun deck, she might be of use there. Close inspection didn't improve her confidence. The guns were unbelievable; what Will would have said of the miscellaneous selection of ordnance she didn't dare think. There was a huge, possibly Spanish, demi-cannon, two sakers of differing bore, a culverin and some falcons. Some of the ammunition was modern, but there were stone balls among it. The powder keg wasn't being treated with respect; it was too near the guns and because, during the voyage, its three constituents of sulphur, saltpetre and charcoal had stratified, Fergal, Grace's master gunner, was stirring it like a baker.

'You should've got that into cartridges,' she told him sharply, remembering Will's methods. 'You ram that stuff agin the wad too hard and you can grow a beard waiting for it to go off.'

Fergal's nerves were on edge and he didn't like women. 'I'll ram you, O'Flaherty, if you're not away from here.'

She left, to find they were overhauling the carrack obscenely fast. Grace had crammed on every bit of sail the galleon could carry. What she had seen below told her, ominously, that Grace would have to get within at least one hundred yards of the carrack if her own guns were to have any accuracy. Perhaps the Hollander would surrender. Perhaps Grace would surrender. Let one of the buggers surrender. Now.

She could see the black pennant of the Sea Devils streaming from the Hollander's stern as she ran before the wind, the dirty brown of her sails. They were too close, too *close*, the streaming water of the two bow waves clashing into spray between them.

The carrack had one chance to fire as the *Grace of God* bellied past her to gain the wind. It took it. Barbary saw flame lick out from the muzzles of the Hollander's guns, had time to see the puffs of smoke, see the black, round shapes get bigger as they travelled at her, hear the rip of torn air, and just time to leap for cover in the canvas locker before they crashed into *Grace*'s rigging, sending the foremast falling against the main yard. Splinters thudded into the deck like darts.

Men screamed orders, screamed with excitement, with fear, with pain, and above the shocking percussion of both ships' guns, cracking wood and slapping canvas was an ear-scraping stridor that went on and on.

Barbary burrowed her head into harsh canvas that smelled of salt and lanolin. She could still hear it, feel the shudders of the ship. Even in this cover she felt naked, as if she was hanging from the yardarm with 'Shoot me' tattooed across her chest.

Somebody was dragging at her feet. She screamed at them, kicked out and huddled deeper. 'Sure, it's not always like this,' somebody was shouting at her through the racket. She kicked out at the fool, whoever it was. God Almighty, what a time to tell her. As if she'd expose herself to this terror again, this noise, those monstrous black bees humming at her through the air. She could put up with a lot, but never this. She was unmanned, unwomanned. Piracy? They could keep it. Get me out of this, God, and I'll believe in you. Get me out, get me out . . .

Hoping against hope, she wriggled round to put her head out of the locker, and shouted: 'FOX!' Nobody heard her.

The ship jumped up in the air, followed by sound so massive it blew the lid off her locker. She fought her way under more canvas.

Then it was over, quiet, a few shouts. 'Drop anchor.'

Drop anchor? She poked her head out into what had reduced itself to calmer chaos. Tangled rigging, tangled men. A crewman was picking bits of wood out of his arm. She crawled out, hugging a sail. The crewman grinned at her. 'That'll teach them to come pirating in Herself's waters.' She nodded indulgently at him, as to the insane, and looked about.

The Hollander was in worse shape than the *Grace*. The explosion she'd heard had been one of its powder kegs going up. Part of its side and all of its stern had been blown away. Black-singed men lay still on its deck. Others were being thrown overboard. Lines had been set up to transfer the contents of her hold to the *Grace*.

Moving her head slowly, as if it might still come off, she looked for her grandmother and saw her kneeling beside a body on the deck. It had a splinter as big as a rail post through its chest. It was still alive and Grace was talking to it in a voice her granddaughter hadn't heard her use before: '. . . And there you'll wait, Myles, and when it's my time I'll join you and we'll sail the sea of heaven . . . Ach, sure there's boats. Isn't St Peter a fisherman? And didn't Christ do a bit himself?'

There was blood coming out of Myles's mouth which was forming a word. Barbary thought it was 'Deirdre'.

'You know I will,' said Grace. 'You know I will. Like me own. Rest with God now.' Myles rested. Grace's dripping hands cupped his face for a moment, before she drew a cross on his forehead in his own blood with her thumb. Then she stood up, put her foot on his chest and yanked the splinter out.

Eoin, the *Grace*'s master, shouted from the carrack's taffrail: 'We have it all now. Her captain's dead, but there's a few quick left. Will we tow the prize in, Granuaile?'

Barbary saw her grandmother shake her head. 'Squall coming. The living can come over, the dead can go to Hell.' Eoin relayed the message in pantomime to what was left of the carrack's crew, indicating that they were free to try to get their wreck home, but that a storm was forecast. Bemused, the Dutchmen looked around at a sea no less and no more choppy than it had been all day, and pantomimed back that they would prefer to limp home, thank you very much. They could scarcely believe their luck.

'You'll be sorry,' Barbary heard Eoin say, shrugging, 'Herself knows the weather.'

Order was being restored, damaged rigging chopped away, a staysail and what was left of the others set. Grace regained the quarterdeck, and gave one, cold glance at her granddaughter. 'Where were you?'

'In there.'

Grace spat.

On the way back the sea began to slap the *Grace*'s buttocks in a familiar fashion, then more violently until they were bucketing ahead of the storm Grace had predicted. Huddled against the bulwark next to the wheel, Barbary shouted to Eoin: 'How did she know?'

Eoin shrugged. 'She knows. An arrangement with the saints, maybe, God rest them. If we'd been towing the Gaul we'd be going down to Hell with her this moment.'

Barbary lifted herself to look back into the rain and wind. No sign of the Hollander, just grey, loutish sea in the place where she'd been. Well, she'd come pirating into foreign waters, knowing the risk. And she'd fired first. Nevertheless, the encounter had been a mess, a royal, pap-puking, piss-pizzler of a mess. She was offended by it.

Eoin glanced at her for a second. 'No need to be shamed now.'

'I'm not,' said Barbary. 'That Hollander wasn't lobbing sponges.'

Eoin went on comforting at a shout over the noise of the squall. 'Herself's so brave she doesn't realise. She was on the high seas when Tibbot was born. A Turkish corsair, the Devil run away with it, attacked her ship and things were going badly, and they called Granuaile up on deck from her birth-bed. She came swearing, bless her: "May you be seven times worse who cannot do without me for a single day." So she said, and discharged a blunderbuss at the Saracens, and her men rallied and she won the day.'

'Wonderful,' said Barbary, flatly.

'And to be sure, it's not often like that,' continued Eoin. 'Usually they give in without a fight. No need to be shamed.'

'I'm not,' repeated Barbary. And she wasn't. Irish piracy might depend on courage, but where she came from courage was way down the list of admirable qualities. The Order advocated guile, not courage, in its exploits. If you had to be brave, you'd done it wrong.

The *Grace of God* was left in Blacksod Bay for repairs, her pirated cargo transferred to two hookers which sailed Grace and her granddaughter back to Clare, separately. Grace was shunning her.

It liberated Barbary from her last restraint. In every situation of her life she had been forced to pretend she was something she wasn't; now she was home on her own territory in her own right, 'and I ain't going to pretend no more'. After a long think, she clambered up to the castle's top room and went in, uninvited. Grace was sitting at a table, smoking, drinking whiskey and giving orders to Manus for the funeral of her dead crewman. Don Howsyourfather bowed and smiled at her from a corner, as impervious as a cat to the way everybody ignored him.

Grace's face didn't change. 'There was never an O'Malley yet that was a coward,' she said. Manus winced.

'Well, there is now,' said Barbary. 'I want to talk to you.'

'Hiding in a locker.' Grace was making a meal of it.

'Yes, well, cannon balls aren't what I'm good at. And I didn't come for to be brave. I came to meet you. But I don't like the way the English are killing babies, so I also came to get O'Neill's cannon for him.' She dragged a stool up to the table and sat opposite her grandmother. 'And while we're about it we're going to pick up a few for you and all. Where'd you get them pop guns the *Grace* was shooting yesterday? The local blacksmith?'

The lese-majesty of her tone was agitating Manus nearly out of his wits. Don Howsyourfather said: 'You don' talk to Hhherself so rude.' But Grace's eyes had a cautious interest.

'And what's wrong with them? Didn't we take the ship?'

Barbary said: 'You took her because you can sail and because you fired a lucky shot. But one of these days an English warship'll come prancing into these waters, and with the guns you got you can line your lads up to spit and you'll get better firepower.' In her anger, she was wagging her finger at her grandmother. She transferred it to the dust of the table – there was plenty of it – and began drawing, showing Grace the design of Will Clampett's latest demi-culverin and sakers, his improved fuse mechanism and his marine gun carriage which gave space for recoil and still allowed easy loading.

Don Howsyourfather was offended. 'Na, na. Not nice gun. You want nice gun.' His long, elegant finger drew a long, elegant and indeterminate piece of artillery mounted on a trailed field carriage. '*Media culebrina*,' he said, fondly. 'Nice.'

'Lovely,' agreed Barbary. 'That's what lost the Armada.'

Grace studied Barbary's tracings. 'Can we make guns like this?'

Barbary relaxed with relief, and began admiring her grandmother again. 'No,' she said. 'But I know a man who can.'

By the early hours the table dust was patterned all over. Manus had long since taken himself off, assured in his own mind that it was safe to leave the two women together, and Don Howsyourfather, having decorated his gun with curlicues, had fallen asleep.

Grace sat back. 'What now then?'

Barbary thought. She could talk grandly about delivering guns, but in fact she couldn't deliver anything without Will Clampett, and whether Will would be prepared to help her provide artillery for his country's enemies she didn't know. After his Irish war experiences, he hated the English Crown, but that was a very different matter from espousing the cause of Ireland. If she went to him she was fairly certain she could persuade him, but there were two or three objections to that. In the first place, she would very much rather, if he did take the huge decision to switch sides, that he did it for the same reason she had, to correct an appalling imbalance, rather than for love of her. For another, she was reluctant to leave her ancestral lands now that she'd found them, and even more reluctant to return to England. Grace's piracy might not be everybody's idea of the honest life, but compared with the piracy committed in Elizabeth's name it was positively saintly. England was oppression, it was Burghley and Spenser and Rob. Already this islanded coast was dearer to her than England had ever been. And, she had to admit it, while she was in Ireland she was in the same country as O'Hagan . . .

She knew one thing: Will wouldn't steal from his employer. He might go over to Sir Henry Sidney's enemies, but he wouldn't steal Sir Henry's guns while he was in Sir Henry's employment. He might prefer, if he did switch sides, to come to Ireland and make guns here. It would take longer . . . 'Any ironworks around here, Grandmother?'

Grace nodded through the pipe smoke. 'Iron Dick was called Iron Dick because there's iron worked on his land.'

'Now your land?'

'Now my land.'

Barbary made up her mind. 'I'll send Cuckold Dick. He can go on one of your cargoes to Bristol.' Ignoring all embargoes, Grace O'Malley and Bristol carried on a mutually advantageous trade. Dick would put the situation to Will in that uninvolved way he had, and Will could decide without his affection for her buggering up his judgement. Would Dick be safe? Where's safe?

'I'll not be putting that scrofulous piece of ill luck on any ship of mine,' said her grandmother.

357

Barbary was tired. 'It's too dangerous by land. Either he goes by ship or I go for good.' She'd known the test would come sooner or later. She was developing affection for this dreadful old woman, her grandmother, but if the price of their relationship was the surrender of her right to think for herself, she wasn't prepared to pay it. She waited to see how much her grandmother valued it.

Don Howsyourfather snored prettily. The shadows of bars from the canary's cage striped the walls. Grace O'Malley took her pipe from her mouth. 'That's a powerful stubborn streak you got from the Gauls.'

Barbary was magnanimous in victory. 'It wasn't from the Gauls I got it.'

Cuckold Dick surprised her by being reluctant to go. With his gift for being at home wherever he found himself, he had managed to absorb himself into the pirate fraternity, even though – or perhaps because – he was banned from accompanying it to sea. He had settled himself into the cottage on Clare's quay where the pirate wives, with typical Irish hospitality, looked after him like one of their own. Every time she entered it, Barbary was reminded of her time on the Lambeth Marshes with Will Clampett. Like Will's cottage, Dick had made this one into a temple to scientific enquiry, and had barely room for his bed among the retorts, tubes, and metalwear which littered it in rackety profusion. Will had been in pursuit of the perfect cannon; Dick was searching for the finest *usquebaugh*, and doing it with the enthusiasm of an alchemist on the track of kitchen-produced gold. He used mysterious terms like 'doublings', 'singlings', 'backing the wash', 'still head', 'worms and worts'.

'Be a shame to leave now, Barb,' he protested.

'Will could help you make an even better still.'

He shook his head. 'It's not a go, Barb. You got to have Irish malt and turf and peat water to give it the flavour.' He brightened up. 'I could smuggle it into England.'

'You wouldn't have to. There's no whiskey tax in England. They don't know what it is. You could be "Cuckold Dick. Whiskey Importer. By Royal Appointment".'

The idea of trading legally was novel and unsettling. Dick considered it, then shook his head. 'They'll tax it,' he said. 'Sure as the Devil hates holy water, they'll tax it.'

'You don't have to stay, you rinse-pitcher. I need you back here.' She was irritable, because she didn't want to lose him any more than he wanted to go. 'Just put Will in the game and see if he wants to play.' She put her hand on his arm. 'It'll be good to see Will again, see if all's beneship with him.'

'All right, Barb.' He was persuaded, but still uneasy at leaving her with Grace O'Malley whom he considered to take the English threat too lightly. 'She's powerful clever, Barb, but she's got green in her eyes. Round here they talk about the Gauls like they talk about the fairies. They don't hardly believe in them. But they'll come after her, Barb. She's tweaking their arse too much for them not to. I don't want you there when they does.'

Barbary knew he was right, and found it all the more reason to get him out of the way. 'You be easy. If I get nabbed, I'll send word to Sir John Perrot. And the O'Neill. Between them, they can stop Bingham stretching our necks.'

'If he ain't done it before then,' said Dick, gloomily. 'That bachelor's baby'd trine as soon as look at you.'

'You take care, Dick. Give my love to Will.'

'You take care, Barb. For Gawd's sake keep out of sea battles.'

There were none. Eoin was right, the exchange with the Hollander had been unusual. Fighting was inherent in the piracy trade, and when necessary Grace O'Malley ordered it done, but it wasted time, men and shot as far as she was concerned and most of the ships she plundered were overcome by the threat of battle, rather than by battle itself. Which was where Barbary came in. Disappointed as she may have been that Barbary's arrival hadn't provided her with another battling heroine, Grace had at least come to recognise her as an element she could use to overcome crews without violence once she'd boarded. Barbary's training enabled her to single out what the Order called the 'barker', the one in a group of potential victims likely to cause trouble, the leader, the one with initiative. Sometimes it was the ship's master, sometimes it wasn't, but once spotted he could be conied out of his impulse to be brave by fear, suggestion or sheer fast talking. Barbary's English was another advantage since the majority of the ships they boarded were English-owned. Irish ships, knowing Grace's reputation, handed over her 'pilotage' without so much as a peep.

Gradually grandmother and granddaughter became a piratical double act; Grace a natural as the 'frightener' prepared to stick at nothing, Barbary playing the 'pleaser'. There were no more deaths.

In early October the *Rose Tremayne* out of Bristol bound for Galway was carrying a cargo such as could console Queen Elizabeth's Lieutenant in Connaught for his lordship of a province which he loathed and which loathed him back. Sir Richard Bingham was looking forward to receiving it. The problem was that the master of the *Rose Tremayne* had missed Galway; not so much missed it as beginning to think the bloody place didn't exist. A storm, and not so much a storm as God's vengeance on man's wickedness directed entirely on this one ship, had ripped her off course and left her adrift off an unfamiliar coastline with her master, still shaking, grateful to Heaven for his deliverance and wondering why he hadn't taken up tannery like his mother'd wanted him to.

With his first mate, he consulted the sea card, a sheepskin on which was drawn a scale of latitudes and what little was definitely known of Ireland's west coast.

'Well, it's not Galway,' said the first mate, who had a gift for the obvious. 'The card don't show no funny-looking mountain like that.'

They could just see the funny-looking mountain, a bare cone, through the driving rain of the storm's aftermath. What they didn't see was the oar-driven galley creeping out from one of the nearby islands towards them, and for that they couldn't be blamed. The galley had no mast to stick up above the sea line and its neutral colour blended into the blurring caused by rain bouncing on the water's surface. It edged towards them like a venomous log.

By the time they'd spotted it, the *Rose*'s tired crew were too late to prime their handguns, and while their ship carried two demi-culverin, they didn't have the man-oeuvrability to shoot down at low-lying craft. But the galley, like a small dog attacking somebody's kneecaps, could send shot virtually into the *Rose*'s waterline.

The first mate and some of his men drew their knives

and rushed to cut away the grappling hooks which were already dropping over the taffrail. It wasn't a wise move. A discharge from four arquebuses – as ancient, ridiculous, and as effective, as the galley's cannon – drove them back, allowing unattractive-looking persons carrying axes in their belts and knives in their teeth to swarm over the side. Most unsettling was the large, grey woman who seemed to be in charge. The master had heard of women pirates; he'd heard of mermaids, sea monsters and the Archangel Gabriel, but he hadn't expected to meet them.

The woman gained the poop deck, shouting in a foreign language, gesturing for her prisoners to kneel on the deck below.

'It's healthier doing what she says,' said a voice in English at the master's arm. Looking down, the master saw he was being addressed by a skinny youth with freckles and an ear-flapped cap. 'The last lot as didn't,' continued the boy conversationally, 'was cut up for fish bait.'

Studying the woman, the master decided the boy didn't exaggerate. Apart from her men, who were terrifying enough, she carried a sense of weight disproportionate even to her big frame, as though she were granite, a monolith with arms and legs. 'See them gew-gaws round her neck?' asked the boy. The master looked at Grace's coral necklace, actually a gift from a Corsair captain. 'Bones,' intoned the awful boy, 'bones picked from the living flesh of men as opposed her.' The master believed him. That this pirate was female and elderly increased the horror. It was like seeing midwives, stall-holders, grandmothers, all the old women one took for granted, pick up an axe and become murderous. She was a domestic nightmare. The master instructed his crew to do as they were told.

'Now then,' said the boy, seating himself cross-legged on the ship's drum. 'Herself wants to know who you are, where you're bound, what you're carrying and who for.'

The master's orders didn't preclude answering questions, especially as the small, efficient-looking handgun the boy carried was aimed at the master's stomach. It seemed unnecessary to list the cargo since some of the pirates were already down in the hold opening boxes, but he listed it anyway.

'Sir Richard Bingham, Lord Lieutenant of Connaught,' nodded the boy, and spoke in rapid Irish to the large grey woman, who spoke stolidly back. 'He's a lucky man, is Sir Bingham. You'd lost yourselves anywhere else, anything could have happened. Wrecked, boarded by pirates, anything.' He seemed to expect the master to express gratitude, which, without enthusiasm, the master did. The boy nodded again. 'Which instead Herself gives a pilot service in these waters. Usually she's pricey, but seeing as it's Sir Bingham, let's say one hundred pounds and I'm a fool to meself. Got a hundred, have you?'

The master's language indicated he hadn't. The boy tut-tutted. 'Herself'll have to take it out in goods then,' he said sadly.

The master watched bales of cloth, silver plate, boxes of spices, furniture, hangings – all amounting to considerably more than £100 – passed down into the galley. There were shouts from two pirates who had opened a small chest. The master groaned: 'Not the tobacco.'

'Smokes, does he, Sir Bingham?'

'Don't know,' said the master, 'but I bloody do.'

The boy grinned and made pleading sounds in Irish. The woman indicated with her axe that beheading the entire crew was still an option as far as she was concerned, but under the boy's persuasion some of the tobacco was tipped into a tin, much to the master's relief, which increased as he saw the pirates preparing to leave, only pausing to empty the ship's cannon balls from its shot locker over the side. His bones might not, after all, decorate this terrible woman's neck. 'Here,' he demanded, realising he still had to find Galway, 'what about that pilot?'

The boy spoke to the woman leader, who took the sea card from the master's hand, turned it over and scratched a rough chart on it with her dagger. The master didn't thank her. He'd paid for the service.

Cull and the crews were admiring of Barbary's efforts. 'She can charm the barnacles off their bottoms,' said Cull, 'and in the English too.' Grace merely snorted and said the English had taught her grandchild to be *plámás*, as if plausibility was an underhand Saxon trait, unworthy of straightforward O'Malleys.

362

She resisted all Barbary's attempts to get her to dress as a man. Barbary had reverted to boy's dress because skirts were inconvenient up boarding ladders and because she saw no point in advertising who she was. 'And why shouldn't they know who *I* am?' asked Grace.

'What's the point,' said Barbary, wearily, 'what's the bloody point in letting these crews we've pirated,' she caught her grandmother's eye, 'piloted, go and tell Lord Lieutenant Bingham as Grace O'Malley's robbed them again? And that's another thing. We should never have taken goods off the *Rose*. I begged you then and there. They were Bingham's goods. Why make Bingham more frettish at you than he is already?'

She was wasting breath. To Grace this coastline was her kingdom by as great a right as England was Elizabeth's, and the pilotage of foreign ships in her waters she regarded as much her due as Elizabeth did her taxes. 'He pays his levy like the rest,' she said, puffing on a pipe full of Sir Richard Bingham's tobacco.

There were times when she drove Barbary distracted with her obduracy, and others when Barbary floundered at the old woman's seafaring genius. Her instinct for weather was mystical. And the signalling system Grace had set up gave her time to calculate which ship of her fleet was appropriate to use against an intruder in the pertaining conditions. She was always right. Sometimes she used a couple of fore-and-aft fourteen-ton hookers, occasionally the *Grace of God*, her biggest galleon which she could sail so as to eat the wind out of the opposing ship's canvas while retaining it in her own. Sometimes she used the fast and manoeuvrable galleys.

The reason the English hadn't come against her so far was because they daren't; their navy was over-stretched already in protecting England's coastline against another possible invasion. Bingham had a small fleet at Galway but, for all the antiquity of Grace's guns, the superior number of her ships could overwhelm it with ease. The only way they had been able to get her into their hands at all was by using her son as a hostage.

Her aloofness was something Barbary decided had been a vital ploy when she'd first begun commanding men, and had now become petrified into her nature. On land she used words as if they cost her money. At sea she encouraged her crews by cussing them with a profanity that opened new vistas of swearing to Barbary. She was especially foul-mouthed to her galleymen.

'Row, you goat-begotten bastards,' she'd roar at them. 'Bend your backs, you turd-licking, crab-catching, double-cunted, donkey-dicked fish-suckers.' And they rowed, contentedly closing their eyes like men encouraged by angels' trumpets.

'No, no, it's a comfort to be cursed by her,' said Cull, who had been promoted to fleet steersman but was still most at home in the galley, which had been Grace's first command. 'We're her boyos, do you see. It was us joined her at the beginning. After Donal-of-the-Battles was killed, the O'Flaherties wouldn't give her rights, God's curse on them.' An Irish chieftain's widow was entitled to a third of her husband's personal estate. The O'Flaherties had reneged on a traditional agreement. 'It was why she had to take up the piloting.'

'But *why* did you join her?' That leap Grace had taken from wronged but respectable widowhood to pirate captain crossed a chasm still unfathomable to Barbary.

Cull looked at the sky, at his boots, stroked his chin and said: 'Ah well, you see, she took us.'

And that, simply, was the explanation. Nobody else had wanted them. The many different clans they came from had disowned them. A few had committed crimes too dire even for the tolerant Irish social system. Others just hadn't fitted in, some had been butts, scapegoats, malformed or merely unpleasant. All of them carried pejorative nicknames which gave a clue to their original isolation. Mooch, slow and ox-like. Gawk, clumsy. Keeroge, black beetle. Haverel, a boor. Kitterdy stuttered. Rap, meaning bad coin, was a name which indicated that its owner had been a cheat. Scalder, 'unfledged bird', had a hare lip. The port side's stroke oarsman who wore jewels on his fingers and tossed his long, fair ringlets as he rowed was known as 'Molly'. Cull himself, even the reliable Cull, whose name meant the weakling of a litter, had done something so terrible that Barbary never found out what it was.

These sweepings from the clans had carried their nicknames and their shame into exile, unemployed and unemployable until Grace O'Malley had gathered them up as a job lot. It was an indication of how low they had sunk that they had been prepared to sign on under a woman, and it was an indication of how extraordinary the woman was that, under her, they had been whipped into the finest sea-going fighting unit in Ireland.

Now they were all rich men by West coast standards. More than that, they carried their terrible nicknames with a swagger. They shouted them as they attacked. 'Granuaile Aboo,' they'd yell, 'Grace to Victory,' and then 'Haverel Aboo,' 'Keeroge Aboo', 'Molly Aboo'. They had become honourable titles worthy to be passed on to successors. The original stutterer had been killed, but his place in the starboard rank was filled by his son, a non-stutterer who answered proudly to the name of Kitterdy Two.

It was Mooch who took Barbary shrimping. Keeroge taught her new card games, and Molly cut her hair. She was recovering her childhood, allowing its seaborne Irishness to infiltrate the sharpness of that other childhood in the London streets, and finding in the combination a way of holidaying from the memories of Spenser Castle.

Her outlook became that of an amphibian's, the sea no more an obstacle between one place and another than a bridge. Surprisingly, they went to church almost every Sunday, walking to the tiny Cistercian abbey on Clare, or sailing to Murrisk on the edge of Clew Bay under Croagh Patrick to join the congregation in the Augustinian abbey in which Grace had been baptised and which smelled of incense and seaweed. In both abbeys was a stone carved with the O'Malley coat of arms and their motto: *'Terra Mariq Potens'*, 'Powerful by land and sea'.

The sight of Grace O'Malley on the first occasion Barbary accompanied her grandmother to church was staggering. A crowd of admiring pirates had turned out to witness what was obviously an event. Instead of her usual outfit of calico and wool, Grace had raided the chests she'd pirated from foreign ships for more womanly attire. None of the items matched. She bore down on her waiting granddaughter like a galleon in full, multi-coloured sail. A massive, farthingaled scarlet skirt was hitched up by gold tassels to show a tartan petticoat. Her purple bodice had a pearl-encrusted stomacher, bombasted bishop sleeves and a cartwheel ruff. Nothing had been left at home in the accessory line. Hanging from her chain girdle was a small book of hours, a pomander, a purse, a fan and a crystal looking-glass. A Spanish comb stuck her coarse, badgered hair into a six-inch contortion which she'd adorned with a billowing black lace mantilla. In a high wind she wouldn't have stood a chance.

How much Grace believed in the tenets of the Catholic faith, Barbary was unsure – it wasn't the sort of thing they discussed. It was more a matter of how much the Catholic faith believed in Grace O'Malley.

As the last grains of sand ran out in the giant four-hour glass that kept the time on the fleet's biggest ships, the watch was changed to the mutter of a short prayer. Each watch was known by the first words of its own special prayer: the 'God grant us' watch, the 'Lord hear us' watch, the 'Watch over us' watch.

When, after a late raid, the galley returned in the dark to Clare, Cull's voice would ring out over the black water with her particular password: 'Before the world was God,' and receive the countersign from the lights on the harbour: 'After God came Christ His Son, born of Mary.'

It was a salty, superstitious Catholicism, bordering on the pagan, and it had its beauty. When a mist came down over the sea, through it could be heard the low, eerie moaning of seals calling to each other. 'I remember me duty,' said Kitterdy Two, and on a glorious October day he took Barbary to visit his aunt who had turned into a seal some years before. They rowed to a cave where light reflecting off the green water wobbled over the matt bodies of seals lying on its ledges. Kitterdy Two's whisper echoed against the rock. 'She was never great with my uncle, and one day she put on the *cohuleen-dru* and dived into the waves off Roonagh Point.'

'Which one is she?'

'With the damaged flipper. It's how we know her for that's where my uncle threw the boiling water over her hand. *Go m-beannuighe Dia dhuit*, Aunty, and God save all here.'

Kitterdy Two's aunt looked at them out of weeping almond eyes before flopping into the water and swimming past their curragh to the sea.

In late November the good weather finally surrendered

to winter. Gales closed the seas and the piracy season was over for another year. If anything, Grace O'Malley became busier. She claimed as much by land as she did by sea and ran huge herds of beeves over her extensive grassland. There were disputes to settle, poachers and raiders to punish, chatelains to reprimand or reward, repairs, judgements, decisions to be made. As tanaist to Grainne's chieftaincy, Barbary was observer to most of these matters. She learned the interests of lordship, much about its boredom, and even more admiration for her grandmother's acumen.

But through all the business there was a recurring discomfort, like the early-warning twinges of disease. 'What is on you?' roared Grace O'Malley at her Burrishoole herdsman. 'Four hundred beeves? You had a six hundred on foot, you miserable sheep-shagger.'

The herdsman wilted, but stood his ground. 'The Gauls came against us and took them and it was prudent to let them, for there was more of them than us, and weren't they armed to the teeth of them.'

'What Gauls, blast your soul?'

The herdsman shrugged. 'Gauls from Galway. They had the death of Rory Conroy and I escaped being killed by the black of my nail.'

They had the same story from the herdsman at Shrule in the east, though this time it was eight hundred beeves that the Gauls from Galway, English soldiers, had stolen.

On top of this, there was no tribute from the island of Arran among the taxes due to Grace. The island was actually O'Flaherty territory, but had found it prudent to pay for Grace O'Malley's protection over the years. This year, however, neither O'Flaherty nor O'Malley was getting anything from it; the island had been occupied by a force of Gauls under the leadership of Sir Thomas le Strange.

Furiously, Grace did her accounting of an empire which was being eroded round its edges like a cheese nibbled by rats. Her income was down; it was still considerable, but it was definitely down. 'I'll make those Gauls smell Hell for this,' she said. 'Come the spring I'll raid the bastards back. I'll feed their bollocks to the pigs. I'll give them steal from Grace O'Malley, so I will.'

Barbary shook her. 'Will you listen to me? It's the

English you're talking about. The English. Not some bloody clan. It's war. England versus Ireland.' But Grace O'Malley didn't understand. There was no Ireland. There was hardly a Connaught. Its people had existed too long as free-wheeling, intersecting tribes, each with its own great history, to have a conception of themselves as part of a whole. For them to think in terms of nationhood was too soon and, Barbary feared, too late.

Christmas was to be spent at Westport in a huge gathering of O'Malleys. But before that, Grace O'Malley was intent on taking Barbary to the secret treasure, the Kishta, an enterprise that meant a march inland to Lough Mask.

The pony Spenser had spent the piracy season in the care of Grace's horseboys, running the grassland with the O'Malley herds of Connemaras, and was fitter than at any time in his life. To be on his back again brought memories of Spenser Castle, good and bad. Her apprenticeship to the pirate trade had rendered her so much a sailor that to be out of sight of the sea was at first claustrophobic. The swooping Partry mountains hemmed them around, blocking every view into the distance with smooth uprushes of thinly grassed rock. There was water a-plenty, falling down clefts so that from far off it looked as though white ribbons were dangling down the mountain faces, feeding the rivers that twirled through the valleys, forming loughs like mirrors of every size, some of them dotted with tiny, tree-sprouting islands. It was a terrain of such difficulty and isolation that she almost caught some of Grace's conviction that no enemy could find them in it. Almost.

It was dazzlingly cold, no snow yet but a metallic iciness which refused to give way to a bright, clear sun and froze the last remaining bolls to the bog cotton and turned the peasants' stacks of cut peat bricks into brittle walls. The owners of the peat were not in evidence; an occasional dead-straight line of smoke issuing from the landscape – the turf roofs were so thick that they looked more like natural protuberances than dwellings – indicated that the hut beneath was occupied, but the only living creatures they saw were sheep. Twice they heard melodious howling from the mountain tops. Cull said it was wolves. 'Greeting Herself with a challenge. Herself loves a good wolf hunt.'

She would, thought Barbary. She looked ahead to where Grace bumped along on what appeared to be a cart horse; her head was wrapped tightly in a scarf and poked up through the splayed fringe of her voluminous cloak so that from the back she looked like a hunched and enormous vulture. Probably tears their heads off. One of the mysteries she still hadn't solved about Grace O'Malley was the secret of the woman's physical strength. 'Doesn't she ever get tired?' she asked Cull.

'Ah well, you see,' Cull said, 'her bones aren't bones, they're ships' spars.'

But did no arthritis twinge the spar joints? Didn't they ever long to be laid up? If there was one constant to pirate life it was its spray-splashed, rain-lashed, hard-benched, rope-burned discomfort. Yet Grace, old as she was, didn't just endure it, she thrived on it. And now, on holiday, she was trotting through bog, over bridges slippy with ice and heigh-ho for a wolf hunt at the end of it.

They were travelling with an escort made up of most of the galley crew, not for protection but for Grace's consequence; no chieftain worth his salt was attended by less than twenty followers. Away from their oars, their muscular upper bodies and undeveloped legs made them look crab-like, but they were enjoying the excursion. Keeroge and Kitterdy Two carried hawks on their wrists, and wolfhounds followed Molly and Cull.

They emerged out of the Partry mountains and onto the western shore of Lough Mask in a sunset that put a spell on even that magical lake, turning its frosted islands apricot, flushing the reeds which stippled its surface and polishing the water itself with a sheen that reflected everything above it, trees, swans, hills, their own selves, in a pellucid gold.

Men and women in curraghs were waiting on a small, wooden pier to take them to their destination. The horses were led off to a corral, the dogs to a houndmaster to await the hunt. Unless you were a bird, an overall view of Lough Mask was impossible; what Barbary thought was the lake turned out to be one of its thousands of inlets, separated from the others by trees, piles of slabbed rock and islands. Even out on the water its bends prevented

Barbary from seeing more than a fraction of the lake's ten-mile length. What she did see as they approached the eastern bank was a giant boot, at least it looked like a boot from her view, a mid-calf boot of stone with the outward curve of its uppers in the water, as if some Colossus had got one of his feet stuck into the mud of the lake, slipped his leg out of his boot and left it there. Nearer, it turned into a fat, looming castle built onto an island just out from the shore. Cull nodded towards it. 'Hag's Castle.'

'Who's the hag? Herself?'

Cull nudged Barbary's ribs for her naughtiness. 'Not at all. It belonged to warrior women. Way back. The time of Noah. It was always a woman's place, a secret place. It suits Herself.'

Like Grace, the castle was old and grey and strong. They were landed onto tiny, lethal steps which led to a rocky surround, and made an even more difficult ascent up a rope ladder to the only door, set halfway up its wall. The ladder was drawn up after them. Barbary was half-relieved, half-alarmed at this precaution. 'Do we expect trouble?'

Cull was reassuring. 'Not at all. Not at all. But Herself took the castle from the Joyces, and you never know if the bastards will try and get it back.'

Considering that it was an O'Malley residence, Hag's Castle was surprisingly comfortable. Its centre was a hollow core which ended at the bottom in a well. Around it were galleries balustraded on one side, serving the rooms leading off it. Grace had furnished it with some of her finest pirated pieces, so each storey had surprises: a Persian carpet hiding an archway to a privy, a gaudy carving of women with too many arms, a square of mosaic with a representation of a peacock, Spanish chairs, beds, chests.

Barbary would have welcomed bed, it had been a long journey, but there was a meal with the crew and lakeland men and women to be eaten first by candlelight at a huge round table set over the well head on the ground floor. She was sloping off to bed at last when Grace caught her: 'Come with me.'

'Doesn't anybody ever sleep round here?'

'Do you want to see the treasure or not?'

She did. She had seen it before a long time ago. It was one of the clearest pictures she'd received once memory of her childhood had returned because it had been in many ways the strangest; she'd been surrounded by women, not in itself an unusual event but their gravity had made it so. Her aunt Margaret, Grace's only daughter, had been there. Odd she should remember her so vividly, for Margaret had little personality, as if her mother's abundance had used up the supply. Her own mother had been there, aloof and beautiful as always, and her uncle's wife and every other woman of importance in the O'Malley clan, all in their best linen and gold. She had been aware of ceremony, oaths of secrecy, singing, silences.

What had imprinted it on her mind had been the sense of illegality. These women then had been defying something. It was no ordinary, condoned feminine ritual, like the Maytime dances, or husband-foretelling on St John's Eve. Whatever it was, they were being audacious and rebellious in doing it. She remembered the scars on Grace's hands as, reverent for once, they had lifted the treasure out of its carved box . . .

The same box was in front of her now, in Grace's room, the candlelight and the glow from the brazier shifting its tortuous Celtic pattern, the same rough hands lifting its lid with the same reverence.

Barbary grinned. Queen Elizabeth should be here this moment, and Lord Burghley. And Walsingham. And Raleigh. And Rob. And Tibbot. All the people whose innards had griped at the word 'treasure'. The smell of what Grace was holding now had reached the nose on the throne of England and sent it sniffing the streets of London for the boy who would be the means of attaining it. That priceless object had worked through agents great and small to discover a poor urchin and, having found her, changed her character and outlook to restore her to her people.

And it was only a book. Not even an impressive book, but a ragged piece of vellum stitched between plain leather covers. The writing was ancient, not just the original Latin-scripted manuscript, but the two translations, one in Irish and one, surprisingly, in a crude mixture of English and Norman French. Perhaps because they hadn't been written in the crabbed style of a professional scribe, the first two were comprehensible to Barbary.

Her grandmother fetched a candle and put it close to Barbary's stool, then sat on the bed to wait. Despite the room's brazier, Barbary found her hands shaking. The air coming through the shutters smelled of icy vegetation, but there was another scent coming from the book, very old, very strange. Perhaps it was sanctity.

'Know all who live now and who will be,' the manuscript began, 'that I am Finola of the clan of Partraige, once Sister Boniface of Fontevrault, once Abbess of Kildare . . .' It told her story.

It was a book by women about women. To the women of her clan it became treasure, the most precious thing in the world because it was unique in the world. Among the millions of volumes that had been written to record the doings of men for the glory of men, there was just one, here, in these pitiful pages, that recorded the doings of women for the glory of women, as if in a universal monastery of chanting monks a single woman's voice had been raised in an unheard female hymn.

Finola, the one-time Abbess, had begun it because otherwise she would have been wiped out of history. She had been Abbess of Kildare in the twelfth century which had made her the most powerful woman in Ireland at that time, and one of the very few who could write. She had come up against the equally powerful, and certainly more ruthless, King of Leinster, Dermot MacMurrough who, to get rid of her, had her raped by his men. It was a successful move. Even more than the Roman, the Irish Church of those days prized virginity. Because, however unwillingly, the Abbess of Kildare had lost hers, a carelessness that besmirched her, she could not be mentioned. History was in the hands of the tonsured monks who sat at their writing boards in cells all over Ireland, and they allowed the wronged, defiled Abbess, like so many other women, to drop through it into the dark. She was unrecorded, invisible. She had never existed.

But she had existed. She had made her way here, to Lough Mask, and with the help of the warrior women who lived in Hag's Castle, she had exacted revenge on Dermot of Leinster. Then she had written her story.

Somehow the document had been preserved. Because of Hag's Castle's feminist tradition, other women had read it and been inspired to write their own history. Finola's quill and ink had become more than a means of making marks on vellum; they had become a torch which cast a tiny light down generations of women who would otherwise have lived and died unknown and unsung.

Barbary looked up at her grandmother. 'Is this why you wanted to get into the Annals of Clare?'

'How will the future know of me otherwise?'

True. Grace could not write. If men didn't record her existence, she hadn't existed.

Every so often there was a gap in the continuity where female literacy had flickered out for a while, as it had now; here and there a cross marked one of the pages as if some woman who could not write had nevertheless shown that she knew the book's value. Hag's Castle had changed hands many times during three hundred years of clan feuds but, miraculously, one woman had always managed to hand the book on to another safely. Word of what Finola called 'The Word of Woman' had got out to become a legend that the women of the western clans possessed great treasure known only to themselves, but even so it had been kept from theft and destruction. It had suffered – some of the pages were scorched on one edge as if it had been snatched from fire – but it had survived.

Not all the stories were as interesting as Finola's. One entry in an appalling script merely said: 'Brigit O'Connor did bake the best bread of all.' Others recorded acts of heroism by women; some had fought in battle, some had commanded their clans, one had found a herbal cure for sore throats, another had given birth to twenty children, another had been childless, some had written their own prayers.

All of them had been inspired by Finola whose story included a great heresy. 'God is not male,' she had written, 'God is at once male and female and more than both.'

Barbary looked up, appalled, to meet the eyes of her grandmother. 'Bloody hell,' she said. Grace O'Malley nodded.

'. . . in that Jesus came to us not in strength but in the

373

weakness of a poor human baby,' wrote Finola, 'not to experience the power of the world but its pain, he was partaking of the common lot of women. . . . In that he loved and forgave prostitutes and adulteresses and rejoiced at marriages as at Cana, and frequented the company of women, he reflected the womanly nature of God as much as the manly. Nor can I find any condemnation of women in his teaching such are heaped on our heads by the bishops . . . Therefore the saints who have regarded Eve and her daughters as evil have done violence to God who is both their father and their mother.'

Barbary looked up again. 'What happened to her?'

'They killed her.'

'I'm not surprised.'

It was a bell-jangler, this. It had never occurred to her before to question God's maleness. He was ultimate authority, which was male. And yet, why not? Just because the Burghleys ruled this wicked world, it didn't mean they ruled Heaven. Had the Church, after all, got it wrong this long, long time? Had men walked along the road of history with their heads stolidly in one direction, taking in only what was happening on their side of the way? Wouldn't they then believe that only their side of the view held importance, and the other none?

No wonder they'd killed Finola, with this clarion call of equality before God. And no wonder the women of Lough Mask had kept the book hidden. In the eyes of the Church this was not just heresy, it was blasphemy and sacrilege as well.

Yet it had produced its effect. This then, these scribbles of ink on a tattered piece of vellum, were the secret ingredient that had transmuted an Irish widow into a pirate chieftain. It was a charter giving her the right to break the rules men laid down for her because they weren't the rules of this new-seen, vaster God. Piracy might not have been what Finola had in mind for her sex when she wrote her heresy, but Grace had interpreted it as a woman's entitlement to survival, and with a female God urging her on she had gone out and survived.

And yet Grace's story was not in the book.

'Who did you get to read you this?' she asked Grace. No man, for sure. A man reading this heresy would combust and the manuscript with him.

'We've tried to keep a woman olave at Lough Mask who could read and hand on the skill. Me mother brought me when I was old enough, like yours brought you. But the last one died before she could remember me.'

So that's why Grace had been so insistent that the Cistercian annalist should 'remember' her. Women were half the world, Finola said. And intended to be so. *Intended*. Not squeezed in at the last moment, curse-endowed, flawed, useful little ovens into which men inserted the next generation.

'So now you'll do me remembrancing,' said Grace.

'You believe what it says here?'

Grace's eyes were steady. 'Why not?'

Why not? Because it changed the world, that's why, sent the planet off course, spinning into a new orbit . . . But why not?

In that moment she was bonded to Grace O'Malley as she had never been by blood. With her, and with generations of women who had gone before her, she shared a much greater matter, an idea.

'Why not,' she said.

Grace nodded. 'Go to bed.'

Barbary went. Even in her sleep she was aware of a shift that changed all perspective. She heard trumpets that blew for the untold heroism of untold women. They went on blowing until they woke her up.

On the shore of the lake, real trumpets were blowing. Outside her door men were running and shouting. 'Is it the Joyces?' She could hear her grandmother's voice swearing and giving commands.

'Light the beacon. I'll shorten Ruairi Joyce's career for him, so I will.'

Barbary leaped out of her bed to the window. In the frosty mist of the morning she could see figures on the eastern bank of the lake, lots of figures, clustered round long dark shapes. Boats. Some were already launched and moving over the water towards the castle. Somebody came into her room and she turned to see Molly, the stroke oarsman, peering over her shoulder. 'Isn't that typical of the Joyces to attack at Advent?' he said. 'They'd tear Christ's body for a piece of silver.'

Barbary realised she was naked, and ran to the aumbrey

for her clothes. 'It's not the bloody Joyces,' she shouted. She'd seen the banner with the Tudor rose. 'It's the English.'

Molly smoothed back his long fair hair in relief. 'And I thought it was the Joyces.' He went to the door of the bedroom and shouted: 'It's only the English.' He turned back to Barbary, aggrieved. 'And how did the English find themselves here?'

It was no time for discussion. And no time to put on women's clothes. She struggled into the trousers and shirt she wore for pirating, rammed on her cap, snatched up the Irish woollen cloak her grandmother had given her, and the snaphaunce. 'Let's go.' But another glance out of the window showed it was too late. Under its thin, low-lying mist the lake was speared with boats, like slow-moving arrows, all centring on Hag's Castle.

From the castle's inner balcony overlooking the drop to the well, she could hear men telling each other: 'It's only the English,' and felt their initial alarm degenerate into disorientation. This was their playland. Even its dangers were familiar. And now they had been disturbed in it by an enemy so alien that they could no more comprehend it than if elephants had appeared on the hills and tigers sprouted in the rushes of the lake.

Barbary was very frightened, not only for herself, these men, for Grace, but for the Kishta. It mustn't be wiped out; it would be intolerable for that new colour she had discovered last night to be withdrawn from the rainbow. Finola had to go on living; it would be very nice if they could all go on living.

Her grandmother was coming ponderously along the passage. At the sight of her everybody, including Barbary, calmed down. Her nod might have been wishing them good morning. 'We've lit the beacon.' Above her head, from up on the roof, came the deep roar of a fire. The message of its smoke would be repeated by the beacon on the Hill of Doon, flashed to the Killaries, then from beacon to beacon along the hilltops to Murrisk and across the sea to Clare.

'How soon will they come?'

Grace considered, and Barbary remembered that all O'Malley and allied forces had dispersed for the holiday.

Trust the bloody English to attack at Christmas. 'Soon,' was all she said.

'They've got art-ill-ary,' called a look-out. Barbary rushed to the window and looked out. Two strings of figures were man-hauling a gun to its position on the shoreside.

'You're supposed to be the expert,' said her grandmother's voice behind her.

Barbary rubbed her eyes and looked again. 'A saker, I think.' It wasn't as big as some, but it didn't have to be. 'Five-pounder. It can hole us, given time.'

'How much time?'

'Depends on the accuracy. For certain before help comes.'

'We've been betrayed,' said Grace, flatly.

'Yes.' They hadn't dragged that thing through this terrain in twelve hours. It had been nearby, waiting for them. Who? A rival clan? Or some poor captured sod saving his life and his family's?

'God damn the bastards,' said Grace, suddenly violent. 'Do they think I'm *made* of lead?'

Barbary looked round in alarm. Was her rock wobbling? But Grace was striding out of the room, shouting orders. 'Strip the roof. Light all braziers. Get the boats ready.'

The parapet round the roof of the tower was only waist-high, and the diameter of the roof itself so wide that to be in its centre meant exposure to the shore's high ground and the musketry of the soldiers swarming over it like ants. Grace's men had to crawl on their bellies to strip off the lead. They had two factors on their side: the lead had been softened by the heat of the beacon, now gone out, and the English musketry was terrible. Haverel was its one victim, and he was just grazed by a ball. He came round from momentary unconsciousness to be told by Rap: 'It's not where it matters. Only your head.' The worst injuries were hands lacerated by torn metal.

Outside, the uppers of Hag's Castle boot were jammed with besieging soldiers and officers. Attempt after attempt was being made to reach the door in the castle's side with ladders and grappling hooks. So far they were being foiled from above by showers of rocks which had been laid up along the various storeys of the tower for just such an emergency. To shoot down at them with a gun meant leaning out of the windows, thus becoming a target. Keeroge, who tried it, took a small steel arrow in his throat from a matchlock. He tore it out.

'Ain't you got cannon?' shrieked Barbary at Grace.

'No.'

'Jesus.' Waiting for the bombardment was what terrified her most. She took a roll of lead out of the bleeding hands stretching it down through the roof hatch and skittered with it into Grace's room where a cantilevered cauldron was being set up over the brazier. The tower began to reek with peat smoke as braziers were lit wherever there was a window or arrow slit.

She ran back to stand beneath the roof hatch and receive more lead. She didn't hear the noise around her. They'd got the saker in position. They'd begin the procedure. The only sound in her head was Will's voice chanting the fourteen commands for firing cannon.

'One. Put back your piece. Two. Order your piece to load.'

Down to the next floor with more lead, this time into Haverel's cauldron. He told her to go down to the undercroft and bring him more rocks 'to discourage the bastards down there'. He had to tell her twice.

Up from the undercroft, this time hauling a net of rocks from the basement store. Dropping it on the first landing. Kitterdy Two, sweating, dragging it towards his arrow slit.

'Three. Search your piece. Four. Sponge your piece. Five. Fill your ladle.'

More hands, more blood, more rolls of lead. Down the merciless steps, wedge-shaped, steep and naked.

'Six. Put in your powder. Seven. Empty your ladle. Eight. Put up your powder.' They were obeying the commands out there on that lovely shore. God damn them. God damn.

Shoving lead at Mooch standing over his cauldron. Down. More rocks into a net. Up the fokking stairs, meeting MacCaudle, the one Scotsman in the crew, coming down and singing. Singing?

'Nine. Thrust home your wad. Ten. Regard your shot.' What would they use? Stone? Iron? 'Eleven. Put

378

home your shot gently.' Gently, gently.

Dropping the net on the second storey. Molly, still managing to mince, bless him, dragging it to his window. Gawk puffing at the peat in his brazier to get a flame. Cull on the inner balcony, overseeing the hauling of curraghs up from the undercroft. If they cleared away the soldiers outside – some hope – they'd throw out the boats and scramble after them and row away, row away, to Myles on his golden sea.

Soon now. Any minute. Up to the roof hatch. More lead.

'Twelve. Thrust home your last wad with three strokes. Thirteen. Gauge your piece.'

Now. 'FIRE!'

The tower rocked. Motes of centuries-old dust and mortar wafted out of the walls and hung in the slants of light. They'd got the range first go. 'Are we holed?' Barbary screeched. Answering shouts in the negative came from all floors; the walls were over six feet thick, but they wouldn't stand too many hits like that. At least the door on the tower's south side was angled where shot couldn't reach it from the shore.

She heard her name and dashed into Grace's room where her grandmother was using a poker on the fire. Keeroge, still bleeding badly from his throat, had collapsed on her bed. 'Get the grissets,' Grace said to her. 'And you, Keeroge, on your feet: you're not dead yet.' Glad to know it, Keeroge hauled himself up by the bedpost. Before he could think, Grace swung on him and thrust the red end of the poker into the wound in his neck. 'You be well now,' she said. Barbary looked at Keeroge, fallen back on the bed, groaning but grateful. If Grace, having cauterised his throat, said he would be well, he'd be well. Grace glanced at her granddaughter. 'Will you go for them grissets?'

Whatever grissets were, they'd be in the undercroft – Grace pointed in that direction. Cull was retrieving them from a corner, shallow, iron vessels for melting things – grease for candles, resin for torches, lead for terror. They rattled in his arms as the tower shook from another explosion. He saw her panic. 'Not to worry now. It worked lovely when we poured it on the Joyces at Corrib. Hen's Castle that was.'

Oh God Almighty, they'd done this before. She staggered back up the steps, clattering grissets into what rooms she passed, swearing, promising God, male or female, she'd abandon piracy, take up good works, tapestry . . .

Grace was at her door. 'Ready, me darlins?' Her deep voice echoed back and forth across the tower as another shot hit it, but even that wasn't as shocking as the endearment. Her grandmother didn't think they'd get out of this.

'Ready, Granuaile.' 'Ready.' 'Ready.' 'Ready.' 'Ready.' 'Ready.'

'Hold the damn thing still, girl.' Dreadful, grey, bubbling liquid tipped into her grisset. She was so frightened. 'Take it to the window. Steady now.' She scarcely dare walk, she certainly didn't breathe; she imagined it over her legs, eating into her flesh, the pain . . .

The narrow window had a peculiarly shaped outer sill, thin at its juncture and widening out, like a fan. It had been manufactured for this. She rested the other end of the grisset on it. Having pictured what it would do to her, she knew what it would do to the men below. Could she do it?

'Hullo the tower.' English-accentuated Irish echoed thinly over the lake from where someone was calling to them. She dragged her eyes away from the thick, soft, silver bubbles for one second; fifty yards out on the water a grandly dressed man was standing up in a boat. 'You are under bombardment,' he was saying, in case they hadn't noticed. 'Surrender in the name of Queen Elizabeth. You will receive a fair trial.'

'Is that the bastard who's been stealing my beeves?' came Grace O'Malley's voice behind her.

She managed to say: 'It's Bingham.' He'd scared her when she'd first seen him; he scared her now. Lord Lieutenant of Connaught, he'd come himself.

'That's your man.' Grace's hand went under the grisset and tipped it. Barbary saw the molten lead pour into the sill, fan out into a sheet, disappear. She heard the hiss and the screams. Men came into her view from under the walls, scrambling into boats, throwing themselves into the water. It wouldn't be any good, cold air, cold water, it would just cool the metal's exterior; where it was

380

against the skin it would go on burning. Helmets welded to living tissue.

'Now we go,' said Grace cheerfully. She had Keeroge's arm round her neck as she made for the steps.

'Where's the Kishta?' shouted Barbary at her.

'Down me boot,' Grace shouted back. Barbary had the snaphaunce down hers.

Getting to the boats was dreadful. The saker couldn't bear on them, but musket fire could, and not all the English had retired to the shore; some were in boats shooting at them. Every part of the tower's side was being dimpled from the musket balls smacking into the stone. Scrambling down the rope ladder after Grace – she was in practice – Barbary was still thinking how Will would have loathed the sloppiness of the soldiers' aim when she saw Haverel, above her, claw at his back, wheel away from the doorway and drop onto the rock with a thump that incorporated the crack of bones. Grace pulled him down into her boat with another bump. Mooch was standing in its stern, and he went down, spreadeagled, still trying to protect his captain with his body.

There were some English lying on the plinth around them, a few still screaming. One corpse impeding the steps to the boats had a completely silvered head. Gawk kicked it out of the way, and it rolled, leaving some of its face sticking to the rock.

Other crewmen were lowering themselves from the window on the other side of the tower. They came running round to the boats. Barbary got into a tiny curragh with Molly, Gawk and Kitterdy Two. They were rowing through the noise of firing, shouts, splashing. Oarsmen all, they heaved and the boats shot away from the tower, heading for cover in the rushes and trees of the opposite shore. Only her boat was going slowly; she saw water sloshing around her feet. 'Mother of God, we're holed,' Molly shouted. 'By *damn* I hate swimming.'

But swimming they were now. It was cold, it was like a pursuit nightmare, effort, panting, getting nowhere. Shots spurted sprays of water around them, then they could hear the creak of oars getting closer. For a second she hoped and feared it was Grace coming back for them, but heard English: 'Grab them.'

A boathook stabbed her back and she was dragged by

her shirt to a boat's gunwale. Somebody gripped her hands. They'd got Molly. And Kitterdy Two. Gawk was away, or drowned. There was a moment of complete lucidity as she saw the far side of the lake and the flotilla of Irish curraghs nearing it fast. Other boats, English, were after them, but unless they'd got soldiers stationed over there, Grace and her men had escaped. Thank God. Somebody else's hand was on her head and pushing her under, once, twice. 'Drown, you young cunt. You killed Tanner.'

The weight of the hand was removed. 'If anybody,' said Bingham's voice, still beautifully precise, 'if *anybody* kills one of these men, he will take his place on the end of the rope. I intend the walls of Galway to display one body per yard at Epiphany. There will be no gaps.'

It was not a voice you doubted. She kept losing consciousness. She heard grinding as the boat's prow met lakeside pebbles. There was some surreptitious prisoner-kicking when they were hauled ashore and along a track. Behind Bingham's back, Barbary stumbled and a neatly placed boot cracked two of her ribs.

There were carts waiting, already full of men, women and children with their hands and feet bound. Bingham's expedition had made a good haul. Soldiers tied Barbary's hands and feet and chucked her into one of the carts. She managed to roll out of the way as Molly then Kitterdy Two were thrown in after her.

Orders were given, whips cracked and the carts began to move. Kitterdy Two snuggled himself comfortable and spat out some teeth. 'Isn't it grand to be taken by the English now,' he said. 'The bloody Joyces would have made us walk.'

Chapter Eighteen

Inscribed into the ancient lintel over the west gate of Galway were the words: 'From the fury of the O'Flaherties, good Lord deliver us.'

Other peoples at other times had begged God for deliverance from other plagues – Huns, Goths, Norsemen, plague itself – but the O'Flaherty clan was Galway's particular terror. Without the pirating O'Flaherties and their allied O'Malleys, the port of Galway, or so Galway reckoned, could have ruled the world. Even with them it hadn't done so badly; virtually a city state, so great was its trading prowess that there had been centuries during which whole tracks of Europe believed Galway to be the name of the country and Ireland one of its cities.

Staggering between Kitterdy Two and Molly, Barbary was too tired to raise her head and see that the city she was entering wanted delivery from her fury, though, for all her exhaustion, fury was what she felt. It was the only thing that stopped her collapsing from fear. Galway was to be the place of her execution and the execution of the hundred or so people with whom she had made the terrible journey from Lough Mask. As the crow flew, it was about twenty-five miles, but the crow hadn't wound along Lough Mask with exhausted, injured companions, nor skirted Lough Corrib, nor suffered the skirmishing as fellow crows tried unsuccessfully to rescue it. It had taken a freezing, mostly foodless, often waterless, week.

Lord Lieutenant Bingham rode ahead to the city on the first day, leaving the prisoners to an escort which had observed his strictures that they should be delivered to Galway alive, though carelessly. Nobody had been beaten to death, but some of the men had been kicked to within an inch of it. Their cloaks, always highly prized by poorly dressed English soldiery, were taken away the moment

Bingham's back disappeared into the distance. So were their boots. The carts had been cleared to make room for the badly wounded and the slower-moving women and children, while Molly and Kitterdy Two made the journey on bare feet. Barbary kept her boots only because they were too small for any of the soldiers, but she lost her good woollen cap. A halter round her neck joined her by rope with the two galleymen and six others, one of whom persisted in falling down and nearly strangling the rest every half mile. The child prisoners wandered beside the file like frightened calves following their mothers to the slaughterhouse. There had been some raping of the women.

There were odd moments of compassion as well. A boy whose foot turned septic from a thorn was piggy-backed by a soldier for two days on end. When the wits of an elderly MacJordan woman began to wander from the effect of the cold, a sergeant took off his own, stolen, cloak and wrapped her in it. 'There you are, Granny. Snugasabuginarug.'

Apart from the fact that their bodies were going to decorate Galway's walls, the prisoners had little in common. Keeping her ears open, Barbary learned that Bingham's advance into Connaught had actually been a punitive expedition against the Bourkes, just recently risen against him. With uncharacteristic inefficiency, he had underestimated the distance from Galway to Bourke territory. Probably he had been misled by the fact that when Connaught men talked about 'a mile' they referred to a measurement twice the distance of an English mile. By the time he'd reached Lough Mask his line of supply and communication was dangerously stretched. Catching Grace O'Malley in residence at Hag's Castle had been an unexpected stroke of luck, about the only one he'd had. And since Herself had managed to evade him, he was left with what he regarded as three unimportant O'Malley kern – one of them a mere boy – a rag-tag collection from various clans who'd tried to impede his progress, hill shepherds, and families he'd taken by surprise.

He'll trine us, thought Barbary angrily, because he's got to get some fun out of the business.

The only common denominator to the prisoners was their courage. Barbary was astounded by it, and made angrier at their oppressors. Poor, bewildered, frightened, they were nevertheless in the hands of Gauls, a species for whom they had as great a contempt as Bingham did for them, and they would not give the satisfaction of showing fear. Fathers and mothers hushed children who cried, telling them to remember they were a MacJordan, a Joyce, an O'Connor, and limped on through the nightmare with the endurance of a superior people who, as they died, would be gathered to the bosom of a superior God.

And, if you had to march with broken ribs, every breath painful, shivering with cold and terror, there were no better companions to do it with than the two galleymen, Kitterdy Two and Molly, though even they infuriated her at times with their perpetual pretence that they were in luxury. 'Isn't it grand to be walking now, instead of pulling a bloody oar.' 'Sure, and I always wanted to see Galway from the inside.' Because the siege of Hag's Castle had caused such casualties among their companions, the soldiers were particularly hostile to the only three prisoners captured from it, but Barbary escaped much of their attention because Kitterdy and Molly drew it on themselves, putting their own bodies between her and the attacks. She tried to regulate her calls of nature to when it was dark, but as the connecting rope was never taken off their necks, the whole of her group was aware of when they had to be made. 'One squats, we all squat,' Molly said, and all the men crouched with Barbary, facing away, while Molly and Kitterdy Two loudly discussed the beauty of the night. She was grateful to them, but her temper grew with the humiliation.

It was an impressive city, Galway, tightly walled to landward, tunnelled by bridges, partly islanded by the branches of its river. Its grey, merchant-endowed buildings and churches were saved from solidity by the thin, sea-washed light of the giant bay, beyond which lay the Atlantic. The fortune it was making confirmed its citizens' good sense in having stayed loyal to the English Crown during the Desmond Wars and other local difficulties. Most of them were Catholic but happy to be as much a part of the English Pale as their rival, Dublin, over the opposite side of Ireland. Galway knew which side its bread was buttered. It was a city with its head screwed on. Except at Christmas.

Nobody in Ireland celebrated Christmas like Galway. At Christmas Galwegians transformed from respectable, hard-working men and women into debauchees, compared with whom Bacchus was an old sobersides. At Christmas they loved everybody, except O'Flaherties, and everybody loved them. Foreigners had been known to leave their own festal, family firesides to keep Christmas in Galway and totter through the alcohol fumes from open door to open door until they could totter no more. By the time the Twelve Days were over, Galway had a civic hangover in which pale, suffering shades bemoaned their wounds, their damaged property, their empty cellars, and vowed not to do it again. Until next time.

Laws had been passed to stop the hospitality to other Irish: 'At Christmas, Easter, nor no feast else . . . on pain to forfeit £5; that neither O nor Mac shall strut nor swagger through the streets of Galway.' Lord Lieutenant Bingham had issued strictures against it. Laws and Bingham, especially Puritan Bingham who sullied proud walls with corpses, had no effect. For three hundred and fifty-three days of the year Galway paid its taxes to the English Crown and cheered the English Queen, but at Christmas England could go stuff itself: Galway was revelling.

A line of drunken dancers came down the street, weaving under and between the roped prisoners as if they were festal poles. Barbary's sense of reality, which was slipping in any case, lurched at the sight of their faces: twenty or so Lady Sidneys from Penshurst waltzed around her. Then she realised. The ancient Irish custom to feast in masks was alive and well in Galway. A male reveller lunged a leather bottle of whiskey at Barbary. 'Have a dram, my bucko, and bugger Bingham.' She grabbed it, drank, and passed it on to Kitterdy Two. 'Got anything to eat?' But he danced away.

The streets were almost warm from the flambeaux on the walls of nearly every house, lighting up decorations of bay, ivy and holly as thick as hedges. Singing, music and chatter came through the windows with a smell of food. Nobody showed surprise at the prisoners – Galway had seen thousands of rebels brought to book – but there was general consensus that this wasn't the time for them.

'The pity of it at Christmas. Will you look at the wee ones,' and from one house came a shower of loaves and sweetmeats which the children fell on like wolves.

When they passed through the entrance to the courtyard behind the landward gate, warmth fell away. There were some people in it, but for Barbary and the others the flares stuck into the cobbles lit up only the stacks of wooden biers on which bodies were taken to the burial pits, and the empty nooses on the gallows stretching the length of the east and west walls. 'Ah, and they've put up the decorations for us,' said Molly.

'Shut up,' whispered Barbary, 'shut up, shut up.' The terror of strangling on the rope – she'd seen it take minutes for an Order victim to die – threatened to consume her. And this wouldn't be like the grand executions she'd heard about in the Tower of London where elegant men and women were allowed last well-chosen words to an admiring crowd, with priests for their confession, ceremony, ritual, a clean axe. This finish would be ugly and anonymous, in a courtyard smelling of urine and her body one of a hundred thrown into a lime pit after.

Their sergeant grumbled as he herded them into a corner. 'If he thinks I'm hanging you lot tonight with my back, he's got another think coming. I'm entitled to me Christmas, same as him. He can order you up easy enough, oh yes, but he don't have to lift you down.'

'He', Lord Lieutenant Sir Richard Bingham, was on a dais at the far end of the courtyard surrounded by dignitaries with whom he was arguing or, rather, who were arguing with him. The raised voices and the acoustics of the echoing courtyard brought the occasional sentence to her. '. . . Cannot be allowed . . . barbarous . . . they're too young . . .'

Centre stage, standing alone in the expanse of cobbles, the obvious subject of the contention, were three boys. The eldest was about fourteen, the two youngest no older than nine and seven.

'God help us,' said Kitterdy Two. 'It's the Bourke lads he took as hostage. He's never going to hang them.'

Ulick Bourke, son of the Blind Abbot, Richard, son of Shane Bourke, and William, son of Meyler Oge Bourke, were dressed like young English gentlemen. The eldest was bearing himself gallantly, but the two little boys were

387

holding hands and one of them was crying.

Molly was watching the argument on the dais. 'Who's that in the fine blue cloak, now. Don't I know him?'

Nobody bothered to answer him; nobody cared. Molly called over to the gatekeeper: 'Would you have the kindness to tell me the name of the gentleman in the blue cloak?'

'Friend of yours?' The gatekeeper was Galway Irish, and unhappy at being on duty at Christmas. 'Fat good he'll do ye. That's the newly created Baron of Waterford. Another bloody Munsterman raised above his station.'

'I know him,' puzzled Molly. He nudged Barbary. 'Don't you know him from somewheres?'

Sighing with irritation, Barbary looked, and stopped sighing. She knew him. Very well.

'I resent that,' Chief Justice Wallop was saying with energy to Bingham, 'soft on the Irish, by God's eyes. You'll not confuse me with Perrot. I've hanged more of the buggers than you've had hot dinners, but I'll not let you hang those innocent mites there. You'll set the whole province by the ears.' Wallop was fat and red and, at this point, extremely sweaty.

The newly created Baron of Waterford looked at the mites standing by themselves in the centre of the cobbles; innocent indeed. But among the prisoners just brought in there was a little girl no more than four years old, not to mention babies in arms, yet Wallop wasn't protesting their doom. It was a matter of class. The Bourke children were nobly born, or as nobly born as Irish children could be, and well educated; they spoke English, qualifying for Chief Justice Wallop's compassion. The children huddling with their mothers and fathers in the crowd of prisoners were mere Irish. Expendable.

The Bishop of Kilmore, the Mayor and other dignitaries of Galway added their voices to Wallop's, but more respectfully. Bingham stood in a silence that insulated him. His thin, handsome face was calm, his eyes fixed on a point others could not see. He would not argue; earlier he had said: 'They are hostages and their lives are forfeit for their fathers' treachery.' There was no necessity for repetition. He knew he was right.

And, thought the new Lord Waterford, he is. That's

what rules are for, to be rules. Bingham rode his orders with the logic of a man who, assured the road ahead is straight, ignores the bends and goes over the cliff edge, taking everybody else with him. 'Anglicise Connaught,' his Queen had told him, so Bingham applied the letter of English Common Law to a people who had operated a different system for a thousand years, showing none of the flexibility of which other governors, and even his own Queen, were capable. This latest rebellion by the Bourkes had been caused by Bingham's abolition of the MacWilliamship, the title to their chieftaincy. It was an Irish title, therefore it did not exist; the fact that it had in fact existed since 1342, and that time and persuasion were needed before the Bourkes would abandon it, was irrelevant because the rules made it so.

Had Bingham been a different sort of man, Lord Waterford could have felt compassion for him. He truly wanted the betterment of Connaught; it just didn't behave as it was supposed to. When Bingham looked at the boys in the centre of the courtyard he didn't see three pitiful children, only an aberration to his pattern. He was going to hang them to make his pattern tidy, and nothing would stop him.

The smallest boy broke away from the other two and came stumbling up to the dais. 'Don't hang me, my lords,' he said. 'I can read. I heard you don't hang people who can read. I can read. A bit.'

His older cousin ran forward and dragged him back. 'Don't beg.'

Chief Justice Wallop's eyes filled. 'Bless the child, he's pleading benefit of clergy.' He turned to Lord Waterford. 'You talk to the bastard,' he muttered. 'We can't have this.'

I could run him through, thought Lord Waterford, I could rally the disloyal element in the town and effect a rescue. And I'd throw away the position I've worked so hard for these last years. He shrugged. 'My lord,' he said to Bingham, 'you know for what services Her Gracious Majesty has seen fit to honour me. By my persuasion, tribe after tribe has been brought in to offer her its loyalty. Let me attempt the same on the Bourkes. With time and some rope we shall receive a happy outcome.'

'No time,' said Lord Lieutenant Bingham pleasantly,

'but plenty of rope. My lords, gentlemen, it is late. Let us to dinner.'

Wallop was seduced. He'd come to Galway for the festivities and the hunting, not for argument, and he was hungry. He'd work on Bingham over the meal. He led the way to the southern gate of the courtyard, patting the smallest Bourke kindly on the head as he passed. Lord Waterford tried not to look at the boys, but something dragged his attention to the common prisoners crowded in their corner. The light from the flare was being reflected back from a head of hair so red that it was like a flare itself. It was of a once-in-a-lifetime redness. With wine in it. He stopped in his tracks.

'After you, Waterford.' Bingham was at the gate, waiting for him, alert and untrusting.

'Will you be hanging this rabble tonight, my lord?'

Bingham had clear, sharply defined eyes, like a raptor's. 'Perhaps.' He did not have to explain himself to an Irishman, even one ennobled by the Queen. They left the courtyard together.

Padraig, who acted as Lord Waterford's personal valet on these trips, was waiting at Lynch Castle, and hurried up the stairs with him. 'We've had word from a friend, my lord. Concerned about a relative.'

'A granddaughter, perhaps,' said Lord Waterford.

'How did you know?'

In the room Lord Waterford kicked the door shut. 'Where's Herself?'

'Out in the bay with three ships. The message is,' Padraig paused because he didn't believe it, 'she's ready to attack when we give the word.'

Attack Galway. Either Grace O'Malley's concern for Barbary was outweighing her common sense, or she'd gone insane. Even at Christmas Galway's walls were invulnerable to the outside. But at Christmas, maybe, they could be vulnerable to the inside. Maybe.

Lord Waterford spoke fast. 'Gather our friends in the city while I'm at dinner. The nightwatchman reaches the landward gate walls every half-hour. Replace him. Kill him and replace him. Mind you get someone who sounds like him. Phelim O'Dowd – he can imitate anybody. I want men on those walls immediately. Any attempt to hang the prisoners is to be stopped. The soldiers have no guns. Just pikes. Get a message to Herself to have small boats near Spanish Arch Quay by midnight. Then I want arms, all you can get. And masks. About a hundred.'

'Masks? There's not a mask available in the city this night. Every bastard's wearing one.'

The newly created Baron of Waterford took his cousin by the elbows and lifted him off the floor to look into his eyes. 'Masks,' he said.

'Mother of God, Conn, I will if I can. Don't hurt.'

Some sanity, though not much, returned to his chief's face. 'I'm getting her out of there, Padraig.'

'I know you are, Conn. I know. Put me down and I'm away this minute.' As he left the room, Padraig added, without hope: 'And God save us all.'

Behind him, Conn O'Hagan kicked a side table into the fireplace, picked up a stool and threw it against the wall where it splintered noisily, adjusted his cloak and went down to dinner.

Barbary watched her lover go, leaving her imprisoned.

'Is it Conn O'Hagan gone over to the Gauls?' asked Molly.

She smiled at him as she hadn't smiled for a week, for months. 'It's Conn O'Hagan come to get us out.' If her brain had been working she'd have called out, 'Don't come back.' She'd seen it in his face, watched it move as he saw her. He'd get her out. He'd got her out before. And if he couldn't, her heels would drum the more lightly because she'd seen him again. 'Don't come back.'

Suddenly she knew how brave she'd been; all this long time, so brave to be without him. Even in her happiness at finding the land of the cherubims, she'd clenched emotional muscles against his loss, missing him so badly she hadn't dare recognise it. Filthy and in pain, a rope round her neck, she leaned luxuriously back against Kitterdy's shoulder and let herself remember a room in a gatehouse at Spenser Castle. They'd been doodles to let each other go. Her as stupid as him. More. What they'd had in that room had been greater than any religion, any cause. Causes and religion were here, in this stinking court. God, Finola's God, had been there. If he did get her out, if she ever got him back, she'd never let him go

391

again. She'd be a penance to him if she must be. O'Neill could whistle for his guns, Ireland could sell itself for dogmeat, but she'd never let him go again.

From the walkway of the wall above them, Galway's nightwatchman stamped his round. He stood on the rampart of the North Gate, a deeper black figure against the black sky. 'Eleven o'clock and all's well.'

Bingham returned. He spoke briefly to the sergeant and went away again. As he left, the soldiers began binding the male prisoners' wrists and legs. Panic broke out. Some of the women, their nerve gone, began screaming. A few of the men fought and the soldiers used their pikes on them. Children ran and were cuffed back to the group.

'Is it now?' She wasn't brave at all. Molly's hand had hers in a grip and she clung to it.

'It'll be quick,' he said. It wouldn't be quick. She'd seen it. One of the soldiers tore their hands apart to rope them, and clubbed Molly over the head when he struggled.

She was almost blind with fear. It took minutes to register that only three of the gallows were being got ready. Three kick-stools placed under three nooses. Dear God, it was to be the boys. Not her and the others, not yet. The Bourke children.

The mere Irish became quiet. Sounds of revelry came from over the south wall. The littlest one's voice rose sharply: 'But I can read.' He was clinging to the soldier taking him to the platform.

Please God, please, prayed Barbary. Whoever you are, wherever you are, please no. They heard the eldest say: 'Be brave.' They were pressed further back into their corner with ten soldiers forming an angle across them, pikes levelled. There was nothing to be done. Except one thing. One of the women fell to her knees and raised her voice in a chant: 'Christ be with me, Christ be before me.'

It was the Faeth Fiadha, the Deer's Cry, St Patrick's own invocation of his God at a time of great peril.

'Christ be behind me, Christ be with me.'

Beside Barbary, Molly's deep voice and then Kitterdy's took up the chant: 'Christ be beneath me, Christ be above me. Christ be at my right, Christ be at my left . . .'

The singing swelled as all the prisoners knelt for the boys.

'Christ be in the heart of everyone who thinks of me. Christ be in the mouth of everyone who speaks to me.'

The soldiers worked quickly for a kindness. The youngest boy's voice shouted once more, 'But I can read,' before it choked away.

'Christ be in every eye that sees me; Christ be in every ear that hears me.'

It was over. At least they hadn't been alone.

The soldiers stepped back and put up their pikes. The sergeant and his team came down from the platform. For some reason the sergeant looked apologetically at Kitterdy Two. 'Orders to leave them up there,' he said. 'And you,' he addressed the gatekeeper, 'get out there and find us some whiskey. There's no more hanging tonight.'

Though nobody looked at them, the quiet of the three bundles on the gallows permeated the courtyard. The living children fell asleep on their parents' lap, the other prisoners huddled together and tried to doze, though it was becoming very cold. Where the boys had stood, the soldiers made a bonfire and sat round it, occasionally grumbling, mostly silent. The gatekeeper came back rolling a barrel. 'Compliments of a grand gentleman.' He stayed to sample it.

Stars came out and frost fell; Barbary could almost see it falling. First the cobbles acquired a sheen and then a gentle sparkle. 'I tell you this much,' she said to the stars, 'if I get out of here I'm going to hunt Bingham down to Hell.'

Molly was awake. 'And I'll be with you.'

The cloaked figure of the nightwatchman thumped its way along the top of the wall. 'Twelve o'clock and all's well.'

Kitterdy Two stirred. 'Strange,' he said. Nobody asked him what was, and he settled down again. Steady tapping of the barrel was going on round the fire, rallying the soldiers into better humour.

A new crowd of revellers was approaching the street outside the courtyard's city gate, shouting and laughing, rattling sticks along railings, clanging cymbals, and singing at the top of its voice the song about Galway's founding, and apparently well-endowed, giant who lived on a

393

rock in the bay. 'It was *long* as the river, and as *thick* as the town.'

Molly started, and began shaking awake the prisoners attached to his neck rope. Barbary wanted peace. 'Leave me alone.' Molly jerked his head upwards. On the ramparts there were shapes like statues that hadn't been there before. Other prisoners were stirring, gently wriggling themselves free of sleeping children. Barbary had difficulty with her breath; frantically she tried to flex hands numbed by the restricting rope.

'And the *poor* maiden quivered as it *went* up and down.'

Kitterdy Two was speaking to the others. 'There's an alarm bell in the gatekeeper's lodge. We get between him and it.'

A soldier by the fire fell forward into it and stayed there. Two more slumped sideways. If it hadn't been that the one in the flames was burning, they might all have been pretending. The sound of whatever had hit them was lost in the noise from the street. Barbary looked up and saw an archaic figure swinging a piece of leather round his head. The sling opened. A fourth soldier fell forward. Another had sprouted a dart in his eye. But the rest were on their feet. Shapes were coming down the walls on ropes. A soldier ran one of them through the back with his pike before it reached the ground.

Barbary felt a tug on her neck as Molly began to crawl to the lodge. She crawled after him with the others, in parallel, awkwardly, so as not to throttle themselves. The gatekeeper, picked for size rather than quickness on the uptake, recovered his wits and rushed for his lodge and the bellrope, to find himself impeded by a twelve-legged, clumsy monster insect whose attack, like a bee, threatened its own life but which, like a bee, was prepared to risk it. He drew a dagger and charged. Barbary was dragged down in a mass of shouting, biting, kicking bodies. She couldn't see which was whose. Agony came from somebody's elbow in her broken ribs, the rope was tightening on her neck. She clawed at it, open-mouthed, rolling in the tangle. Her last, strangled, irritable thought was that she was saving Bingham the trouble . . .

Of all things, somebody was putting a hat on her head. She flapped at it feebly and somebody slapped her.

'Leave it on. Get up.' Her hands were apart, they must be free. She could breathe but wished she couldn't. Her lover's voice was unloving. 'What the hell are you doing here?'

'Just passing through.' She was in a lot of pain.

The gates to the town were open and her fellow prisoners were being ushered through them, each having a mask slapped on his or her face by men who were themselves masked. 'Remember to revel now,' they were being told. 'Come on, you can revel.'

'Whyn't we go that way?' She nodded her way towards the gate leading to open country.

'Barracks.'

The courtyard was littered with bodies, more bodies than there had been soldiers. O'Hagan had had his losses. There was another body at her feet. 'Molly. Oh not Molly.'

Kitterdy Two put Barbary's right arm round his neck. 'He's dead, bless him. And took the gatekeeper with him.' O'Hagan took her other arm and they half dragged her to the gate. A cheery rescuer tied mask strings under her hat. 'Don't forget to revel now.'

They joined the gang which had been making such a noise outside the gate; it continued making it as it wound its way back down the street. 'It was *long* as the river. It was *thick* as the town.' Some of the men and women were fantastically dressed, carrying torches, waving bladders. A couple had drums, one a whistle. They jigged along before, behind and on the edges of what was now a huge snake of people, most of them as festal as death. Barbary saw the eyes of a fisherman's wife who'd been captured at Lough Corrib staring in terror from the holes in her mask as she tried to jiggle her baby like a Christmas puppet.

Barbary wasn't sure whether some streets were brightly lit and others dark or whether she kept losing consciousness. In the bright bits she prayed for dark. They didn't look like revellers; except for O'Hagan and the other rescuers, they were too ragged and radiated too much fear. Besides, the streets were quieter now. Galway had drunk itself into stupor. What gaiety there was had locked itself into the houses, leaving the streets to the dead drunk and night prowlers who, in turn, were attracting patrols of the portreeves. And they were losing people. Every time she looked behind to the rest of the snake, it was smaller; some weren't keeping up with the pace O'Hagan was setting.

'Wait,' she shouted at him.

'No.'

Her hand which was clutching the back of his cloak was wet. He was bleeding. He let go of her for a moment to clout a MacJordan shepherd. 'Revel, you bastard.' The man attempted a caper, shook a bladder he'd been given, and resumed the lope of a hunted dog.

They were approaching a square by a church; across its entrance were a string of men with a ship, Galway's arms, blazoned on their tabards. They were shouting something. Barbary dropped to her knees as O'Hagan let go of her again and drew his sword. Kitterdy Two and some of the other rescuers joined him in a rush forward. There was a rasp of steel. She struggled to her feet and ran forward over bodies. Some of the portreeves had got away. Kitterdy Two and O'Hagan were alive. They grabbed her hands, running now as the great bell of St Nicholas Church began to toll the alarm. The crowd behind them was smaller than ever, and at its far end there was shouting and some kerfuffle.

She woke up because they'd stopped again. They were at a wall, gates. A stout man in front of her, holding a huge ring of keys which jingled as he hopped up and down, was the best dressed she'd seen this night. She recognised the type, aldermanic. 'Will you ruin me, O'Hagan?'

'Get the bloody gate open.'

There were more bodies around, presumably the gate guard. As the alderman-type fumbled with the locks, she heard O'Hagan say, 'She's O'Neill's agent. She's important.'

'She'd better be.' The city was rocking with the clanging of bells. The gate creaked open, panicking men and women poured through it. They were through into a parade, the gate slammed behind them, the keys turned. An arch, lots of arches, very few people. Those who weren't out now wouldn't get out. But there was the smell of river, the moon reflecting off water. Not enough boats and still a long, dangerous way to go; men and women in the water clinging to gunwales as they moved off. Cull was in her boat. In the next one a massive figure was swearing at the oarsmen. 'Bend your backs, you swag-bellied, donkey-dicked fish-suckers.'

Beside her, Kitterdy Two gave a great sigh. 'Listen to Herself. Did you ever hear such music?'

Barbary considered before she passed out again. She hadn't.

A burst of musical bubbles woke Barbary up, Through one eye – the other wouldn't open – she glared at a caged canary trilling with what she considered unnecessary force. The unopened eye hurt, her head ached, her throat was sore, breathing was painful, there were rope burns on her wrists, her nose was cold, the rest of her was clean and warm in a clean, warm bed. There were lobster pots in the corner of the grey-lit room, a Spanish chest, the sound and smell of the sea, and a man with his back to her, a cloak thrown over his shoulders, looking out of the window. She was on Clare, and as near Heaven as she ever wanted to be. She was washed by gratitude for him, Grace O'Malley, Cull, Kitterdy Two, Molly, above all Molly, masked men and women she didn't know.

'Are you hurt bad?' she asked in English.

'Not much.' He turned round. Under his cloak his chest was bare except for a bandage. His face was older than the intervening absence since Spenser Castle should have made it and it wouldn't ever be as amused as it once had been. At the moment it wasn't amused at all. 'You're awake then.'

'How many got out?'

'Thirty-five.'

Sixty or more fate unknown. Not to be thought of. 'You did well.'

'Did well?' He was mocking her in his temper. Apparently she was at fault. 'Did well? I threw away years, *years*. Mine and O'Neill's. Planning, quietening the clans till we were ready. I had the bloody English eating out of me hand. In London Elizabeth was flirting her goggle eyes at me.' His mouth pursed into a rictus alarmingly reminiscent of the Queen of England, and his voice went high. ' "Rise Baron of Waterford and be a good boy." Thank you, your bitch Majesty. For nothing.'

'Thirty-five people would have hanged else.'

He turned back to the window. 'Christ forgive me, I've not even the excuse I did it for them.'

She thought: we're never going to get it right. Men are a waste of time. She went back to sleep.

When he woke her up it was dark outside the closed shutters, a brazier had been lit in the room and he had a bowl of porridge and a spoon.

Wincing, she pulled herself up and obediently opened her mouth to the spoon. 'Gawd help us, what is it?'

'Stirabout. I made it meself.'

'Don't take it up for a living. Where's Herself?' Outside the shutters the sea was roaring and banging, but the respondent echo in the tower indicated emptiness.

He shoved more stirabout in her mouth and scraped off the surplus, still angry. 'The bloody woman wouldn't leave one servant, not one. Stayed long enough to see her precious granddaughter would survive, and went to the mainland to prepare her inland defences. There's a crone called Katty in the cottages who leaves bread and milk and dresses people's wounds. And the look-out on the other side of the island.' His irritation was giving his English an unusually heavy Irish accent. He put down the porridge and went back to his damned window, opening the shutters again. 'I should be with O'Neill, making new plans now that you've destroyed my position with the English.'

'I destroyed it? *I* destroyed it? That beats the Dutch, that does. Nobody asked you to come interfering. I'd have got away, never you mind. They weren't going to trine Barbary Clampett. And I don't want to be here any more than you. I've got plans of my own, thank you.'

He turned round. 'It's plans now, is it? What plans?'

'Don't you mock me, you bastard. I've got a place in this war just as big as you.' She paused and quietened; it was true, she had. 'I'm going to get O'Neill his guns. And I'll bring Bingham down if it's the last thing I do.'

'Bingham? You? Bingham? Don't bank on me rescuing you next time.'

'You . . .' Epithets failed her. 'If you remember, the last time we was in a tower it was *me* rescued *you*.'

'I do remember.' She looked up because his tone had changed. 'There's the hell of it. I've remembered every second of it every day since. I'd go to confession to be rid of it, and remember it over again. And I'd think: there was nothing to that red-headed, skinny woman, nothing at all.'

'Oh, good.'

'A married woman who'd have forgotten me long ago. And I'd persuade myself I was only grateful for the saving of me life. And then, there you were among the prisoners. Skinnier than ever and dressed like a scarecrow.' He came back towards the bed, and as he passed the firelight it gave a sheen to the skin over the muscles of his chest. 'Why in hell get mixed up in this? Why didn't you go back to your husband where you belong?'

She was snuffling. 'You mind your own business.'

He picked up the stirabout. She could see he was in pain; how much of it was physical and how much mental she couldn't tell. 'And here we are again.'

Tears were running down her cheeks, and she got porridge over her face as she wiped them away. 'I'm sorry, O'Hagan.'

'Ah, now.' He ran his finger over her mouth and put it in his own. 'Maybe God'll not notice. With all the ugly old evil going on out there, maybe He'll wink at the bit of time we can snatch together.' He smacked his lips. 'This is grand stirabout and you're an ungrateful Saxon, so you are. Did you remember me at all?'

'No.'

He leaned forward and licked her face and then he was kissing her, his arms so tight round her that involuntarily she gasped in pain. He sat back, wincing on his own account. There was blood coming through his bandage. 'God damn. How are we going to manage this now?'

'Carefully.' She rubbed her cheek against his. 'But somehow.'

In the morning the room was freezing and snow had piled up on the windowsill and made a small drift on the floor beneath it. It was still coming through in thick flakes. Such a winter was rare in western Ireland and she could have sung at the weather's complicity in their isolation. He was still asleep and she winched herself painfully onto her side to study his face. No wonder it had gained lines since Spenser Castle; the man had balanced his life on a blade edge and only nifty footwork had kept him from a nasty death at the hands of the English.

In between making love, he had talked of the mission he'd carried out. Tricking the English into trusting him as their pacifier of the clans had been marginally less difficult than persuading the clans to cohere. 'Some wanted to rise quicker than yesterday. Others saw no reason to rise at all. Others wouldn't join O'Neill's army, just kill their landlords.' He lifted himself up to look at her. 'You'll not go back to Munster, promise me. Nobody will hold the MacSheehys from slaughter when it comes.'

'When will it come?'

He shrugged. 'Whenever it is, there'll be no winning of it. Even if we beat them, Gaelic Ireland is lost.'

She didn't ask him whether, in that case, there was any point to a war because she had seen enough to know that people pushed to the brink, as the Irish were being pushed, had to fight, if only to find a more survivable way of losing.

He amazed her. Organising the escape from Galway alone had required such nerve as made her gasp, and he'd done it for her. Being loved by him was astounding not just for itself but because for the first time in her life she could throw away physical and mental reserve. Last night she hadn't felt a fool in using her body, within the limits imposed by its battering, to show him how much she loved him, and telling him so over and again. She wished she could command erotic Irish such as he used so she could tell him better. Or erotic English for that matter. She wished she remembered the love poetry Philip Sidney had taught her. Order love language was strictly limited, its most romantic phrase for the sexual act being 'mattress jig'. There weren't words for him. 'You're a dimber cove, O'Hagan,' she said at last.

He kept his eyes closed. 'I'll bet you say that to all the boys.'

She kissed him. 'Let's get that wound seen to.'

'I've other priorities.' He reached for her. She grimaced with pain, and he said: 'Ouch. God help us, how do hedgehogs work these things?'

'I told you . . . ow . . . carefully.' But, again, manage they did, and afterwards she soaked the dressing away. He was still a baby in physical affliction.

'Mother of God, woman, will you skin me?' The

400

wound wasn't near as bad as the one that had nearly killed him in Munster; not a thrust through this time, but a slice that had colloped a portion of flesh away from the back of his waist.

'It ain't good,' Barbary said. 'Why can't you stay out of trouble?'

'Red-headed women keep getting me into it.'

They were driven out of the room eventually by hunger. O'Hagan had got it into his head that she should be recompensed for missing Christmas – 'Bingham's version of it being unfestal' – by a feast of their own. But he wouldn't allow Barbary to send for Katty to cook it. 'No outsiders. You cook it.' He didn't believe her protestations that she couldn't. 'All women can cook.'

They hobbled downstairs – she was still discovering her injuries, and one of them was a sprained knee. They picked out a goose from Grace's cold house and found her cupboards contained everything from basic flour, oats and beans, to exotic durables. 'Sugar, my God,' said O'Hagan. 'Where did she get the sugar?'

'Piloted it,' said Barbary.

Her ineptitude at making forcemeat and shoving the unappetising result up the bird's wrong end convinced him there was at least one woman who couldn't cook, and he took over himself, becoming edgy and preoccupied with pan sizes and weights, in a self-imposed, brow-furrowed responsibility which couldn't have worried him more if he'd been formulating a political constitution rather than a dinner for two. Redundant, Barbary wandered the tower, investigating her grandmother's chests and boxes. Manus, the steward, had taken the more important valuables to be available to Herself on the mainland, but she was able to adorn the table with exquisite Dutch tankards of colourless glass mounted in silver-gilt, pewter bowls, and gold, Spanish, dolphin-shaped ear-picks which she set out because she thought they were spoons.

The shock was in discovering the hand mirror, in itself a lovely thing of polished steel set in embossed leather, but reflecting a face that had seen too much wear. Its skin was tightly stretched. She had a cut across the bridge of her nose, a dark-blue, moon-shaped bruise under one eye and a scar through her top lip. Had he been making love to *that*? She'd seen prettier pack saddles. And her hair . . .

She tried lugging an iron laundry boiler to the top room, and had to give up. She wrapped herself up in a cloak and hurried down the slope to the quay to beg Katty for a bath. While the water heated, she returned to the tower and ransacked it, putting her loot into a handcart.

Back in Katty's kitchen, which smelled of baked bread and lye soap, she poured the unguent contents of strangely shaped glass bottles into the steaming wooden cask that was Katty's bath and washtub. With a vague remembrance that Philip Sidney had known somebody who bathed in asses' milk, she added a couple of quarts from the milk churn. She stripped, clambered in and, using a loofah from the unguent box, sat up to her neck in hot water and nearly scrubbed her freckles off. She washed her hair, dried it by sticking her head in the still-warm bread oven and burnished it with a pair of Grace's silk drawers.

Eventually, smelling like a bawdy dairy, she paraded in front of Katty in jewelled, satin, high-heeled shoes somewhat too large and a child's bodice and skirt slightly too small of sea-green plush stitched with pearls. She had Colombian emeralds in her ears and round her neck, hiding the rope burn; in her hand was a peacock-feather fan.

'As beautiful as Herself on Sundays,' Katty said, 'though smaller.'

Going back up the hill to the tower, Barbary said goodbye for ever to boy's attire. She might don male dress for convenience's sake, but never again as a disguise; the mirror said she couldn't get away with it much longer. Her body was still unsatisfactorily boyish in its thinness, but her face had lost its youth; not lined, not sadder, but set in awareness. It had always been knowing; now it had gained the ageing element of wisdom. She didn't like it, but how old was she now? Twenty? Thereabouts. A mature woman; time to dress like one.

She posed in the doorway of the tower's undercroft, the fan coquettishly over her lower face, waiting to be noticed. O'Hagan glanced up from his oven and came abstractedly towards her. 'What'll I do with all the goose grease?' he asked.

She snapped the fan shut, and told him.

If she had to say once that the goose was the most perfectly cooked bird that ever graced a board, she had to say it twenty times. If it had been raw with feathers on she'd have said the same. The meal, the warmth, the candles, the furniture of the room, its lobster pots and cobwebs, the bloody canary, the sea and snow acting as sentinels outside, were all subsumed in enchantment. He was wearing one of Don Howsyourfather's fine linen shirts, ruffled at the wrists and open at the neck, and when he'd stopped preening himself at the goose's perfections, he became aware of her. Even then he didn't seem to notice the dress or the emeralds. He put down his tankard of Grace's best Bordeaux and leaned his elbows on the table, staring. 'Hair like that should have special dispensation from the Pope.' He was slightly drunk, but so was she, and neither of them on the wine.

'Admit it, O'Hagan, you wouldn't love me if I was bald.'

'I would not.'

'Stop looking at me like that.'

'I can't help it. God help me, I can't help it.'

The bawds had never said that there could be this sort of passion between men and women, so desperate it was a form of despair.

After a week or two of this intimate living, she supposed the passion she felt would become domesticated into something more comfortable and everyday.

It didn't. She knew every inch of him but he could still come back into the room from fetching peat or water, and his long-bodied shape in the doorway unsettled her breathing as badly as it had back in Spenser Castle gatehouse.

Her breathing was unsettled anyway. She wasn't getting better as fast as he was. He'd healed nicely and she'd lost her bruises, but the pain in her chest kept coming back. At first the illness lurked, like an eavesdropper at the door, so that she was only uneasily aware of it. She waited for it to go away, but gradually the lurker came in as real and unwelcome as a third person. She had more

403

and more difficulty waking up from sleeps that resembled delirium. She didn't tell him because she couldn't believe that her happiness wouldn't cure it. With the poignancy and joy of this spring-in-winter, she must get better. She was in a spice-scented Hy Brazil floating on azure waters, sprinkled with flowers that to the less enchanted were frost crystals on dead stalks of grass. When they went for a walk, their frozen breath made lambs'-tail clouds.

'The Order would say this was my bunting times,' she said, panting, to O'Hagan, dislodging the aftermath of a snowball from her neck.

'Bunting times?'

'When the grass is high enough to hide the loving of swain and maid.'

But on the next walk she fell down and couldn't get up. He carried her back to the Tower. 'Why didn't you tell me?'

'I'm all right.'

She was aware that he nursed her, as she had nursed him. Through terrible dreams, his voice was the only causeway leading her back to solid ground. Sometimes it bullied her back, then it pleaded. 'Will you die on me?'

Chapter Nineteen

It was the coldest winter anyone in Ireland could remember. Starvation forced the mere Irish, who had hoped to stay clear of both, to join either the rebels or the English army. In neither camp did they find more in the way of food and warm clothing than if they'd stayed where they were, though things were marginally better among the rebels who were not subject to a royal parsimony that forced the Queen's Irish administrators into corruption which began at the top and filtered down to the bottom where soldiers had to sell their weapons in order to eat. It was a time of inactivity and complaint and therefore a time to look for a scapegoat. Among the constant despatches from Ireland landing on Lord Burghley's desk requesting supplies, uniforms, arms and money, he began to notice increasing mention of O'Neill, Earl of Tyrone. Spies were bringing information, for which they were paid, that O'Neill was treating with Spain, with Scotland, with rebels. He was still protecting shipwrecked Spaniards. He would not move against neighbouring Irish clans who refused to pay their taxes. It was he who had been behind the escapes from Dublin Castle, he was in cahoots with the pirate Grace O'Malley, he was in cahoots with the O'Donnell who was once more ensconced in the fastnesses of Donegal, defying Her Gracious Majesty Queen Elizabeth.

For the Irish huddled round their peat fires, equally inactive and with even more complaint, it was time to look for a deliverer. And there, too, men and women mentioned with increasing frequency the name of the O'Neill. They passed around among them the ancient prophecy of the Two Hughs who, when they came together, as Hugh O'Donnell and Hugh O'Neill were now contemporaneous, would bring about the reinstatement of the High King of Ireland, and banish from thence all foreign nations and conquerors.

And in Ulster O'Neill himself bent and resisted, doubled and dodged, in his attempt to be all things to all men and still keep Ulster free. On the east he had an angry and reluctant brother-in-law, Henry Bagenal, trying to bring him forcibly to court on the grounds that he had married Mabel Bagenal bigamously. He had commands, exhortations, enquiries and bans arriving every day by snow-covered English messengers from Dublin. From the south-west, also every day, he received pleas for help from clans writhing under Bingham's oppression. He was trying to keep his westerly neighbour, Maguire, from all-out war with England and to control the even more westerly, even more hot-headed Hugh O'Donnell, his kinsman. Struggling against calumny, prophecy and snow, the O'Neill went to Dublin and cried as he answered the charges against him. He cried so hard his accusers were embarrassed. 'I acknowledge myself most bound to Her Majesty for her great goodness and bounty extended towards me,' he sobbed. 'Let me go to London that I may kiss her feet and tell her how I am hounded on all sides.'

He didn't go, he had no intention of going, but he was playing a strong card, because the Dublin administrators didn't want him to go either. For all they knew, O'Neill might be in the right; the only evidence against him was based on the word of unreliable spies. If they could have requested one gift from God that winter, it would have been the ability to see into O'Neill's mind. But though God might be holding the lantern that cast light into such a dark labyrinth, He wasn't giving it to anybody else.

It was not to be expected that a man like Bingham would suffer prisoners to be removed from under his nose without reprisal, and he didn't. While Barbary was fighting for breath at Clare Castle, her grandmother arrived to say that an English fleet was on its way from Galway and that Clare itself must be evacuated.

'Bingham's enough ships with him to choke Clew Bay,' she told O'Hagan. 'Maybe we'll beat him off, maybe we won't. Either way the girl must be got out.'

O'Hagan panicked. 'She'll die. She's dying now. I'll not move her.'

Grace O'Malley was unmoved. 'Will we ask Bingham to let her get better before he hangs her?'

'Where to, then? Where do we send her?'

'To the O'Neill. Ulster has the only safety now. The sea's calm and I've a good little merchantman waiting to take her. Katty and Kitterdy Two will go along with her. I'll be needing you here.'

The two escapers from Dublin Castle looked hard at each other. Grace was right, O'Hagan knew she was right. He wrapped Barbary in a large, warm cloak and carried her to the landing stage. She felt the cold on her face, tasted the sea air, and put what energy she had into clinging onto his neck. 'Don't send me away.' She was only safe when she was with him. Losing him now would be losing him for ever.

'I'll get you back. Avourneen, listen to me. If Hell comes between us, I'll get you back.' But he wouldn't have put money on the chance of either of them surviving the next few days. Carefully he handed her over to Kitterdy Two.

'She'll come through,' Grace told him. 'She's got the O'Malley blood with her.'

The O'Neill castle on its hill at Dungannon commanded the north's River Blackwater. It was of so many architectural periods that from a distance its towers and steep-pitched mansards resembled a collection of stalagmites. It would have grieved Lord Burghley to see that not one of them was roofed with the lead he had so kindly permitted the O'Neill to import from England, that same lead having long ago been moulded into bullets.

However, O'Neill had paid his patron the compliment of building on a new section that was a pastiche of Burghley's home of Theobalds, a jumble of cinquecento and Tudor styles. It had a gallery a hundred feet long, a magnificent staircase rising out of an enormous hall, parapets and porticos carved into grotesque shapes, black and white stone floors, side walks in the gardens, and statuary everywhere. But whereas the risk of siege was a thing of the past in Hertfordshire and Theobalds could face the world unprotected, Dungannon was curtained by walls.

The room where Barbary was nursed back to health,

though not without difficulty, was high up in one of the modern turrets and looked over the battlements to woodland and Lough Neagh. It wasn't a restful room. Every inch of wall was tapestried with hunting scenes. Its ceiling was vaulted into a roundel depicting a scantily clad Artemis aiming a bow at an equally naked Actaeon, somewhat needlessly, thought Barbary, since he was being torn apart by hounds anyway. She spent listless days staring at it from her pillow. It was a sign she was getting better when the scene began to get on her nerves. And on the day she was heard to hiss at Artemis: 'Oh, go ahead and shoot him,' was the day that Katty informed the O'Neill her patient had turned the corner and could be visited.

He came into the room tiptoeing absurdly, one hand holding a pomander to his nose and the other proffering a posy. 'Are you better?'

Katty took the posy and put it in water. 'Sure, I could blow her off me hand, but she's better, thanks be to God.'

'Grand. I hate sick women.' Everything about him was exaggerated, his beard – he was dyeing it – his over-colourful clothes, his gestures. Even the fact that he knew he was verging on caricature was exaggerated; his long black eyes looked sideways to measure his effect. The room became doubly unrestful.

'Any news?' Barbary asked.

'None.'

She sank back. There had been a perfunctory sea battle between Grace O'Malley and the English fleet outside Clew Bay, but the overwhelming superiority of Bingham's numbers and firepower had been such that Grace had used her own superiority in seamanship and knowledge of the waters to make her escape with few losses. Since then, there'd been no word of either her or O'Hagan. It was only O'Hagan Barbary worried for; Grace O'Malley had established herself in her granddaughter's mind as immortal. They wouldn't get Grace O'Malley. But for the vulnerable O'Hagan she prayed barbaric prayers. 'Just keep him safe. I'll never see him again if that's what You want, so long as You keep him safe.'

The rest of the news was not reassuring. The settlement of Connaught, which had never been as successful as Munster's, was being renewed. Bingham's army was evicting the Irish, there was fighting and starvation.

The O'Neill perched himself on the window seat and opened the casement to the falling snow outside. Katty promptly shut it. He went on staring out through the glass. 'They're plucking geese in Connaught,' he said, 'that's what we used to say when it snowed. Plucking geese in Connaught. It's Bingham plucking them now.' He slid his eyes towards the bed. 'It's gone, Connaught's gone,' as if western Ireland had slid into the sea. 'I'm the man in the gap.'

'They're dead, aren't they?'

'Not at all. We'd have heard. They'll turn up one day, dead or alive or a-horseback.' He came over to sit on the bed. 'Do you want other news?'

She shook her head.

'Then I'll begin. Did you know Sir Walter Raleigh is in the Tower for having made a secret marriage to one of Elizabeth's maids of honour?'

'Never.' He'd caught her attention. 'What'd he do that for?'

'I imagine,' drawled the O'Neill, 'that he got bored. Pouring out passion for the Queen and staying celibate can only be done by a Christopher Hatton, and he's dead now, poor bastard. The intelligent find it wearing. Perhaps our Walter wanted legitimate issue. He's forty-one years old, after all.'

She pondered on it, and the O'Neill, watching her, thought she'd fallen asleep until she said: 'Poor old Edmund. What price his poem now?'

'Spenser's back in Ireland.' He looked at her curiously. 'Are you interested in your husband at all?'

She'd known this would come. 'I suppose so.' It wasn't as her husband she remembered him; her mind had rejected the interlude of marriage and reinstated Rob as the real Rob, the lover of ships and books, Rob of her childhood, the only Rob for whom she could feel any affection, and even that as someone far removed.

But O'Neill kept insisting on the relationship. 'He's rising, your husband. He came well out of the recent campaign, the only one that did.'

The expedition to pursue the Spanish fleet to its home

ports had proved disastrous. Its leaders, Sir Francis Drake and Sir John Norris, had refused to risk their ships on a difficult crossing to the Biscayan ports and disobeyed Elizabeth's orders by sailing on to the Azores to look for prizes among the New World fleets, knowing the Queen's displeasure could be assuaged with gold. They hadn't found it. Eleven thousand men lost their lives and the condition of the returning ships was lamentable.

'But your husband had the good luck. He took a prize stuffed with spices, much of it pepper. Do you know what pepper fetches in England? Elizabeth sneezed her pleasure at him. She likes a well-built young man with good luck. He's at court now, an object of jealousy to the boy Essex, so I'm told. Drake's in disgrace and poor Norris is back in Ireland.'

He was still looking at her for a reaction, but it was like listening to fairy tales, something happening in another world. 'Well,' she said, and went back to sleep.

She spent much of her convalescence on the window seat, and much of that time straining her eyes towards Lough Neagh, looking for a ship flying the O'Malley pennant, which never came. When the waiting became unbearable she would distract herself by looking down into the formal garden sixty feet below her turret where men and women were reduced to the size of chess pieces. It was a bird's eye view on the dangerous game the O'Neill was playing, so dangerous that if some of the pieces encountered others, his life was forfeit.

There was the bearded, cloak-swirling Maguire, a figure out of myth and head of the English-hating clan that bordered O'Neill territory, brandishing his fists at the O'Neill and bawling his wrongs in Irish. There were the Catholic priests remonstrating in Latin, come from Rome to urge on O'Neill the Holy War which would restore the True Faith to Ireland.

Once, and it made the palms of her hands sweat, a servant came running to clear them out in the nick of time before a deputation of English officials from Dublin came stalking into the garden to give orders to the O'Neill in high, commanding voices that came up to her like the cawing of rooks. The hats of the English passed along one side of a hedge, while the tonsured heads of the

410

priests, a bobbing row of spring onions, skulked along the other.

She watched the small figure in the centre of it all caper, talk, reason, argue, switch from command to petition, from Irish to English to Latin and back again, stand straight, bow, give and receive homage, and wondered when it would go mad. There were times when he came to her room and she wondered if he wasn't mad already, so violently did he rail, as much against his own people as the English. But it was the madness of a visionary who sees what others are too shortsighted to glimpse.

'All they can grasp is that Elizabeth offers them abasement. They'll go out and fight in individual, heroic despair, grand idiots that they are, knowing that they'll fall. And all the time there's an alternative, *my* alternative. A confederation of Gaelic clans which, given time, could be so mighty that Elizabeth would be powerless against it. But they've never united before, so they don't see it. God damn them. God damn them.'

Even on unharassed days the O'Neill was never still, and walked the garden dictating to his English secretaries interminable letters to Burghley and the Queen and in the next breath to Philip of Spain.

'Why use English scribes?' she asked him once. 'Didn't one of them betray you once?' Katty got a lot of information from the servants.

The O'Neill flicked his fingers. 'I only trust the devious, Lady Betty, being a devious man myself. It's the straightforward give me trouble. I never know what bulls like Maguire and the O'Donnell are going to do.'

On another day she saw two beautiful girls quarrelling as they pulled him in two different directions. 'Sure and he's got to have mistresses,' Katty told her. 'Would he keep the respect of his people if he didn't have women?'

'But where's Mabel?'

'Who?' asked Katty.

And there was the ghost. Barbary knew it was a ghost because, although she could see it from her eyrie, nobody else did. Sometimes it was alone, drifting through the early spring garden, sometimes it made its appearance when the garden was crowded, moving through conversing groups that obliviously went on talking. It was elderly, thin and female. Nobody addressed it or looked at it. Barbary was relieved it cast a shadow.

On the night after his physician had pronounced her well, the O'Neill came up to escort Barbary down to the hall for dinner. She was reluctant. Her window had become a waiting place, suited to the limbo she existed in.

'It's only family,' O'Neill said. 'Nobody controversial tonight. A small feast in your honour'. His idea of a small feast was two hundred people; the entire clan felt free to pop in to sample O'Neill hospitality any time it was passing, often staying for months, sometimes taking up permanent residence. To Barbary, used to the quiet of her room, it looked, and sounded, as if half Ulster and its dogs had come for dinner.

'I'll not toast you,' said the O'Neill, 'for there's no need to let the secretaries know everyone who stays here.' The chair on his other side was empty. 'They'll think you're a new mistress and that I'm a lucky man.' He was smiling as he said it but his eyes were on the far end of the hall where a figure had come in to drift along the tables. It was the ghost. It leaned over a guest, who appeared not to notice, and picked up a leg of chicken which it gnawed as it continued its invisible progress.

'Excuse me, my dear.' O'Neill left his seat and walked towards the ghost, courteously taking its hand to conduct it to the empty chair beside his, but it moved away from him and went out.

Now Barbary knew who it was. She ran outside after it and caught it up among the geometric flower beds of the garden where she had so often watched it walk. 'Mabel. It's me. Barbary. You came to see me once. At the Spensers' house in Dublin. I was going to be married and you were . . .' She gave it up.

'Did I?' Mabel didn't remember. She was fairly interested, but no more than in the chicken leg, which wasn't much. How could somebody young look this old? No, not old. Age was something positive, and everything positive had gone out of Mabel O'Neill. She was dressed in Irish clothes, but wasn't wearing them; somebody else had stuck them on her and the shoulder seam sagged at the front of her chest, the head-roll had been jammed ridiculously far down on her forehead. Youth, health, emotion had gone but there wasn't enough in her to say she was ill. Her face, which had been so round and pink-cheeked, merely lacked definition. Some remnant of manners remained. 'So pleased you could come.'

'The O'Neill was kind enough to shelter me.'

Mabel patted her on the shoulder. 'You must make sure he doesn't kill you,' she said. She might have been advising against the prawns.

'Does he kill people?'

'I think so. I think he killed my brother.' She dropped the bone, regarded her hands as things not belonging to her and wiped them on her skirt.

'Mabel.' Barbary put her hands under the woman's chin, so that she would look at her. 'Mabel, Henry Bagenal's alive. O'Neill hasn't killed him.'

Mabel nodded, 'I expect so,' and began to move away.

Barbary held on to her. 'Would you like to see your brother? Mabel, we can go now. I'll take you now, this minute.' And she would have done; anything to reverse this lethal wilting. Sod O'Neill. Him and his bloody table napkins, what had he done to the girl? 'What's he done to you, Mabel?'

The Countess of Tyrone glanced up at the moon like someone estimating the time and disengaged Barbary's clutching hand. 'He kills people.'

Barbary watched the ghost of Mabel Bagenal waver away. She found the O'Neill beside her and turned on him. 'What in hell have you done to her?'

He shrugged. 'She didn't transplant well.'

'*Didn't transplant well?*' She could have hit him. As if Mabel Bagenal were a cutting refusing to flourish. 'How did you ever think she could?' The loneliness of the girl. Dropped into what she must have seen as Dark Age society where the barbarians regarded her manners, her language, her people and her religion with contempt.

'You did,' said the O'Neill.

That was different. She'd been prepared by the Order's own form of barbarism. Besides, for her it had been a coming home and her eyes had been opened to its beauty and comradeship.

'My dear,' said the O'Neill, 'I should like you to come with me on a little boating trip. There are some people out on Lough Neagh I want you to meet, and it would be as well if nobody else saw their faces. Horses are being got ready for the ride to the loughside, if you feel well enough.'

She forgot Mabel and clutched at him. 'Is it O'Hagan?'

'I fear not, though I have received word of him.'

'Is he safe? Where is he?'

It was chilly in the garden. Absentmindedly the O'Neill took her hand and held it high so that they walked in the attitude of dance as they once had in the garden of Penshurst a long time before. 'He is well,' he said, 'and on his way to Spain.'

She couldn't understand him at first. 'Spain? *Spain?* Why's he going to Spain?'

'Because I ordered him there.' He turned and, still prancing, led her back the way they'd come. 'My dear Lady Betty, our mutual friend O'Hagan is possibly the most able lieutenant I have. His action in rescuing you from Galway must be applauded, but it finished his usefulness here. In my position I cannot afford to waste talent and, since King Philip knows and likes him, he is to be my unofficial ambassador in certain negotiations I am conducting.' He glanced up at the moon. 'It's time we were going.'

'I don't believe you.' She was stumbling to keep up with him as he led her through an archway towards the stable block. Somebody wrapped her in a riding cloak and helped her up onto a horse. 'I don't believe you.'

'We must be quiet now. Wait until we're in the woods.'

They rode through gates, courtyards, more gates, a lane and along a green road through woods. For all Barbary was aware of their progress they could have been standing still. Misery hadn't caught up with her yet, only disbelief. Yes, O'Neill. Three bags full, O'Neill. Off to Spain at once, O'Neill. He wouldn't have done it like that. Abandon the most precious thing either of them had ever experienced without so much as a wave?

She shouted: 'How do you know he's gone to Spain?'

O'Neill slowed his horse and came alongside her. 'I sent him his orders last week. This morning I got word his ship had sailed from Donegal.'

'You're lying.'

He caught hold of her horse's bridle. 'Do you know him then? A couple of encounters and you know the

414

man? O'Hagan is my foster brother, and there's no closer relationship in our culture. Did you know he intended for the priesthood? Why do you think he never married? Was he easy with you?' He stopped in a patch of moonlight and examined her face. 'I see he was not.' Suddenly he leaned over and embraced her. 'Let the man go to his work and his conscience. We're facing annihilation.' He let her go and they rode quietly on. 'The time for love is over.'

The ground sloped to a small stone jetty where a barge waited for them, its riding light casting a yellow, wavering path on the water; there was no other light, except from the moon which outlined the barge's elegant shape. The O'Neill handed her along the gangplank. Her numbed mind had to go back years to recognise the combination of bilge water, holystone, polished wood and the metallic smell given off by gold braid on the uniforms of sweating men. The O'Neill's barge was an ornamented, gold-leafed copy of Queen Elizabeth's royal barge on which she had first encountered Burghley and Walsingham, on which one chapter of her life had closed and another opened.

The poop deck was covered by an awning beneath which had been set a table. On one side of this sat four hooded figures. The awning shut out the moonlight so that their shapes were only degrees of blackness in the dark. The O'Neill gave the order to cast off. Phosphorescence, the colour of burning brandy, was ladled up by the oar blades. Barbary put out her hand to touch the unmistakable bulk next to her. 'Thank you, Grandmother.' She hadn't been in any condition to express gratitude for her rescue from Galway since it had happened.

'Captured by Gauls,' Grace O'Malley hissed at her. 'You're not fit to mind mice at a crossroad.'

Barbary was in no mood for that game. 'It is right O'Hagan's gone to Spain?'

Grace shrugged. 'We split up when we were being hunted. The last I saw he was for Donegal.'

'Hunted?'

Her grandmother said, as the O'Neill had said, 'Connaught's gone. Most of me fleet's gone. The people are in hiding and Bingham's killing everything that lives.'

Barbary woke up. Since her illness she had been drifting in personal misery of which O'Hagan's defection had been a terrible extension. But he was alive when thousands were recently dead, when an entire culture had disappeared, when this indomitable woman beside her had lost her home and her empire.

Barbary had become too mature and was now too hurt to pretend, as she would have once pretended, that, to hell with him, she didn't care. But there were other things and people that mattered to her and those, as the O'Neill had pointed out, were facing annihilation and the time for love had passed. She shook herself and became aware of the strangeness of being on a boat at night with hooded figures round a table. 'What are we doing here?'

'I don't know about you, but I've come to get me country back.'

Barbary looked around. They were heading out into the centre of the lough. She could just see dark slivers, either seals or curraghs, lying on the white strands behind them. The slight breeze carried the scent of blossom from the land and massaged the water into wavelets.

A servant brought a live coal from the fire bucket and lit lanterns hanging from the awning. 'We won't be seen now, lady and gentlemen,' said the O'Neill, 'if you would like to unveil. One at a time, perhaps.' He loved theatricals. The first hood slipped back off a red head, and immediately a charge like an invisible St Elmo's fire played around the table from the man's inherent energy. It was O'Donnell. How he'd managed to sit still and quiet for so long was a miracle. He smiled and bowed to Barbary. He had an engagingly snub nose. 'It's to be hoped you've overlooked the unpleasantness after Dublin Castle,' he said.

The second unveiling was Cuckold Dick. Barbary sighed with comfort, and then went wild. 'Dick, did you . . . ?' She could see he was full of himself.

'I did, Barb.'

And he had. The third man was Will Clampett.

She flung herself across the table to clutch his neck and kiss him. 'Oh Will, I missed you awful.' His answering pat on her back was a reminder that she'd lived among emotional Celts for too long, this wasn't the way the foster daughters of cannon masters behaved.

416

'All right, girl,' he said. Barbary wriggled back, rebuffed and happier.

Grace O'Malley lit a pipe, bottles and tankards were put on the table. O'Neill said: 'I would not choose to greet honoured guests in this manner but, between you, you make up a combination that would hang us all. The English, as usual, might get the wrong impression. For this is not a council of war, it is a council of . . . well, a council of eventuality. Master Clampett, one question. Are you prepared to make guns for me?'

'I come for two reasons,' said Will, the familiar voice sounding weighty against the rapid speech of the O'Neill. 'One, for that I wanted to see that maid there again. Two, for that I wronged your country once and wish to right it. Then again, I'm out of a job. That's three.'

'What's your man droning?' asked Grace O'Malley, whose shaky grasp of English was having trouble with the Devonian accent.

Barbary ignored her. 'Why'd Sir Henry Sidney let you go, Will?'

'He's dead, girl. There's a new lord at Penshurst didn't want me.'

'Dead?'

Will nodded. 'Lady Sidney, too. Seemingly they didn't want to live after they got the word about Sir Philip. I'd thought you'd heard. He was killed fighting the Spanish in the Low Countries.'

There was a tree in front of her eyes with a young man leaning against it reciting poetry. The sun came through its branches. She heard O'Donnell say: 'That's one less damned Gaul to kill.'

There was a silence. 'O'Donnell,' said the O'Neill, 'still your filthy tongue before I cut it from your head.'

The young chieftain was blustering, Grace O'Malley was pouring wine and talking – she'd met Philip. Only O'Neill and Barbary were silent. He had known, of course, but perhaps he hadn't wanted to pile on too much sadness, strange man that he was. They sat quietly, joined in watching a golden English gentleman dance out of their sight, taking light with him.

'Don't even have to steal 'em,' Will was saying to O'Donnell, 'more a matter of crossing the right palms with silver. The Weald turned out two thousand ordnance last year. Near two hundred pieces never got fired by English gunners. Went missing.'

The O'Neill shook himself. 'Can you set up a foundry here?'

'If you've got the iron, I got the skill,' said Will. 'Take time, mind.'

'Do you hear that, O'Donnell?' asked the O'Neill. 'Time.' He banged the table suddenly with both fists. 'Now then. The English have demanded that the Maguire come in to pay his rents and make his submission to Her Gracious Majesty's deputy in Dublin. They want *me* to bring him in. *I* want to bring him in. But last week the Maguire left my table, spitting brimstone, to declare war on Bingham who is harassing his southern border. The English will demand that I join their expedition to suppress him, and join it I shall, or be attainted. And when we've wiped out Maguire we shall continue westward to wipe out the O'Donnell.'

'You'll not wipe me out, O'Neill.' O'Donnell was on his feet, his head into the awning and his hand on his sword hilt.

'No, my dear, I won't. Because you are coming to Dublin with me to make your submission.'

'I'll not.'

'*You will!*' The O'Neill screamed, he threw bottles into the river, tears spurting out of his eyes. It was an appalling exhibition. The only one who wasn't immobilised by it was Grace O'Malley. She put a massive hand on his shoulder and forced him back into his seat, then patted him.

'Your nerves are in flitters, me boy.'

The O'Neill went quiet. That was rehearsed, thought Barbary, but it's real for all that. The O'Neill's nerves were in flitters all right, but from anger; anger at a war he dreaded being forced on him, and, most of all, at his own people's connivance at conflict in refusing to bend to the English wind.

A servant put out more bottles. O'Neill raised himself and poured wine for them all. 'You will come with me to Dublin,' he said softly to O'Donnell, 'and you will bend your back to the Lord Deputy, confess your misdemeanours, especially your insolence in escaping from gaol, promise that you will be a loving subject of Her Majesty from here on, pay her taxes, and tuck her soldiers up at nights. If they produce the Bible, you will swear on it. You will do this because I have had to do it for twenty years. You will do it because it will give us *time*.' The bottles on the table bounced nervously again.

O'Donnell's large and handsome head turned from one table companion to another. His eyes were screwed up. 'A sort of game, you mean?'

O'Neill expelled his breath. 'Yes, my dear, a game.'

'To give us time to form an army.'

'Yes.'

'Trick them.'

'Yes.'

O'Donnell beamed. 'I can do that,' he said. They drank to him.

O'Neill turned to Grace O'Malley. 'How many ships have you got left, Granuaile? If it comes to it, can you transport guns and gallowglass?' Gallowglasses were Scottish mercenaries whose inclusion in Irish wars went back centuries.

'If I get me price.' Grace put her pipe down. 'Now do you know what I'm going to tell you. You buggers have Bingham yapping on your borders, but it's Connaught the bastard's ravaging. Time, you say. But my people have no time left. I'm making me peace separate and I'm making it now.' It was the longest speech Barbary had heard her grandmother make. O'Donnell hissed: 'You're making peace with Bingham?'

Grace shook her head. 'With Elizabeth of the Gauls.'

'With the Queen?'

'I've written to her,' said Grace, picking up her pipe again. 'Cut out the middleman. One woman to another. Didn't the O'Malleys and O'Flaherties submit to her? And didn't she promise her protection in return? Well, now she can deliver it and prise that bastard off me back.'

All at that table had reason to consider themselves audacious in their various ways; only Will Clampett was unamazed by this old woman who gave new meaning to the word, and that was because she'd spoken in Irish. They stared, Cuckold Dick with his what-an-Upright-Man-she'd-have-made gaze, Barbary, a Jill the Baptist beholding the half that had not been told her, O'Donnell as at the Medusa, and O'Neill like an alchemist at the

419

pupil who's come up with the formula for gold. 'You've written to Elizabeth for protection from Bingham? Asked Attila for protection from the Hun? What of pirating her ships these forty years?'

Grace puffed out a long stream of smoke. 'Pilotage, would you mean? Forced into it, so I was. It's a fine, sweet letter. Manus has the English and wrote what I told him. I'll not be surprised if she asks me round to England to split a bottle with her.'

The O'Neill passed his hand over his eyes. 'By God,' he said, quietly, 'I think she might.' They were so used to the thump of oars in the rowlocks and the grunt of rowers that the sounds of the night, a dog's sudden bark a long way off, the splash of a disturbed swan, fell on apparent silence.

'Lady Betty.'

Barbary stirred uneasily. It was her turn. 'What?'

'Last and most important.' His dark eyes were tender as he took her hand. 'We've known each other a long time.' It's going to be nasty, she thought, but he digressed. 'How was it Philip Sidney died, Master Clampett?'

'Gangrene,' said Will. 'Place called Arnhem. A hard death, but borne like a Christian, so they say.'

'Yes,' said O'Neill gently, looking back at Barbary, 'it would be.' He was deliberately resurrecting Philip Sidney as a link that only they shared.

'What do you want, O'Neill?'

'You, my dear. Back in England. Getting my guns. Putting in the right word at the right time. Destroying Bingham. You did swear to destroy Bingham, I believe? Back in the good graces of Our Gracious Majesty.'

The request was so outrageous and so impossible she was relieved. 'The Queen? O'Neill, she wouldn't look at me. Sir John Perrot said she wanted my head off. She'll never forgive me.'

'Whether she does or she doesn't, my dear, you have a direct link to her court which could be of the utmost use.'

She'd gone white. She knew what he was asking, knew he knew his own enormity in asking. He wanted her back with Rob.

'No,' she said. 'I won't.'

'There's nobody else can do it.'

'No.'

He didn't throw a fit. Or bottles. The conference was over. But after a while in the general movement she found herself standing in the barge's stern with the O'Neill beside her, though how the manoeuvre had come about she wasn't sure. There was an almost imperceptible lightening of the sky as they headed back to the lough-side, though the shore was still some way off, a confused mounding of dark shadows. They had come a long way out in the O'Neill's search for complete secrecy. You couldn't blame him, she thought; on this barge there's an arch-renegade in O'Donnell, an arch-pirate in Grace O'Malley and an English cannon master. Just being seen in such company would condemn him to the block.

The O'Neill leaned companionably on the gilded scroll-work. 'And how will you occupy your time now?' he asked. He knew her too well, always had.

'You can save your breath, O'Neill. I'll fight. I'll spy. I'll do anything you want. But I can't go back to Rob.'

His hands spread out in amazement that she could think he'd force her to. 'I understand. You love another. Don't I know about love? Haven't I been in it often enough? It's just, well, a matter of function. For many a woman a man is her function, and good luck to her. But for Barbary O'Flaherty? I thought you'd want to do work only you can do. No matter. We'll find something else.'

'You're a bastard, O'Neill.'

'So they tell me, so they tell me.'

They stared down, hypnotised, at the bubbles of their wake. 'I always had hope while Philip Sidney lived,' said the O'Neill.

She knew what he meant; not hope for anything specific, just a possibility that the world held marvels. And it had gone. She put out her hand to ringed fingers which clutched at hers.

Ahead water rose up in a white, untidy column. The barge reared, then rocked. Barbary's body knew they were under fire and threw itself down before her brain caught up. The O'Neill landed on top of her. There was another explosion, this time forward. They were bracketed. Her fingernails tore at the planking, trying to burrow through it. The next shot would be a direct hit.

It didn't come. A voice used to hailing over distance

shouted: 'Ship oars and surrender in the name of our sovereign Queen Elizabeth.'

Barbary dragged herself up and peered over the gunwale. It was difficult to see the ship, even though she knew it was there; it had hidden itself, waiting, in the shadows of the lakeside until the barge, as conspicuous as a beetle on a white carpet, was in the middle of open, moonlit water. The O'Neill hadn't cared who saw the barge as long as they didn't see her passengers. Like Grace O'Malley before him, he had considered himself inviolable in his own country. Like Grace O'Malley, he'd been wrong. And he'd been betrayed; this was no chance entrapment.

'I have information the traitor O'Donnell is aboard. I'm coming alongside in a boat. One false move and you'll be blown out of the water.'

The O'Neill's face was green. His trickster's eyes shifted in the search for a way out. Her own brain was racing. Make a run for it? Get blown up clean and fast? Bluff? Say they were bringing in Grace and O'Donnell for their submission?

Beside her the O'Neill said: 'And me so full of promise.' He'd tested every bar and found no way out. The only thing left to him was to show courage.

Barbary said: 'Get out of sight, O'Neill.'

His mind was on other things, so she kicked his shin to wake him up. 'Take the others, get into the bilges or whatever, and keep out of sight.'

'Doomsday must be met with dignity, my dear.'

'It ain't Doomsday yet. We might still catch this cony. Send Cuckold Dick down with a pack. Clothes, anything that looks like luggage.'

He kissed her hand. After he'd gone, she moved to the taffrail gate and waited, wishing she was dressed as an Englishwoman and not in Irish fashion. For what it was worth she took the Gaelic roll off her head. This was going to have to be a good catch, the best. Will's life depended on it. They'd hang him for sure, consorting with the Irish. And Grace. And O'Donnell.

A longboat was coming out of the shadows into the moonlight. The voice she had recognised said again: 'One false move and I'll sink you. Yield the traitor O'Donnell.'

Cuckold Dick was standing beside her. 'Have you got a pack?'

He whispered back: 'Yes, Barb. What we been doing in O'Neill territory?'

What had they been doing? She hadn't thought it through. Jesus, her mind was a blank. She could hear the clunk of rowlocks in the oncoming boat and she hadn't an idea, not an idea . . .

'Haven't we been visiting your old friend, Mabel Bagenal, Barb?'

'God bless you. That's what we've been doing. I forgot.' She was opening the taffrail gate as the longboat bumped alongside, welcoming its commander in her best court English. 'This is a most happy chance, Sir John.' Order rule: get in first. 'I'd heard there was an English ship close by . . .' Why not? If the O'Neill had been betrayed to them, they could have been betrayed to O'Neill. '. . . and I said to my lord of Tyrone: "If I can get aboard her, she can take me home," I said. And so he very kindly lent me his own barge. Help me down, Dick. Pass my pack carefully now.'

'Stay where you are.' She blinked as a torch was held up by the man standing in the boat. 'Identify yourself.'

'Oh, Sir John,' she said reproachfully, 'and I recognised your voice at once. You know me. And most certainly you know my husband. Don't you remember? We met in Munster, just before the Armada? I am Lady Betty.'

She saw the battered, kind, and now very worn face of Sir John Norris lift with recognition. 'God bless us. Lady Betty. What do you do here?'

'I'm wanting to get home.' She fluttered her eyelashes at him. 'I can't tell you how sick of Ireland I am. But I could hardly desert poor Mabel, could I? The Countess of Tyrone and I are old friends.' She prattled on, settling herself in the boat, passing her pack to sailors, beckoning Cuckold Dick to join her. 'My servant . . . Now, I want to hear about Rob. I hope my letters to him have got through more regularly than his to me . . .'

She was rocking the man, she could see. Dick was in the boat now, and the barge's taffrail gate closed behind him, its oarsmen sitting still as death.

'Is there nobody else aboard that barge, Lady Betty?'

She raised her eyebrows. 'Only some very stupid rowers. They took me out to the lake, and of course lost the way. These Irish . . .'

She'd done it. He had to take the word of a woman who was wife of his expedition companion. He had to because he was a gentleman of the old school. It was what she'd banked on. He signalled to his own rowers to fend off and turn round.

She kept talking, hearing her words skip across the distance to the barge until it grew too great for them to reach it. Until then she hadn't had time to realise the consequences of what she was doing. It had been necessary in order to save the lives of people who were vital to her, but for her own life it was disastrous. For a moment her voice faltered. She was doing what the O'Neill wanted. To the letter. She had cast herself off. She was going to be taken back to England, the Queen – and Rob.

Chapter Twenty

The mere Irish did Sir John Perrot no favours when he was recalled to England. They lined his route to the harbour in their thousands, weeping and calling out that their only friend was deserting them. They stood on the dockside, still weeping, to wave him off.

Sir John shook his fist at them. 'You bastards,' he shouted. 'You've wept me into the Tower.' He wiped his eyes. 'And you too, mistress,' he said.

'They're not weeping for me.'

'You're their friend, so I'm told. That's enough to loosen one's head on one's shoulders, eh, what say you?'

Barbary said nothing. She was returning to England as she'd set out: with Sir John Perrot and at the behest of Lord Burghley. The order to Norris had been sharp. The State required the answers to many questions concerning Lady Betty, who was to be closely attended and sent to London on the next available ship, which had turned out to be the same one taking Sir John Perrot, also to answer 'certain charges' against him.

Neither's future held promise. Barbary assessed her chances of escaping severe punishment and didn't fancy the odds. She had tricked the Queen into believing she was a boy, she had married without the Queen's permission, she had absented herself, and – though, with luck, they wouldn't know this – she had been in the company of notable rebels and committed piracy. People had gone to the block for less.

It couldn't be said she didn't care, more that there wasn't a lot left to care with. The bit of her that mattered stretched beyond the low, green hills of Dublin across the central plain to a land of sea and rock where it sailed with pirates, swam with seals and loved a man in a tower. She had, she realised with irony, become typically Irish in

425

loving Ireland not in its entirety, as a country, but a region of it. She was in exile. She had no lover. She had no child. All she could do with what was left over, if they let her, was to protect her kingdom by the sea. A confusing pain across her chest was either a breaking heart or a return of illness.

If she'd been accompanying anybody but Sir John, she'd have curled up in the cabin for the voyage and slept, but Sir John was ill and because of his kindness to Ireland and herself she felt a weary duty towards him, and kept him company during the terrible attacks that he put down to 'stones', and during the equally terrible drinking bouts with which he anaesthetised them. Drunk or in pain he raved against the 'yapping weasels' in Dublin who had hampered his every attempt at reform and gained his removal by telling England that he was a traitor, encouraged rebellion, corresponded with Philip of Spain, and spoke contemptuously against the Queen.

And of those charges the only one with truth to it – and the most serious, thought Barbary – was that of speaking against the Queen. He was furious with his sister's mismanagement of Ireland, and when Sir John Perrot was furious he was loud. Looking exactly as an enraged Henry VIII must have looked, he stamped about the ship's cabin, foulmouthing Elizabeth as a 'filthy hypocrite, more at the mercy of those frisking courtiers than her wise men'.

'For God's sake, Sir John,' Barbary told him, alarmed, 'with your tongue you don't need enemies. Take it quieter.'

'Quieter? While Bingham hangs for the pleasure of it? While those Dublin weasels line their own pockets? While Loftus corrupts the word of God? I tell you, mistress, the meanest hedge priest is a better archbishop than that son of a whore. I'll not be quiet. God's wounds, what's in here,' he pointed to his enormous codpiece, 'is a better sword of state than the paltry thing my sister wields.'

'That'll go well at your trial.'

'There'll be no trial. Even that base, bastard, pissing, kitchen woman will pause from arraigning her own brother.'

Barbary wished she could be so sure. Of all treacheries,

the greatest in the view of the Queen was disrespect.

Sir John clutched his back and moaned. Barbary helped him to his cot and ran for his attendant and some medicine. He waved both away. 'Where's that potato-faced varlet? His is the only physic to aid me.' Cuckold Dick had employed their short wait in Dublin in acquiring ten barrels of whiskey which he was shipping to England to begin his new career as liquor importer, though Sir John's newly acquired taste for it had already reduced the ten barrels to nine and a half.

'And he's welcome, Barb,' Dick said earnestly when she demanded more, 'but if he tears the Queen's body to the revenue men when we gets to England like he's doing on this ship, they'll impound us, whiskey and all.'

Barbary was worrying along the same lines. 'When we get to England you slip ashore without us, whiskey or not. If I'm for the Tower, I don't want you there with me. And somebody's got to get those guns.'

Elizabeth's new Master of Ordnance, the man responsible for the country's cannon manufacture, was the Earl of Essex. The young favourite had clamoured for the post for months and finally got it, to O'Neill's relief. 'I feared she would give it to Robert Cecil, Burghley's son,' he'd told Barbary, 'for he is an efficient man. Essex is more to my liking, capable of great industry, but never for long. We'll whisk more guns from under his nose than Cecil's.'

And Will had told Dick that the cannon master who had replaced him at Penshurst's foundry was bribable. 'If we can't grease him, Barb, we can do a crossbite,' Dick said.

But would they get the chance? The very ship they were aboard indicated what bad odour she and Sir John were in with the powers-that-be. It was a studied insult to Sir John; old, leaky and much too small to accommodate the large retinue which was his due. Now he was laid low in its none-too-clean cabin, his huge, swollen legs sticking out from the end of its cot, breathing oaths and whiskey fumes. 'God's wounds, no other prince in Christendom would deal with me so. But she'll not curb Old Harry's son, silly woman.'

Barbary bathed the great flat, red face. 'Go to sleep.'

He couldn't. Even dozing, anger spurted out in expletives. 'Pissing woman. Bastard Bingham. Sniveller Loftus.'

His light, protuberant Tudor eyes glared at Barbary. 'If I go down, they'll come with me.'

Barbary adjusted his pillow. She was remembering three small bundles hanging on the gallows at Galway. This at least she could do. 'My Lord,' she said, 'if you were to bring Bingham down, how would you do it?'

Used to the clean, bare outlines of the Connaught coast, Barbary found England's late and pretty spring almost oppressive. As if making up for the aloofness of winter, the landscape on the banks nestled close in a glut of foliage, constricting the sunlight into a million dapples, blooming with such energy that even the wattle fences round the sheep folds and small fields were in bud. There was too much of it. The distortion, she knew, came from her state of mind, but she felt suffocated. The Thames was busy all the way up, and near London it was crowded with traffic. She was amazed at the growth that had taken place in her absence; areas along the river which had once been dotted here and there with villages were now an almost continuous waterfront down to Stepney.

They were landed at Wapping; immediately the gangplank was in place a contingent of breast-plated men-at-arms marched aboard, politely but firmly funnelling the passengers onto the quayside. There was no opportunity for Cuckold Dick to slip away; with everybody else he found himself ushered towards a closed, gilded coach waiting with some baggage carts. The door opened and Sir John and Barbary were helped into it, Dick still standing outside.

For a moment Barbary, adjusting from the glare of sunlight, thought the coach was empty; the one man in it was dressed in black, like its hangings, and sat in its most shadowed corner blending quietly with his surroundings. It wasn't until the coach had stopped rocking from Sir John's collapse onto the bench, that a light voice revealed the chameleon. 'My lord,' it said, 'and Lady Betty, this is an ignominious welcome home, but it was thought in the circumstances that discretion . . .'

Sir John Perrot peered blearily into the corner, then sighed. 'Ah lad,' he said, 'is even your father afraid to greet this old pariah?'

'The Lord Treasurer is ill, my lord,' said the pleasant,

insubstantial voice, 'or he would have been here, expressing his friendship and support.'

So the man Sir John addressed as 'lad' was the Queen's new Secretary, for Walsingham was dead. He was Robert Cecil, Burghley's son, and now holder of England's third great seal. O'Neill, when he was bringing her up to date on court matters, had described him as 'the coming power in the land'. Coming or going, he didn't look a power. He looked a puppet, not necessarily one to be manipulated, but unreal, a doll. First glance showed a bright, interested, wide-eyed little face, second glance showed the same expression, its perkiness carved as permanently as gravity was chiselled into a stone crusader. Elizabeth had nicknamed him her 'Elf', which was clever as far as it went, but gave no reflection of the stillness behind the spritely exterior. The head moved, the mouth talked, the eyes blinked but the jaunty mask was fixed on something very deep indeed. It turned on Barbary. 'Dear madam, our Sovereign Lady sent your husband on an embassy to the Low Countries some weeks ago, and he is as yet unaware that you have . . . reappeared. He will be overjoyed to know you are alive, as are we all.'

Had they thought she was dead then? She supposed they had. The relief of knowing that she didn't have to encounter Rob right away lessened some of the dread that had been making her feel ill. She could face punishment, but she couldn't face having marital relations forced on her again. Belatedly it occurred to her that perhaps Rob couldn't face them either.

'Her Majesty has been graciously pleased to grant him the honorary position of Keeper of the Tilsend Light,' continued the Elf, 'which carries with it the manor of Tilsend in Kent. No doubt that is where you will wish to make your main residence. His house in the Strand is as yet unfinished. So while you are here, perhaps you would do my aunt, Lady Russell, the honour of lodging at her house.'

Nice touch that, as if she had the option. She inclined her head graciously, wondering if this mannikin realised the smartest place she'd ever lodged in the London area was Will Clampett's hut on Lambeth Marshes. And Rob had certainly gone up in the world. He now had a manor in Devon, another in Kent – that might be useful – and another in the Strand. Highly salubrious.

'And you, my lord,' said Mr Secretary Cecil to Sir John Perrot, 'would you do the Lord Treasurer the honour of lodging at Burghley House?'

Sir John swatted the invitation with an unsteady hand. 'I'm for my Welsh estates, lad. Keep out of the bitch's way.'

There was another blithe blink. 'Later perhaps, my lord. Until then, my father would be most happy . . .'

Dick was making faces through the coach window. 'My lord,' said Barbary, quickly, 'my man there has imported some barrels of a new, Irish drink he is hoping will find favour in England. Can he have permission? It's distilled from malt.'

'*Usquebaugh*?' said Cecil, perfectly. 'One has heard of it. One might be interested . . .' The crook of a small finger brought an official, a word sent him off, unloaded the barrels, and set all of them under way with Dick perched on top of his whiskey on the luggage carts behind them. And that, thought Barbary, impressed, is power. O'Neill was right.

Within its walls, too, London was changing. The Tower was its old looming self, but nearly everywhere else gaps that had been fields were being filled by tenements and warehouses. Despite runners clearing its way, their coach was obstructed time and again by crowds, drays and flocks.

Barbary's nose went further and further out of the coach window, twitching at the ancient, remembered smells, while, despite herself, the city ground her senses down to the narrow sharpness that had kept her alive in its streets. Rip me, twice as many chairmen as there used to be. Twice as many sweeps – probably twice as many chimneys – and still mistreating their boys from the look of the poor little sods. That was never Pinky Annie still selling garters at Paul's? It was. 'Strong scarlet garters, tuppence a pair.' Older than God she must be. And Harry Oaksey at the Lud with his 'Chickweed for your singing birds'.

London was like nowhere else in the world. It buzzed with joy in itself. The old statute that citizens' wives should wear flat, white, knitted caps unless their husbands could prove themselves gentlemen was still being flouted. Ungentle wives strode the streets in hats of all shapes and material with an air suggesting that if the law tried to stop them the law would regret it. Why did Elizabeth deny to her Irish this splendid English freedom?

Another generation of maidservants gossiped with the water-carriers at each conduit. Same old washerwomen, round-shouldered and lopsided, staggered along with their tubs. Same old prickle-basketmakers squatted by the Fleet, weaving their prickles for the wine merchants' bottles. Smells from the tallow-maker and cat-gut cleaner in Fenner Lane, sewage, cow-heel broth, horse manure, hot pudding. Old Santander staggering along under his basket: 'Old chairs to mend . . .' Wait for it. Sure enough, every urchin in Fleet Street shouting back: 'We don't want to mend any old chairs.'

She peered back to the cart with Dick on top if it. He looked right as he never had in Ireland, seedily in tune with his surroundings. They were nearing Temple Bar. There were the grotesquely carved brackets of the King's Head on the corner of Chancery Lane, and off to the north, behind the shop fronts and houses, lay the putrefying alleys of the Bermudas. She could smell it. Cuckold Dick waved to her, and directed his carter to turn into the Lane. Then he was gone, back to the Pudding-in-a-Cloth and home. And she'd have gone with him if she could.

Her best was in Ireland, her meanest was here, and since they'd dragged her back to it the meanest was what they'd get: Barbary Clampett, purse-cutter, verser, crossbiter extraordinary, a lady whose bib they were not going to wet. Let them do their worst, she'd wriggle out of it somehow.

She sat back in her seat, chin forward, to meet the brightly interested gaze of the chameleon. And what the chameleon saw was not the wan Irish lady from the boat, but a London streetfighter.

They passed out of the city into the Strand and more change. All lords worthy of their title were desperate for an address here. The Savoy was still in picturesque decline, and between the Savoy and Durham House there was a gap, but everywhere else great houses, many with scaffolding still in place, obscured the waterfront.

'Where's Rob's house?'

'Much further down. The old Rounceval site.'

They were held up by congestion outside Leicester House where, most unusually, the great gates were open to welcome the world and his wife, who had accepted the invitation. Inside, a band played to petitioners awaiting audience in a queue that went round the courtyard. Under an oak in the centre, beggars were feeding at a long table bent from the weight of dishes upon it. Sight-seers wandered everywhere, picking keepsake-leaves off the bushes, gawping up at the windows in the hope of seeing the provider of this largesse. 'What's going on at Leicester House?'

'It's Essex House now,' said the Elf.

Of course. Leicester was dead and his mantle had fallen to his stepson, the Earl of Essex, the new royal favourite, the man of whom O'Neill had spoken slightingly. Well, O'Neill might not think much of him, but he was winning London's heart, that was for sure.

Leicester dead. Sir Christopher Hatton dead. Philip Sidney dead. Walsingham dead. Raleigh disgraced. Burghley ill. A new generation had moved onto the chessboard where the Queen was the only unvarying piece. For the first time it struck Barbary that even this constant was mortal. Despite everything she'd come to hate in Elizabeth's reign, she felt disorientated by the thought, and frightened; Elizabeth had been there for her lifetime and almost everybody else's. How would the world spin without her?

'How is the Queen?' she asked.

Mr Secretary Cecil's gaze was fixed on the north and less fashionable side of the Strand. 'It seems, mistress, you are to have the opportunity to see for yourself.' Barbary hitched herself along the seat to look where he was looking. Another crowd was up ahead at Burghley House which had its gates decently closed, but standing outside them, attracting the attention, were four tabarded trumpeters, the royal arms on a square of gold cloth attached to their trumpets. The Queen of England was paying a visit to the sickbed of her Lord Treasurer.

Barbary glanced at Sir John Perrot, who had fallen asleep and was snoring. Oh Jesus, if he saw her and began a harangue . . . 'I think, my lord . . .'

432

'I think so too. Excuse me.' He leaned over to open the flap to the coachmen. 'Cecil House.' He gave the order mildly, but they were thrown to one side as the coach swerved instantly to the right under an archway. Gates opened at once and they were into a courtyard fronting a small palace of a house, steps, ornate doorway, and oriel windows set in gleaming grey new stone. Cecil House: another addition since she'd been away. A fountain played in a newly planted flower bed. On the left, over the garden wall, loomed the roof and chimneys of Burghley House's eastern wing. She didn't have time to look around, the Elf's fingers were fluttering orders, servants were helping Sir John Perrot out of the coach. Cecil dismounted and handed Barbary out, and managed to get to the top of the steps before his guests in order to bow them indoors. The manoeuvre was deft but not without difficulty, for he was crippled. His furred cloak couldn't disguise the crookedness of his shoulders, nor the way his feet splayed out as he walked. He was very small, which made him look more gnomish than ever. Barbary didn't like to think what emotion the child he had been had suppressed to perfect that unwavering cheerfulness, or what bullying and jeers had made it necessary.

In pain again, Sir John was persuaded into the bed of a temporary apartment, but Barbary was taken to another room and left there. It was a beautiful room, the room of an educated and busy mind, and Barbary, wishing to know that mind, had no qualms about investigating it.

Everything in it, except a portrait of Elizabeth, was functional. The books that lined the walls were of every language known to Barbary, including Irish, and many that weren't. Sea charts were in one drawer she opened, diagrams of the human skeleton in another. Astrolabes, globes, measuring compasses, a framed map of the heavens.

A servant came in bearing a tray of wine, meat patties and fruit for her, and through the door he opened she could see an anteroom full of clerks writing with the energy of digging badgers.

When the man had gone she munched a pattie and crossed to the more interesting door on the other side of the room. It was very small, Cecil-sized, and very strong. It was locked – she tried it – and somebody was knocking on it. A code knock. Rap-rap. Tat-tat-ta. Rap-rap. She said: 'Who's there?' but there was silence.

She went to the casement, opened it, and leaned out. The room was at the end of the house and the little door led to a staircase which came out into a covered walkway. It ran the length of the garden to its end wall beyond which – she orientated herself – must be Covent Garden. She thought she heard a crunch of gravel as whoever it was made his or her disappointed exit.

Well, well. It would be nice to think that Cecil entertained exotic women in this room; nice, because the little man scared her and she'd have liked him to have a human weakness. But it was unlikely; the room wasn't furnished for dalliance. And the complicated knock had taken her back to the night all those years ago when she'd followed the barnacle that had followed Rob. That covered walk, the staircase, the door, were for Mr Secretary's secret informants.

When Cecil returned she was surprised all over again by how small he was. He'd already gained greater stature in her mind. He climbed up onto a chair behind his desk and beamed at her. 'We do not have as much time as one would like. My people will send word when Her Majesty is ready to leave my father so that we may waylay her.'

'My lord,' said Barbary earnestly, 'it's really not a good idea to bring me in front of the Queen.'

'There's no denying,' said the Elf, still beaming, 'that Her Majesty holds grievances against your good self and Sir John Perrot, though the grievances are more personal than is warranted by both your political services. And it is hoped that she can be disabused of them in each case.'

'Eh? What political services?'

'Perhaps it should be said,' the Elf said brightly, 'that one is cognisant of the reasons why the Lord Treasurer sent you to Ireland in the first place. It is true he was unaware at the time of your . . . ah, sex. Nevertheless, the results you have achieved are as good as any man's and worthy of your country's gratitude.'

Barbary was cautious. 'Oh?'

'Indeed.' He shuffled through some papers. 'There is here a gratifying letter from your kinswoman Mistress Grace O'Malley offering to surrender herself and make full and honest submission to the Crown. There is another from the Earl of Tyrone acquainting us of his intention to bring in Lord O'Donnell for the same purpose, in which he mentions that he was persuaded by your advice on the matter. You have done well.'

Barbary sat back in her chair, thinking. Grace, fortuitously, and the O'Neill, deliberately, had managed to put her in a good light with this powerful little man and his father. She saw it from Burghley's and Cecil's point of view. They had cast her, like bread, upon the waters. She'd disappeared into them – she was pretty sure they had no idea of what had gone on in Connaught – and after many, many days the bread had been returned, very nicely.

The Elf interrupted, suddenly sharp: 'Was there treasure?'

She shook her head. 'It's called The Treasure. But it's a book. A history of Connaught women.'

He surprised her by believing her, though wistfully. 'Nevertheless you must have gained a rare and unusual and *valuable* view of Irish affairs which would be of use in our administration of that unfortunate country. Indeed, with your own, special . . . ah, sources over here, it is to be hoped that you will continue to serve the State.'

'What sources are those?'

'It's known as the Order, is it not? The presumption that you kept up the, ah, connection was enforced by the fact that you still have in your employment the man, Dick Robertson.'

So Cuckold Dick's surname was Robertson. Mr Secretary Cecil knew something she never had. He knew a lot. She took another pattie to give herself time. He was going to use her, just as his father had used her. Which meant she could use him. But this was no ordinary cony. You caught conies as quick as this one by telling the truth, or at least, part of the truth.

He clambered down from his chair to pour her wine, and while he was doing it, she said: 'But as far as the Queen goes, I'm still in the shit.'

She watched his reaction. This little power-in-the-land would trust her more if she didn't put on airs and graces and pretend to be a lady. The father had sent off a Cockney sparrow to Ireland, the son would be reassured if it was the same Cockney sparrow that had come back. Cecil's pouring hand wavered for a moment, but didn't spill a drop.

'There are certainly problems,' he said, 'but one has made representation to Her Majesty of your work on her behalf. And if there is to be a reconciliation it must be now, before your husband comes back from the Low Countries, since she will require the monopoly on his attention.'

Barbary mentally translated. Rob was a favourite. The Queen didn't like favourites to have wives. If they did have a wife, she must be invisible. If the Queen was to forgive her, it must be before she was forced to become invisible. But why was Cecil so anxious to endear her to the Queen?

He returned to his desk and interrogated her on Ireland. The mask remained inexorably perky as he asked his questions and scratched notes of her answers on a wax tablet in hieroglyphics she presumed were his own shorthand. At once she realised at least one reason why she was of value; she had what virtually no other living soul could give him, a two-sided view of the Irish situation. He hoped she was English enough to be loyal, yet Irish enough to tell him what was actually going on. He didn't trust her, she doubted if he trusted anybody, but he could weigh her evidence with the rest of his enormous knowledge – and how much he knew about Ireland surprised her – to come to a balanced appraisal.

Knowledge is power, she thought.

She told him the truth, not all of it, but truth nevertheless. About Munster she said: 'If the undertakers don't stop treating the Irish like they do, there'll be trouble. There's hatred there.'

He knew that already. Tut tut. After a few questions, he passed on to what interested him more, Connaught. What was the extent of O'Malley power? What sort of woman was her grandmother? Was her proposed submission genuine?

Again, Barbary was honest. 'Grace O'Malley is no traitor. She's an old woman out for herself and her people, she's had to be.' She found it difficult to communicate and encapsulate Grace's non-patriotic, localised, self-interested, law-disregarding form of private enterprise, so

436

she said: 'As a matter of fact, the person she reminds me of is the Queen.'

For a moment the carved smile on the face of the Elf went into something genuinely astonished and amused. Then he nodded and scratched another note. 'Perhaps it would be as well not to draw the parallel when you meet Her Majesty. Now then, Mistress O'Malley's fleet. How large would you say it was?'

She gave an estimate considerably less than the true size and added: 'Smaller than it was before bloody Bingham attacked her.'

Ah, Bingham. She'd really got his interest now. 'There'll be no peace while Bingham rules Connaught,' she said, and told him about the hanging of the three boys at Galway. 'And the youngest was still protesting that he could read as he was hanged,' she finished, wiping unfeigned tears from her eyes.

The Elf made another note.

She added: 'And he holds the castles of Roscommon, Athlone and Carrick, all without warrant.'

'That's the way,' Sir John Perrot had told her. 'Hint at corruption. Connaught should be worth four thousand pounds a year to the Crown, and yields only one thousand. If the cheeseparing bitch thinks he's withholding her dues she'll have her teeth in his neck faster than a ferret.'

Every instance of Bingham's butchery and self-seeking she'd ever heard about was scored into the wax. Through the big door to the anteroom she could hear the scratching of quills, and from the open window behind the Elf came the equally insistent splashing of fountains.

Cecil put down his stylus and bounced his fists up and down on the desktop, like a polite little boy showing enthusiasm for a present he was about to receive. 'And the Earl of Tyrone?'

She'd known this was coming. 'He wants to be a good Englishman and he wants to be a good Irishman, and neither side'll let him be either.' Cecil might as well know the situation; he was one of the few men in the world who had some influence on it. Besides, if he was intelligent, he knew it already.

'Do you find yourself in that position, mistress?'

Crafty, he was a crafty little cove. She had to be

437

credible, and if she swore unthinking loyalty to the Crown he'd know she wasn't. 'Just seems to me there's something wrong when a man like Sir John Perrot's recalled and a Bingham left at large,' she said. 'If peace is the object.'

'Peace *is* the object,' he said. Was there a moment of commitment there, reassurance? Perhaps, but she'd never really know. She'd noticed that during the interrogation he'd rarely, if ever, said 'I'. Always the passive, 'one might think . . . it could be said that . . .' What Mr Secretary Cecil felt and thought was locked away inside a box in a guarded interior. The tidiness of his questioning, like the tidiness of the room, showed abhorrence of chaos. His peace wasn't her peace. He wanted peace for Ireland because the alternative was too expensive, because cruelty exacerbated a dangerous situation. But it still made him a better ally than those to whom slaughter was the only solution.

He was opening a drawer in his desk. 'Are you familiar with Sir John Perrot's writing, mistress?' She was. She'd received notes from him while she was staying with the Spensers and his signature had been on proclamations all over Dublin. 'Then be so good as to look at this.'

He passed over a page from a letter. She had only to glance at it. 'It's a forgery.'

'How do you know? It resembles his hand.'

'I wasn't taught to read and write by the best jackman in England for nothing.'

'Jackman?'

'Counterfeiter.'

He nodded as if she said she'd been taught needlework by her mother. 'You should know,' he said, 'that Archbishop Loftus came to England last week expressly to give this letter to Her Majesty. It purports to be written by Sir John offering assistance to the King of Spain.'

'Then it's definitely a forgery.'

'Nevertheless, it is to be feared that it will be used against him at his trial.'

'There'll be a trial?'

'Her Majesty is intent on it.'

'And you don't want that?' Commit yourself, you little bugger.

The Elf's happy little face remained happy. 'It may be

438

that Sir John's Irish policy, despite his, ah, indiscretions, has been less damaging than most. And it would be useful to his friends to know exactly where this letter originated. Perhaps with your connections . . .'

'You want me to find out who forged it?'

'Can you?'

'I'll try.'

A servant knocked and came in through the door to the scriveners' room. 'Her Majesty is taking leave of the Lord Treasurer, my lord.' He went out.

The Elf produced a ring of keys and climbed down from behind his desk. He went to the secret door and unlocked it. 'I'll lead the way. Quickly, mistress, if you please.'

She followed him, reluctantly. 'Mr Secretary, it's *really* not a good idea . . .' But at the bottom of the stairs he actually took her hand and limped her along the covered walk and through a gate halfway down into the confines of Burghley House, all lawns, fountains and courtyards, then into the house itself. The gallery was full of heralds, ladies-in-waiting, attendants. Cecil hirpled through the crowd, gesturing Barbary after him, until they were in another, quieter wing, panting outside double doors.

The doors opened. Cecil knelt. Barbary went into a deep curtsey and stayed in it. 'Ah, little man,' said a voice, 'I have been administering calves'-foot jelly to your father. I have told him to be well. Even my Elf cannot replace my Spirit.' She wanted to be the magician everybody told her she was, to put health back into the only man she'd ever been right to rely on with a command and a bowl of calves'-foot jelly.

Cecil was weeping and bobbing, calling her *'Victrix orientis'*, this year's favoured address. Barbary, her eyes close to the Queen's long, narrow shoe, saw that the skin under the silk stocking was wrinkled like dry, ribbed sand. She dreaded the moment of recognition, if it came. In the years since they'd met, Elizabeth had come to be the focus of so much evil done in her name that in Barbary's mind she had diminished into a cypher, sitting on her faraway throne like a virulent toad on a stone. But here, now, in her presence, the woman had more than absolute political power; her personality was so over-riding that gaining its approval was all that mattered.

Perhaps she'd forgotten. God, let her have forgotten.

She forgot nothing. 'May I present Lady Betty . . .' began Cecil.

'We've put on petticoats now, have we, Mistress *Boggart*?' The word was practically gobbed onto the floor. 'Abandoned our lewd male attire? You dare to re-enter the presence you fouled with your dishonour? Take this . . . this thing away, Cecil. You have earned our displeasure for bringing it.'

The long shoe kicked Barbary's skirt aside as it moved off, scraping her knee. Something happened to Barbary with that kick. Physically, the sting was nothing; mentally, it reacted into an indignation so overwhelming that she was helpless in its grip, not for Ireland, but for the child Barbary, and all children who scrabbled just to keep their noses above the sludge that underlay Elizabeth's golden reign. The spasm of anger was so strong that Barbary shook from the terror of being unable to stop signing her own death warrant.

She stood up. 'Do you know what it's like?' she said clearly to the retreating back. 'Have you any idea what goes on in the back alleys of your precious city? Men like wild beasts on women? On little girls? Honour? I tell you, madam, if I hadn't dressed like a boy I wouldn't have *had* any honour. I survived as best I knew how.'

Cecil had closed his eyes in apparently happy prayer.

The Queen turned round. She had a silver bowl and spoon in her hands. Barbary stood where she was. And she saw a woman who did know what it was like. Linenfold oak corridors had been the young Elizabeth's back streets and she'd been hunted through them as viciously for the power she could give as any little girl lost in the Bermudas. Her eyes looked through Barbary to wild beasts who'd worn velvet and silk, then they focused.

'Ireland didn't improve your manners,' she said mildly.

Barbary dropped then and crawled forward to hug the skinny ankles in true obeisance. 'I'm sorry, I'm sorry, I'm sorry.' And at that moment she was.

Cecil was skipping about them. The mention of Ireland had given him his cue. Lady Betty had done sterling work in that country . . . carried out the instructions Burghley had given her to the letter . . . bringing in Grace O'Malley, pacifying the pirate . . .

reconciliation . . . loyalty to the Crown. 'Nor do I mistake me if I see her influence in the Earl of Tyrone's bringing in of the O'Donnell.'

The Queen was tapping Barbary's head with the spoon. 'There, there. Is it still a loyal little Boggart? Well, we shall see. These matters shall wait till you come to court.' She was gone, with her Elf hobbling along beside her.

Barbary crawled to the wainscot and sat with her back against it, exhausted and ashamed by the emotion that had shaken her. How could she love that woman? After all the hangings, all the horror that had been committed in her name? But she did, had. Just as she'd wanted her grandmother's love, in that moment she had wanted Elizabeth's.

And had apparently got it; she was to be received at court. She couldn't have manoeuvred it better if she'd tried.

After a while, Mr Secretary Cecil came back. He held out a small hand to help her to her feet. 'It appears, Mistress Barbary,' he said, 'that the, ah, shit is not as thick as we thought.'

Chapter Twenty-One

'Yes, Lady Russell,' shouted Barbary backwards from the street door into the house at Blackfriars. 'No, Lady Russell. I will. Not far, Lady Russell.'

Lady Elizabeth Russell, Cecil's aunt, was old and busy and had instructions from her nephew to allow Lady Betty to come and go without question, but every time Barbary went out she was put through a catechism: Was she warmly wrapped? Was she sufficiently attended with just one footman to guard her? Would she be safe? Where was she going?

Since the summer was warm, and since, so far, her forays had only been along the crowded quaysides of Blackfriars to Cuckold Dick's Thameside warehouse at Puddle Dock, these precautions seemed to Barbary to be unnecessary, but Lady Russell lived in the conviction that London was populated by footpads and assassins of which the weather was a climatic accomplice, ready to kill by jumping out in a shower of rain or a cold breeze. Andrew, the footman, pushed aside a couple of the more aggressive creditors who were in permanent attendance on Lady Russell's door and Barbary was at last walking along the lovely colonnade, the old monastery's cloister, which led out of the close. It wasn't that Lady Russell couldn't pay, though she pleaded poverty, but that she disliked paying any bill she thought too high, and since most bills she regarded as iniquitous, her relationship with her tradesmen was stormy.

At first Barbary had been surprised that the Elf, if he wanted her as a secret agent, should place her in the care of a woman who invariably attracted attention. But he said he needed her respectably established and Lady Russell, for all her raging eccentricity, was respectable and most certainly an enthusiastic upholder of the establishment. She attributed all the crosses she had to bear to the fact that her second husband, John, Lord Russell, had been careless enough to die while his father was still alive and before he could inherit the earldom of Bedford, thereby granting his wife her dearest wish, to be a countess. 'Had I been a countess, my dear, this would not have happened,' she would say to Barbary every time a tradesman presented an outrageous bill. Despite her advanced age, she was still determined to be one and had her eye on the Earl of Kent, 'for though he lacks four of his five wits, my dear, I have enough for both'.

Tiresome though she was, there was something endearing about Lady Russell; she was as eccentric and entertaining as the English public, eccentric themselves, expected their aristocracy to be, and by riveting attention on herself, Barbary's own somewhat erratic comings and goings were overlooked. It was, Barbary realised, just what Cecil had wanted: that she be established yet disregarded. She went to church with Lady Russell, enduring the long ranting sermons of the popular Puritan divine, Stephen Egerton. She accompanied Lady Russell to the more decorous court occasions which nowadays mostly consisted of long, Latin eulogies addressed to the Queen. Barbary was official yet unremarked – a most excellent situation for passing on information to Cecil as she did.

There was another, more ominous, reason why the Elf wanted her to be an accepted part of the court scene. 'Perhaps you should know, mistress,' he'd told her one day, 'that some months ago Sir Rob applied to the Archiepiscopal Court to prove your death.'

She had been shocked to the core. 'Why?'

Cecil shrugged. 'Doubtless he genuinely thought you were dead. Perhaps he wished to marry again. He is a young man.'

And then she had realised that in Cecil's tortuous mind was the suspicion that unless her existence was well known, Rob might attempt to get rid of her. 'Rob'd never Amy Robsart me,' she said, more stoutly than she felt. After all, it was odd that rising men who had made disadvantageous marriages in their youth were almost invariably free to make an advantageous one later on. Doubtless some of the first wives were paid off, or died naturally, but what happened to the others?

'Perish the thought,' said Cecil. But she knew he thought it and was protecting her, not from friendship, but because she was useful. It had caused her to put Cuckold Dick on to making certain enquiries. And today she would, among other matters, learn the result of those enquiries.

When she was out of the close, she turned to the footman who walked behind her. 'Take the day off, Andrew.'

He was reluctant. 'Lady Russell wouldn't like it.'

'I would. Cut off.' She watched him slouch away, every line of his back suspecting an assignation with a lover. Better that than the truth. There must be no connection between Lady Betty and the place Barbary intended to visit today. Halfway up Fleet Street she turned into Red Lion Court and in a well-remembered gap between an apothecary's shop and the inn, took off her silk cloak and hat, folded them into her basket and took other items from it.

The servant who eventually emerged from a narrow alley into Fetter Lane was well but not showily dressed in a plain buff gown over a red kirtle. A white coif under a grey felt hat concealed her hair, and there was a white tippet round her shoulders. That she came from a house of rank was displayed by her gloved hands and the scarf that hid her lower face – high-class servants took precautions against bad air as seriously as their masters and mistresses.

She walked through Long Acre to Covent Garden with its view across woods and fields to the windmills on High Gate Hill. Here she dawdled, frequently turning round. Confident that they could provide it, the traders called: 'What do ye lack, mistress, what do ye lack?' On offer was anything from fennel to a firescreen, from cabbage to cheeseparers. The servant appeared to lack a capon, for she bought one, then wandered on.

'What do ye lack, mistress? What do ye lack?' She paused, interested, at a stall selling strange implements. The stall-holder exhaled smoke and patter. 'Artillery for the new fashion, mistress. The ladle for assisting cold snuff to the nostrils, the tongs, the priming iron. Here's woodcock heads of the best, and tobacco boxes. See me, mistress, I have taken no other meat for twenty weeks

but the fume of best Trinidado. It assists the expulsion of
rheums, and sour humours, a specific against asthma,
scabs, breast afflictions and flatulence. I can teach you the
trick of it in two easy lessons at my smoking academy.'
She shook her head and walked away.

A catchpole was lounging at the corner of Ship Lane,
where the Ship Inn was still decked in black mourning
ribbons for its late owner, Sir Christopher Hatton. He
stopped her. 'Don't go down there, mistress. There's no
place for respectable young women in the Bermudas.'

The respectable young woman pushed past him, the
gently spoken words that emerged through the chin-
clout sounding remarkably like: 'Piss off.' Bemused, the
catchpole watched the prim figure disappear into the
overhung shade at the end of the lane. Here she paused
and pulled the chin-clout down for a moment to whistle
three notes. A figure that had been waiting in a doorway
to snatch her basket withdrew and allowed her to pass
unmolested.

In another familiar doorway she changed again, taking
off a further layer somewhat crossly. If there'd been a
barnacle, she'd thrown it off at Red Lion Court, but Mr
Secretary Cecil insisted on every precaution. 'Not all
enemies are overseas, mistress.'

Spy mad, she thought. They've all gone spy bloody
mad. It had always been recognised that ambassadors and
men like Walsingham, and now Cecil, should have a
network of agents, but in the England Barbary had come
back to, even the most insignificant courtier employed
spies. It was a growth industry. And not just to keep
themselves informed on international affairs, but on each
other. Jealous rivals tried to find or fabricate evidence
to prove the other was a Papist or in some other way
disloyal.

The Queen's increasing senility brought an added complication for courtiers looking to their future. Whom
should they support for the succession? King James of
Scotland? The Infanta of Spain? Lady Arabella Stuart?
The roads and ports of England were crowded with
agents, some carrying secret, tentative messages of good-
will to a prospective heir to the throne, others trying to
intercept them to find out who was backing whom.

In this labyrinth of mistrust Barbary, with her Order

445

training, was in her element. Her campaign to get Bingham recalled was doing very nicely. In front of the Queen one day, Cecil had given her the opportunity to re-tell the story of the three young hostages hanged at Galway. The Queen wept, then became angry: 'God's death, is this the way to win Irish hearts?' She'd become even angrier at Barbary's hints at corruption, though it wasn't Bingham's corruption that was the issue as far as Barbary was concerned – he was no more corrupt than any other of Elizabeth's generals – it was his systematic brutality. And because Cecil regarded brutality as counter-productive, he was her ally. In return, she had become his creature.

What alternative did she have?

There were two main parties vying for power at court. There was the one which was in favour of everything the Earl of Essex stood for, and there was the one which wasn't. The Earl of Essex himself led the pro-Essex party; the anti-Essex party was more diffused, but rummaging down into it, tossing aside the front men, what you came to was the unassuming, crooked little shape of Mr Secretary Cecil.

Essex. For a moment in that dingy doorway in the Bermudas, Barbary's fingers paused in their tussle with hooks and strings. Like everybody else, she'd caught her breath on seeing him first. It was at the Grocers' Hall. The Mayor of London was making a boring loyal address to the Queen, and Essex had rushed in late, apologising, and bearing a basket of sweet grapes he'd had brought post-haste from France so the Queen should taste them with the bloom on. Immediately Grocers' Hall became a forest glade, the Queen a maiden beset by goblins, and Essex the rescuing medieval knight, turning the whole thing into a celebratory picnic. He had that power. Even the Mayor was charmed.

Before she set eyes on him, and from the way everyone talked – and it seemed to Barbary they talked of little else – she imagined a handsome but sub-standard Philip Sidney. But Essex was both more and less than Philip. Beautiful, God, he was beautiful, blazing, tall, leonine head, cheekbones, jawline, lovely hands – and unaware of it. That was the thing, he didn't care. He paid no attention to his dress, he frequently had mud on his boots and cloak. And this glorious, elemental *thing* stroked and petted Elizabeth's mummified old body as if it was a young Cleopatra's and he an Antony.

He dragged admiration after him, men's even more than women's, like a comet. And if he'd been content to be what he was, an event, Barbary would have felt the same spell that had put the Queen under her midsummer enchantment. But he wanted power, over Elizabeth, over England. His foreign policy was as lacking in frills as his dress. The Irish, bog-trotting savages, must be subdued by the sword once and for all. The Spanish, Papist heretics, must be subdued by the sword once and for all. She had looked from the irrational splendour of the Earl of Essex to the paltry body of Cecil and decided she was in the right camp. She knew Mr Secretary Cecil no better now than the day she'd met him, despite frequent encounters since. She didn't know if he liked her, didn't like her, whether he preferred dogs to cats. But it didn't matter. He was for peace with Ireland. And in a comparison of brain size, Essex's was a pea and Cecil's a prize vegetable marrow.

However, at Elizabeth's court, brains didn't always win out against beauty. Cecil could fail; he was failing in the matter of Sir John Perrot who was being sent for trial, despite all that his friends could do.

So here she was, Cecil's last resort, now dressed in a red kirtle with the tippet tied like a skimpy shawl over an equally skimpy bodice, a feather stuck in her hair. A pawn on the Cecils' bloody chessboard, that's all you are, Barbary Clampett O'Flaherty.

She bundled the servant's outfit into her basket and stepped out from her doorway. She gave another whistle and set off for the Pudding-in-a-Cloth. 'Rip me, what's happened to the Bermudas?' How had it gone so far downhill? It was darker, filthier, smaller than she remembered. Rot nibbled at its shutters and doors, sewage ran sluggishly along the gutters in which ragged children floated boats made from twigs. Women with black eyes and sores at their mouths sat listlessly in their doorways, suckling thin babies from thin breasts.

Jesus, it had always been like this. She had expected to be washed by sentiment when she came back here, but it was only the child she had been who'd invested it with energy and romance. From the vantage point which had given her so different a view, she looked down to the red-headed, ignorant little ghost galloping through these terrible lanes, and felt compassion.

A new sign swung on a bracket above wide, decaying, once-beautiful doors declaring that the old inn was now the 'House of Pity', but otherwise the Pudding-in-a-Cloth hadn't changed.

The glamour of the Pudding belonged to the night-time; daylight exposed the bones of its business. A pot boy was polishing the carefully placed mirrors which would later reflect the gulls' cards. A pedlar – it was Wilkin – was checking his dice. Damber the Filch was polishing a nice-looking ring on his sleeve and examining it with the air of one who hadn't had it long. The bawds, of course, would still be in bed preserving their strength for the night to come. The place smelled of candle grease, cheap scent, old ale, basting chickens and new sawdust. And on the dais at the far end an enormous figure was stacking coins into piles and clicking the beads of an abacus.

At Barbary's entrance, Wilkin, the dice, the ring and Damber disappeared like magic. The figure on the dais raised its head and told a pot boy: 'Throw that bawdy basket out. She's not one of ourn.'

Barbary side-stepped. 'Oh yes I am. Hello, Bet.'

'Gawd's buttocks, it's Barb.' Galloping Betty heaved herself to her feet and stepped massively down from the dais, obviously such a rare event that the pot boys stood staring. Barbary found herself enwrapped in Galloping Betty's flesh, a substance that had not diminished over the years, though her laboured breathing heaved it about more alarmingly. 'I should've known that poison pate anywheres. It's Barb, lads. Barbary as was a dell all those years when we thought she was a kinchin co.' She raised Barbary up and shook her, 'You naughty pigsney, whyn't you tell old Betty?'

'Never fancied the Upright Man,' Barbary said through rattling teeth.

'None of us do, dear. And he's still at it, the old dog-bolt, though there's not the powder in his pistol that there was, thank Gawd.'

Barbary was put back on her feet to be hugged and

slapped on the back by Wilkin and Damber who'd re-appeared from the woodwork. 'Don't she speak holiday?' 'High in the instep now, in't she?' With exquisite regard for Order etiquette nobody asked her what she'd been doing in the intervening years; Cuckold Dick would have informed them as much as he considered necessary.

Barbary gave the capon she'd bought in Covent Garden to Galloping Betty who said: 'No need, pigsney,' but took it anyway, and to mark the occasion ordered up her best malmsey. The four of them sat round a table to drink it, Barbary being pointed out to the pot boys as an example to them all: 'Best crossbiter's aid in England, she was.' Damber held up her hand. 'See that? That little white famble could nimble the reds out of a miser's purse.'

That she was still alive and healthy was a success in itself. So many colleagues were not. 'Foll? She's a doner, dearie.' Galloping Betty wiped a tear from her eye. 'Of the pox. Not all suitors of my Venuses will wear a Mother Phillips.' Mother Phillips lived, appropriately, in Cock Lane and supplied the Pudding with condoms made of sheep gut. And Doll was a doner. Rafe the Rifler also, having had the misfortune to murder a nightwatchman and be nabbed for it. And Limping Billy had fallen off a roof while farcing a ken. They called the role of the dead with a gloomy satisfaction and drank to each honoured name. There had been losses, but others had filled the gaps. The Armada had come and gone, houses risen and fallen, but London of the Order was still Rome-ville and very much the same.

Eventually, Galloping Betty poured more wine for herself and Barbary only, indicating that Wilkin and Damber could take themselves off.

'Seen my boy, Barb?' she asked idly.

Barbary hadn't been looking forward to this. 'You know we was married, Bet?'

Betty nodded so that some of her white-rooted gold curls tossed into her tankard. 'Irish Harry brought the news.' Her international network was better than any courtier's. 'That was a night, Barb. When we heard. We whipped the cat that night, all right. Wilkin got so drunk he opened his shirt collar to piss.'

'In the middle of the ceremony, Bet, he said: "If only

my dear mother was here to celebrate with us." That's what he said.'

Galloping Betty nodded, appreciating the lie. On the wall behind her was a tattered fly-sheet mentioning Rob as one of the heroes of the Armada.

'Only a-course,' continued Barbary, 'being so warm with the Queen, he's been busy ever since.'

Galloping Betty wept at Rob's neglect of her, but not too much. She had reached the age where pleasure and loss, kindness and unkindness had a similar tenor. She grabbed Barbary's hand and her eyes, sunk deep in puffy flesh, scoured Barbary's. 'You want anything, Barb. Strike, stalls, skew, anything, you come to old Bet. I never forgot that day my boy was seek-we'd. You was a hero. Stood there in your little jallyslops and said: "I'll save him for you, Bet." And save him you did. Old Bet ain't forgotten. You come to old Bet.' It was a powerful offer from a powerful woman. 'Now then, Dick'll be down the dancers in a minute. Keeps his bed these days, said he did enough dew-treading in Ireland.'

'Has he found the Jackman for me?' Having promised Cecil she would find out the forger of the treacherous letter Sir John Perrot was purported to have written, it had been concerning to find the Jackman gone from his usual haunts.

Betty showed her gums. 'Hylles found him. He was sleeping in the pure out Hampstead way. So drunk he couldn't see a hole in a ladder. He was flapping away pink snakes when Hylles stumbled over him. He's not got long, Barb. Pitiful he is. But he should be sober now.' She raised her voice. 'Hugh, bring out the Jackman.'

A pot boy opened the door of one of the Pudding's many cupboards, fished about in it and dragged out a brown-habited skeleton which he propped up on a bench. The skeleton opened its eyes and called for wine.

'Had to put him there, Barb,' apologised Betty, 'for he was lowering the tone something wonderful, and no lodgings'll have him. But I'll keep the old flick vitty as long as he lasts.'

Barbary went over to sit by the old man who'd taught her to read. He smelled of urine and vomit and he wouldn't impose on the Pudding's hospitality much longer; his skin, even his eyeballs, were as yellow as his hostess's hair. Gently, Barbary tried to make him remember who she was, but he stared at her, mewed, and tried flapping her away as if she were cobwebs. 'There'll be no sense from him till he's had his milk,' called Betty. 'Hugh.'

A blackjack of wine was set on the table, the Jackman grabbed it and managed to spill most of it into his mouth before his weakened hands let it fall onto the table. He sneered. '*Pax vobiscum.*'

'Do you know who I am?'

His head swayed with drunken dignity. 'Knowledge is power,' he said in Latin.

'Look at these.' She put two pages in front of him. One was a genuine letter, mundane business that Sir John Perrot had penned to Mr Secretary Cecil. 'This is from a friend of mine.' She let him examine it and then held up the forgery. 'And this is another supposed to be from him.'

The Jackman barely glanced at it. 'It's a forgery.'

'I know it is. But who forged it?' She steadied the Jackman's shaking hands as he held it to his eyes.

He belched. 'Char . . . Charles Trevor. Wouldn't gull a jackass. Lives in Cheapside. Disgrace to a noble profession.'

She stroked his sticky hair and said goodbye, then Hugh picked the old man up and carried him upstairs. Galloping Betty had gone back to counting her money on the dais. Charles Trevor, eh? A freelance, not one of the Order. She hoped for his sake that he responded to Mr Secretary's questioning promptly or he'd find himself giving his answers on the rack.

'Glad to be back, Barb?' Cuckold Dick flopped down beside her.

'Yes.' And she was. 'How's the whiskey business?'

Dick sighed. 'He done me, Barb. Mr Secretary done me.' It had surprised them both when Cecil, in return for his help in easing the liquor through customs, had appointed himself the enterprise's senior, though secret, partner and put in his own man, a former purveyor by the name of Rattray, to oversee sales and distribution. It had surprised Barbary less when she realised that Cecil received only £800 a year for the maintenance of his intelligence service when, in fact, it cost nearer £3,000.

Like his father, he lacked inherited wealth, and had to subsidise his salary, and his spies, by other means.

Dick still retained control over the shipping side, which was the important bit as far as Barbary was concerned, but the fact that he was not sole recipient of the profits had caused him to relapse into semi-inertia, which Barbary suspected he would have relapsed into anyway. Like most of the Order, Dick was better at dreaming success than achieving it.

'I could a been a rich man,' he said with the gloomy satisfaction of one who no longer has the responsibility of exertion, 'but he done me.'

'You wouldn't have liked it,' Barbary told him impatiently. 'Think of all those fathers trying to foist their daughters on you. Did O'Neill send the ruddock?' They couldn't move on their own account until they had some gold. As it was, she was living and dressing on a small allowance from Cecil.

Cuckold Dick brightened and put a finger to the side of his nose. 'The way we're doing it, Barb,' he said softly, 'is there's a small barrel among the rest on the ship marked for me personal. I got it agreed with Mr Secretary as I could supply the Pudding direct. It comes straight ashore and into Dirty Kate's handcart, and she pushes it round here.'

Dirty Kate was a pie-seller whose dropsy, facial carbuncles and personal habits affected her trade to the point of never selling a single pie. The Order used her to carry goods it preferred officialdom not to see.

'How much?'

Dick splayed two hands, with three fingers turned under. 'All gold coin of the realm, Barb.' Dick's whisper was awestruck. 'I was frit the dockers unloading would notice the weight.'

Seven hundred pounds. She'd expected the O'Neill to be generous, but the hugeness of the amount, and O'Neill's willingness to pay it, jerked her into a horrified realisation of what she was doing and, more importantly, what she was asking Cuckold Dick to do. She saw herself and Dick, travellers in a long and tortuous full circle which had brought them back to the inn they'd started out from; two conspirators. Only this time they plotted not a crossbite, but high treason.

The journey had changed her so much there was hardly a point of contact between the Barbary who'd left the Bermudas and the Barbary who'd returned. But Dick was untouched, exactly as he had been, vulnerable and innocent.

'I want you out of it, Dick,' she said briskly. 'Your bit's done. Some of that ruddock's yours. Take it and cut off.'

He was hurt. 'Why, Barb?'

'Dick, I'm a traitor.' Was that what she was? Could pity and indignation for all the inequality, all the babies hanging from their hanging mothers, be reduced to that simple, terrible word? She had been vouchsafed the imbalance of things and put in the way of fumblingly, perhaps hopelessly, trying to right it. But Dick had gone through no such process. 'And you ain't,' she said. 'They don't whip you at the cart's tail for smuggling guns to the Irish. They cut your tripes out.'

Dick stared thoughtfully into the middle distance. She got up and retrieved what was left of the malmsey. Tenderly, she poured him some. What would she do without him?

He sipped, thoughtfully. 'You see, Barb,' he said, as if he'd already made a statement, 'I'm in it. Separate from you, like. O'Neill, he said to me: Dick, he said, I'm like a gravedigger, up to my arse in business and don't know which way to turn. You're the expert, Dick, he said, and it's an expert I need. Barb's the contact, he said, but you're the beater. I need them guns bad, he said, and you're my Upright Man. You in or out, Dick? he said. And I said "In" and he said "Oatmeal" and we shook fambles on it. I don't call it treason, I call it business.'

Barbary was silenced. Even if it had not been conducted in those terms, the O'Neill and Cuckold Dick had come to their own understanding. Useless to tell Dick that the O'Neill was an astute and manipulative bastard; for the first time in his life somebody had ascribed to Dick the quality of upright manliness he so admired in others, and, tripes cut out or not, the injection of dignity it had given him was irreversible. And perhaps the O'Neill was not so wrong after all. She'd been the one patronising Dick when all along such strength as she had came from him. She had to do some reassessing.

'Suit yourself,' she said. There was an awkward pause while they both absorbed Dick's new independence. 'Where'd you stow the ruddock?'

He smiled with relief. 'Under Galloping Bet's bed.'

There was nowhere safer. 'Any news from the walking morts?'

'Nan Nevet come in yesterday to report. That gunmaker's a rogue right enough.' It was a word Order members never used about themselves and described a dishonest man in ordinary society. 'Friends round Panningridge has it that for every three ox-loads of cannon leaving the gunworks is one the Master of Ordnance never gets to be h'aware of.'

'Who's he selling to?'

Dick shrugged his dandruffed shoulders. 'Sea Beggars, maybe. The morts don't know yet. Word has it the ox-carts leave the foundry afore first light, but one cuts off from the train. There'll be some inlet along the coast where they load the guns aboard some rock-creeper. Could be he's trading with Low Countries Spanish. It don't matter much.'

Barbary agreed. If the cannon master at Will's old iron works was a rogue, it was going to take at least some of the sweat out of her mission. He could be blackmailed if necessary but he was more likely to respond to a straightforward bribe which, thanks to the O'Neill's provision, they could make unrefuseable. 'Tell Nan to set up a meet,' she said.

Cuckold Dick put a hand on her arm. 'Not you, Barb.'

'What do you mean, not me?' Dick's sudden uprightness was giving him ideas above his station. It had always been understood that she should handle negotiations for the cannons.

Dick stuck his thumb in the air. 'One. It don't do for ladies as are warm with the Queen of England to be oiling cannon masters.' His forefinger went alongside his thumb. 'Two. The walking morts say Bumboy should do it.'

Barbary stared at him. 'I don't believe it.' Bumboy was a slim, attractive and, according to his story, bastard scion of a noble house – he hinted at Leicester's – whose work in the Order was a highly specialised form of crossbiting. Research into the etymology of his nickname delivered everything it suggested. 'Cannon masters aren't like that.' Cannon masters were like Will.

'This one is,' said Cuckold Dick, 'so the morts say.'

Well, the walking morts would know. They were the peripatetic females of the Order who, rather than take up the life of a bawd – though they were prepared to niggle if the occasion called for it – tramped the highways and byways of England using the various skills of the Order to gain a dishonest living: glimmering, ring-falling, dummering, rifling, milling, figging, prigging, bung-nipping. Some were accompanied by their children, a few by a man, but their common denominator was their knowledge of the countryside; it was said of a walking mort that if she reached the age of fifty, there wasn't a bush in England she hadn't piddled behind. Above all, even more than the rest of the Order, they had contacts everywhere. And they knew human nature. If the walking morts said the cannon master of Panningridge was a homosexual, then that's what he was.

'Will Bumboy do it? Does he know the risk?'

'Barb.' Dick's tone was reproachful. 'Bumboy's life's a risk. I sounded him last night. He'll do it for a leopard.' Fifty pounds. Worth every penny. 'You tell him what you want. He'll be in later. And Barb, while they was about it, the morts kenned Rob's place at Tilsend. What the Queen gave him. It's ideal, Barb. On the coast. Got a stone jetty. Need a stone jetty, Barb. Them cannons' heavy.'

'I'll go down tomorrow if I can. We need to get off at least one consignment before Rob gets back.'

Cuckold Dick coughed, gently, behind his hand.

'What is it?'

He wriggled uncomfortably on his bench. 'Well, Barb, there's a complication.'

Barbary sighed. In Order cant 'complication' referred to a specific set of circumstances. 'I thought there might be.'

By the time she left the Pudding-in-a-Cloth that evening, she had made arrangements with several of the Pudding's clientele and renewed her acquaintance with many more. Whistling herself safely back out of the Bermudas, transforming herself as she went from bawdy-basket to servant to Lady Betty, she reflected sadly on what her absence had done to her and them. The Order had been pleased to see her, would help her for old times' sake – and money's – but it knew, as Barbary knew, that she didn't belong to it any more. What excluded her from it, oddly enough, was her esteem for it; not, as it once had been, a desire to emulate its higher members, but a profound yet distancing admiration for the indomitable, interlocking, elaborate structure they had made out of their own survival.

The Cistercians had positively rejoiced in making life hard for themselves. Not for them chummy township monasteries such as Blackfriars; chumminess and the corruption that went with it was what they were reacting against. Instead, the twelfth-century monks spreading out from their mother abbey of Citeaux in France searched for remote places to keep themselves to themselves.

And one of the sites they chose for the smallest of their foundations was a rise on the deserted, swampy, inhospitable flats of Kent's foreland where wading birds and the common gull, which is not common at all, were the only witnesses to their rule.

But as the monks prayed and worked, people would wash up on their beach and they had to keep stopping, either to pump sea-water out of some half-drowned mariner's lungs or, more frequently, perform a burial. These interruptions were so frequent that the monks set up a beacon to stop ships wrecking themselves on the shoals which lay off their shore.

As the centuries went by, the Tilsend Light became an important navigational aid to shipping making its way in and out of the Thames estuary, and keeping it lit became the abbey's *raison d'être*.

When Henry VIII abolished the monasteries, the Abbey of Tilsend and its Light went dark, and the Ship Swallowers, as the shoals were known, began claiming their dead once more. In response to protests, Edward and then Mary Tudor leased the abbey to anyone who promised to keep the Light burning, but as it consumed something like eighty tons of coal a year, the lessees either didn't bother, or demanded a toll to defray costs.

Elizabeth brought in Trinity House to decide the matter. Merchant shipping was for the Light; local people were against it, they gained considerable income by acting as pilots. 'We have our own sea-marks more trustworthy than any light,' they said. The clinching argument against the Light, however, was national security. If merchant shipping was able to find its way easily into the Thames, so could piratical Sea Beggars and the Spanish.

The Tilsend Light stayed out but, with good English logic, the title of its Keeper remained and was bestowed from time to time on whomsoever Elizabeth wished to favour with a manor.

Which was Rob. Which was why, one heavy evening in June, bitten by midges, muddied from leading their horses through marsh, a party consisting of Barbary, Cuckold Dick, Nan Nevet, Walles the water pad, and one of Galloping Betty's frighteners, Winchard, cursed and scratched their way across their hundredth sand dune on the Kentish foreland.

'Thought you knew the fokking way,' Cuckold Dick said to Nan Nevet.

'This *is* the fokking way,' said Nan. 'It's remote is Tilsend.'

'Why didn't we come by bloody boat?' asked Barbary.

Walles, not for the first time, answered: 'We'd a needed a pilot, Barb. Dangerous waters, these are.'

'We need a bloody miracle,' snapped Barbary. She turned on Cuckold Dick. 'And you said the place was ideal. Ideal for what?'

Nan took up the cudgels. 'It *is* ideal, Barb. There's a causeway leads to it, but we come this way so's not to be seen.'

'Durr,' said Winchard, indicating he was about to make a statement. They waited for it more in hope than expectation. 'Don't like the flies,' he said. Unlike his size, Winchard's contribution to intellectual thought was small.

They tramped on, pulling at their horses' reins as marsh sucked at hooves and boots alike. Nan's bare feet wearing socks of mud moved as easily as if they were cloven. She came of a long ancestry of women who had been 'born on the tramp' as the Order called it, and used her race memory on her town-bred colleagues to recount things only her great-grandmother could have known.

'The monks was best,' she said, 'always a dry bed and a wet bottle when the monks was here. Good, them Cistercians.'

'You all right, Barb?' asked Cuckold Dick.

'Yes.' For a moment the heavy air had let in a breeze from a different sea. Cistercian. A monk hanging upside down, a dear, ridiculous scene. Peat smoke, lobster pots, the amber air of a Connaught evening. It kept happening to her. Some casually spoken word and she would wince with the cramp of exile. She'd heard his name the other day. Essex had spoken it in a list of proscribed traitors to show Elizabeth how much he knew about Ireland. 'O'Hagan,' he'd said.

'There she is,' said Nan.

To their left, marsh ran imperceptibly into the grey, flat estuary which in turn ran to a horizon pierced here and there by shafts of setting sun coming through cloud. Ahead was the only rise in the landscape, the first indication of the chalk to come, and on its top was the one-time abbey.

Erosion had taken away its seaward wall so that its frontage was now perilously close to the white drop, but what had once been the monks' refectory and dorter stood in placid grace against the darkening sky. Behind it were other buildings and ruins covered with ivy. Further away, on the highest point, was a stone column topped by a large, square grate. 'The Light,' said Nan.

'Where's the bloody jetty?' asked Barbary. She was tired and nervous.

'Other side,' Nan told her. 'There's a inlet there. They call 'em "Gates" round here. Good, deep water.'

'How do we get in?' On the landward side were substantial walls.

'Usual way. There's a shepherd'll have left the gates open while he rounds up his sheep for the night. And taken his dogs with him, thank Gawd.' All Order members had good reason to dislike dogs.

'Mount up then.' With Nan riding pillion, Barbary's horse scrambled up the rise to the causeway leading to the gates. She had intended to rush them, but there was no challenge so she paused. The marsh had gone quiet with the onset of evening, only the eternal midges danced in the last rays of light. Now she was closer, she saw that the manor was mouldering. A crack through the Latin-inscribed lintel above the gates looked dangerous, the house roof lacked several tiles, a gutter and pipe had come away from a wall which was splashed with green, heaps of manure and dog turds interspersed the weeds growing through the courtyard cobbles.

She became angry on Rob's behalf. Cecil had told her Rob had been given little time to set the manor in order before his mission to the Low Countries, but had left a steward in charge to do it for him. Nan, with a life's experience of sizing up servants, had said the steward was 'a troll with', a lazy, corrupt bully. On this evidence the man must be planning to decamp before Rob's return. Rob would surely kill him, else.

Once inside, Winchard shut the gates to keep the dogs out. They were rusty and creaked, but even so the manor remained silent, except for a small boy who came running round from the back.

Barbary gasped. The child was dressed in good velvet though his feet were bare. He carried a fishing rod in one hand and a line of mackerel in the other. And he was the image of Rob. Reincarnated was her childhood's Rob, energetic, healthier, less sulky perhaps, but just as aggressive. 'Who are you?'

She took in a breath. 'Friends, my lord. Anyone at home?'

The boy ran to the arched front door and stood on tiptoe to hammer its knocker. 'Lambert shall attend you while I make myself ready,' he said grandly. He knocked again. 'He may be in his cups,' he added. 'He usually is.' At last the door was opened. The boy said: 'Lambert, see to our guests,' and darted inside between the legs of the man who stood in the doorway.

'Who are you?' Lambert's best feature was his scowl, the rest went downhill from there, apart from his clothes which included a fine, though dirty, linen shirt, soft leather trunks, and silken hose over his bulging calves. Either Rob was overpaying him or he'd raided Rob's wardrobe.

'Friends of Sir Rob, calling on the lady of the house,' said Barbary.

'I been in Sir Rob's employ years,' Lambert said, 'I was his bosun on the *Speedswift*, and I don't know you.

459

The lady of the house ain't receiving. So cut off.' Another man appeared behind him, holding a pike. She was aware of a couple more coming menacingly into the courtyard.

Poor Rob, still new to the life of a landed gentleman, employing a sailor as steward. Probably a good bosun, but as a steward he lacked finesse. And she was tired. 'Lambert,' she said kindly, 'I've got a snaphaunce trained on your stomach. Are you going to call your mistress or not?' To back her argument Winchard stepped forward, and, as most people did, Lambert recoiled.

Barbary and Cuckold Dick dismounted and, followed by Winchard, entered the house. Walles and Nan took the horses to a trough.

The refectory, now the hall, was beautiful and belied the rotting exterior. Somebody had taken trouble with it, though dust was prevalent. Dying light came through long windows onto bowls of roses on a table. Eyeing the Clampett, and then Winchard, Lambert took his men off. She could hear him calling: 'Mistress, mistress,' somewhere out the back.

Walles and Nan came into the refectory. Barbary sat down on a bench. Nobody said anything.

A woman appeared in the doorway and stopped. She stood in a graceful droop, Lambert glowering behind her. She was dark, beautiful and taller than anyone in the room except Winchard, but managed to give the impression of looking up at them all from under her long black lashes. A victim, thought Barbary at once. Lambert bullies her, probably even Rob bullies her. And into her head with that familiar, exquisite pain came O'Hagan's voice telling her what sort of women were his type: 'Soft, dark-haired, compliant, fragile, grateful to me. Not women with hair like a toasted carrot.' Well, that was Rob's type. Reacting against the tough females of the Order, Galloping Betty, herself, he'd chosen someone completely vulnerable.

The woman waited, then as nobody spoke, said shyly: 'I am Lady Betty.' She was Rob's 'complication'.

Barbary stood up. 'Now there's a coincidence,' she said.

Her name was Helen. She had no objection to Barbary's sending Lambert packing. 'He wouldn't do what I told him,' she said, mildly. The man had traded on her being only Rob's mistress, hinting that the Queen would hear of their liaison every time Helen tried to stop him rifling Rob's clothes and cellar. 'But will Rob approve?' was her only worry.

Lambert even tried to blackmail Barbary: 'Suppose I tell the Queen as her beloved Sir Rob's got a wife turned up.'

'Winchard,' said Barbary, 'explain to this gentleman that the Queen and I are good friends.' Half an hour later, with his pack on his back and his eye closing from Winchard's explanation, Lambert left Tilsend Manor.

The other servants were instantly amenable, and a decent enough meal was served for them all, Helen acting as hostess and her son, Henry, as host.

She was a Devonian, the daughter of a prosperous innkeeper who'd had her educated for a lady, and – she blushed; she did a lot of blushing – she'd met Rob when he'd taken possession of Kerswell, the manor in Devon Elizabeth had given him for his part in the Armada battle.

Whether Rob had intended to marry her when he'd proved Barbary's death, Barbary refrained from asking. She thought it likely. Rob no longer needed to marry wealth and position, he was gaining those on his own, and from what she'd seen of modern, strong-minded society women at Lady Russell's, they wouldn't suit him. He needed dependence. And Helen was the most dependent female Barbary had ever met. She had immediately accepted Barbary's authority as Rob's legal wife; she was aware that he had one and she didn't seem to be jealous – doesn't need to be, thought Barbary, ruefully. Helen immediately fell in with Barbary's arrangements, only asking from time to time: 'But will Rob approve?'

'He'll have to,' said Barbary. 'The Queen expects me to be in residence here. You go back to Kerswell. I won't interfere there, I promise. You liked Kerswell, didn't you?'

'Oh yes,' said Helen, 'But will—?'

'Yes, he *will*,' shouted Barbary. The inclination to bully Helen was infectious.

The only fight was shown by little Henry. 'Why do we have to go? It's our manor, Father said it was.' He had a pugnacious lower lip, like his father's.

'Well, it isn't, so there,' said Barbary. 'I'll let you visit, though.'

Henry considered. 'I might,' he said, 'if Mother doesn't need me.' And that was Helen's other attribute; when men weren't actually oppressing her, they were protecting her. Walles kept pushing dishes to her side of the table and asking her to eat, as if he were her host. Dick, even the asexual Cuckold Dick, wanted to know if she felt a draught. Nan Nevet, her elbows square on the table, caught Barbary's eye and raised her own with the impatience of one woman who'd never been protected in her life to another.

Helen showed no surprise at the curious collection of guests she'd suddenly acquired. They were just happening to her, as Rob had happened to her, as her baby had happened to her, as Tilsend had happened to her and was now being taken away.

The next day Barbary gave her money, helped her pack, and sent her and Henry off, with Walles and Winchard as escort, towards Deptford where she could get a ship for Devon. Barbary stood under the dangerous lintel of Tilsend's gates and waved them out of sight, discovering she felt guilty at dispossessing Helen. And what the hell for? she asked herself angrily. The woman's got everything else. She's beautiful, she's got Rob's love, and she's got young Henry. She was welcome to the beauty, and Rob's love, but very much, very much did Barbary envy her young Henry.

Chapter Twenty-Two

The unarmed ship sailing up the Thames on the tide was small, not more than a hundred tons, and of a type unknown to those waters, a cross between a balinger and a Galway hooker. Grace O'Malley had designed her to double as transport and merchantman. She was expendable; if this was a one-way voyage, Grace wasn't going to deprive her fleet of a fighting ship. Nor, as a supplicant, could she prance into English territory in anything as magnificent as the *Grace of God*. The name alone would have hanged her.

The battering from the Atlantic breakers past Land's End and the Isles of Scilly, along the Channel and through the Straits of Dover had left the ship salt-stained and unpolished. The slight breeze fluttered a somewhat tattered pennant showing the tusked boar and sail of the O'Malley arms.

She dropped anchor in the Pool of London where word that the Irish woman rebel-pirate had come to visit the Queen attracted an immediate crowd. The first person ashore was Sir Murrough na dTuadh O'Flaherty, whom Grace had brought along to make initial contact with the Queen because he was one of the few pro-English relatives she had, and because he looked impressive. He was impressive, tall with snow-white beard and hair. But his rich, unexceptional, English clothing disappointed the crowd which expected native Irish to wear loincloths and bones in the nose. Murrough's soubriquet 'na dTuath', 'of the Battle of Axes', had been earned before he settled for the quiet life. The crowd hung on in the hope of something more savage.

Pushing through the press, Barbary heard adverse comments: 'My old mother's washtub's a likelier pirate. Papist traitors. Squalid, them Irish.' A contingent of

463

small boys marched up and down the quay holding their noses to illustrate the universal truth that all Irish smelled. But a man from one of the boatyards was admiring the hull's apple-cheeked forequarters which ran from its deceptively sharp, clean entrance to the raked transom. 'They can build, all right. Hardly a flat plank in her.'

Mr Secretary Cecil had sent a small detachment of his personal guard to keep the over-curious off the ship, and its captain, recognising Barbary, allowed her through. The gangplank's length was a time-bridge. She had never worked out why the lanolin which permeated Irish ships' ropes and sails smelled different from English lanolin, why the resin in Irish spars was distinct from that in English wood, but if she'd been blind she'd have known she was aboard a Connaught vessel, and the effect of that familiarity here in the midst of this other familiarity was disorientating. So was seeing the crew.

That man on the poop deck coiling ropes with a preoccupation that quarantined him from the English catcalls was Cull, the three sailors holystoning the deck on which the crowd was spitting were Rap, Keeroge and Scalder, shapes known in another world and now set against the London skyline. Seeing her in her court clothes was just as strange to them; they were almost remote in their greeting until Cull, lovely Cull, looked into her face, as he had once done on a strand in Connaught, and gathered her up. 'No need to be homesick now. Sure and we're here.'

'Oh, Cull.' She clung to each of them, showered by whistles and more catcalls from the quayside, then pulled herself together. 'Where's Herself?'

'Below. Making pretty.'

She stepped down into the captain's cabin. Ireland again. Lobster pots. Grace's pipe, the smell of tobacco and seaweed and stirabout, a crucifix. And Grace O'Malley herself, as sturdy as Croagh Patrick, but a Croagh Patrick rigged out in bunting. She was in her Sunday best, all her Sunday bests. With extras. Farthingaled, tasselled, mantilla-ed, accessoried almost into a stoop, whaleboned, buckrammed, slashed, embroidered, belaced, be-furred, be-jewelled and bedecked. She looked like an ironmongery stand. Catching sight of Barbary in the doorway, she picked up an ostrich feather fan and added it defiantly to her already weighty chatelaine. 'I'm appearing me finest to the Saxon queen,' she said grimly.

'What are you trying to do, *outrank* her?' It took time and high words, but at last Barbary had battled Grace down to her shift and started again. 'Irish, that's what you've got to be, for Chrissake. Dignified and Irish.'

In an excellent linen robe of saffron surmounted by her cloak and with a fine Irish roll on her head, Grace's height showed off the sweeping lines of a culture as sure of itself as Elizabeth's. 'No jewels,' said Barbary firmly, 'you're not going before the Queen in stuff you've piloted from under her nose.'

'I'll be selling them while I'm here anyways,' Grace told her. 'That black-hearted bastard Bingham's cessed his troops on the Two Owels and they're eating me people's food like maggots.' She looked at Barbary. 'There's famine.'

Oh God, not Clare, nor Murrisk, not all those confident people bewildered and dying. 'Tell her.'

'I intend to. And I'm wearing this.' Grace picked up something from her cabin table and put it round her neck. The beautiful and barbaric torque that had been Barbary's mother's, that Lord Burghley had once held, the cause of everything that had changed Barbary's life, glowed its Gaelic triumph round the sinews of Grace O'Malley's throat. Barbary wiped her eyes and nodded.

It would have been quicker and, Barbary thought, more appropriate if Grace had been carried to Whitehall by boat, but the Elf had sent a coach. The crowd on the quay jeered as they went ashore but Grace stalked through the path cleared for her by the guard, paying no more attention than if the sound was the wind on her quarterdeck. In the coach she sat upright, refusing to turn her head to look out of the windows, though her eyes slid sideways from time to time.

She's amazing, thought Barbary, she's never seen a city like this before. Has she seen a city at all? Aloud she asked: 'What do you think of it?'

Her grandmother put her in her place. 'Seville's prettier.'

As they left the city, Barbary began to panic. 'You've got to sweeten her. Play the poor old woman. None of this you're an uppity Saxon barbarian and I'm a descendant of Noah. I've put Bingham in her bad books, but you're the one can finish him off if you play your cards right. Remember Connaught.'

'I'll not be likely to forget. Katty died of starvation.'

'Katty? But I left her with the O'Neill.'

Grace's voice was inexorable. 'She went home, never being happy away from it. I was off at Rockfleet, and the Saxon soldiers made a surprise raid on Clare. They took away all the harvest and the animals and then destroyed the boats so the people could not fish. Katty gave her food to her grandchildren, much good did it do them for they were dead with her when I got back.'

That comfortable, comforting woman who'd nursed her at Dungannon, dead. The community that had been Clare, dead too? Like a vulture, the reality of what had been an amorphous word flapped onto Barbary's shoulder. Famine.

'And it was your woman killed her.' An inclination of Grace's head cited London and its Queen. 'So hold your breath for I know what I've to do.'

'What?' But questions, advice and pleading glanced off granite.

She's no idea what she's dealing with, thought Barbary. There was no parallel in Ireland to English court life which was dominated by the shifting mood of one person. Had Elizabeth been continually tyrannical everybody would at least have known where they were, but she could lull her people into relaxing and then switch. One of her women had been cast into outer darkness for playing the Queen's favourite tune when, in mid-phrase, the Queen had sickened of jollity. The court danced, as it were, to a measure that had no rhythm. The problem was the Queen's age and the Queen's love. Miserable as they were when they were apart, Elizabeth and Essex had begun to get on each other's nerves when they were together and their tantrums and reconciliations were eruptions that caught others in the lava-flow. Essex had looked with flirtatious eye on Lady Mary Howard; Her Majesty had said nothing but had Lady Mary's best dress secretly taken from her wardrobe and stalked into court wearing it herself. The effect was awful; Elizabeth was several inches taller than Mary Howard. 'If it's too short for me, it's too fine for you, so it fits neither of us well,' she'd shouted at the cowering maid of honour.

Undoubtedly the Queen was going mad, but Essex was madder. He wanted to invade Spain, the Indies, put down the rebels in Ireland. Why was the Queen not filling the vacant command of Ireland? It was on this matter that he had ruined himself, or so it seemed at the time. The Councillors who witnessed the incident came out of the Council shaking. Essex had drawn his sword on the Queen, or at least would have done if the Earl of Nottingham hadn't pushed him back and held him. He'd been insolent, she'd boxed his ears and he'd clapped his hand to his sword: 'This is an outrage. I would not have borne it from your father's hands.'

They had waited for the order to take Essex to the Tower. It hadn't come. Essex vanished into the country and Elizabeth did nothing. Nobody could believe it. He *couldn't* survive this. But he did, had. After a hideous month, he was back at court as charming, and apparently valued, as ever. As usual it was the onlookers who suffered and one of these was Barbary. Like so many people before her, she'd thought she'd got the Queen's measure; having once told the Queen the truth she continued to speak it, pressing Bingham's atrocities, the need for a kinder hand on Ireland's helm. But the Queen had turned on her suddenly: 'God's blood, Boggart, I am sick of your Irish plaguing.'

Since then she had not been invited to any court occasions. And now here she was, at the Elf's urging, accompanying an Irish pirate to court to translate that pirate's plea for mercy. We'll both end up in chains at Wapping, she thought.

A courteous, chirpy Mr Secretary Cecil met them at Whitehall Yard, and if he noticed that Barbary was sweating, he didn't mention it.

The heterogeneous mass that was Whitehall Palace extended from Scotland Yard to Cannon Row and inland from the river to deep countryside. People rash enough to refuse a guide had been known to wander about it for days. The Elf hopped along at Grace's side, to Barbary's relief treating her grandmother as an honoured visitor and not a captured warlord, indicating architectural and historical points of interest. Grace behaved well; not too impressed but inclining her head graciously.

They had to wait at the entrance to the hall where Elizabeth was receiving. The hall itself was so vast that from where they stood in the doorway the group of people around the Queen's chair at the other end looked as if they had been constructed to a smaller scale than human. A single monotonous voice which might have been clarity itself down there lost its lower register as it travelled back along the tapestries to the doorway so that it came to them in cheep-cheeps.

'The Venetian ambassador,' Cecil explained. Nervously, Barbary wondered if the man was doing Venetian bird impressions.

At last the cheeping stopped and the Queen's High Steward came up the hall to escort them into the presence, sweeping his ivory staff so that its point clicked on the marble with every step. They followed him, becoming dwarfed by the immensity of the avenue that led through the gold and silver tapestries. They were still ten yards away from the Queen when there was an interruption. Essex. He came swirling before them, accompanied by two of his acolytes, and barred their advance. 'No Irish savage shall near Her Gracious Majesty without I am satisfied for her safety,' he shouted. 'Search the pirate.'

He was showing off to the Queen. That was the nice thing about Essex, thought Barbary, when he acted the fool he did it without prejudice to sex or rank. Then she thought, oh Jesus, *is* Grace armed?

'Search her,' shouted Essex again, and one of the acolytes, Sir Gilly Merrick, moved in on Grace with outstretched hands. Then he doubled up, yelping, clutching his testicular area where Grace had kneed him with a movement so fast Barbary hadn't seen it. When she caught up and transferred her gaze from the gasping Sir Gilly to Grace, her grandmother was smoothing down the front of her gown. 'Tell young Cuchulainn there,' she said, tilting her head at Essex, 'if he wants to try it I'll cure his hiccups as well.'

Barbary said nothing. The man was out of control, reaching for his sword as he had done against the Queen. 'My lord.' Voices were shouting warnings, the loudest of them Elizabeth's own. Barbary watched the other acolyte, Essex's secretary Henry Cuffe, hang onto his master's sword arm, whispering. There were times when the insanity that lurked in the caves behind the Earl's beauty came rearing into the daylight and this was one of them. If she'd had her Clampett with her then she'd have produced it. The only thing that could stop this monster was a bullet. But there was one thing else: the high, insistent voice of Elizabeth. 'For shame, my lord. For shame.'

For a moment he was petulant and white, and then he allowed himself to be led away. He would retire for days now, ill.

Shaking, Barbary looked around. The courtiers were showing horror; genuine horror on the part of the Essex adherents, pleasurable horror if they belonged to the anti-Essex party. The Earl had done it again.

She looked at the Queen, and nearly collapsed with relief. Elizabeth was laughing. This was better than bear-baiting. The royal humour favoured the prat fall, and if the prats being fallen on belonged to a young man who mesmerised her to a point where she resented her own enthralment, so much the funnier. The Queen wiped her eyes. 'Tell the old woman that if she does not intend to kill me she may approach.'

Elizabeth was sitting in a chair by the corner of a massive marble fireplace surrounded by her ladies and several men. Barbary saw the Earl of Ormond was among them, no doubt to check on her translation of what Grace might say. She was wearing a dress that must have taken an army of seamstresses years to make, black satin criss-crossed with thousands of seed pearls. Her ruff was diamonded and diamonds were stitched into her orange wig. As usual when Essex was around, her bodice was open almost to the waist, showing the loops of her breasts.

Grace's bow was no lower than she would have given to one of her fellow chieftains on the Connaught shore, but Elizabeth was so amused that she ignored the lack of obeisance. She had decided to treat Grace as an ignorant old fisherwoman, and Barbary prayed Grace wouldn't spoil the indulgence.

'You have injured one of my courtiers, to say nothing of killing some of my ships, old woman. Would you now kill me?'

Barbary translated.

'No.'

'For God's sake say something else,' begged Barbary. 'She expects compliments.'

'The crone is overwhelmed,' said Elizabeth over her shoulder. 'Come, Boggart, ask what she thinks now that she meets her Ard Rí face to face.'

'She wants to know what you think of her.'

Grace considered. 'The dress is good,' she said, 'but she must be whipping her dressmaker for cutting it too small to cover her tits.'

Barbary glanced at Black Tom Ormond, the only other Irish-speaker in the hall. Both these women were his kinswomen. Would he betray Grace by intervening with an exact translation, or betray Elizabeth by keeping quiet? At the moment his mouth was curved, but shut. She swallowed, prayed for inspiration and found it in the memory of a song the galleymen had sometimes sung as they rowed. 'Were it not that full of sorrow from my people forth I go,' she said, 'By the blessed sun, 'tis royally I'd sing thy praise, Great Queen.'

Grace understood a little of it and sniffed. Lady Mary Howard, only just back in favour and watching her chance to stay there, moved forward and proffered Grace her handkerchief. 'Tell her that civilised people blow their noses on this. We don't sniff.'

Grace blew her nose on the laced cambric, then threw it in the fire.

'No, no,' said Lady Mary, wriggling with pleasure. 'Tell her, then we put it in our pocket.'

'Tell her that where I come from we don't keep soiled linen on our persons,' said Grace.

The Queen was smiling again as Lady Mary retired hurt. Was it instinct, wondered Barbary, or sheer luck that Grace was offending all the right people today?

'And what about my ships, old woman?'

'Ah well, d'ye see,' said Grace, 'tell Herself that I'm just such a one as she is. The O'Flaherty bastards wouldn't give me me dues. I was cast out into the world's sea in me shift. Either I drowned or I swam, so I swam. If it was her ships I sank it was nothing personal, and you can give her me apology. I never fired on one that didn't fire on me first. Tell her I sank Spanish alongside hers, and if she'll take Bingham off me back it's only her enemies I'll fight in future. Tell Herself that.'

Barbary told her. Word for word.

Elizabeth stopped patronising. She leaned back in her chair, her long fingers tapping its arms, suddenly grim. 'Does this pirate equate herself with our majesty?'

'Different spheres,' said Grace, 'and we survived in our each, though the men tried to stop us.'

'*Omnia venalia Roma*,' quoted Elizabeth.

'*Quis nisi mentis inips oblatum respuit aurum?*' answered Grace.

Elizabeth's head came forward like a pointer's. '*Nascimur pro patria*.'

Grace nodded. '*Mallem non esse quam non prodesse patria*.'

Barbary was redundant. The two women were in conversation, mouthing Latin platitudes at each other, Grace with less fluency than the Queen, but without the need of an interpreter. Barbary moved away and joined the Earl of Ormond. 'How in hell did Granuaile learn Latin?'

'We are not ignorant, Mistress Boggart, despite a general view to the opposite.'

We. She looked up at him. He was watching Grace with something like tired pride. He had always thrown in his lot with the English, he'd fought more of Elizabeth's battles against his own countrymen than any of the men she'd put in charge of Ireland, yet one word in defence of those countrymen, one act of mercy, and he'd been castigated as a traitor. Time and again he had been downgraded only to be called back to sort out the mess his superiors had caused and could no longer handle. Here at court he heard anti-Irish jokes and racism pour from those who had never been to the country as unthinkingly as the air came from their lungs.

'Well, she put Essex in his place.'

'She did, Mistress Boggart, though Essex was less concerned with showing Her Majesty how he can deal with the barbarian Irish than showing her that Cecil can't. That little exercise was directed against Mr Secretary.'

'What's he want the Irish appointment for?'

'He doesn't. Even Essex isn't that lunatic. He just doesn't want any of Cecil's men to get it.'

471

The Queen had stood up now and the two women were walking together, Elizabeth glittering, Grace matt like a seal.

'What's happening?'

He listened. 'I gather Granuaile is suggesting they sail away together to the New World where they will subdue the natives and carve out a dual empire, England and Ireland being too small for their combined talents. She overlooks the fact that our Glorious Maritime Majesty has never actually been to sea.'

At the far end of the hall where other petitioners and envoys were impatiently silting up the doorway, the two women turned, Elizabeth listening as she hadn't listened in years. One of the thousand facets of which she consisted was at that moment seeing herself leading a ship-borne invasion of a new continent. She had no intention of doing so, but she was enchanted by the idea, and that the female by her side should think her capable of it. They're both pirates, thought Barbary. They have options which nobody else is ruthless enough to take.

'Will Grace get her to recall Bingham?'

Ormond shrugged. 'It doesn't matter. Bingham is not the problem.'

'He's a problem to us in Connaught.'

He looked down at her. 'I don't know if you are aware of it, Mistress Boggart, but I was the one indirectly responsible for sending you to Ireland.'

'You were?' She was surprised.

'And my responsibility in that regard urges me to give you one piece of advice. Don't go back. Forget that country. Renounce it. Live in peace with your husband, breed children. And never go back.'

Elizabeth and Grace passed them, still talking. Elizabeth ignored the courtier who held the back of her chair and stepped up onto the dais, leaving Grace alone at its foot. She moved to stand before the throne and raised her voice. 'Let it be known that Mistress Grace O'Malley has persuaded us that what she did against us was out of force of circumstance and not malevolence.' The adventurous moment had passed, and she was Queen again, dispensing mercy on an old woman who was, in fact, exactly her own age. 'Lord Lieutenant Bingham will be recalled and put in the Tower for the answering of many wrongs done

472

against Mistress O'Malley and her people.' She looked grandly down at Grace. 'Go, good old woman, and use your remaining years to prosecute my enemies as you have promised.'

Grace bowed and, to Barbary's relief, moved away backwards. Elizabeth smiled them out of the hall.

'Aren't I the clever one?' said Grace O'Malley.

At Deptford there was an uncomfortable incident when the Ballast Master came aboard as they waited for the tide, demanding to know why a ship that had come upriver laden – Grace had brought hides to sell on her own account and more whiskey for Cuckold Dick – was returning downriver empty and without ballast, since to do so would make her dangerously light, not to mention depriving the Ballast Office of a toll. He was unimpressed by Grace's passport which had been signed by Elizabeth herself. 'You still need ballast.'

"Tell the bastard we're loading guns further down,' called Grace in Irish.

'Oh, thank you,' said Barbary. To the Ballast Master she said: 'We're picking up a cargo of corn at Tilbury given by Her Majesty to the starving people of Connaught.' The corn was going to cover the guns. 'Also whiskey,' she added after a thought.

'What's whiskey?' asked the Ballast Master.

He was helped ashore an hour later and they went on their way.

'You're too damn full of yourself,' Barbary told her grandmother. 'Just because you've got the Queen of England eating out of your hand.'

'Haven't I though,' crowed Grace. 'Now there's a woman understands the piloting trade.'

'No, she doesn't. And she wouldn't understand you picking up guns, either. She thinks you're going to fight the Spanish for her.'

'And don't I need guns to do it? Not all that art-ill-ary will go to the O'Neill. She's getting Bingham off me back and for that I'll sink all the Spanish she wants, and the Hollanders, and the—'

'The Hollanders are on her side,' pointed out Barbary.

'Ah well, you can't have everything.' Grace was in fine form.

It was a hot day and apart from a fitful breeze in its flapping sails, the ship's progress depended solely on the tide. Traffic going upriver had come to a stop, but the two women leaning on the gunwale to watch it experienced the illusion that a frieze painted to represent the world's shipping – there was even an Arab dhow – was moving gently past them.

'Ah well,' said Grace, 'it's time to give you the letter.'

'What letter?'

'Come down to the cabin.'

'It's from O'Hagan, isn't it?'

'Keep her centred, Cull,' said Grace.

'I got her up, I'll get her down," called back Cull.

'Is it from O'Hagan?'

The cabin was warm and its open window allowed in the reflection of sun on water to waver over the bulkhead. Grace opened a familiar box and gave Barbary a small roll. The seal was unrecognisable; a ring had stamped into it so hard that it had gone through to the parchment, spattering the wax. The same anger had distorted the scrawl of the short sentences.

'The O'Neill says you have returned to your husband to save your soul and mine. Could this salvation not have waited two more days? Were you afraid I would not let you go?

'As it is, take your English soul. I take mine to Spain, and God have mercy on them both.'

It was dated from O'Neill's palace at Dungannon, two days after she'd left it. Even as O'Neill had been telling her O'Hagan was on the sea for Spain, he'd actually been on his way to join her.

Grace's arm stopped her before she got to the cabin steps. 'Where are you going?'

'I don't know.' Catch him, that's all she thought. Catch him before he goes. But he'd gone. He was already in Spain by now. The letter was nearly three months old. The fury and hurt in it were ancient now, for him. Not for her.

She stared up at her grandmother. 'He tricked us. O'Neill tricked us. He lied to me and he lied to him. Why didn't you tell O'Hagan why I went? I was saving you. You, not my soul. I don't give a damn for my soul. Only him.'

Grace caught her hands in one fist. 'Stop it.' She forced her down onto the cot. 'Stop it now. I'd gone from Dungannon before O'Hagan arrived. He gave the letter to Katty. I found it among her possessions.'

Barbary went on staring, as if Grace held relief from her misery. 'He tricked us.' They hadn't suited his purpose. Love hadn't suited his purpose. 'O'Neill lied to us.'

'Sure and he lies to everybody,' said Grace, comfortingly. 'He's promised me more money than he's ever put down on the nail. Wipe your eyes for the sake of God. It's only a man.'

'He tricked us.' She wanted to bawl to alleviate the pain, lie down on the cabin floor, drum her heels and bawl like a calf. 'I saved the bastard's life and he tricked me.'

'He's the grandfather of all trickery,' said Grace. 'I thought you'd known that.'

That lovely thing they'd had. She was in agony to think O'Hagan believed she'd returned to England voluntarily. O'Neill's lying disregard for them both . . . 'I'll see the bastard dead before I get him his fokking guns.'

'If it's him you're getting them for,' said Grace calmly, 'I should.'

The reflected wavelets danced uselessly against the wood of the bulkhead. Barbary hammered her fists on the cot edge in her helplessness. God damn them all, what could she do? Of course the guns weren't for the O'Neill. Never had been. Her grandmother was right. They were for shapes hanging in a dawn in a Munster forest. And she would supply them to a man who had versed her with a brilliance that put him high in the Order's role of honour. His lie to her had been clever, but his lie to O'Hagan, that she had gone back to save his soul and hers from the sin of adultery – what adultery? what soul? – had been a perfection of the verser's art, lancing into her lover's damned bloody conscience. But the O'Neill would get his guns because he was all that stood in the gap to save his people, O'Hagan's people, *her* people, from annihilation.

Wearily she said: 'What happened to Don Howsyourfather?'

'His loving would have held me back, with a war on,' said Grace, 'so I returned him to Spain where he wouldn't get damaged. Maybe I'll get him back when it's all over. Or maybe I'll get another one prettier.'

Grandmother and granddaughter looked carefully at each other. Grace had saved Don Howsyourfather from being caught up in the hell that Ireland had become. Perhaps, after all, thought Barbary, it was better as it was. O'Hagan would be safe in Spain. 'You're no fool, are you, Granuaile?'

'Fools go under. Will we go and get the guns now?'

A trap within a trap within a trap. 'What else can we do?'

When they'd discussed the matter during Barbary's convalescence at Dungannon, the O'Neill's strategy for war if it were forced on him would, he said, resemble all his dealings with the English. 'No pitched battles. We'd not win. Hit and run, stay unseen, so they'll think the trees are killing them. Lead them like marshlights into the bog and watch it suck them down.'

For years he'd been supplying clans all over Ireland with small arms and getting instructors, most of them taught by the English themselves, not just to shoot accurately but to shoot accurately on the run. His greatest weapon was the English contempt for the Irish soldier who, propaganda had it, was an inefficient coward. Where English propaganda got it right was that the Irish invariably ceded a held position, not because they were cowards as the English believed, but because they lacked cannon or, if they had cannon, couldn't use it. O'Neill's own knowledge of ordnance was sketchy. 'Consult Will Clampett,' he said. 'I want guns powerful enough to breach a ten-foot wall, light enough to float over bogs and willing to skip up mountains.'

But there had been no time for Barbary to consult Will. She knew that the O'Neill intended to use Will to set up his own foundry for larger cannon, therefore her job was to supply manoeuvrable pieces. She had primed the Bumboy to negotiate with the cannon master at Panningridge accordingly. It had been a needless exercise. The cannon master had indeed fallen for the Bumboy, and his money, but he couldn't fulfil a special order in the

time she had given him. She would have to content
herself with pieces creamed off from the legitimate,
government order. In effect, she'd have to take what she
would get. And that had turned out to be four robinets
which, though carriage guns, were light, twelve two-and-
a-half to three-pounder falcons – ideal for the O'Neill's
purpose – and a saker, a six-pounder, needing a team of
oxen to drag it.

When the wagons bringing the consignment to Tilsend
had creaked out of a dawn mist along the causeway, she'd
taken one look at the monstrous shape pinioned by ropes
to one of them and said: 'Take it back.'

Despite the impenetrable Wealden accent of the leading wagoner, she gathered from the number of four-letter
words expressed in it that he wasn't prepared to do so.
Carrying that lot through uncharted Kent forest had not,
it appeared, been enjoyable. As it was, all he wanted to
do now was dump the guns in her courtyard, get his
money and return whence he came. It took four-letter
words of her own to persuade him to proceed with his
train to the buildings which had once been the monastery's grange and sheep-shearing barn. They stood on the
hilltop above the chalk steps that led down to the inlet's
jetty from which the monastery's lay brothers had sent
their corn and fleeces by ship to London markets.

Her idea had been to hide them under the bales of
straw which half filled the grange. But there could be no
hiding the saker. They managed to get it inside and left it
there in the charge of Walles, Cuckold Dick and Winchard until her return from London with Grace O'Malley.
Her constant fear was that Rob would come back to
Tilsend before the guns could be got away. Cecil had said
he wasn't due back for another two weeks, but a week of
that had already passed.

Just manoeuvring the saker through the grange's great
double doors had presaged some of the difficulties
entailed in getting the thing into the hold of Grace's
balinger. On the return trip down the Thames Barbary's
mind, already sore from O'Hagan's letter and the
O'Neill's betrayal, had grown tired wrestling with the
problem of gantries, cranes and winches, the tide, the
weather, weights and waterlines.

Now, as they stood in the doorway of the grange and

477

looked at the dinosaur within, her grandmother lifted some of her worry. 'Sure, it's no problem. I've piloted bigger buggers than that. Did I tell you of the time I piloted the dome of Akbar's mosque?'

This was no time for Arabian reminiscences. 'It'll take some getting along a gangplank.'

'Gangplank me arse,' said Grace. 'We'll drop it into the hold.'

'How? Toss it?'

'There's an overhang to your inlet. Put a winch on the top of the cliff and lower the bastard down.'

Cull and the Irish crew went up to the headland with the Order men to look. Grace was right. Some hundred yards along the cliff edge from the outbuildings was an overhang. From here the swell of the rise behind them hid the house. Only the Light was visible, looking like some gawky, helmeted sentinel. It was a calm, hot day, and by lying flat on their bellies they could see down into the water some thirty feet below them where the white sea bottom gave it the colour of a chalky emerald. There was a rock-free basin there, certainly wide enough, and at high tide deep enough, to take a ship of the balinger's size. After a long discussion involving tide and the balinger's draught when fully loaded, it was decided to load the guns right away. Barbary was driven by an urgency that made her restless. It was noon already. They could load the lighter guns this afternoon from the jetty and be ready to lower the saker from the cliff when the tide was at its peak, even though by then it would be dark. 'There'll be a moon. We've got flares. Let's get on, before some shingle-tramper surprises us,' she said. Revenue men made irregular patrols of the Kent coast, which was where a large proportion of the country's smuggling took place.

They began work at once. One by one the falcons and robinets were trundled to the top of the steps where the barrels were dismantled from their carriages, the carriages from their wheels, and each piece carried separately down to the jetty and stacked for the Irish sailors to carry on board. The falcons needed three men per barrel, the robinets four. The steps became smooth as ice under the wear of their boots, and they had to fix a winch at their top.

All the time the heat made the cast iron almost unbearable to handle. Sweat, flies and the glare from the sea blinded them when their hands were too full to wipe their eyes. The marshes on either side clicked with stridulating insects like a million ratchets, bees buzzed in the sea-pinks on the chalk.

Barbary drove herself and everybody else like a slaver. All the light in the world seemed concentrated on this headland and what they were doing; how long could it be before someone spotted them doing it? She kept glancing round, unable to rid herself of the idea she was being watched, but apart from some sheep and the occasional sail out in the estuary, there was nothing to see.

Walles and Cuckold Dick were not good at hard labour, hard labour being what they had joined the Order to get away from, and they had to be shouted at. It was Winchard who won her heart that day, Winchard who carried on like an uncomplaining ox, except for the periodic mention of his dislike of flies, Winchard whose great hands blistered and went on carrying. Winchard, she thought, a pearl among men, a lamb in wart-hog's clothing, a dependable man. Winchard wouldn't believe the first lie he was told and go off to Spain . . . She tried to bring her brain under control. It would soon be dark and they had yet to get the saker into position.

Twice she went up to the house to fetch something for them to drink. She began winching up some water from the well to pour over her sweating body, but the winch made such a noise in the silent courtyard that she stopped, as if somebody might hear it. Was that a creak in the house? She went in, but nobody was there. She went down to the cellar to fill some jugs from the ale barrel.

The bad state Lambert had left the house in hadn't been improved by the occupancy of Winchard, Walles and Dick while they awaited her return from London. Before she'd gone she'd paid off the remaining servants and sent them away. Had they come back to spy on her? Were they watching her now? On her way out she stood and looked round the courtyard again, as swallows ricocheted across its cobbles picking up insects from the ordure. Nothing.

Earlier that day Grace had asked her, nonchalantly:

'Are ye coming back home with us?' And she'd said: 'Yes.'

It would be going against the O'Neill's wishes that she play the spy for him in England, but, once she'd delivered the guns, she owed O'Neill nothing.

She'd done her best for Ireland, but she'd sickened of intrigue, Mr Secretary Cecil's, the O'Neill's, her own. She would get away from this stifling place back to clean, green Connaught, however war-torn and starving it was.

Above all, she must be away before Rob came back. She'd betrayed him, not by her adultery with O'Hagan, but by using his house for his enemies. He was still, after all, her legal husband.

And she was uneasy about the guns. In her brain beat Mabel Bagenal's words: 'He kills people.' O'Neill had betrayed her. He'd betrayed his best friend, O'Hagan. Who knew whether he wouldn't scruple to use these guns not in defence of the Irish way of life, but against some clan that annoyed him. 'He kills people.' O'Neill killed people. These guns killed people. 'What else can I do?' she asked aloud. Trap within a trap within a trap. Well, this was the last trap this cony would get caught in. She would go home.

She took the jugs down to the jetty and was cursed by Irish and Order alike for bringing cider, not ale. She hadn't noticed.

It took all of them, roped like mules, to pull the saker up the rise. There was a moment of terror as they neared the overhang when the thing threatened to roll on into the sea, dragging them with it. Somehow they brought it to a halt and pegged its ropes into the ground. The ropes creaked, but held.

It was dark by now and the moon hadn't come up high enough yet for them to dismantle the gun by its light. Barbary sent Cuckold Dick and Walles back to the manor to fetch flares.

Grace and the crew went to get the balinger ready. With no wind, they were going to have to sweep the ship from the jetty to the basin.

They'd just gone when the two shapes of Walles and Dick appeared out of the darkness behind her. 'There's glims up at the house, Barb,' said Dick quietly. 'Shingle-trampers.'

480

'How many?'

'Couldn't see. Enough.'

She thought hard. Caught in the act of smuggling guns aboard an Irish boat, not even Cecil could save them from execution; nor would he want to.

'Coming this way, Barb,' said Dick, gently. She could see for herself the glow of flares advancing towards the rise.

'Get down to the ship,' she said. 'Tell Grace to get the sweeps to pull her out into the estuary, far out. She can drop you further up the coast.'

'What about you, Barb? And this bugger?'

'It's going over. Run.'

Dick wouldn't leave her. She screamed: 'I'll be safe as long as I don't have to explain away you lot. It's my house, remember? Run.'

They ran. Barbary ran, towards the overhang. She could see the mooring light on the balinger which, thank God, was still by the jetty. She waited until she heard the pounding of the Order men's boots on the jetty. Good. She ran back to the saker and began pulling up the pegs that roped it. One of them was stuck deep. She pulled and pulled, glancing behind her. The flares were over the rise, she could hear men calling to each other. Would they see the saker outlined against the lighter dark of the sky? With luck their flares would blacken anything outside the range of their light.

Got the swine. She ran round the other side of the gun, kicking out the rest of the pegs.

And the saker didn't move. She ran round to the left wheel and shoved. She felt a tremor, but the swine stayed where it was. She pushed again with everything she had and reluctantly, with desperate slowness, the saker shivered, then moved, gathering speed, heading for the overhang with the ropes around it flailing a desperate goodbye. She saw the back of its carriage rise in a huge, saucy kick as its front end tipped, then the ground opened at her feet. The weight had been too much for the overhang and part of the cliff followed the saker into the sea. She threw herself backwards, clutching at grass. There was too much pounding in her ears to hear the crash of chalk and iron against water, but she saw the white of spray, felt it on her face.

With nothing to obstruct her view she could now see the balinger, drawn by its sweeps, like a coach dragged by mice, roll as the shock wave hit it. But it was clear of the jetty and moving, though hideously slowly, out to sea. Thank God, Dick had persuaded Grace to be sensible.

Somebody kicked her. 'Got you, you bastard. Stand in the name of Queen Elizabeth. God bless us, it's a woman!'

'What you been smuggling, you slut?'

She lay in a circle of flares, dazzled, but one of the figures said: 'Jesus,' and she turned her head to the voice.

'Hello, Rob,' she said, and fainted.

When she came round she was still on the ground. The shingle-trampers were trying to make sense of what was happening by questioning Rob who was answering in the short, weighted sentences of a very angry man. 'I told you. I have been abroad on the Queen's business. After I reported to Her Majesty, I came here. This is my home. I saw men on my jetty loading guns aboard a ship. They were too many to tackle alone. I rode to fetch you.'

'You told us your wife had been kidnapped.'

'Well, obviously she has not. This is my wife.' It cost him something.

Oh, Rob, she thought. You missed a trick there. Too honest for your own good. You could've done an Amy Robsart. Let the shingle-trampers hang me.

Then she woke up properly. No, he couldn't, could he? He'd already been to London, seen Elizabeth who would have mentioned her. She was official. What he hadn't known was that she was here at Tilsend; nobody had known. She'd told Cecil she was going to visit Penshurst. Rob was having to protect her because anything she did would reflect on him. A Queen's favourite couldn't have a criminal for a wife.

'I tell you I returned to find my house empty and my, my wife gone, and men loading guns – I thought they were guns – at the jetty. Which was why I rode for you. Obviously, it was a mistake. I'm sorry.' The apology was a spit, almost more than he could bear. 'You can go now. It was a mistake.'

'Mistake, was it? There's a ship down there all right. She's moving under sweeps, but she won't move far, not in this calm. We can get launches from Rochester and go after her.'

Barbary pulled herself up. 'That is my grandmother's ship,' she said in her best court English. Grandmother was a respectable word. She needed respectability. 'Why should you go after her?'

''Cause he saw guns.' The leading shingle-tramper, a big man, nodded his head towards Rob. 'Gun-smuggling's penal, grandmother or not.'

'It was timber.' What a marvellous liar she was. 'She's transporting timber to my husband's estate in Ireland.' She turned to Rob. 'It was for you, Rob. You always said you wanted English oak furniture at Hap Hazard. Remind you of home.' She stared at him, willing him. Would he back her? He was staring at her too, loathing her. 'I expect it looked like guns,' she was jabbering frantically. 'We had the trunks mounted on wheels. That's what made you think it was guns. I expect they looked like gun barrels.' Come on, Rob. Let Grace go. You've gone this far.

She heard him groan. He was no actor. He'd never fitted into the Order. But his lips moved. 'Might have been timber,' he muttered.

'What?' asked the chief shingle-tramper.

She saw Rob make up his mind. He was trapped. A gun-smuggling wife would ruin him. 'I said it must have been timber,' he said loudly, 'I made a mistake. I'm sorry, gentlemen.'

They weren't satisfied. 'What was that wunnerful great crash as we come up then?' Oh God, if they looked over, would they see the saker sticking up?

'Part of the cliff gave way,' she said. The chief and a couple of his men went to the edge. She peered with them. The moon was casting light now. The sea was as flat and black as silk, but there was still froth floating on the basin and, here and there, pieces of chalk like geometric fish.

'Does that,' said one of the men to his chief. It was an eroding coast.

'I know.' He still wasn't happy. A hero of the Armada was telling him one thing and his smuggler-catching instinct was shouting something else, even if he couldn't prove it. But if he sent boats after Grace, he'd catch her,

Barbary knew. The balinger's crew couldn't sweep her far.

They discussed it among themselves for an age. But nobody fancied riding back to Rochester to get boats out on what might prove a fool's errand. Eventually, they turned landwards towards the house. She couldn't walk, her legs had melted with relief and fatigue. Rob grabbed her arm and pulled her along, not from kindness. He hated her, she could feel the hate in his grip.

Back at the house the men paused outside the door, not welcoming the thought of the journey back to Rochester in the dark, waiting for the hospitality they had a right to expect. Rob gave them none. And that was another reason for hating her; his house was too shameful to entertain even these petty functionaries. Rage pulsated in him like a bull pawing the ground. 'Goodnight,' he said, yanked her inside the door and shut it.

There was a single lit candle on the table next to the bowls still holding Helen's dead roses. Barbary limped over to the table and leaned on it. Behind her she heard him shooting the bolts on the door, then his boots advancing across the tiles. Her head was yanked back and he hit her across the face. 'Where's Helen, you bitch?' Her head snapped to one side and another whack snapped it back. She tried to run away from him, but his hands kept finding her and hitting. Only the Upright Man had ever beaten her like this. Rob was the Upright Man. He'd got used to beating people.

It was righteous anger, she had to admit it. She'd come back from the dead. She'd turfed his mistress and son out of his house. She'd smuggled guns to the Irish. She'd endangered the good name of this great man.

'Where's Helen, you bitch?'

Her spirit came back. Who said he was right? What gave him the right to say what was right? Who'd asked him to marry her? His own gain, that's what. If she didn't suit him, that was his fault. She was sick of being hurt by men she didn't suit.

'Where's Helen, you bitch?' The beating didn't give her time to answer. He was going to kill her. Terrifying. *Stupid*. She would *not* be killed by a stupid man.

She pulled away from him and ran for the press where she'd put the snaphaunce.

For the second time in his life Rob found himself staring down the wrong end of the Clampett. 'I'll shoot you, Rob, I swear.' And she would. He knew. She kept it primed. Whether it would fire after all these years she didn't know. He didn't either.

He managed to drag back his anger, though it took as much effort as hauling a saker. They were both panting. In a minute she'd drop. 'Let's sit down.' She lowered herself into a chair at one end of the table and gestured with the Clampett for him to sit at the other end. He was calmer now.

'What have you done with Helen?'

That, to do him justice, was his greatest worry. Helen obviously meant more to him than she, Barbary, ever had. Helen was his sort of woman, adoring, dependent and helpless. He'd thickened. He was the successful venturer and courtier, but something had gone out of him. He was still handsome, but his jowl and belly were fleshy and he'd acquired the brutal air which came to self-made men.

'Now then,' she said, 'Helen's at Kerswell. She's all right. I sent her to Kerswell. Her and Henry.' Keep talking, she was as powerful as he was if they could talk. 'She's a nice lady.'

'You bitch.' He couldn't think of anything else to call her.

She kept talking, she was still in danger. 'I know it's a shock, Rob, when you thought I was dead. But circumstances . . .' God, what an inadequate word, '. . . circumstances brought me back to England.' She tossed great names at him to show how official and respected she was, that she had done his reputation no harm. 'I've been working with Mr Secretary Cecil, and staying with his aunt. I sent Helen away because the Queen expects me to live here. She's fond of me.' Tiredly, she added, 'The Queen, not Helen.'

'But you're still prepared to betray her, you bitch. You Papist spy.'

She opened her mouth to argue what was and was not betrayal, but she didn't have the energy. 'Not any more,' she said wearily. 'I'm too tired.' Too tired, too old, too betrayed in her turn. 'All I want now is peace.'

'By smuggling guns?'

485

'Timber, Rob. It was timber.' He knew what he'd seen, but timber was her story and he was stuck with it. 'First and last time.'

'You're a traitor, you bitch.'

How they used the word. Their assumption that Ireland was theirs because they said it was. 'I'm Irish,' she said wearily. 'I didn't think it mattered when we married, but it turned out it did.'

'Irish bitch.'

She was prepared to be reasonable but she was getting to the limit. 'You're married to this Irish bitch. I'm official. You can't Amy Robsart me.'

He lifted his head and she saw, despite everything, he hadn't even thought of it. Ponderous, a bully, a self-seeker, within those limits he was still a decent man. He'd never fitted into the Order. Beneath the fleshing face she saw an honest, sullen boy. 'I'm sorry, Rob,' she said, 'I'm so sorry. I'll get out of your life. I'm going back to Ireland. I'll disappear. You can marry Helen and become Lord Rob. Do whatever you like. I won't bother you again.'

He'd started to think. Rage was ebbing. He was probably as tired as she was. No, there was nobody as tired as she was.

The big shape at the other end of the table became Tibbot ne Long. Tibbot of the Ships. Uncle Tibbot, the bastard, bless him. Even that terrible meal she'd eaten in that tower on the edge of Clew Bay was bathed in gentle starlight because it had been on the edge of Clew Bay. The next day the ship had come floating in on insect wings to take her into the cherubims. She was crying as she dozed. Oro and Welcome Home, sang the oarsmen. Take me home.

Her head jerked up. She'd drifted off for a second, but he hadn't moved; she couldn't be sure because he was on the edge of the candlelight's range, but some change had taken place in him. Waves of aggression had stopped coming at her down the table's length. In her exhaustion just then she'd displayed vulnerability, and that had always disarmed him. She'd forgotten. He was looking at her without hatred now; not much liking, but without hatred.

'Is there any wine?' he asked.

486

It was a relief to hear a sentence without 'bitch' in it. Was there wine? Had the Order boys drunk it all? She went to look, taking the Clampett with her – she wasn't sorry enough for him to leave that behind. She'd gone out of the door before she realised she hadn't got a candle and went back to light one from the candle on the table. 'Wine,' she said. If she didn't concentrate, her brain would splinter and lose her purpose. She found the kitchen and looked around the debris, stumbling against a pot that spilled porridge onto the tiles. The place stank. No wine. 'Wine.' Could she sit down and sleep? How far had the ship gone by now? She was so lonely. The only people she loved were on a ship edging out to sea. O'Hagan didn't love her. He wouldn't have left her. She'd left Ireland. Ireland was leaving her. 'Wine.'

There were barrels in the cellar, one of them still containing some wine. She got a jug, filled it. Needed tankards, but the Clampett was in one hand, jug in the other. 'Tray,' she said and found one. She went back to the hall. 'Wine.'

He didn't look up. She poured him wine and some for herself. She went back to her place, realised she'd left the Clampett on the tray by his elbow, went to get it and at last sat down. He didn't notice. He seemed to be calculating. He'd drawn Helen's bowl of roses near him and was gently rubbing a dry petal between finger and thumb. If she wasn't so damned tired, she'd be touched.

'I don't mind about Helen, Rob,' she said. Who was she to mind? But she wanted him to know she didn't.

Still holding the Clampett she drifted back to Tibbot's tower on the edge of the bay and waited for the cherubim ship to come and take her home.

'I don't want you to go,' said Uncle Tibbot. She looked up. Rob sat in Tibbot's chair, thought given, decisions taken. 'I want you to stay here.' He'd gone mad, poor man, like Tibbot.

'What?'

'Do you mean it? You've finished with all this Irish chicanery? Do you promise?'

Chicanery. Perhaps it was. At least she and Grace had managed to free Connaught of Bingham. She'd supplied the O'Neill with the guns she'd promised him and, through Will Clampett, the means to making others. He

487

could kill more than enough people with those, and she couldn't be responsible for killing any more. She'd come to the end. 'Yes, I'm telling the truth.'

'Does anyone know you are childless?'

'Eh?' The question was extraordinary in this situation. He really had gone mad.

'Does the Queen know, does anybody know you've not had a child of mine?'

Obedient in its fatigue, her brain tried to think it through. 'I don't think so. The question's never come up.' Her court appearances had been at formal occasions where there'd been little gossiping. Certainly the courtiers had shown curiosity about her, as they did about everybody who ventured into their circle, but Cecil had told her not to talk too much about her past, and discouraged questions, even from Lady Russell. As far as most people were concerned, she was Sir Rob's wife with a mysterious Irish past.

'You know I can still get that ship brought back, don't you?'

She nodded. The sweeps could only take her so far before the rowers needed to rest. The revenue launches could overtake her without trouble.

'If I let her go, you must stay. You promise. Now. On the Papist Bible if necessary.' His mouth went into disgust as if he'd mentioned the Koran. 'Swear on your life.'

'Swear what?'

'That you stay. As my wife.'

'*What?*' Definitely mad. She made her words soothing. 'You're tired, Rob. It's been a bad night. You don't want me. You don't love me. You love Helen. A nice lady. You let me go and let Grace go and I'll disappear and you can marry Helen and you'll have ever such a nice life. You see.' Her words were so soporific she almost nodded herself off.

'Oh no. I'm not having you run off only to bob up again and ruin me. You're my legal wife and you will be my legal wife. Lady Betty. Margaret Betty. You will bring up my son as your own. No more Ireland. No treachery. If you swear it, and if I believe you, I'll let the ship go. If not, the whole stinking crew, grandmother and all, can hang in chains.'

She was confounded. So that's what he'd lacked in his

wonderful life, a lawful spouse to give him the final respectability, the start of a line of Bettys. If he could have proved her death, Helen would have taken the role, even if the Queen didn't like it. He'd achieved great power, only to find, as other men had, that it was ashes if it could not be passed on to his son.

Raleigh, Leicester, Essex, and now Rob, all prepared to risk losing their position at court to achieve that most primitive right, an heir. Raleigh had gone to the Tower in order to marry and gain his, even if he had managed at last to charm his way out. And Rob was one up on Raleigh; he had a wife and, moreover, one who was in better odour with the Queen than poor Elizabeth Throckmorton Raleigh.

'But if I disappear, you can marry Helen and she's more your type.' Oh God, why couldn't she forget O'Hagan that night when he'd told her his type of woman? She couldn't stay here, in this loveless place with this unloving, calculating man.

'No.' He was quite firm. He'd thought it all out. 'I'd have to slide down the ladder of the Queen's favour and begin again. Somebody might find out, you might reappear, even if you didn't intend to. I'm not risking a charge of bigamy and having Henry declared bastard.'

'Suppose somebody finds out he is anyway?'

'Margaret.' The word brought back an old suffocation. 'How can he be declared bastard if you say he isn't?' He leaned over so that his face was in the candlelight. 'I'm offering you your grandmother's life, Margaret, in return for your promise that you will take up your position as Lady Betty, wife of a famous husband, mother to a fine son. Is it so bad a bargain? You've acquitted yourself well in society for your own ends. Acquit yourself well for mine, and your grandmother's. We got on well enough before, we can again. You'll live in luxury. Is it a bargain?'

He was brutal, she'd been right when she'd seen it in his face; the self-made man who bought and sold, offered this one a bribe, that one a threat to get what he wanted. He was prepared to put away a woman he loved to gain from a woman he didn't. And he was capable of handing Grace O'Malley to the hangman.

'I'm not taking that child away from Helen,' she said.

'If it's for his advancement she'll want you to. And it is.'

How strange men were. She leaned back in her chair with fatigue. What in hell made him think he could trust her once Grace O'Malley was safe? She almost smiled. 'Are you putting me on my honour, Rob?'

He scented weakness and became charming. He still could be. 'No. I want you to say dibs.'

'Dibs?' It was Order cant for bargain. He was condescending to speak in a language she understood. The Order broke oaths, but no member, ever, had betrayed a dibs. What a stupid man. Give in, say you'll do it, save Grace, get some sleep, then run away when his back is turned, and Oh God, she couldn't. Grace O'Malley's life meant too much to her to purchase it with a promise she intended to break. She had, in truth, come to the end of herself.

'I couldn't be your wife in bed,' she said.

He shook his head. He didn't want her to be. 'It won't be that sort of marriage.'

Christ, this was ridiculous. But perhaps, after all, she owed him, for their childhood together, and the words that she'd said to the preacher when they married, for Grace O'Malley.

'Rob,' she said, 'I really don't want to.'

'Can't you see I'm saving you from yourself? How long can you run with Irish trash? I'm offering you a chance to live in the best society. You can take it, or I ride for Rochester this minute. Is it dibs or isn't it?'

'It's dibs.' She felt nothing momentous as she said it, just fatigue. She'd sort it all out tomorrow when her brain worked.

'Then give me the snaphaunce, Margaret.'

She could have laughed if she'd had the energy. He wanted a symbolic capitulation. She looked at the beautiful lines of the Clampett and he was right; it was a symbol. It was the key to freedom and independence; without it she was locked away from Barbary Clampett O'Flaherty O'Malley of the cherubims, and into Margaret Betty of English court society, housewife and mother.

'Please, Margaret, bring me the snaphaunce.'

She got up, the Clampett in her right hand, her left helping her to edge along the table. It seemed a long walk. At the end of it she stood before him. He reached over and took the Clampett away from her.

Chapter Twenty-Three

She'd sold out. Never mind that she'd done it to save Grace O'Malley and her crew, to say nothing of Cuckold Dick and the others; in doing it she'd given up Ireland, traded her birthright. She was bereft, and she grieved for her loss. The shapes of the dead who had hung in the Deer Park at Spenser Castle returned to haunt her.

But in her bereavement were to come compensations which, to begin with, made her more guilty than ever. Rob had promised her luxury, and, like the excellent merchant-venturer he'd become, he would make an honest trade.

She resisted it at first and stayed down at Tilsend, working to clear the place up. It salved her conscience to be busy and uncomfortable.

Nan Nevet arrived one day to tell her that Cuckold Dick, Walles and Winchard were safely back in the Bermudas and that Grace had got away. Barbary was grateful for their safe deliverance, but with the going of Grace she felt marooned. She'd lost touch with Ireland, Connaught, O'Hagan.

But gradually the relief of not being involved became restful, silence after a lifetime's clatter. She'd done what she could. She had nothing left for trickery and subterfuge.

There was no responsibility. There was time. She went for walks without having any other object than to enjoy walking. Rob, who'd shown his trust in the dibs by going back to London, sent servants to help her put the manor into shape, and she began to enjoy letting them wait on her.

Whenever she felt trapped, she told herself that she could go any time she liked. Grace was safe, no longer hostage to a dibs. Anyway, it was childish of Rob to think he could bind her by a dibs. She *could* go. If she wanted. Cuckold Dick was still in the whiskey trade, she could board one of his ships to Ireland any time. But Ireland didn't have O'Hagan. Ireland had the O'Neill.

She might stay on here for a while and rest. Hadn't she earned some rest, for God's sake? So she stayed, made free to do so by the thought that she was also free to go.

Then Rob came down to see how she was getting on and take her back to London with him. He was awkward and stilted, but trying hard. 'You have done well here, Margaret. But it is time for you to see your new home. I have sent for Henry.'

'Can't I look after him here?'

His face set heavily. 'He must be introduced into society. I should prefer it if you would accompany me to Betty House.'

In London she would be nearer Cuckold Dick and her means of escape when she wanted it. 'Very well, Rob.'

Standing at the Strand entrance, the magnificence of Betty House took her breath away. She'd known Rob was doing well – he was now a gentleman of the Privy Chamber – but not as well as this. Betty House stood on the site of the old Abbey of St Mary, Rounceval, which had decayed after its suppression into messuages and allotments.

'The Queen granted me the land for the house,' said Rob.

'Did she grant you the ruddock to build it?'

For the first time since they'd made their bargain he smiled. 'No.' He didn't even correct her use of Order cant.

It must have cost thousands, tens of thousands. They passed through gates surmounted by armorial stone lions carrying shields on which were entwined the letters RB and into a courtyard some eighty feet square. She cricked her neck staring at towers and turrets and an oriel window, three storeys high. It took the entire morning to show her both house and gardens. Despite everything, she was touched that he wanted to impress her.

'You see, Margaret. All the way down to Scotland Yard in that direction. Lean out, you can glimpse Whitehall. And down there to the old Lady Wharf. Betty Wharf now.'

The furnishing was not completed. 'There'll be tapestry here, of course.' But the bare rooms were lovely with their gracious dimensions and their carved foliated friezes with the entwined RB medallions. Even the cisterns were leaden works of art into which were impressed Tudor roses and more RBs.

'And this will be your room.' A private staircase led to it, high in one of the towers, circular, panelled, with a great bay window overlooking the river. She fought against being overwhelmed. 'Oatmeal this is, Rob.'

She'd gone too far. 'Will you help me or not? I'll not have my son speaking cant or being shamed by a mother who talks it.'

A mother. She would be a mother. She would be mistress of all this. She supposed she could put up with it for a while at least, just to keep her bargain. 'My dear Sir Rob,' she drawled beautifully, 'I can most certainly try.'

And she did. The shapes in the Deer Park receded as this new luxury became first a novelty and then a drug.

She went to Lady Russell and hired her services as adviser. Armed with Rob's purse and Lady Russell's taste, she called in furniture makers, bed suppliers, statuary and porcelain importers, needlewomen and ironworkers. She took on servants and entertained. She went to dressmakers and hired a dancing master. She was astounded by her own enthusiasm and told herself it was a hiatus. 'Just to swim *with* the tide for once.'

It was conying really, using the swank, all the old Order pretences to be accepted as a lady. When she'd attended court functions during Rob's absence, she had, at Mr Secretary's suggestion, kept in the background. Now that Rob was back she was, of course, no longer invited to court, but beneath the royal circle existed another consisting of women, wives and mistresses who were not acceptable to Elizabeth but who nevertheless formed a high society of their own. And it was into this scene that she now stepped, and enjoyed it.

So she stayed. She told herself it was for Henry's sake, and partly it was.

Ebullient little boy though he was, he was disturbed by being taken away from his mother and woke up at nights

494

crying for her. Rob, probably because he'd never cared for the woman who had been the only mother he'd known, couldn't understand it. 'Jesu, boy, can't you see this is for your profit?'

'Rip me, Rob, he's only six years old.' A year younger than when she'd lost her own mother. She put her arms around the child. 'There, pigsney. When the season's over you shall go back to Kerswell and holiday with your mother. Look, I'm writing her a letter to tell her you've met Mr Secretary Cecil, and how well you look in your russet doublet.'

Elizabeth, according to Rob, took with resignation the news that this favourite of hers was a father. So was Essex. So was Raleigh. She could not imagine why the men in her life should wish to breed, but it seemed they must. She asked how old was 'the little fellow', wondered without much interest why she had not heard of him before, and did not ask for him to be presented.

In the sub-culture that existed outside court, however, Henry was taken to every household of note and introduced with a flourish by his surrogate mother. 'Lord, but he was so sickly. We felt it better to leave him in Devon to be raised by his wet nurse until now.' If it was marked that Henry was the least sickly child and, despite warnings, occasionally referred to the wet nurse in Devon as 'Mother', nobody commented on it; in that society there were too many skeletons in the cupboards to point out anyone else's.

Barbary was corresponding regularly with Helen who, to her relief, seemed to have taken the loss of her son with the glazed equanimity with which she accepted all situations. Barbary knew Rob had other women, and that during his frequent trips to Bristol to oversee the outfitting of his merchant ships he also journeyed to Kerswell and Helen, and was always surprised at his reluctance to admit it. She didn't mind. Well, next time he could take Henry as well. The boy was getting over his grief, but he was still homesick.

To alleviate it, she began to attach the child to herself. She couldn't out-mother Helen, nor did she want to, but she had skills that Helen didn't have.

'How do you do that?' asked Henry, running down the

walkway to retrieve the dagger which still quivered through the heart of a rose.

Barbary was modest. 'I'm rusty. I was aiming for the bud.'

'But how do you *do* it? I want to do it. I want to do it. Show me.'

She had plenty more tricks up her sleeve, not all of them pleasing to Rob: 'Margaret, I will not have Henry taught to cheat at dice.'

'It is not cheating, Rob. I was merely demonstrating how to put them in with the four-side down and flick the shaker, like this, so terces come out every time. It's something to stand him in good stead in later life.'

'His later life will be in honest society, not the Order.'

'Have you diced in honest society lately?' asked Barbary, who had.

With servants and a tutor to take away its drudgery, she found parenthood immensely worthwhile. Henry had all the character and strength of will necessary to carry him into successful adulthood and she did not fret, as Rob did, over trying to mould it. What the child felt for her was not the love he had for Helen but friendship, and the greater friends they became the harder it was to make the effort to abandon him.

Rob said: 'You have behaved excellently, Margaret. I thank you,' and presented her with a diamond brooch in the shape of a dragonfly. Because she was prepared to say it was, Henry's legitimacy was beyond question, a line of Bettys could be established. She had fulfilled the dibs. And still she stayed.

Then she found that she had acquired not one child, but three.

Roland, the steward, entered what Rob had somewhat optimistically called the 'sewing chamber', and which Barbary, being unable to sew, used as her private sitting room. She was doing accounts.

'A visitor, my lady. I have put him in the gallery.'

'Who is it, Roland?'

Roland's swagger left him. 'I have forgot the name, my lady.'

Servants. 'One of these days, Roland, I'm going to take that staff of yours and stuff it up . . . the chimney.' She'd

496

had to promote him from footman because there wasn't a steward to be had in the whole of London and Whitehall.

'I'm sorry, my lady.'

'I'll be out in a minute, tell him. Sweetmeats and malmsey, Roland.'

'Yes, my lady.'

She went to her looking-glass and dallied. One did not rush to greet unexpected visitors, apparently. 'One's steward makes him comfortable in some spacious apartment,' Lady Russell had said, 'that he may examine its riches. One's butler brings him sweetmeats and malmsey, while you, the hostess, make yourself *point-device* in your boudoir. Then you go to him, taking him into some other grand apartment . . .'

Was that grey in her hair, or a trick of light? Was it time to call in the dyers? No. The light, thank God. Should she put on a patch? The hell with it, patches might be the rage, but she still couldn't put one on without getting mastick all over her fingers.

The plunket samite had turned out well with billiment lace. The face in the glass smiled as she thought how far she'd come in dressing since the O'Neill had sent her one of his mistress's outfits all those years ago when she'd been staying with the Spensers. The Spensers, Maccy, the children, Dublin, Munster, Rosh, the hanging woman, O'Hagan . . . Think of something else.

Tomorrow she must call in the ruff-maker and get another rapato; she'd worn this one at too many events for it to be seen again, and Rob insisted that she keep up appearances. Which suited her down to the ground; she had succumbed to a weakness for wearing beautiful things, as she had succumbed to having servants, entertaining, living in a house where every turn brought beauty to the eye. She had never been privy to riches on this scale, not even at Penshurst, and there was no doubt of its seduction. She might linger lovingly over thoughts of the good old days in the Bermudas and Connaught, but they'd been bloody uncomfortable. Every time she climbed the steps to her four-poster bed with its needle-point hangings and goose-feather mattress, while a maid hung away the clothes she'd taken off, the prospect of exchanging it for a ship's cot or a palliasse became that tinge less inviting. After all, Rob was keeping to his promise and letting her sleep in it alone, and a bargain *was* a bargain. Henry really couldn't afford to lose her yet. Dammit, Ireland had cost her enough, for Jesu's sake. A wiser head than hers had told her not to go back.

A pair of startled eyes stared back at her. Why should she? What was there for her now? O'Neill? He'd tricked her. O'Hagan? He'd left her. Her grandmother? Will? Well, yes, but there was no rush . . .

Lord, the visitor. Etiquette or no etiquette, one didn't leave somebody waiting this long. She went out into the gallery.

Like the rest of Betty House, the gallery imposed dignity on its occupants, and Barbary's progress along it was a stately rustle of silk. Its 120-foot length on the south side was nearly all windows, 1,500 separate panes of glass, looking out on the Thames. It might be draughty when there was a southerly blow but the effect was superb. Every recess in the opposite wall had a table covered with Turkish carpet, or contained statuary and other *vertu*, while the spaces between were lined with tapestry. They'd economised here; the tapestry was actually by Hicks of Warwickshire, not Gobelins of Paris, but it took an expert to tell the difference.

A figure at the end of the gallery stood up at her approach. Barbary's acquired fashion sense assessed it. Fairly well dressed, though the copotain hat was a mistake and, oh dear, the marquisetto beard was no longer the *ton*. And whoever it was was impressed by his surroundings, it showed in the way he stood, and nobody in the right circles *ever* showed he was impressed . . .

'Edmund.' She stumbled over her high heels as she ran towards him. It was as if thinking about Munster had summoned him up.

'Lady Betty. How well you look.'

Suspiciously she squinted at him under her lashes. Did he mean how well she looked compared to the mess she'd been when first put in his charge in Dublin? Better than she'd looked in a muddy potato field in Munster? Was he going into an I-remember-you-when? No, he wasn't, bless him. Edmund Spenser was thrilled by acquaintance with the great. Barbary's dress, jewels, her husband, her house declared she had achieved greatness. Therefore she was one more with whom he could be thrilled to be acquainted. He wouldn't belittle her because he didn't want her belittled.

'Forgive me, Lady Betty, for the intrusion. But with Sir Rob away . . .'

'My dear Edmund, we're old friends,' she said with grandeur. 'Sir Rob is in Bristol for the moment.' She sat him down and handed him sweetmeats. 'How are things at court?' It was kindness to assume he knew, though now she came to think about it she'd only heard vague references to him, as if he'd been running around on the edges, tugging at people's attention.

But it was a sore point. 'Ah, Lady Betty, what times of envy and detraction we do live in.'

'Do we?'

They most certainly did. 'Our peerless Majesty herself was so graciously pleased with "The Faerie Queen" as to grant me a pension of fifty pounds a year, but there are those who put difficulties in my way of getting it.'

She gathered he meant Burghley, or, more likely nowadays, Mr Secretary Cecil who couldn't stand Spenser any more than his father did. She saw his sudden recollection of her connection with both gentlemen. 'Though doubtless it is obstruction by the petty functionaries of great men too busily involved in affairs of state . . .' His retrieval of the mistake took time.

Poor old Edmund. He'd hitched his star so firmly to Raleigh's wagon that it had been extinguished when Sir Walter went into disgrace – and the Tower – for his marriage to Elizabeth Throckmorton, and though Raleigh was slowly working his way back to acceptance it looked as if his protégé wasn't enjoying the same rehabilitation. And the protégé couldn't think why. Sadly, he was saying: 'I had hoped my poor rhymes would have found favour with those having the virtue to hear them.'

God knows he'd tried; she couldn't enter a noble house without seeing a prominently displayed dedication by Edmund to its owner. Being new to the grovelling of the patronised for the patron, most of them churned her stomach. He hadn't missed anybody out. Just to make sure, he'd even addressed one 'To All the Gracious and Beautiful Ladies in the Court'. But it hadn't worked. The nobility was pleased to receive the poetry but not the poet.

She watched him as he talked, trying to reason why. His work left her numb with boredom, but, then, she wasn't educated; those who were said it was the greatest thing since Chaucer. (And a little of *him* went a long way, and all.) The thing was, you could know that Edmund had genius, but when you were with him you couldn't see where he kept it. It was as if it was something completely separate from the anxious, stubborn, obsequious, unremarkable little man himself.

His soul wasn't big enough, she decided. Now Philip Sidney – there was a poet if you liked – had been able to see all points of view, even the Irish. You couldn't imagine Philip standing by and watching while his side slaughtered unarmed men or hanged pregnant women. Spenser had. A blinkered little bugger, she thought. And boring. All she really wanted to hear about were his children.

'How are Catherine and Sylvestris?'

He was delighted. 'How kind of you to remember, Lady Betty. And you recall me to the point of my visit.' He paused. 'I'm getting married again.'

'My felicitations.'

He was blushing. 'An Irish country lass with the freshness of the dew about her.'

'Irish?'

'Anglo-Irish, of course. A Paleswoman from Youghal. Elizabeth Boyle. We are wedding at Cork. I shall leave wanton extravagance and false standards of worth and return to that savage land where yet there is simplicity.'

'Very nice. And the children?'

His hands clasped. 'Lady Betty, would you, would Sir Rob take them into your household? With you they can receive affection and introduction into the highest society I could wish for them. Your tenderness towards them and their poor mother emboldens me to ask it . . .' He was going on at length, something about the sacred Muses being the nurses of Nobility, or vice versa, her and Rob being immortalised by the poem he would dedicate to them. She stared at him, remembering the agony it had been when he'd taken the children to London and she'd had to tear their hands from her neck.

She shook herself. Would Rob agree? He might, he'd probably be flattered to contribute to the tradition where the children of a good family were sent to learn their manners in great households. And he admired Spenser's work; he might like to be immortalised. And he was beginning to rely on her judgement.

She gathered that dew-fresh Elizabeth Boyle was nervous at starting family life with two stepchildren, that Spenser wanted peace and quiet in which to compose a new poem, a wedding ode 'Epithalamion' which would far surpass . . .

'I shall speak to Sir Rob,' she cut in, 'but I think you can take it that he will agree.'

She accepted his gratitude graciously. She could have kissed him. He found her worthy to entrust her with the most precious things he had because it would lead to their betterment. She was no longer Barbary of the Order playing at being Lady Betty. She *was* Lady Betty.

Nineteen English companies of foot and six troops of horse, 1,750 men in all, set out from Dundalk under the command of Marshal Henry Bagenal on a routine march to take supplies to the fort at Monaghan. The size of the force was merely to show the Tudor flag along the Ulster border and to discourage any clan that was feeling disaffected.

Monaghan was the most central of a line of English garrisons along what the Dublin administration liked to think of as a Hadrian's Wall dividing the north of Ireland from civilised territory; except that there was no wall, just isolated forts, and very few of those. Nevertheless the Irish, and especially the O'Neill, whose territory they encroached on, found their presence an insult; the Armagh garrison, for instance, occupied one of the country's oldest and most sacred cathedrals, a hill site presented to St Patrick himself by Queen Macha. And in the last ten years the English had been edging the invisible wall northwards. Another fort had been built above Armagh on the River Blackwater, and others were planned to fill the gaps, when and if Elizabeth sanctioned the cost of building them.

Lately the clans had been giving more trouble than usual.

The Marshal was marching in the usual three divisions of vanguard, battle and rearward, with himself and other officers in the rear. The vanguard, the point of least danger, if there was danger, consisted largely of raw recruits fresh out from England, but to counteract their inexperience the column contained some of the two thousand veterans whom Elizabeth had recently recalled from Brittany to stiffen her Irish army.

On the second day's march the howling began. Even the Brittany veterans, used to battle, were unsettled by an apparently empty countryside wailing as if the hills and trees had voice; the recruits were badly shaken. From nowhere a band of Irish shot appeared ahead of the van, firing with rapidity and accuracy. The English recruits crumbled at once and a company of veterans, musket and pike, had to rush forward to steady them. As fast as they'd come, the Irish disappeared.

The column reached Monaghan without further incident. The fort was built with the stones of an abbey the English had pulled down for the purpose. Supplies were carried into the quartermaster's storehouse, wounded seen to, the dead buried, weapons cleaned. They'd already burned a good deal of their powder.

The next day, at ten in the morning, the English left a fresh company in the garrison and began their return march. This time there was a better distribution of officers and men. Bagenal moved up to the vanguard, and two of the Brittany officers took command in the battle and rear with the recruits.

Without heavily laden wagons to slow it down the column stepped out briskly into a sunny morning and a nightmare. Three miles out from Monaghan the howling began again. There was nothing to be seen except echoing hills and the trembling reeds of bog, but from either side of the column the bog began to spit fire. Suddenly up ahead were what appeared to be three hundred English soldiers, red-coated, firing English calivers. To be attacked by doppelgangers broke the already stressed recruits who ran and had to be replaced by the battle division. Then the red-coats had gone, as if a mirror had shattered. Silence fell over the pretty countryside, birdsong came back. Bagenal ordered the march to continue.

Ahead was a stream and on its far bank, in full view, was a horseman. They said later he shouted: 'Let it be

502

seen today whether the Queen or I own Ulster.' The O'Neill had finally declared himself.

The place was called Clontibret.

Most of the English stood still, but a Palesman called Seagrave spurred forward into the attack with forty troopers. As if by magic Tyrone cavalry appeared behind the O'Neill, shooting. They missed Seagrave, who reached O'Neill, knocked him off his horse and fell on top of him. O'Neill was saved by one of his subsidiary chiefs, O'Cahan, who cut off Seagrave's arm. O'Neill managed to reach his dagger and finished him off.

From then on the column was under continuous attack. The Irish horse was worked forward by troops, each troop protected from English fire and cavalry by a formation of shot. It was a manoeuvre that brought them right up to the English ranks. Weighed down by its wounded, but showing courage, the column stopped, fought, staggered on, fought, staggered on. Irish horse and foot came screaming out of the scrub time and again, the kerns whirling along at the cavalry's stirrups like acrobats, firing, stabbing, and then being whirled back out of danger by the horsemen. Any soldiers foolhardy enough to pursue them were never seen again. There was no clear front. Ammunition was low. Bagenal gave the only order he could, to press on with the march, suffering loss, men dropping around him. It went on for eight hours.

By dusk the English had covered fourteen miles to a moorland height where they fell down in battle formation. Bagenal's pewter dishes were melted down for bullets and one of Bagenal's servants – an Irishman, Felim O'Hanlon – was sent off to make his way to Newry and bring help.

The next morning the relief column came marching over the moor to find weary and wounded Englishmen encamped in an empty countryside. The Irish had gone. The O'Neill, too, had run out of ammunition.

Back at Newry Marshal Bagenal, humiliated and ashamed, recorded his losses as merely thirty-one killed and one hundred and nine wounded. In fact, the English casualties had been something like seven hundred.

Numbers, however, were not the point. The point was that it had happened. The O'Neill had used Irishmen who had been trained by Elizabeth's own officers in the time when she'd trusted him, and, moreover, used them in a new kind of warfare. Contrary to what everybody had been led to believe, the enemy was not rabble. One of the Brittany captains privately wrote to Cecil saying that the O'Neill had proved himself a skilful commander of troops as disciplined and accurate as any he'd faced before, brilliantly using familiar terrain, and that it would take a better-trained, better-equipped army than had so far been put in the field to defeat them.

Marshal Henry Bagenal had one cause for triumph, however. The shifting shape that was sometimes the Earl of Tyrone, Her Majesty's loyal subject, and sometimes the O'Neill, Gaelic chieftain and backer of rebels, had stopped flickering and resolved itself into a figure on a horse directing troops against the English. He had shown himself as the arch-rebel his brother-in-law had always said he was.

Neither the English nor the Irish bothered themselves with why he had chosen that moment to cross his Rubicon. For the Ulster clans which had grown sick of his shifting, it was a joy to be celebrated in savagery. As if somebody had trailed gunpowder along the invisible Hadrian's Wall and lit it, flames exploded in colonial fort, castle and homestead along a line from east to far west, killing and burning military and civilian alike. Humiliation and cruelty were revenged in humiliation and cruelty. Sir Richard Bingham's brother George was murdered in the library of his Connaught castle.

The rising in response to Clontibret was so immediate that it was happening while letters bearing the news of the defeat were still on their four-day journey to England.

'We shan't be too long, Rob. Sylvestris is at his Greek with the new tutor. Catherine is spending the day at the Cumberlands.'

'I don't like Henry going to the Tower.'

'He won't be coming into Thomas's. He can go off with Winchard and visit the menagerie.'

Rob looked up from his desk. 'It does my consequence no good, Margaret, for my son to be accompanied by an ape whose knuckles brush his shins. When Winchard opened the gate to Sir James Harington the other day Sir

James refused to enter until he heard him speak.'

'That's Winchard's job, to frighten people off. Nobody's going to attack me, or the children, with Winchard about.' Sometimes she herself wondered why she'd hired Winchard, but he was one of her naughtinesses, the deliberate lapses to remind Rob, when he became over pompous, that his past too lay in the Order and even if he was ashamed of it, she wasn't, and that she still had a will of her own. Winchard was her new Clampett.

'They wouldn't attack you anyway,' said Rob. He was still sulking from the incident at Paul's churchyard two days before when his purse had been cut. The loss of the purse hadn't upset him as much as having it returned a few minutes later by a figure who muttered: 'Didn't realise you was Barb's husband,' before disappearing into the crowd.

'Who was it?' Barbary asked, interested. 'Damber the Filch or Harry Poyning? Harry works Paul's.'

'I have no idea who it was,' said Rob, 'and I could wish you didn't.'

'Anyway,' said Barbary, pursuing the Winchard argument, 'Henry likes him. And if you think you can find a better you are most welcome to try.'

Both statements were clinchers. Henry was the apple of Rob's eye, and good servants were so hard to come by that acquiring them was a specialist business.

'Very well. Very well.' He generally gave in nowadays.

With Winchard and Henry she went down the garden, where the under-gatekeeper unlocked the gate onto the wharf and Winchard called up an eastward boat. Strictly speaking, they should have kept a barge of their own – Essex kept two – but, as Rob pointed out, the Earl of Essex was in debt to the tune of £20,000; he even owed the Queen £3,000, *and* she'd asked for it back.

As the boat sculled under the raised portcullis into the basin of the Tower of London's watergate, a guard she hadn't seen before asked for her authority, but his sergeant came bustling out of the postern to hand her up the steps. '*Good* afternoon, Lady Betty. Can't stay away from us then? Hot for May, in't it, Lady Betty. Brought the little lad today? Arternoon, young gentleman. Mind your step, now, Lady Betty. No need to show you the way. Good day to you, Lady Betty.'

He looked after her, appreciatively watching her progress into the ward of St Thomas's. Her kirtle and bodice were of emerald satin embroidered on stomacher and bodice in a bold coral pattern; round her neck was a gold carcanet; her hair was uncovered except for an audacious, nodding ostrich feather. She left behind in the river-smelling basin a whiff of best Italian scent. Even though she was attended by a servant who looked like a gorilla, she was the glass of fashion. 'That's Lady Betty,' he said.

'I gathered,' said the guard.

'I do not wish to hear, Henry,' Lady Betty was saying, 'that you have been poking sticks at the lion through the bars. Nor you, Winchard. It will be a hot lion today and it might get angry again. Do you hear me?'

'Yes, ma'am,' said Henry.

'Yes, Barb,' said Winchard.

'Winchard.'

'Yes, Lady Betty.'

'And then you may go to the Ordnance Tower and look at the guns. Tell Sir Roger you have my lord of Essex's permission. I shall come there.'

'H'ray,' said Henry.

Winchard winked. 'Guns, eh, Barb?'

'Winchard.' She watched the two disparate figures walk away, one lumbering, one skipping. Winchard's nods and winks to her past were rare and so impenetrable as to be comprehensible only to those in the know, but she tried to cure him of them, mainly to prevent Rob from dismissing him.

She stood where she was for a while, gloating, looking towards the centre of the grey complexity of buildings where she had once been incarcerated. Her visits to the Tower were occasioned by tragedy, but there were moments when the contrast between her consequence then and now made her want to shout: 'Look at me. Look at me, you key-clankers. Recognise me?' They didn't, of course. Two visits previously she had passed Keeper Morgan and, although he'd been one of the kinder warders during her imprisonment, she'd been unable to resist a petty revenge for it: 'Do you not salute a lady when you pass her, my fat fellow? I shall inform your superiors of this discourtesy.' Kept her happy all day, that had.

Oh well. Barbary turned into St Thomas's tower gateway. She nodded to the guards, who saluted, not even bothering to examine the basket she carried, and made her way through the hall that Edward I had built, to the turret staircase leading to the gallery that in turn led to the chamber above the watergate. It was a beautiful room with a tiled floor, vaulted ceiling, and windows fitted with coloured glass that looked out onto the river and today were open, letting in the sunlight and the calls of watermen, a room unusually sumptuous and escape-worthy for a prisoner, even if he was a king's son. But the prisoner, who lay in a great bed facing the windows, wasn't going anywhere.

'How are you today?' asked Barbary, leaning forward on tiptoe to kiss him. His breath smelled of urine. She opened her basket. 'I've brought you apple jelly mixed with port wine and a receipt of my cook; he makes it from elicampane roots, whatever they are, and—'

'Whiskey.'

'Sir John, you'll get me hanged. The doctors—'

'Abortionist bastards. Whiskey, woman. What say you?' He'd grown thin and was as yellow as the late Jackman had been, but he was still in command.

Barbary looked at Cutress, Sir John's valet, who shrugged. She brought out a bottle from a locker, picked up a feeding glass from beside the bed, crossed to the window, tipped out the medicine and filled it with whiskey. She had to hold the glass while he sucked greedily at its tube. The Queen, conscience-stricken by what she had done to her half-brother, was sending her own doctors every day, but it was too late. Sir John Perrot was dying.

All Barbary's and Mr Secretary Cecil's efforts to prove the evidence against him false had gone for nothing. Despite pleas from Burghley, his son and even Essex, whose sister was Sir John's daughter-in-law, the Queen had been determined to have him arraigned for treachery. Her Justices sitting at Westminster refused to allow Cecil's and Barbary's findings to be taken into account, the forged letter was accepted as prima facie evidence, and Sir John was condemned to death.

His arch enemies, Loftus and Wallop, had come over for the trial. Barbary, watching them from the ladies' gallery, could see that even to them the verdict was a surprise. By then it wasn't a surprise to her. Sir John's supposed treating with Spain was not the issue; the thrust of the charges were Sir John's insults to the Queen. In effect he was on trial for hurting Elizabeth's vanity. The jury buzzed with horror at hearing Her Majesty referred to as a 'filthy hypocrite', 'a base, bastard, pissing, kitchen woman', and, with Sir John shouting even juicier epithets from the dock, they returned a guilty verdict after only three-quarters of an hour.

It was then that the whole point of the travesty became apparent; the Queen declined to sign the death warrant and refused to sanction the usual custom whereby a traitor's property was confiscated. Sir John's heirs would be able to inherit. Mr Secretary Cecil had been as near anger as Barbary had ever seen him. 'Just to teach him a lesson,' he said, slamming his small hands on his desk. 'That's all it was, to teach him a lesson.'

'Well, she's done it,' hissed Barbary. 'Now she can let him out of the Tower.'

'She will,' the Elf had said, soothingly. 'She will.'

But by the time she did, Sir John was too ill to be moved.

'Fill it up again, mistress,' he told Barbary when he'd finished his bottle. 'I'll keep it under the bedclothes. Quickly, the doctors are coming.'

But it wasn't the doctors, it was the Lord Lieutenant of the Tower, Sir Owen Hopton, in a sweat. 'Forgive the intrusion, Sir John. I hope you are better today. But I have need of your Irish knowledge . . . ah, and Lady Betty. Excellent.' Sir Owen always became distrait when he saw Barbary, as if he was trying to remember where he'd seen her before.

'What is it?' snapped Sir John.

'And hold your voice down, sir,' said Barbary sharply. 'You are in a sickroom.' Keeping Sir Owen off balance was another of her revenges.

'Do you think it's a prelude to invasion?' whispered Sir Owen, taking a chair by Sir John's bed, 'because if it is, the work involved in putting the Tower back into war readiness should be taken in hand at once.'

'What say you, blast you?'

'Haven't you heard? No, of course not, I've only just heard myself. Clontibret, a place called Clontibret in

508

Ireland. Half of Bagenal's force wiped out in the Earl of Tyrone's ambush. The Queen is publishing a—'

'Are you sure it was the O'Neill?'

'How do they know it was the O'Neill?' Sir John's and Barbary's questions were simultaneous.

'Most certainly it was him. Stood across a river and jeered that he'd be King of Ireland within the month. His kerns cut off our soldiers' heads. The cur, the treacherous cur, after Her Majesty raised him from the dust.'

'Tell us what happened, man,' said Sir John, quietly. Barbary went to the window as Sir Owen told what he knew. One of the guild barges was rowing by, its pennant so long that it trailed in the water. Watermen, waiting for a fare, were gaming with dice on the steps of the wharf. Had he used cannon? 'He kills people.' *She* killed people. If you supplied a man with guns, he'd use them. She'd known that. Ordinary people, like those men down there, men who joined the English army to get away from poverty at home, men no more responsible for Ireland's past than she was. Metal came flaming out of gun barrels and cut bits of them off. It had seemed so indefinite, the O'Neill had temporised so long that it had seemed as if nothing would make a difference, certainly not a few guns.

Oh God, Will. He was in the midst of it, and making more guns for the O'Neill. She'd get him back. She'd send a message through Cuckold Dick's whiskey boats to Grace O'Malley and tell her to get Will out of it. Grace could do it, she could do anything. But then her grandmother must return to Connaught and stay there, where she'd be safe.

Still with her back to the room she said: 'Why did he move now?'

'Because he's a cur, a treacherous cur.'

Sir John said: 'Because they demanded his son.' She turned round. The old man in the bed was crackling a letter between his weak fingers. 'James, *my* son, wrote to me. Dublin demanded O'Neill send in his eldest son as a hostage. It showed him, d'you see. He'd never be an Englishman to the English. They treated him like a chieftain in a wolf-cloak, not an Earl in doublet and hose.'

'And quite right too.'

Barbary turned on the Lord Lieutenant of the Tower.

'Out.' Sir John was crying, she wouldn't have a fool like Sir Owen see him cry.

'But there's the matter of my lord Bingham. Will the Queen release him now, do you think?'

And that was the best of Barbary's revenges. Though Sir John was in the Tower, so was one of his greatest enemies. Sometimes she would stand beneath the window of the small, uncomfortable cell in which Elizabeth had ordered Sir Richard Bingham to be confined, and imagine for her pleasure what fear and humiliation he was suffering. She wanted him hanged so that she could watch him on the gallows, hear him beg as a little boy who could read had begged.

But she couldn't be bothered with all that now. 'Out with you.'

Sir Owen went, and she crossed to the bed and wiped the yellow, waxy face with her handkerchief. 'Don't now, don't. God knows you did your best, my lord. It would never have happened if they'd listened to you.' Why didn't he swear and rage? How could he be this ill and still care so much? 'You were the best Englishman Ireland ever had.'

Cutress was in distress on the other side of the bed. 'Do I go for the doctors, my lord, my lady?'

The wrinkled eyelids opened and the pop-eyes of a Tudor glared at him. 'Whiskey.' They gave him whiskey and he rallied. 'Well, well, it's begun. The end has begun.'

Barbary began repacking her basket. 'Maybe it's not the end.'

'What say you?' His hand took hers in a suddenly strong grip. 'You think he'll beat her, do you?' He was still shrewd.

'Well . . .' Something might happen. Elizabeth might sicken of her rebellious Irish, might withdraw, pigs *might* fly. Anything was possible.

'I tell you, mistress, it's the end of the Irish. He's offended her, d'ye see. She'll never forgive him. I know. Don't *I* know? She'll go all out. Watch the old cheese-parer spend the cash on arms now.' He fell back on his pillows. 'When she might have spent it on peace.'

She wiped his face. The flesh was falling away from the flat plane of its bones. As she kissed him his hand tight-

ened once more on hers. 'Barbary.' It was the first time
he'd called her that.

'Yes?'

'Don't go back. D'ye hear me? Don't go back.'

Henry, most definitely his father's son, wanted to return
home by river, as they'd come. 'I don't want to go in a
chair, it's eff, an eff word.'

'Effeminate, you mean – I hope. Maybe, but my shoes
hurt and I must call in at Paul's.'

He studied her. 'You do look tired.'

Two of the chairmen on Tower Hill, waiting to take
sightseers home, jumped for her custom. Henry balked
again. 'I can walk.'

'Very well, I'll have Winchard ride with me, and *he* can
tell me about the lion.' Grinning, Henry clambered into
the chair. He was aggressive and occasionally a bully,
but, young as he was, his humour gave him a flexibility
his father had never possessed.

The middle aisle of St Paul's had a different sound to it
today; usually it rang with young bloods shouting their
conversations to each other over the noisy trade of the
stalls to attract attention. But today there was the low,
concentrated buzz of discussion. Winchard cleared a way
for her through the crowd round one of the pillars so that
she could read the news sheet. It was long and full of
invective against O'Neill – among other things it called
him the 'Great Satan' – but it contained no more facts
than Sir Owen Hopton had given. Below was another
sheet declaring 'Her Majesty's grief at the loss and death
of so many good soldiers'. The mood around the pillar
was bellicose with a touch of panic. 'It's a cockatrice den.
Always was. Wipe out the lot of them, I say.' 'Gad, the
Queen should make me Lord Deputy, I'd show them.'
'She should send Essex. *He'd* show them.' 'What if the
bastard joins up with the Spanish?'

She felt very tired. Back in the chair she closed her
eyes listening to the new note that came into the voices
outside as the news of Clontibret spread. At the top of
Ludgate Hill she and Henry were bounced by their chair
bumping to the ground. 'Trouble, m'lady,' said one of
the chairmen.

She leaned out of the window, pushing Henry back.

Coming up the hill was a running footman. By some unwritten but immutable law nearly all running footmen were Irish. Livery-suited, wiry-bodied, thick-accented men, they were the butt of Londoners' jokes as they jogged through the crowds with their employers' letters and their shouted 'Shtand aside now. Will ye shtand aside dere.'

This one was really running. He'd outstripped the crowd pursuing him, but his legs were beginning to wobble while the mob was gathering fresh recruits as it came on. She could hear the yells: 'Paddy bastard. Irish murderer. Death to O'Neill.'

She leaned further out and shouted to the chairmen: 'Put me down near that door. Quick.' And then, 'Grab him, Winchard. Shove him in here.'

The chairmen were glad to veer out of the mob's path. As the man staggered past, Winchard took hold of him by his crutch and his belt and threaded him neatly into the open offside door of the chair so that he slithered across Barbary's knees. She shut the door and opened the near side. They were right across the entrance to the Black Bush. She pointed into it, pushing the footman off her. 'Through that passage there and down the steps. There's a back door.' It was an escape route she'd used more than once.

The man squirmed an agonised face towards her. 'Tank you, your ladyship, tank you.'

'Try running.'

She got out. At her side Winchard was making growling noises. Some of the men were trying to enter the Black Bush but were getting entangled in the chair's long handles. The footman had time to get away. She faced the mob, stallholders mostly, a butcher with a cleaver, women with broomsticks, the usual preacher – cause of all the trouble – still baying for Irish blood.

She couldn't have made herself heard over the shouting so she didn't try, just stood there, prepared to trade her soul, if she'd had one, for the confiscated Clampett. After a moment the chairmen joined her; they didn't want to lose their fare. The mob stared at the four, the four stared back. If Barbary had known it, the look on her face, her red hair, was reminiscent of a younger, shorter Elizabeth.

512

'Thinks herself a queen, don't she?' One of the women was trying to get her comrades forward. 'Cut off our heads, eh?'

The fancy tickled the crowd, the mood changed. She was bowed ironically back into the chair and cheered all the way down to the City gate.

'That was exciting, wasn't it?' asked Henry, not quite sure.

'Yes.'

'An adventure?'

'Yes.'

'Did you know that man?'

'No. The crowd didn't either.'

'Why'd they want to beat him then?'

She rubbed her eyes. 'He was a scapegoat. It means they're blaming him for something somebody else did.'

'Why?'

'I don't know. Let me sleep.'

'You're very brave, aren't you?'

'Yes,' she said, 'I bloody well am.'

As he always was when she'd been out, Sylvestris was at the door to greet her. They looked at each other anxiously.

'How have you got on with the new tutor?' The previous tutor had been thrashing him regularly but the boy had never said a word. When at last she'd seen the marks, she'd gone after the man with a riding whip and Rob had been furious at her unladylike behaviour.

'Very well, ma'am, I thank you.'

She said to him in Irish: 'You prevaricating little anatomy of barebones, if I see a thrush's ankle of a lie from you I'll bate that skinny carcase of yours into frog's jelly.'

He grinned and answered in the same tongue: 'His breath smells, but he knows a lot and he's kind.'

'He'd better be.'

He'd been worrying on his own account. 'There was trouble out on the streets and I was afraid. With you being Irish . . .'

'Lord, boy, they wouldn't dare. I'll tell you about it later, but first I must see Sir Rob.'

'He's in the library. The Lord Chamberlain came and upset him, I think.' Sylvestris picked up emotional

513

undercurrents as a deer scented danger. Rob tried to be patient but considered the boy a milksop and said so. Barbary thought he was the bravest child she'd ever met; he'd kept quiet about the tutor's over-enthusiastic cane because he'd been anxious that Barbary's reaction would get her into trouble with Rob – as it had.

The depth of her affection for Edmund Spenser's son had taken her by surprise, as had his for her. He'd been too young when he left Spenser Castle to recall much about it consciously, but, perhaps because he'd been miserable at his aunt's house in London, he attributed to the period when his mother was alive every possible happiness. Somewhere at the back of his memory existed a sun-drenched Irish paradise which, because she'd been part of it, bathed Barbary in gold. His father had somewhat shamefacedly told her the boy insisted on studying Irish alongside his Latin and Greek, 'though it may be no bad thing for his inheritance that he comprehends what the serfs are saying'. But whereas, like most of the undertakers, Edmund loved the land and not the natives of Ireland, Sylvestris made no such distinction and pestered his sister to tell him stories about Rosh and her family, and what she could remember of Irish legend.

He was an unremarkable-looking child with his father's straight, fairish hair, a weaker physique than Henry's but a mind much older. His perception attributed a vulnerability to Barbary which she didn't understand, but which made him constantly concerned for her, and because his sensitivity made him vulnerable, she was constantly concerned for him. She loved all her foster children but for Sylvestris the love was ferocious in its protectiveness. When he'd nearly died of the measles she never left his bedside, in a panic obeying every remedy the doctors suggested, wrapping and re-wrapping the feverish little body in new red flannel, praying. His recovery gave her more relief than she'd ever known, but worry for the child remained.

As she entered the library she was expecting to find Rob upset over Clontibret. She was wrong.

'Margaret,' he said, turning to her, 'disaster. She wants to come to supper.'

She didn't ask who; there was only one 'she'. 'Rob, all hell's broken loose in Ireland, there's mobs on the streets of London. It's a disaster the Queen wants to come to supper?'

'Yes,' he said coldly, 'it is.'

She slumped down onto a chair, trying to concentrate on his problem. She supposed it was a disaster. Elizabeth ate frugally, but her court didn't. The cost of feeding it was phenomenal and it was a cost Her Majesty frequently liked to put on somebody else. Her hosts were supposed to be flattered, but the favour could bankrupt the favoured.

'At least she hasn't asked to come and stay,' she said, remembering Sir Henry Sidney's sufferings during the royal visit to Penshurst.

'It's bad enough.' It wasn't just the horrendous price of the food, it was the pageantry to go with it. Elizabeth was easily bored, and more than one courtier had cracked his brain trying to think of magnificent novelties that would predispose the Queen towards him so that he would get at least something, a barony, a remunerative position, as reward for his outlay.

'Let's fob her off with a picnic.'

Rob's mouth tightened. 'Since only Ireland seems to interest you,' he said, 'perhaps I can gain your attention by telling you there's a chance I may be its next Lord Deputy.'

'Rob!'

He couldn't help smirking. 'Cecil's putting me forward.'

Cecil had put a lot of men forward for the post, so had Essex, and both had cancelled out each other's. She couldn't see it happening, and was glad not to. Rob responsible for the continuing genocide was something she couldn't face. 'But are you—' she was going to say 'are you up to it?' and amended it to 'Are you sure?' He was deluding himself; he was a sailor, not a general. Elizabeth would never send him. 'It destroys everybody. Look at them – Grey, Sir Henry Sidney, Sir John. And now with the O'Neill . . .'

'I know.' He himself was awed by the prospect. 'But I'm the man. I could do it. The curse is from political back-stabbing when one's not at court to counteract it, but I should be freer of that than most.'

That was true. It might happen, oh God, it might

515

happen. Rob had shown wisdom in avoiding the court's factions as far as it was possible. He'd attracted Elizabeth's favour by his bravery against the Armada and, once at court, he kept his place not by trying to out-charm Essex, at which he would have failed, but by being the Queen's honest, reliable sea-dog. His admiration for Raleigh had given way to caution when he saw how extreme the rivalry between him and Essex had become. Rob disliked extremes and distanced himself from his old friend. Raleigh had been hurt, but Raleigh, who had the self-preservation of a lemming, had gone down, and Rob had stayed up. He'd carried out his embassy to the Low Countries with cunning – there were times when Barbary thought Rob owed more to his Order training than he'd admit – and won Cecil's respect. Although the Elf manipulated him, it was done, like all the Elf's manipulations, so nobody would suspect, least of all Rob, that he was Cecil's man. It might happen.

'You're not as compromised as most,' she said, 'but—'

'I *am* compromised. You have compromised me.'

'How? For Jesus' sake, I've worked my buttons off—'

He held up a calm and irritating hand. 'I do not reproach you, Margaret, nor do I try to stop you doing what you doubtless consider your Christian duty, but your visits to the Tower have been a reproach to the Queen. She is tender on the subject of Sir John . . .'

'So she bloody well should be.'

'. . . and Ireland, and the slightest tarnish can affect her decision on this matter. Which is why a successful supper is vital.' He put his head in his hands, sententiousness gone. 'Help me, Margaret. I don't know how to do it.'

It was the first time he'd ever admitted powerlessness. She was shaken. 'I don't either. Can we afford it?'

'No. And we can't afford not to.' He got up and began striding about. 'Jesus, given time I could bring peace to that wretched country. I could. It isn't the aggrandisement, not even the place in history. I should like to earn God's grace as well as the Queen's before I die.'

He meant it. This Rob was a revelation, and she was amazed that she could have lived under the same roof with him without finding him out. And suppose he could do it? Suppose he was the man? She was light-headed with discovery. Dreams assembled themselves before her dazzled mind's eye. Reasoned government under a reasonable mind, the assimilation of two peoples into one happy nation.

'Rob, I must know. Do you really intend peace? And I mean peace for the Irish, not just for the English?'

'My dear Margaret, the two are indivisible.'

Only Sir John Perrot had known that, or at least he had been the only one to demonstrate that he knew it.

'Then we must have the Queen to supper.'

The noble ladies' gambling nights rotated between their houses, and tonight's was at Essex house in the 'small gaming chamber', a room in which the Pudding-in-a-Cloth could have been accommodated comfortably, And felt at home here, thought Barbary. The only difference between the cheating and plotting which went on in both establishments was that the Pudding's was professional.

She had been shocked the first time she realised Penelope Rich was palming cards. As did most of the lower orders, she'd assumed that high-born ladies led a life of uplift and good works. Then she'd sighed a comfortable sigh. Just like home, this was. If cheating was to be the order of the day, Barbary Clampett was their woman. So far it hadn't been necessary, their usual game being cards, especially Post and Pair which depended on bluff, what they called 'vying', and none of them could bluff their way out of a bucket. Rich's eyes sparkled if she got a pair, Frances Essex looked tragic if she didn't, Elizabeth Vernon bounced up and down if she drew a one or a two.

Barbary always played a catcher's game, losing some, never winning too much, waiting for the stake to be worth versing for. And tonight was the night. In the hours since her conversation with Rob she'd been flexing her fingers.

She was shown in and went into a deep curtsey, peering against the blaze of candles that concentrated light on the tables, and left the rest of the room in a rich darkness. 'Lady Essex. Lady Leicester. Lady Southampton. Lady Rich.' It was always tricky getting the precedence right; she was never sure whether a dowager countess, like Lettice, who was Essex's mother and now the widow of the Earl of Leicester, took priority over Essex's wife, Frances, or not. Or whether Penelope Rich as Essex's sister and daughter of the house should be above Essex's mother. But since Frances Essex was her hostess, Barbary put her first. That was one of the few things they were touchy about, their titles. Curtseying over, kissing began. 'Lady Betty. Welcome.'

'Lady Betty.'

'Lady Betty.'

'Lady Boggart.'

That was Penelope. Barbary grinned at her. 'And how's the rich Lord Rich? Still up nórth?'

Penelope Rich put her beautiful hands into an attitude of prayer. 'And long may he remain there.'

Barbary sniffed. 'Fee fi fo fum. I smell the blood of an Englishman. Where's Lord Mountjoy?'

Elizabeth Vernon squeaked with joy. She thought Barbary's jokes funny. Barbary liked her. 'The men are at bowls. How did you know?'

'My father was a necromancer.' Actually the smell of tobacco still in the air had told her he was visiting. Mountjoy was a chainsmoker. You could always tell when he and Penelope Rich had been consummating their illicit affair: she stank of Trinidado.

'Last week you said your father was a highwayman.'

'That'll teach you to believe the lower classes.' The moment she'd taken their measure she'd abandoned any pretence of being a lady. Rob had been horrified that she exalted not just her commonalty but her criminal commonalty. But she'd known what she was about. She couldn't have fooled women like these for long in any case; better to make a virtue out of something like the truth. They weren't sufficiently interested to investigate further; she was a novelty to them, and they loved novelty above everything. The two degrees, highest and lowest, were able to share a luxury not available to those in between – she remembered the rigid, watchful etiquette of colonial society in Ireland – the luxury of being what they were.

Actually, they reminded her of the bawds, though they were not so promiscuous. They didn't have to be. But they showed the same defiant shamelessness which, as with the bawds, arose from being isolated into a society of their own by the peculiarity of their circumstances.

All of them were banned from Elizabeth's presence; Lettice for having taken as her second husband the Queen's late favourite, the Earl of Leicester; Frances for having married the present favourite, the Earl of Essex; Elizabeth Vernon for marrying Wriothesley, Earl of Southampton; an absent Devereux sister, Dorothy, who'd married Sir John Perrot's son without permission. It was said there was more blue feminine blood outside court than in it.

Well-educated, witty, afraid of nobody except the Queen, they were forced to put their splendid energy into pranks, infuriating the Puritans by their fashions – their current rage was for men's doublets – scandalising foreigners by kissing visitors, male or female. Preachers railed against the power they had over their husbands, because, with no other outlet, they channelled their considerable political ambition through their menfolk.

Penelope Rich was the only one of them still in Elizabeth's favour, although she was openly carrying on with her brother's friend, Lord Mountjoy, and even she had been temporarily suspended from the Privy Chamber for being 'naughty' to the Queen. 'Well,' she'd said in explanation, 'what can you expect when I, an heir to the ancient aristocracy of England, have to put up with tantrums from a descendant of a Welsh butler?'

Barbary could see what it was that had enthralled Philip Sidney; her Devereux colouring was still lovely, but the 'Stella' of his poems had gone. Being sold off to the highest bidder against her will had coarsened her. She had a frenetic quality. Her indiscretions, like her cheating, were so blatant that they seemed designed to provoke challenge.

But she was a genius at gossip. 'How are the Northumberlands?' Barbary asked her, settling down. The atrocity stories about the Earl and Countess of Northumberland were as enjoyable as they were incredible. 'Does she still threaten to eat his heart in salt?'

'My dear,' drawled Penelope Rich, 'they made up. The Earl wants an heir to spite his brothers whom he says, next to his wife, he hates above any. But I think it must be off again because he went to that ferret Cecil the other day and said his wife was plotting to have James on the throne and that it would be a good thing if Cecil told the Queen who would have her beheaded.'

'What did Cecil say?'

'He said he didn't think it would enhance the Earl's reputation to be known as the man who had betrayed his own wife. The Earl was puzzled; he couldn't see anything wrong in it.'

They all plotted. In this very room she had overheard supposedly cryptic conversations between the Earl of Essex, Mountjoy and these women, which she'd have been an idiot not to understand. It was the Queen's fault, of course, for refusing to name her successor; they had to consolidate their position in advance with whomsoever that might be. But they did it so *carelessly*. Amateurs, thought Barbary. And if they believed Mr Secretary Cecil wasn't aware of what they were up to, they were mad.

'Dice or cards tonight?' asked Frances.

'Dice,' said Barbary. But Elizabeth Vernon was not staying and Lettice had a headache, so dice was overruled for cards and they settled on Gleek which could only be played with three. A pity. Very difficult to cheat at Gleek, which was a game of memory, patience and bluff. However, Frances had no memory for cards, and as for Penelope, patience was not a quality the Devereux possessed.

'And the wagers?'

'The usual.' They played for servants, a good butler or maid being more priceless than rubies. In a recent game of Ketch Dolt, Barbary had managed to offload the dreadful Roland onto Vernon, and replace him with Rich's Philip.

Penelope broke out a new pack and handed round counters. 'I warn you, my dear Boggart,' she said, 'that tonight I intend to play for Winchard.'

'Winchard?'

'I love Winchard. He's *so* ugly. I'll put him in a pie and get him to jump out at the Queen. That should finish the old hag off.'

This was what she'd wanted. Barbary feigned reluctance. 'Winchard is a man among men. He held an entire mob off my coach today.' She gave an edited version of the running footman story. They shrieked with laughter. 'But I'm no pinch-buttock, as we say in the Fleet. I'll wager Winchard if you put up Joseph.' She said it idly.

520

Everything was resting on this. She needed Joseph. Badly.

Frances looked alarmed. She was, after all, mistress of the house even though Penelope acted as if she was. 'Please, please not Joseph, Boggart dear. What about Daniel?'

Barbary shook her head. 'I've got Philip.'

'Janet?'

'No, I've got Maria. But if the stake's too high . . .'

'Very well. Joseph.' Penelope Rich's chin was up.

So far so good. Joseph was what she'd come for. With Joseph, a Leonardo da Vinci of marchpane, she could rule the world, certainly put on a supper to knock the Queen of England's eye out. Now for it.

They played, they stopped for refreshment. Wine in winking glass, plovers on beds of sallet, lobster, tarts and creams from the magical Joseph. Barbary was two up, Frances one and Penelope three. Winner would be the first to reach the best of seven. She dare not let Penelope take another game, but her own cards were krap. With every wit she possessed she couldn't win unless the luck changed. At the moment it was with Penelope. Why hadn't she insisted on dice?

Essex, Henry Cuffe and Mountjoy came in from the bowling alley, smelling of sweat, a summer night and, from Mountjoy, the inevitable nicotine.

'Will you stay for supper?' Frances was suddenly intense.

Essex kissed his wife's hair. 'Sweetheart, this weary knight must drag himself to the palace in a moment. She too wants to play cards.'

Frances looked tragic, she had the right sort of face for it, thin and dark. Unlucky at cards, she ought to be lucky in love, thought Barbary, but she wasn't. She'd married Philip Sidney not long before his death, knowing that his true love was Penelope Rich. Then she'd married Essex, knowing that his love, true or not, was the Queen's. Poor old Frances was a natural martyr.

'Robert,' said Penelope, 'what do you say to having the Bettys' Winchard on the staff? He's as good as won.'

'Excellent. We can put him on the roof as a gargoyle.'

'You haven't won him yet,' said Barbary.

As the women began to play again, the men drew off to

521

a corner. Barbary could hear some of their muttering: '. . . send to Victor . . . sign of Venus failing . . .' Amateurs. She'd latched on to their code weeks ago, enough anyway to realise that 'Victor' was James of Scotland and 'Venus' was the Queen. Well, if they wanted to dice with death, that was their business. She needed to concentrate on the cards in hand. She was playing for stakes higher than theirs. She was playing for the soul of Ireland.

They kept trying to refill her glass so that she'd get muzzy, and when she sipped they accused her of cheating by keeping a clear head. Still, they were tipping back their wine faster than she was. The calls were coming louder. 'Tib. Fifteen to the dealer.' 'Tim.' 'Towser.' 'Tumbler.'

'The Ruff.'

'I'll vie the Ruff,' said Barbary. Frances had surprised herself and everybody else by taking two games. Each of them was three up. This was the last hand.

'I'll see it.' Frances was getting cold feet.

'I'll see and revie,' said Penelope.

Now then. She had six trumps, the knave, the ten, the five, the six and the two. Frances had drawn the king and the four some time back, and Barbary was pretty sure she had some more – but not as many as herself. She'd won, unless bloody Penelope Rich had the four aces, which took the game regardless of trumps. She certainly had two. Her eyes were sparkling, but that might be the wine. She was damned sure it was the wine.

Here goes Ireland. 'I'll see it.'

Frances laid down her hand. Only four trumps. But no aces.

Slowly, holding Barbary's eyes with her own, Penelope flicked a card onto the table. The ace of trumps. She flicked another. Ace of hearts. And another. Ace of spades. Then she smiled, and spattered the rest onto the table, a motley collection without an ace among them. 'Will you take Joseph now, or shall I have him sent round?'

'I'll take him,' Barbary said, 'wrapped.'

The supper was a triumph. From the moment in the garden when the Queen put up her hand to the branches of the apple tree above her head, picked an apple and exclaimed: 'It's marchpane,' its success was assured. It had been a dreadful risk. Rob had sweated at Barbary's choice of theme which was Robbery. 'A play on your name, see, Rob.'

'A play on my neck. She'll hate the reminder that crime is rife.'

'She won't. I've written to Spenser to write us a masque in which she steals everybody's hearts. She'll love it.'

'What about a naval theme?'

'Essex did that.' He'd set three hundred artificers to dig a lake in the shape of the Channel, filling it with wine and gilt model ships with guns that exploded scented powder in a mock battle. For a finish he'd given the Queen a gold fishing rod and she pulled out a golden trout with pearl eyes. They couldn't compete on that scale.

Rob gave in because he couldn't think of anything cleverer. They'd have to gamble on the novelty of it. Joseph nearly killed himself to crown his career and created a complete orchard out of marchpane. It used up a shipload of sugar that Rob had been hoping to sell. It was a hot September and stopping the damn thing from melting, let alone keeping the flies off it, nearly killed Barbary as well. Rehearsing the staff, ordering the food, hiring enough silver for one hundred and fifty – it was a small supper by the Queen's standards – acquiring sufficient seamstresses to make the costumes, finding composers and musicians, consulting the Lord Chamberlain on precedence and etiquette, she became thin and doubtful. 'Oh, Rob, it's all wrong. It's the wrong theme. I'm sorry, Rob.'

With the die cast, he'd become amazingly calm. 'Whether it sends me to Ireland or the Tower, I'm grateful for your trouble, Margaret.'

Edmund Spenser did them proud. From Munster he sent a masque that began with Eve stealing the apple, went through allegorical and mythical thieves like Pandora and Prometheus, including a lot Barbary had never heard of, and ended with a hundred stanzas of such grotesque flattery to the 'Lovely Arch-Robberess Who Has Stolen Her Nation's Heart' that, translated into material sugar, they could have made another orchard from it.

Parts were written into it for the three children; another risk. Elizabeth had made no reference to Henry since she'd first acknowledged his existence. By this time Rob was so numbed by the enormity of his gamble, he said: 'I have only one son and one neck. Go ahead.'

And Henry, dressed as a playing card Knave, stealing tarts away from Catherine, the Queen of Hearts, very nearly stole the entertainment as well, especially when he gave the tarts to 'Her Majesty, the true queen of hearts' in the audience. Elizabeth said: 'His gallantry gives us cause to wonder at his years, God bless him. He will be a singular man.'

Whether they should make a topical reference to Ireland cost Barbary and Rob sleepless nights. The situation over there had calmed down but . . . Eventually they included it in the buffoonery. Winchard, dressed as an asinine O'Neill, lumbered onto the stage; Rob, dressed in an English soldier's uniform, made of silk, stole the Irishman's trousers, revealing Winchard's backside to be wearing a target through which emerged a forked tail. Archers appeared from behind the marchpane trees and shot blunted arrows at it.

Elizabeth laughed until she cried. Barbary closed her eyes with relief. She felt no guilt at exposing the O'Neill to ridicule; he could hardly incur more hatred than he had already, but she'd had a momentary qualm about exposing Winchard – needlessly as it turned out. Winchard was so happy at his performance he refused to leave the stage and had to be dragged off.

The peroration went down beautifully. The buffet – for which half the wildlife of the home counties had laid down its life – spread from one end of the hall to the other and went down even better.

As she left, Elizabeth smiled maliciously at Barbary: 'Did you draw on your own experience, Boggart?' Then relented and kissed her: 'We have enjoyed ourselves.'

Cecil helped his hostess to the gallery's oriel window from which they watched the final rehearsed surprise of the night. Elizabeth's coach was being waylaid by silver-clad highwaymen, led by Rob, in order to steal a kiss from its royal occupant.

'I congratulate you,' the Elf said. 'A most entertaining evening.'

'Does it get Rob Ireland?'

Mr Secretary Cecil's small face beamed at her. He loathed direct questions nearly as much as he hated direct answers. 'I believe it will. Her Majesty was graciously pleased to suggest that Sir Rob should first reconnoitre the ground, as it were, and join Marshal Bagenal to see for himself the problems of its warfare. She has just whispered to me to prepare the necessary orders.'

'And then will he be Lord Deputy?'

'I see no reason why not. God willing.'

Chapter Twenty-Four

Rob left for Ireland within the week.

'All that trouble,' Barbary moaned, 'all that money and you're still not appointed.' With the building and furnishing of the house, and with the supper, they were in debt to the tune of £30,000.

Rob was less displeased than she was. 'It will be no bad thing to gain experience of this form of soldiering at first hand. If I were appointed without it, Ormond and all the Dublin men would be telling me to do this or that and I should be unable to gainsay them.'

'Shall we come with you? We can stay at Hap Hazard, or with the Spensers.'

During all the time they'd been living together, he had never asked her about her time in Ireland.

'No,' he said sharply. Then he softened. 'There is too much to be seen to here.'

'Very well.' She'd had to offer, but it was a relief that he had refused; she was getting too old to be badgered with uncomfortable memories and confusion. She was very nearly middle-aged, a woman with responsibilities; sometimes nowadays she looked back and wondered where the girl she had been had found all that emotion.

She would miss Rob, though. Their relationship had become equable; if anything, his reliance gave her the upper hand. As he had come to trust her, he had become less guarded, more able to drop formality and display something of the real man behind it. And a very considerable man that was, she'd decided. The desperation for advancement which had panicked him in his early days had eased as advancement had come. He was still ambitious, but ambition had begun to include his soul, not just his fortune. In those early days in the Order, she thought, he must have dreamed of righteousness as well as riches and was now carefully attaching it to his reputation. He took pride in being known at court as bluff, honest Rob. One night, as they sat together over supper, he had confessed that he was disappointed by the morality of the society in which he moved: 'In all honesty, Margaret, there are times when one could believe oneself to be back in the Bermudas.'

Not that such realisation had softened his dislike of the Order. He'd severed the professional connection between Barbary and Mr Secretary Cecil, telling the Elf he did not wish his wife to carry out any more assignments, especially those which returned her to her old haunts. Unperturbed, Cecil agreed.

Even when Cuckold Dick turned up to inform them that Galloping Betty was dying and asking to see them both, Rob had refused to go. 'The woman may account herself my mother, but I have never done so,' he said.

Barbary hadn't gone either. 'You may go if you wish, Margaret,' Rob had told her, 'but I should be sorry to see the improvement between us jeopardised by a return to those people.' She'd thought about it, but it had been when Sylvestris was recovering from the measles and by the time he was fully better it was too late.

The days before he left passed in a tumult of packing interspersed with instructions. 'Henry is now too old to have the maid sleep in his room.

'The wharf should be reinforced. Tom Motte must see to it.

'Do not neglect family prayers either at morning or night. Any servant who does not attend to be fined twopence.

'The cochineal from the Indies should be at Bristol by the end of the year. See Martin sells it for not a penny under forty shillings a pound. It will cover the debts with sufficient left over for the household and the fitting of more ships. I shall write to Martin, but you must oversee the matter.

'In my absence I would rather you do not gamble any more. Especially at Essex House. It is a dangerous place and has served its purpose.

'A copy of my will is with John Forber of the Scriveners' Company, another at the Archdeacon's Court. Effingham and Cecil are its executors and Effingham is

527

also Henry's guardian. I have included in it an instruction that he is to consult your advice in matters concerning Henry's upbringing.' He frowned. 'Though not necessarily take it.'

'Very well, Rob.'

In leaving he lingered uneasily at the door. 'I have been gratified, Margaret, by your conduct since you became mistress of my household . . .'

She knew him well by now. His pomposity was due to worry about Helen and because he didn't know how to say so. 'Rob,' she said, equally pompous, 'we have become what we always should have been, friends. I shall watch over Helen, and Henry, and Tilsend and Betty House and the cochineal for you. You watch over Ireland for me.'

She stood in the oriel window to get a view of his ride up the Strand. He was in his splendid plum velvet, his entourage following behind in blue livery with Rob's badge, an anchor, on their left sleeve. She felt very proud. A small crowd of Londoners, always attracted by a to-do, were cheering. Barbary opened a pane to wave a handkerchief, and the loyal wife seeing her brave lord off to war got a cheer for herself.

Yet there was no war. Almost as quickly as he'd set fire to the north of Ireland, the O'Neill damped it down and went back to his old tactics, suing for peace and pardon, protesting his 'dear wish to obtain Her Majesty's favour'.

Nobody really believed him, but the colonial administration was in disarray and needed its own time to recoup. It advised the Queen to give assurances to the rebel 'which later may be cancelled and forgotten'. And hope still flickered that O'Neill meant it; it was his genius that those to whom he made promises always believed against the evidence that he might keep them.

In an England which had been badly shocked, there was reassurance at the return to his old game. He was the Running Beast again, the cowardly, shape-shifting prevaricator. The Great Satan of Clontibret had been an aberration.

Rob's letters always began 'My good wife Margaret' and ended with 'Your affect. husband, Rob Betty, Kt.' The pages between reiterated his instructions, with others he'd remembered since. Apart from the fact that Marshal

Bagenal had received him with honour and it was raining in north-east Ireland, she had no indication of his condition.

But that winter he wrote:

'You should not be amazed that Her Matie has freed Sir Richard Bingham from his imprisonment and sent him once more to Ireland. He is known everywhere for a good soldier and she will have need of such, a matter to far outweigh promises which, you say, she made to a common Irish pirate.

'You tell me his gains were ill-gotten but were you here, which I thank God for your sake and Henry's you are not, you should see such base dealing by Her Matie's servants in this place as to make you wonder if she were not better to employ common rats.'

After that his complaints against those who lined their own pockets in Dublin while the army went 'naked and weaponless' were constant. She learned of the vicious circle which sustained revolt, of officers kept short of supplies and pay being forced to commandeer the harvest of loyal clans, leaving them starving and in rebellion.

From Elizabeth's point of view, millions had been poured into Ireland and gone nowhere. But Rob said that the supplies, uniforms and arms which arrived in Dublin were frequently half the amount on the requisition orders, or sometimes didn't arrive at all. Much of the corn, powder and match which lumbered on the sixteen-day journey to Chester disappeared while it was in the sutlers' warehouses, was frequently spoiled during the crossing, and dwindled even more on reaching the other side.

The levies of men who'd been snatched from English and Welsh villages for an army in a country many of them had never heard of were ragged. They deserted as soon as they could, looted in order to eat, or died of disease. Captains kept short of money put in for the pay of a command up to full strength, then filled in the blanks with starving Irishmen who rode pillion on other soldiers' horses and whose weapons were no more than cudgels.

'We fight rabble with rabble,' Rob wrote. 'God help us if O'Neill should break out again.'

On the day of Lord Burghley's funeral, Betty House was draped in mourning cyprus crepe like all the noble residences in the Strand; even Charing Cross had been tied with black ribbon out of respect for a nation's grief.

The tiltyard stand had been bedecked in black and carried to the open gateway so that Barbary, Catherine and Sylvestris could watch the procession on its way to Westminster Abbey. The great bell was tolling.

'My legs ache,' Catherine said. The August had turned hot and humid, and under an overcast sky they all sweated in the funeral clothes which enveloped every area of skin except the face. They had been standing there for an hour as the muffled drums beat on and on, timing the slow march of city archers, infantry, shot and gunners, the livery companies, ward beadles and watches, foresters, infantry, and heralds.

'Bear it,' said Barbary. 'The hearse hasn't gone by yet.' But here it was, coming down the hill by the Cross, pulled by black horses caparisoned to their fetlocks, with pennants over their manes and tails. By its side walked gentlemen pensioners with pikes reversed. Behind it a herald led Burghley's horse, riderless.

'Kneel.'

They knelt, but at this height they could look down under their eyelids and see the statue lying on the coffin.

'Was he a good man?' asked Sylvestris.

'He was a great one.' She thought back to the barge going down to Greenwich that night very long ago. What she remembered most was his fatigue. Even then he'd had little more colour than that marble down there, but it was not so much physical tiredness as erosion of a personality that had worked too hard, known too many secrets. The brain had manipulated her, blackmailed and schemed as it had gone on blackmailing and scheming all these years since to keep his Queen's peace. Goodness or not, she didn't know, but it was greatness.

His last appearance in the Council Chamber had coincided with another outburst from Essex denouncing peace with Spain and the Irish. Barely able to speak, Burghley had taken his prayer book from his pocket and pointed silently to the twenty-third verse of Psalm 55: 'Bloodthirsty and deceitful men shall not live out half their days.'

And now the old crossbiter was dead, and the streets were massed with silent people who felt less safe without him. Elizabeth, they said, had gone to pieces.

'He must have been good,' Catherine was saying, 'to warrant all this.'

The two sons walked alone behind the hearse. Thomas, the new Lord Burghley, was the one who looked the statesman, whereas in fact he did everything the hobbling, stunted figure at his side told him to do. Mr Secretary Cecil's expression was so habitual that, even now, he couldn't rid himself of it and stared ahead in a cheery rictus that caused the crowds to murmur in disapproval. Behind them came the dukes, the earls, the viscounts, a walking black forest of England's notables, foreign princes and ambassadors.

'There's Henry.'

Barbary clamped Sylvestris's arm. 'Don't wave.'

Henry was too young to be at the Abbey, but Garter King of Arms had agreed that he could represent Rob in the procession as far as Betty House. He was behaving beautifully, matching his short stride to the Lord Admiral's. Now he bowed to the hearse and cut away from the lines, the crowd opening to let him through.

He squeezed between the gatepost and the stand and looked up at Barbary, wriggling. 'I'm desperate.'

Oh dear. 'Go behind the rose bed, then come up here.' He'd been waiting for hours at Paul's while the procession assembled. She could hear the splash of a tiny stream above the slow shuffle of the five hundred poor and needy going by, all dressed in their new black gowns and hoods.

She hoped Elizabeth in her grief had agreed the Treasury should pay for all this. What it must be *costing*. She could think of nothing but costs nowadays. Ominously, the cochineal boat still hadn't put in; she was only holding off creditors by persuading them that Sir Rob had great expectations. She'd had to pawn her diamond dragonfly brooch to pay for their mourning dress and these all-encompassing, stifling Mary Stuart hoods she and Catherine had to wear.

'My lady.'

She looked down. 'Yes, Philip?'

'A visitor, my lady. Lady Penelope Rich. Come by boat.'

Stupidly she asked: 'Are you sure?' Everybody who was anybody, and Penelope Rich was somebody, was either taking part or watching the funeral.

'In the library, my lady.'

The servants were all clustered on the stages of the oriel window, enjoying the procession. It was quiet in the library. Penelope was in a baroness's weeds, a coronet over her mourning hood. Later, Barbary was to remember her kindness, the hug, how she made her sit down and sent Philip for a restorative.

'There is no easy way to tell you, my dear. Sir Rob is killed.'

Barbary put out a reproachful hand to pat her. She smiled. 'Lady Rich,' she said, 'I had a letter from him this morning.'

'Please, Boggart, don't. I'm from Whitehall. The Queen gave me permission to come and will come herself by and by. We have it firsthand from Captain Wingfield who has ridden day and night from the boat. He was there. A place called Yellow Ford. Somewhere near Armagh. An ambush by O'Neill and O'Donnell. Terrible, so terrible. Three thousand men dead and injured, the rest defeated. I thought the Queen would go lunatic.'

It was still a mistake. She had read out Rob's solid sentences to the children just this morning; she could still hear them. Penelope's sporadic phrases were irritating; if the woman would only go away, everything would be back as it was.

'Marshal Bagenal too. Ulster is lost, perhaps Ireland.'

Crossly, Barbary turned her head to find Penelope down on her knees beside her, clasping her hands. 'But I tell you this, Boggart. He'll be revenged. They'll listen to Essex now.'

That night Lady Russell relieved Lady Rich. They spoke in low voices outside the door of Barbary's sewing chamber. 'She's very calm, except to keep asking whether it was cannon that killed him. As if it mattered. Perhaps it matters to that class, how can one know?'

'How did he die?'

'They think he was blown to pieces. It was all such chaos apparently. Two barrels of powder in his section were hit and exploded. Charles Percy, Northumberland's brother, did well to retrieve the body. They knew it was his from the quality of the uniform pieces. I've told her he died like Bagenal, a musket ball in the forehead as he lifted his visor. It seemed to quiet her. Great God, who would believe this could happen.'

'Well,' said Lady Russell stoutly, 'I have made my arrangements. I have written to my nephew, demanding he give me a detachment of halberdiers to defend my house. I shall kill as many Irish as I can before they cut me down. And Spanish. They say the Spanish have already landed on the Isle of Wight.'

'They always say that. I give it no credit. Who'd land on the Isle of Wight if they could help it?'

Guilt took up occupation like some monstrous tumour. As she made arrangements, took decisions, received condoling visitors, she dragged it around with her. She was her own battleground; nothing that had happened at Yellow Ford altered her feelings one jot for the three men she knew who had been involved in it. She recoiled from understanding why the O'Neill and the O'Donnell had attacked the English column, but understand she did and there was an end of it. She knew with what high ideals Rob had gone to Ireland and approved them, but they had not given him the right to be there in somebody else's land. If there was any right in the business, it was the historical, male, right of conquest. And if conquest was a right and Ireland had originally been won for England by conquest, then the O'Neill was exercising the same right to get it back.

But Rob was dead and she had helped to kill him. Friends, she'd told him, versing him like some cony she was planning to catch. 'We've become what we always should have been, friends.' They hadn't been friends. They had come to an amicable arrangement to preclude the truth.

He'd never asked why she'd run guns to Ireland, and she hadn't told him. As he'd grown in stature and revealed the maturity that had come to him in these last years, she had wanted to explain the complexity of

Ireland, the O'Neill, Grace O'Malley, the hanging woman, Will Clampett and the reason for his defection. He hadn't even known Will *had* defected.

Once or twice she had broached the subject but he had become unsettled and angry, and she was so comfortable with things the way they were she hadn't persisted. He'd gone away unarmed by knowledge he should have had. If he'd understood the O'Neill and the O'Donnell, the Ireland she had discovered, it might have made a difference. It might have helped him. It might have saved his life.

And here she was, tenant of this beautiful ostentation that wasn't paid for, widow of a marriage that had been no marriage at all, mother of children who weren't hers. She had achieved standards the Upright Man could only dream about. She was a credit to him.

Fraud was everywhere. The official placebo being handed out by Elizabeth's government to try and stop panic was a fraud. Two surviving commanders of regiments at Yellow Ford, Sir Thomas Wingfield and Sir Charles Percy, came to see her to express their sympathy and, however good their motives, they were fraudulent too. They told her Rob had ridden gloriously into the mêlée at the head of his loyal men, and their accounts were so stilted and, under questioning, so conflicting, she'd known they were lying. It was probable that in the confusion nobody still alive had seen Rob die.

Nevertheless, she called Henry into the room and watched his face as they gently fed him the same story, seeing it help him. He had the right to be proud of his father, but one day he ought to know more than the fact that a bad man called O'Neill had lain in ambush and slaughtered good Englishmen for no better reason than that he was wicked.

Busy as she was, she called in Cuckold Dick. She hadn't seen him for months. As a result, ten days later she put on a plain cloak and took a boat with Winchard down to Nell Bull's waterside tavern at Deptford. Cuckold Dick was waiting for them. 'There ain't many, Barb. Most of them's being offloaded in Wales and finding their own way back, and a lot more's deserted and in hiding. But there's him. Name of Brent. Brittany captain. Been here two days.'

And hadn't stopped drinking from the look of him.

Captain Brent was holding up Nell's doorpost and obstructing anyone trying to go in and out. He was also shouting. 'The Great Satan, eh? Hang O'Neill high, shall we? Eh? Eh? Let's blame good old Irish Satan. Eh?'

Cuckold Dick spoke to him, and the captain focused on Barbary with difficulty. 'Lost your husband, lady? There's a pity. What a pity.' He dragged off his cap and threw it on the ground. 'Stamp on that. That's O'Neill's head. Stamp on that.' He snatched Dick's hat off and threw it next to his own. 'An' I'll stamp on this. Know what this is? It's Bagenal's head. This is me stamping on it. See? Eh? See me stamping on the Marshal's head? Poor old good old bloody old Marshal.'

It took time to calm him down and get him to sit in Nell's private room where nobody else could hear this sedition. 'Bloody Bagenal,' he kept saying. 'Bloody Bagenal. I'll tell you about bloody Bagenal. Him and his bloody sister. Glad he's dead. Glad *she's* dead.'

'Is Mabel dead?'

'That her name? Never knew her name. Dead as a rat. An' took my lads with her. Bloody Bagenal.'

They managed to gather that when Marshal Bagenal had heard of his sister's death he'd pestered Dublin to send him the two thousand newly arrived, newly levied recruits for an attack on O'Neill, who was blockading the Blackwater Fort. Dublin said no; it was still negotiating terms. Bagenal persisted. Worn down, suspecting Bagenal to be too unbalanced, Dublin asked Ormond to command the attack if attack there must be. 'But Black Tom's got too much sense. Wanted to protect his own property in Leinster. Got a lot of property in Leinster. He said no.'

Bagenal went on persisting. As usual the recruits were receiving no pay and, also as usual, turning into looters and deserters who terrorised the city, so at last the administration agreed and sent one thousand of them to Bagenal.

'Sweepings,' Captain Brent hiccuped, 'that's what they were. Didn't know their pikes from their pricks, pardon the expression.'

So Bagenal marched four thousand men out into the little hills of Armagh that, even in August, were islands in wet meadowland. 'A bloody mile of us, strung out in

535

bloody bog, lifting boots stuck with half of Ireland, pulling the bloody horses, pushing the bloody saker. You ever seen a saker, lady? Bloody thing. Never fired a bloody shot as far as I know. And guess what bloody Bagenal did. Eh? Go on, guess.'

She shook her head.

'Left one hundred and fifty paces between each regiment.' Captain Brent spread out his arms and knocked over his tankard. 'Bloody great gaps. But correct. Routine. Very sound on procedure, our Marshal. I went back to him. "Look, Marshal," I said, "I don't want no bloody great gap at my bloody rear when I'm marching through enemy territory," I said to him. Did he listen? "Get back to your position, captain," he said. And I got back. And it came.'

She ordered more ale. 'What came?'

He shook his head. 'You don't want to know, lady. You may think you do, but you don't. They howl, you see. Did you know they howled?'

Yes, she said, she knew they howled.

'But these weren't savages. Savages don't sustain attack for hour after hour after hour after hour. Savages don't shoot like that. Know how my men died? Shot. It pissed bloody shot. More shot than air. They got in between the gaps and poured shot up our arses. Bloody recruits. Threw down their arms and ran like bloody rabbits. Never fired a bloody shot back. And my men,' he smeared his tears over his face, 'been with me all through the Lowland wars. Good men. Too good for bloody Ireland. Snapped down like wasps.' He peered up at her. 'Know why they're bringing us home? Because we're no bloody good. See that?' He held up a filthy fist with a tremor like a palsy. 'Afraid? I'm still afraid. All bloody afraid. So you go home, lady. Don't think about it. Bury him like a bloody hero, whoever he was. You go home and blame bloody O'Neill. I'm staying here and blaming Bagenal.'

After he'd cried himself to sleep she slipped a mark in his purse and told Nell to look out for him.

On the dockside she said to Cuckold Dick: 'I've ordered a headstone for Galloping Betty.' There'd just been enough cash left after paying the servants.

'That's good of you, Barb.'

'I don't want you to say that. I don't want you to say anything.'

'What you going to do, Barb?'

'I don't know.'

Edmund Spenser wrote from Ireland asking for his children back because, with Rob dead, they would no longer benefit from his position in society. The letter didn't put it like that; it was full of sympathy for her, anger at O'Neill, gratitude, but she must not be further burdened in her grief, and in these dreadful times a family should be together.

When she told them, neither Catherine nor Sylvestris wanted to go. Catherine had always liked life in London and her move to Betty House and its higher society had put her in her element. Barbary had been unable to become as close to her as to her brother, though the girl was affectionate enough; they talked clothes together and enjoyed shopping trips, but gradually Catherine had made her own niche among her contemporaries, well-born girls who were also nearing womanhood, and had been invited for long, gossipy stays at the Cumberlands' and at Penshurst and Wilton, the home of Philip Sidney's sister, Mary, the Countess of Pembroke.

Catherine was desperate at the thought of being returned to Ireland: 'But it is so dangerous.'

'Munster is a long way from the north.' The question of danger was one of the things that kept Barbary awake at nights, but Spenser's letters assured her that Munster was so well defended and, now, so settled that there was no possibility of trouble.

'But my lady Pembroke has invited me to stay at Wilton.'

Barbary thought about it. Mary Sidney was a scholar and a level-headed woman, a much more suitable guide and companion for Catherine than most, and because of the old connection between Edmund and the Sidneys, it might be that she would take Catherine in, for the time being at any rate.

'I'll see. I must write to Lady Mary. And to your father, of course.' Catherine kissed her and ran off to the kitchens where she and the cook were concocting a specific against freckles.

Sylvestris was re-reading his father's letter: '*Are* we a burden to your grief?'

'No.' In fact they were. The world was shaking and she was terrified for all of them. Henry she could barely look at without wanting to shield him, and if Sylvestris had been vulnerable before he was doubly so now. But Edmund Spenser had been particular in stressing that his son should return to the 'sylvan simplicity' of Spenser Castle and learn to manage the very considerable Munster estates he would one day inherit. She put her arm round his shoulders. 'Haven't you had any invitations, Sir Stayon?'

He tried to smile. 'Perhaps the Lord Admiral's men will ask me to join their playhouse.'

She smiled back. He'd been given one line to speak in the masque, 'Stay, sweet Sir Actaeon', but had been so nervous that it had come out as 'Act, sweet Sir Stayon'. She said: 'But you've wanted to see Spenser Castle again. And put flowers on your mother's grave.'

'You're my mother,' he said.

She left the room quickly; she was so powerless to help him or any of them now. All her consequence had gone with Rob's death and she was dependent on the fair-dealing of men over whom she had no control. She was working like a demon to safeguard Henry in her dreadful shame at having so complacently and wickedly waved his father off to war. He should be safe, she thought, Rob had chosen well in making Lord High Admiral Effingham his guardian, but guardians didn't always guarantee a ward's happiness. Penelope Rich's father had wanted her to marry Philip Sidney as much as the two young people had wanted to marry, but after Lord Essex's death her guardian, the Earl of Huntingdon, had sold her off to the dreadful Lord Rich.

It's a judgement on me, she thought. She had become so used to power, playing for servants at cards as if they were counters and not human beings who might resent being uprooted at a whim, using Winchard as a curiosity. Jesus God, coming from a class even lower than the servants, she should have remembered what powerless-ness was like. She had used her background to amuse the Essexes and their like, occasionally strutting out her Cockney and Order phrases to make herself and everybody else believe that there was no reason to despise it. But if she hadn't despised it, why had she dropped Cuckold Dick and made excuses not to go to Galloping Betty's deathbed? She had betrayed them and herself to be noticed by a society where novelty was everything.

Well, she was yesterday's novelty now. The initial sympathy had worn off quickly. The Queen had not called or sent for her, although Barbary had received a royal letter of condolence. She was a commoner's common widow without money or consequence; she was dependent on Henry for the clothes she stood up in, and until Henry reached his majority, he was dependent on his guardian who might, or might not, look after his inheritance for him.

Not that there was too much for him to inherit. She was doing what she could. She had sent for Helen to help the boy through his misery over his father's death. She had sent for Martin, Rob's agent in Bristol, to present the shipping accounts. The Archdeaconal Probate Court had proved Rob's will surprisingly quickly, and she was due to have a meeting with Mr Secretary Cecil, one of its co-executors, this very day.

They sat together in the library. As they went through the household accounts, the Elf's legs dangled over the edge of Rob's chair which was too big for him. The same awful brightness with which he looked on a summer's morning, or his own father's funeral, was clamped on his face. Burghley's death had affected him, no father and son had ever been closer, yet it was difficult to pinpoint the change in a man whose whole life had been an exercise in revealing nothing of himself. But there was a tightening there, a sense that all the closed doors leading to the inner chamber of Mr Secretary's feelings had now not only been locked, but bricked up.

He closed the household book without comment and she gave him the agent's books dealing with Rob's maritime ventures.

The remains of a merchant convoy had limped into Bristol bearing the news that the cochineal boat had foundered in a storm on its voyage home from the Indies, but she had been hugely relieved to find that among the surviving ships were three in which Rob had a part interest, one carrying sugar, one spices, another tobacco.

539

'Martin tells me the sale of Rob's share of the cargoes should bring thirty thousand pounds,' she said. 'But at least ten thousand of that will go in other ventures which my Lord Admiral has promised to oversee on Henry's behalf.' She stared at Cecil meaningfully. 'And I could wish that you will oversee my Lord Admiral in this matter.' Keep each a check on the other. Of the two executors, she trusted Effingham more than Cecil, but she didn't want any of Henry's future going into the Lord High Admiral's pocket.

'Certainly, most certainly.' His eyes were still on the figures. When he'd finished he looked up. 'Correct me if I'm wrong, Lady Betty, but that still leaves a deficit of another ten thousand.'

'Debt,' she said. 'It leaves us still in debt for ten thousand.' She was drowning in all these euphemisms, wholesale defeats that were 'setbacks', 'He didn't suffer', when they didn't know whether he had or not. There was no need to shrink from the word 'debt' when the entire court lived on credit.

'And what steps do you propose on this debt?'

I'd hoped that miserable old bitch who's your mistress might propose steps on it, she thought. But, having paid for Rob's funeral and buried him in Westminster Abbey, the Queen obviously felt she had discharged her duty to her late courtier and hero.

Out loud Barbary said: 'I propose to sub-let the lease on Tilsend.' That would bring Henry some income and still leave him and Helen with Betty House and Kerswell. 'And I propose to sever my son's connection with a country that has already cost him his father. I want to sell Hap Hazard.'

He considered. 'That seems satisfactory. Would you conduct the sale yourself?'

'With your permission. I must take Edmund Spenser's son back home to his father, though his daughter is staying on in England with the Countess of Pembroke.' She leaned forward. 'How safe is Munster?'

'Oh my dear Lady Betty, there is no question—'

'I want to know.' Left to herself she wouldn't go near the place, but if Sylvestris had to be delivered back to his father, accompanying him would postpone their separation for a while at least, and she could judge for herself

540

how his new stepmother received him. Ellis was leasing Hap Hazard and Spenser, in his letter, had indicated the man was eager to buy. She'd enjoy squeezing the highest possible price out of that one.

'As I was about to say, my dear Lady Betty, Her Majesty has determined to put down this insurrection once and for all. She is asking questions as to why there are more regiments on Irish paper than on Irish soil . . .'

'She could have asked that before. Rob told her. He told me.'

'. . . and she has ordered the levying of twenty-five thousand new soldiers to accompany my lord of Essex when he takes command.'

Not even a wince disturbed the bland happiness of his face, but if she'd had any sorrow left she would have felt it for him then. The long conniving of his father, his own straining to keep that complicated peace had gone for nothing and in the end the 'bloody and deceitful men' of the psalm had won the Queen's mind for war.

'Sir John Norris is in command of Munster,' the Elf went on, 'and he is, as you know, a proven general. His brother, Sir Thomas, commands a strong garrison at Mallow – the nearest town to your estate, I believe – and he writes to me that just one of his men can outweigh three Irishmen in battle.'

'That's what Bagenal said before Yellow Ford.' She was too sick to be polite. She very nearly told him she didn't care whether it was the O'Neill or Norris who held Munster; she could survive equally well under either. All she wanted to know was whether she and Sylvestris were going to be there when they battled it out.

He persisted. No danger. Dear Lady Betty. Let him assure her. She could see he wanted to get away, and there was still the will to be read.

The will brought tears to her eyes. It began with Rob's profession of faith: 'I bequeath my soul to Almighty God, my Maker and Redeemer, fully trusting to be saved by the death and passion of his only Son Our Lord Jesus Christ when the last trump shall blow.'

She could hear Rob's sonorous voice under the Elf's pipe. Basically it was very simple: with the exception of some bequests to servants and friends, Rob had left everything to Henry. But it was weighted with meanings

Rob had known she would understand.

'To Henry my son,' read the Elf, 'all my movable goods unbequeathed upon condition that he be a comfort to his mother that she shall have free liberty of my house at Kerswell, with good and sufficient apparel, meat and drink and servitors in sickness and in health for the term of her life—'

'Mr Secretary,' interrupted Barbary, 'I have taken into the household my husband's cousin, a lady by the name of Helen Westacott. Sir Rob was kindly attached to her and has let her live at Kerswell these years. She had the rearing of Henry through his babyhood and was to all intents and purposes his mother. While I am absent, or in the event of my death, the terms of that section of Sir Rob's will must apply to her.'

The Elf flipped her a quick glance. It left her with the feeling that he guessed the situation. Like his father, she thought, he knows everybody's secrets. Would he question Henry's legitimacy? He might if it served his purpose, but she couldn't see how it would, not while she would deny it.

'I see no reason why that cannot be arranged,' he said. He went back to reading the will. 'I also command my son to suffer my good and trusted wife to occupy for her lifetime and as she will all the hall and her especial chamber in each of my houses of Tilsend and of that in the Strand known as Betty House with all commodities as befit a lady who has been so dutiful, and that she shall have for her own keeping the object she shall find in the desk of the library at Betty House.'

This was provision for her, Barbary.

He squinted at her over the parchment: 'That is all, apart from the witnesses.'

You did well, Rob, she thought.

He coughed. 'As executor, I fear I shall have to ask what that last-named object may be, Lady Betty.'

She didn't know herself. It occurred to her that whatever it was, it would be the only thing she actually owned in the whole world; everything else was on sufferance. Well, what had she ever owned except her wits?

He passed her the great ring with Rob's keys on it which she had ceremoniously presented to him on his arrival. She selected the desk key, crossed the room with the Elf skipping along at her side — he was taking his responsibility to the limit – and opened it.

Inside lay the Clampett.

Chapter Twenty-Five

She would have been reduced to tears when she said goodbye to Henry if she hadn't seen that the boy was having to use all his courage to hold back his own. Until then she hadn't realised how much she'd come to mean to him. He was still grieving for his father; now she was compounding the loss.

'I'll be back,' she said briskly, but Henry only clenched his jaw harder. His father had also said he'd be back.

She put her hand on his shoulder. 'You do see, pigsney,' she pleaded. 'I've got to go. Hap Hazard must be sold well.'

The sale of Hap Hazard would put his finances in good fettle, and she didn't trust anybody else to get the price she wanted for it out of Ellis. If it hadn't been for that, she would have had to choose between the two boys whom she loved as much as true sons, between staying with Henry or accompanying Sylvestris to Ireland.

Probably, she thought, she would have accompanied Sylvestris anyway. It was a matter of who needed her most. Sylvestris was the more vulnerable and, for all his distress at their parting, Henry *would* be all right. His was the more resilient character, he had Helen and great men as his guardians. And, although he didn't know it, he would also have less exalted, secret guardians; Cuckold Dick had instructed the Order to look out for him.

But at this moment of parting, with Henry's chin wobbling, hardly able to control her own voice, all the reasoning in the world didn't ease the pain.

'Look after Helen,' she said quickly. 'Keep Winchard out of trouble. And I love you very much.' She turned and ran down the steps to the coach, leaving him standing, suddenly very small in the enormous doorway of Betty House.

Cuckold Dick saw them off at Deptford. It was one of his ships they were sailing in, although he complained, 'Well, not mine, Barb, as you know. More like Mr Secretary's. He's still doing me, Barb.'

'Don't come the dead-lurk with me.' She rubbed a pinch of his cloak between her fingers to feel its quality, and then reached up to touch his hat: 'That beaver cost twenty shilling or I'm a Dutchman.'

He smirked. 'More like thirty.'

'You're in oatmeal, you old scobberlotcher.' His whiskey trade was flourishing. Thanks mainly to Rattray, whom Cecil had put in to organise the business, Dick and his partner now owned a small fleet and had warehouses at Deptford, Bristol and Milford Haven. Dick's cassock was of best grey linen and underneath it his heavy thighs were in silk Venetians down to his buskins. There was still something seedy about him – perhaps the dandruff – but it was seediness with a gloss. And he had grown into the age he always should have been. Barbary realised with a shock that the Cuckold Dick she'd known in the early years had been a comparatively young man who looked middle-aged. Now he was middle-aged and looked no older; he would stay middle-aged into his seventies.

And he was still worrying about her. 'Don't like you going back, Barb.'

There was full-scale war in Ireland now. Dick had lost touch with the O'Neill, whose armies were rampaging over the north and east, and, accordingly, with Will Clampett, although he was still trying to make contact with him.

She smiled at him. 'I'll be oatmeal. Munster's calm, ain't it?'

As they went up the gangplank she asked: 'What's this cargo we're going with?' The whiskey trade, after all, came only one way.

'Gunpowder.'

She stopped. 'Oh, thank you.'

He urged her on, comfortingly. 'Safe as a mouse in cheese, you'll be, Barb. It's stowed proper, and my lads here are famous lads. Not a fumer among 'em.' The tendency of sailors to smoke had already sent more than one ammunition ship to the bottom. 'Legally requisitioned, an' all.'

She looked at him suspiciously: 'Legal?' There wouldn't be much profit if it was a legal supply for the army.

'You see, Barb . . .' He paused and said to Sylvestris, 'Want to go and look at the nice sails, young shaver?' He steered Barbary to her cabin. 'You see, Barb, the Rome-Mort pays us to take it to Ireland, but when it gets there somebody else pays us for letting them send it somewhere else.'

'Where?'

'I don't ask, Barb, and—'

'Where, Dick?' Had gunpowder from Cuckold Dick impelled the shot that killed Rob?

'Barb, I don't ask. It may go to the O'Neill, it may not. English nobs come aboard and buy it afore the army sutlers do. They speak nice and they pay nice. That's all I know.'

She nodded. She could hardly condemn Dick for doing what she herself had done at Tilsend, especially as he seemed to be doing it under English sanction. She wondered if Mr Secretary Cecil knew where his profit came from.

'Well,' she said, 'as long as the boy and I don't arrive in Dublin before our ship does.'

Dick looked shocked. 'You're not going to Dublin, Barb. You're headed for Kinsale. I wouldn't land you in Dublin. As soon send you to Paltock's.'

'Is it as bad as that?' Those whom the Order expelled from its ranks, and the Order wasn't generally fussy, gathered at Paltock's inn. Unwary drinkers who ventured in were never seen again.

'Worse. The rude and licentious is running amok there. And O'Neill's advancing, got as far as Drogheda. Now I yields to nobody in my respect for O'Neill, as you know, Barb, but I wouldn't want to be in Dublin when his merry lads march in. No, we deal through Kinsale now. Munster's quieter.'

She tried to remember where Kinsale was. She'd heard of it once. It occurred to her that Cuckold Dick knew more of Ireland than she did now; he certainly was more up to date on the situation there. Mr Secretary Cecil

546

hadn't mentioned the O'Neill being at Drogheda.

'Kinsale's on the south coast,' Dick told her, 'well away from the fighting. Round to Cork and left a bit. One of the Pale towns, though it's a wonderful sharp place, Barb. I reckon they call it Kinsale because the citizens will sell you their families if you ask 'em. They'd sell a dog fleas would the Kin-sellers.'

He looked round. 'They even trade with the Dons, they do. Bible, Barb. Saw a ship in the harbour there last month. Remember Don Howsyourfather? Your gran's fancy? Well, it was full of coves as looked just like him. Did everything bar fly the Spanish flag. And the Mayor talking them pretty an' all.'

'Get off.' No English town, even an Irish English town, would be trading openly with Spain.

He shrugged. 'What I'm saying, Barb, is Kinsale's got imagination. Not restricted like. Any trouble, Barb, you head for Kinsale. One of my boats'll be in there sooner or later and pick you up.'

'Is there going to be trouble?'

'Maybe, maybe not. It's quiet enough. The undertakers is happy, but I don't think the Irish are.'

'No news of Will yet?' She knew there wasn't; he'd have told her, but she kept asking. Apart from her affection for him, Will was another of her guilts. He'd gone to Ireland because of her.

'No. You got the message about Herself?'

'Yes, bless you.' One of his whiskey ships had ventured to Connaught – Cuckold Dick always maintained the whiskey made from Connaught streams was the best – and Grace O'Malley had intercepted it. The moment he'd heard, Dick had sent a runner round to tell her that her grandmother was alive and kicking. It had been on the day of Rob's funeral, the only bright spot in it.

'Demanded pilotage same as ever,' Dick said, shaking his head. 'What an Upright Man she would have made, Barb.'

'Is Bingham harassing her?'

'Bingham ain't harassing nobody. Dying, so they say.'

'Good.'

'Red Hugh O'Donnell's taking back all what Bingham took away. Connaught's as good as Irish again.'

'Good. I suppose there's no news of . . .'

'O'Hagan? No. You asked me that yesterday.' He patted her shoulder.

The last news she'd had came, by chance, from Cecil. He had happened to say that the O'Neill's ambassador in Spain was still trying to persuade the Spanish King to send troops to help the Irish. 'A man called O'Hagan,' he'd said.

The captain put his head round the door. 'Ready to cast off, sir.'

They moved out onto the deck. 'You're a prize, Dick. Or should I say "sir"?' She couldn't get over seeing him in a position of authority.

He exaggerated a sigh. 'It ain't easy, Barb. I got to go back and tell all them quill-drivers what to do.'

'What's a quill-driver?' asked Sylvestris, who'd over-heard, as they stood together on deck to wave goodbye to Cuckold Dick.

She watched the distance between her and the stout figure on the quayside widen as the ship began to move. 'A clerk. Wave.'

'Why do you talk funny when you're with him?'

'He's my oldest friend. We were in the Order together.'

'What's the Order?'

She told him. While the ship ran to Ireland before a light breeze over a tranquil September sea, she told him practically everything there was to tell, about the Order, about her relationship with Ireland. She was literally putting her life into the hands of a ten-year-old boy, but it was important to her to arm this future Anglo-Irish landholder with knowledge she had withheld from Rob. He should be aware of another Ireland than the one his father knew, and the only way she could explain that Ireland was to unfold it bit by bit, as it had been unfolded to her. They would take him away from her once they arrived in Munster; she had to tell him now.

He listened quietly, occasionally asking questions. 'Why did you want to save the man who saved the priest?'

'They'd have killed him. There'd been too much killing.'

'Is it wrong to kill Catholic priests? It's legal.'

'I'm beginning to think it's wrong to kill anybody.'

The next day, when they were spinning for mackerel, he said: 'You love a lot of people, don't you? Cuckold Dick, Grace O'Malley, this O'Hagan, even the O'Neill, for all he tricked you.'

'It's not rationed.'

'But I only love you and Catherine.'

'That's not bad. When I was your age I only loved myself. And you love your father.'

Sylvestris stared down at the twirl of silver cloth on the hook in the water. 'I don't know him very well.'

'You don't have to know people to love them. Look at me and you. I think you're very peculiar.' But she saw the trap she'd put him in. 'Look, Sir Stayon, you shouldn't have secrets from your father. You can tell him all this when I've been and gone.'

She squinted at Sylvestris; perhaps she had been unfair to tear off the blinkers through which he'd inevitably seen the world all his life. She remembered when Philip Sidney had told her that bell-jangler about the man in Italy who'd said the world went round the sun rather than the sun round the world. For a moment, before dismissing the idea, she'd tried to encompass it and felt dizzy, as this boy must be feeling dizzy, from seeing established things somersault into a different position. In one lesson he'd been shown legality through a criminal's eyes, great men at great crime, an adulteress excusing adultery, and rebellion from the point of view of the rebel. Accepting it, if he did accept it, would be hard. Well, she thought, it was hard for me living it.

'Phew,' he said.

She was pleased with him. That just about summed it up.

The rocky southern coast of Ireland opened to the great River Bandon, and the gunpowder ship had to stand off from the estuary, waiting for the tide, before it began its voyage up the river's long, sickle-shaped progress between the hills. They passed through the high points where the guns of two big English forts, Rincorran on the east, Castle Park on the west, commanded the approaches, and along a stretch of cliffs with spits of beaches at their base. It was a beautiful day. Terns followed their wake. Anglers waved to them from the rocks, while far above them, on the hills, tiny oxen plodded ahead of ploughs turning patches of harvested fields into furrows like corduroy. The earth was reddish.

She remembered now. Kinsale was where Will, a wounded soldier, had been reminded of his Devon home; this was Will's Road to Damascus. Here he had seen the light that exposed the Irish to him as a people like any other. It was here he had rescued the child that had turned into Barbary Clampett. She looked around, interested to see what Will had seen.

Then she was down on the deck, retching. One of the cliff faces had leaned over and sucked her into its own perspective so that she was the child clinging to it, looking back over her shoulder at the river, afraid of the drop, afraid of the soldiers running along the top above her. A man in a boat was beckoning to her. She wouldn't make it. They'd shoot her before she could get to him. Fear was using her up. Fear and grief. They'd hanged her mother. How long had she been running and hiding? Too long. She'd drop and let them shoot her.

'Aunt Margaret. Oh please, Aunt Margaret.' Sylvestris was leaning over her and she clung to him, sobbing.

By the time they rounded the long bend where the river turned to go south again, nearing the quays of Kinsale, she had gathered herself up and was cross. 'The name's Barbary,' she told Sylvestris.

She could see what Cuckold Dick had meant about Kinsale. The curve of the hills round its harbour was terraced with cottages washed in different colours. There were plenty of grand houses as well, but, grand or common, their windows all looked down onto where ships of diverse nationalities discharged and loaded cargo. The town's warehouses and offices were pushed back as far as possible, as if they'd skipped out of a flood's path, to make more room on the vast quays which were crammed with goods and people.

She didn't wait to see who came aboard to buy Dick's gunpowder. They were rowed ashore and picked their way round trays of fish, linen and bales, hides and dockers who asked her to 'Mind your back dere, please, madam', in the Pale accent which owed more to Irish than English. There were other accents in the crowds of shouting, bargaining men and, Dick had been right, one group of brightly-dressed gentlemen were speaking exactly as had Don Howsyourfather. Nobody but her blinked. Kinsale was, as Dick said, a selling town and it didn't mind who it sold to.

One export dominated all others – wood. Sawn timber lined an entire quay, and more was being offloaded from barges that had just come up river from the interior. There were more new wine barrels than she'd ever seen, stacked for loading with their staves loose at the top, and beside them piles of the finishing hoops. A docker hammered the lids on boxes containing hundreds of wooden pipe staves and on each lid was stamped the crest of Sir Walter Raleigh. Crates being handled with more care than most contained glass, and glass needed massive amounts of charcoal for its manufacture. Somebody, somewhere was using up a lot of trees.

'There's Father,' said Sylvestris.

Edmund was attended by various dignitaries, the least of whom was the Mayor of Kinsale. Edmund was, after all, an important man: Clerk to the Council of Munster. Opting to be a big fish in this provincial pool had been a wise choice on his part, Barbary decided, even though he'd been given little choice. He was a provincial man. Here, where he was looked up to, he had gained authority. It was she, in her modern court mourning, who looked outlandish among the Munster ladies who tended towards the conservative styles more suited to their figures. Munster ladies, at least the ones who had come to greet her, ran to width, like their cows. In Connaught, she remembered, the phrase for a fat woman was 'thick as a Munster heifer'.

She was surprised she warranted such an exalted welcome, and assumed that it was extended to all of Edmund's visitors as a compliment to him, but the same reception awaited her in Cork that night after the long drive in Edmund's coach. Here she was given a corporation dinner. She was Lady Betty, widow of brave Sir Rob of the Yellow Ford's glorious dead who had laid down his life fighting the Great Satan, and in paying respect to her they were paying respect to Rob. 'He'll be avenged,' she was told, time and again. 'The Queen and Essex will avenge him.'

The two names were synonymous. The loyal toast was 'To Our Gracious Majesty, Queen Elizabeth, and Our

Lord of Essex, God bless them'. Essex's policy to exterminate the Irish threat was one they had been urging on the English government for years, and now it was about to be implemented they were cock-a-hoop. The Mayor of Cork, wittier than most, spoke of the O'Neill as having embarked on a course that would wreck him 'on the Essex coast'.

Barbary listened for any sign of panic beneath the laughter and could detect none; there was less worry here than in London. By the very act of colonisation they had proved the Irish to be inferior. Clontibret and Yellow Ford had been hiccups in a status quo as ordained as the Ten Commandments, to be blamed, saving her presence, on an ill-equipped army having been taken by ambush. The north and Connaught had never been settled like Munster, they explained, O'Neill would never reach Dublin, and Essex was coming . . .

The same certainty awaited them at Mallow Castle where they spent the next night with Sir Thomas Norris, Lord Justice of Munster, and his wife, and by this time Barbary had begun to accept it. The town had grown in the years she'd been away, its slope down to the river now a street of prosperous houses and shops. The coloured and very English inn signs, the stone bridge, the chunky garrison whose doors were patrolled by slow-marching, red-coated soldiers, the castle above it with its gardens gave out a sense of rooted stability. Everything Irish had been banished, except the accent of some of the shopkeepers and soldiers, but such shopkeepers had a portrait of Elizabeth in their window and such soldiers shouted 'God Save the Queen' as they opened the gates to Edmund's coach.

The welcome here was more muted than at Cork. Rob and Sir John Norris, Sir Thomas's brother, had been venturers together and there had been genuine shock at Rob's death. Sir John was ill upstairs, making it no occasion for feasting. And besides, Barbary herself was remembered as having arrived in the district trailing a disreputable history, something about being dressed as a boy, and then disappearing in peculiar circumstances. Out of courtesy to her late husband and to Master Spenser, and to the fact that she had been consorting with some of England's highest nobility, even if she was of

Irish birth, Sir Thomas must entertain her, but he did it at the family table with no other guests.

Lady Norris, particularly, was in contortions as to how to behave to this upstart whose behaviour – Lady Norris was vague about what form it had taken – disqualified her from sitting at her table but who was at the same time qualified to be there, if Master Spenser was to be believed, through having been a familiar of the Queen's and Mr Secretary Cecil's. Lady Norris did not approve of Mr Secretary Cecil and his feeble policies towards the Irish, any more than she had approved of his father for the same reason, but she had all the colonial woman's reverence for Her Gracious Majesty.

It took Barbary, who was tired, two courses of the heavy supper to realise that verbal darts were flying at her over the venison. Her hostess was trying to take her down a peg for airs which she had not been aware of putting on, while at the same time trying to impress her with her knowledge of the English social whirl.

'My brother-in-law, Sir John, was amazed when you popped up out of Lough Neagh, Lady Betty. Quite Arthurian, he said. The Lady in the Lake.'

'Yes,' said Barbary. 'I had been to visit the Countess of Tyrone. How is Sir John?'

'Not well, I fear. Sir Thomas is acting Lord General at the moment.' Lady Norris picked up another dart. 'Ah, poor Mabel. Quite mad at the end, they say. But what can you expect from a mixed marriage?' She smiled, having scored a nice inner. 'Of course, my dear Lady Betty, that does not apply to yours. I am sure you and Rob were of the happiest, though you were so many times absent from each other.'

Oh krap, thought Barbary, I'm too old for this. Nevertheless she began mentally to turn up her sleeves. 'Indeed. How wise you are, Lady Norris, to stay at Sir Thomas's side, even if it does mean exile from fashionable life at court.' An outer, but she was beginning to get the range. Further down the table she saw Sylvestris imperceptibly lift his thumb.

Lady Norris shifted her grip. 'Nevertheless, dear Lady Betty, we are in the closest contact. My mother-in-law, as you know, is the Queen's dearest friend and has never had the shame of a falling-out with Her Majesty and

553

being excluded from it.' A good inner; old Lady Norris even had the distinction of a royal nickname, being the Queen's 'Crow'. Before Barbary could take the next throw, Lady Norris went on: 'She has suggested Her Majesty should make her first visit to Ireland on the occasion of the masque we intend to give in the spring.'

'You must allow me to advise you on it; Sir Rob and I gave one for her not too long ago.'

'Its theme was criminality, was it not? I wonder why?'

'I know Her Majesty's humour, and she was graciously pleased to say it was the best of any she had been to.'

By the end of the dinner Barbary had lost count of the score, but she found herself, to her own surprise, invigorated as she had not been for a long time.

The next morning, back in the coach, Sylvestris said: 'You won.'

'Are you sure? She got a couple of golds.'

'Who got golds?' asked Edmund. 'What do you two talk about?'

The five-mile journey to Kilcolman was one she knew well, but she was shocked by the view out of the window. 'What have you done with the trees?' An old and handsome friend had suddenly become bald. The countryside was sleek under rich September sun, hedges edging fields in which stooks of corn leaned against each other, but to Barbary these were mere wisps of hair left by a galloping alopecia; Munster's crowning glory had gone. What had been mysterious was exposed as suburban as the countryside around London; where glades had rung to the hunting horns of the Fianna, cows now grazed in uninterrupted meadowland.

They passed the lane that led to Hap Hazard. Edmund Spenser fell back in his seat as Barbary turned on him: 'Where's my bloody woods? You let that bastard Ellis cut down my woods?'

'Compose yourself, Lady Betty. Deforestation has had to be deliberate policy, a matter of security.'

'Krap.' She had no deep feeling for the Hap Hazard estate, but there'd been a view of it against beechwood enhancing the light falling through branches into slanting columns. And bloody Ellis had cut down the lot, so that the house was just another English residence in orderly parkland.

'I beg you to remember the boy, Lady Betty. It is true. The trees harboured the rebellious Irish and became our enemy as much as they.'

'How can a tree become somebody's enemy?' She remembered the quays at Kinsale. 'Became somebody's ship, you mean, somebody's wine barrel, somebody's bloody pipe stem.'

'Lady Betty, *please*. It is true again that much of the province's wealth has derived from its timber, but the profit was unlooked-for and arose out of a greater expediency.'

She sat back, muttering. The trees had differentiated Ireland from England, giving it a touch of Eden which was now prosaic and tamed, lost for ever. They'd take the sea away from Connaught next. She was wholly Irish again, rebel against the Lady Norrises, the Ellises and other such woodsmen. She remembered with poignancy the wonderful evening when she had barnacled Rosh through the wooded Ballyhouras to the place of the Mass, the evening that had led to O'Hagan.

And Spenser's Deer Park had gone, or at least a real deer park replaced the woods which had flanked the road to Kilcolman's entrance. Selected oaks stood in carefully casual groves, dappling their section of sward. A herd of fallow deer feeding and whisking their tails gathered in the ornamental shade. Probably nailed their hoofs to the ground, thought Barbary, but she did not complain; the old Deer Park had contained Maccabee's 'namelesses', and Captain Mackworth, and the hanging people. Perhaps there were some trees that had to be erased. But as they turned into the drive to the house, she looked back and saw that, behind the Deer Park, the Ballyhouras had gone too. There were mountains there sure enough, but they were shorn down to their bones, the great canopy of varying green ripped away to display bare mounds on which, at this distance, some sort of moss or fern glowed a dull red as if they were embarrassed.

'You've worked hard, Edmund,' she said grimly.

'Thank you,' he said. 'You will see some changes.'

Like the rest of Munster, Spenser Castle had the patina achieved by prosperity. No weeds surrounded the gatehouses, now connected by a lintel and large gates instead of solid wooden doors. They swept between clipped hedges flanked by lawn, glimpsing the cupolas, green with the verdigris of real brass, and twisted brick chimneys. The miserable sticks of yew along the path from the bawn, where she and Rosh had dragged the unconscious O'Hagan that terrible night, were now marvels of topiary. The gravel led to steps on which stood great stone pots containing geraniums. This was no castle, but it was a very fine mansion.

Edmund was rightly and quietly proud. 'An improvement, I think, Lady Betty. You will remember your first sighting of it.' She stopped being cross with him, remembering how brave he had been on the morning they had both seen the ridiculous stumps and stones of what he had expected to be a great keep. It was the last time she and Edmund made any reference to the past: Elizabeth Spenser saw to that.

Edmund's new wife was a big young healthy Paleswoman, fair-haired and already pregnant with her and Edmund's second child. She came from middle-class undertaker stock – her uncle was the Mayor of Youghal – and had no pretensions to be other than she was. She threw herself in a buxom welcome on her new stepson and her visitor and for a while Barbary thought: Uncomplicated, bless her. Sylvestris will be all right.

Later she mentally kicked herself for believing that the world contained an uncomplicated anybody. Elizabeth Spenser, though much younger than Edmund, adored her husband, thought herself the luckiest woman in the world to be married to such a great man, and was eaten away with jealousy of the time when she wasn't.

Whether Edmund had represented his previous marriage as idyllic, Maccabee as a paragon, and the time since her death as a period when he had walked, admired but sorrowing, with princes, Barbary couldn't be sure. Whatever its cause, Elizabeth tolerated no mention of any of them. If the conversation so much as veered in the direction of England or any time pre-dating her and Edmund's meeting, she waded into it like a master of hounds sorting out a dog fight and commanded it back into behaving itself with interruptions such as: 'My Lady Norris has commended her own children's wet nurse to me, Lady Betty. Should I accept her?' Or, 'Would you look at the tetters on this baby's forehead, Lady Betty, and give me your opinion.'

Barbary absolved her from triumphing at her own fecundity and her, Barbary's, childlessness; it was jealousy pure and simple. Elizabeth was a good wife and mother, but the cosiness of the family circle she had created included her, Edmund, and their baby boy – whom Edmund, with what Barbary regarded as singular lack of imagination, had christened Sylvanus – and no other. Barbary resented the fact that no enquiry was made about Catherine, and even more the deliberate tendency to exclude Sylvestris.

She was taken on a tour of the house and grounds to have not only their new features but their old pointed out as if she had never been there. She was even introduced to Rosh. 'Allow me to present my invaluable housekeeper, Roisín.'

Barbary flung herself on her old ally, and was rebuffed. Extricating herself from the hug, Rosh dropped a curtsey and acknowledged her with a polite: 'Lady Betty.'

Elizabeth was gratified. 'Rosh is always a little wary with visitors, but you will find her the salt of the earth. We know Roisín's little ways, don't we, Roisín?'

Obviously she did, and obviously Barbary didn't, not the ones she had now developed, at any rate. After dinner she excused herself and ran Rosh to earth in the kitchens. 'Well, old salt of the earth,' she said, 'what's this with you and your little ways?'

Rosh looked up with disinterested courtesy. 'Can I get you something, Lady Betty?'

Retiring hurt, Barbary wondered what had happened. Was Rosh offended that she had never sent her word from Connaught? But she had sent her a letter via Edmund, a noncommittal letter, true, but showing that their old relationship was not forgotten. Did her clothes, her reputation smell of that oppressor, the English Queen? Or had Rosh indeed transferred all her attachment to her new mistress and family and, following Elizabeth Spenser's example, shunned all outsiders?

Unlikely. The old friendship between them had been that of equals, something Rosh could not share with Elizabeth who, however good an employer, was patronising and spoke of the mere Irish as if they were breeds of dogs. She was doing it now, as she sewed her embroidery, sitting on a stool as near Edmund's chair as she could get it, with the baby Sylvanus in a cradle at her feet. 'I'm not sure we should employ Nuala's son for the cows, Edmund dear. His father was a MacBrian and the MacBrians are never trustworthy. We should look for an O'Hanlan; they have the proper herding strain.'

'What happened to Rosh's father?' asked Barbary. 'And Lal?'

'Dudley died, poor old man,' said Elizabeth, 'and Lal was a disappointment. Went off. Just disappeared. Rosh was so upset; she felt he had let us down.'

'Where did he go?'

Elizabeth shrugged. 'Nobody knows. They do that occasionally.'

'And do you still get trouble from the MacSheehys?'

'Oh my dear, the MacSheehys were rooted out years ago.' Elizabeth changed the subject which might lead back to a past she hadn't been involved in. 'Edmund, do read Lady Betty your "View of the Present State of Ireland".' She looked towards Barbary. 'It's the answer to all those on the mainland who still think you can pat the Irish on the head without getting your hand bitten. Edmund points out that there can be no lasting peace until all the mere Irish are wiped out, don't you, Edmund?'

'It's not quite that, my dear.' He put his finger in his book to mark his place. 'My plan, Lady Betty, is that to Anglicise this country for once and for all it should be properly garrisoned. The rebellious septs would receive twenty days' warning, and if they did not submit after that, they should be hunted to extinction, their crops destroyed and their cattle killed. It would only take one winter; there would be little trouble with them the following summer.'

He warmed to the theme. 'That policy *must* co-exist with enforcement of the old Kilkenny statutes, so lamentably fallen into abeyance, to banish Irish customs and dress and the Irish language. No intermarriage.'

'Definitely not,' said Elizabeth.

Edmund held up his hand. 'It may sound harsh, Lady Betty, and I know you have a sympathy for them, but we who live among them know them to be an evil race which must be extirpated. Legally, of course. I hold no truck with those who suggest assassination of their chieftains.'

'You're such an old softy-boots, Edmund,' said Elizabeth fondly. To Barbary she said: 'He quite rebuked Sir Walter Raleigh's suggestion that the O'Donnell be sent poison. Sir Thomas Davis has offered to worm himself into O'Neill's presence and stab him to death, but my lord here would have none of that either. Personally I see nothing wrong in it. Well, let's hope the Queen will read and take note of "The View".' She looked up at her husband. 'You'll show it to my lord Essex when he comes, won't you, Edmund?'

'He'll love it,' said Barbary. She stood up: 'I'd like to go to bed.'

Elizabeth lit a candelabra. 'Edmund has it in his head that you should like to occupy the old gatehouse during your stay. I said you'd be more comfortable in the house, but when my lord speaks . . . We have made it fit for you, I hope. I'll light you to it.'

She turned in the doorway: 'Don't pick the baby up, Sylvestris. He's unused to strangers.'

As she stood on the old familiar steps of the gatehouse, candelabra in hand, and said goodnight to her hostess, Barbary supposed it had been thoughtful of Edmund to remember her previous fondness for the place, but she felt a reluctance to go inside and, once inside, to go upstairs. She didn't think of O'Hagan every minute any more, she didn't think of him every day; whole weeks had begun to go by without her being surprised by that beautiful, terrible pain, until, eventually, it had lost all its terror and some of its beauty. The anger in his letter, even the O'Neill's lie, had become mossed over by time.

The candles made shadows on the wall and her footsteps echoed as she passed the door to the well, awaking other memories. She had crawled back here after seeing the hanging mother and child. Time hadn't managed to blur that; it had been the watershed of her life. She climbed up past the first storey to the bedroom more briskly. Men came and went, mostly went. What were they? Mere machines to provide women with the generation that came after them, and in order to disguise the fact that they had no other purpose than this one, they blustered about, making war on each other, thereby endangering the reason they were here in the first place.

With something like bravado, she swung open the door to the top room.

Elizabeth had refurnished the room for her, a single bed with a tester from which hung sprigged lace curtains, a most beautiful clothes press, a side table on which was a pot of sweetmeats and a crystal glass. A lamb's fleece was on the floor to greet her feet when she arose in the morning, a warming pan sticking out from a lace bed-spread, another small table with a bowl and ewer. There were shutters on the window, open to the autumnal night. This was not the room where a man had cursed her for nursing him and muttered that her hair had the colour of wine in it. And a good job too.

It was as she was getting into bed that she saw the bat. It hung in the corner its ancestor had made its own, looking at her from the same wicked, upside down little eyes, a dark and atavistic reminder in the prettiness of the room that some things were unchangeable. Time, after all, had mossed over nothing. Certainly not pain.

Somehow Ellis had managed to become Mayor of Mallow, a member of Munster's Council, a fellow of Cork's Guild of Merchant Venturers, Commander of the Awbeg Militia, a magistrate, and remain as big a boor as ever.

He'd learned to put a flimsy veil of joviality over his aggression, but only in order to complain of those who took offence that they couldn't take a joshing.

His greeting to Barbary on the steps of Hap Hazard was: 'You've done well for yourself. Who's going to be husband number two?'

'I see success hasn't spoiled you, Master Ellis.'

He was complimented. 'That it ain't. Ellis didn't get where he is today by fancy talk and beating about the bush. I'll pay you three thousand pounds for this house and land which is what your better half paid for it, Ellis knows, and not a penny more. But come in. Come in and welcome to some vittles. Wife! Get along and fetch our fancy lady here drink and meat.'

Concealed somewhere in Ellis's hoglike soul, Barbary decided, there must be taste. Hap Hazard had flourished under his tenancy, if you discounted the rape of its woods, and he had been wise enough to make no alteration to the crazy, chevronned black and white exterior of the house, which had been an innovation in Ireland when Rob's mason built it, and was now the vogue in the towns, although it was still the only one of its kind in the countryside that she knew of. Ellis's furniture, which she had expected to be ostentatious, was limited to good, black oak pieces redolent and softly shining with beeswax. The white plaster was expertly moulded. Bowls of potpourri, late roses and holyoaks were reflected in the sheen of an old refectory table. The portrait of Ellis over the white stone fireplace, while kinder to his nose than it deserved, had been painted after the manner of Holbein.

Mrs Ellis, another example of Ellis's good choosing, had lost the worn look which the hard work of the first years had imposed on all the undertakers' wives and blossomed into a handsome, happy woman.

It was Mrs Ellis Barbary kept her eye on while they sat down and listened to Ellis boast of his plain common sense and bluster about what he would pay for and what he wouldn't. She was the card-mirror which had overlooked the conies' hands back at the Pudding-in-a-Cloth. Barbary needed to know Ellis's cards if she was to get her £10,000. How much did he desire Hap Hazard? At first she had been surprised that he desired it at all; it was a gentleman's residence undoubtedly, but she could have expected Ellis's ambition to covet a castle; he could certainly afford it. Munster undertakers, however, had become to some extent victims of their own success; all land that had once been available when it had been taken away from the rebel Irish was now occupied, either by the new settlers or by such old Irish aristocracy as had made its peace with the Elizabethan regime. The inflation that was rampant in England, where the Treasurer was anxiously calling in Crown debts to subsidise Essex's new army, was affecting Ireland no less. The realisation that the Irish forests were actually a goldmine had shot up the price of timber, and at the rate it was being cut down that same timber was becoming scarcer. Ellis in his early days had managed to acquire more land than his original parcel, but to build on it now would cost him a fortune.

Mrs Ellis wanted to stay at Hap Hazard; she was showing alarm at her husband's protestations that there

561

were hundreds of greater mansions he could move to. She'd reached the sphere that suited her; she didn't want to rise to heights where she would be forced to compete with, and be patronised by, the Lady Norrises of the next stratum up. And Ellis placed a great deal more reliance on his wife than he pretended; he kept looking at her for approval.

It was a quietly confident Barbary who clambered onto horseback and trotted off with Ellis to be shown the estate's apparent shortcomings. That field over there was too wet, that hill too dry. Look at them bloody fences, he'd have to repair the lot and did she know what chestnut paling fetched nowadays?

The only real dilapidation was in the houses of the Irish tenants. The roofs on at least three cottages were so bare of thatch that rain could get in. She was shocked; Edmund Spenser, whatever his opinion of the mere Irish, kept them carefully housed. 'They're too bloody lazy to repair 'em,' said Ellis, and added unguardedly, 'besides, a new roof puts the rent up.' Each garden was given over to a potato bed indicating that its cottager was either too overworked or, according to Ellis, too bloody idle to grow anything else. 'You like 'em, don't you?' he shouted at a collection of women picking the last of the apples in his orchard. 'Eh? You're a lot of spud-diggers, aren't you?'

It was obviously a regular pleasantry. The women smiled and curtseyed, and one of them answered him in Irish. 'Yes, yes,' said Ellis, waving, and turned to Barbary: 'Never could get the hang of their lingo. But we understand each other, me and the bog-trotters.'

Barbary doubted it. The woman had said: 'What can you expect from a pig but grunts?'

Back at the house they went to the library and Ellis made his offer again: 'Three thousand, not a groat more. It's not as if a fancy lady like you needs the money.' All along this had been his theme, that Barbary in making an astute marriage had done very well for herself and, by making another, could do even better. Like those who had never been to court, Ellis laboured under the belief that everybody who had was possessor of an endless supply of fairy gold.

Barbary took a tablet and stylus from her placket. 'Master Ellis, I shall expect twelve thousand pounds to be paid within the week or your vacation of Hap Hazard at the end of the month when your lease expires.'

'You're mad, woman.' He folded his arms. 'You'll not get it.'

'I think I will.' She made a note. 'Item. Ninety-four acres of beechwood cut down without permission, say, two thousand pounds.'

'Assart,' bellowed Ellis. 'Improvements. National security.'

'Also sold to Sir Walter Raleigh without permission. Item. One hundred acres of hornbeam coppiced and sold to Master Slade of Kinsale for struts etc. without permission. Item. Three hundred acres of oak sold and sent to Bristol shipyards. Without permission. Item. Two hundred yew trees felled and supplied to the army. Without permission. Seven hundred tons of charcoal sent to Waterford glass manufactury. Without permission.' She looked up. 'That's what I have proof of; of course there may be more. Item. Extra rents raised from tenantry. Without permission.'

She sat back in her chair. 'I am being lenient in putting it at twelve thousand pounds. The court may adjudge it more.' Neither on her journey up through Kinsale and Cork, nor in the two weeks since, had she been wasting her time. Ellis, bless him, might think she was unpopular in the district, and so she was, but there had been plenty to come forward with information that would do Ellis down and help Sir Rob's son get a fair price.

He got it that day. Ellis blustered but gave in with a suddenness which made her wonder whether the old cliché that a bully backed down when faced by a bigger bully was true, or whether he'd become so rich from the timber on this and his other lands that money wasn't really an object with him. She had even gone up in his estimation. 'We commons understand each other.'

They agreed that the sum should be paid in one thousand gold pieces now, and the rest made up in the transference to Henry of Ellis's interest in three boats at Bristol, the papers to be prepared by a notary at Mallow. He fetched the money from some fastness in a cellar, counted it into a chest and had it put in her cart. 'It's people like Ellis as made it safe for a woman to tote gold through Munster,' he grumbled, but he was affable enough when he saw her off. 'Tell Edmund to stick his books away,' he said. 'I'm calling out the militia for extra training.'

She paused on the step. 'Why?'

He spat. 'Bloody Dublin's persuaded the Council to send most of the Munster army to Sligo under young Henry Norris and Clifford Conyers to halt the O'Donnell. Some idea of diverting O'Neill away from their precious city. Essex is coming, they say. We don't need the men we got, they say. But I say let Dublin find its own men. Ellis knows.'

As she drove away, Barbary felt that, for once, Ellis did. The peace that reigned over the fat fields of Munster was extraordinary considering what was going on elsewhere. There was no insurrection; not so much as a lamb belonging to the undertakers had been killed in months. The gleaners who passed her at the bottom of Hap Hazard's drive waved their rakes at her not in revolutionary fury, but a cheery good-day. Around her the hedges were full of rose-hips and late blackberries, the trees were still leafed in their autumnal colours, and she told herself that her unease was because it had been on just such a lovely day that she'd found the flayed body of Captain Mackworth.

No, it wasn't that. There had been small flickers in this even seasonal tenor; nothing dramatic, happenings that would have passed unnoticed in the early undertaking days, which the undertakers themselves were brushing off as unimportant but which, to an Order nose, smelled of fish.

On the Sunday before last, there had been no Irish in the congregation at Effin where Edmund still preached occasionally to make up for the deficiencies of the pleasure-loving Prebendary Chadwick. Edmund had worried about it but when, this Sunday, the church was full again he had decided not to fine the recusants, which as a magistrate he was entitled to do, and submitted them instead to an extra long sermon on the hellfire awaiting those who ignored the Sabbath.

And Ellis had just told her there had been no single case of drunkenness brought to court in three weeks. 'What about Prebendary Chadwick?' she'd asked. 'I thought he was always sheets to the wind.'

'I mean mere Irish, woman.'

'And what does Ellis know about that?'

'Ellis knows that he's confiscated all their damned poteen and they're too bloody idle to make more, that's what Ellis knows.'

But all the way home to Spenser Castle, through the tang of leaves, dusty lanes and horse manure, Barbary's nose twitched at the scent of something else.

There was a horse by the mounting block, and the schoolmaster from Buttevant on the steps, talking to Edmund.

'What's the matter?'

The schoolmaster turned on her, holding a child's primer. 'Lady Betty, look at this. I ask you. I've been saying to Master Edmund here, it's disgraceful, and as a magistrate he should proceed against the children. Flogging means nothing to them.' He shoved the book under his nose. 'Look.'

'It's a primer.'

'And where's the first page? The one with the style and title of the Queen on it?'

'Torn out.'

'Exactly. And so it is with all the others. Thirty-four most excellent books vandalised of Her Gracious Majesty's sanction. They've had the same trouble at Doneraile. Savages we found them and savages they remain.'

She and Edmund stayed on the steps after he'd gone. 'Something's brewing, Edmund. Isn't it time you paid another visit to your sister?'

His lack of surprise showed he'd actually considered it. 'But it will not be of any great moment, Lady Betty. Of course they're infected by the doings of Tyrone, but this isn't the north. They've been subjugated too long; treacherous they may be but they are also enfeebled.'

'The army's pulling out.' She told him what Ellis had said.

He shrugged. 'We have a strong militia. All our houses are fortified and our own Irish are loyal. We withstood the MacSheehys, we can surely withstand a little rioting.' She had the uneasy feeling that she had interrupted a process that might have ended in his temporarily evacuating Kilcolman if his stubbornness had not been aroused by her suggesting it. They walked round the ornamental garden towards the lake which was now paved round its banks, the delineation emphasising its strange, crescent shape more than ever. 'Did you get rid of the frogs?'

'Indeed. I had the marsh drained of the beasts, though they have begun to be troublesome in the evenings again.'

'Edmund,' she said, 'I've got my price for Hap Hazard and would like to get the money to England as fast as possible. My friend's ship should be arriving again soon, so I intend to set off for Kinsale tomorrow. I wondered if Sylvestris might accompany me?'

'To England?'

'Just to Kinsale. I shall come back for a while if I may.'

He pretended to consider, but she knew instantly he wouldn't let the boy go with her. There had been several indications that he resented the closeness between the two of them; in his own way he was as jealous as Elizabeth. 'I am grateful to you, Lady Betty, but perhaps it is time that Sylvestris settled down to knowing his new mother somewhat better than he does. He will stay here.'

While she was in the gateroom packing, she heard Sylvestris running up the stairs. 'Did you get it?'

'I did. And two thousand more.'

'Oh, well done. Henry Croesus. And can I come with you to Kinsale?'

'No. Your father says you should stay with your stepmother. And he's right.' There was silence behind her. He was being brave, damn him.

'You'll go on to England, won't you? You're not coming back.'

She swung round. He was trying to smile at her though tears were coming out of his eyes. 'I'm coming back. Listen to me, Sir Stayon; today's, what, the first of October. I'll be back by the fifth, certainly the sixth. You be here in this room on the sixth of October and I'll come straight here. If I don't, it's because the boat's delayed and I have to wait for it. Understand?'

'Yes.'

'And I smell trouble. Stay in the grounds and don't go out unless your father tells you.'

He nodded and helped her downstairs with her wicker hamper. Passing through the hall was Rosh, who paused. 'Are you away now?' It was the first time she'd spoken as if Barbary wasn't a stranger.

566

'Just to Kinsale. I'm coming back.' She was sure Rush was about to say something else, but at that moment they were joined by Edmund in his riding clothes and a high humour.

'I'm accompanying you as far as Cork, Lady Betty. I received the summons last night. I understand I'm to be made Sheriff of Munster.'

'Congratulations.'

'Congratulations, Father.'

She could wish the appointment had been made at some other time. She and Edmund were being accompanied by two of the ex-soldiers he employed as guards; it would leave the house short of valuable men. But Edmund had made up his mind. 'You trouble yourself too much, Lady Betty. Our people are loyal, the walls are stout and the militia is patrolling the roads.'

Again, once she was ambling through it, the countryside's look of permanence reassured her; it was difficult to believe in danger among fields and hills that resembled Kent, where a drover taking cows to Mallow knuckled his forehead amiably as they passed through his herd, and a girl milking a goat by the side of the road was singing.

As they neared Mallow they had to go up on a bank and wait as the garrison, reinforced by others, marched along the road north to Limerick to join up with Conyers and proceed against Connaught. Young Henry Norris saluted as he trotted by at the head of the column: 'Fine day, Master Spenser. I'll bring you back Red Hugh's head and you can write a poem on it.'

'A fine lad,' said Edmund, looking after him. 'A fine family. Six Norris sons, all in Her Majesty's service, and one already killed for it in Brittany. Their mother must be proud.'

It took time for the soldiers, about six hundred, to march by. They must have drained the country of every regular, thought Barbary. Edmund waved his cap and cheered until they'd gone and the pipe and drum faded to be replaced by the shuffle of women following their men to war.

Ellis was waiting for her at the notary's. Riding on once again, she realised how much she had been worrying about the transaction; now it was completed and Henry was provided for she felt considerably better. She enjoyed the journey to Cork, and the one on the following day to Kinsale, although there she had to wait two irksome days before Cuckold Dick's ship came in. It was the same ship and captain who had brought her to Ireland three weeks before.

'You're late,' she told him irritably as she stepped aboard. At Kinsale prices, the lodging of herself and the escort had been very expensive. 'I want this case put in the special whiskey barrel for Master Dick's special attention, and hand him these papers. Is he trading with Connaught any more this year, do you know?'

'He'll have to be quick if he does,' the captain told her, sniffing the weather. 'Another month and the seas will be closed. But I'll tell him.'

'He can send a message to me at Kilcolman.' If it was this year, or next, it didn't matter too much. She was a free woman. For the first time in her life she wasn't having to react to circumstances, wasn't cony-catching or being cony-caught. Life's sea which had tossed her about like an empty bottle had finally entered a calm. There was no urgency about returning to England. She might make a visit to her grandmother first. She could try and contact Will.

She extracted thirty gold pieces from the case for her own use – after all, she'd negotiated more money for Henry than he could have expected and she needed some for herself. She returned to the inn and paid its damned bill, and then in the euphoria of freedom was tempted into shopping. She might as well buy clothes for Connaught here; it wouldn't be any use turning up there in court dress and high-heeled shoes. She had difficulty in finding what she wanted, Kinsale had English-style clothing for all classes but scorned to cater for mere Irish. Eventually she ran down a stall in the market that sold Irish cloaks and bought herself a good one in warmest wool with a high fur collar, a head-roll, some trews – they were better on shipboard than skirts – and a strong knife. The market tempted her into buying some presents; a rattle for Sylvanus, lace for Elizabeth, a fine handkerchief for Edmund and a book of Irish poetry she unearthed on a stall selling bric-a-brac for Sylvestris. As an afterthought she bought some comfits for Rosh.

On the journey back to Cork a westerly breeze came

up. Good, she thought, Henry'll get his money the quicker. As it got stronger she began to worry; a lot of the boy's eggs were in that one maritime basket heading back to England, to say nothing of a crew. By the time they were getting near to Cork, she and the escort had to tie their cloaks round them to stop them flapping, but by then there was more to worry about. The roads were heavy with traffic, mostly large coaches containing well-to-do families and luggage carts, and important-looking horsemen with escorts of household guards. She saw the Bishop of Cork, who had been at her corporation dinner, heading into the city with a train of twenty or more. She dug her heels into her horse and rode alongside him: 'What's happening, my lord?'

The rings on his fat hand sparkled as he raised it in automatic blessing: 'Be at peace, my child.' Then he recognised her. 'There's nothing to worry your little head with. Some insurgents have invaded the province further north and we leaders of our flock are gathering to decide on the appropriate measures.'

'Is it the O'Neill?' The appropriate measure the flock leaders seemed to have decided on was getting themselves inside city walls as quickly as possible.

'No, no. Our information says it's merely one of his jackals. A renegade beast named Tyrrell. God will judge and defeat him, my child.'

They were swept on into the city. At the gates, she was stopped by a guard of the city's militia. 'We'll need your escort and your horses, lady. Requisition. Take them to that post over there.'

She was bewildered. 'What's happening?'

'Council orders, lady. All able-bodied men and horse-flesh to be transferred to the militia.'

She nodded and rode towards the post where there was a chaotic queue of coaches, horsemen and angry notables. She took one look at it and slipped past to go into the city. They were having no horse of hers; let 'em take the Bishop's. She glanced behind her. They were.

There was feverish activity everywhere, but no panic. She was relieved to see that requisitioning was only going on at the gates; there were still plenty of horses around, though most of them were dragging carts of supplies and ammunition to the wall towers. In one of the squares, pikes and firearms were being handed out to a crowd of apprentices. Housewives were crowding the shops and coming out loaded as if for a siege. Good God, they were *expecting* a siege. She had to find Edmund.

She ran him to earth in the municipal council chamber, though she had to brush aside functionaries who said he was too busy. He came to the door when she called to him.

'Thank God, Lady Betty, at least you are safe.'

'What's happening?'

He was white and tired, but he too wasn't panicking. 'Tyrrell's arrived in the Aherlow at the head of a strong force.'

'Who's Tyrrell?'

'One of O'Neill's captains.' Edmund's self-possession broke for a moment. 'And God curse him, he's an *Englishman.*'

'I don't care if he's Chinese. What are you doing about the family?'

'Messengers have been sent to Norris to take them into Mallow. God preserve them, I can't leave here. There's danger the Geraldine clan will rise now. There's a pretender to the dead traitor Earl of Desmond's title; if he can raise the Irish, insurrection will break out all over Munster.'

Sod Munster. 'I'll ride to Kilcolman now.'

'No.' He was stern. 'Sir Thomas will see to them. We can't spare Peter and Oswald to ride with you. Go to Richard Boyle's house, he's Elizabeth's uncle and will give us shelter. Wait for them there.'

'Very well, Edmund.' In a pig's eye, she thought. Whoever this Tyrrell is, he's a damn sight too near Spenser Castle. The Aherlow was the terrible valley where she and Rob and the undertakers had been led by Captain Mackworth through the howling MacSheehys all those years ago. It was the route to the Ballyhouras and Spenser Castle and Sylvestris. She should never have left him, she should have listened to her nose which had more sense to it than these pillocks and their strong militias and loyal Irish. If everything was so strong and loyal, why were so many of the bastards scurrying into shelter?

What racked her was that she'd promised him she would return. 'I'll get you back,' O'Hagan had said to her, and hadn't. So much for men. A little boy was expecting her to get him back. And, Jesus, she would. Organisation was breaking down. Who knew what was going to happen now? She did. She was going to go to Sylvestris. Her horse was still outside, although there was no sign of her escort. She rode to the north gate and smiled at the guards who barred her path. 'I know you need my horse, good fellows,' she said, 'but I believe I dropped my purse a furlong back, and my cousin, the Mayor, has given me permission to venture outside and quickly look for it.' It had to be something frivolous. Order rule: when all else fails, revert to the ridiculous.

'You got your head, lady, don't worry about your purse.'

'Just a look? I'll be back immediately.' She fluttered her eyelashes. And they let her through with the amused, chin-jerking exasperation that men bestowed on the reassuring female persistence to be feather-headed in times of war.

It was late and dark by the time her horse limped her into Mallow, but there had been no trouble keeping to the route; as evening had come down, she'd been lit by the flares of carts and coach lamps going towards Cork, and, for the last ten miles, by flares and lamps going in to Mallow. She was amazed at how easily the provincial nobility were beginning to abandon their homes on the basis of a rumour. Nobody knew anything, just that a renegade called Tyrrell was come to the Aherlow Valley, and that the Geraldines of the south might rise.

She stopped at Mallow Castle long enough to ascertain that the Spenser family wasn't in it. A crowd of men were questioning the guard. Should they be bringing their families into the walls? What was happening? What was happening?

The guard was reassuring. Sir Thomas Norris was out with the militia, bringing in such families as felt in need of security, but there was no need for panic. He said it so often, Barbary began to panic. 'Has he gone in the direction of Spenser Castle?'

'No need to panic, lady,' said the guard again. 'Yes, he's heading for Kildorrey and sending out scouts to see what's happening in the Aherlow. No need to panic.'

She calmed down. She could head across country by the bridle path that led through the Roche estate, past Ballybeg Abbey and Hap Hazard, join the Buttevant road and get to Spenser Castle that way. The militia would be between her and the insurgents; if Kilcolman had been evacuated, she could come back.

The wind kept cloud scudding across the moon, darkening the way, but she knew it well. It was a short cut she'd used often going back and forth to Mallow market, and besides, the tired horse would have to be walked for most of it. She supposed she was tired too, but her anxiety drove her on.

Leaves leaped up in her path like small animals writhing in agony. Hedges leaned back and forth. The wind was distracting, making branches clack together in dry applause at her progress, sometimes sounding like distant screaming. There was a light burning in the ruins of Ballybeg Abbey. Was the old poet, Tadg O'Lync, still alive and living here? She didn't care enough to find out, but she stopped in the circle of light outside an ivied wall and took the Clampett out of her bag and primed it. Whether the cartridges had any explosive power left she couldn't be sure, but she felt safer. While she was about it, she took off her court cloak and wrapped herself in the new Irish cloak. Now she was safer *and* warmer.

The damned horse had rested long enough, she was more tired than it was. She clambered up onto its back and rode along the track to Hap Hazard, emerging near the back of the house where the beechwoods had once stood. The wind was screaming again, more lifelike than ever. Oh God, it was a woman. The sound led her round the inner wall that, a long time ago, she had bullied Rob's mason into building and to the gates that were open, banging with a soft thud against each other, their ironwork casting some solid, some curled patterns onto the light gravel of the drive.

You pillock, it was nothing. It had been the wind all along. There was no light anywhere. Yes, there was. Somebody with a flare was coming up on a mule. She took the Clampett from under her cloak and put it away again as she recognised one of Ellis's boys. 'Richard, is it?'

'Robert.' He held the flare to her face to see who it

was. 'I'm looking for my ma and da, Lady Betty. I thought Father'd be out with the militia, but it's just passed me – I'm farming my own place over Buttevant now – and Sergeant Clancy said as he hadn't reported.'

'Have you seen the Spensers?'

'Passed me minutes back. The militia was taking them into Mallow.'

'All of them?'

'Yes. Mistress Spenser said as she'd go on to Cork and join her husband.'

She could have kissed him. 'I shouldn't worry about your pa, Robert.' Men like Ellis were always all right. 'He's taken your mother to safety and is out there somewhere telling the Irish to sit up straight. There's nobody at the house, it's dark.'

She saw his teeth in a flash of grin. How Ellis had produced a nice family like this she'd never know. 'Better lock up the gates then,' he said. 'It's not like Da to leave them open.'

'It's a lot of fuss about nothing,' she said; her relief that Sylvestris was all right extended a security over everything. She got off the horse to shut the gates for him while he fumbled for a key, but they wouldn't meet together. She ran her hand down the flange to find the obstruction and touched cold flesh. She jerked away from it and the gate swung back. It took an effort of will to push it open again and walk round. It had to be Ellis, she knew, but the moon was behind a cloud and all she could see was a lump, an extra emblazonment against the one he had been attached to. Then the cloud passed.

In many ways it was worse than finding Mackworth, because whoever had killed him had been playful. They'd wired Ellis's ears to the ironwork, passed wires through his hands and feet, and stuffed an apple in his mouth.

She closed her eyes and heard Robert Ellis step to her side. After a minute he began turning round and round, screaming: 'Ma! Ma!' She ran after him up the drive to search. The moonlight intensified the black and white frontage of the house out of its pleasantry into something ferocious. The door was open. She should have gone in with him, but cowardice held her back; she didn't want to find Mrs Ellis. Instead she made herself wander busily round the house, the Clampett held uselessly in her shaking hand, and saw the livid shape of a white sack lying on the tilled black earth of the vegetable garden. 'I don't want to look. It's just a white sack.' But you didn't stick carving knives into sacks.

She took the knife out and put her court cloak over the body before she went to fetch the lad. In death the woman's face had relaxed into the same nice intelligence it had worn in life, a woman who had followed the wrong man to the wrong country.

While the boy was carrying his mother down to the gate, she unwired Ellis so that his son wouldn't have to do it, trying to detach her mind. Just a fiddly job. The body slithered further down the gate as each wire was detached until it slumped at her feet. The boy was in such shock that he dithered about whether to put his father or his mother over the mule, and for a moment she didn't know either; a mule was less honourable than a horse. Her horse was the more tired, and Mrs Ellis was the lighter, so they put her on it and Ellis on the mule and led them back to Mallow along a road deserted of everything but the wind.

The body of its Mayor and his wife were taken into the castle to await services and burial, if a priest could be found to do it. The household had gone. There were more refugees, Sir George Bouchier with his wife and grandchildren, the Aylmers, some others, and the hall sounded with fear-pitched indignation that the Norrises had fled. When the bodies were carried in, the place fell silent except for crying babies. Barbary sat on a bench with Robert Ellis, holding his hand as much for her own sake as his.

He only said one thing during the whole of that long night. He looked round at her and said: 'I was going to marry an Irish girl.' It was an outburst of guilt before he began to cry, a confession that he would have defied his father and the Queen, who had railed against intermarriage. And now he thinks they were right, thought Barbary, and that most reasonable solution to all this isn't an option any more.

Sir Thomas Norris and a strong force of militia turned up in the morning, and they were all transferred to carts for the journey to Cork. Sir Thomas had already taken his family there, but he said he would be making a continuous patrol of the road between to keep it open.

But it *was* open, that was what bothered Barbary. There were some trees down from the wind, but the only danger was from others falling and the whipping of torn branches across the open carts. No people, no bullets, no howls except the wind's. The militia had reported that there was indeed an enemy force concentrating in the Aherlow, but so far it hadn't moved outside the valley.

She understood now. It wasn't the enemy army the English settlers were afraid of. What they were afraid of was exemplified in the two bodies now lying quietly in Mallow Castle's chapel. The enemy at home. It was why the aristocratic undertakers had been so quick to abandon their castles and their residences, because they had always been afraid, even if they hadn't known it, of the people they had dispossessed; even as they had subjected them, turned them into servants and labourers, raised their rents, shown them cruelty or sometimes even kindness, denied them their language, their dress and their customs, shamed them into inferiority and then made jokes about them, they had feared that one day these domestic animals would lower their horns and turn on them. Neither army nor militia could save them from their own livestock, and they'd known it. She fell asleep.

She woke up as they arrived at Cork and passed through gates into Hell. What had been an alarmed but functioning city – yesterday? It couldn't have been only yesterday – had deteriorated into a vast refugee camp. The carts from Mallow had trouble getting through the streets, not just because of the crowds but because angry residents kept trying to turn them back. Two well-dressed men, merchants by the look of them, leaped up onto Barbary's cart and wrested the reins away from the driver. 'Turn round and go back. There's no more room.' They were trying to back the cart, and merely getting tangled up with those behind, when Norris who'd been riding ahead came back. 'What's all this?' One of the merchants recognised him.

'The city's overflowing, Sir Thomas, we can't take more. There's no food. We'll get the plague.'

Thomas Norris drew his sword. 'Get down.' They got down. The carts went on, bumping over packs which overflowed into the street out of the press crammed into its sides. Barbary had never seen so many people in one place, families hunched stubbornly onto flights of steps that had become desirable perches and put them above those having to squat in the mud of the street. Window-sill flower boxes were cots for babies whose mothers squatted underneath, one arm up to hold their child in place. Open doors showed hallways carpeted with sleeping bodies. A finely robed woman was hammering on the knocker of a large front door which refused to open.

A beadle barred their way. 'Sorry, Sir Thomas. Orders. The Council says you'll have to go on to Kinsale or Youghal. There may be room there.'

Sir Thomas focused noble, bloodshot eyes. 'The Council can go and fuck itself,' he said. He turned round to his charges. 'Out. Get down.' To the militiamen he said: 'Circle round the town and back to the North Gate. Rest in the carts. If anybody tries to take the horses, kill them. We'll go back when I've had some sleep.'

Lady Bourchier clung onto his stirrup. 'But where shall we go?'

Sir Thomas flung out an exhausted, expansive arm. 'Take your pick, madam.' And rode off.

Barbary got down, clutching her pack. It still contained the presents she'd bought for the Spensers. Gifts for when she found them. Boyle, that was the name Edmund had said. Richard Boyle, Elizabeth's uncle. She stopped a man who seemed to know where he was going. 'Where can I find Richard Boyle's house?'

He raised his fist as if to punch her, but paused. 'Was that English you spoke? Ach, I thought you were Irish in that cloak. I'd take it off. We'll be hanging every Irish bastard in town this night, if only to make room. Over by the East Gate and ask again.'

She didn't take the cloak off, the wind was increasingly cold, but she turned the distinctively Irish fur collar under and made for the East Gate. Some of the side streets were too blocked by people to get through and she had to make detours, wondering again and again at a fear so strong it had driven men and women and children out of their warm country homes to crouch in the wind-tunnels of a city.

At one point she found herself down at the quays of the river, and paused to watch English soldiers disembarking

576

from a transport. A boy, typical of dockside boys every-where, was pestering them for souvenirs. 'Have you any English pennies, sorr?' One of the soldiers kicked him so that he fell. The last, tiny straw of viciousness broke Barbary's back.

'You bastard. What did you do that for?'

The soldier turned, surprised. He was very young. 'He's Papist Irish, ain't he?'

'He's a Palesman, for God's sake. He's on your side.'

'Is he? What's he talk like that for then?'

Wearily, Barbary said: 'His family's probably been here for generations. Protestant, as you are. Or loyal Catholic.'

'Oh.' The complexity was beyond him, but he meant well. 'Sorry, son.' He fumbled in his pack and threw the boy a penny.

'Are you one of Essex's men?' she asked him.

'Advance guard, lady,' he told her cheerily. 'Arrived in the estuary before the wind got up and been tacking up the bastard ever since. Old Essex'll still be stuck in Wales waiting for an easterly to Dublin. What's this here Cork like anyway?'

'Crowded,' she said.

Richard Boyle's house when she found it was imposing, but full. Stepping over people who were camp-ing in his hall she enquired for Elizabeth. 'Oh, the niece. Upstairs,' a woman told her, tartly. 'Got a room to her-self.'

It was a small, pretty room with rattling windows looking out to the eastern hills. Elizabeth was sitting in a chair feeding her baby, but Barbary's attention went to a table which had bread and cheese and a ham on it. She said crossly: 'I went back to look for you,' sat down and immediately began to eat. She couldn't remember when she'd last tasted food. As she munched she waited for questions, sympathy, some praise and petting. It occurred to her she wasn't getting any of them. She looked round. Elizabeth was staring at her. 'You're all right, aren't you?' Barbary asked her. 'Where's Sylves-tris?'

Elizabeth shrieked and covered her face with one of her hands. 'Oh Lord, oh Lord. When I saw you I hoped . . . Haven't you got him?'

577

Barbary stopped eating. 'What do you mean?' All, Robert Ellis had said. He'd seen them. All the Spensers. Oh God, he'd only seen the family he knew and he didn't know Sylvestris. It was her fault, she should have questioned the man. God, oh God, it must be all right. He's here, he must be here.

'Barbary, he'd gone somewhere. It happened so fast, it was so frightening, and I wasn't used to him being around. I only thought of the baby.'

She was still trying to understand. 'You forgot him?' Then she did understand. 'You stupid, stupid bitch. You forgot him.'

'Please, Barbary.' Explanation and excuse chattered out of her mouth. A suddenly dark, empty Spenser Castle from which all servants had disappeared. Creakings. Whisperings. Terror. The arrival of the militia as scared as she was, hurrying her. Her and the baby and the unborn child, the most important things in her world, and that world collapsing. 'I didn't think of him until Mallow. The militia went back then, but they said he wasn't in the house.'

'Where had he gone?'

'I don't know.' Elizabeth wiped her tears on her baby's head and her voice was muffled. 'He never liked me.'

'I don't either. Does Edmund know?'

'He's so angry. He'll get Sir Thomas to go back. Barbary, don't look like that. He can't leave here with all his responsibility. But he's afraid the boy will be hostage, or worse, because of . . .'

'Because of what?'

'Smerwick.'

The sins of a poet who'd stood by and approved slaughter visited on the head of one, grave little boy. Ellis wired to his gate with the apple in his mouth, the knife in Mrs Ellis's stomach. Debts called in, with torture as interest. She began snatching up the food and stuffing it into her pack.

'Please, Barbary, Lady Betty. Where are you going?'

'Back.'

She heard Elizabeth crying to her as she left the house. She made her way through the town and waited by the carts until Sir Thomas Norris returned and led them out through the gates to Mallow.

They passed more refugees heading for Cork, but their class had changed. The noble families and gentlemen farmers had either got inside already or were fortifying their homes. These were the common undertakers, the plumbers and plasterers, shopkeepers, schoolmasters, ex-soldiers, coopers, the people who had answered Elizabeth's call for settlers and sailed to Ireland for land and a better life. They had furniture, grandparents and children on haywains, they held onto poultry crates to stop the wind blowing them off their pushcarts and drove their milch cows along with them. These people hadn't left their land on a rumour, they were being driven out. They called up to Sir Thomas as he went by and said their homes were burning, they'd been attacked by their own labourers.

As they got further north, the condition of such refugees they encountered changed again as the Irish who were rising against them grew in confidence and cruelty. The people they met now had no possessions, except their lives. Many of them were naked, all of them injured, some with ears hacked away, their nostrils slit or lips cut off. One group consisted of women and girls stripped, who crouched on a bank holding each other's hands. They screamed and shrank away as Sir Thomas and some of his men got down to wrap cloaks round them.

Sir Thomas ordered them put in one of the carts. 'Oh my God. Are we past the halfway mark? No. Here, Francis, and you, George, drive them back to Cork. Are you armed? Then go, and stop for nobody. Oh my God.'

He'd already sent two carts back with some of the worst cases, and Barbary heard him say: 'I'll send no more. We need every one for our own now.' He said no word to her; there'd been no problem persuading him to take her. For one thing he was too tired to argue and for another she disgusted him, he didn't care what happened to her. She was Irish.

She didn't blame him, and she didn't care either. All she wanted was to find Sylvestris. Each fresh atrocity they came across was an intensification of what she could imagine being done to him.

The road became empty; it was getting dark, but here and there the sky was lit up by the flames of a burning house. The wind screeched and tipped the carts like hands trying to turn them over. It bent the flames from Hugh Cuffe's lodge across the road so that they had to back the terrified horses and turn into a field to avoid the elemental barrier, while sparks and glowing splinters showered down on them. Sir Thomas stared to the left until they could see up the drive and to the house. Hugh Cuffe had been a friend of his, a friend of Spenser's. The house had two walls still standing up out of a bonfire. 'Oh my God,' said Sir Thomas quietly. 'Oh my God.'

There was a tree down further along, a thin elm. The militiamen dismounted and began dragging it out of the way. A shot rang out and one of them dropped. Crouching, they got the tree to the side, and lifted the man into Barbary's cart, urging the horses into a canter. She couldn't see where he'd been hit because it was so dark and the rocking of the cart wobbled him about in her arms. Anyway, he died a minute later and when it was too late she saw the bloodstain on his chest.

She held onto him to stop his body flopping and another bullet passed over her head. The cart behind her was hit by two spears and they were still joggling out of its side as they crossed the Blackwater. Militiamen on the bridge had their guns trained ready to shoot, and lowered them in relief when Sir Thomas called out to them. 'Thank the Lord, my lord.'

As they turned in past the garrison and began the pull up to the castle, Barbary stood up, frightened. She had to shriek against the wind. 'We've got to go on. We've got to get to Kilcolman.'

Sir Thomas turned his horse and came alongside her. 'If he's not here, he'll have to take his chance. We're going no further.'

'But he's a little boy. I promised him.'

'To the Devil with what you promised. I've got to hold this place and try to keep the road to Cork open, and I've few enough men to do it. I'm losing no more.'

She couldn't see anything except a ten-year-old boy. In the castle hall she ruthlessly questioned tired, injured men and women. He wasn't there. Nobody had seen him. Some of them just stared at her in the stupor of horror. She followed Sir Thomas to his room. He was having his boots pulled off.

'Sir Thomas, there's a child out there . . .' She tried to be calm; the man was exhausted. He became aware that he was being pestered.

'What?'

'Please, Sir Thomas. Just let the militia take me five miles more to find the boy.'

'No.'

'But he's only a child.'

Sir Thomas stood up suddenly so that his servant fell over. 'God's wounds, woman, if it was my own son I couldn't venture further north. It's collapsing, don't you see? Ireland is collapsing around us and all I can do is keep the road to the sea open so that we can get an army to build her up again. And a damn great army it's going to have to be.' He sat down on the stool and put his head in his hands. 'My God, my God, why have You forsaken us.'

Barbary stared. This was more than the strain of coping with one desperate emergency after another. He could do that; the Norrises came of stock that had coped with Her Majesty's emergencies in more than one part of the world, and were prepared to give their lives in doing it. But Sir Thomas was weeping at the overthrow of a hope that had sustained his country for four hundred years: security from an island that was too close and too alien for England's comfort. The other great landowners were concerned about their personal ruin; Sir Thomas was in terror that the dream of two Englands side by side, twins floating in comradeship on a sea beset by enemy nations on one side and the Unknown on the other, was evaporating before his eyes.

It was only then that the events she had witnessed in the last twenty-four hours linked together for her. This could be, might be, the end of English Ireland, a massive, world-shaking event. And it was still nothing compared to the danger facing a vulnerable little boy.

She didn't have time for tricks of persuasion. She said: 'I don't care who God's forsaking, but you're forsaking Edmund Spenser's son.'

His voice came muffled from between his hands. 'So be it.'

'I'll go then. Let me have a horse.'

'No.'

581

'But it's five miles. I might be killed before I get there.'

He looked up at her and she saw that in his eyes she deserved to be, because she was of the treacherous race that was upsetting his Queen's plan.

'Not you,' he said. 'You're one of them. They won't kill *you*.'

'I hope you die,' she screamed at him.

He closed his eyes. 'I probably will.'

Before she left the castle, she took the Clampett out of her pack, made sure it was primed, and put its cartridge belt over her shoulder under her cloak. Down in the empty kitchens she found a small, sharp knife and stuck it up her sleeve. She threw away her hat, shook out her hair and put on the head-roll.

The guards on the gate, coping with the influx of refugees, didn't give her a glance as she walked past them and up the hill leading north which was filled with the same pitiable traffic she had seen on the way from Cork. But less than half a mile further on it stopped and the road became as empty as if the wind had blown everything off it.

Keep to the road this time, she thought; easier going and more likelihood of getting news of Sylvestris. Besides, the road still seemed to retain some vestige of normality and was in any case less dreadful than the deserted dark which had contained the Ellises. After all, she'd been away from Munster a long time and she was looking very different from the fine English lady who'd kept company with the hated undertakers, so it was unlikely, at least until she got to the vicinity of Spenser Castle, that she'd be recognised. If she was, well, that would be her going to Heaven via Weeping Cross. The insurgents wouldn't be open to long explanations of her association with their overlords.

Well, she still had her wits; Barbary of the Order could trick a small boy from under the noses of country bumpkins; Grace O'Malley's granddaughter could stare down the mere Munster Irish if she had to, even if they had gone mad.

She had no idea. She realised that later. The road was clear because a mile further on a long convoy of undertakers fleeing into Mallow had been ambushed. And the wind that had brought the promise of delivery by the great O'Neill had ripped away everything that tethered the ambushers to coherence. She walked into a dimension where the capacity to commit atrocity had become as infinite as the atrocities which had given rise to it. There was no satiety. A group of men had dragged a farmer out of his cart and were kicking him, had been kicking him for so long that they were exhausted; one of them was holding onto the cart pole so that he could stay upright and keep on kicking, although the farmer was dead. One staggered over to the horse, which had been killed by a spear through its neck, in order to kick that as well.

They were still kicking as they watched her go past. 'Do you want a go, mavourneen?' the man clinging to the pole asked her.

'Me man's at the Aherlow and I wouldn't be sorry to join him,' she said, 'but God save all here.'

The man smiled and kicked again as she walked away.

'Keep on,' she said to herself. 'It's the boy who matters.' But they mattered enough to make her stop further on and weep and be sick.

She'd seen bears baited in her time, hangings, quarterings, but her resistance to cruelty had broken down when she'd seen the hanging mother and child, and it broke down further now under this uncontrolled and uncontrollable surfeit of it. Fifty yards on a naked man – she thought it was Prebendary Chadwick but she couldn't be sure – was being hanged until he choked, brought down to be revived and hanged again until he choked, brought down . . . 'Ye'll want to see this,' called a woman who was helping some men pull the rope. 'They'll have done it to one of yours, like they did it to mine.' She nodded, and stood to watch the cycle, astounded they didn't tire of it and that the man didn't die, only released when at last he did.

The woman came out from under the tree, brushing her hands in satisfaction. 'And who are you, now?'

'Me man's at the Aherlow. I'll be joining him.'

She went on. She was in an Irish cloak, her Irish red hair illuminated by fire, blown about by the wind under its Irish roll, a pack in one hand and an Irish knife in the other, speaking good Irish, indistinguishable from other Irish madwomen who roamed the road, except that her knife had no blood on it.

Further along, a bonfire lit up a place of execution where an anvil stood for a block and a cleaver was serving as a headsman's axe. Again she was invited to watch, kindly, as if they were offering to pay for her to see the strong man at a fair; again, to refuse would have been to court suspicion. The anvil was bloody and some of the young men were out in the road rolling heads along it in a game of bowls and swearing because the heads bumped and rolled out of true.

Two men, one middle-aged and a young one, were decapitated in front of her and in front of the woman whose husband and son they were, who held another child to her side, a young boy, about Sylvestris's age; but it wasn't Sylvestris, it was the youngest Biddlecombe. She recognised Mistress Biddlecombe. Years ago, on another wild night, she and Rob and the other under-takers had accompanied the Biddlecombes to their hold-ing. She remembered one of the children, perhaps the young man whose head now lay on the ground, saying he wanted to go home, and Mrs Biddlecombe saying: 'This *is* our home.'

The man with the cleaver turned to the woman and her child, and Barbary's hand went automatically inside her cloak to the Clampett in her belt. The man nodded to the little boy. 'Does he speak the Irish?' His mother tried to say he did, he spoke Portuguese, Arabic, anything they wanted him to, but nothing came out of her mouth. 'Speak Irish to me, lad,' the man persisted.

The boy had courage and hatred. His face said he was going to survive to grow up and kill the people who'd killed his father and brother, but his mouth said clearly in Irish: 'A windy day is not for thatching.'

The people around the anvil laughed. 'Apt, my boyo, very apt. This windy day's for killing, so it is.' The cleaver man put out his hand to pat the boy, but blood was dripping off it and he looked round for something to wipe it off. With an unthinking gesture born from years of cleaning men up, Mrs Biddlecombe proffered her apron, and cried as the man used it and thanked her.

'If your daddy and your brother had been as sharp as you, they'd be alive this minute. Take your good mother into Mallow now, and tell anyone who stops you that Ruairi Mac Dowd gives his permission.'

The entertainment over, Barbary turned and went on. She never did find out whether or not the Biddlecombes got to Mallow.

She stopped to retch. You're killing the wrong people, she thought; it's not the Biddlecombes who dictated the policy that brought this about, it was the Raleighs, the bishops, the Wallops, Loftuses and Norrises, the Spensers and Elizabeth the Queen, opportunists with disregard for anything but their own greed, who inspired this hatred and left victims like the Biddlecombes to face it. The wrong people were suffering.

Spenser Castle was burning, she saw it as she crept through the Deer Park and heard the full roar as the wind lifted the flames seventy feet up into the sky. There was an impression of figures moving about it, but she couldn't see clearly. The gatehouses were still undamaged, black squat shapes outlined against the orange glare. Careful now. On this territory she'd be a scapegoat as much as the poor people killed back there. She dropped her pack behind a tree and hared across the road to run beside a hedge across the field leading to the walls, but ploughed earth slowed her to a tramp. She walked bent to keep her head below the hedge's skyline, but if anyone was looking in her direction they could hardly fail to see her. It was as light as day.

She gained the wall and shuffled along it to the gates, Clampett in one hand, knife in the other.

Somebody was coming out of the gates, pushing a cart loaded with objects. The figure stopped to pile them on a heap of small furniture and silver already in the drive. It was Rosh.

Barbary shuffled further along the wall and hissed. 'Rosh. *Rosh.*'

The woman turned and came scurrying towards her. 'Is it yourself? Mother of God, have you no sense?'

'What are you doing?'

'Saving some of me employer's fine belongings.'

Barbary clutched her. 'Rosh, is Sylvestris here? Have you seen him?'

She saw Rosh's face go blank. 'Didn't he get away with the rest?'

'No. I've got to find him, he'll be so frightened. Help me, Rosh.'

The light reflected off Rosh's eyes as she squeezed Barbary's arm. 'You're not to worry now. I'll find the small gentleman. Stay here and I'll look.'

'Be careful. The others might see him.' The roar of the flames from the house included laughter and shouting.

'Ach, they're too busy looting. To every cow its calf and to every book its copy, as the proverb says.'

'Certainly.' She leaned back against the wall, watching Rosh walk away into the glare of the drive. Now that she'd shared her burden, she was aware of how much it weighed. I'm going to die, she thought. Let me get him safe and then I'll die. I'll be back, she'd told him. October the sixth, and what was it now? Time had become dateless, stopped in another dimension the world had transferred to. Christ, that's where he is. Where she'd told him to be. If he was anywhere, he was there.

She ran to the edge of the gatehouse and peered round. No sign of Rosh, still sound of activity up on the burning hill, but nobody in sight. She ran as fast as she could to the steps, up them, and pushed open the gatehouse door. She called quietly: 'Sir Stayon.' There was no answer. She looked in the well house, in sudden dread down the well itself. She went up to the next floor. There'd been no looting here, but there was no boy. She heard a step on the gravel in the drive outside, and crept up to the door of the top room and moved it a fraction. There was a gasp from inside. She stepped in. 'I'm sorry I'm late.'

He was crouched on her bed. He flung himself on her and she hugged him. 'There, there. It's all right, I'm back now. I've got you back.'

From outside Rosh's voice called softly: 'Where are you?'

Still holding Sylvestris, she leaned to the window. Only Rosh stood below. 'Up here. I've found him.'

'Stay there. I'm coming up.'

'Don't let her.' The boy's hands were squeezing into her shoulders. 'She's the one. She's been telling them what to do. I saw her.'

He'd been through a lot. 'It's Rosh,' she explained to him.

Rosh stood in the doorway which shaded her figure from the glow that pervaded the rest of the room, but not the carving knife she held in front of her. 'I'll be thanking you to give me the boy,' she said reasonably. 'You can go or you can stay, but we'll be destroying the seed of Smerwick, if you please.'

Barbary gaped, disbelieving her ears, still trusting in the Rosh with whom she had once saved a life, her friend, but instinctively she pushed Sylvestris behind her. 'What are you talking about?'

'I came to this house for that,' said Rosh, still reasonable. 'I stayed for that, I've worked for it. There was Irish at Smerwick as well as Spanish, and my man and my elder son among them. Surrender they said, and they surrendered and they hanged them. And your man was there and wrote that it was a good thing done. His father.'

This was impossible. Nobody could have spent years being pleasant, being Rosh, the worker, Rosh of the funny proverbs, and concealed the secrets that were coming out of her mouth now. An artificiality had descended over the three of them in the room that kept Barbary unafraid. She was just as reasonable as she said: 'You can't hate that long. Not a little boy.'

Rosh smiled. 'Oh, they topped it up. They kept topping it up.'

Outside the window a man's voice called. 'Where's yourself, Roisín MacSheehy?'

It took seconds to sink in. 'Oh Jesus Christ, you're a MacSheehy.'

Roisín nodded pleasantly. 'They never ask your name. Did you know that? In their wickedness and stupidity they hang your people and never so much as ask your name. Good old Rosh I was, and good old Rosh I've stayed for this day.' Light flashed from the knife as she edged to the window. It was the twin of the one that had killed Mrs Ellis. Rosh shouted: 'Up here. And quick.'

She believed it now. She was afraid now. 'You won't have him, Rosh. Lock the door.' She lifted the Clampett out of her belt. 'Lock the door or I'll kill you.'

She'd pointed the gun so many times in the past and it had always done the trick. It would work again, one Irishwoman to another.

'No,' said Rosh and moved forward.

Barbary shot her. Her finger pulled on the trigger, the unused flint scraped against the rough steel plate to spark the powder, and the steel ball Will Clampett had shaped so carefully in its mould went through Rosh's dress and into her lungs. She leaned back against the door, still standing, the smile still grimacing on her face.

Barbary stepped across, pushed her aside so that she fell, and locked the door. 'You,' she said to Sylvestris, 'out of that window.' The percussion had temporarily deafened her, she seemed to be speaking into wool. 'Use the ivy and get to the Deer Park.' Someone was hammering on the door, throwing themselves against it so that upper and lower panels came momentarily away from the frame.

'I won't leave you.' Cycles completed themselves on this night; she'd cried that to her mother and her mother had stayed to get killed by the English. She was her mother now and, by Christ, the Irish wouldn't kill her. 'Out. I'm coming too.' She began priming the Clampett again as he got up on the sill and squeezed through the open shutters. A good thing they were both undersized.

Something was hitting the floor in regular thumps. She looked down. Rosh was lying on her side, stabbing the knife into the floorboards. She leaned down and took it away from her. 'I'm sorry, Rosh.'

'Ach,' said Rosh, as if it was nothing. 'We shouldn't have gone to the Ellises first.' Blood came out of her mouth.

Barbary went over to the window facing the Bally-houras. The boy was halfway down, but the man on the landing had left the door to get help, she could hear his feet running down the steps. She went to the window overlooking the drive and as he came into her view, shouting, she shot him, a bullet into the back. 'God bless you, Will Clampett, for the artist you are.'

Carefully she put the gun back in her belt. The barrel scorched her flesh through her dress into a scar that never went. She clambered out of the window and climbed down the ivy, picking the best footholds. There was no hurry, she could do anything, she could kill people. She even spared time at the foot of the wall to prime the Clampett again. 'They won't have heard,' she said. 'Wind and fire's too strong. Now then, where shall we go? I must get my pack and then it's the back way, I think. Stay here.'

He wouldn't, so they made a long detour to get to the Deer Park, spent an age finding her pack, and went through the trees until they were out of the light of the flames to cross the road again.

They crawled along bending, whipping hedges, over a wall, past the crescent lake flapping with water turned gold from the flames of Spenser Castle, and into the bridle path that led behind Hap Hazard to the Roche estate.

She had no feeling at all, she could walk and walk and kill and kill.

'Is Father safe? And Stepmother? And the baby?'

She just said yes, they were. The transparency coming up in the east was a surprise, as if the wind had gained a special virulence from all the night's deaths to blow daylight out. 'It's the dawn,' Sylvestris said. 'I never thought it would come.'

Could it make a difference? Perhaps horror was the monopoly of darkness and day would send everybody back to their homes, and bring all the dead back to life and make Rosh into Rosh again. Hap Hazard was burning away in the distance, out-lighting the dawn.

'There's something up ahead on the path.'

She peered to where leaves were jumping about a long protuberance on the track. 'It's just another body. Don't look.'

'Something moved. It's alive.'

It wasn't, she knew the inertness of the dead by now, it was just the wind moving a cloak, but she couldn't stop him. 'Oh poor lady, poor lady. She's got a wound in her back.' She wondered how anybody retained enough emotion to feel pity any more. A dark path of bruised grass leading away from the woman's feet showed that she'd crawled from the direction of the road, which was only a field away at this point. English killed by the Irish? Irish killed by the militia? It didn't matter, she was dead. 'Leave it. It's another corpse. There's lots of them about.'

'No. She's alive, she's moving.'

She sank down as he struggled to turn the body over. There was satiety in the night after all, and hers had been reached; if there was a God, and they crucified Him or Her in front of her, she wouldn't blink an eye. She heard

589

Sylvestris sob and pick something up that the woman's body had concealed. He came over and put a baby in her arms. 'It's alive. She's dead, but she hid the baby, poor lady, poor lady. Is it alive?'

She supposed it was; it was warm. Involuntarily her arms clutched it to her, but when she tried to get up she couldn't. 'I can't move.'

'You've got to.' Pushing, pulling, pleading, he got her to her feet.

'Where are we going?' She had lost all authority, lost everything.

The boy said: 'Ballybeg Abbey. It's not far now. Tadg the poet will take us in, he's a friend of mine. He won't betray us.'

She shook her head at him. 'He will.' But she had no volition of her own, and he tugged her.

'Please, Mother. Please.'

Somehow they reached the ruins of Ballybeg, ruins that had gone cold long ago after the English set fire to the abbey. Sylvestris ran ahead while she cradled the baby and crooned to it, and then there was an open door, light, and an old blind man saying he had orphans enough there already, but come in, come in and rest.

English Munster died overnight. The civilisation that had grown up out of the ruins of the Desmond Wars was uprooted and turned back to ruin not by enemy armies, but by the people who'd been forced to help build it.

O'Neill's forces had barely arrived in Munster and certainly had not properly begun operations by 6 October, yet the whisper that they were on their way was enough for men and women who had been in subjection too long. Every bit of their long suffering rose up in their throat and vomited out in violence. All over the province gates opened from within to admit figures carrying torches, axes and knives. Livestock was driven off, its owners killed.

The same whisper sent the English lordship galloping to the safety of the Pale towns. Not one wealthy land-owner lost his life at the hands of the rebels, though most lost the land itself. The greatest names in the counties of Cork, Kerry, Limerick, Waterford and Tipperary, Sir Henry Ughtred, Edward Fitton – Kerry's Sheriff – Sir

George Bourchier, Aylmer, Sir William Courtney, Justice Goold, the Bishop of Cork, Chief Justice Saxey were only a few of those who left their residences behind to be guarded by retainers who either died defending them or handed them over to the rebels without a fight. One hundred of Sir Henry Wallop's household servants were killed at his home in Enniscorthy, while he himself struggled through to Waterford with his family and a few possessions. Old Warham St Leger got to safety but his property was destroyed. The seignory of the absent Sir Walter Raleigh was razed.

The physical casualties were among the middle and lower classes, the less aware and more isolated families. Anglo-Irish clerics who had forbidden the Irish their religion were automatically put to the sword; so were Anglo-Irish schoolmasters who had forced an alien culture and language on their pupils, and Anglo-Irish magistrates and lawyers with their contempt for the native Brehon laws and their insistence on enforcing statutes which worked against the people who had to obey them. Their wives and children either died with them or were raped and sent naked into the cities with their nostrils slit or their tongues cut out as an example of what lay in wait outside.

And in places like Waterford, Cork, Youghal and Kinsale, overcrowded, insanitary and short of food, the survivors lay in the streets and public buildings as the October winds dropped and the rains of November became incessant. Town criers passed among them calling out names to try and reunite separated families, while searchers studied faces in the burial pits to see if they could recognise a lost wife, father or child. The quartering on the Cork townspeople of one thousand newly arrived English troops only added to the misery.

The extent of the devastation was so awesome that the first reports arriving in England were disbelieved. When, finally, they could no longer be dismissed as exaggeration, the Queen put the blame on the colonists themselves; had they but obeyed her strictures to employ only English this would not have happened. Having never visited Ireland, she refused to listen to those who said that if the colony had not used Irish labour there would have been no colony.

Edmund Spenser's letter to the Queen written 'out of the ashes of desolation and waste of this your wretched realm', begged for understanding and help. He excused himself and his fellow undertakers and laid all blame on the obduracy of the Irish. He had thought that by putting the civil example of English life before the native Irish they could be converted out of their savagery. 'But it is far otherwise, for instead of following them, they fly the English and most hatefully shun them, for two causes: first, because they have ever been brought up licentiously and to do as each one liked; secondly, because they hate the English, so that their fashions they also hate.'

Help us, he wrote, for now we 'have nothing left but to cry unto you for timely aid'.

It was the last letter he ever wrote, and its cry went unanswered. By now Tyrrell's forces had established themselves and were besieging the cities. The O'Neill raised James FitzThomas FitzGerald, the late Desmond's nephew, to be the new Earl of Desmond in the south and although the clans called him the 'Hayrope Earl' because his only possession had been straw, they followed him as the clans in the north of Munster were following Tyrrell, with a discipline which was new to the Irish experience. All the secret training of the last years came into its own and the chieftains of Munster cohered for once under the leadership of these two new generals who, in turn, took their orders from the O'Neill.

The old Irish aristocracy, who had been regranted their ancient land and given new English titles in return for swearing allegiance to the Crown, saw which way the wind was blowing, broke their oath and went over to the O'Neill's side. Mountgarrets, Cahirs, Devereuxs, Kavanaghs, the men of whom Elizabeth had boasted, turned their coats so fast that by December Sir Thomas Norris in a letter to the Queen could list only four principal men not in revolt. The country, he said, was 'impassable for any faithful subject'.

Black Tom, Earl of Ormond, stayed loyal but he also stayed in Leinster, fighting to protect Dublin and his own estates and unable to maintain contact with the embattled English of Munster.

The thousand English troops in Cork sallied out of the city to be dissipated in the new warfare that O'Neill had perfected. There was some isolated fighting, but in trying to come to grips with the enemy the English were led into bog and mountain ambushes or lost their numbers from desertion and ague. Munster was sacrificed, at first out of helplessness and then deliberately, to gain time for Elizabeth to raise for the Earl of Essex the greatest army that had ever been sent to Ireland.

The interval was the occasion for the deaths of famous men. Sir Richard Bingham died in Dublin, unfit to have his old duties put on his shoulders. Sir John Norris died, worn out. His young brother, Henry, was killed in a Connaught ambush along with his men and Clifford Conyers. Sir Thomas Norris, still trying to keep the Cork road open, received an Irish spear through his breastplate and died of gangrene at Mallow before the castle there finally fell.

King Philip II of Spain died, to be succeeded by King Philip III.

Leaving his family in Cork, Edmund Spenser brought the last despatches from Sir Thomas Norris to England and delivered them to Whitehall where the Queen stayed in residence throughout the New Year, having daily emergency meetings with her Council. He was paid eight pounds for acting as courier, and badly needed them. Such patronage as he'd had was gone or being bestowed on new poets and, like the other refugees from Ireland, he told a story nobody wanted to hear. Once he mentioned a child that had been lost in the sack of Kilcolman.

He found a room at a crowded inn a few yards beyond King's Gate at Westminster, and fell ill. It was a winter in which the Thames froze from bank to bank for the first time in thirty years, and it took ten days before any of his friends heard of his condition. He died on the morning of Saturday, 16 January, attended by the inn's landlady.

When the winter was over, the Earl of Essex was ready to sail with sixteen thousand foot, nearly fifteen hundred cavalry and the promise of two thousand reinforcements every month, so that the whole thing could begin again.

Chapter Twenty-Six

The greatest misfortune in the world is to be a civilian rooted to the land for which two opposing armies are contending. Whether the armies are liberating or conquering, when the dust settles the civilian has either been killed, starved or made pregnant.

And to be in the Awbeg and Blackwater valleys of Munster as the sixteenth century drew to its close was to be continually occupied (or liberated) by one army, and then liberated (or occupied) by its opponent.

From the point of view of the contestants, the area was desirable because it formed a crossroads giving easy access to both the coast and west Ireland. It was also fertile, and the war degenerated into which army could feed off the harvest over the coming winter while denying it to the other.

From the point of view of civilians trying merely to survive – and they became fewer and fewer – it was like being a beetle stuck to a tray into which first red and then green paint was poured; as the two colours sloshed back and forth, the beetle ended up drowning in a dirty and somewhat familiar brown.

Standing on the duckboard which kept him above the mud outside the elegant pavilion, Lord Roche heard his title inaccurately announced by the liveried servant who had fetched him from the gates of the camp: 'The Lord Maurice Roche, my lord,' and heard equally clearly the answer: 'Let him wait.'

Maurice, Viscount Fermoy, studied the scenery and the weather which had just become fine but frosty after the rainy summer and was nipping the leaves on the few remaining trees into gold and red. This had been a valley of trees, he thought, one's trees, one's valley. Apart from the tents and movement of the camp which spread in an untidy sprawl along nearly half a mile of the Blackwater from Mallow, the landscape was deserted. No, there were some rooks circling and cawing around the elms on the hills which swept up on either side. Amazing birds. One had personally fed on enough of the buggers last winter to have wiped out every nest in Munster, yet here they were back again. Survivors. Filthy eating, but survivors. Maurice, Lord Roche, approved of survival.

His gaze fell on his gloves bought in 1598, last year, before the unpleasantness; Cordovan suede, 12s.4d, and one would have thought for that money they'd have lasted somewhat better than they had. Caitlin had wanted to boil them and serve them with vegetables for the servants' dinner, but one had dissuaded her from the idea by a black eye. A good cook, though, when she had the wherewithal.

The whole question of appropriate attire for this audience had perplexed one considerably. One's violet taffeta sleeved cloak with the standing collar, £18.7s, was too rich and would set the English into thinking one could contribute supplies to their army. Besides, one had an idea that the fashion for cloaks hanging to the fork had gone out in the last year. On the other hand, too poor and the bastards would disregard one.

'You may go in, my lord.'

Maurice, Viscount Fermoy, entered the pavilion and flung himself onto the Earl of Essex's dress boots, cream doeskin, gold-buckled, five pounds if they were a penny. 'Most magnificent and redoubted lord, pillar of my life, eternal praise for thy chivalry in rescuing from the savagery—'

'Get up.'

Maurice Roche rose, glancing up at the beautiful face as he wiped the tears from his beard. It was showing disdain, but one could tell one had been on the right lines. And one had been right about cloaks; Essex's swirled down to his ankles. Velvet. Gold-tasselled. All of £24 by today's prices. 'Pardon my emotion, my lord, but to my poor eyes you are emperor of the sun, the summer's nightingale.' He gave a sob. Definitely the right lines.

'You are protesting your loyalty to Her Gracious Majesty, are you?'

Good God, what did he think one was doing? 'It has

never wavered, my most noble lord, in thought, word or—'

'Then where is your son?'

'Laid low, puissant lord, from a wound received fighting our lonely battle.'

'Who for?'

'Eh?'

'I said who for. For whom? Which side was he on?'

Could the noble Earl have possibly glimpsed David during that last skirmish between the English and Tyrrell? No, it had been an ambush and David had sensibly refused to wear Irish colours, and kept his visor down. If one had been dealing with a man of sense one would have explained that to send one's sons to fight for the Irish, while keeping in with the English oneself, was the only way one could survive this hell and still come out with credibility for whichever side won in the end. But one doubted Essex's sense. If he'd had any he'd have stayed at home tucked up in bed with the Queen, bony old besom though she was.

Maurice made his eyes steely with resentment. 'The Roches claimed Ireland for the Crown when they landed with Henry II in the twelfth century . . .'

'Very well, very well.'

Well, they had. Well, not Henry II exactly. They'd come over with Strongbow in the hope of easy plunder, but the moment Henry II had shown he was the stronger they'd declared for him. Time for the gifts. 'My lord, to mark this glorious deliverance at your hands, may I present . . .' A really lovely chalice some of his kerns had taken from Effin church before they'd burned it, and a kid-bound copy of Spenser's 'Colin Clout Comes Home Again' that his MacSheehys had looted from Kilcolman. Mother of God, what a title. But the noble Earl seemed touched.

'I am touched, Viscount.' Essex stroked the soft cover. 'Our greatest poet. He died in poverty, which is the lot of poets. I sent him money at the last but he said he was too ill to spend it, so he was buried at my charge in Westminster Abbey, as he deserved to be.'

'Indeed, my lord, you have acted the Mycaenas to a great poet and a great loss.' And a great pain in the arse. It was Roche land the damned rhymster had been granted, and one had spent £279.4s.8d. in litigation, to say nothing of setting on the MacSheehys, trying to get him off it. Well, he was off it now.

'But I warn you, my lord,' Essex was saying, 'Her Majesty will countenance no temporising by her Irish nobility.'

Would one be offered supper? There was half a juicy venison pasty on the camp table and a silver gilt drinking cup weighing forty ounces of silver if it weighed anything, and some Bordeaux still in it. How long had it been since one had tasted good wine? Or venison for that matter?

'. . . would command your aid in this matter,' Essex was saying.

Maurice tore his eyes away from the table. 'Alas, my lord, would that one could aid your great endeavour, but one's beeves were driven off by the rebels, may their souls be damned, seed, breed and generation.'

'Your attention wanders, Viscount,' Essex said sharply. 'As I have just explained, one of the many duties I have been given to perform in this unhappy land is to discover whether or not this lady is still alive, and if so, where.'

'Which lady is that, my lord?'

'God's teeth, man, I've just told you. Lady Betty.'

Barbary, eh? What did they want with her?

'It is unseemly,' Essex went on, 'that the widow of an Armada hero, and moreover one who has been received by the Queen, should have suffered death at the hands of barbarians and lie dishonoured in some unknown grave.'

Barbary? 'Rejoice, my lord, for she is not dead. Perhaps you will inform our great Queen that on the dreadful night of the massacre, and at great personal risk to oneself, one sheltered this poor lady and shelters her yet.' Not *exactly* that night, of course; that night one had shut oneself up and listened to the screams of the English peasants. They should never have come to Ireland and taken land which wasn't theirs in the first place. Good riddance. But Barbary . . . One's Christianity to that obstinate female had been unsurpassed.

'Then I shall send to your castle to fetch her.'

Ah. 'My lord, she does not *exactly* live at the castle, it being unfitted at rebel hands, but on Roche land. Ballybeg Abbey is where you will find her.' And good luck to you. Maurice's heart fell to his rubbed buskins, Spanish leather, 14s. two years back, as he heard the audience come to an end with much about loyalty, Her Majesty's determination to defeat the Great Satan etc., etc., and not a bloody word about inviting one for supper.

The Earl of Essex was subject to fervent, though passing, bouts of pity in the same way as menopausal women are subject to hot flushes, and he suffered one as the woman who'd once played cards at his house was carried into his pavilion that evening. She'd aged ten years in the last two; the amazing red hair was frosted here and there with grey, she was skeletal, lined, and with a sore by the side of her mouth. Hard green eyes stared, but didn't seem to see him.

'Night blind, my lord,' said his sergeant, unhooking her arms from his neck and settling her tenderly in a chair.

Essex winced. Night blindness was a symptom of starvation. 'Bring more light.' He bent over the figure in the chair. 'Do you remember me, Lady Betty?'

'Yes. Is there anything to eat?'

The Earl snapped his fingers for supper. To save the lady's shame, he ordered all his officers out while she fell on it; she stuffed food into her mouth as if they'd set a time limit on it. 'How's Henry?'

'I beg your pardon?'

She emptied her mouth just long enough to repeat the question. 'How's my son? Henry Betty.'

'In fine spirits when last I saw him. Her Majesty shows continuing interest in his welfare.' He watched her until she'd finished eating, spilling pastry and gravy down her none-too-clean cloak. 'We shall soon send you back to him.' The woman's capacity for food was small; she had actually eaten very little, but she stared suspiciously at the servant who tried to clear the wreckage away: 'I'm taking that home.'

'Lady Betty,' said Essex gently, 'my army may be on short commons, but you shall take home as much food as you please. Now, have some wine.'

She made an effort to smile. 'Won't you join me, my lord?'

Some vestige of the woman she had been was still

there. He sat down opposite and poured them both wine:
'How bad was it?'

'I've had better times. How are you enjoying Ireland?'

The Earl had received many women in his pavilion
since the campaign began, most of them progressing into
his bed, but none of them had been conversant with the
life he'd left in England as this woman was; however
much of an oddity, she knew the people he knew,
appreciated the magnificent position he'd held. And he'd
missed conversing with intelligent women; his wife and
sister were the repository of every plan, every ambition
he held. He need not over-confide in this poor wreck
whose connections with the Irish were questionable, but
her vulnerability demanded that, for sheer courtesy, he
display his own. Besides, he required information from
her.

So he answered her question, and got carried away as
he usually did. This moist and miserable country that
dwindled his army with its agues and plagues and lassitude, he had never wanted to set foot in it. He'd prophesied doom before he set out. Before God and His angels,
he was badgered with commands from upstarts who had
no idea of conditions that beset the man in the field.
'There is not food enough, either for horses or men, and
the cattle too lean to be driven or eaten. How *can* I go
north against O'Neill until Munster and Leinster have
been pacified? Yet the Queen's despatches yap go north,
go north as if they require my life and not my success.
Well, by God, she shall have it. She may mislike the
course of my actions, but she shall be pleased at
the fashion of my death. I shall charge the arrows of the
enemy, fearing them less than the knives plunged in my
back by those who call me friend.'

He strode the tent, his boots kicking up the scent of
grass to mingle with other smells of beeswax and leather
and calico while her eyes followed them, interested and
sympathetic.

'She doesn't understand, my lord.'

'By God, she does not. Do you hear what she writes?'
He brandished a letter. ' "If sickness prevails why did
you not move when the army was in a better state?" But
didn't I rout Tyrrell at the Pass of Plumes, even though
he escaped at the last? "If winter approaches, why were

the summer months of July and August lost?" Didn't I take Cahir Castle?'

He sat down and leaned across the table, stabbing the letter at Barbary. 'Do you guess who writes this? Not her. Raleigh. Raleigh dictates to her while I wage a war against savages ignorant of its etiquette, who stab and run like cowardly rabble, who promise fair battle and attack our hindquarters.'

'Unfair, my lord.'

Essex wiped the froth from his lips. 'Only those like you and I, who suffer it, plumb the full damnation of this forgotten waste.' His eyes were kindly and cunning. 'Lady Betty, you know something of Tyrone, you knew his wife. If he should offer truce . . .'

He could retrieve the situation yet. The secret emissary from the O'Neill had offered a way out: a meeting between the two of them, face to face. He was in touch with James of Scotland and his spies told him O'Neill was in touch with James of Scotland. There was common ground there; neither of them wanted to precipitate a situation that might change drastically if James could be set on the throne. Why fight each other when, if they waited, they could become the actual rulers of their respective countries under the figurehead of James? They could patch up a truce, he could get out of this awful place and go home to counteract the damage evil-wishers were wreaking behind his back. Elizabeth would rant, but he could pacify that old carcase into doing what he wanted, he always had.

But could he trust the O'Neill? That's what he needed this woman to tell him. '. . . if I met him face to face. For all his lack of true nobility, he bears the title of earl. Should I meet him if he offers?'

He tried to read the expression that came into the frozen green eyes, and if she hadn't been such a tragic object he might have thought it was amusement.

'I wouldn't if I was you,' she said.

He sat back. He loathed wrong answers; he shouldn't have demeaned himself by asking. What did a slut like this know of high politics? Well, but she was famished, her fingers round the stem of his cup were twigs, grubby twigs.

'How can I serve you, mistress?'

600

She became alert enough at that. 'Can you take me and some others to Kinsale?'

'Kinsale? Mistress, I couldn't take you through to Cork, let alone Kinsale. Both are heavily besieged. It would need all my army to win through, and tomorrow we march north.'

She looked down again. He heard her muttering: 'Must get to Kinsale, must get to Kinsale.'

'Endure a little longer, mistress,' he told her. 'You will be safe enough here with the garrison I shall leave behind to protect the area.' He terminated the audience. There was much to do. 'Go with my sergeant here and order what supplies you need from the sutler to see you through the winter and they shall be carried with you to . . . where was it?'

'Ballybeg Abbey.' She got up and crouched down on her knees, clutching his boots with her twiglike hands. 'I am grateful, my lord.'

He stood at the flap of his pavilion, watching her being led along the duckboards. Pitiful, pitiful.

His officers rejoined him, men of rank and title, many of them knighted by himself. He'd added another quarter to the English knighthood since he'd been in Ireland; his detractors were saying his sword never left its sheath except to tap some acolyte on the shoulders, but, by God, these friends who endured this place of torment with him should have loyalty rewarded. They played cards before he decided he was tired, and flung himself on his cot, noticing with irritation as he did so that his boots had lost two of their gold buckles.

The soldiers staggered back and forth from the cart to what remained of Ballybeg's refectory, unloading the provisions, three barrels of flour, two flitches of bacon, dried herring, sacks of beans, match, a tun of ale. The sergeant was bitter at the advantage the woman had taken of his commander's generosity. 'Sure you got enough, lady? Didn't fancy our eyeteeth?'

She shook her head, being too intent on her loot to say goodbye or thank you. The sergeant spat and ordered his men back to the cart, glad to get away. The morning was misty and the ruins were blurred shapes dark with ivy. There was no movement or sound, not even birdsong,

601

but after a year in Ireland the sergeant knew when he was being watched and he knew it now. If they got back to the camp without being sniped at they'd be lucky.

Barbary listened to the hoofbeats and creak of wheels fade away down the road. Eyeteeth. If eyeteeth were edible she'd have taken them.

She'd listened to what Essex had to tell her about the situation in Ireland, but she'd only taken in the situation as far as it affected her. Ireland had dwindled to the few square miles around Ballybeg Abbey, her trap, and once she'd understood that it was still impossible to get out of it, she'd lost interest.

She'd been here . . . how long? She couldn't remember. Months and months. At first, she and Sylvestris and the others had cowered in the comparative safety of Tadg's house in the ruins while the massacre of the undertakers went on around them. The small house had been constructed above the crypt and it was in the crypt she and Sylvestris and the other English children Tadg had taken in hid when the MacSheehys rampaged into the abbey grounds, looking for Rosh's killer. Tadg had denied all knowledge of them. The blind old Irish poet was one of the greatest Christians Barbary had ever met, determined not to abandon his English refugees to their enemies.

When, later, a long time later, a phalanx of English cavalry had managed to battle their way through to Mallow and had come to the abbey looking for Irish to kill, it was Tadg and the Irish children who hid in the crypt, and she who'd saved them.

'I am Lady Betty,' she'd told the English captain. 'I should like you to escort me and my family to Kinsale, if you please.'

He'd looked at her as if she was mad. 'I couldn't escort you round the corner, madam. I've lost half my men getting this far. The bastard Irish army's to the south and north and pressing hard.' He looked at her suspiciously: 'How have you survived, if you'll pardon my asking? You're the only Englishwoman in the area that isn't a corpse.'

'Luck,' she'd told him, shortly. 'But we can't stay here. We've no food.'

The captain had lacked sympathy and time. 'You managed to last this long, you'll have to hang on a bit longer, till we've wiped this murdering scum off the face of the earth.'

But it was the captain and his men who were wiped off, the next day. An ambush by Tyrrell's men killed them all. After that, it was the Irish back in occupation.

The Irish were out to slaughter anyone who couldn't speak Irish, the English anyone who couldn't speak English. And Tadg, blast him – she began to hate his Christianity – took in more and more orphaned children, so that Irish-only speakers joined the English-only speakers he'd rescued during the massacre.

Even so, at that stage, as the only two who were completely bilingual, she would have taken Sylvestris and left the rest to their fate while she attempted to get through to Kinsale and Cuckold Dick's promised boat. Kinsale was still in English hands although it was besieged on three sides by the Irish. But, she reckoned, they couldn't besiege the sea and Dick would rescue her somehow if she could only reach it. The journey would be hideously dangerous, she knew, but it was worth the risk if she could get out of this butchering ground.

She waited for a lull in the fighting that never came. At one point they had to evacuate Ballybeg completely and take to the open countryside while a battle for possession of the abbey raged across its pitiful ruins. When the dust settled and they were able to return, it was to find that Tadg's house had been destroyed, and they had to move into the crypt for shelter.

Gradually, inevitably, the day came when she realised she couldn't go, not unless Tadg and all the children came with her. They'd become her children, nearly as precious as Sylvestris himself. She'd keep the little buggers alive somehow. They must become bilingual so that they wouldn't be killed by whatever army was in occupation, no matter whose lines they had to cross to get to Kinsale. More than that, they must learn to steal and cheat as she had. They must survive.

Alone, hungry and desperate, in the ruins of an Irish abbey, Barbary had begun creating an Order of her own.

She counted again the barrels that she'd brought from

Essex's camp. 'Three barrels of flour . . .'

A knifepoint pricked her spine and a voice hissed: 'Your money and your life.'

She stood still. 'Or,' she said. 'Your money *or* your life. Give them a choice, Gill.'

'Not me. And the name's Giolla.'

She squinted into the mist and pointed to a scrap of material that hung above the remains of the abbey bell-tower. 'Is that red?' Sulkily, he nodded. 'Then today you're English, so speak it. We didn't have nationalities in the old Order, and there won't be any in this one. Get the bigger boys and hide this food. Tell Nanno to put a pan of beans to soak. Bacon and beans for breakfast.'

He loped beside her as she headed for the chancel. 'Ye didn't hear me creep up though.'

'No,' she said, tiredly, 'you did well.' He was nine years old and she didn't like him much, but she supposed that stabbing to death when he was eight the English soldier who was raping his younger sister had stifled much of his natural charm. The real Order would have thrown him out as too unstable, sent him to Paltock's.

Outside the empty jambs of the doorway to the south aisle she paused to get her breath and whistle the pass-notes. The nave was bare and open to the sky, the only shelter being the chancel's half-roof, kept in place by bramble and creepers. A hand held back one of the elders that had grown up by the cracked steps and hid the chancel from view, so that she could go through. The mist coming through the light at the east end was beginning to show yellow, but it was cold and the children sitting on tussocks in front of the altar were huddled together. Apart from craning their necks to look at her they didn't move. Tadg, like an elderly, white-haired, blinded Samson, was standing behind the altar, teaching them their catechism, and Tadg could hear a feather fall. She nodded assurance that she'd brought food and they turned back.

'Is the Son God?' asked Tadg.

'Yes, certainly He is,' they chorused.

'Will God reward the good and punish the wicked?'

'Certainly; there is no doubt He will.'

She'd told him and told him; what was the bloody good of teaching them in two languages if, when they spoke

604

English, they did it in typical Irish manner and used four words where one would do. She wasn't up in the catechism but she was damn sure English children just answered 'Yes' or 'He will', not 'Certainly, there is no doubt He will'.

The elders moved and Sylvestris beckoned her to join him out in the nave. 'Did you get any food?'

'Yes. Gill's putting it in the crypt. Not enough though.'

'We'll manage.'

'We won't. We've *got* to get through to Kinsale before the winter.'

'We can't.'

'I know that, don't I?' Her scream echoed round the bare stone walls; starvation temper. From the chancel, Tadg's deep voice shouted: 'Quiet out there.'

She pushed back her hair. 'I got these too.' She opened her hand and showed him the gold buckles she'd removed from Essex's boots. He grinned and nodded. He was in better shape than she was; he hadn't grown much, but his voice had broken. She and Tadg kept their rations down to leave more for the children, but Sylvestris was beginning to notice and insist on an adult's right to go without as well.

He said: 'Roche's Caitlin said she heard there were some sheep for sale over at Doneraile. These'd buy two.'

'Buying them's not the problem. It's getting them back without Roche taking them off you.'

'What did Essex want with you anyway?'

She tried to remember. 'Oh yes, he's moving out with the army tomorrow. The O'Neill must have got word through to him. He said did I think he could trust O'Neill if he met him face to face and made a truce.'

'What did you say?'

'No point in saying anything. He's desperate. He's frittered away the army Elizabeth gave him without achieving anything. If he agrees to meet the O'Neill, and he will, he'll be chewed up and spat out in whatever sizes O'Neill wants him to be. He's not clever.'

'A truce, though.'

She supposed it was his youth that kept him hoping. 'If Essex doesn't succeed, Elizabeth'll send somebody who will. It's never going to end.'

'Have faith in the love of God. Did he have news of Henry?'

'He's well. The Queen's watching over him.'

'Praise God and his saints. I'd better see about breakfast. I'm teaching them the *Iliad* later, but I can't remember much of it.'

'Teach them what you can.' They were all handing on what they knew; Tadg taught the children Irish poetry, and how to find their way in the dark. Sylvestris taught them English. She taught them survival.

As he left, the boy genuflected in the direction of the altar and crossed himself.

'Don't do that,' she screamed at him.

He turned on her. 'I'm going to. I meant what I said. You can't stop me.' He'd said he wanted to become a Roman Catholic priest.

Oh God, she thought. He does mean it. Even if we can ever get away from here, we can't go back to England. He'd only have to open his mouth to give away his conversion to Papism. In his own way, and for his own beliefs, Sylvestris was fearless. He'd be martyred in England.

Nearly all the children's experiences on the night of the massacre and since had led to some form of obsession. Six-year-old Tabitha, who'd been hidden by her mother under a woodpile, had heard her parents and brothers being hacked to death. The family had been strongly Puritan, and now she continually repeated, parrot-fashion, its invocations of a stern, militant God in an attempt to keep its memory alive, so that her shrill little voice rang out with 'Praise the strong arm of the Lord' and 'He shall trample sinners under His feet'.

Peter counted everything, branches, stones, steps, the number of beans on his trencher. Gill told rambling stories in which the hero killed armies of English soldiers, and his little sister washed and re-washed her doll.

What Barbary found wonderful was that the hatreds and fears they had picked up in the past did not extend to each other. Irish or English, they were too young, too hungry or too much in need of a community to see one another as symbols of the divide that had destroyed their parents. Gill did not equate English children with his sister's rapist, Tabitha did not recognise that Tadg was

606

teaching her a catechism which would have made her mother and father despair for her immortal soul. In the early days they'd trotted out the shibboleths – all Irish smelled, the Queen of England was a bitch from Hell – but gradually their suffering and mutual dependence had bonded them.

In Sylvestris's case the memory of his abandonment on the night of the massacre had developed into a desperate grudge against the woman who'd left him. It wasn't the Irish who'd burned his home he held responsible, but Elizabeth Boyle. Thanks to Barbary, he had some insight into what had caused the uprising, but his stepmother's had been a personal betrayal, and he refused to extend any understanding to her panic for her baby and unborn child; she'd left him, his father had been absent when he'd needed him most, no militia had come back for him, the whole structure on which he'd relied had let him down. He'd had to find a new one to fit into, and Tadg, with his Catholic litany and ritual, had provided it; he had fallen in love with the holy mother who had not deserted her son at His crucifixion.

When, months after the event, they'd heard of Edmund Spenser's death, Sylvestris had shed few tears. It was ironic, thought Barbary with despair, that the appreciation of beauty which he'd inherited from his father should respond to a religion his father had loathed. It wasn't that she cared a damn what he believed in as long as it made him happy, but he didn't have to go to extremes. And he did. He prattled about the priesthood, vows, about going back to England one day to lead it out of its heresy and return it to the Only True Church.

'You just want to get your own back,' she'd shouted at him. 'They'll kill you. They killed Edmund Campion, cut him into bits while he was still alive.'

But he'd merely looked at her as at some lesser mortal whose clumsy, plebeian feet were muddying the pure waters of his soul. Sometimes she was saddened that their old communication had gone; at other times it made her want to clip him round the ear. Mostly it terrified her. If she'd known on the night of the massacre that Tadg would create an oasis for the boy, providing through Catholicism the only beauty he could find in the hideousness around him, she wouldn't have taken his hospitality.

Yes, she would. There'd been nowhere else to go.

She'd have to stop him somehow, if only because it cut down their options for the day when they could get out of here. If they reached Kinsale and Cuckold Dick came in with his boat, they couldn't go to England with a budding priest on board. She could still see the tortured Campion tied to his hurdle on the way to his death. Where else could they go? Spain? France? With little Tabitha Longman parroting her anti-Papist rubbish? The Inquisition would love her.

'Help me. Isn't there anybody to help me?' The longer they stayed, the worse the mess they got in, and the worse the mess they got in, the longer they had to stay. She believed in God as firmly as Sylvestris and Tadg; only God could have created such a beautifully consistent trap. She could see Him, staff in hand, daubed with pig's-blood wounds; Upright God of Upright Men, rapist, killer and cheat. He'd sent her children so that He could watch her watch them die. He created a perpetual layer of armies between her and Kinsale and made sure that if she ever got there she wouldn't have anywhere to go.

If there was a female God, as Finola had said in 'The Word of Woman', she was in abeyance, as all women were in abeyance in this mad, male world.

If Essex moved out tomorrow, the Irish would move in and kill the garrison he'd left, the green would flow in as the red flowed out, and the only change would be that the conies her children had to steal from would speak a different language.

In February their neighbour and landlord, Maurice Roche, Viscount Fermoy, arrived bearing gifts. Just as astonishing, he and the man leading two mules waited politely at the abbey gates for permission to enter.

Barbary trained the Clampett on him. 'Get out, Maurice. There's nothing here for you.' In fact, they'd survived this winter better than last; the Ballybeg Order was getting into its stride.

'You pain me, Lady Betty. I bring a Christmas feast for you and the children, belated but welcome, I trust.'

Bemused, she allowed him in and watched him and the servant unpack the first mule's hampers, flap a tablecloth and lay on it wheaten loaves, four cooked chickens, a leg of beef, another of mutton and a hog's head with an apple in its mouth, beakers, ale, dried plums and honey. From the second mule came a brazier which they lit with coals, and a churn of milk. The milk nearly undid her; the children hadn't tasted any for a year, but still she didn't call them. 'It's poisoned, isn't it? You're finally going to get rid of us.'

He dipped a beaker in the churn and drank a little, carved a small piece off the comestibles and stuck them in his mouth. 'I-u-er-ood', he said, from which she gathered that he felt misunderstood. She whistled and the chancel was filled with small, furred – they'd held up a consignment of pelts on its way to the besiegers at Cork – and unfriendly looking children, all of them armed with knives or hatchets. The older ones had handguns, a present from an unwitting sutler in Tyrrell's army.

Viscount Fermoy shuddered. Even the tiny hedgehog of a child, it couldn't be more than three, and one was unable to guess its sex, carried a useful-looking dagger. 'The dears,' he said, 'may one not bestow a little charity on such innocents?'

She surprised him by taking the apple out of the hog's mouth and throwing it away, then she nodded to the Order. The tablecloth and its contents vanished under a heaving pile of fur and leather. It was like peering down into a large nest of squirming rats. Maurice averted his eyes. 'One gathers your curriculum does not include table manners.'

'No.' But for all their hunger, she noticed with pride, not one of them turned their backs on either the Viscount or his man. She grabbed a drumstick, said ''Ware hawk' to Sylvestris and took Roche out into the nave. 'What do you want?'

'One abhors such suspicion in a woman, Barbary.'

'Maurice, you've charged us, you've stolen from us, you tried to sell my older girls to the army brothels. Jesus, you tried selling the boys. Every baby that's landed on your doorstep you've handed to me, even when you knew I couldn't feed it.'

'The exigencies of war lead all of us along paths we should prefer not to follow.'

'Don't I know? What do you want?'

'Let us walk.' It was freezing. The branches of the

trees were as ossified as the tumbled stones of the abbey, and as they stepped out onto the grass it crackled beneath their boots. Barbary chewed on the chickenbone in her left hand and kept her right inside her sealskin court muff which, as Maurice Roche knew, concealed her snaphaunce.

'It's the O'Neill,' he said. 'He's touring Munster, a royal progress. He is everywhere acknowledged as King of Ireland. It is said the Holy Father is sending him a Bull with which to excommunicate all heretics, and having a crown made ready for his coronation.'

'Well, well.' She no longer cared. Besides, she'd already heard it from Sylvestris who was in cahoots with Caitlin, Maurice's cook. Unknown to the Viscount, the scraps of food that had helped to feed them in the early days had come from the Viscount's own kitchen.

'Did you know he intends to visit Roche Castle?'

She shook her head. She did, but it would be unfruit-ful to betray Caitlin's friendship. 'Why?'

'Why? Because he wants one to commit oneself to his cause, that's why. Isn't it enough that one's sons ride with him? Does he want the head *and* the body? Oh, that troublesome man. His visit will so compromise one in the eyes of the English if they win this war.'

'You still think the English might win then?' Maurice's judgement was worth having.

'How can one tell? One can only say that so far the O'Neill has not. And delay is fatal in Ireland. He has done marvels in uniting the clans, but cracks are begin-ning to show. One imagines he is waiting for the Spanish to come help him administer the *coup de grâce*. Or for Elizabeth to die, of course. How that woman does hang on.' He paused. 'Yet she had the energy to cut Essex's head off.' He looked down at her and gave an elaborate sigh. 'It's a lesson to us all not to be hasty. I wager that the young man died neither for his disobedience nor his rebellion, but because he galloped home and surprised her in her bath.' Lord Roche shook his head. 'A high price to pay for glimpsing a queen without her wig.'

It was very cold. 'Are you going to tell me what you want?'

'Well, can't you stop this visit? You have influence with the man.'

She stared at him. 'I've got influence? Over the O'Neill? You're mad.'

'You must have. He knew you were here. He has informants everywhere. The message from him specifically states that Lady Betty née O'Flaherty is to be among those present to receive him. Send to him. Tell him one has got the plague. Tell him something. The cost alone—'

'No. He won't listen to me any more than to you. He never has.'

Maurice sighed. 'One was afraid of that. Well then, the least you can do is propitiate him to oneself. One feels he may have misunderstood one's stance during the last few years. Inform him of one's protection to those little ones, what a guardian one has been to you . . .'

'Maurice, what you've been to me is a bastard, and if you think a piece of chicken will make me treacle you to the O'Neill, you can think again.'

'One may not have been able to do all one liked, it is true.' He stopped and put a hand on her arm, looking down into her eyes. 'But one thing, Barbary. One never told the MacSheehys who shot Rosh MacSheehy at the sack of Spenser Castle that night.'

She stood still. 'And you know?'

'One could make an educated guess.' He'd never seen her smile before and it amazed him. Despite everything, she was still an attractive woman.

'Maurice, I never told you that I admire you above any man I've ever met, but I do.'

She watched him walk away, knowing he thought she'd been ironic. But it's true, she thought. You've obeyed the precepts of the Upright God with total honesty. You've guided yourself and your family through Hell and come out alive, and whoever wins or loses, you'll stay alive. And nothing is more admirable than that.

As the O'Neill came into view, the chieftain standing next to Barbary said involuntarily: 'He's Moses.'

The comparison was not inapt. The child who had been plucked from Irish bulrushes into the house of the English Pharaoh had become the leader taking his people out of captivity. In manoeuvring to keep Ulster free, the man found himself the saviour of a nation and symbol of its hope. More than that, one of the tiny pennants he had once waved for expediency had become a banner in his hand and streamed behind him so that not only the Irish but all the Catholic nations of the world cheered him on. The O'Neill was now the holy warrior who defended the True Faith against the machinations of a heretic Queen.

As he trotted past her, his eyes on Roche Castle, Barbary looked for a vestige of the trickster she'd known and found none. He'd let his hair and beard go grey and on his face was the astonished calm of one who has been overtaken by destiny. The diminished population of the Blackwater and Awbeg put out its hand to touch his horse, his stirrup, his boot, it threw handfuls of precious wheat over him, it cheered and sobbed, and it ran along before him, scattering his way with oak leaves instead of palm.

The cavalcade that followed him was almost imperial. Apart from more Os and Macs than could be counted, gallowglass and Scottish chieftains, every province belonging to Philip of Spain was represented. Castile, Aragon, Leon, both Sicilies, Jerusalem, Portugal, Navarre and the Indies, as well as a cardinal from Italy, Jesuits in doublet and hose and brown-habited Franciscans. The cardinal was waving his biretta and encouraging the onlookers to cheer louder. '*Viva*,' he was shouting. '*Viva Ugo, Conte di Tirone, Generale Ibernese.*'

And all Barbary could think was: How's Maurice going to feed them?

Maurice Roche was thinking the same thing. When she struggled into the hall and glimpsed him kneeling before the O'Neill, she saw his face was screwed up into what others would see as exalted penitence and was actually worry for his larder.

The O'Neill's voice was clear and cold. 'You,' he said, 'it is you, and those like you, who are the reason why Ireland is not joined together to shake off the cruel yoke of heresy and tyranny. Join us in our holy action, deliver us from the most miserable tyranny and enjoy your religion, safety of wife and children, life, lands and goods, which are all in hazard through your folly.'

Maurice, Viscount Fermoy, said one didn't have many goods left to enjoy, but one would do one's best.

All the local chieftains swept up to do homage. Then it

was Barbary's turn to be led before the chair that had been set up on the dais as a throne.

He questioned her courteously, like royalty briefed to ask the right questions of an overawed subject. And she was overawed. She had expected that he would expect to be berated for having tricked her, that there would be, not apology, but side-stepping, a nudge, some self-conscious banter to get her back into a good mood. And there was nothing. The old channel that had always allowed them to understand each other was not just stopped up, it might never have existed; he was his own hagiography so completely that history had been rewritten. She and other victims of the doubling, weaving strategy, like the strategy itself, had been sponged from his memory. The divide was terrifying and so impenetrable that she heard herself answering his questions with the bashfulness of a new courtier.

'We understand you have gathered many of our local orphans into your care,' he said.

'Yes, my lord, I have.'

'How interesting. Did you seek the task, or was it thrust upon you?'

'They just came.' Where there was war there were orphans. Babies conceived by rape on mothers whose husbands, and sometimes they themselves, couldn't bear to countenance them. Children whose parents were dead. Children whose parents couldn't feed them. Children who'd just got lost.

And as surely as war created them, it destroyed the institutions that cared for them. No Protestant Poor Laws, no Catholic monasteries. Perhaps because Tadg's reputation and the ruins of Ballybeg Abbey still retained some odour of sanctuary, it was there that they were taken or found their own way. In those early days after the massacre when she and Sylvestris had been hunting for food, they had heard others crying in the woods. One day she'd found three babies left before the altar where some desperate, devout soul had entrusted them to a miracle by the Mother of God. They'd all died from exposure.

As chief man of the district, many were landed on Lord Roche. And he'd landed them on her: 'They need a woman's care, Barbary.'

'They need food,' she'd told him. 'I can't take them. We're starving.' But take them she had to, because he wouldn't. And starve they did.

'How many do you have?'

'Twenty-six alive, my lord. Fifteen died.'

'Not too bad a proportion,' he said encouragingly.

A good word, proportion. Practical. There was no vomit in it, or dysentery or haemorrhaging. A word that muffled screams, choking, coughing and the calling for their mothers, and obliterated those that had died making no sound at all.

Pleasantry out of the way, he proceeded. 'It has been brought to our attention that you may be acquainted with the Englishman Charles Blount.'

Blount? Blount? That was Lord Mountjoy, Essex's friend and Penelope Rich's lover. 'I can't say acquainted; I've played cards with his mistress.'

'What sort of man would you say he was?'

Why did he want to know? 'In what connection, my lord?'

'He is the next to be sent against me by Elizabeth.' This time his condescension was not for Barbary but for the poor Protestant Queen who kept kicking against the pricks.

Mountjoy. White and black satin against one of the tapestries in Essex's card room, a puff of smoke, a light voice that spoke a great deal on the subject of food, a whisper in Essex's plotting. She shrugged. 'A great smoker and a fop. I can't speak for his generalship.'

The O'Neill nodded. 'You confirm what we have heard.' He turned to the chieftains around him. 'We will beat him in the time he takes to finish breakfast.'

While they laughed, she was thanked, blessed and dismissed. Only as she turned obediently to go, did she realise what was happening and turned back. 'For God's sake, O'Neill, don't treat me like this,' she said. 'At least tell me about Will. How is he? Where is he? Where's Grace O'Malley. Where's O'Hagan?'

Why hadn't any of them come to rescue her?

The hall hushed; was the woman going to commit that worst of lèse-majesty, a female scene?

The O'Neill raised his eyebrows. 'Mistress O'Malley is well, I believe. And if you also refer to my ambassador in

Spain, then I have word that he, too, is well.'

Still in Spain. He probably believed she was still safely ensconced in England.

Men moved in from all sides and ushered her away. She was taken to a room and found herself alone with Hoveden, the English secretary, his face composed into official sympathy. 'My lord wished me to tell you privately,' he said, 'and to express his sympathy that Master Clampett died last month.'

He waited but she was quiet, so he went on. 'An accident, I believe. A cannon that was being inefficiently loaded onto a trailer overturned and fell on him. He died the next day.'

Will.

Hoveden coughed. 'Though indeed my lord has found less use for cannon in his warfare strategy than he first envisaged, Master Clampett was buried with all honour due to a man who worked usefully for our cause. A priest was with him and tells us that he made a good end.' Hoveden coughed again. 'I can't tell you his last words, because the priest didn't understand English. But he made a good end. You were related in some way, I believe.'

'He was my father.'

She walked back to the abbey through fields that were returning to the wilderness from which they'd been created, and Will Clampett walked with her every step of the way. Mostly he was silent, but sometimes she heard his Devon voice propounding scientific theory. She'd brought him to this country in her heedless pursuit of balance and left him to die in it attended by some priest pestering him with mumbo-jumbo he didn't believe in and couldn't understand.

'Oh Will,' she said to him. 'why didn't you leave me to be shot by the English soldiers? Then you could have died in your bed of old age, and I wouldn't be lost without you like I am now.'

Being a personal, he didn't answer the question.

Chapter Twenty-Seven

Elizabeth's new general arrived in Ireland with the new century.

Mountjoy's father had ruined himself and his family by a dogged pursuit of the Philosopher's Stone that would turn base metals into gold. He left his son four things, an ancient name, doggedness, the ability to know a fool like his father when he saw one, and the knowledge that there was no such thing as a Philosopher's Stone.

Though Dublin and the Pale towns were screaming for him to relieve them of O'Neill's besiegers, as they had screamed at his friend and patron Essex, he refused to make Essex's mistake and listen to them. He was here to win a war, not make friends. 'The baseness and dishonesty of the English-Irish inhabitants have been the chief causes of this kingdom's hazard,' was how he dismissed them. And with that statement time switched from being on the O'Neill's side to being on his.

He had one great advantage in a Queen as dogged as himself and prepared now to bleed England to death if by doing it she could defeat O'Neill. For a while Mountjoy sat quietly in Dublin and did his groundwork. His allies, he decided, were going to be Famine, Time and the Irish themselves. Then he took off his black and white satin, put on a heavy jerkin, four pairs of woollen stockings, three waistcoats, a cocoon of scarves, packed a plentiful supply of pipes and tobacco, and went to war.

Leaving Munster, Leinster and Connaught with little more than their English garrisons to defend them he marched north and began what Elizabeth had always been too mean with her money to do before, make the invisible Hadrian's Wall into a reality. Forts went up in a long, defensible line. Sooner or later, Mountjoy reasoned, he was going to pen the O'Neill behind them. Wherever he found livestock he killed it, and cut down and salted each field growing corn.

It wasn't done without loss. 'Every day we did work and almost every day fight,' he wrote. O'Neill opposed him all the way, but O'Neill's forces were diffused throughout the country, and Mountjoy concentrated his on one objective at a time.

His single-mindedness, a trait the Irish did not possess in any great measure, was frightening. The chieftains were not used to someone who couldn't be distracted, and they were tiring of this long and hungry war. Their overlords, the O'Neill and the O'Donnell, inevitably had to make choices between the interminably contested leaderships of the clans, selections that equally inevitably led to powerful men being passed over and not liking it.

Where he heard of such men, Mountjoy wooed them. 'Return to your allegiance,' he said, 'and you shall be regranted your lands and leadership.' Some refused, but those who didn't amazed him by the speed and energy with which they turned their coats. Chief among them were members of the O'Neill's and O'Donnell's own families, both typical would-be dynasts who were incapable of rising above their tribal concepts, Sir Arthur O'Neill and Niall Garv O'Donnell. Mountjoy wrote home almost in horror at the eagerness with which they gave him food and helped him deny it to their former allies.

The O'Neill sobbed with rage and misery, recognising that it was not so much weakness of character that took these men away from him as the diseased system which had made Ireland useless against invasion for centuries. He could heal it, for a period he had done away with it, but for a complete cure he needed time, and he didn't have any. If the whole structure was not to crumble around him he needed one of two more miracles to come about: the death of Elizabeth or the arrival of the Spanish.

The death of Will Clampett brought Barbary to realise that she had been waiting. Always into the blackest moments of her life a *deus ex machina* in the shape of Will, or Cuckold Dick, O'Hagan or her grandmother had appeared out of the shadows and in these, the blackest times of all, she had been unable to rid herself of the idea

that one or other of them would do it again. Now Will
was dead and the others weren't turning up. There was
no hope left. Sylvestris watched in panic as she lost more
and more energy.

'We're managing,' he said, trying to urge her to eat. 'In
the spring we can get to Kinsale with the help of God.
Cuckold Dick might be there. Perhaps O'Hagan will
come and marry you. We could steal a boat and get to
Connaught.'

There was no Cuckold Dick, no O'Hagan, no Grace
O'Malley, and there was certainly no God that would
help. 'I'm just not hungry.'

'You're useless,' he shouted at her. 'You're a coward.
You took us on and now you're leaving us.'

But before she could die, Treasa did. She was the baby
Sylvestris had found hidden beneath the dead woman on
the night of the massacre, and his pride and joy. For
some reason Barbary had never fathomed he'd called her
'Trees', which the Irish children of the Order had
adapted to the ancient Celtic of Treasa. Whatever
nationality her parents had been, the child had inherited
from them a natural humour; she'd grown into the
Order's clown, shaping words as she learned them with
a mouth that had crawled up into infectious smiles or
downwards in mock horror. For her Sylvestris had disobeyed Barbary's instructions never to steal from Lord
Roche – Order rule: don't foul your own doorstep – and
filched an old wolf's pelt from the Roche ancestral wall to
make into an all-encompassing garment for her. The
small face blinking from under the animal skull had been
reminiscent of a hedgehog's.

In the autumn, when they were gathering, she fell out
of a hazelnut tree and broke her hip. Tadg set it, Barbary
spooned extra rations into the little mouth, but incipient
malnutrition made her defenceless to pneumonia, 'the old
man's friend', which befriended her sixty-five years
before her time.

Sylvestris's grief was terrible. Instead of helping Barbary fold the hands, as he had done so many times with
other small hands, he picked the body up and rocked it,
refusing to let her take it away from him. 'Leave her
alone. Why didn't you stop it? You could have stopped
it.'

She put her head in her hands. 'Don't say that.'

'You could. You're clever. You rescued me. And now you're giving up and leaving us here. And she's dead and we're all going to die.'

They were in the crypt surrounded by the whole Order because it was the only complete, secure shelter they had. From the corner where Tadg slept they could hear his voice, praying. The rushlight showed pinched, frightened faces, even Gill's mean eyes were full of tears. And they looked to her.

She hadn't wanted them, any of them; even Sylvestris had been landed on her in a way. They had no right to demand what she couldn't give. She'd done everything possible. How could she have done more? There had always been fighting in the countryside that lay between here and Kinsale, and how did they expect her to usher through it twenty-six children, of whom at least a couple had been seriously ill at any one time? And what if they got to Kinsale? Cuckold Dick wouldn't be there, or he'd have managed to contact her by now. Reports from all the besieged towns spoke of overcrowding and refugees begging in the streets for money to buy themselves a passage back to England. What 'proportion' of these twenty-six would survive that?

Twenty-five. They were twenty-five now.

Christ, she envied them the luxury of being helpless. They could die without the agony of responsibility that was here, with her, in the centre of this pathetic circle. She had been like them once, suffering in a cold London cellar with Will trembling from ague, dying of starvation and innocence, and it had been better as that child than it was now as this woman.

It was then, looking back to her tiny self, she saw that into the London cellar had walked the greatest *deus ex machina* of them all, the Upright Man, an angel sent by the Upright God to teach her that trickery was the most useful of all human accomplishments and survival the only good. Brute beast though he was, the Upright Man wouldn't have given way as she was giving way.

Aching, she got to her feet and went over to Sylvestris. 'I'm going to stop it,' she told him. 'Give me Treasa.'

Next day they buried the child in the section of the monks' graveyard where they had buried all the others, and then they started the training.

Until now their survival had depended on crude robbery from the armies encamped along the Blackwater; English or Irish, they were always guarded but their Achilles heel as far as the Order was concerned was their camp followers, because camp followers had children, which meant that guards seeing a few children, more or less, tended to ignore them; they'd chase them away from the food stores such as they were, but they didn't question their presence in the camp itself, and once in camp the Order could hide, watching and waiting, until dark. Two of its members, Tabitha the Puritan and ten-year-old Coughlin, were promising pick-locks; Seamus, who was big for his eleven years, could carry large quantities under his cloak, and under the direction of Barbary they could smuggle food out of camp to where the others were waiting with handcarts.

Tadg disapproved of the Order's enterprise – though never to the point where he refused to eat its results – but he had contributed his expertise in showing them all how to quiet a horse, nick a vein in its neck and suck the blood, as Irish herders on a long journey did with their cattle. Barbary and the older English children were squeamish at the idea, but hunger stopped them being finicky when they saw the Irish children taking sustenance from the cavalry horse lines with considerable benefit to themselves and apparently no harm to the horses.

The Order could barnacle, pick locks, steal and, so far at any rate, talk its way out of trouble. Now the training became more sophisticated.

'Tadg,' said Barbary, 'I want you to stand here and walk about a bit.' They were on the grass outside the chancel. 'And I want you to put these pebbles in your cloak pocket and shout out the moment you feel someone taking them out.' She attached a rag purse to his belt.

'If it's teaching these little ones to pick pockets, I'll have no part of it,' boomed Tadg. 'Woman, have ye never heard of being poor but honest?'

'You ever heard of being honest but dead?'

'Ah, but Barbary, we've managed without this. I'll not help ye hang a millstone round these children's necks, better they go to the Kingdom of Heaven.'

'Treasa's gone there,' said Barbary, 'and I wanted her

here. If you won't, I'll do it myself, but you'd be better.'
Tadg's blindness had been from birth and he'd developed
his other senses to the point where he could feel the
movement of air from a passing bird. If they could pick
Tadg's pockets successfully they could pick anybody's.

Tadg was silenced; Treasa had been his favourite. 'I'll
allow the indignity,' he said, 'for the sin's on your
shoulders, not mine.'

He even began to enjoy the game, though he roared
that he could hear them before the children were even
close. 'You don't know you're born,' Barbary told them
when they got discouraged. 'The Upright Man used to
beat me if he felt a touch.'

That night Tadg called her to his corner. 'It's not just
the sin of it, Barbary, it's the danger to them.'

'Tadg, if we're going to get them out of here we'll have
to move into the towns, and I don't know any other way
to survive in a town than this.'

'But there's no law in the towns any more, so they tell
me. And where there's no law, men will take it into their
own hands. Will you consider what they'll do to a sneak-
thief, however young?'

'Jesus Christ, don't you think I know?' She'd lain
awake sweating at the thought. It had paralysed her into
staying in the abbey longer than she should. Being caught
by soldiers who believed them to be merely naughty
camp children was hardly a risk at all in comparison.
Seamus had been stopped when he was carrying four
loaves from the sutler's store of Essex's army, and
explained in good English, as Barbary had taught him to,
that he was stealing for his sick mother. Sick mothers
always went down well, and there were plenty of them.
The sutler had given him a hiding, but let him go, and
even given him a loaf to take with him. A Cork or
Kinsale merchant with his purse cut wasn't going to be so
benign. 'But fearing that is what's keeping me keep them
here. And if we stay here they'll all die. This war's not
going to end, Tadg. We've got to get away. I don't
know where to, but somewhere. The Upright Man never
worried if one of us got caught.'

'A lovely character, your Upright Man, then.'

'He kept us alive. Most of us.'

Sylvestris who, from Barbary's point of view, was

becoming more and more obstructive, also disapproved of the new training. 'I won't do it, it's stealing. "Thou shalt not steal." '

'What the bloody hell have we been doing all this time?'

'That was different. This is . . . personal. God will provide.'

'He hasn't done much of a job so far.' She tried to be calm. 'Look, Sir Stayon, I can't sew, or cook or make anything. I don't know any other way to survive.'

'But if we get through to Kinsale, you can go to Henry. He'll look after you.'

'He can't look after twenty-four assorted orphans.'

'Are we going to keep them then?' Despite his rebellion against her authority, he still regarded their relationship as special and was occasionally jealous of the others.

'What do you suggest we do with them?'

He hadn't thought. 'There are places.'

'And I've been in them. There's the streets, that's all there is. I know. The girls becoming bawds, the boys too maybe. This is the only skill we can survive on until we can work something out for all of us. And, yes, I'm going to keep them. Perhaps we'll all go to Connaught and become pirates, but your bloody God landed them on me, and unless somebody better comes along, I'm their mother.'

It was autumn again before the Order was ready.

The summer had been good in one way, bad in another. A lassitude had fallen over the area as more and more Irish troops were pulled back to protect the north. The sieges of the Pale towns were more or less over, though none of the enfeebled refugees who'd been trapped within them dared venture out and reclaim their settlements, and probably never would. Every now and then a force of English arrived in the Blackwater Valley only to leave it again a week or so later under the threat of an Irish attack. Very rarely was there an actual engagement.

Rumours that the Spanish were on their way to take up O'Neill's cause were repeated up and down the roads as people began to move cautiously about again; an Armada had been seen off Connaught, off Donegal, it would land in the north, in the west, the south, but such rumours had been common currency for too long, and men passed them on almost apologetically.

With the eternal optimism of the peasant, Irish churls began to gather in a pitiful harvest in the hope that this would be the year when it wouldn't be taken away from them. Their greatest, sometimes their only, sustenance over the past few years had been provided by one of their greatest oppressors: the potato patches they had planted to feed themselves when they worked for the English undertakers had not only flourished, but had been frequently overlooked by marauding soldiers who did not recognise the tuber as a source of food. Barbary and Sylvestris had made a night raid on Hap Hazard's cottage gardens and stolen some from under the noses of the MacSheehys to plant them in a lazy bed dug within the walls of the roofless abbey refectory.

'Say what you like about Sir Walter,' Tadg had said, as day after day their only meal consisted of potato soup or boiled potatoes, potato pie or potatoes roasted, 'but he did the Irish a great service when he brought this damned thing to our shores, God rot him.'

On the other hand, the summer's weather had been chilly and wet and now, as they prepared to leave, one of the English girls, Priscilla, was coughing.

'It may be the lung sickness, Barbary,' Tadg said. 'She shouldn't be travelling.'

'She's got to. She won't improve if she stays here for the winter. We've got the handcart, Seamus shall push her. I wish you were coming, Tadg.' He had frequently driven her mad with his principles and his religion, she blamed him bitterly for filling Sylvestris' head with priestly nonsense, but he had gone without when the children starved and wept when they died. He'd been the only adult with whom she could consult, and had at least given her the illusion that she wasn't bearing the burden of responsibility totally alone.

'I'm too old. I'd be useless on roads I don't know and don't know me. Maurice will provide for me when you're gone, as he did before. You'll be fine.'

'Fine.' She sat down beside him and leaned her head back against the crypt wall. 'I'll be fine. I don't know where we're going, or why, or what we're going to do when we get there. I'm scared to go and I'm scared to stay. And I'm so bloody tired. I didn't want this . . . this being out of control. Did you know, Tadg, I once thought I could save Ireland? Get O'Neill his guns, get rid of Bingham, trick this one, verse that one. What a pillock. I can't even save a bunch of starving children.'

Sylvestris, who'd developed adenoids, was snoring slightly in his corner, Priscilla was coughing, the rest of the Order was asleep, except Gill who was on guard up in the bell tower watching out for marauders. Muffled by the weeds and elders which hid the top of its steps, the screech of the owl from the refectory reached them in the crypt as it went hunting.

Tadg's hand patted down her arm until it found her hand and held it. 'I've been thinking lately that maybe it's not by chance that you called these children the Order. There's Gaels and Gauls here, Celt and Saxon, and though it's stealing they combine at, combine they do. Stolen it may be, but they share their food without thought of ancestry, or country, or even religion, God pity them. Save Ireland, you say, and maybe you will, and England too. You're no pillock, Barbary O'Flaherty, whatever that may be.'

She didn't understand what he was on about, but the sonorous old voice was comforting. She rubbed his veined hand with her thumb, and went to sleep on his shoulder.

First stop was Mallow. Though only five miles away, the journey would be quite long enough for the smaller children to manage. If the town was deserted, they'd cross the river and try and find shelter on the south bank, ready to press on in the morning; if it was occupied then the Order might as well start work there as anywhere. Barbary felt her stomach churn at the risk, but it had to be taken.

The last time she'd visited Mallow had been between the town's occupations to fetch some of the water which issued warm from the limestone rocks around its Lady Well and was reputed to cure rheumatics, ague, and the flux. Since most of the Order suffered from one or the other, she and Seamus had risked the journey, although, for all the good the water did, they could have saved their trouble. The town had been completely deserted except for an old woman rootling among a pile of stones who'd hidden when she heard the rattle of their handcart. Where shops had lined the street going down to the river there were now mere oblongs of walls, not higher than three feet, and you could look over them to the stumps that had once been the castle.

But today Mallow had function; from a mile away they could hear trumpets blowing, and some Irish country-men, always ready to satisfy curiosity even if it killed them, were heading towards the sound. 'Sure and it'll be grand to see a bit of life, even if it's English,' they called to Barbary. 'And it's under a fair number of gooseberry bushes you've been finding all those children, missis.'

'I told you,' Barbary said to the Order as the men went ahead, 'we're noticeable. We're going to split up like I told you. We'll skirt the town to the west and cross the river near O'Callaghan Castle and decide on a rendezvous where we can meet up later. What don't you do?'

'Never find your way into town, inn or prison you can't find your way out of,' they chorused.

'Damn right.'

So when they approached Mallow eventually it was from the south. They broke up to cross the bridge in unrelated twos and threes, mingling with the surprising number of people who were crossing it with them. Bar-bary pushed the handcart, talking to Priscilla, whose coughing subsided under the interesting happenings around her. Red-cloaked English soldiers with pikes were on the bridge, urging on the traffic. 'Come on, come on. Stretch those bandies. Don't you want your free ale?'

An old man beside Barbary said: 'What are the Saxons shouting?'

'They're going to give us free ale.'

'Free ale, is it? A free hanging is all we'll get from them.' But he hurried forward just the same.

A gaunt-looking woman with a baby showed Barbary her basket which was full of damsons. 'Will the Saxons be buying these off me, now?'

Barbary felt one, hard as stone. 'You can try.'

Up the hill, past the castle entrance, was where the town's half-timbered town hall had once stood in the middle of the street. Nothing was left of it, even its rubble had been cleared away, and on the site had been

erected a large platform. Soldiers were in evidence everywhere though she'd seen no sign of baggage carts or
tents, so presumably they weren't going to set up camp.
More worrying was the large crowd of Irish men, women
and children which milled around the platform with the
look of herded cattle. 'They rounded us up,' a woman
replied to her questioning. 'Free ale, they said, and no
harm to us, but I'm not liking it.'

Barbary wasn't either. Was Elizabeth adopting the late
Master Spenser's final solution to the Irish problem and
beginning a programme of genocide? She looked round
desperately, but the Order had dispersed among the
crowds. God, what had she brought them to?

She stopped panicking. Living like a rat for so long,
she'd forgotten that she was in a privileged position with
either side; if necessary she could command whoever was
in charge of these soldiers to transport her, and the
children, to Mountjoy, saying with perfect truth that they
had mutual friends at court. He might raise his eyebrows
at her number of children, but she could say they were
English refugees she'd saved from the massacre, as
indeed many of them were. She'd rather not spend too
much time in English company, where Sylvestris' conversion to the Catholic cause, to say nothing of Gill's hatred
of English soldiers, would get them all into trouble
sooner or later, but it would do as a short-term escape
route.

Anyway, there wasn't going to be a massacre. Tuns of
ale were being lifted onto the platform and tapped. Soldiers knelt, offering a drink from iron cups to the bewildered queue, like priests administering the sacrament of
wine at a Mass. Anyone with a beaker of their own
was having it filled. Barbary rummaged among Priscilla's
blankets and brought out two of the cups she'd packed
for the journey. A jocular soldier filled them for her.
'There you are, missis, drown your sorrows. There you
are, young 'un, that'll bring the roses to your cheeks.'

'What's it for?' she asked him.

'What for, what for? 'Cause we're your friends, missis.
We're the best friends you Irish got. I bet bloody Tyrrell
never give you no ale, did he?' She shook her head.
'There you are then. Now you go and drink it and we'll
have a nice surprise for you after.'

With Priscilla holding the cups, Barbary pushed the handcart to the side of the square where some booths were being set up, and sat down. 'Drink up, pigsney, it'll do you good.' It was fine ale and it did them both good.

She tried to work out what was happening. Presumably the political and military situation had become so finely balanced that, somewhat late in the day, the English had decided to try and win the hearts and minds of the common Irish. 'Do you think a cup of ale'll do it?' she asked Priscilla, who grinned back at her, coughing. 'I don't either.' After drinking nothing but well water for so long, the ale was making her light headed. And the sun had come out for once, giving a mellow September glow to red and brown cloaks alike, taking the pallor out of the Irish faces and ageing the ruins around them into interesting relics.

Nanno and Peter strolled past her, Peter whistling. All clear? Barbary whistled back. All clear.

Both of them were thirteen. Nanno's Irish parents had starved to death in the first winter after the uprising, Peter was a massacred English settler's son. Nanno had organisational ability, had become their cook-general. She was looked up to by the others, among them those who, in their great need, disregarded that it might have been her mother and father who'd orphaned them.

Barbary settled herself into the begging posture, one leg crooked flat on the ground, the other knee raised, and began the spiel of the mendicant. 'Have pity, sorr, I'm kilt for want of food for me and me little ones.' She might get a penny or two, but above all she gained protective colouring; the square was filled with other beggars, mostly women and children, with nobody taking any notice of them.

Things were happening on the platform. An English officer with a plume in his hat had climbed onto it, while soldiers hushed the crowd. He had a carrying voice. 'Good people, I am Captain Price, representative in this place of Her Gracious Majesty, Our Gracious Majesty, Your Gracious Majesty, Queen Elizabeth. I am here to bring to you your true lord, the Earl of Desmond.'

He'd got the attention of the crowd, and puzzled it. Barbary heard the buzz as people questioned each other. Had the English captured James FitzThomas FitzGerald then? Why was this feathered Saxon proclaiming a man whom the O'Neill declared an ally and the Queen declared a traitor? A voice with a nice mixture of boldness and humility shouted: 'Pardon, your worship, but is it the Hayrope Earl you're meaning, for we thought you had no liking for the man?' Whirr, whirr went the Irish in agreement. James FitzGerald was their Hayrope Earl, who rode with Tyrrell against the English.

'Nor have we.' Captain Price's high accent cut the air above the crowd's head. 'That man is a false earl and a renegade. No, no, good people. I am here to give you your true earl, the son of Gerald, Earl of Desmond.'

A trumpeter standing at the back of the platform blew a fanfare, but it wasn't necessary. The name was a fanfare. The crowd drew in a deep breath and roared it out: 'Gerald.' Munster had been his earldom and for fifteen years the man had embroiled it in rebellion against the English until his head had been cut off in 1583. No matter that he'd been as cruel a lord as the English themselves, he'd been their own, his seneschal a Mac-Sheehy, his bastards begotten on Munster women, and by his rebellion and death his peccadilloes were washed away, leaving his memory clean for the imprint of a legend. Though he was being superseded by the Great O'Neill, he had a special place for them, his Geraldines. And he was come again in the shape of his son.

There were merchants with the soldiers, watching the crowd as intently as the crowd was watching Captain Price; taking the first opportunity they'd had to see what pickings were to be found in the Blackwater Valley.

Barbary looked around for the Order. Now for action. If she'd told them once, she'd told them a hundred times: 'A public event is what a man's watching who's not watching his purse.' The Order in London had made its best filches at processions and hangings. If they were distracted by this earl-whoever, she'd been wasting her breath. Like a mother duck seeing her ducklings take to water, she watched Dorren, Gill's young sister, look trustfully up at one of the merchants. He looked down at her, smiling, before returning his attention to the crowd. She cut his purse so fast even Barbary missed the movement. The child had little enough reason to smile at any man, but she'd done it.

Another fanfare rang out. Captain Price pointed to the ruined doorway of St Anne's Protestant church. 'Behold, good people, behold the Queen's Earl of Desmond.'

What they beheld was a thin, hunched man in his thirties who snickered as the crowd's eyes turned on him, and who needed some urging from those about him to sidle out of his doorway to the platform. Barbary, who'd just seen Seamus botch a filch on a merchant who hadn't noticed, flicked a glance at the Earl as he was lifted up, glimpsing a pallor so deep it looked green. 'We used to call that complexion a Fleet Flush,' she confided in Priscilla. She looked up again. 'My God. It's him.'

Up on the platform, his head down to look at some notes on a page before he made his speech, was her old companion from the Tower, the pudding-puller.

Barbary beamed. What a day. So they'd let the poor little devil out at last, hoping he'd lead his father's people back to Elizabeth's fold. Unless he'd improved, he couldn't lead a lamb to its mother.

'GoodpeopleofMunster,' he said. Captain Price whispered in his ear, and the Earl raised his drone a decibel or two. 'GoodpeopleofMunster . . . um, I come among you today . . . ah, as an assurance and a sign that, um, the ancient title of this, um, province . . .'

Barbary lost interest. Her ducklings were coming back. She kept her head down as a purse dropped into her lap. She closed her knees and shifted, patting Priscilla's blanket straight. Two coins. The blanket needed straightening again. A nice handkerchief with another coin wrapped in it.

In the crowd an English merchant who'd just been relieved of his purse watched the child who'd taken it dance prettily away towards a beggar woman squatting next to a handcart. He followed her.

The Irish were being patient with their Earl. 'Sure, any minute he'll be knocking the seven divils out of 'em,' Barbary heard one woman say.

'And I want you to, um, come and give thanks to God with me.'

Certainly, they'd go anywhere with him. But why was your man shambling off towards the Protestant church?

Three buttons dropped into Barbary's lap from George's hand. Good boy. She closed her knees on them quickly.

A pair of boots strode into her field of vision and stopped. She kept her head lowered and whined: 'Me and the little one are kilt for want of food, good sorr.' The boots were hard, brown leather; she'd seen a hundred like them in her time, beadles' boots, watch boots, the boots of authority. They tilted as their owner sat down beside her: 'You ain't half given me trouble, Barb.'

Joy wrenched her, loosening the fear and loneliness of years. She didn't turn or look or say anything, just stayed as she was and sobbed like a baby.

Cuckold Dick sat quietly while she cried herself out. 'Bib's a bit wet meself,' he said, wiping his eyes, 'but we better go, Barb.'

Gasping, she quieted Priscilla who'd become distressed and was yelling, 'Baa-baa.'

'Baa-baa's all right, pigsney. Don't cry.'

'Who's the kinchin?' asked Dick. 'Bit big for a cart, in't she, Barb?'

'She's touched.' Her injuries when they'd found her as a baby indicated that somebody had bashed her head against a wall. She was four years old and said nothing but Baa-baa. 'There's lots of them, Dick. Oh, Dick, old scobberlotcher, how'd you find me?'

'Followed my purse. That little mort took it beautiful, same style exactly as when you were a younker, Barb. Hello, Dick, I said, she's been taught by the Order or I'm a Dutchman.

'You glimmed her, though.'

'Well, one professional to another that was, Barb.'

They were talking for the sheer pleasure of hearing each other speak, but they were beginning to be drowned out by the crowd which was getting disillusioned and angry. The pallid Earl was standing on the steps of St Anne's church, irresolutely trying to gesture for the Irish to follow him, soldiers were urging them more forcibly with the butt end of pikes, but they weren't moving. They'd have followed his father into Hell – they had – but if the son thought to get them into a Protestant church, he could think again.

'You're no son of Gerald's,' somebody shouted. 'Go whistle a jig to a milestone.' A woman was singing the old song: 'Unless that you turn a Roman you ne'er shall get me for your bride.' And somebody else yelled: 'There's a

Roman Hell for you, my Protestant boy.' These were
from the courteous, the less polite were looking around
for missiles. A ball of horse dung landed at the Earl's
feet. A stone-hard damson just missed his nose. He
shrieked and retired.

Captain Price was ordering his men to push the crowd
back. He had the look of a man who'd been acting on
some superior's idea that he'd known wouldn't work.

'They'll riot any minute,' said Dick. 'Let's go. Where's
the rendezvous?'

'The old castle, west on the other bank. See you there.'
She whistled the call-in as Dick disappeared, but in a
commotion getting louder and louder, few of the Order
could hear her and the rest were getting carried away
with their own success. She managed to struggle through
to Sylvestris and told him to contact the others.

As she pushed Priscilla over the bridge, ten of the
Order passed her without a sign. She looked back to
where a cloud of dust and shouting indicated that the riot
was in full swing, but one by one the rest of the Order
was emerging out of it. 'What a day, Priscilla,' she said,
and Priscilla smiled.

She introduced Cuckold Dick to the Order as, in twos
and threes, it announced its arrival by a whistle and
slipped into the shell of what had once been O'Callaghan's hall. Outside on the river bank the grass was touched
into yellow by the setting sun, some moorhens clooped in
the reeds. Occasionally, a sound like a faint cawing came
upriver on the evening breeze to tell them that there was
still disturbance in Mallow.

'Sylvestris you know. This is John Hapgood. Priscilla
you've met. Barnaby, Seamus, Coughlin, Aileen, George,
Orlaith – Orlaith, this is the gentleman whose purse you
cut – Benen, Harry, Mary, Peggy, Tabitha, Fergal and
Festus – they're twins – Nuala, Percy, Alsander, Clod-
agh, and up there is John Smith.' She tried to see them as
Cuckold Dick must be seeing them; dirty faces, ragged,
all ages from four to fourteen, all heights, all thin, some
remembering their manners and some scowling. She saw
just the richness of diverse personalities, different forms
of courage and ways of coping with what had happened to
them, the proportion who'd survived. Just as clearly she
remembered the faces and names of those who hadn't.

'Pleased to meet you, I'm sure,' said Cuckold Dick, insincerely. 'Bloody hell, Barb, I know you said a lot, but this is overdoing it.'

'There's four more to come.' She looked up to where John Smith was clinging like an ape to some ivy. 'Any sign, John?'

'Not yet.'

'They'll have trouble fitting in the wagon.'

'Wagon? You've got a wagon?' She'd almost forgotten there were other forms of transport than a handcart. 'With a horse?'

'Two on 'em. But, Barb, the rude licentious is going back to Cork tonight. Why don't we all travel in safety in their baggage carts?'

'Nanno and Dorren and Peter,' sang out John Smith.

Nanno was carrying Dorren and puffing. 'It's Gill, Barbary. One of the soldiers patted Dorren on her bottom and Gill stabbed him in the arm.'

'Have they got him?'

'Not sure. He ran away and they ran after him.'

Barbary's eyes met Cuckold Dick's. 'That's why,' she said, 'I daren't stay in English company too long. Order, I'm going back. When it's dark you get into Mister Dick's wagon and go with him to Kinsale. I'll join you there.' She paused. 'You *have* got a boat at Kinsale?'

'Yes, but . . .'

'Gill swimming the river,' called John Smith. 'No pursuit.'

Gill crawled in, dripping water and weed, and then began posturing. 'That'll be teaching the bastard to keep his hands off my sister.'

Cuckold Dick regarded him for a moment. 'I'd throw him back, Barb.'

'I know you would, but I'm not going to. Just get us to Kinsale.'

Chapter Twenty-Eight

Cuckold Dick had been unceasing in his attempts to find her. And so had Grace O'Malley. Busy as she was in trying to keep her people alive in a starving Connaught, she had sent some of her men to Kilcolman to try and find out what had happened to her granddaughter, but whether they got there or not nobody knew. They hadn't come back. Certainly they had been killed, but how, or why, or by whom, it was impossible to say. The Connaught men had become a few extra butchered carcases in the Munster shambles.

Such information as Dick and Grace could gather indicated that Spenser Castle was a deserted, burnt-out shell, and that Barbary was probably dead.

'But she wouldn't give up, Barb. She gave O'Donnell hell for not invading Munster to find you, and she gave O'Neill hell for the same, and then this spring she sails to Spain to give King Phillip hell for not invading so's to find you. *What* an Upright Man she would have made, Barb.'

'Spain? Will she see O'Hagan?'

'Such was her intention, Barb. She was due back a month ago, but she's probably gone to Connaught afore coming here. She still brings me a whiskey supply when she can, though you'll never guess what them bloody Kin-Sellers have gone and done, Barb.'

She couldn't. She was too tired, just content to sit beside him on the cart and hear him talk as it pulled them south through the Munster countryside.

'Put a port tax on whiskey. I ask you, Barb. Mr Secretary Cecil wasn't best pleased either, him making a nice thing from the trade. But we got a way round it. There's a deserted cove with an old cottage in it over the other side of the Old Head of Kinsale eight miles away. I put in there when I'm meeting Grace, though there's precious little whiskey about. Been bad years for barley.'

Bad years for barley, she thought.

Dick chattered on. He hadn't changed. Even during the siege of Kinsale, he had spent much of his time in attempts to find her.

'Bought a nice ken there now, Barb, prices being rock-bottom. And another boat. Called her *The Barbary*.'

Obligingly, he handed her a handkerchief to wipe away her tears.

'And Henry, he's been trying to find you. Growing like a weed and the image of his pa.' Both Henry and Cuckold Dick had harassed Mr Secretary Cecil into instructing the Earl of Essex to locate Barbary. 'And he sent back he'd seen you, Barb, but the pillock never said where, and by the time he'd rushed back to England against the Rome-Mort's orders he was as crazed as Connolly's cat. I was there when he tried to raise the city against the Queen. Him and his friends rushing about shouting, and us lookers-on not moving, just staring. Pitiful it was. And under questioning ratted on everybody, even his sister what you played cards with.' Dick sighed. 'But they say he made a good end, though we wasn't allowed to watch it. He'd asked the Queen if he could be beheaded private, and she gave him that much.'

Barbary didn't really care. Essex, the Queen, Cecil, they were remote. She gathered, although Dick wouldn't actually say so, that after this one attempt, Cecil hadn't bothered himself with the task of discovering what had happened to his one-time agent. Her usefulness had gone. The Queen wasn't interested in the widow of a dead favourite. Her troubles with Essex had taken her mind off everything else.

'Everybody thought she'd be a doner after his death,' continued Dick, 'with grief like. But when the Commons got uppity about her monopolies, she goes to the House and makes a speech as had them wetting their bibs.' He shook his head with admiration. 'Upright material there, Barb.'

He was Upright material himself. He got them into Cork, through it and settled in an inn. He saw the children fed as they hadn't been for years and helped

Nanno put them to bed. Then he sat down with Barbary, urging her to eat more: 'I seen fatter pea-sticks.' He touched her hand with one finger. 'Was it bad, Barb?'

'Yes.' There was no point in telling him, nobody unless they'd been through it could imagine how bad it had been. And she was almost blind with fatigue; she just wanted to sit with him by the fire and look at his beautiful mutton-fat face and let him take over all responsibility. But she did tell him about Sylvestris and his conversion to Roman Catholicism.

'Wants to be a patrico?' Dick was shocked. 'That's bad, Barb.'

'I don't know what we're going to do, Dick. I daren't go back to England with him. He'll land himself in the Tower, or worse. And young Gill . . . What am I going to do, Dick? Where can we go?'

'We'll come up with something, Barb. Battle the watch.'

He helped her to the long, communal, plank bed she was to share with the girls and tucked her down between Dorren and Priscilla for warmth, but Dorren had nightmares and Priscilla coughed and both conditions flowed into Barbary so that she had a bad night. She was back on the Kent foreland and ropes were holding her to the ground so that she didn't go over the cliffs; one by one somebody was loosening them. She was losing her hold.

The next morning she managed to get up on the cart next to Dick for the drive to Kinsale. Dick intended to drive straight through the town and along the left bank of the River Bandon, which cut Kinsale off from the headland that protected its harbours, to the ferry, cross the river and on over the headland to his hidden cove and *The Barbary*. But by the time he reached Kinsale it was raining and Barbary was muttering with fever, so he drove to his house instead.

The next morning a Spanish force under the command of Don Juan del Aguila landed at Kinsale with four thousand men.

The Spaniards' choice of Kinsale for their landing was argued all over Europe then and after. When he heard of it the Venetian ambassador in Paris reported the French

635

belief that, by landing on the south coast so far from his allies' strongholds in the north, King Philip had thrown his men away.

The Spanish reasoning was that it was not an invading army but a support group to help the O'Neill and the O'Donnell sweep the English out of Ireland and that Kinsale was a convenient jumping-off point for the secondary objective which was to be a later invasion of England. As well as that, King Philip had not forgotten the fate of his father's Armada on the hostile west and north coasts.

The O'Donnell would very much have preferred the landing to be nearer to his lands in Donegal. He knew that by leaving his own territory at this stage he risked having no territory to come back to; his cousin Niall Garv would see to that. But he was not a man to squawk. He moved immediately and came south in bad weather on what one of Mountjoy's generals, Carew, later described as the 'greatest march that was ever heard of', avoiding the army Mountjoy sent to cut him off by crossing the Slieve Phelims, usually a quagmire, when they had become frozen with ice.

The O'Neill was less precipitate. More than anybody else, he knew the dangers and considered them with his usual care. But he had pleaded for Spanish help and it had come. Slowly, gathering his men, he moved south.

The fastest mover of all was Mountjoy. He heard of the landing when he was at Kilkenny in Leinster on 27 September. Within the week he was outside Kinsale. This was his opportunity. The war as it was being fought at the moment would never come to a conclusion to satisfy his Queen, but if he could entice his enemies out onto the open, sweeping hills behind Kinsale, he would have the chance to meet them in pitched battle instead of the bogs and woods they used so well.

After considerable fighting he managed to dislodge the Spanish from the two strongholds of Rincorran and Castle Park which dominated the Bandon River to the south, forcing the Spanish into the town itself. There he bottled them up.

Dublin squealed that it was being left undefended, even Elizabeth expressed concern that her entire Irish army was concentrated in one place, but Mountjoy was unmoved. He demanded more men and supplies and stayed where he was.

Barbary's illness was compounded by malnutrition, exhaustion and relief; handing over her responsibility to Cuckold Dick robbed her of the energy that had sustained it and she gave in to the luxury of being ill in a feather bed. The journey to Kinsale had been equally hard on the children, many of them in no better state than Barbary, and several of them succumbed to a variety of coughs, fluxes and fevers. Always a man to respond to a crisis, Cuckold Dick hired two Irishwomen to assist Nanno in looking after them, transferred his goods from his warehouse to his own cellar and gloomily retired to a nearby inn until the situation should resolve itself.

Had the Spanish landing taken place in an English port town, there would have been immediate wholesale evacuation to get away from an enemy believed to have a forked tail and smell of sulphur. In England, Don meant Devil. Most of the well-to-do and important citizens of Kinsale, including the Mayor and Corporation, fled the moment they saw the Spanish ships sail into the bay, but a considerable proportion of the population, shopkeepers, innkeepers, brothel-owners, decided to stay rather than become refugees dependent on the charity of their trade rivals in Cork and Youghal. Her Majesty's loyal Anglo-Irish they might be, but they were also more cosmopolitan than most. They had been trading with the Spanish Don for years, all through the war, and had found him a willing and courteous customer. Trade, after all, was trade.

Barbary woke up to hear Priscilla screaming, the only sound that could have activated her limbs into moving. She found herself scrambling out of a strange bed in a strange room, hobbling out onto a strange landing and looking down over a balustrade into a typical merchant's hall. A large group of children were cowering away from the front door in which stood a man with darker complexion than any man's had a right to be, a turban on his head, barbaric gold earrings, and huge, bat-winged pantaloons. He was also wet.

'Baa-baa's coming, pigsney.' Omnipotent, because she

thought she was dreaming, she managed to get down the stairs and stand between Priscilla and the apparition. She waved it away. 'Cut off.' The man's teeth gleamed in a grin. 'Cut off, I said.'

Entering from outside, also drenched in rain, Cuckold Dick squeezed past the Saracen and showed him a piece of parchment from which dangled a large seal. The man grinned, saluted and disappeared. Barbary sank to the floor and gathered up the sobbing Priscilla. 'That showed him.'

'Showed a good deal of you and all, Barb,' said Dick. She was staring at a pair of thin, bare legs; her own. She was in a skimpy night shift and the Order were peeking and giggling.

'What's happening?'

Nanno and Dick helped her up the stairs, into a cloak and a chair by the window which overlooked a square, talking all the while. This was Kinsale, Dick's house, Spanish in occupation, not to fret, everything well. Barbary took in some of it, but mostly she stared at Nanno. 'You're fatter.' The girl's hair had acquired a sheen and her cheeks were rosy.

Nanno preened. 'Isn't it grand? Two square meals a day, Barbary. Two. And a fire in the hall, and warm clothes and boots, Barbary, oh beautiful boots that Uncle Dick rescued from Spanish occupation, like the grand gentleman he is. Will you have this blanket round your knees now? Priscilla says Daa-daa now when she sees him. I'll run and fetch you a nice cup of milk.'

Barbary watched her go and turned her gaze slowly on Dick. 'Uncle Dick?'

He shuffled. 'Cut it, Barb, it wasn't my idea.'

'What was that black man doing downstairs?'

'Requisitioning. One of Don Aguila's Afriques. But I got an order from him says we can stay. Beneship is Don Aguila, and a good taste for whiskey.'

It was these two attributes, he explained, that had permitted him to keep his house when so many of the Irish were being turned out of theirs to accommodate Spanish officers, and having to make do in the town hall opposite. 'I took him round a case right away, Barb, no point in not being friendly even if he is a Don. And his men behaving beautiful and all. Don Aguila's told them if they so much as stare at a lady's ankles, he's going to have their nutmegs off.'

'So we're trapped.'

'Unless you fancy crawling over the defences and getting shot by the English, Barb, which I don't, I reckon we are. Don Aguila's tried to parley with Mountjoy to let the women and children go, but Mountjoy said no.'

He would. Mountjoy was an exponent of total war, and total war meant leaving as many mouths as possible in a besieged town to eat up its supplies.

'But I tell you this, Barb, I'd rather be tucked up here nice and warm than out there on them hills with Mountjoy and his trenches filling up with water. You never see such rain, Barb. And so far we got plenty of food.'

But for how long? Eventually a besieged town must run short or there would be no point in besieging it. 'I'll not let the Order starve again, Dick.'

He soothed her. ''Course you won't, Barb. 'Course not. Something'll turn up. But there's not much we can do till you're better.'

Getting better took longer than it had before. The image of the saker and the loosening ropes haunted her; death had moved closer than her years warranted. The period since the massacre had taken time away from her that she would never get back. She minded for herself, but she minded even more for the Order whose anxious faces appeared round the door every morning to see if she was improved. For their sake she tried eating everything set before her, sleeping when she was told and spending her days resting in a chair while she looked out of the window.

At least she had entertainment. Despite incessant, driving rain, the square was the centre of social activity in Kinsale. Spanish officers in their flanged helmets, rich doublets and sawdust-stuffed wide breeches moved in and out of their requisitioned houses, pausing at the stalls which still sold fish – part of the harbour was out of the English snipers' view – and the last of the fruits from the Kinsale gardens. She watched them visiting the 'Mercy Me' brothel at the back of the square, which, with typical Kinsale enterprise, had changed its name to 'The Conquistador' the moment the Spanish had landed, or flirting with the maidens who leaned from the town hall balcony despite all that their scolding mothers could do to prevent them.

Priests and monks were everywhere, readying themselves to bring their services back to spiritually starved Ireland. Dominicans, Franciscans, Jesuits, Benedictines touted for business and the church at the top of the square was re-consecrated with ceremony and a procession of reliquaries and the gilded statues of saints, while its bells rang joyfully for the reinstatement of the True religion. Barbary was too irreligious to care that a church which had once heard prayers for the health of Queen Elizabeth now rang with pleas for her damnation, but she sensed an artificiality, as if the priests themselves were conscious that the colour of their ritual and their foreign, alien saints did not belong in the neutrality of this rain-washed Irish town.

What she minded was that Sylvestris, although he regularly enquired how she was, visited her less frequently than the others and was to be seen more often going into the square's church in priestly company. She waited until she felt strong enough, then opened her window as he passed and called him. Somewhat reluctantly he spoke to the man he was with, who nodded, and brought him to stand beneath her. 'May I introduce my mother, Father Dermot?' She noticed it was she who was introduced to the priest, rather than he to her.

Father Dermot was one of the new Jesuits, black velvet doublet and hose and worldly eyes. The only sign of his religion was the large gold cross on his breast. 'Ah, mistress, I am having the pleasure of instructing this lad of yours in the Faith.' His Irish accent was overlaid with Spanish emphasis. 'And a promising subject he's turning out to be. I've told him he'll be welcome in the seminary of the Society of Jesus in Madrid as soon as we can get him there.'

She was too weak for the subtle approach. 'He's not old enough to make up his mind about such a thing,' she said, and saw how hideously she'd embarrassed Sylvestris. He blushed and opened his mouth to protest, but Father Dermot put a warning hand on his shoulder.

'The females don't understand these matters, my boy. Leave it to me.' He turned his face up to Barbary's.

'You'll not interfere, woman. The boy hears the call of God and to God he shall be given. He has work in his own country to bring the heretics back to Holy Mother Church.'

They walked away, Father Dermot's arm round her son's shoulders. 'You shan't have him,' she found herself saying. 'You shan't have him, you bastard.' Sylvestris had the nicest mind of anyone she'd ever met, and if she could do anything about it, it was going to pass on to his children. She'd rather die than have it warped into thinking that suffering was a good, or have it obliterated by some executioner's disembowelling knife. She flopped back onto her chair. They had to get out of here, they had to.

The air screamed in echo of her mental agony, there was a noise as if two hills had thumped together, and plaster from the ceiling came down in a dust on her head. She knew what it was and had hit the floor before the plaster settled. Mountjoy had brought up his cannon and was bombarding the town. She heard cries from downstairs. 'Oh, for God's sake,' she said, 'it's too much. It's too bloody much,' and went down to shepherd the Order into the cellar.

The bombardment, like the rain, was incessant, slowing up a little at nights, but incessant, and the town suffered, mainly through the loss of its larger stone houses which provided bigger targets and were more vulnerable to shot than the wattle and daub cottages which could take a cannon ball through their walls without falling down. There was surprisingly little loss of life; Kinsale was riddled with vast, vaulted underground cellars and into these the shopkeepers, publicans and prostitutes retired to carry on life and business as troglodytes. One inn collapsed on top of its cellar, which was full of customers at the time – luckily, as it turned out, for they helped the landlord to dig through the wall into the next cellar and get out.

Barbary was impressed by the high morale among the townspeople and her own Order, wondering sometimes whether it was the novelty of this extraordinary life which kept them going. It was no novelty to her to be under bombardment and she had to fight panic in order to appear calm in front of Priscilla, the only one apart from

641

herself who loathed the whole business. Peter and some of the other boys became fascinated by artillery as a subject and, when Dick told them she was an expert, pestered Barbary with questions about calibre, trajectory, weights and powder until she yelled at them.

But she got used to it, a person could get used to anything. After a fortnight it was possible to tell from the scream of displaced air where the cannon ball would land, which areas were out of range and which unsafe. Even the unseen gunners became familiar in their habits, so that the townspeople knew when it was safe to go out and draw water because the crew of the saker on the north-east hill always took a break at noon, that the battery situated across the river in Castle Park was lazy and didn't get up early. It was wearing; people's faces became haggard from the sense of vulnerability, rather as if they were parading constantly nude in the presence of a rapist. But they got used to it.

The girls had the sense to be afraid of the guns, but Cuckold Dick's cellar was better equipped, more comfortable than the crypt at Ballybeg Abbey, and smelled of whiskey. In the lulls, Dick took them out for what he called 'liberating' and other people called 'looting', occasionally finding an overlooked sack of flour but more often bringing back chests of clothes which had been left behind by their owners. Barbary couldn't see the point of it, but the girls spent long, happy hours ignoring the explosions as they dressed up.

Food was beginning to run short at last; the church in the square had provided a daily soup kitchen for the other residents, but one night Dick reported that the Spanish military had ordered its cessation. 'This Don says to me: "When do your Irish come to save you? Where are your Irish?" And I says: "They're no Irish of mine, but I wish as they'd hurry up." And so I do, Barb, because we're going to be on marvellous short commons soon.'

'Did you see Sylvestris?' It was the reason he had gone, to find out why Sylvestris hadn't come home.

'Saw that Father Dermot. He said it was easier for the lad's instruction if he stayed over there.' He patted her back. 'He'll be safe enough, Barb, the church's out of range.'

'We've got to get out before we lose him altogether and we all starve anyway. We've got to.'

'How, though, Barb?'

There must be a way. The old young Barbary would have thought of a plan to cony her way out, and make a profit at the same time. The new old Barbary could think of nothing, especially in a cellar crowded with playing, quarrelling children settling down for the night. She took a rushlight and went up into the empty house for some peace, and stood in the street doorway breathing the fresh wet air.

It was too black to see anything except the rain glistening in the circle of her rushlight as it slanted past the door, but she knew what was out there in the darkness – the ruins of the square's west side which had been hit over and over again by the saker's shot on a trajectory that just missed Dick's roof every time. There was rubble where the town hall had stood and under it, living in its cellar, were families that would soon be starving.

Poor Kinsale. It was a town she'd grown to admire. Dick had told her that after the massacre it hadn't waited for refugees to start dying as had Cork and Youghal. Instead, its merchants, recognising the risk of plague, had voluntarily paid for them to be shipped to England where they could be somebody else's problem. The motive was self-interest, but the ends had been worthy; at least in England the penniless settlers would have relatives who could take them in. And now what had been a prosperous, enterprising community was being reduced to just another devastation in a devastated country.

Something hopped over her feet and she lowered the rushlight to see two frogs hop away down the streaming gutter. Nice weather for frogs. She wondered if they were edible.

The slant of rain was hypnotic and she stayed crouched where she was watching it and listening to the wind coming in from the west. The west. She ran to the trapdoor of the cellar and poked her head down through it. 'You got any tobacco, Dick?'

'Taking up the fume, Barb? Good for damp in the bones, so they say.'

'Have you *got* any?'

'Two kegs. I bring some for your gran every trip. Proper tobacconist she is.'

'Is it here?'

'Never leave it on the ship, Barb, in case the crew smokes it.'

She went down the ladder and joined him. 'How long's the wind been in the west?'

'Oh, I don't know, Barb. Weeks. One of the Dons was laughing that the wind wasn't helping the English like it did against the Armada and that poor old Mountjoy wouldn't be getting no supplies from England till it dropped.'

She poked him in the chest. 'And no tobacco, either.'

'Probably not, Barb.' He was patient, as with a child. 'I should get some sleep if I was you.'

'But that's the beauty of it, Raleigh was telling me. Tobacco's add . . . add something, once you start you can't do without it, and Mountjoy goes from one pipe to the other without a rest in the middle. I've seen him.'

He squinted at the idea, and liked it. 'Worth a try, Barb. I'll go and see Don Aguila.'

'Not without me, you're not.' She wasn't as old as she'd thought. 'What can I wear?' She'd been going about in her old cloak and a pair of boy's boots liberated from an absentee cobbler's shop.

'There's a nice chest of duds belonging to the Mayor's family.'

She remembered the Mayor's wife. 'I want to wear it, not live underneath it.'

'The Mayor had slim daughters,' said Cuckold Dick.

Nanno was still awake and helped them rummage. 'Isn't this the darling robe now with its purple and popinjays.'

'You wear it. I'm too old for purple popinjays.' Eventually they pulled out a neat, close-bodied gown of sea-green with a Medici collar and trunk sleeves edged by grey ribbon. Barbary cursed the Mayor's daughters for being nearly thirty years out of date but, with the judicious use of pins, it fitted.

Ignoring Nanno's effusions, she looked in the tiny mirror attached to its ribboned waist band and groaned. The skin of her face stretched so tightly over her bones

644

that it made her eyes slant, and was so white that her freckles looked like scattered toast crumbs. Her hair had gone grey at the temples, but as the Mayor's daughters' taste in hats was unspeakable, she let Nanno play it under a silver-filet, snatched up the nearest decent cloak and left it at that.

The Spanish were relaxed about the curfew as long as nobody showed a light; the easing of the bombardment at night-time meant it was safer for their girls to visit the barracks then, but she and Cuckold Dick were stopped twice by patrols as they made their way to the harbour. Each time they were allowed to pass. 'Ah. Señor Whiskey.'

'How much have you been selling them, for God's sake?' asked Barbary as they hurried on.

'Got to think of future markets, Barb.'

Don Aguila had sensibly made his headquarters out of the Port-Reeve's house, which nestled so closely under the north-east hill that the battery on the top could not bear down on it. But if it was safe it was noisy. Waiting on the doorstep while a guard took their names to his commanding officer, she looked up and saw the sky light up from flame belched by a cannon. She ducked as shot screeched towards the west end of the harbour; Dick had learned not to flinch when he knew there was no danger to his vicinity; she never could.

They were taken up a nice staircase to a long, imposing room hung with Spanish arras – Don Aguila had obviously brought his comforts with him – where supper things were being cleared from a table. The number of dishes indicated that it had been for a large number of people, while the smell of cheap scent suggested they hadn't all been male.

Dick introduced her. 'Ah, Doña Offlarty, how you grace these poor apartment with your beauty. You are Irish, yes?'

'Yes.'

Don Aguila was small, dark, with a nose like a bowsprit and heavy brows over amused eyes, an ugly man with charm. 'Do me the honour to taste these wine. Is good?' It was lovely. 'How do I have the honour to serve you?'

She sipped some more. 'Don Aguila, I understand that

Lord Mountjoy refuses to allow women and children here to pass through his lines.'

'We have parley,' explained Don Aguila, 'but I regret. The man is without chivalry. Perhaps if he see your beautiful face . . .'

It was flim-flam but, like the wine, it was lovely. It had been a long time. 'I also understand that he cannot be receiving any supplies from England.'

Don Aguila smiled, showing nice white teeth. 'Is a Spanish wind. Not like English wind in eighty-eight.' Then his face went into a ridiculous grimace, like a sad monkey. 'On other hand, he does not let me have any too. When do the Irish come, do you think?'

'I've no idea.' She refused to be sidetracked. 'The thing is, Don Aguila, that Mountjoy is a smoker. Do you know about tobacco? To-back-co?'

'Beautiful lady, we invented it.'

'Oh. Well, if he's not getting his supplies, he's not getting tobacco. And I should imagine he's wanting some. Very badly. My friend here happens to have two kegs and we thought that it could be offered to him on condition that he lets the women and children go.' Dick had his passport given to him by Cecil, and would be able to go too, but she didn't mention it, not knowing where Don Aguila stood on the subject of Mr Secretary Cecil.

'You believe him to be such a fool?'

'I believe him to be such an addict.' She'd remembered the word.

'Is good,' said Don Aguila. 'We do it.' She was taken aback by how swiftly he adopted the idea; she'd expected argument or, at the very least, discussion, but Don Aguila had called for an aide, *'Pronto, Don Abruzzi,'* and was giving instructions for the trumpet to be blown for a parley.

'Isn't it a bit late?' She didn't want Mountjoy to receive the offer while he was irritable from disturbed sleep.

'No, no. He likes the parley. He is bored, like me. It is monotonous, a siege. And he has no beautiful lady to visit him.'

Better strike while the iron's hot. 'Don Aguila, there is another matter on which I should be grateful for your assistance.'

Don Aguila spread his hands to indicate that he had

landed with four thousand men on this foreign coastline merely to be of use to Doña Offlarty.

'It concerns my son. He is very young and has fallen in with one of your priests who wishes him to go back to Spain and take his vows or whatever it is. He is too young yet. I beg you to tell this man to let him alone.'

Don Aguila frowned. 'What is these priest?'

'A Father Dermot.'

'Father Dermuchio. The Jesuit.' His eyebrows said extraordinary things about the Society of Jesus. 'I regret, Doña Offlarty. I cannot help you in these. I dare not. I am military, I cannot come between Holy Mother Church and her souls.'

'But I'm his mother.' It wasn't Holy Mother Church who'd sat up nights with him when he was ill, who'd stolen for him, *killed* for him.

'I dare not. I regret.'

She sank back in her chair, angry and desperate.

He's prepared to let me relieve him of the burden of his dependants, she thought, but he won't lift a finger to help *me*. He didn't know she wasn't Sylvestris's real mother; he was quite prepared, as the Church was, to let the boy be taken away from her, and she was helpless. If I'd been his bloody father, she thought, that'd be different. A father has rights, a mother none. And you've done it now, Barbary Clampett O'Flaherty. If the Order is allowed to leave Kinsale and Sylvestris stays behind, what are you going to do? Kidnap him? She considered it, imagining trying to smuggle a resisting potential young priest through Spanish and English lines.

Don Aguila was pressing more wine on her and trying to include her in his conversation with Dick, as if she was a girl sulking because she hadn't been allowed a second helping. 'When Señor Robertson come to Spain with his whiskey after the war, Doña Offlarty, I beg you come with him. I will introduce you the *corrida des toros*, the Alhambra, our lovely haciendas.' She was too angry and upset to reply.

It was a relief to them all when Don Abruzzi came back to announce that the parley had been arranged and would take place at once under a ceasefire.

'You may come,' said Don Aguila, suddenly stern. 'But you watch. I talk, you say nothing.'

They put on their cloaks and followed him out into the rain and down to the harbour and the East Gate. It had been immensely fortified by banks of earth on either side, but it had received a direct hit earlier in the day and men were hammering a sheet of iron over the hole. Torches were lit, and she realised how long it had been since she'd seen blackness lit up by anything but cannon fire. Trumpets blew, drums beat and then the gates opened to show a group of men on the other side.

Don Aguila bowed to a figure made squat by the fact that it had left nothing at home in the muffler line. Good God, was that Mountjoy the Fop? He was bowing with less ceremony, and she was concerned that he was irritable. But no, he was standing there, patiently listening in the rain.

Perhaps Don Aguila was right. Sieges were so boring that any break in routine was welcome. She could imagine what it was like out on those bare hills in the rain and she found it awesome that a man such as Mountjoy, used to comfort, had been prepared to endure it for weeks on end, his army dwindling with the inevitable desertion and disease, waiting for the Irish to come up on his rear. Awesome to the point of frightening. The Irish had never faced an opponent like this before. She gave up hope for her plan; someone as single-minded as that wasn't going to allow his enemy an advantage just so that he could smoke a pipe.

But Don Aguila was talking and talking, putting it nicely, using his Spanish guile to disguise the fact that he was offering a bribe. And, by God, the muffled figure was nodding. Had this ridiculous plan worked? Perhaps Mountjoy had a regard for his reputation and wasn't prepared to let women and children who were, after all, his Queen's own subjects, starve to death. Or perhaps in these long days of mud and monotony the idea of a smoke was overwhelmingly attractive.

Anyway, the parley was drawing to its end. More bowing. More trumpets. The English contingent was turning away to go back up the hill.

And something was coming down it. They heard hoofbeats. A rider and horse were galloping down the hill at a speed which risked both their necks. They didn't slacken as they reached the group of Englishmen which had to scatter to avoid being run down.

She saw the horseman's cloak blow out behind him as he jumped over a Spanish soldier who'd fallen down in his haste to get out of the way, and then he was through the gate and the impetus was carrying him past her.

Don Aguila screamed at his men to shut the gates. '*Pronto, pronto. Esta Don Haguenne.*'

The gates banged shut and hid the astonished, angry face of Mountjoy and his aides. Spanish officers were running after the rider to accompany him back to where Don Aguila stood waiting, his arms spread out in welcome. '*Olé, Don Haguenne. Olé, Don Haguenne. Bravo. Bravo.*'

She caught hold of Cuckold Dick's hand. Nobody noticed them as they walked away.

Dick was disgruntled. 'I don't know who that bugger was, Barb, but he's scuppered your idea. Mountjoy'll be so fokking cross that some bastard got in while he was parleying, he'll never let nobody through, not for all the fume in the Americas.'

'It was O'Hagan,' she said.

She'd known him on the instant. She'd tucked the thought of him away in some fenced-off part of her mind where it couldn't hurt her any more. Then a mud-spattered shape crouching low over a horse's neck had leaped out of the darkness, and in mid-leap the old, beautiful agony was back in her life. He was all right. He was here in the glorious rain of this wonderful place.

For a second she'd stood in an enchanted garden, and then she'd taken Dick's hand and walked out of it. She couldn't cope with the emotion; better to stay in limbo than risk knowing he'd married, or forgotten her, or even that he loved her but, sorry, he was just on his way to somewhere else and couldn't stop. Above everything else, she couldn't bear his seeing her, watching his face change as he saw what she'd become or, worse, not recognising her at all.

There were running feet splashing through the puddles behind them. She urged Dick on, but two soldiers stood in front of them. 'Don Aguila,' they were shouting. 'You, señora, and you, Señor Whiskey.' They had to go back.

As they went up the stairs, the cannon on the clifftop roared out. If its cannon ball had exploded her into smithereens at that moment, she'd have been a happy woman. She pulled the hood of her cloak down over her eyes until she could only just see, and stood in the shadows.

For a moment she thought the room was empty apart from Don Aguila, but then she glimpsed a figure lying on a couch over the other side of the table with its muddy boots crossed and its eyes closed. She felt a desperate surge of tenderness; he had a right to be asleep, riding through the English lines to get here. Why did he have to be in the thick of it? Why didn't they give the dangerous jobs to someone else?

'Is Don Haguenne come back to us,' explained Don Aguila, beaming. 'Don Haguenne, these is Doña Offlarty and Señor Robertson. Oh, he sleep.'

He turned back to them. 'I can trust you, Doña Offlarty? You are Irish, yes? You wouldn't betray me to the English, no?'

'No.'

'And Señor Robertson is your friend, a man of all the world. He won't betray me to the English?'

No, Dick said, he wouldn't either.

He took their word easily. He's careless, thought Barbary, or perhaps he's a good judge of character.

'Don Haguenne come back to us,' Don Aguila said again. 'Brave man, he bring me intelligence the Irish have arrived at last. Now then.' He dipped a finger in a wine-glass and made a shape on the table that resembled half an onion with only two skins. The core of the onion was Kinsale town. 'These,' the inner skin, 'is Mountjoy. And these,' the outer skin, 'is Don O'Neill and the armies of the Irish. Soon O'Neill and his army, and me and mine, we meet up.' His fingers squeezed through the half-onion at three points. 'But first Don Haguenne must return to the Irish with my message.'

With his thumb he jabbed a line from the core through the inner to the outer skin. 'He goes with you and the ladies and the children tomorrow. Maybe we dress him like a lady so Mountjoy don't see him.'

Cuckold Dick looked at Barbary to point out at least one or two of the most glaring flaws in the plan and, when she said nothing, did it himself. 'The Kinsale ladies ain't up to much, I grant you, my lord, but I reckon as

650

even Mountjoy's going to notice one as is six foot tall and sports a beard. And then again, will Mountjoy let us through anyway? Don . . . er . . . Haguenne was very brave, undoubted, but he buggered up the parley and spoiled a ceasefire. Mountjoy won't be best pleased.'

Don Aguila shrugged off Mountjoy's displeasure. 'Already I have sent Don Abruzzi with my apologies. I tell him Don Haguenne was one of his own deserters, an English soldier coming over to Spain.'

Dick raised his eyes to heaven. 'Even if he believes it, he'll play the rules of the parley and want the deserter back.'

'He can have him.' Don Aguila saw no problem. 'I send one of my English prisoners to him. I took many in fighting. Mountjoy hangs him instead.' To conceive the plan was the thing, not whether it would work.

'Oh. Well. That's all right then.' Dick looked hopelessly at Barbary, but she was preoccupied, and moving towards the door. The figure on the couch was as still as a stone crusader, perhaps she could still get out without his seeing her.

'These is good,' said Don Aguila, happily. 'We drink some more wine and then we sleep. Soon be dawn. You are content, everybody? No questions?'

No, nothing. Just let me get out of here.

Without opening its eyes the figure on the couch said: 'I have a question, Don Aguila.'

Don Aguila looked at it fondly. 'What do you wish to know, Don Haguenne?'

'I wish to know if Doña Offlarty will marry me.'

Chapter Twenty-Nine

They were left alone in the room while around it officers bawled orders, soldiers were sent out to gather Kinsale's women and children, trumpets blew, drums beat and Mountjoy showed his displeasure at the violation of the parley by a full barrage from every gun he had.

Occasionally Don Aguila tiptoed through the room, which connected the hall to his map room, with exaggerated pointed toes, like an elf. He whispered progress as he passed. 'Mountjoy accepts the apology. You go at noon.' Or: 'I see to the wedding. Before you leave, uh?' But he doubted if they heard him. They disappointed him by merely sitting across the table from each other, chins propped on hands. He would have offered them his bedroom if they had shown an inclination for it, but it seemed the Irish were as passionless as the English. What he could catch of their muttering as he went by had no romance, no fire.

'O'Flaherty, you look terrible,' O'Hagan said.

'So do you.'

'It's time I made an honest woman out of you.'

'I thought you'd make an honest woman out of one of those lovely Spanish haciendas.'

'Ach, I never met a hacienda with red enough hair.'

And hers was, still was, red enough for him. He didn't see how old she was; his eyes went over her face as if he was licking it. Neither could she see how old he'd become; at least, at moments she glimpsed for the first time what he would look like when he was very old, at other moments he was younger than he'd been in Spenser Castle's gatehouse. They weren't in love with each other's age, just each other.

'Why didn't you get me back?'

'I didn't know where you were. I thought you were in England. I didn't enquire too closely, I didn't want to hear about you if you were back with your husband. Then Grace O'Malley turned up in Spain and told me you'd been in Munster at the time of the massacre.' He passed a hand over his eyes as if trying to eradicate a memory. 'Jesus Christ. Why do you do these things? Even then I couldn't leave. And either you were dead by then, or you'd survived.'

'Your hair's quite grey,' she said.

'That's your fault. And Ireland's affairs in Spain. They wouldn't move, and the O'Neill needed me there to bang my head against their damned bureaucratic wall and get worn down by officials and their damned etiquette, to wait for days in corridors in the damned Escurial, to eat my heart out, begging for invasion, begging for help, begging for bread. It seemed important at the time.' The deep lines down both his cheeks had been carved by years of attrition.

'The O'Neill tricked us.'

'I know. Grace O'Malley told me.'

'He *tricked* us.'

He grimaced, but only as at a forgiveable sin by a loved child. 'He's the O'Neill. I've thought about it, and would we have done any different? Wouldn't you have gone to England to spy for him? And wouldn't I have gone to Spain?'

'It's not been worth it.'

'Don't say that.' He leaned across the table and shook her, the first time he'd touched her. 'You'll not say that. Ireland's worth everything we have to give her. Christ help me, if I start kissing you now I'll never stop. I'll have you on the floor.'

'Why don't you?'

Don Aguila tiptoed into the room again. 'My apologies. Not long now.'

They went back to chins on hands. 'Tell me how bad it was,' he said.

Everybody asked her that, as if it was describable. 'It was bad for the whiskey trade.' They were so close, knowing what they needed to know, that it was disconcerting to be informing each other of things that had

653

happened when they were apart. Almost reluctantly, she gave him a precis, dwelling mainly on Sylvestris and the amassing of the Order.

He was the man for her; he thought it was funny. 'No time to consummate the marriage and already I'm the father of twenty-five children.'

'Get me Sylvestris back, O'Hagan.'

'Ach, he'll be my wedding present. You stopped me becoming a priest, I don't see why he should have the privilege.'

'Did I?' She was enchanted.

'I considered it. But no man who spends his nights thinking of a woman the way I thought of you is fit for the priesthood, I can tell you that.'

'My friends, it is time,' said Don Aguila.

The wedding procession dodged its way to the church through puddles and a cannonade. The eastern battery had got the range of the square's south side and was staggering its fire so that the bombardment was almost continuous; the marriage party sheltered in the doorways of the road leading to the square, waiting for a chance to sprint. O'Hagan clutched her against him as part of a roof on the opposite corner fell majestically down, and shouted in her ear: 'Why can't the bastard throw rice like everybody else.'

She knew how he felt. Mountjoy was going to get them sooner or later; he might let them marry first. At last there was a pause in the firing and they raced through the rain to the church.

Cuckold Dick, she knew it was Dick, had worked wonders. The interior glowed like an illuminated manuscript with candles that lighted up the foreign, painted and gilded saints the Spanish had brought with them. By the pulpit the flames of massed offertory candles were a blinding white against the reredos, sending out warmth. The Order stood at the front on the bride's side of the nave looking smart in their looted clothes. Dick had also liberated evergreens from somewhere, so that each of the girls carried a posy. Priests in gold-threaded copes moved back and forth across the altar.

On the groom's side were the Spanish officers with shining cuirasses over their doublets and their helmets tucked in the left arm. The prostitutes from 'The Conquistador', who would be going with them through the lines, clustered round the door, wishing her good luck, a few of them dabbing their eyes with scented handkerchiefs. They screamed as a cannon ball hit the far side of the square.

O'Hagan left her side to stride up the nave and take his place at the chancel steps. Don Aguila joined him. Cuckold Dick joined her. He put a wreath of silk flowers on her damp hair. 'All right if I give you away, Barb?'

'Nobody if not you, Dick.' But she thought of Will Clampett as slowly, holding Dick's arm, she walked up the nave to the altar. 'Baa Baa.' Priscilla broke away from the restraining Nanno and walked with them, holding Barbary's other hand.

Sylvestris was acting as server, dressed in a white surplice, and smiling at her. It didn't take long, there wasn't time for an address, and Father Dermot as the officiating priest rattled through the service in a speedy monotone, drowned out from time to time by the cannonade. Later, she found a ring on her finger and could only remember O'Hagan's face as he put it there. When the ceremony was over, he kissed her, and Don Aguila had to pull them apart. 'A little time to drink and then we go.'

'One moment,' O'Hagan said. He took Father Dermot to one side and talked to him. The priest nodded. O'Hagan put an arm round Sylvestris's shoulders and took him into the vestry.

Barbary sat down on the chancel steps and disappeared under the hugs of the Order. Don Aguila and other officers were distributing wine from a side table to the congregation. Sylvestris was standing in front of her: 'I've promised I'll look after you until the battle's over.'

She held him tight. 'Thank you.'

It was as if bliss had been accumulating somewhere, building up until it couldn't be contained and poured down an overflow pipe with its outlet coming through the roof of the church; she tried to absorb details which would enable her memory to come back here and wander around in a perfect re-creation, but all she could fix were certain scenes with no links between them. O'Hagan and Dick were shaking hands. It was astounding to hear Dick say: 'I've heard a lot about you.'

'And I you.'

Dick held out a piece of parchment with a seal. 'Wedding present.'

'Thank you. What is it?'

'A passport.' He was so proud of it he knew it by heart. 'Entitling Mr Robertson, whiskey merchant on behalf of Mr Secretary Cecil, and a servant, to pass unhindered by any of Her Majesty's subjects. You speak proper English, Mr O'Hagan?'

'I can sound the "th", Mr Robertson, when pushed.'

'Well, you be Mr Robertson and I'll be the servant.'

Barbary watched them quarrelling and wondered if any of the plaster saints in the church had ever performed such miracles as St Cuckold Dick, now giving the clincher: 'Well, I look more like a bloody servant than you look like a bloody woman.'

Don Aguila was ushering them out into the grey square and she heard the doors of the church shut behind her to keep out the rain. All the way to the East Gate O'Hagan argued that they should be given a horse and cart. 'Do you expect my wife and children to walk in this weather?'

'Pardon. We have no horses.'

'You've got the one I rode in on.'

Don Aguila shrugged. 'I fear not. At this moment the cooks stew him.'

'Mother of God, that was a good horse. Mules then. Come on, Juan, you haven't got the fodder to keep them anyway.'

'Very well. Two. But you Irish must attack soon.'

'I've told you.'

Cuckold Dick wanted to take what was left of his whiskey barrels alongside the two kegs of tobacco but Don Aguila's generosity had been exhausted once the mules were harnessed to a cart. He waved them through the East Gate as if they were going on an outing into the countryside and would be back soon.

Nearly three hundred women and children were going with them. Barbary watched wives kissing their husbands goodbye, girls clinging to their sweethearts, some of them Spanish soldiers. It would be her turn soon. She made the oldest women get in the cart with the frailest of the children, and would have walked up the hill by the side of O'Hagan, but he lifted her up and sat her down so that her legs swung over the open tailgate.

She stretched down her hand and he held it as he walked. 'Aguila worries me. You're sure he'll back you up when you attack?'

'My good woman, he hasn't come to Ireland to sit on his arse in Kinsale.' He picked up Priscilla who was running after Barbary, wanting to get into the cart, and put her on his shoulders. 'Isn't that a stupid woman? That lady there, the one I've just married.'

'You're sure?'

'It's not Aguila that bothers me. It's the O'Neill.' He settled Priscilla's skirts so that he could look around, but the women in the cart and those following were too sunk in misery to be listening. 'Your man's never faced a pitched battle before and if he was open to my advice he wouldn't now. Hit and run is his line, and brilliantly he's done it. Mountjoy's cut off from supplies, and this weather's losing him a hundred men a day.'

'So what would you do?

'What I told O'Neill. Let Don Aguila stew, literally. Pick off Mountjoy's men with quick raids, and starve him out the while.' He tickled Priscilla's knee. 'But what do I know, eh? I'm the man who spent the war safe and warm in Spain.'

And thank God for that, she thought. But his face had relapsed into its deep lines; Spain had been his penance when he could have been having a nice time in danger among the bogs with the O'Neill.

'He's going to show off and that's the truth of it,' he said, suddenly. 'He wants to show King Philip and the Holy Father and all the rest of them that he can win a great battle, and he's been training the army to use the *tercio* formation.'

'What's that?'

'Ach, an idea the Spanish have used to good effect on the battlefields of Europe. But it's not Irish, O'Flaherty. Our lads don't know a *tercio* from the Ten Commandments.'

'Is he going to lose?' She meant: are you going to get killed?

'Not at all, not at all. There's more of us than there is of them. If necessary we'll mass ranks and push the bastards off the cliffs.'

657

'When's it going to happen?'

'Tomorrow maybe, or the day after. Aguila's been told to listen for the sound of firing and then charge.'

She looked past him down the hill they'd been climbing to the ruined town, the white Spanish flags with their red saltires flapping prettily from the remaining rooftops, and to the long, drab tail of women and children winding away from it. All over the Christian world men would be waiting for the result of this coming battle, tallying dead men as 'losses', the limbless as 'casualties', not categorising these homeless walking behind her at all. Love him as she did, she felt an impulse to lean over and take Priscilla away from him.

'I want my honeymoon,' she said hopelessly, 'and I want it now. Let's go straight to Dick's boat, and sail away to Clare Castle.'

'The wind's wrong just now,' he said, and smiled at her. 'I'll meet you there after the battle.'

She'd known it. 'I'm not going without you. I'll wait for you at the boat. It's in the cove over the headland.'

'You'll wait for me on Clare.'

'I'll wait for you. At. The. Boat.'

He addressed Priscilla: 'I should never have married the woman.'

They'd be at the English lines soon. She must tell Sylvestris to keep a close eye on Gill. 'How did you work the oracle with Sylvestris?'

'I became his father, and therefore his absolute ruler. Old Dermot and the Holy Church can't come between a man and his son.'

'I mean what did you say to Sylvestris?'

They were about to round the last bend. Time to separate. 'That's between a man and his son.' As he helped her down, he said: 'You're not to worry now if Mountjoy wants to question Dick and me.'

She watched him climb into the driving seat beside Cuckold Dick and whip the mules into a reluctant trot towards the log palisade and gates that marked the beginning of the English lines. He showed the passport to one of the sentries, who glanced at the seal and nodded the cart through.

Although they were high above the sea, the rain blocked out any sense of altitude, cutting down visibility, holding down the heads of the women and children as they trooped towards the gate in a long gaggle, dripping from hair, noses and fingertips. As usual, the English soldiers didn't differentiate between loyal and rebel Irish. If it hadn't been for an officer watching from his horse, the Kinsale women would have been attacked; as it was they came in for verbal abuse. 'Trollops.' 'The Don ain't choosy who he shags, is he?' 'If it was me, I'd hang the lot o' yous.'

'Here,' said a soldier to Barbary as she passed by. 'What's *meschini* mean?'

'I don't know.'

'That's what them Papist bastards called us during the trumpet. Thought you'd be fluent in Don by now.'

The officer was urging the women to quicken their pace. 'You're not wandering where you like, you know.'

'Where are you taking them?' Barbary asked him.

'We're not taking you anywhere. You've got an escort as far as the Cork road and then you're on their own.'

'But it's twenty miles to Cork.'

'And the Irish army in between. That's what you get for opting to stay with the Spanish. Now get those damn kids in line and move.'

'We're with that gentleman there. We're going west.' She could see the mule cart standing outside a tent with a Tudor pennant flapping wetly on its roof. 'He's got business with Lord Mountjoy.'

The officer snorted and spat. No true gentleman would sink so low as to adopt a draggled woman with a score of equally draggled children, but he let them stay where they were as the Kinsale women trudged off through the mud.

Barbary wondered how many of them would see hearth and home again. Not many. But she had worries enough of her own; the Order had reverted to their fur cloaks, as she had to her filthy but warm Irish one – under it was the Clampett – and had managed, thanks to Cuckold Dick, to become well shod at Kinsale, but some of them were shivering. They stood uncomplaining and quiet, like small oxen. Even Gill had stopped glaring about him. The incessant, driving rain took away initiative; she supposed she should be glad that it was affecting the entire camp in the same way, and that they were being spared the curiosity and questions the energy of a bright day might have subjected them to, but she wished she could get the children into shelter. She was desperate with relief when she saw her two men emerge from the tent. Dick had a lantern which he'd already lit and put it carefully underneath his driver's seat. The smaller children piled into the cart and covered themselves with the tarpaulin that had kept the kegs dry. Mountjoy had taken them both. Barbary got up on the driving seat next to O'Hagan, and Dick shook the wet off the reins. Sullenly, the mules moved off, the older Order walking alongside. They followed a mounted officer who was to take them through the camp to the west.

'Did he question you, Mr Robertson?'

'No.'

'That's good.'

'That's bad. It means he knows everything he needs to know about Aguila's force. There's a traitor in Kinsale for sure.' The lines were back in O'Hagan's face. He was looking about, estimating numbers, calculating dispositions. Barbary could see only mud, and miserable men baling out trenches, droop-headed, half-starved horses, unending stumps of trees that now burned on camp fires where soldiers tried to dry their boots and cloaks, more mud, cannon protected by canvas while their crews sat in the rain, clusters of gallows on which hung the bodies of recaptured deserters, their amputated hands stuffed in their mouths.

'For God's sake, why don't they all go home?' she said.

'Don't underestimate them. Look carefully, they're all on alert.' He flicked a finger to the right. 'See that squadron over there? Under the reed thatch. It's saddled ready.'

She was getting frightened because he was; he'd been disturbed ever since he'd left Mountjoy's tent. 'What's Mountjoy like nowadays?' she asked.

'Impressive.'

They were approaching banks of sharpened stakes made into hedgehogs for the impalement of charging horses. Further off, the ground began the slope towards the Bandon, an untidy grey gleam in the grey distance. Their guide spoke to a sentry who called some companions to help him shift one of the hedgehogs and let them through. The officer saluted. 'If it's the foreland you're heading for, you'll have a job crossing the river. But cross it you'd better. The Irish lines are further up on this side. Long live Her Majesty.'

They long-lived her and set off down a track towards the bank. It was better going in every way; though the rain didn't let up, the track was rocky and gave some purchase to the mules' feet; there were growing shrubs and trees again and birds calling. Dick said there should be a ferry further along.

'Should be,' said O'Hagan gloomily. He was the only one unaffected by the freedom that existed beyond the camp; Barbary knew he was still back there, working out plans of attack. He'd left her already.

The ferry was a raft with two thick nets attached to either side of the base and stretching up to ropes which looped through pulleys set into stanchions on both banks. On the far bank was a ferryman's hut, but in its owner's absence passengers pulled themselves, hand-over-hand, across what was normally a narrow part of the river. Now the rains had caused it to overflow, and the jetty on their side was washed by enough water to make the mules nervous about stepping onto it, and even more loath on boarding the swinging raft. They all had to haul on the ropes to counteract the smooth, weighty pull of the current. The cart swayed, Priscilla cried, everybody shouted and prayed, and eventually, somehow, they were across.

They said their goodbyes. O'Hagan was going back immediately. The weight of knowledge that he might be killed inhibited what they wanted to say rather than released it, and they had their separate responsibilities; he must find the Irish lines before daylight went, just as she and Dick had to get to the cove or let the Order spend the night in an open cart. So the moment was transient, its importance slipping helplessly away from them in a cold, rainy kiss. An impotent 'Look after yourself' and he had stepped back onto the ferry. 'I'll see you at the boat,' he said.

'You'll see me here. The day after tomorrow.'

They hauled at their end of the ropes until he was safely on the opposite bank, and then pulled the raft back to their side. He waved once, but the intensity of the thin, tall figure as it splashed along the bank leading upriver showed that its mind was occupying itself on other matters than the group that watched him go.

'Come on, Barb. Soon be black as the Earl of Hell's riding boots.'

They got on the cart in silence, except for Dick's oaths at the mules, who were getting grumpier by the minute. To lighten their load she got down to walk with the older children and found Sylvestris walking beside her. He was taller than she was now and had spoken very little since leaving Kinsale and she had a sudden realisation of her own impertinence in overriding his wish to become a priest. Using O'Hagan as her instrument she had manipulated him as if he were just another cony. The boy was no longer a boy, he had been her tower of strength through terrible years and she had treated him as if he were in the grip of an adolescent obsession. She would do it again if she had to, but she was sorry for having had to. She took his arm. 'I'm an interfering old woman,' she said.

'You are.'

'I'm sorry if O'Hagan forced you to come with us. What did he say?'

He looked at her, surprised. 'He didn't force me. He asked me if I was sure I wanted to enter the priesthood and that if I did he would respect my decision.'

It made her blink. Without consulting her, O'Hagan had risked giving her son the benefit of making up his own mind. 'And?'

'And I decided not to.' He frowned. 'I suppose I'd wanted certainty.'

She could sympathise; there'd been as little of that about as of everything else in the last years.

'But talking to Father Dermot, he was *too* certain. He said God willed the death of Treasa and all the others, the Pope was infallible, all Protestants were heretics, everybody who didn't belong to Holy Mother Church would go to Hell. I listened to him and it was like hearing my father talk. He said all Roman Catholics would go to Hell, the Church of England was the only true church. Just the same, only the nouns were different. They'd

662

both taken out a monopoly on God.' He took a deep breath. 'And I decided that whatever God was He was bigger than that.'

She should have trusted him. She had the sense of admiration and loss that comes to mothers when they realise their children have gone beyond them. 'Or She is bigger than that,' she said.

'What?'

But she didn't have the energy to pursue it. The foreland was miles of deserted, wind-blown grass and they trudged on in silence, tranquillised by fatigue, while sea-gulls hovered above their heads in an effort to make way against the wind and gave up, to be swept off towards the east. Cuckold Dick's swearing was becoming more ferocious and she knew that if he'd been taking bets on whether his boat would still be where he'd left it after all these weeks the odds would be long. He'd only been to the cove by boat, never overland, and was using guess-work to find the track he'd seen leading down its hill. He told Sylvestris to put a new candle in the lantern, but the light decreased their ability to see through the murk, so he put it between his feet again. At last Sylvestris spotted a grassless patch between some trees, and they'd found the track. Fergal and Fergus got out of the cart to lead the mules down, Fergus holding the lantern high. They could smell sea somewhere out in the blackness. A difference in the sound of hooves and wheels told them when they'd reached sand. The other boys got out to help pull the mules towards a defined blackness on a rise to their right. 'Welcome to Dick's ken,' said Cuckold Dick. The cottage was damp, cold, empty and stank of animal. 'The lads'll be tucked up cosy on the boat somewheres out there,' Dick said. Nobody believed him.

Whoever had been last in the cottage had conscientiously laid in dry tinder and logs, and they got a fire going which showed two bare cots, an equally bare cupboard, some stools and a fox which spat at them and bolted out of the door. 'No food,' said Nanno.

'Brought it with us. Peter, you go and rummage under the cart. You'll find a cauldron of stew a-hanging underneath it. Gill and Fergal, there's a hut round the back should have some hay in it. Put the mules in there and rub 'em down. Spread the cloaks out to dry, girls. Where'd you put them cups you had, Barb?'

She stirred herself from immobility caused by fatigue and admiration. 'Where'd you get the food, you old scobberlotcher?'

'Told Don Aguila's cook where he could find the last barrel of whiskey afore Don Aguila did.'

When they'd eaten, they settled down to sleep, uncomfortable but warm, with their stomachs full of part of O'Hagan's horse.

Dawn showed sleeping children, rain coming through a broken window, and Cuckold Dick standing at the open door, looking out. 'No need to stir, Barb,' he said. 'There's no boat.'

She squeezed herself carefully out from between Priscilla and Dorren and joined him. It wasn't so much a cove as a sizeable bay formed by high hills on either side and with mist and cloud bringing the horizon close. Rain was dimpling sand and water alike. 'I wonder what happened to 'em,' said Dick. 'They was good lads.'

She put her arm round his shoulders. 'There was no sense in them staying,' she told him. 'We always knew that.' With a bit of luck, the crew had sailed back to England before they got captured by the Spanish or requisitioned by the English. Oddly, she was less concerned than he was at their own position; they were in a limbo anyway until the battle was decided. Her mind had needed a night's sleep to absorb the fleeting enchantment of the day before and had now lodged it there, where nobody and nothing could take it away. What her dreams had been about she couldn't remember but they'd been more beautiful than any she'd ever experienced. And she felt better; loving and being loved was definitely good for the health. 'They're not going to wet our bib, are they?'

'No,' he said, less sure.

'Let's go fishing.'

In its short years the Order had never done anything for the fun of it. Trapped between battle lines and sea, with no rescue in prospect, with rain falling, its members had the nicest morning they could remember. They took the pins out of Barbary's wedding dress, found some line curled up on a shelf in the cottage, discovered more abandoned on the beach, and used shells to scrape for bait.

Barbary's illusory wellbeing faded as the day went on; she kept hushing the Order so that she could listen, driven mad by the unceasing sibilance of the rain. Would she hear guns, with the westerly wind taking the sound away from her? He'd said they'd start the attack today or tomorrow. The future might be being decided right now, hers, his, Ireland's, and she was spending the time putting worms on bent pins, and waiting, with a crick in her neck from looking up at the cliffs behind her.

Cuckold Dick was looking in the opposite direction. He sat on a rock, refusing to fish, and stared constantly out to sea, wiping the rain out of his eyes. 'I keep thinking *The Barbary*'s out there somewheres,' he said. 'I keep thinking I see something.'

Bless him, he'd been through enough. 'We'll get away, Dick. When O'Hagan comes back we'll get away somehow. Time we were going in to get dry.' The tide was out and mist was obscuring the entrance to the bay; there could be nothing out there but cormorants, and even they would be having a problem with the visibility.

George, who was Cuckold Dick's admirer and rarely left his side, squeaked that he could see something too. 'So can I,' said Nanno. 'Something.'

She concentrated until her eyes watered. There was an impression that some areas of the mist were more dense than others, but it cheated any definition, and her sight wasn't as good as it was. 'Nothing.'

'Listen.'

She recognised the creak of oars, lots of oars. 'Get into the rocks.' She ran to pick up Priscilla. Whoever this was might be as harmless as they were, or might not. The Order had survived by its ability to hide, fast; within seconds the beach was empty and so silent that some godwits and oystercatchers, frustrated from their feeding routine, came back, did aerial acrobatics, and settled down to such sandhoppers and lugworms as the tide had uncovered.

The creaks became louder. Barbary gave Cuckold Dick her cloak and Priscilla to hold, took off her cartridge belt and began priming the Clampett. 'There's too many of them, Barb,' he whispered.

'Just in case.'

The boats came in with the eeriness of a manifestation, invisible one minute, then an outline, then solid shape. Ten long curraghs, each of them crammed with about thirty men, some in full armour, some with helmets, some without, some in ancient leather cuirasses and caps. As they grounded, they leaped out and unloaded the boats of their arms, as assorted as their dress: pikes, arquebuses, slings and swords. For a military unit they lacked uniformity, but as sailors they were experts; they had rowed against an outgoing tide with effortless precision, yet they let the boats drift unsecured behind them as they waded up onto the beach. They formed up into untidy ranks. Their leader was a huge, grandiose man who carried an ornamental helmet to match his ornamental armour, but still wore a high, plumed hat.

'Who's he remind you of?' Barbary whispered.

Cuckold Dick was being teased by a memory, as she was. 'Somebody.'

The man's voice ran richly along the beach: 'Gentlemen, we join the final battle,' and then, with less confidence: 'All we've got to do is find it.' The accent was unmistakeable.

Barbary handed Dick the Clampett. 'Shoot him only if necessary.' Nobody had better cause than she did to know the man was untrustworthy, but she was drawn into making contact because he belonged to a period when she'd been happy. Anyway, she was curious. Stiff with crouching, she hobbled along the beach, whistling to the Order to stay hidden. The man in the plumed hat saw her and didn't recognise her. 'Ah, a crone. Where's the battle, my good woman?'

She waved towards the cliffs. 'Keep north until you cross the river, English on your right, Irish on your left. Uncle Tibbot.' When he peered at her she peered back so that he could see her well. He hadn't changed one jot, though there was even more of him than there had been; a greedy, insecure boy still looked through his eyes over their debauched bags. 'What are you doing here?' she asked, somewhat unnecessarily. 'Where's Grace O'Malley? Is she out in the bay?'

'Do I know you?' His face changed. 'Madam, I really cannot stand here clacking to beachcombers. I have a war to win.' He drew his sword as if the enemy were only a hundred yards away and he was about to charge. 'On, men.'

They shambled off after him, more like mummers who cantered around on May Day than an army. She was unoffended. He'd known her; the lack of recognition had been his way of punishing her, though for what she wasn't sure; she hadn't proved the threat he had once suspected her to be, but perhaps the mere fact that his mother had shown affection for her had been enough to set jealousy simmering in the dark stew of Tibbot-ne-Long's brain. It had been nice to see him, partly because the meeting had been so peculiar and, for a moment, her mind had been diverted from anxiety, but mostly because he'd left her so many boats. Cuckold Dick and the Order were already dragging them up above the tide mark. There was a cry of triumph from Peter, who was waving a loaf of bread – somebody in Tibbot's army had left their provisions behind.

Chattering with excitement, the Order gathered in the cottage with the day's booty: the loaf, seven sea trout, a flounder and four crabs. There'd be fish stew tonight. She began answering their questions about Tibbot when Dick, standing by the window, said: 'I'm seeing it and I don't believe it.' Everybody rushed to join him. Barbary looked and, like Dick, didn't believe. Her head swam; undoubtedly some great jester in the sky was laying on an entertainment, attempting to take their minds off the lunacy of war by providing the ludicrous. Coming out of the mist of the bay was an enormous washtub and standing up in it, propelling it by planks of wood, were Grace O'Malley and Cull.

Barbary raced down the beach, splashing through the shallows as the thing grounded, tipping its occupants out onto their hands and knees. Barbary hugged first one and then the other. Cull hugged her back. Grace O'Malley said: 'Get off.' They were less surprised to see her than she to see them. 'We thought if Whiskey Dick found you he'd be bringing you here,' explained Cull. He picked up a leather bag and swung it over his shoulder.

Barbary had a hundred questions, but the most urgent seemed to be: 'What the hell are you doing in that washtub?'

Grace O'Malley took a cutlass and a pipe out of the tub and put both in her belt. She shook her fist towards the cliffs and, presumably by extension, towards her son: 'Forced to the indignity, so I was. That young bastard took every bumboat from off me fleet, the Devil fly away with him. This was the only bugger that would float.' She turned and waved her fist at Barbary: 'And not one word from you about it, either.'

'You've got your fleet out in the bay?'

'I have. And every decent O'Malley from the Two Owels aboard it.' She began striding towards the beach, snatching her heavy, wet skirts away from her legs. She was thinner and there was no red left in her hair, but apart from that she showed no sign of age. She kicked the impeding water away from her like a man booting his way through a dog fight.

Cull, on the other hand, had become an old man since Barbary saw him last, as if he'd taken on the burden of Grace's ageing as well as his own. 'Herself's leaving, Barbary. I think she's leaving Connaught.' Saying it was so terrible that his eyes screwed up and his mouth widened like a baby's. He began to sob. 'She's brought her people with her.'

'Cull.' She took his arm and led him towards the shore.

The Order was staring at Grace as at some geriatric Venus who'd risen from the foam on a domesticated and very Irish form of seashell. Grace ignored them. 'Is there transport, blast ye?' she demanded of Cuckold Dick, who told the twins to go and fetch the mules. 'And where's me weed?'

Dick swallowed. It was Barbary who said: 'We had to give it to Mountjoy to get through the English lines. Where are you going, Grandmother?'

Grace nodded her head towards the cliffs and Tibbot. 'After him.'

'Why?'

'To give him a mother's blessing,' snarled Grace. 'Why else?'

Barbary glanced at Cull, who shook his head. She made up her mind and took Cuckold Dick, Sylvestris and Cull to one side. 'I'm going with her.'

'But where's she going, Barb? And why?'

She had no idea why, and in this mood Grace wasn't

668

going to tell her, but it was towards the battle. 'I was going anyway. I promised O'Hagan I'd meet him at the ferry when it was all over, and I might as well go in her company as any other.'

Sylvestris shook his head, but Cuckold Dick blew out his cheeks: 'I'd back her against Irish, English and Don combined,' he said. 'If we got to go, we got to.'

'Not we. Me.' She took off her cloak, wriggled out of the cartridge belt and handed it to him with the Clampett. 'I want you and Sir Stayon here to take the Order, get them into the curraghs and paddle out to the fleet – it can't be very far off. Whoever wins or loses this battle, Ireland's going to be no place to bring up the Order, not for a long time.'

She was impatient that they looked doubtful; couldn't they see that Grace O'Malley was a miracle and that they weren't likely to be vouchsafed another? They had to get away from this place, all of them. 'For God's sake, we'd agreed we'd go in Dick's boat, what's the difference if we go in Grace O'Malley's?'

She looked at Cull and he nodded: 'Sure and there's room a-plenty. Tibbot paid for a one-way passage for him and his men, he said nothing about a return journey. But you'd better ask Herself.'

Dick sighed. 'The difference is, Barb, we don't know where she's sailing.'

'We didn't know where *we* were going to sail.'

Grace was disputing with one of the mules which, remembering its labour of the day before, was showing a disinclination to be ridden. 'Hold still, you shit-rumped, scab-bellied bastard till I mount ye.' Cull made a stirrup with his hands and they heaved her up.

'After the battle, Grandmother, where are you and the fleet going?'

The mule tried a circle and got a thump in its flanks that dissuaded it from doing any more. 'Where the wind takes us,' Grace said. Barbary looked at Cull for help and he shrugged back that he had none.

'Will you give us all passage?'

'Who's all? I need to be off with your questions.'

Barbary indicated the crowd about her. 'And O'Hagan. After the battle.'

'Is the O'Hagan in the battle now? And me thinking he

was in Spain.' For the first time she seemed to notice that she was being stared at by a large number of children. 'Where did you find all these grawls? Well then, I've no time to argue, but it's an imposition and we'll be seeing about their passage money after.'

'She means yes,' said Cull. 'She's pleased to see you.'

'I'm away,' said Grace and headed the mule towards the track. Cull scrambled onto the second mule – wherever Grace O'Malley went he was going with her – and leaned down to pull Barbary up in front of him.

Sylvestris stopped her. 'All right, we'll do it,' he said, 'but you've got to come back.'

'I'm going to come back.'

'I mean it. It's not for me, not for you, but the Order. They've had too much to bear, and they love you. You shouldn't be going. If you got killed, they wouldn't survive it. They've been abandoned too often.' He was speaking with an authority that weighted her down.

She looked around at the faces turned to hers. Only Sylvestris was trying to stop her going because the others had no hope that she would stay; their faces were set in the endurance she had grown up with, among children whose idea of normality was the abnormal. They had no expectation that life held anything other than what they could filch from it; it bore no rights for them and they didn't even know that it should. She and Tadg and Sylvestris and Ballybeg Abbey had been the only blessing they'd received after the massacre but the very nature of the blessing had taught them to put up with its loss. They could bear it, she thought, they could bear anything. But I'll be damned if they have to.

'Whatever happens,' she said, 'I'll be back.'

Chapter Thirty

Even Grace O'Malley was incapable of urging speed out of a mule that was against it; Cull's and Barbary's hastened itself enough to catch up its companion once it had gained the hilltop, but after that both animals settled down into the heavy amble of their normal pace. Tibbot and his army had disappeared into the mist and rain and Grace had become resigned to mulish inevitability; apart from rousing herself to kick her mount from time to time, she rode in preoccupied silence.

'Why is she chasing after Tibbot?' Barbary asked over her shoulder. 'Didn't they come in on the same ship?'

'They did, but it's a long story.' He told it to her, his body protecting her back from the wind and his breath coming strong into her ear with the syllables of great names of clans and chieftains she remembered from her childhood. Dermot O'Connor of the O'Connor Don of Roscommon, O'Connor Sligo, the MacWilliam, the Bourkes of Mayo, the Bourkes of Clanrickard, the MacJordans, MacDonnells, Clandonnells, the complexity of interbred, interwarring septs whose age-old battles had turned more monstrous under English interference.

Grace's old friend and fellow prisoner, Red Hugh O'Donnell, had gone in strength into Connaught to lead the Irish resistance against the English. 'He's the great young man, Barbary, hasty and headstrong but the greatness has come upon him these last years with the influence from the O'Neill, and Herself gave him recognition for it. But he decided to force through the election of the MacWilliam which has caused such discord among the clans these years, and the one he chose for the title was Theobald, son of Walter. Well, Barbary, as you know, Tibbot of the Ships has always laid claim to the

MacWilliamship, and he was not pleased. He went to the Saxons and they promoted him to be a captain in the Saxon Queen's pay, for they are crafty in playing one man against another.'

She shifted, not just because riding a bony mule without a saddle in driving rain was uncomfortable, though it was, but because Cull's voice had fallen into rhythm with the mule's pace and achieved the sing-song quality of the reciters from her childhood retelling the old myths. He couldn't bear what he was saying so he was distancing himself from its immediacy by speaking of it as if it had happened to the long dead. And he's right, she thought. These are my people, relatives of mine, alive now, and they are the past. He was recounting the destruction of Connaught and she was hearing the destruction of Ireland.

'Herself was not pleased either and she upbraided the O'Donnell, but she stuck with him.' For a moment Cull dropped into his everyday voice. 'I know she plays the battleaxe, Barbary, but she is the wise one nevertheless. She has been to Spain and to the African coast and she went to England with you and met the Saxon Queen, and so she went to Tibbot and said there would be time enough to fight over the MacWilliamship when they had driven out the Saxons and they would not drive out the Saxons by fighting among themselves. "We are wolves in a trap," she told him, "and if we have to gnaw off our own leg to get out we must not gnaw each other's."'

'Did she?' Barbary looked towards the vulture's shape of her grandmother sitting stolidly on its mule, the fur collar of her cloak drawn up.

'She is a doorful of woman,' said Cull, and relapsed into his sing-song. 'And she went on working for the O'Donnell. But Tibbot is clever only for himself and he played the old game, drawing his pay from the Saxons the whiles ambushing the enemies of the O'Neill when the O'Neill told him to. And when the O'Neill sent word that he would be obliged if Tibbot would bring an army to help him fight in this great deciding battle to drive the Saxon out of our land, Tibbot agreed and he hired his mother to transport him. Old as she was, she said she would fight alongside him, and so would I have done, and others. But, Barbary, this morning when the fleet was still asleep after the voyage, and it was a difficult one, Tibbot took his men and stole all our curraghs and came ashore. And when we discovered it Granuaile said: "I am of the opinion he has gone to fight for the Saxon and not the O'Neill and I must go after him, so launch the bloody washtub." And the rest you know.'

'Will he? Fight for the English?'

'He will fight for whoever he thinks will win.'

In between darker cloud the sky was an unhealthy mustard and the rain was varying between merely falling down and bursts of such violent intensity that it seemed to be commanded by a god who'd become deranged.

'I think Herself is Noah,' said Cull.

'What?' The entire world was hissing.

'Noah,' shouted Cull. 'She has brought all her people with her because she could not let them stay behind to starve, and she says if the Saxons are winning she will be leaving Connaught. But I think she heard the voice of God telling her the second Flood was at hand, and here it is.'

He was probably right. The mules' hooves were sinking into ground that had reached saturation point and the surplus lay in sheets as big as lakes, so that raindrops hit and bounced up again in a blur of dancing water that reached the mules' withers.

'Do I see something?' Cull yelled at Grace and pointed. Barbary shielded her eyes to look but the wet on her eyelashes distorted her vision. They had been travelling for what seemed like hours, relying on Cull's sense of navigation to keep them going north. Grace nodded and kicked her mule again, hopelessly; with her weight on its back it was having difficulty pulling its legs out of the mud at all. 'I saw something,' Barbary heard Cull mutter. 'It was the Tibbot's foolish hat.'

If it was, they didn't see it again until they reached the hill above the Bandon and worked their way west along it, watching for the ferry point. Barbary's eyes were on the opposite hill, looking for signs of battle, but there was nothing.

'There he is,' shouted Cull. They were still some way above the ferry and along from it, but a large cluster of men stood on the far side, helping to pull the last load of Tibbot's men across. There was no mistaking Tibbot's hat, although its feathers were flattened down onto his shoulder, and no mistaking the grandiloquent wave of his sword as, without waiting, he led his way up the hill opposite theirs. They couldn't catch him now, and Grace didn't try. She sat on her mule and watched.

'Where are the Irish lines?' Cull asked Barbary.

'To the left.'

The men had assembled now at the top of the hill, a hunched little group at this distance, all concentrated on the matchstick figure of their leader. A last mustard glow from the miserable sun came through a lessening in the cloud behind them, and they could see him caper in it as he addressed his men. Then he wheeled and marched off, with his men loping behind him. To the right. Tibbot of the Ships was throwing in with the English.

The most shocking sound Barbary ever heard came from Grace's mouth then. In it was none of the hatred and rising madness of the MacSheehy howl, it was a linear wail of despair, piercing enough to travel the winds of the river to the sea reaches, issuing from a fissure in the past and widening into the future. It went on and on, the ullagone, the song of grief, not for herself, not for her son, not for anything except an unlocalised, undirected agony for the human condition.

The strange thing about it was that it was not strange; apart from the surprising source from which it came, it seemed natural, assimilating itself into the rain and the grey-green, wet-streaked, desolate country as if it had been expected. Even after Grace had closed her mouth, the water in the air and ground appeared to go on vibrating from it.

When it released them, Cull and Barbary ran to her grandmother. Grace's eyes were quite empty. She took a deep breath and said: 'That's that then. We'll have to be spending the night in that *sean-tigh* down there.'

Barbary walked alongside her as Cull led the two mules down the slope towards the ferryman's hut, patting her like someone trying to shape back together an ornament that had fractured.

'We'll need to be leaving early in the morning,' Grace went on. 'There is a lot to do before we catch the tide.'

'Oh Granuaile.' Barbary did some more patting.

'Because Tibbot has joined them it doesn't mean the English are going to win.'

Grace looked offended. 'Do you take him for a fool? He would not have joined them if they were not going to win. If he cannot be the MacWilliam, he will be a lord among the Saxons.' If it hadn't been for the ullagone still ringing in her ears, Barbary would have thought Grace was proud of him.

It was getting dark as they reached the ferryman's hut and the wind was getting up. The traditional courtesy of the Irish had again left dry sticks and logs by the hut's central fireplace, though some of them had been wetted by rain forcing itself through the louvre in the roof. Cull hobbled the mules under the most sheltering tree he could find, and came in to get a fire going. The draught roared it upwards so that after a while they could take off their cloaks and boots and begin drying. The two women spread out their skirts. Barbary had long, stinging weals on the inside of her thighs where they had rubbed raw on the ride. Grace put her empty pipe in her mouth and sucked it.

They sat round the fire, hardly able to see one another for steam from their clothes and the smoke being tossed back into the hut by a burst of draught. They kept the door open so that they could breathe, but they would have kept it open anyway; it faced the river and gave them a pathetic illusion of being in touch with what was happening on the hills beyond it.

The wind hit the back of the hut with a force that made it rock, lifting the river into waves that lashed the opposite bank in white spray. There was a flash of light and, seconds later, a grumble of thunder. Oh, for God's sake, thought Barbary, this is ridiculous. The Upright God was getting carried away by his own theatricals, like some off-stage manager in a playhouse shaking a sheet of tin. It was all there, the blasted heath, the battle lines waiting for the charge, it didn't need thunder as well. You're overdoing it. Then she thought: the Irish are bound to win now; this sort of drama's just up their alley.

Why did they have to fight at all? Cut out the middlemen, all those husbands and fathers and sons, valuable and beautiful middlemen, like O'Hagan, and just have Mountjoy and the O'Neill playing chess for it, or dice, and charge admission. Grand prize: Ireland. If wet, indoors.

It was a long night. In the early hours it became impossible to think as the Upright God showed what he could do when he got down to it, stabbing lightning into the river and hills with a frequency that displayed the three of them to each other in ghastly flickers. The thunder cracked so loud that they flinched. When it moved away to position itself over the battlefield, the comparative silence it left them in had to be filled by talking. At least, Barbary and Cull talked; Grace stayed silent. 'Why are you leaving Connaught?' Barbary asked her, and then, to Cull: 'Why's Herself leaving?'

Cull said reluctantly, 'There is no Connaught. There's a place where if something grows, Saxons or Irish cut it down, if a man builds a cottage, somebody burns it, if a calf is born, it is eaten as it leaves the womb. We are chased from island to island; if we land, the Saxons kills us, if we sail, they sail after us. A fleet, she says, but we've only the *Grace of God* and two ships else left to us.' His mouth widened again into the terrible baby's grimace. 'They even killed Kitterdy Two's aunt.'

'Oh no.' Extra, tiny tragedies were almost unbearable.

He nodded. 'Even though it is bad luck, they eat the seals. And the seals come to be killed when they are called, for they are not used to being killed by men.' He leaned over and took her hand. 'Don't cry now, maybe Herself will return to Connaught one day. Tell us what happened to you. Herself sent some of the O'Malleys to find you, but they did not come back.'

She told them, at greater length than she had told Cuckold Dick and O'Hagan, in order to fill up the silence that was preluding dawn. 'I'll have to wait here tomorrow. For my husband.'

Cull hit himself on his forehead with the heel of his hand. 'And I have the whiskey in my pack to drink you joy.' He rummaged and passed round a leather bottle. Grace O'Malley stirred herself and lifted the bottle to Barbary before she drank. 'Here's to your man and to you, Barbary Clampett, O'Flaherty, O'Malley, O'Hagan. Maybe we'll wait with you till he comes.'

It was amazingly comforting. She thought: Clampett, O'Flaherty, O'Malley, *Betty*, O'Hagan. It was fitting that the mother of so many, variably parented children should have so many racially varied names. I am an Anglo-Irish relation, she thought, and took another swig from the bottle. If ever there was a time to get drunk, it was now.

Grace O'Malley sobered her up: 'Something's happening.'

They crowded into the doorway. There was still lightning across the hills beyond the river, as well as some far-off thunder, but there was an impression of other light, the diffusion from thousands of glow-worms, and a noise that lost its distinction in the wind.

Somewhere out there men bent their backs to the wind and applied match to their fire pots and swore as the priming powder blew out of their muskets and calivers. Disciplined against the natural instinct to run away, they were running forward to meet the enemy, so frightened that some of them were evacuating their bowels as they ran, or micturating without knowing it. Horses were neighing to the cavalry drums as they cantered towards pikes that would disembowel them and hedgehogs on which they would hang, screaming, until they died. Arms, fetlocks, heads, tails were disintegrating in explosions from cannon.

Miles away, three people in a doorway saw the pretty twinkling of glow-worms and heard a fitful thrumming.

It was useless to watch it and when the sun came up, miserable apology for a dawn though it was, it leached away the distinction between light and dark and made the glow-worms fade out, but they stayed where they were. The fluctuating murmur that came from the hills was overlaid by thunder. Tucked down in the pocket of Kinsale, would Don Aguila have heard the guns, or was the wind taking the sound away from him? The impulse to go and see was overwhelming. 'I'm going across the river.'

Grace's hand gripped hers. 'You'll not.'

No, it was stupid; there would be no chance of finding O'Hagan among the thousands of men who were struggling out there. She didn't want to join in on either side any more; she just wanted O'Hagan not to be killed, none of them to be killed. Grace's son was there somewhere, her own husband, the O'Neill, Red Hugh, men she had met at Elizabeth's court, men who had fought with Rob perhaps. Among the Spanish there might even be relatives of Don Howsyourfather, or Don Howsyourfather himself. All trying to kill each other. Wait, just wait with the rest of the world, to see if this part of it will assume a different complexion. Wait for one of the balancing scales to go down.

'How long's it been going on?'

'Three hours about.'

There was a change. The morning had become marginally brighter and very much colder, the rain was coming straight down instead of at a slant. The battle sounds came more clearly, but they contained no drums or trumpets, only yelling.

A group of men appeared on the opposite skyline, running along the hill and straight over towards the river, not stopping at the slope but hurling themselves down it, clinging onto bushes to break their tumbles, dropping like clusters of plums. The first dozen to reach the ferry immediately began to haul it across and the men behind them had to jump to get aboard. Their weight rocked the raft, tipping some of them backwards still holding on to others. Those who couldn't get back on grabbed the planking and allowed themselves to be dragged through the water. One couldn't reach, and was swept downriver by the current.

Every man on the ferry was hauling to make it cross faster. It was fearful, not because the three figures watching them approach felt in danger but because the fear generated by the men themselves was infectious. They had no object that would imperil the women and Cull, they weren't going *to* anywhere for anything, just from. Sobbing with effort, swearing, they bumped the ferry against the landing stage buffer and scrambled ashore. They took no more notice of the three than if they'd been a cluster of trees. Without pausing they turned upriver to go running along the bank. One man had stayed behind and began hacking at the rope going through the stanchion pulley.

Grace drew her cutlass. 'Leave it,' she said. 'For the others.'

He stopped and stared at her, he was so swathed in mud it was impossible to tell what he was wearing, or if he was wearing anything. 'Where were the bloody Spanish?' he asked. Then he turned to run after the others.

678

The hills on the opposite bank were sprouting men along their skyline, lots of them, becoming an avalanche of sliding, falling bodies funnelling down to the ferry. Cull looked anxiously at the partly severed rope: 'God help it hold for the poor devils.' There was no time to do anything about it, the raft was pulled back to the opposite shore where at least one hundred men jammed themselves onto it. No faulty rope was going to stand up under weights like that for long. 'Tie her up when she's in,' Grace told Cull. 'We'll lash it.' Barbary was amazed at their self-possession, that they had the wit to be sensible in this flood of irrationality.

The second ferry-load came ashore, eyes showing white through masks of mud with the fixed stare of stampeding animals. Cull and Grace grabbed the ferry's painters and hitched them to their bollards while Barbary guarded the stanchion. One man raised his dagger to the fraying rope, and she stepped in front of him. For a moment she thought he would bring the knife down anyway, but he shrieked at her and ran off. On the other side of the river men were already trying to tug the ferry back, hampering Cull as he worked on the jerking rope. Their shouts came through the rain in ferocious pleading and swearing. Some were stripping off their boots and armour and diving into the river, and being swept away. 'Hurry, hurry, Cull.' There was no sign of the first man who'd fallen into the river; downstream was empty except for a small tree dwindling into the distance, twisting with the curl of the current. Cull's steady hands worked with the care of the one-speed craftsman, but men were drowning. Eventually he was ready: 'I'll be doing it again after the next trip if they overload,' he said. 'She'll not hold for hundreds.'

Grace unhitched the ferry and stepped aboard. Barbary joined her. It'd need two to restrain this stampede; it would need an army. Even so, she had to fight the impulse not to approach whatever terror was chasing these men.

They had to fight to get off the ferry on the other side against the press of men getting on it and then struggle to try and stop the excess. Barbary screamed at them, 'The rope's fraying. Not so many,' grabbing at muddy arms that slipped through her clutch or shook her away. Grace was laying about her with the flat of the cutlass. 'Stand off, you bastards. Wait.' Both of them might have been gnats dancing up and down; Barbary was pushed down into the mud and a man's boot crushed her hand in his eagerness to get aboard. She crawled out of the way, hauled herself up and stood watching. It was hopeless. The men kept glancing up the hill behind them, but only more like themselves came pouring over it.

So this was a rout, this touch from the horned god that blinded men's eyes and screamed into their ears, turning them into sobbing, panting animals who'd lost the power of reason. Time and again they silted up around her as Cull held the ferry back to work on the rope, and she was lost in a jostling crowd of terror. She shook them, shouted at them: 'Wait, wait. Have you seen the O'Hagan?' but they were stupid with horror and dumb. Some asked her back: 'Where were the Spanish?'

There were wounded being not so much helped as pulled along, yelling as broken bones were bumped, but in as great a panic as the rest that they might be left behind. Some trailed blood. A corpse still had its arms around the shoulders of two comrades who were unaware they were rushing a dead man onto the ferry.

These men scattering like quail had been soldiers only a while ago; some were veterans wearing the O'Neill's red-handed badge of Ulster. On their own ground they had outwitted and outfought the best that Elizabeth could send against them; enduring homelessness and starvation, they had remained undefeated. But that was on their own ground, and they'd stepped out of it.

There were riders on the hilltop lashing out with their swords at the men who still poured over the drop. She caught hold of Grace and began to drag her towards the ferry, as terrified as those around her. 'The English cavalry.'

Grace shook her head. 'Irish,' she said, 'trying to stop them.'

Barbary looked back up and saw one of the running men go down under a slash from an officer's sword. It made no difference to the stampede, it was just another man killed and this time by his own side. Leave them alone, leave them *alone*. It's over, they can't fight, they won't. They're beaten. They weren't meant for this.

680

Nobody was meant for this. Leave them alone.

The ferry went, came back, went, came back. How long she and Grace had been on this bank she couldn't remember. Time and again they tried to help one of the wounded and were pushed away. The river was a barrier against the English and the men's eyes were fixed on the opposite bank like souls in Hell glimpsing water. Nothing was going to keep them from it.

Perhaps because they'd come from a farther part of the battlefield, the men coming down the hill now were quietened by a tiredness that anaesthetised panic. They asked the same question: 'Where were the Spanish?' The same uniforms were distorted with the same mud, but they stood without complaint as they waited for the ferry while Cull worked on the rope again. Barbary noticed they avoided looking at her and Grace, even at each other; they slumped and rubbed their faces like shy girls. One boy, no older than Sylvestris, went past her with his face buried in his hands.

Christ, wasn't it enough that they'd been beaten? Why did they have to feel ashamed? 'You lost,' she told the boy on impulse. 'It's no crime, you just lost.' But he shook his covered head and joined the others.

Her word echoed back at her: 'Lost.' Absorbed in separate tragedies, she'd forgotten what they accumulated into. Was Ireland lost?

Three hours. It wasn't possible to obliterate the freedom of an entire race in three hours. They'd regroup or whatever it was that shattered armies did. But more was needed than to collect these men together; unless it was possible to stick broken souls back in place one by one, Ireland had died in three hours.

She turned to her grandmother for help and saw a bowed woman leaning on a cutlass stuck in the ground as a crutch, her head quivering with the palsy of the very old.

Barbary ran along the bank and up the hill, dodging weary horses and riders who told her to get out of the way. She had to find O'Hagan. In this total disintegration, she must find her husband. She clung onto stirrups and boots. 'Have you seen O'Hagan? Please, have you seen O'Hagan?' She was a woman who hadn't been there; they treated her like an outsider trying to intrude on the exclusivity of their misery. Most of them pushed her away, one of them kicked out his boot and sent her back into the mud. She struggled up and ran on to the next horse. 'Have you seen O'Hagan?'

She was looking into the face of the O'Neill. The shape she knew so well was there but nothing else. The man was dead. He was breathing, and holding the reins of his horse and considering the sight down at the ferry, but he was dead. If she could have brought him back so that he could take O'Hagan away from her again, she would have done it in that moment. Now that she saw the shell, she comprehended for the first time the greatness that had inhabited it. Not a good man, sometimes not a nice one, all his chicanery had been to provide the cement that had stuck one brick to another in the colossal edifice he had created from nothing. That he'd built it on too ancient, too rotten foundations hadn't been his fault, they'd been all he'd had to build on.

In the course of his masonry he had become Ireland and Ireland had become him and now they were both dead. He was hatless so that raindrops fell off his nose and drenched his beard. His eyes were the driest things about him, gazing like stones into the rest of his life in which he had been left nothing to do but save it.

The O'Donnell rode beside him, the one vivid man in the landscape because he was angry. He was shouting, she'd heard him from a distance over and over again: 'I'll go to Spain, so I will. I'll have a new army and an explanation from the bastard Philip if it kills me.' She watched them both go down the hill, O'Donnell still shouting.

More men went past and then a thin figure leading a horse. He scooped her into one arm as he went by and she trotted beside him, wiping the mud from his face with her hands. She asked the same inadequate question he'd asked her on their wedding day. 'Was it bad?'

'No,' he said reasonably. 'No, not bad. A thousand dead, maybe, but we'd anticipated more if we'd won the day.'

'Where were the Spanish?'

'I don't know. Maybe they didn't hear us. It doesn't matter. They'd have made no difference.'

'What about the English? Are they coming after us?'

He was still reasonable. 'I don't expect so. They were harrying towards the north when last I saw them. You see, we tired them out by running away so fast. It's a grand new strategy. Have so many of us run, the enemy kills himself trying to catch us.'

'Stop it. Stop it. What happened? O'Hagan, look at me.'

He wouldn't. He shrugged his shoulders. 'We weren't ready for it. Not the bloody *tercios* or the treelessness or disciplined cavalry on open ground. They charged, our men tried to fight – and didn't. It was like watching knitting unravelling. Somebody took a thread and ran it back and forth along the rows and the stitches all came out. All came out, all of them. We tried to stop them, God help us, and killed a few, but they trampled us down.' He doubled up, retching. She knelt down beside him and held him. He wiped his mouth. 'The whole bloody world waiting for the rebirth of Ireland and we have an abortion.'

She put his arm around her shoulders and helped him up. 'Come along, pigsney. One foot, that's right. And the next. I love you so much.' She got him down to the ferry which had already gone over. Grace had crossed with it. She was standing by the ferryman's hut watching the O'Neill and the O'Donnell riding away from her up the bank. The O'Donnell was still shouting.

Jesus, let me pick them all up and tell them they're wonderful and it will all come right. They wouldn't believe her and it wasn't going to be all right. If the Upright God had been a good God He would either have let them get rid of their despair through victory, or killed every last one of them; instead He'd created the perfect balance of hatred, tamping it into the soil and the air so that treading it, breathing it, English and Irish would forever poison themselves.

'Isn't there any hope?'

'No.'

Cull was bringing the ferry over for them. There were very few on their side of the river now, one load would do it. The hills had become exhausted of men and high up above them two buzzards were circling in the lessening rain.

'Hello, Cull,' O'Hagan said.

'My lord.'

They crossed in silence except for the rush of the river.

As they landed, O'Hagan looked back once more and, with a violence that made them jump, drew his sword and cut through the ropes holding the ferry to the stanchion. The raft became another piece of jetsam, dragging its rope out of the stanchion on the far side and floating free, turning round on an eddy in a pirouette like a clumsy dancer performing totally for his own pleasure. The river assumed a nakedness and though Barbary was in no mood for symbolism she thought that however many ferries or bridges would be laid across it in the future, the barrier it formed now would never be mentally crossed again.

A new breeze brought the far-away, long drawn out yelping of seagulls. 'They're laughing,' said O'Hagan. 'Mother of God, listen to them laugh.'

'It's seagulls,' she told him. 'You're imagining it.'

'By God I am,' he said. 'I always will.'

What was wrong with them all? They'd escaped with their lives, and instead of thanking their God and getting on with living, they acted like men who wanted to change places with the corpses they'd left behind. They invented honour and chivalry, shame and disgrace, and worshipped these concepts as if they were realities. At the age of seven she'd known more of how the world turned.

Well, she would get him away and make him glad he'd survived.

O'Hagan was kissing Grace O'Malley's hand. 'We're for Inishannon,' he said. 'Will you come with us, Granuaile?'

Grace shook her head.

'Goodbye, then.'

'But you're coming with us,' said Barbary. 'You're coming with me. Grace has her fleet in the bay, and the Order are on board. You said you'd meet me by the boat, it was arranged.' He was turning away from her, and she turned him back, babbling.

He didn't understand. 'Woman, I'm not leaving him now. Neither of us, we can't leave him now. He's defeated. Don't you see your man's defeated?'

'He's dead.' She grabbed the sleeves of his doublet with both fists. 'He's dead, he's dead, he's dead.'

'It doesn't matter. If he's going into Hell, we're not leaving him to go down alone. He needs us. He needs me and I need you.' He tucked his arm through hers, as if they'd made up a quarrel. 'Come along now.'

'No.' She dragged away from him, 'No, I can't leave the Order. I promised.'

'Grace will look after them.'

'No. They're my children.'

'They're not really yours.' He said it as if she'd been playing some game for which time was now up.

'They are. They're yours as well. You said.' Her voice was puny with despair. 'They're alive and the O'Neill's dead.'

He glanced upriver where the figures who'd gone on were dwindling into the mist. He didn't have time for this. 'Listen to me. It's for my honour. He is my foster-brother and there is no greater loyalty than that.'

'There is.' She was screaming. 'You've made it all up, these traditions, these rules, but they're not real. Your loyalty's children. It's what we were put here for, to look after life. These things you play about at, they don't matter. Wars and rituals . . . all the time you're wasting children. You fought as well as you could, but you've lost. Let it go. Please, O'Hagan, please. Come with me.' She was dragging him so hard towards the ferryman's hut that he was pulled a little way and then stopped to look back. She put up her hands and turned his head to hers. 'Don't look at him.' The deadness of O'Neill would go on down the generations, always dividing, into infinity, while on Grace O'Malley's ship was the untidy mixture of breeds that was the only reasonable answer to the whole mess.

He had to come with her. She tried to quieten her voice. 'We've given most of our lives to the O'Neill, he can spare us what's left.' She would die if she lost him again. He was the one rope left holding the saker from going over the cliff.

'You're my wife,' he said. 'I want you to come with me.'

I want it too, she thought. Being with you for the rest of my life is all I want, even if it means being hunted; maybe there'd even be romance in playing outlaws, they could love each other at least, and when they were dead

685

people would make legends about them. In the end that was what he and the O'Neill and the O'Donnell wanted, to have their names live on in stories. There would be no romance in going back to her children and taking up the burden again, there was no material for legend in keeping children clean and fed. Even when she'd been telling him how important children were, she hadn't really felt it, the words had come down through some chain of command that was older and stronger than she was.

'O'Flaherty,' he said, and she remembered every moment when he'd called her that. 'I'm sworn to him. I have to go.'

'You're sworn to me,' she said.

'Are you coming or not?'

She opened her mouth to say yes. More than anything in her life she wanted to say yes. She said: 'No.'

'Well,' he said, 'I tell you what.' And she knew she'd lost him. 'You go on now with the children. Send me a message when you get to where you're going. But I have to go with him at this minute.'

He loved her as much as he could. It was in his face that he was in pain. He would sit with the O'Neill by a fire when they had a pause from the pursuit, and somebody would sing a love song and he would feel the pain again. But not enough.

She said: 'I'll leave word where we're going in the hut in the cove. When the O'Neill's dead, will you come after me?'

'You're the pulse of my heart,' he said, 'but you don't need me like he does. You don't need anybody. Do you remember me telling you?'

She remembered. 'Will you come after me?'

'Yes.'

'Take care of yourself.'

'Take care of yourself.'

The mud from his face was on hers, the mud from her dress where she'd fallen down was on his cuirass. He took his horse's reins and walked away, after the O'Neill. He wouldn't look back, there was no point in waiting.

On the ride over the headland she considered dying. It was an attractive option. She couldn't remember any more why she hadn't gone with him. She was heading in the wrong direction and she couldn't remember the reason. She didn't feel Cull's body behind hers on the mule. She didn't know if Grace rode beside her. Time passed and they were looking down over a bay in which the *Grace of God* and two other ships were anchored close inshore on a full tide.

'The wind's changed,' said Grace.

'Has it?'

'Pull yourself together, for the sake of God.'

'Will you give me directions for him, Grandmother?'

'I will. Now sniff the wind, girl.'

Like a dog she did as she was told, a cold, easterly wind. From England. Mountjoy would get his tobacco. One curragh had been left on the beach for them. 'Where are we going?' He might change his mind, even now.

'Will you listen to the woman. Hear me, Barbary. We're going where the wind takes us. We're going west.'

'Tell me the course so I can write it and he can see it.'

Grace told her the course and she scored the directions over the lintel of the hut with Grace's knife, making them deeper and deeper until Grace pulled her away. 'We'll miss the tide.'

They sculled out to the *Grace of God* where a long row of heads lined the gunwale, cheering at their approach, though some of the faces were green with sea-sickness. Barbary looked at them as she climbed up the net. Sylvestris, Priscilla, Nanno, George, Gill, Peter . . . She counted them, all present and correct in their Order which, she supposed, had to matter more to her than the man she'd just parted from or she wouldn't be here.

Other women were on board with their children, Grace's people, and they were trying to minister to her unseaworthy Order, but as she came aboard they were pushed aside. Priscilla staggered towards her and vomited down her dress. Gill clutched at her: 'Am I going to die?' Nanno's round face was pinched and green, staring at her with the hopelessness of the living dead.

Perhaps, later, she'd have time to dwell on tragedy, on men who preferred honour to real life, but not now. She couldn't blame men. Reality was vomiting children; the process of cleaning them up would never get into song or go down in legend that could be recounted around flickering fires to remind its hearers of past glory. Where was the romance in a sick, snotty, crying child?

But here were her ropes, twenty-five of them, twenty-six if you counted Cuckold Dick, twenty-eight with Grace and Cull, to hold the saker back. Enough to keep her alive for a bit longer. And here with the smell of vomit were other familiar smells, lanolin, sailcloth, Connaught.

Grace had regained herself and her ship. She was giving orders, men were pulling on ropes. Barbary glimpsed old friends among them, Keeroge, Kitterdy Two – they were too busy pulling up the anchor to greet her but they waved, bless them, and smiled.

Like a mother pelican the *Grace of God*'s canvas flapped and bellied out and, with the two smaller galleons beside her, began moving towards the mouth of the bay.

She wanted to go astern and watch the shore in case, at the last minute, there was a thin figure on it waving at her to come back, but spray was whipping onto the deck and wetting her children. She caught a glimpse of the shore as she took them down to Grace's cabin under the quarter-deck and it was empty.

Her grandmother came in, pushing back her wet hair: 'Did I tell you I'd brought that bloody pony of yours along? He's down in the hold, bad-tempered quadruped that he is.'

'Spenser?' Another rope, well, more a piece of string, but she was glad of it. 'I thought you'd have eaten him by now.'

'We might yet. It's going to be a long voyage. And while we're about it . . .' Bad-temperedly, Grace hoisted Dorren off a chest she'd been sitting on, opened it, and brought out a tattered parchment. 'Can ye still write? Then you can employ yourself on the Kishta. If men won't do my remembering, a woman will have to.'

Barbary was fully alive now, back in touch with worries and responsibilities. 'Where did you say we were going?'

'If you listened instead of mooning,' said her grandmother, 'you would know. The wind's right and we're making for the New World. I said to your Saxon Queen would she go with me, but the woman has no initiative. Ireland's too small for the likes of me, and I'm hoping the Americas will be bigger.'

The full realisation came to Barbary at last. The course directions had meant nothing to her. 'Grace,' she said, 'we won't make it. The Americas are thousands of miles of ocean away. Raleigh told me. We'll run out of food and water, we'll founder.'

'I've never foundered yet and we've provisions a-plenty. And what does Raleigh know? Has he been there?'

'No,' said Barbary slowly. 'No, I don't think he ever has.'

'There ye are then. And with that bloody Cuckold Dick giving me weed to the Saxons, I've nothing to fill me pipe, so I'm having to go to the source. Cut out the middleman. Will ye stop worrying? We'll make it well enough. And if we run out of provisons, we can always stop another ship and pilot some more.'

Barbary regarded her grandmother. The woman's losses were greater than her own and she was cutting them. Here, perhaps, was the truth of Finola's She-God. Here was true legend, the implacable, the unforgiving strength of female survival. If Grace O'Malley was heading for the Americas with her shipload of pirates and versers and pickpockets and cony-catchers and cross-biters, a Noah's Ark of tricksters, then the Americas had better look out.

'Why not?' she said.

The course directions would remain on the lintel of Cuckold Dick's hut, and she hoped one day her man would read them. Maybe he would.

The *Grace of God* and its fleet sailed away from Ireland before an east wind which plucked up the sea into dapples like a million-strong shoal of mackerel, heading for the New World.

Epilogue

Trickery was pursued to the end.

The O'Neill was hunted up and down a famine-ridden north and in March 1603 was at last forced to surrender. He was given the promise of terms and came in, to Mellifont Abbey, where Mountjoy kept him kneeling before him for an hour. The English negotiators were already aware that their Queen had died, but the news was kept from the O'Neill in case, knowing that a more sympathetic James was now on the throne, he should ask for better terms. They told him afterwards.

He dragged out a few more years in Ireland but, on 14 September 1607, with ninety-nine companions, he sailed away and died in Rome in 1616 aged sixty-six.

Immediately after Kinsale, Red Hugh O'Donnell had gone to Spain, still hoping to enlist more help from King Philip. He was poisoned a few months later, it is said by an English assassin named Blake who'd been sent after him.

Mountjoy returned to England and enjoyed a happy, though short, reunion with Penelope Rich. He died in 1606, aged forty-three.

The legitimate Earl of Desmond, having spent most of his life in the Tower of London, was sent back to it, and nine months later, died there, as did his cousin, the 'Hayrope Earl'.

Grace O'Malley's son, Tibbot, fought against the Irish so well during the battle of Kinsale that he was knighted and was eventually created the first Viscount Mayo. He died in 1629 and tradition says he was murdered by his brother-in-law, Dermot O'Connor.

Although Grace O'Malley herself has become an Irish legend, she was never mentioned by her contemporary Irish annalists, and it is only because she was such a nuisance to the English that there is considerable record of her activities among the Elizabethan State papers. When she died or where she is buried is a mystery.

More Historical Fiction from Headline:

FAY SAMPSON
BLACK SMITH'S TELLING
Daughter of Tintagel

Any smith's a man of magic, but I was a cut above all the rest. I was a king myself in our craft. If she was truly the Lady I took her to be, she would know me for her equal.

She turned my head when she came, riding to her own wedding like that. I'd never thought of a queen as a woman before. Black hair tumbling loose over her breasts; eyes, when I got up my nerve to look at them, a truer green that ever I'd seen. When she got close her eyes turned away from her sister's and met mine. There was something quickened in them then. She looked full at me, till she seemed to suck the being out of me into herself, and all my secrets with it. Then, in front of all those kings and the lords and ladies, she bowed, very gravely. Yes, once, Morgan of Tintagel bowed to me.

I should have run while I had the chance.

Uther Pendragon has been dead of poison for many a year. He left kings aplenty – each too busy raiding the other to banish the Saxon invaders from Britain – but no great emperor to lead them. His only son disappeared with the wizard Emrys Merlyn when a baby.

Now Morgan comes to be wed to King Urien of Rheged. Merlyn moves in secret, disguised as the bard Silver-Tongue. Deep in the fells, the lovely Nimue and her band of warrior women teach a young man and his followers the art of war, before endowing him with a magical sword and scabbard and sending him out to unite the scattered kingdoms. How long can they keep brother and sister apart?

Morgan draws to her her wise and dangerous sisters: the sensual and amoral Morgawse and the brooding, future-seeing Elaine. Each of them has reason to seek revenge against the son of the man who killed their father. Trapped between these two forces in their currents of love and hatred is Teilo, once a proud and powerful Smith and wise man of the Old Religion, now condemned by Morgan to play the part of a woman because he failed to understand the balance in which the world must be held – the marrying of sword and scabbard.

Also by Fay Sampson from Headline
WISE WOMAN'S TELLING   WHITE NUN'S TELLING

FICTION/HISTORICAL   0 7472 3400 0

RUTH NICHOLS

The Burning of the Rose

A
**compelling
fifteenth
century
love story**

In the Florence of the Medicis and the
Renaissance painters, Claire Tarleton, beautiful
and talented musician, artists' model and scholar,
is brought up by the foster parents who have
cared for her since her real parents died in the
plague of London.

Despite her elegant surroundings and protected
upbringing, Claire is conscious that she lives in a
world of adventure and danger, born into the
knowledge that war is permanent. Even as the
Hundred Years' War is ending, the Turks are
advancing on Italy and Claire and her family flee
to Normandy. For Claire the move from a city of
beauty and culture to a grey coastal village proves
traumatic . . .

Here, English by birth but French by nurture,
Claire discovers half-denied questions about her
true parentage, and about where her own future lies.
Trapped within the violently divided loyalties of
the community, she betrays and is betrayed by the
man she loves . . .

FICTION/HISTORICAL   0 7472 3512 0

A selection of bestsellers from Headline

FICTION

RINGS	Ruth Walker	£4.99 □
THERE IS A SEASON	Elizabeth Murphy	£4.99 □
THE COVENANT OF THE FLAME	David Morrell	£4.99 □
THE SUMMER OF THE DANES	Ellis Peters	£6.99 □
DIAMOND HARD	Andrew MacAllan	£4.99 □
FLOWERS IN THE BLOOD	Gay Courter	£4.99 □
A PRIDE OF SISTERS	Evelyn Hood	£4.99 □
A PROFESSIONAL WOMAN	Tessa Barclay	£4.99 □
ONE RAINY NIGHT	Richard Laymon	£4.99 □
SUMMER OF NIGHT	Dan Simmons	£4.99 □

NON-FICTION

MEMORIES OF GASCONY	Pierre Koffmann	£6.99 □
THE JOY OF SPORT		£4.99 □
THE UFO ENCYCLOPEDIA	John Spencer	£6.99 □

SCIENCE FICTION AND FANTASY

THE OTHER SINBAD	Craig Shaw Gardner	£4.50 □
OTHERSYDE	J Michael Straczynski	£4.99 □
THE BOY FROM THE BURREN	Sheila Gilluly	£4.99 □
FELIMID'S HOMECOMING: Bard V	Keith Taylor	£3.99 □

All Headline books are available at your local bookshop or newsagent, or can be ordered direct from the publisher. Just tick the titles you want and fill in the form below. Prices and availability subject to change without notice.

Headline Book Publishing PLC, Cash Sales Department, PO Box 11, Falmouth, Cornwall, TR10 9EN, England.

Please enclose a cheque or postal order to the value of the cover price and allow the following for postage and packing:
UK & BFPO: £1.00 for the first book, 50p for the second book and 30p for each additional book ordered up to a maximum charge of £3.00
OVERSEAS & EIRE: £2.00 for the first book, £1.00 for the second book and 50p for each additional book.

Name ....

Address ....

....

....